Dear Arabesque Reader,

Thank you for choosing to celebrate ten years of award-winning romance with Arabesque. In recognition of our literary landmark, last year BET Books launched a special collector's series honoring the authors who pioneered African-American romance. With a unique three-books-in-one format, each anthology features the most beloved works of the Arabesque imprint.

Sensuous, intriguing, and intense, this special collector's series was launched in 2004 with *First Touch,* which included three of Arabesque's first published novels, written by Sandra Kitt, Francis Ray, and Eboni Snoe; it was followed by *Hideaway Saga,* three novels from award-winning author Rochelle Alers, and the third in the series, *Falcon Saga,* by Francis Ray. Last year's series concluded with Brenda Jackson's *Madaris Saga.*

This year we continue the series with Donna Hill's *Courageous Hearts* collector's edition, Felicia Mason's *Seductive Hearts* series, Bette Ford's *Passionate Hearts* collection, and the book you are holding, Shirley Hailstock's *Magnetic Hearts*—which includes three of this pioneering author's most cherished Arabesque romances—*Whispers of Love, White Diamonds,* and *Legacy.* We invite you to read all of these exceptional works by our renowned authors.

In addition to recognizing these authors, we would also like to honor the succession of editors—Monica Harris, Karen Thomas, Chandra Taylor, and the current editor, Evette Porter—who have guided the artistic direction of Arabesque during our successful history.

We hope you enjoy these romances. Please give us your feedback at our website at www.bet.com/books.

Sincerely,

Linda Gill
VP and Publisher
BET Books

SHIRLEY HAILSTOCK

MAGNETIC HEARTS

BET Publications, LLC
http://www.bet.com
http://www.arabesquebooks.com

ARABESQUE BOOKS are published by

BET Publications, LLC
c/o BET BOOKS
One BET Plaza
1900 W Place NE
Washington, DC 20018-1211

ISBN 1-58314-661-X

First Printing: November 2005
10 9 8 7 6 5 4 3 2 1

Printed in the United States of America

Contents

Whispers of Love

To Marilyn McGrillies and Patricia Hahn, who believed in Robyn and Grant from the beginning and who helped in ways even a wordsmith cannot express.

PROLOGUE

Most people came to Las Vegas for the gambling, but Robyn lazed outside the casinos in the arid heat of the desert. The pool had emptied since she'd done her fifty laps. Susan was inside at her rehearsal, and Robyn had been given free rein to use the hotel facilities for any of her needs while she was in Las Vegas. She stretched out on one of the blue-and-white lounge chairs that framed the pool of the Mountain View Resort. Huge sunglasses protected her eyes from the glare bouncing off the still water. Her one-piece bathing suit gave her a modicum of decency. In the quiet, her mind went back to Washington and her job. She pushed the thought aside. She wouldn't think about the Major Crimes Bureau now.

Closing her eyes, she rested a moment. Then, instinct told her she was no longer alone. She could feel someone looking at her, staring at her. Without removing the lenses, she searched the rows of chairs. She saw him at the end of the pool: a man in a blue uniform, his arms casually folded over the back of a lounge chair, and his eyes staring directly at her. Robyn stared back. She felt compelled to. She was used to seeing uniforms, due to her work at the FBI, but this was not a military man. His uniform was that of an airline. She couldn't make out which one.

He pulled his gaze away and let it be caught by the beauty of the distant hills. He was so still, like a bronze statue. Suddenly, Robyn wished for her camera to capture his solitary profile. Few people, who came to this gambling mecca, took the time to notice the awesome beauty of the landscape. She followed his gaze, entranced by the burnish gold and red colors that painted the rugged horizon.

He must be a different kind of man, she thought as she gazed at him openly through her concealing glasses. He was lean and tall, over six feet. His shoulders were straight and broad, giving him an athletic look. His hair was cut short and capped by a captain's hat.

"There you are, Robyn." She jumped, not expecting to hear her name. "You've been out here entirely too long." Susan plopped down on the chair beside her, still in her leotard and footless stockings. Her body completely blocked Robyn's view of the man who'd stared so openly at her.

Robyn checked her watch. "It's only been an hour."

"An hour here is vastly different from an hour in Ocean City, Maryland."

"Just a few more minutes and I'll be in," she sat up, shifting to see if the man was still there. He was gone. Robyn checked the area, but she didn't see him. He must have left as quietly as he'd arrived.

"There isn't time," Susan was saying. "We have a lot of work to do."

"Work? I didn't come here to work." Her mind was still on the uniformed officer. Where had he gone? She wondered if she'd see him again.

"I've got you a job in the chorus line," Susan announced.

Robyn stared at her for a moment then burst into laughter. Susan's face was sober and after a moment Robyn's sobered, too.

"You *are* kidding," she stated positively.

Susan shook her head slowly.

"Susan, I can't dance."

"Yes, you can," she contradicted. "We were in the same dance class for five years, and I know you still go twice a week."

"I don't mean I can't dance. I mean, I can't dance in a show."

"Why not?"

"I'm on vacation."

"That's not a reason."

"I don't want to dance."

"Of course, you do." Susan rejected her reason.

"No, I don't," she protested.

"Well, you have to. I've just spent half an hour convincing Bob Parker you're the best person for the job, and you can't let me down."

"Susan Collins," Robyn shouted, coming to a sitting position. "We are no longer in school. You can't keep getting me mixed up in sophomoric pranks."

"This is not a prank, sophomoric or otherwise. One of the dancers came down with something."

Robyn thought she was being intentionally vague.

"She'll be out a day or so. We only need you for one night, maybe two."

Robyn knew what that meant. Susan had been her roommate through four years of college. They had shared the same apartment until Susan left to get married almost eighteen months ago. When her marriage broke up after a year, she gave up her teaching position and came to Las Vegas. She got a job as a dancer and had been here for the last eight months.

"Why can't you go on without her?" Logic rallied to Robyn's aid.

"This routine requires that we pair off."

"Then, why doesn't one of the girls sit that dance out? Like you. If you could get the night off, we'd have time to talk before your date." Robyn pulled her glasses off, excited at her counterplan, but Susan was already shaking her head.

"A missing pair would create a hole. It would be obvious something was wrong. We'll have all day tomorrow to talk. I don't have a rehearsal until five o'clock." Susan's large brown eyes pleaded with her.

Robyn knew before she said it that she was going to agree. If she didn't, she knew Susan would argue until she got her way. "I'll do it, Susan." Robyn stopped her friend's happiness with a restraining hand. "But I promise you, if I make a fool of myself, I'm holding you responsible."

The darkness of the lobby was a stark contrast to the brightness of the sun. Grant stood a moment to let his eyes adjust. He turned back to check the two women by the pool. They had the same color hair, although copper highlights bounced off of the hair belonging to the one in the bathing suit. Soft, natural curls flowed over her shoulders to the middle of her back, moving like synchronized swimmers as she bobbed her head up and down. She was sitting up now without the glasses that had covered her face like a mask. He stopped in his motion of turning around. She was beautiful. He'd seen her body while she slept, and her face was just as ravishing. Yellow roses came to his mind. Yellow roses that have been tanned a golden brown, exactly as he liked it. A discovery he'd made this very day.

She sat straight, and her legs were long and shapely. Suddenly, she smiled, and Grant was swept away by the intensity he felt. The two women got up and walked toward another entrance. He watched them with a smile—one in a striped dance costume and the other in a bathing suit of bright red. Her legs seemed to go on forever. The angular jut of the building blocked his view as they rounded a corner and disappeared.

"There must be a woman out there," David greeted him with a slap on the back.

Grant moved around to face his friend who leaned toward the door. He knew David wouldn't see anyone. The woman he'd been watching was well out of sight.

Grant didn't tell him about her. For the moment, he wanted to keep her a secret. He didn't know why. He and David had been friends since the air force, and there was little they didn't know about each other. But when he'd seen the woman from his balcony methodically swimming lap after lap, he'd been fascinated by the beauty of her brown body slicing through the water.

Without changing his uniform, he'd gone to the pool. And there he'd found his nymph lying on a lounger in the afternoon sun. Why he hesitated in approaching her he didn't know. He had no problem with women. They seemed to flock to him. But this one looked so serene, as if life hadn't wiped the idealism from her features yet. For the time being, he only wanted to look at her.

"I got the tickets," David said.

For a moment, Grant didn't know David had been speaking to him. "What tickets?" he asked.

"For the show tonight." Four red tickets extended from David's hand like flat fingers. "It's the best show in Vegas. Lots of girls and singing and girls and dancing and girls and girls and girls," he repeated the litany.

Grant laughed as they headed for their room to get out of their uniforms. The show was hours away. They had time to shower and get in some gambling before David saw *his* girls. And Grant knew he had a date with one of the stewardesses but now couldn't remember her name. He also knew David had set him up with someone and would feign surprise when she suddenly showed up. He didn't care, he told himself, but when they reached the elevator he looked back toward the pool and thought of dark brown hair with copper highlights.

This was certainly a better place to work than the Assassination Bureau. Robyn Warren stood backstage, a three-pound headdress of pink fur balanced on her head. In moments, she'd be on stage for the second time in her twenty-five years. The first time had been two hours ago. She rubbed sweaty hands down her hips and waited. The curtain went up, and the lights rose, bathing sixteen scantly clad women in a blinding white light.

With a smile plastered to her face, Robyn listened to the music and counted the beats, as she performed the memorized steps. A single sound of tapping feet worked in unison to the music of *42nd Street.* It was exhilarating. Blood pumped through her system, mixing with adrenaline, restoring the energy her afternoon of rehearsal had depleted.

She felt the nervousness leave her. She could tell by the twinkle in the eyes of the other dancers when they passed each other forming a set of four circles that blended into one larger circle and finally opening into a straight line that she was a part of the group. The audience applauded in the middle of the routine. The sound was deafening to her ears. For the first time she looked beyond the footlights, wondering if the man from the pool was somewhere out there. It was hard to see anyone with the lights in her eyes. Besides she didn't know anyone here, except Susan, who was dancing on her left. She'd only been in Las Vegas two days. The man by the pool had been a stranger. They hadn't even said hello.

The dance ended much too soon, and she followed the line of bobbing fur backstage to change for the next number. There wasn't much time for musings; for as soon as they had switched from pink to white lace, she heard the call of five minutes. It meant they were to line up backstage, according to a preset system. She stood between Vera and Susan, the three of them were the same height.

The second outing on the stage seemed shorter than her first visit. She was breathless from the exhilaration and excitement. Susan had been right, she loved being out there. Almost before she knew it, she was back in the dressing room. The noise level was high as everyone tried to get dressed for their dates. Robyn moved aside. Susan had quickly dressed and was the first to leave the room, smiling at her and telling her she'd see her back at the apartment. She disappeared through the door, her dress changed and her face remade without the heavy greasepaint that they wore against the harsh lights of the stage.

By the time Robyn was dressed, the room was clear. She flipped the switch, throwing the room into darkness and leaving behind the smell of sweat, perfume, and makeup. From the top of the stairs, she saw him—the man from the pool. While there were people moving around him, carrying scenery and lights, he stood still. His black suit, distinctive against the surroundings, made his presence commanding. His white shirt made his skin darker by contrast. Robyn smiled when he looked up at her.

"You must be lost," she said, as she came down the steps.

"I don't think so." His voice was deep and dark like a warm night.

"If you're waiting for one of the dancers, I'm afraid you've been stood up." She could not imagine anyone forgetting about a guy whose brown eyes were so warm they could melt ice. They followed her all the way to the bottom step.

"I'm waiting for you," he said quietly.

"Me!" She didn't know this man, although she wouldn't mind getting to know him. From the distance she had to look up, she confirmed his height to be just over six feet. His hair had been picked until it circled his head like a small halo.

"I saw you by the pool . . . and on the stage, both times."

She smiled, pleased that someone had come to see her one and only performance. "We were staring at each other," she said directly.

"My name is Grant Richards." He stood up slightly straighter, as if he were coming to attention.

"I'm—"

"Robyn Warren," he finished for her. "I asked one of the other dancers," he explained to her questioning look.

"We don't know each other."

"A situation I'd like to remedy." His smile exuded charm.

He took her arm and locked it through his elbow. Several minutes later, Robyn found herself sitting in the casino's restaurant and having a late dinner with one of the most gorgeous men she'd ever met. He told her he'd been a copilot for Trans-Global for nearly four years. By the time dessert and coffee were served, she'd learned he'd grown up in a series of foster homes, before going to stay with an aunt. He and his friend, David, were here for a few days before they had another flight. She told him she worked for the government.

"I didn't know the government had a need for long-legged girls in bejeweled pink tights."

Robyn laughed. "They weren't bejeweled. They were sequined." She told him how Susan had convinced her to replace a sick dancer in tonight's show.

"Well, since you don't dance for a living, what do you do for the government?"

Robyn dropped her head. "I'm nobody important. I'm an analyst in a small Washington department." She was deliberately vague. She'd been taught to reveal as little as possible about her true purpose at the Federal Bureau of Investigation.

"Washington, D.C.!" Grant seized the word. A large smile displayed his even teeth.

"Yes," she nodded, lifting her coffee cup. The liquid was lukewarm.

"I live in D.C., too."

The thrill that shimmied up Robyn's spine couldn't be stopped. She'd only met Grant a few hours ago, yet she was sure she could fall in love with him.

"So where's Susan, now?" he asked.

"She had a date." Robyn came back from her musings. "And where's David now?" she asked, as the waiter served more coffee.

"He had a date. I lost him when I went to the second show."

"Why did you stay?"

He leaned forward, taking her hand in his. "After I saw you, I was devastated. How could I leave?" His eyes twinkled with mischief.

Robyn blushed, knowing he was teasing. "How could you tell us apart. Up there, we all look the same." It was a common complaint of the dancers. With the makeup and costumes, it was difficult to tell one from the other. And with her coloring, she blended in easier than Susan's milk chocolate complexion did.

"I could argue that." This time there was no teasing in his tone. It was deadly serious.

Robyn's throat constricted, and pulling her hand free, she picked up her water glass. The cool water helped only slightly, for Grant's eyes were fixed on her. She felt as if he were setting her on fire. It was all around her, defining her shape, and any effort to break free would cause the flames to incinerate her. But the overwhelming emotion that rocked her more than the thought of burning was that she didn't want to break free. She wanted this new sensation to continue.

"Why don't we go to the lounge and dance?" he suggested.

They had finished eating long ago, but had lingered over the coffee to talk. Now, they rose and went to the small lounge. The soft music played by a combo filled the room, and many couples were on the dance floor.

The hostess led them to a table, and Grant ordered drinks. Without waiting for them to arrive, he pulled her into his arms, and they began circling the floor to the slow beat of the music. Robyn thought she could die now and not be happier. He smelled good, of lemon soap and after-shave. She raised her hand to the back of his head and touched his soft hair. His arm tightened around her waist, pulling her closer to his body.

They moved in perfect rhythm, each matching the steps of the other as if they had always danced together. She didn't think, after the grueling afternoon she'd had learning the steps to the routine, she'd ever want to dance again. Yet, now resting in Grant's arms, her feet barely touched the floor. She was dancing on a cloud.

They spent the evening there. When most of the other couples had opted for the casino and thoughts of striking it rich, she had found her fortune. She swirled in Grant's arms to the sexy sound of a saxophone that played on and on into the small hours of the morning. When he took her back to Susan's apartment on the outskirts of the city, light was just breaking behind the distant hills.

Robyn didn't move when he pulled the rental car in front of Susan's building. It was one of the best days she'd ever had, and she was reluctant to have it end.

"It'll be daylight soon," she said, prolonging his departure.

Grant looked at the pink color spreading in the sky. It reminded him of the early morning horizon when he was flying.

"It's going to be a beautiful day." He knew that, even without the clear sky. Robyn had entered his life, and for some unexplained reason, he knew all his days would be beautiful.

Robyn turned to him and smiled. His arms snaked around her and pulled her unresisting body closer to his. He kissed her slowly, something he'd wanted to do since seeing her asleep in the sun. She moaned slightly in his embrace as she circled his neck with her arms. She played with his hair, her soft fingers combing through to his scalp. Sensation rocked him. He'd never known anyone to make him feel the way she did. He'd loved having her in his arms when they had danced, and now, his body strained for her. When the kiss ended, he kept her close, hugging her tightly to him.

"Do you suppose it's true that you can find anything open in this town at any hour?"

Robyn leaned back to look at him, her eyes dazed. "Is there something you need right now?" Her voice was thick with emotion.

"I know we only met today. All I know about you is that you work for the government, live in Washington, and like to dance. But I was wondering if we could find an open chapel, would you marry me with the sunrise?"

CHAPTER 1

Grant was coming!

Robyn squeezed her eyes closed and massaged her temples with the tips of her fingers. Pain throbbed against her hands. Dr. Elliott thought he was delivering good news when he'd told her the blood was on its way and the donor with it. She never dreamed he'd come. Never thought when she'd given information about Grant to the doctors that he'd do anything except go to the nearest hospital and have the blood drawn. But now he was on his way.

Robyn pulled the hair lying on her back into a ponytail, then stretching, she let it go. Marianne came back at that moment with two cups of coffee in her hands.

"I saw Doctor Elliott in the hall." There was a large smile on her face. "He told me they found a donor who's not too far away." She put the two cups on the table and came to face Robyn. "Why don't you try to get some sleep, Brooke. When Kari wakes up, she'll want to see you. And you don't want to have those dark circles under your eyes."

"I'm all right, Marianne." She patted her friend's hand and wandered back to the window. All she could think of was that Grant was coming. He was coming to save his daughter's life. What if he came to see her, too? What if he didn't? She didn't know what to think. It had been five years. Five long, solitary years of thinking and dreaming about him. And now he was going to be in the same building with her.

She longed to see him. See what he looked like now. How he'd changed. Did he weigh more? Was his hair gray? And his smile, was it as she remembered? But she knew she couldn't see him. She knew she couldn't stand being near him the way she felt now—tired and afraid.

"Brooke, are you listening to me?" Marianne asked.

Robyn turned around, at this moment unused to her new name. She hadn't heard anything. Her mind was reeling from the news of Grant's impending arrival.

"I'm sorry, Marianne. I'm afraid I'm not good company. Why don't you go home? You must have a thousand things to do."

"I'm not going anywhere. Now, why don't you lie down here? I'll get a blanket from the nurse." Marianne motioned toward the sofa. "A few minutes' sleep won't hurt you."

Robyn knew she wouldn't sleep, but to please Marianne, she lay down on the sofa.

"I'll be right back," Robyn heard Marianne say and saw a nurse meet her at the waiting room door just before she closed her eyes.

She didn't sleep. She remembered. Remembered her wedding in the Las Vegas chapel, the house in D.C., and the photos she used to develop. So many pictures of Grant. He was her favorite subject. They'd get up early in the morning and go to Rock Creek Park while the mist was low to the ground. She had to leave them all behind. She wondered what Grant had done with them. Was he still living in their house? Had he remarried? Her mind bubbled over with questions but the one that plagued her the most she had no answer for—would he know her? Under whatever cover the Witness Protection Program had draped her, would his heart still recognize her as the woman who'd loved him with all her heart?

Jacob Winston eased his suit jacket off as he entered the red-brick house with white shutters that he alone occupied on Tamarach Street in Washington's Rock Creek Park. He found it convenient to his office downtown and to the park's quiet solitude that he often needed. The central air conditioning had kicked on at three o'clock, making the dwelling blessedly cool after the sweltering heat of July in the nation's capital.

He headed for the den to check his messages. It was a normal routine whenever he entered his house. The den was set up as an office. While the rest of the house was clean enough to satisfy any mother-in-law's prying eye, his office was cluttered with books stacked haphazardly on the built-in shelves and piles of old newspapers separated into the three languages he read fluently—English, Spanish, and German. Flipping on the switch of his computer, he headed for the kitchen and a cold beer. The refrigerator looked like his office—cluttered with plastic containers of leftovers, Chinese food boxes, and several bottles of imported beer. He'd acquired a taste for German beer when bumming around Europe the year after he'd graduated from Stanford.

Using the bottle opener he'd mounted on the wall between the kitchen and the utility room, he caught the metal cap and tossed it with an exaggerated jump shot into the trash can nearly six feet away. Then, taking a long swig of the dark liquid, he headed back to the den.

Jacob had left his office before noon, spending the rest of the day in meetings. It was unusual for him to come home without checking in with his secretary or calling his electronic mail to any network computer within the FBI confines. But it was well past nine when he'd left, and tonight he'd wanted to get home. He had the urge to go out into his garden, darkness be damned, and spend the rest of the night in the pool.

Sitting down, he rested the bottle on the coaster he'd assigned permanent duty next to his color monitor. Choosing a menu item, the machine automatically dialed him into the FBI network. Typing through three levels of security and waiting while the remote messages traveled to the central processor and back, he finally saw the *access granted* message blinking on the screen.

Quickly, he accessed electronic mail, knowing his efficient secretary had entered his messages on-line. He took another swig of his beer and then stopped with the bottle midway between his mouth and the coaster. The name on the screen paralyzed him. Robyn had called him three times today, using the name Brooke Johnson. *Urgent* flashed like a danger sign next to her name. Robyn had never, in the years since he'd left her at the FBI headquarters in Atlanta right after Kari was born, ever called him. And to add to his paralysis were four messages to call Marianne Reynolds, each with the same urgent light flashing next to her name.

"Damn," he swore, his blood pounding in his ears. Something had to be wrong for both of them to call. Jacob snatched up the phone, punching the clear button for the unused line. He beat out the digits next to Marianne's name. It wasn't her home number. He knew that by heart.

"Buffalo General Hospital, ICU," a soft female voice greeted.

Jacob was jolted. He could hardly speak to answer the greeting. "I'm trying to reach Marianne Reynolds. She left this number." He didn't identify himself. Years of training had made subterfuge an unconscious act.

"One moment, please," the voice went on calmly and efficiently while his blood had begun to boil. In seconds, Marianne came on the line.

"What's wrong, Marianne?" he asked, wasting no time with a greeting or identification.

"You're too late," she whispered. Her voice sounded resigned and tired.

"Too late for what?" His temper was rising along with his voice level. Fear crowded in, making his heart tight.

"I think she's called him." Marianne's voice was stronger. Jacob could tell by the static that she was speaking into a cordless unit. She must have found a secure place to talk.

"Called who?" he asked unnecessarily. He knew she meant Robyn had made contact with her ex-husband. At least that meant *she* was all right.

"Tell me what happened?" He leaned forward, resting his head against the heel of his hand and closing his eyes.

"There was an accident. Kari is in critical condition. We've been here for two days." Marianne kept her words to a minimum. Jacob knew she realized this was an open line.

"What kind of accident?" Robyn had breached security with her phone call. He needed to know how deep the breach went. Marianne had been trained, but she was obviously attached to Kari, and Jacob knew she loved Robyn like a sister.

"An automobile accident, a stupid, purposeless accident." Her words told him there was no reason to suspect foul play. "Broken glass cut through an artery in Kari's arm. She lost a lot of blood."

"What about Brooke?" Jacob tensed, his mind forming pictures of red-stained bandages and broken bones.

"She escaped with minor cuts and bruises. She's been released, but we needed blood. None was available."

"What?" Jacob stood up, remembering a long ago argument he had with the then Robyn Richards over Kari's possible rare blood type.

"The supply is outdated, and no donors could be located."

Breath left Jacob's body in one long exhale. "Why didn't you call the center in Atlanta," he snapped.

The center was the Center for Disease Control. "I did that, Jacob." There was censure in her voice. "Their records showed that the supply is outdated. The closest supply we could find is in Los Alamos, New Mexico. It won't arrive before morning. She'll die by then."

Jacob heard the sob in Marianne's voice. A lump rose in his throat as he thought of the black-haired child. Although he hadn't seen her since she was born in a maximum security center four years ago, he had a fondness for her unlike any other he could define. He supposed it was due to his being Robyn's Lamaze coach for her delivery. After that experience how could anyone not love a child?

"How long has she got?" He spoke slowly, dragging his mind back to the present problem.

"I don't know, but minutes count at this stage."

"I'll take care of it from here. Keep me informed," he said resolutely. "In the meantime, stay with her."

Marianne handed the phone back, giving a weak smile to the nurse who replaced the receiver. "Thank you," she said absently as the perpetually smiling nurse handed her a blanket. She hoped Robyn was asleep. She'd known Jacob would help.

"Jacob would do anything for her," she muttered to herself as she walked toward the somber colored waiting room. Marianne had learned that the first weekend she'd reported to him. She'd been assigned to protect the newly created Brooke Johnson and her infant child. She quickly learned to address her only as Brooke and Robyn never knew she was her guardian angel. It was an easy assignment and Robyn and Marianne got along well together.

But Jacob was in love with Robyn. Marianne wasn't even sure he knew that. But she could tell by the way he gave in to Robyn whenever he disagreed with whatever she proposed. Usually, the outcome was that she got her way.

But in this case Jacob was too late. Robyn had given her ex-husband's name to the doctor, and he'd already been called. There was nothing else she could have done, and Marianne knew, in her heart, if Robyn hadn't done it she would have called herself.

When she entered the room, Robyn wasn't asleep, but had taken up her position in front of the dark window. She was staring out, looking at nothing, seeing nothing. Marianne knew she didn't even hear her come back.

"Brooke," she called softly. There was no reaction. She went to her friend and stood next to her. Robyn continued to stare through the glass.

"Brooke," she said again, her voice slightly louder. Robyn was still lost. Taking her arm, Marianne shook her lightly. The dazed eyes cleared to a somber brown. "I took a call for you," she said, letting her think Jacob had called her. Robyn didn't know that she was Marianne's assignment. Jacob insisted Marianne not tell her.

"Who was it?" Robyn turned, her face blank, her eyes wide.

"His name was Jacob. I told him what happened. He said he could get the blood."

"It's too late." Tears rolled down her face again. Marianne grabbed a tissue from the box on a nearby table and pushed it into Robyn's hand.

"Don't cry, Brooke. It'll get here in time," she told her, being more positive than she truly was. "Kari will be fine."

Robyn nodded. "Yes, Kari will be fine," she repeated, as a fresh batch of tears shook her body.

Marianne couldn't do anything. She guided Robyn to a chair and sat across from her, allowing her friend to sob tears as large as her swollen eyes.

"You should be at the restaurant," Robyn said.

"I'm not leaving until I know you and Kari are all right. The restaurant can survive without us for one night."

Marianne knew it was true. She'd called Yesterdays, the turn-of-the-century eatery they owned together, and found out things were running smoothly.

"Why don't you try to get some sleep? Just lie down here." She tried to get Robyn back to the sofa.

But Robyn was shaking her head. "I couldn't sleep. I keep thinking about when Kari was a baby." A smile flitted across her face, and Robyn began telling her anecdotes about Kari when she first learned to crawl. Marianne let her continue although she had either heard the story before or been there when the incident happened.

Finally, Robyn's eyes were so heavy that she was falling asleep while she talked. Marianne helped her to the sofa and pushed her down.

"The blood is here." Dr. Elliott came in, and Robyn was up immediately.

"Wonderful," Marianne said. "How's Kari?"

"It'll be hours before we know anything," he said. "But I expect God has given us the time we need."

He left them then, and Marianne immediately hugged her friend. "She's going to be fine, Brooke. I'm sure of it."

"I'm sure of it, too," Robyn said, her voice strained. "Now I think you should go."

"Brooke, don't be silly," Marianne protested.

"I'm not being silly. I'm scared and relieved at the same time. But most of all, I think I'd like to be alone for a while."

It wasn't the truth. What Robyn needed was assurance that Grant had come and gone. She didn't expect to see him. He didn't know Brooke Johnson. Then why was she so nervous that she needed Marianne to leave?

"I don't think being alone will do you any good."

"Please, Marianne." Robyn rolled her eyes to the ceiling. "I'm much too tired to argue the point. Go home and get some rest. In the morning, go to the restaurant. I promise if I need anything, you'll be the first person I call."

Marianne gave her a sober look and nodded. "Use the blanket," she said, reluctant to leave her alone. "Things will be better in the morning."

Robyn smiled as best she could. After Marianne left, she sank into the nearest chair and folded her arms across herself in a protective gesture. She waited. Dr. Elliott would come back when Grant had gone. Tears rolled from her eyes. Five-year-old tears spilled onto her cheeks, reminding her of a time when she'd left everything she loved behind—including her husband. The only thing she'd taken was Kari, and now she might even lose her.

CHAPTER 2

"You've saved her life," Dr. Elliott said, as he entered the emergency room's curtained cubicle. "The sample matches so perfectly you could be of the same bloodline." A nurse carrying the life-giving liquid passed him, carefully holding the sterile plastic bag that contained the Richardses' ancestry.

Grant smiled at the white-coated doctor. He donated blood often but this was the first time the recipient of his rare type was waiting for the extraction as it left his body. "What's her name?" he asked. All he'd been told was that it was for a child.

"Kari Johnson, a beautiful, black-eyed four-year-old with long dark braids and a smile to twist a man's heart."

"Sounds like she's got yours, Doc." Grant laughed a clear, hearty sound.

"Oh, she has. Her mother is in the ICU waiting room, fourth floor. I'm sure she'd like to see you again."

"Again?" Grant slipped off the examination table, rolling his sleeve down and rebuttoning his cuff.

"She gave us your name and told us where to find you. I naturally assumed you knew each other."

"Mrs. Johnson?" Grant slipped his arms in the blue uniform jacket the doctor held out to him. His brows knitted in confusion. Johnson was a common name, but it brought no images to mind.

"Mrs. Brooke Johnson," Dr. Elliott prodded.

The name meant nothing to him. "I'm not sure I remember a Brooke Johnson. Maybe it's her husband I know."

"She's a widow. Her husband died as a result of some military accident before they moved here. I never met him."

"It doesn't matter. I'll say hello before I leave." Grant smiled. Generally, he was good at remembering names and faces. And if he did know Brooke Johnson, it would be rude to leave without seeing her.

"Good-bye, Mr. Richards and thank you for coming."

Grant shook hands with the thin, long-legged doctor whose height matched his own six-foot, two-inch frame. Frank Elliott would have had all the earmarks of a country doctor if it hadn't been for the rush of brown curls that fell over the collar of his long white coat and the diamond stud that pierced his left earlobe. Dr. Elliott thanked him again, as the doors of the elevator slid open. Grant clasped his hand and with a smile, stepped inside.

The hall was clear when the doors opened onto the fourth floor. Grant whistled softly into the quiet as he walked toward the waiting room adjacent to the doors leading to the intensive care unit. Pushing the door open, Grant's heart suddenly stopped, then hammered so hard against his ribs that he thought the woman facing the windows would certainly hear it. He gripped the glass-paneled door. Robyn was dead. His mind told him that, but everything about this woman screamed her name. The way she stood with her arms wrapped across her body as if she were warding off something. The bow of her head and the soft curve of her hips and legs could be duplicates of the woman he'd loved with all his being. The hair falling down her back was the same color as Robyn's had been. The darkness of the outside prevented any highlights from showing, but instinctively he knew they'd be golden, like the copper pennies he collected in the glass bowl on the desk in his den. His heartbeat shot to his throat and lodged there. Beads of sweat popped out on his forehead despite the comfortable temperature of the room. He didn't know how long he stood there, rooted in position. It was like seeing Robyn again, being in the same room with her.

Then she turned. When she did, his heart stopped again. This time in relief. Color drained from his face, and he dropped his head for a second to gain control of his rioting emotions.

When he looked up, sad swollen eyes looked into his as though they could see into his mind. But not even the shape of her face had any resemblance to his dead wife's. In the five years since Robyn died, he hadn't reacted to a woman as violently as he did to the one standing ten feet away. When she spoke, her voice was throaty and choked. Robyn's had done that when her emotions were close to the surface. He braked his thoughts, telling himself he was reading more into this than was really there. Hundreds of women have that hair color. Don't make more of this than is necessary.

Robyn had her back to the door, but she felt the soft rush of air as it opened and closed silently. The goose bumps rising on her arms and legs and the cold fear running the column from her neck down her spine told her that Grant had entered. Even though she knew he was coming, she was not prepared to see him again.

"Mrs. Johnson, I'm Grant Richards." The deep voice that had whispered words of love in her ear had not changed. She didn't move. Her body seemed frozen except for the hot blood that sang in her ears. Five years ago, this man had been her husband. His vital good looks were as she remembered them before his plane had been hijacked to Beirut, and he'd been held prisoner.

His tall, athletically toned body looked more like he spent his days on some California beach than cutting through the air thirty-thousand feet up. His black hair was slightly longer than airline regulations allowed, but his eyes were still sepia brown with dark flecks of gold. The cleft in his strong chin added sex appeal to a winning smile.

There wasn't much different about his appearance. His eyes looked tired, but that could have been due to having extended his day by immediately boarding a flight to Buffalo after his plane had landed at Washington's National Airport. Dr. Elliott had given her this information when he'd located Grant. Several strands of gray had sneaked into his hair near his temples, and a small vertical scar bisected his right eyebrow. The scar added a slightly sinister look to his face. It hadn't been there when she'd last seen him. It had to be a reminder of the time he spent as a Lebanese captive, she thought. Some sixth sense made her ball her hand into a fist behind her to keep from smoothing the separated brows.

"You didn't have to come. They could have flown the blood up. I didn't expect its owner to come with it," Robyn continued. She looked directly at him but made no attempt to move.

Eyes without a glimmer of recognition appraised her from her high cheekbones and shoulder length, dark brown hair to the generous curve of her hips, down her dancer's legs to end at her sandaled feet. She hadn't left the hospital since they brought Kari in. Now, she was aware of the rumpled shorts and blood-stained T-shirt that she still wore from their trip to the beach.

"Doctor Elliott was insistent on the urgency. There was a plane standing by—and here I am. Your daughter should be receiving the blood right now."

Relief pierced through her like physical pain.

Grant saw her step back and brace herself against the window frame.

She turned away from him as she began to tremble. Her body shook violently, and no amount of self-determination could stop it from completing the course it had begun.

He watched her fight the fear that the accident must have caused in her. And now that Kari would be all right, delayed reaction to the pent-up stress was setting in. He had seen it before, in Beirut, when they were finally released. Men, who had been paragons of strength for many months, even years, had collapsed in tears when they reached safety.

Grant touched her lightly on the shoulder, then turned her toward him. She went easily into his arms, and he closed them around her as if they had a right to be there. He lowered her to one of the sofas.

"It's all right, she'll be fine now," he said, comforting her, unable to keep himself from stroking her hair.

"Thank you," Robyn said moments later as she pushed herself up. Grant took her hands and held them. The gesture, she was sure, was to comfort her, but what she felt was a magnetism which wanted to push her farther into his arms. "Mr. Richards . . ." she began.

"Grant," he corrected. "Everyone calls me Grant, and we are practically related," he added, a smile crinkling his eyes. "We have a child between us."

Grant had intended the comment to make her laugh. But when the color drained from her already pale face and fear replaced the sadness in her eyes, he was sorry for the joke. His hands squeezed the suddenly cold ones in his grasp. "I'm sorry. It was a poor joke."

Robyn tried to smile, but his words had caught her completely by surprise. "I understand," she managed. "I was . . . I just wanted to say that I appreciate what you've done for Kari. It must have been an inconvenience for you . . . and your family to come all this way." She stood up and walked aimlessly about with no particular destination in mind. The brief moment in his arms was too close to heaven for her to withstand his nearness.

"I don't have a family. I had a wife." He hesitated for the space of a moment. Robyn noticed it. "She died five years ago."

No she didn't, Robyn wanted to scream. "I'm very sorry." Robyn was relieved but somehow sad, too. If he had remarried his leaving wouldn't have been any easier to take than knowing he was still single. It might even be harder knowing there was another woman who had taken her place.

He stood up and came to stand behind her. "How long have you been here?" he asked, moving the subject away from the past. Robyn didn't know why she'd brought up the subject of his family. She knew he thought she was dead. It was how Jacob Winston and his force had manipulated the situation.

"The ambulance brought us in yesterday. No-no, it was the day before."

Robyn had done that, that little quick repeat of the word no, Grant noted with shock. "And I'll bet you haven't had anything to eat except these cups of coffee."

For the first time, Robyn noticed that the table was littered with partially emptied cups of vending machine coffee. Eight tan-and-white striped cups were scattered about the low table, several more looked at her from the wastebasket.

"I'm hungry. Let me buy you a good dinner," he offered.

"No, I need to stay here. Kari . . ."

"Is in good hands." Dr. Elliott spoke from the door. "You need to get out of here and get some sleep." He came toward them. "Kari is sleeping comfortably. She won't wake up before morning."

How could she explain? She couldn't have dinner with Grant. She didn't want to feel the way he made her feel. Spending time in his company wasn't part of the bargain she'd made with Jacob. In fact, it was in direct violation of the Witness Protection Program of which she and Kari were participants.

Dr. Elliott bent to pick up her sweater from the chair while Grant took her elbow and nudged her toward the waiting room door. She was too tired to struggle, allowing herself to be jockeyed by the two men. One part of her wanted to give in, but somewhere inside a part of her shouted to stop before things got out of hand.

"Could I see Kari before I go?" She turned back to the pediatrician.

"Of course, but only for a moment." Dr. Elliott took her hand and spoke seriously. "Kari is taking the blood now. We won't know much until tomorrow. Get some sleep. If there is any change, I'll have the hospital call you."

Robyn nodded, her eyes flooding with tears that she blinked away. The three of them walked down the hall to the room that housed her small daughter and several shelves of monitoring equipment. Grant followed Robyn as she entered the room and stood at the restraining rail. Kari slept quietly. The precious liquid dripped slowly through its plastic tube, linking Kari's fragile existence to the preserver hanging above her.

Tears sprang to Robyn's eyes as guilt filled her heart. Grant, misunderstanding her action, turned her into his arms and rested her head on his shoulder. She savored the moment. He was so warm and solid she wanted to hang onto him. His child lay so close, and her mouth was bound against telling him of her existence.

Grant didn't know what was happening to him. He had her in his arms now for the second time in the half hour since they'd met. She was so soft. Her hair smelled like sunshine and fresh air. He wanted to crush her to himself, let her know her child would be all right. Brooke Johnson was making him feel things he hadn't felt in years, but he couldn't tell her. Her mind was totally on the child in the bed behind them. She was only clinging to him because she was tired and scared.

Robyn gently pushed herself away from him and moved back to the bed. She smoothed back Kari's dark hair. Her bangs had lost all their curl, and her barrettes looked unnatural against the pillows. She was pale. Her skin, usually a golden brown, was a pale gray. Her arms were bandaged, and there was a bright red gash on her cheek. Lowering the railing between them, she leaned over and kissed her daughter. Carefully, she examined the arm where the exploding glass had severed her artery. When she straightened and repositioned the barrier, she stared at Kari until Grant put his hand on her shoulder and slowly turned her toward the door.

"Are there any good restaurants close by?" he asked at the High Street entrance as they waited for a taxi.

"Of course," she said, thinking of Yesterdays for the first time in nearly two days. Although Marianne had been at the hospital, Robyn had not thought of the restaurant. "I'm not very hungry. I don't really want anything to eat."

"Then, I'll see you home."

Robyn nodded. Her head lolled on her neck. Grant put his hand on the small of her back, guiding her down the steps. The taxi arrived, and he helped her into the backseat.

Robyn leaned against the upholstery, her eyes closed. Grant hated to disturb her. "We need your address, Brooke," he whispered.

She was instantly alert. As much as she wanted to fold herself against him, she sat erect.

"This is lovely," Grant said twenty minutes later as they entered the house she and Kari had occupied since coming to Buffalo. A large L-shaped sofa in a soft dusty rose faced the fireplace in her oversized living room. In front of it was a square mahogany cocktail table holding an arrangement of gray and mauve silk flowers. Two wing chairs completed the grouping. At the opposite end of the room was a baby grand piano.

"Thank you," she smiled, somehow glad he liked it. "We find it comfortable."

"It looks more than comfortable." He went to the mantel and lifted a gold-framed photo of a smiling child. Dr. Elliott had been right. He could see how she could twist a man's heart. Except for her eye color, Kari looked nothing like her mother, he thought. Grant looked at the wedding photo on the opposite side of the mantel. He didn't see much resemblance there either.

"My husband," she explained. "He died before Kari was born."

"I'm sorry," Grant said, feeling at a loss of what to say.

Her hands squeezed into fists behind her as Grant compared the doctored wedding photo of her and a man she'd never met to the one of Kari he held in his hand.

"She's got your eyes," he said.

Robyn nodded. And everything else she got from you, she silently amended.

He turned back to Brooke. Grant liked the decor. The room told a lot about its owner. It was cool and serene with a quiet charm. Although the furnishings were modern, the accents revealed a definite traditional flavor. As he looked around further, he saw everything was neatly stored in its proper place, yet there was an air about it which said *you can live here.* He could imagine toys scattered about the carpeted floor or see colored packages radiating from a tall Christmas tree.

It's home. The thought knocked him off guard. He hadn't thought about a home since Robyn died. He'd sold their old house. He couldn't live there without her. Her mother's piano was the only thing he hadn't put in storage, and he couldn't bring himself to sell it. Robyn had loved it too much.

And here was another woman whose placement of inanimate objects had caused him to remember what it was like to live in a home. After the many foster homes he'd lived in before he was twelve, he couldn't remember anything as being permanent, rooted. He was as sure as he could be that this was his idea of what home should look like. He replaced the photo and turned back to Brooke. For a second their eyes locked in a momentary stare. Heat sprang up in the lower regions of his body, a heat he couldn't control. He felt like he was back in high school, but he had turned thirty-seven on his last birthday. Yet, his body was acting as if it had only today learned about puberty. There was no doubt he wanted Brooke. But the signals he got from her were mixed. He felt there was a guard in front of her, someone who edited everything she thought before allowing the words to come from her mouth. He could almost see another presence behind her sad eyes. He wanted to pass through that invisible being and touch the woman behind it.

"Do you play?" He indicated the piano to cover his discomfort. Taking a seat at the keyboard, he ran his fingers lightly across the keys.

"Only enough for my own satisfaction," she lied.

Robyn, sitting at the piano, suddenly intruded. She had played well. Often, her private concerts led to them making love.

Color rose in Robyn's face. She, too, thought of where her piano playing had led. Suddenly, the danger of his presence hit her. It had become natural for her to play the role designed for her, but with the way her emotions danced out of step each time he looked at her, she had to get him out of her life. And before Jacob Winston learned what she'd done.

"I'm not very hungry, Grant," she began in her it's-time-for-you-to-go-tone.

"I understand." He stood, preparing to leave. "Will you be all right?" His voice was quiet, laced with concern.

"I'm fine—really," she reassured him.

After a slight hesitation, he started for the door. Invisible hands squeezed her heart until she thought she'd scream. Robyn clutched her chest, trying to calm it. She reached into herself, searching for some of the courage and reserve that Jacob had promised would be there when she needed it. And she needed it now.

She watched him walking toward the door. The room suddenly seemed bigger, longer. He moved in slow motion, getting smaller as he got closer to the far side of her life. Just a few seconds, she thought. Just a few more seconds and he'd be gone, out of her life. She'd be safe.

"Gr . . . Grant . . ." she stopped him with a stutter. "Don't go."

CHAPTER 3

Jacob hung up the phone and slumped back in his chair. He grabbed his beer and drained the glass bottle. Usually, he enjoyed his beer, but Marianne's call had his stomach churning. Something didn't sit right.

Suddenly, he sat up in his chair as if propelled. His fingers flew over the computer keyboard, racing against an unseen force. Seconds later, he'd passed security and was in the computer of the Center for Disease Control. The records on the screen confirmed what Marianne had told him.

Why didn't he believe it? It was just too coincidental that all the hospitals in the area were out of stock. Jacob didn't like coincidences. He pulled the phone toward him, setting it on his thigh. He dialed the number he knew by heart but hadn't called in years.

"This better be good," a voice gravelly with sleep barked into his ear. Jacob would have smiled if he hadn't been concentrating so hard.

"Carl, this is Jacob," he said.

"I won't ask if you know what time it is."

Jacob could almost see him turning the clock toward himself to check the digital dial.

"It's important, Carl. I need a favor."

"All right what is it?" he asked, seriousness entering his voice.

Carl Logan and Jacob Winston had been partners on the police force. They'd worked homicide in Chicago for six years, until Carl's wife, Amy, was kidnapped and killed by a serial killer who took their investigation personally. Carl had become a computer jockey. Jacob had gone to the

FBI, a different kind of law enforcement. The Cynthia Affair had been his reason for needing a change of location.

"I need you to go and check the blood supply at the center."

"What?" Jacob knew Carl was climbing out of bed. He was the closest thing to a best friend Jacob had. Over the years, the two of them had used their respective skills to help each other whenever they could, and Jacob knew Carl wouldn't let him down. "Why don't I just dial in and check the stock? On second thought, why don't you?"

"I've already done that. It says the supply of AB negative is exhausted."

"And you have reason to believe something different?"

"It's just a hunch." Jacob had no concrete evidence that anything was wrong, just a gnawing feeling in his gut.

"Jacob, we keep extremely accurate—"

"Carl," Jacob stopped him before he began a lecture on the methods of making sure the physical stock matched the records. "This is very important."

"All right, Jacob. I'll go over right now and check it out myself. What are you looking for?"

"AB negative. How much have you got?"

"I'll call you back when I get there. Where are you?"

"Home."

Jacob hung up and waited. Suddenly, everything was quiet. He could hear the crickets outside and the quiet hum of the refrigerator in the kitchen. The clock in the hall, that had been his mother's, chimed out the hour. But the phone did not ring. He stood up and went for another beer, dropping the empty bottle in the recycling container.

There were three bottles in the yellow container before the phone rang. Jacob lunged for it, snatching it off the wall before it finished the first ring.

"Yeah," he said.

"This is really weird, Jacob," Carl said.

"How much have you got?" he asked, trying to control his anxiousness.

"Enough to supply a small war if every casualty was AB negative. None of it's outdated. I'm standing in the refrigerator, and the supply is here. Yet, the machines say we're out. I don't understand."

"Try finding out what happened, and let me know." Jacob knew he didn't have to ask the favor. Carl would search without direction. He couldn't leave a puzzle until all the pieces were in place. "Thanks for your help," Jacob continued. "I owe you one."

"Anytime, partner."

Jacob replaced the receiver and leaned his head against the arm that he had propped on the doorjamb. He'd been tracking anything that might jeopardize Robyn and Kari for five years, but something had started with Robyn's accident. He could feel it. Tomorrow, he'd verify the blood at the other hospitals. But he already knew, before he'd placed one call, that the Crime Network was back in action.

Robyn stood frozen. Grant's hand was on the doorknob when she'd stopped him. She hadn't realized the strangled cry had come from her until Grant turned. For a heartbeat, there was a sign of recognition, then it was gone.

"There isn't much food here," she said. "But the least I can do is make you an omelette and some coffee."

"It sounds wonderful, I'll help," Grant said. A smile lit his face as he came back into the room. Robyn thought she saw relief in his eyes. Maybe she just wanted to see it, she told herself.

"That won't be necessary." She needed time to compose herself and understand why she'd stopped him. She knew it was safer to let him go through the door, yet she'd called him back. It didn't matter that it wasn't a deliberate act. She'd asked him to stay.

"Don't worry," he smiled. "I'm very good in the kitchen."

"I'm sure you are." She knew how much help he could be. Many nights they'd spent, side by side, preparing dinner or loading the dishwasher.

"I am, I promise." He raised his right hand in the Boy Scout salute, then took off his jacket and folded it over the back of the sofa before following Robyn to the kitchen. He stopped short at the door. It was a huge airy room, brightly lit and outfitted for a gourmet cook.

"Maybe I should take that back," he groaned.

Robyn laughed for the first time. Both of them noticed it but neither commented. Filling the coffeepot with water, she poured it into the well of the automatic machine. Her kitchen was a cook's dream. Copper pots gleamed from a rack above the butcher-block counter, two sinks strategically placed for functionality, and a side-by-side refrigerator and freezer still allowed room for free movement.

"I'm sure you'll be able to find the eggs," she said.

This was where her business had begun. She had a degree in history and had thought she'd follow her father into government work, but Jacob steadfastly asserted she could never use it.

"Absolutely everything about Robyn Richards has to be forgotten. She won't exist. Brooke Johnson does not have a degree in history." She could still hear the adamant tone in his voice.

Robyn chose cooking as a career. She loved making art out of food. Since it was a relatively unassuming profession, and Robyn wasn't one to sit around doing nothing, Jacob had few objections.

At first, she and Marianne catered parties and weddings, fashioning elaborate designs with sweetbreads. Fruits and vegetables were transformed into statues. But her trademark was the spectacular one-of-a-kind wedding cake scenes. She met people who recommended her to their friends. Her reputation and fortune grew until she had saved enough money to buy a run-down Victorian mansion that she'd renovated and turned into a restaurant.

Grant found the eggs, and Robyn handed him a bowl and a silver whisk. He began breaking them as she found cheese, onions, peppers, celery, and ham and started dicing them into small pieces. She worked quickly and efficiently.

He watched in amazement at the lightning manner in which she used a knife. "You *will* tell me if you ever decide to use that on me?" he asked lightly. "Should I ask how you learned to use a knife with the skill of a Japanese master chef?"

"There's nothing mysterious about it. I practiced a lot." She smiled at the fun she had playing with him. "I used to own a catering business, now I have a restaurant in town. For a while my partner and I were the only cooks. And practice does . . ." She left the cliché hanging, allowing her proficiency to finish the sentence.

Robyn took the eggs Grant had whisked into a yellow fluff, added the diced vegetables, and then poured them in the omelette pan. Minutes later, they were seated at the breakfast nook where she and Kari usually began their day.

Grant ate hungrily, obviously enjoying his food. Robyn, too, finished a meal she hadn't thought she was hungry enough to eat. They talked quietly about life in Buffalo, the theater, the latest world events. Robyn knew it wasn't important conversation. She also knew he was trying to help her take her mind off Kari. For the most part, it worked until finally all that was left were dirty dishes and memories. She wanted to cry.

"I should call the hospital," she said tears apparent in her voice.

"She'll be fine." Grant put a restraining hand on her wrist. A regiment of electric shocks galloped from where his hand lay on her wrist up to her shoulder. Her eyes found Grant's and held. She pulled her arm away, rubbing it gently to restore normal feeling.

"I'm sorry. I didn't mean to hurt you."

"I'm not hurt," she said a bit too quickly, then tried to hide it by taking a drink from her coffee cup.

"I'm sure Kari's fine. Doctor Elliott promised to call if there was any change in her condition."

"I know. It's just that I feel so helpless." She stood up and began moving the dishes from the table and stacking them in the sink. "If only I'd listened to Kari. She wanted to stay at the beach longer. If only . . ."

Grant came to stand behind her. "Don't do this to yourself." He turned her to face him, dropping his hands quickly. "It was an accident. You can't blame yourself for circumstances."

"I know, but I keep feeling, if only I'd seen the other car . . ."

"It wasn't your fault," he said more forcefully. "There was nothing you could have done to prevent it." She looked at him, her eyes wide and tired. She wanted to step into his arms and let him hold her but she couldn't. "You know, you should get some sleep. You'll feel much better tomorrow." His voice was quiet as if he could no longer argue with her.

"I don't think I could." With Kari in the hospital and Grant within holding distance, she was sure sleep for the night was not an option.

"Why don't you try a hot bath? It will relax you."

"Tonight, I don't think it would work."

He nodded, understanding. "All right, talk to me. Tell me where we know each other from."

Grant's instincts were excellent, yet he didn't need them to tell him Brooke Johnson was familiar. He recognized the tenseness in the way she held her shoulders, the nervous way she wrung her hands, and the way her eyes widened. She dropped her head for a moment. The smell of her shampoo wafted through the air. He knew it, had smelled it before, but where? A millisecond of memory flashed through his mind, but flitted before he could capture or record it.

There was no single thing about her that leaped forward to force his memory, but the collection of small things, like the way she moved, tipped her head to the side, or held her fork when she ate. He wondered where they had met and if she remembered.

"We haven't met before," Robyn told him.

"Doctor Elliott said you gave him my name; told him where to find me."

"Oh," she laughed, turning back to the sink and busying herself restacking dishes that were already stacked. "It's your blood type. I memorized the names and addresses of everyone with Kari's blood type within a four-hundred-mile radius. When Doctor Elliott explained all the local supplies were exhausted or outdated I gave him your name."

Lie number one, Robyn thought. Thank goodness she'd devised a reason for knowing who he was without telling the truth. If he'd asked her to name another donor she'd be hard pressed to think of one. If she'd done something practical like finding the names of possible donors and committing them to memory, Grant would still be in Washington, and she would be inside the protective world Jacob had set up for her. She'd used Kari's blood type as a reason to settle so close to her former husband, but she'd hadn't considered the real need to contact him. When Jacob told her there would be a blood supply if needed, she believed him. It unnerved her that his promise proved untrue.

Robyn turned on the water and opened the dishwasher. Methodically, she began rinsing and placing the soiled dishes in the dishwasher. Her thoughts went back five years to the days after the trial. She'd been blackmailed into this elite prison. She was angry, and Jacob took the brunt of her bereft feelings.

She and Jacob argued over everything: where she would live, what she would look like, even the color of her hair. The two of them were a battle looking for a war. It erupted the night she told him she was pregnant.

The last saucer had been placed in the rack, yet the water ran unheeded over her hands. Jacob had been angry. He'd told her it was against the law to break up families. Robyn hadn't known she was going to have a baby when she chose to go in without Grant. His life had been uprooted too many times, and he'd have to give up flying, a sacrifice she wouldn't want him to make. Yet, it might not have had an impact if it weren't for Project Eagle. After she found the camouflaged microchip, Grant had been forced to tell her about it.

Robyn had regrets, but she knew she'd done the right thing. Without Clarence Christopher's fatherlike influence, she'd have chosen to help her husband and the nine other men being held prisoner in Beirut.

"Brooke, where are you?" Grant reached around her and stopped the flow of water. She snapped back to the present. It had been a long time since thoughts of how she got into the program intruded on her life.

"I'm sorry. I'm tired." She grabbed a paper towel and dried her hands. "Since the accident, I've been at the hospital." She fumbled for something to say. It seemed the past and present were colliding, and she had lost control over what would happen. Why hadn't he just given the blood and let it be flown up? Why did he have to come himself?

"Why don't you get some sleep?"

"Maybe you're right. I think I will take a shower and try to sleep."

"Good idea. Go on. I'll clean these dishes and see myself out."

Robyn hesitated a moment.

"It's all right." He knew she was thinking they had only met. He was a stranger, and how could she leave a strange man in her kitchen and go to bed. "I promise to lock the door behind me."

Robyn was struck by how much she still loved him. She walked to the door, then turned for one last look. "Thank you, Grant. I'll never forget what you've done for Kari. Good-bye."

Robyn stepped into her shower minutes later, hoping the water cascading over her tired body would be enough to wash away the aching need she had for the man downstairs. She hadn't thought her feelings would be this intense. It had been five years, and she had been out with several men since Grant. One of them she'd actually considered marrying. She had thought there would be a dullness to her feelings if she ever saw Grant again, but she was wrong. Her feelings had not changed. Her love was as bright and new as it had been when she saw him standing at the bottom of the stairs in Las Vegas. Her heart beat just as fast now. Her throat was dry and her hands were as cold as when he'd asked her to marry him.

She thought of him washing dishes as the two of them had done countless times. She smiled remembering his playful nature as he'd teased her that they'd still be washing dishes together when they reached sixty and their children were grown and gone. A lump rose in Robyn's throat at the bittersweet irony of the situation. Grant was in her kitchen, five years after she'd walked out of his life.

Tears mingled with the running water. This was her fault. It wasn't that Grant was downstairs because of the accident. It had begun years ago, when she had almost begged to get the part-time job at the FBI while she was in college. A fresh batch of tears racked her body. It was impossible to know at the time, but her happiness that day had paved the road to the misery that she felt pouring from her body like the water spurting from the showerhead.

After graduation, she was offered a permanent position as an analyst in the Major Crimes Bureau. She worked hard and had a good memory. It was because of her memory she realized she had seen a dead man, a man presumed dead. Several witnesses, who claimed they had seen the body of this international assassin, had reported him dead. Word had it that he was killed when trying to execute a contract against a drug lord. But she had seen him—alive—at a Washington restaurant. She had instantly recognized him when he bumped into her as she made her way to the ladies' room.

Four years later, she sat across the courtroom and identified him as Alex Jordan, code name: the Devil. She'd known his life as well as she knew her own, including the assassinations credited to him, like the baffling case in Sicily where six American men had died inside a room that had been locked from the inside.

Alex Jordan had only been the beginning. Everything about him made her suspicious, and every piece of information she uncovered drew her closer and closer to her own agency. It was a Pandora's box and she had sprung the lock.

The shower had gone from hot to tepid when Robyn's memory returned her to the present. Reaching for the crystal dials, she switched them off. The plush white towel that soaked the water from her body was thick and soft. It was not at all like the scratchy one she'd used in the dingy motel room only weeks after Alex Jordan was killed, and McKenzie Cranford was exposed as a mole in the department.

Grant watched Brooke go up the stairs. She had a strange mixture of hurt and trust in her eyes. Trust had won, and somehow that made him feel good. Naturally, she assumed he'd fly back to Washington. What else could he do? He didn't know her, yet he felt a strange pull toward her. His body wanted hers. He resisted the tightening of his stomach muscles that the thought produced. But more than that he also wanted to get to know her. He wanted to know what made her eyes so sad. And why did they give off such ambivalent messages? But the feeling that had passed between them when he touched her was shocking. He knew it shot from his fingers into her arm with the same erratic force that scampered up his own arm. Even if she hadn't rubbed it away, he'd have known she felt it.

When he finished the few dishes she hadn't rinsed, he went back to the living room. It was still in the same neat order he'd left it, but he felt he knew it better on second sight. This time he lifted a picture of Brooke, who smiled from a frame which matched the one of Kari. He noticed her eyes. They held the same sadness he'd noticed when he'd first seen her standing in the backlight of the hospital window. She reminded him of someone else, but he couldn't quite focus on who. But of one thing he was certain, Brooke Johnson *would* see him again.

He liked the feelings she evoked in him. He hadn't felt them in a long time. Not since that day he was finally home, back on U.S. soil and moments away from seeing his wife. His best friend had pulled him away from the throngs of reporters, who were shouting question after question about his release, to tell him there had been an accident. His beloved Robyn, on her way to the airfield to greet him, was in a car that had collided with an oil tanker. In his mind, images of billowing black smoke spiraling above the city and the ensuing fire that had burned her body beyond recognition crystallized as vividly as they had done on that clear day in April five years ago.

He replaced the gold-framed photograph and hooked his jacket over his shoulder, preparing to leave. He listened to the silence and assumed Brooke had fallen asleep. His hand was on the doorknob, before it occurred to him to look in on her and make sure she was all right.

He found her asleep in a room at the top of the stairs with muted yellow walls and beneath a blue-and-white bedspread. She looked like a little girl. Feelings he thought were long buried surfaced, making his body warm. Suddenly, he was a knight in shining armor, standing ready to protect her against whoever had taken the light from her eyes and replaced it with an ever-present sadness. Carefully, he replaced the coverlet over shoulders that he had to resist caressing. She stirred slightly but didn't wake.

Closing the door quietly, he stepped into Kari's adjacent room. Switching on the light, he found the room to be a bright, happy one with pink curtains and stuffed toys filling every available corner. One grouping had six baby bears sitting around a toy table. Miniature cups and saucers sat in front of each bear, indicating an end of a good meal. Grant thought of the impromptu meal he'd just had. It was simple but satisfying.

A hutch with children's books graced one corner. He picked up *Cat in the Hat,* remembering he'd had this book before his parents were killed, and he was left alone. He put it back. The top shelf had more stuffed bears on it. There was a model of an old train. Inside were two bears dressed as nurses. They had their backs to each other as if they were walking in different directions. Another arrangement had seven bears dressed as knights. They were lined up on a replica of the Brooklyn Bridge.

Above his head was a shelf which circled the room. Books and toys stood behind a small, pink newel post fence. Grant smiled as he picked up a small brown teddy bear and placed it on the shelf overhead with others of its size and color. As he turned, he noticed the photo albums. Pulling one from its place, he flipped through it, finding the pages filled with pictures of the child he had seen but once.

Robyn, too, had loved taking pictures. He remembered building her a darkroom in their basement. She'd spend hours there, developing the film she'd taken of everything from flowers to portraits. He hadn't seen it in years, but the person who took these pictures had the same style as Robyn. He noticed how well each one had been framed before the shutter opened to freeze the moment. Anyone of them could have *made the wall,* Robyn's phrase for the best pictures. "This one," she'd say. "This one makes the wall."

Grant wanted to look closer at them. He took several of the albums downstairs so the light wouldn't filter under Brooke's door and disturb her.

When Robyn woke, sunlight streamed through her windows. She looked at the clock next to her bed. Kari would be in anytime now, bouncing on the bed saying, "I'm hungry." Robyn rolled over smiling, then memory flooded her consciousness. Kari was in the hospital. Rapidly, she jerked herself upright and dialed the direct number to Dr. Elliott's office. The nurse assured her Kari was all right. She had slept comfortably through the night, awakened briefly at six AM, but immediately had fallen asleep again.

Robyn felt a new optimism as she pulled on the matching robe to her full-length gown and pushed her feet into her slippers before heading downstairs to start the coffee maker. Afterward, she would dress and go to the hospital. She wanted to be there the next time Kari woke. Mentally, she made a note to call Marianne and Will, her closest neighbor and Kari's surrogate grandfather. They had taken turns staying with her. She would check in with Marianne at the restaurant. But first the coffee.

Halfway down the stairs, her heart leapt into her mouth. Grant was still here. He slept silently on the long side of the sofa. The coffee table was scattered with volumes of Kari's baby pictures. For a long moment, she stared dumbfounded. Her hands with a strength unknown to her gripped the wooden banister.

She didn't know how long she stood there nailed to the step or what ghosts carried her across the room, but she found herself wedged between the coffee table and the sofa. Slowly, she dropped to her knees. Grant didn't move, but Robyn's world tilted. Suddenly, she was Robyn Richards, and this was her husband.

"Grant," she said in a small, hoarse voice barely audible. She swallowed the painful knot in her throat and tried his name again. He didn't stir. Robyn savored the unguarded moment. She enjoyed watching him sleep. For the first time in five years, she could gaze upon a real person, not the elusive image she was forced to create during the long nights she endured alone. But why was he here? What made him stay? For a moment, fear that he knew who she was crept into her brain. She rejected the notion immediately. After the elaborate plastic surgery and implants nothing about her face physically was the same. Jacob wouldn't allow it.

Grant shifted. His arm fell off the sofa and into her lap. Robyn caught her breath sure her presence would wake him. After a moment, she relaxed, sitting back on her legs. She stared at him, remembering their honeymoon and the nights he'd wake her when he came in from a late flight. A dreamy smile curved her lips. When his hands moved to her arm, she froze. His eyes opened but didn't focus. "Robyn, I love you." She knew he was dreaming, but when he pulled her into his arms, her body had already decided to go. His mouth found hers in a soft brushing motion. Tentatively, it probed, tasted, cajoled. Whatever metaphysical forces kept time and space continuing in a forward motion seemed to have stopped as he continued his slow exploration. One hand found its way into her hair, combing through it with long sensitive strokes that ended in gentle caresses against her shoulders. Warm waves, like the gentle lapping of a calm sea, washed over her melting body.

Then, with sudden swiftness, passion flared, and his tongue pushed past her teeth to taste the wet nectar inside. Her body arched, straining closer to him. Arms she'd forgotten were hers wrapped around his frame. Excitement flowed through her fingers as she felt the play of sinew, bone, and muscle that rippled in response to her searching hands. His chest crushed her full breasts in a wonderfully erotic pain as he shifted position and slid to the floor. Fervently, he ravished her mouth, her neck, and her shoulders. Dark brown, erect nipples pushed back against him with unbridled restraint. Her head fell back, allowing him access to the full column of her neck. Torrents of heat invaded her body.

She felt herself dissolving into him. She wouldn't be able to stand this assault on her emotions much longer without screaming for him to make love to her. Already her body was hot and longed for him to push her back into the soft carpeting and give her the fulfillment she'd waited five years to experience again.

CHAPTER 4

"Oh, my God!" Grant said forcing his mouth from hers. He slumped against her as he buried his face in her hair. "I'm sorry, Brooke. I had no intention of doing that."

Robyn's breath came in ragged gulps. She was conscious of everything about her body, even feeling the blood rush through her veins. She tried to speak, but opening her mouth only provided an additional vessel for the air she craved. Grant rolled away from her, but the confined space kept them touching from chest to toe. Finally, control returned to her muscles. Robyn pushed herself up.

"You mentioned your wife last night." Her voice was breathless, and she rested her head on the sofa. "It's only natural you would dream of her." Forcing herself to look at him, she continued, "When I woke you, you thought I was her." She was amazed how calm her voice sounded, almost clinical.

"You must be the most amazing woman in the world."

"Why?"

"Anyone else would have slapped my face for calling her by someone else's name and kissing her the way I kissed you."

Color crept up Robyn's face to her ears. She hadn't completely recovered from being lost in his arms, and his comment brought back graphic images of them from moments before. "I thought you were asleep when you did that."

"I was, but you weren't."

"I didn't . . . I mean . . ." She dropped her eyes, at a loss as to what to say.

"Why did you let me go on?" The softness in his voice made her want to tell him the truth.

Robyn looked him in the eye for a silent second, then dropped her gaze to her hands. She couldn't tell him she was his wife and wanted nothing more than to be held in his arms and smothered with his kisses.

"It's all right," he paused, lifting her chin with one finger. "You don't have to answer. But I do apologize for calling you Robyn."

"Apology accepted." She managed a smile. "Now, how about some breakfast?"

"Sounds good to me." He helped her up, and they entered the kitchen together. "Have you called the hospital?"

"Yes, Kari is doing well." Robyn busied herself preparing the food. She usually sat with Kari, laughing during their breakfast ritual and listening to her excited conversation about the day before. Since beginning life as Brooke Johnson, widow with child, she'd changed significantly.

"Ah, maybe I'll get to see the real girl before I go back. I guess by the look of the living room, you noticed I glanced through a few albums."

"I must admit I did notice one or two." She laughed, realizing it seemed like years since she'd last laughed.

"I planned just to look in on you and leave, but then I saw the photo albums. My wife was an amateur photographer. The pictures reminded me of . . ." He stopped as if the memory was too painful. "Anyway I must have fallen asleep."

"It's all right. I don't mind you talking about her. Robyn, right?"

"Yes, she liked photography. Did you take the pictures in the albums?"

"It's a hobby of mine. Unfortunately, I don't have much time to really get into it."

Grant was quiet a moment. Robyn was sure he was thinking of the Robyn he lost. A pang of guilt hit her. "Tell me about her?" Robyn asked, putting a cup of coffee in front of him, but keeping out of his line of vision as she continued frying bacon and eggs. "How long were you married."

He lifted the morning potion to his lips and tentatively tested the hot liquid. "Two years. We were technically still honeymooners. We had a house in Washington. She'd done all the decorating herself."

Robyn remembered that house. She could still see the beige curtains that hung from the windows of their bedroom. On breezy days, the wind played hide-and-seek with them. Grant had found the house before they were married, just off Connecticut Avenue. She smiled, remembering the two of them walking to the Washington Hilton for Sunday brunch, then her face clouded when she thought how short their marriage had been.

"Do you still live there?" Robyn dragged her thoughts back to the present. Her eyes were smarting, but she kept them averted from his by giving her full attention to the work she was performing. Jacob hadn't given her any information on Grant. He said a clean break was best for all concerned.

"Not anymore. I tried it for a while, but there were too many memories. I kept expecting her to walk into the bedroom or find her in the kitchen at dinnertime. Finally, I sold the house and moved into a condo."

Robyn's heart sank. She had imagined him living in their house. But now she was glad he had moved. He was only thirty-seven, a virile man. She'd hate to think of him and another woman in the house where they had shared so much love.

Giving him a plate and taking the opposite chair, she said, "You must have loved her a great deal."

"I did. I admit it. What we had in the two short years is more than other couples get in decades of marriage."

Something caught in Robyn's throat. For a moment she couldn't speak.

"How did she die?"

It was a question Robyn had asked Jacob, but his answer had been she didn't *need to know.* She could still hear his cocky reply. "The details of Mrs. Grant Richards's demise are on a need-to-know basis, and you do not need to know." End of discussion, file closed. No manner of coercion could get him to release any details that he had not been specifically ordered to divulge.

"She died in an automobile accident. A plane I was flying was hijacked to Beirut. We were held prisoner for five months." He touched the scar above his eye. Robyn noticed the gesture. "On the day I returned to Washington, the car Robyn was riding in hit an oil tanker."

Robyn flinched. All the air threatened to leave her body, but she forced herself under control. For months, she had taken classes, brainwashing lessons, that taught her how to act and react under unexpected situations. So that was how they'd done it. The story they told him must have included her body being burned beyond recognition. Oh, Jacob, she thought wryly, you are thorough.

"Excuse me," Grant interrupted her thoughts. "I didn't mean to surprise you."

"That's not it. I'm so sorry for you. It must have been terrible, being a prisoner. Then, just when you were free, to have your wife die when trying to reach you." She reached across the table and took his hand. The static electricity which began snapping along her arm wasn't at all unpleasant. His hand tightened.

"You're a very perceptive lady. I like you. And there's more meaning in that phrase than the words convey."

Robyn took her hand away, raising her coffee to her mouth. It was cold. She took both cups and moved to refill them. "Do I remind you of her?" she asked when she sat down again. She wasn't afraid of the answer. The changes made to her included everything—even her voice. The implants in her face elevated her voice while eliminating the almost husky quality she'd had when she and Grant first met. However, of all the alterations forced on her, she did like her new voice. Now, when she sang each night in the lounge she owned, she discovered her range had been increased by several high notes.

"Not much." Grant was saying. "Seeing you yesterday, I was taken by your hair color, but today I don't think it looks like Robyn's at all.

"But I can see a warm, sensitive, and sad person." He went on with her character analysis.

"I'd better get dressed now." She could feel the attraction he had for her. She knew it couldn't go on, wouldn't be allowed to grow and blossom into the love she'd locked safely away never to be taken out and held again. "If you'd like to clean up, there's a bathroom Kari's grandfather uses when he stays the night. I believe he keeps a razor there." Robyn remembered she still needed to call Will.

Grant's hand scratched across the stubble on his chin. "I could use a shave."

She showed him to the room that Will sometimes used when he spent the night with Kari, then went to her own room to dress.

Just as she was putting the finishing touches on her makeup, she heard the doorbell.

Robyn slipped the remaining earring through her ear and pushed her feet into the blue pumps which matched her navy suit. She was halfway down the stairs when she saw Will and Grant locked in a bear hug.

They separated but grasped hands and shook them like two ex-soldiers at a reunion. "I haven't seen you in ages. What the hell are you doing here?" Will asked. Robyn noticed that the corners of Will's eyes were moist.

Grant explained Kari's need for blood. "And how do you happen to be here?"

"Been retired now seven years next May. I got tired of wandering about the world and settled here," Will explained.

"Hello, Will," Robyn interrupted, as she reached the bottom step.

"It's a small world, Brooke." The smile on Grant's face showed obvious happiness at finding a lost friend. "This man is a near father to me."

William McAdams was a six foot, silver-haired retired colonel from the U.S. Army. He was Robyn's closest neighbor and had proved to be an anchor after he moved in next door last year. Will was there to fix any inconvenience that needed attention. He'd taken care of Kari when Robyn spent late nights at Yesterdays. Kari thought of him as her grandfather, and Will encouraged it by allowing her to call him "Graffie." Robyn remembered the long conversation her three-year-old had had with Will before they settled on "Graffie" as a name.

Kari was very proud of her Graffie and introduced him to all of her friends at nursery school on Grandparents' Day. Will, too, reveled in delight at having a small child around. He had three married children who did not visit often, and none of them had children or seemed to be interested in making him a grandfather.

Robyn was grateful for his help and attention when she needed a friend. She also thought of Will as the father she had lost.

"I called the hospital, Brooke." Will addressed her. "They told me Kari's much better this morning. I came by to give you a lift."

In minutes, they were seated in Will's LeSabre. Robyn took the backseat to allow the men to talk without having to crane their heads over the front seat. She sat quietly, listening to them. Something about this meeting seemed out of place. Why had Grant never mentioned Will when they were married? Even though their courtship was whirlwind, they were married for two years. In all that time, he'd told her only about his Aunt Priscilla, with whom he finally went to live, and about a special friend he called Ace, but not that there was a man close enough to him to be his father.

Stop it, Robyn. She braked her thoughts. This is some of Jacob's brainwashing filtering into your mind. There is probably a simple, logical explanation for Grant's silence. And she'd be interested in finding out what it was.

When they reached the hospital, Robyn went directly to ICU. Kari opened her eyes as she came through the door. "Mommy," she called, opening her small arms and reaching for her mother. Robyn fought tears. She'd thought she'd never hear that word again.

"Good morning, darling. How do you feel?" She reached over the restraining rail and took her hands.

"My head hurts."

"Well, it won't hurt for long. Doctor Elliott is here, and I'm sure he'll want to know everything that bothers you."

Kari smiled. Robyn knew she liked the pediatrician. Kari was very pale and weak. Robyn smoothed the wisp of hair that sleep had loosened from her braids.

"Can I have something to drink?" Kari whispered.

Robyn looked around at the nurse. Almost imperceptibly, she shook her head. "Doctor Elliott will be right in," the white-clad woman whispered.

As if on cue the tall brown-haired man entered. His right hand held onto the stethoscope hanging from his neck. "And how is my favorite patient this morning?"

Robyn couldn't help smiling at the exchange. To think, Kari was almost dead yesterday, and this morning she was alive and active as if the accident had never happened.

Dr. Elliott examined her silently, before asking questions that Kari answered in her clear soprano voice. When he finished, he smiled and told her she could have some juice and a light breakfast of Jell-O.

"That's great, Doc," Kari agreed but appeared sleepy. "I like Jell-O."

"I'm going to tell the nurse to give you something for your headache. It will make you sleepy, but sleep is good for you right now."

Kari frowned. "Can I eat the Jell-O first." A pout that would melt any heart crept across Kari's face.

"Yes, darling. You can eat the Jell-O, first." Dr. Elliott ruffled her hair and winked at her.

When he left, Robyn told Kari about Grant bringing the blood she needed and how he wanted to meet her. For a moment, she stepped out to allow him to visit Kari briefly.

He came back smiling. "We're blood relatives now." Two pairs of eyes looked at him. "I had to show her my bandage. She's a wonderful kid."

"I know. No granddaughter of mine would be anything else," Will said, he passed a stunned-faced Grant and went into the intensive care unit.

"Will is not your father." Grant made a statement, turning his attention to Robyn.

"Will is a very close neighbor and the best friend I've got. He's like a father to me and a grandfather to Kari. But, in actuality, we are not related."

"He does have that kind of effect on people."

In the life she'd been given, Will had no part to play. "Kari and I met him on his moving-in day. That's what Kari called it," she explained. "I liked him on sight." He was the first real person to come into her life since Grant's buddy, David, and her friend, Susan, had dealt her the heart-crushing blow that Grant was being held in a Beirut prison. She supposed she grabbed hold of Will as an anchor. They had been family ever since. "He's been a constant help whenever I've needed him." She finished. "How do you two happen to know each other?"

"I grew up with his family. We all lived in the same neighborhood. Will was a father to all of us, especially the ones prone to trouble."

"You were prone to trouble?"

"Oh, yes. My parents were killed when I was seven. For five years, I went from one foster home to another."

Robyn knew this. Grant had told her about his Aunt Priscilla. She loved the old woman and remembered how they relied on each other for strength during the five long months of Grant's captivity. "Finally I went to live with my mother's aunt, a woman I'd never met," he continued. "She was too old to handle an active teenager. So, like most boys raised by a single parent, I had more freedom than kids with both parents. Will would pull rank whenever he thought I was getting out of hand. Now, I thank him for keeping me on track. I think it made me a better man."

"How come you lost touch?"

"I was flying by then. Will's children married and left. His wife died. He was reassigned to the Philippines. I was flying the New York to London route. Our lives got busy. We just forgot to write. We lost touch." He hunched his shoulders and spread his hands in a gesture of unexplained reasoning. "I did hear a few years ago that his son from his first marriage had died. I never did get the details."

Will joined them after Grant's comment, preventing Robyn from saying she hadn't known about a son. "Kari's asleep," he said, taking a seat next to Robyn. "I'm sure she'll be out of danger soon."

"I can't wait for her to be well and back at home, playing with her stuffed animals and pestering me to take her to the park."

"I'm sure it won't be long before that happens," Grant assured her. "Unfortunately, I'm afraid I have to leave now. I have to be back in Washington this afternoon."

Robyn's eyes met his directly. She steeled her reflexes so as not to give away the turmoil erupting inside her. This was the last time she'd get to see him. And it was a stolen moment. She'd seized the prolonged interlude that she knew had to end sooner or later.

"Will, could you give me a ride to the airport?" he asked.

"Of course. I'll get the car and meet you at the main entrance." Then, directing his glance to Robyn, Will told her he'd be back to pick her up.

Grant stood, nodding at Will as he left them.

Robyn left her seat to walk to the window she'd stood before nearly twenty-four hours earlier. The pale blue walls were designed to be soothing. For her, they were anything but, although outwardly her appearance could have rivaled that of the best secret agent.

"Grant," she began hesitantly. "I . . . Kari wouldn't be alive without you." She heard the unintentional double meaning in her words. "We'll never forget you."

He came up behind her, taking her shoulders and turning her around to face him. "I want to see you again."

"No, Grant, it isn't a good idea."

"Why not? Is there someone else?"

"Someone else? No, there's no one else." No one except Jacob Winston and any number of hit men, courtesy of Alex Jordan.

"Then why?"

"I can't explain it. Let's just say I'm busy. I have a restaurant to run and a daughter to care for. There's no place in my life right now for a man."

"That's not what your kiss said this morning."

Color began to steal under Robyn's skin tone. With incredible control, she forced it to stop before it broke through the neckline of the white tube top she wore beneath her suit jacket.

"You weren't kissing me. It was Robyn you held in your arms. Maybe the man I held wasn't you."

Grant was stunned. "You just said there wasn't anyone else."

"Even though there isn't, I have reasons."

"What reasons?"

"I can't explain them."

"You're a real puzzle, Brooke Johnson. I'll admit you're doing things to me I'd forgotten existed between a man and a woman. I can't walk away with no hope of seeing you again without knowing why."

"Please, Grant. You've only known me one day. We shared a kiss—a kiss that I enjoyed fully and without reservation. But it was only a kiss. It's not like we're in love."

Robyn didn't recognize her own voice. Was that controlled speech coming from her? Was she telling this man, whom she loved with her very breath, that she didn't want to see him again and not falling to pieces?

His shoulders dropped. The hands gripping her arms fell to his sides. "Good-bye, Brooke Johnson." He turned to leave.

"Fair winds, Grant Richards," she said.

"Fair winds, Mrs. Rich—" he answered automatically.

Abruptly, he stopped. Both of them stared at each other. Grant's eyes widened in surprise. Robyn steeled her expression. She knew it had been a mistake, but the words were out before she could stop them. It was an expression they had used to say good-bye whenever he had had a flight.

"Why did you say that?" he asked, coming to stand in front of her.

She made herself giggle. "You'll laugh if I tell you."

His features relaxed. "I promise I won't."

Robyn hesitated just long enough to make it seem as if she was embarrassed. "I heard it in a movie. It was about a ship captain and a Russian princess. Whenever he left her to go to sea, she'd wish him 'fair winds.' " She paused a moment. "You remind me of the captain."

Robyn gave him a tentative smile. Her acting was better than she thought. She hoped that it would work and that he would buy her story.

Suddenly, he smiled. He and Robyn had seen that movie. And they'd picked up the phrase as their personal message. He was sure it was because she reminded him of Robyn that made her comment suspect.

"Well, fair winds," he said.

"Fair winds," she repeated softly.

Grant turned abruptly, leaving her alone in the room. The same quiet rush of air that foretold his arrival accompanied his departure. Robyn sank onto one of the sofas. Her legs had grown weak with the effort of keeping her body erect and now refused to support her frame any longer. The tight rein she held over her emotions fractured, then crumpled. She buried her head on her knees and softly cried.

"Tell me about her, Will?" Grant asked, as Will drove expertly through the light traffic on the expressway.

"I met the two of them a little over a year ago when I moved into the house next to them. What in particular do you want to know about her?"

"Everything."

"Ah, ha, she's got ya, huh?" Will teased.

"Never could hide anything from you." Grant smiled. "You've still got a mind like an active volcano." Grant knew Will was remembering a conversation they'd had years ago when he was a young boy in which he vowed never again to let a girl get under his skin. This was after Mary Beth Armstrong dumped him for the captain of the football team.

"I'm afraid there isn't a lot I can tell you. She doesn't talk much about herself."

"I gathered that. This morning I told her all about Robyn and Beirut, but I don't know anything about her except that she has a daughter with a rare blood type and that she owns a restaurant."

"Robyn? Beirut?"

Grant relayed his story. Years had separated them, but he still felt close to Will.

"My God! I didn't even know that you had married. When I retired, I took a long cruise, went to the Caribbean. It was almost a year before I returned. I didn't read any newspapers or watch television while I was there. I knew about the hostages. The papers were full of them for years, but I never heard about your capture or release."

"It's ancient history now." Grant shrugged off memories of his captivity. He didn't want to go into the hardship it had imposed on his life. He knew Will understood that a man could not go through the experience without it having an impact on his life. "And in the last five years, I've learned to live with Robyn's death."

"And now, Brooke." Will was entering Williamsville. Grant noticed the small black-and-white sign that strained against the wind created by the constant flow of cars moving at the fifty-five mile an hour legal speed limit.

"I asked to see her again. She said there was no one else, but refused me."

"Did she say why?" Will glanced sideways at him.

Grant noticed a change in Will. He was leaning closer to Grant as though probing for specific information. "She said she didn't have room in her life for a man."

"Is that all?"

"No, she said there were other reasons, but she wouldn't explain what they were."

"In the years I've known her, all I can tell you is she had a husband, Ensign Cameron Johnson, U.S. Navy. He died of an embolism on his way to the naval base at San Diego. He had the same rare blood as Kari."

"Kari almost died under the same circumstances. No wonder she keeps a list." Grant whispered the last. He saw Will's frown. "Brooke has memorized a list of people with Kari's blood type. It's essentially how I came to be here." There was that subtle interest coming from Will again. "Will, is there something you're not telling me?"

"What do you mean?"

"Twice, now, when I've repeated something, you've reacted as if it were a surprise."

Will was quiet for a moment. Grant knew he was making up his mind whether he should tell him something. "I just wonder why, if Brooke knew the names of several people with the same type, she waited so long to tell Doctor Elliott." He related the search for Kari's blood type.

"There's something else." Will frowned. "I was in military intelligence a long time, and I can see things the average person would miss."

"You think she's hiding something?" Grant shifted to look at his friend.

"I'm not sure. I can't quite focus on anything specific. It's the way she talks about her past. As if she had learned it, not lived it."

"What are you saying? You're losing me."

"I don't know what I'm saying, and believe me I'm lost, too. But it's like Cameron Johnson is made of cardboard. If I hadn't actually checked him out, I'd say the man never existed or at the very least Brooke never knew him."

"But why would she make up something like that?"

"I haven't a clue. I don't know that she did make it up, but I can tell you that Brooke is a smart cookie. I've dealt with some pretty ingenious characters in my career, and I'd match Brooke against any of them. She thinks well on her feet. When I talk to her, I feel like she analyzes every word she plans to say before she allows it to escape her mouth. She's always on guard—against what or whom I can't tell you."

It was strange that Will's assessment was the same as his own. He, too, felt that Brooke planned her words before saying them. "Where did she live before coming here?"

"Atlanta, Georgia."

"Was Cameron with her there?"

"No, he died five years ago, just before Kari was born."

"Kari was born in Atlanta?"

"Yes."

"What about before Atlanta?"

"Texas. It's all there in its proper place. There is nothing that can't be traced. Her entire life is available through public information sources. Like I said, it's nothing that you can pick out. Just in talking to her you get facts, no stories from childhood, no anecdotes on life in general."

"Will, you worked in intelligence. Are you sure you're not making more out of this than there is?"

"Maybe, maybe not. She's a mystery. I guess it's the training in me, seeing spies where none exist."

"Come on, Will. Spies?" Grant grunted a laugh.

"I won't be that melodramatic. I don't think she's a spy."

"Good. But why would someone leave the warmth of Atlanta to move to snow country?"

"I asked her that. Her answer was that she likes snow." He paused. "It's true. I've seen her walking after a heavy snowfall. Once she even fell down like a child and created angels in a fresh drift."

Grant smiled at the image of Brooke's dark hair and her hourglass figure, which her suit fit like a custom-made glove, contrasted against the whiteness of newly fallen snow. He must drag his thoughts away from her body. It made him harden just thinking of her.

No matter what she said, he had to see her again. She'd awakened something in him, and even though it was Robyn he'd begun kissing, he was fully aware of the woman in his arms long before he broke off the hold she had on him. And she, too, had been affected by the kiss. She had lain against him for several exquisite minutes, her breath ragged, her body out of control.

"Grant, I love Brooke and Kari as if they were part of my own family." Will's voice pulled his attention back to the present. "I'd never do anything to hurt them. Brooke has already suffered through a deep hurt."

"I know, I can see it in her eyes." Grant remembered the photograph he'd held. The saddest eyes he'd ever seen had stared back from a face smiling at an unseen camera. "Did she ever say who caused it?"

"No, and I never asked. She's a fiercely independent woman."

Grant agreed. "I could tell that by the way we had to practically carry her out of the hospital to get her to rest."

Will paused a moment. "Don't get me wrong, Grant. I don't mean to sound as if Brooke is hiding anything more than any other person. It's just that she has boundaries she's erected. I'm careful to stay on my side."

"What do you think I should do about them?" They had reached the airport entrance. Will stopped the car at the light. When it switched from red to green, he guided the powerful vehicle into the airport complex, following the directed paths to the terminal entrance. Parking in front of the automatic glass doors, he faced Grant.

"I can't answer that one, Grant. What do you feel?"

What did he feel? Grant turned the question over in his mind. He wasn't sure how he felt. He only knew that she'd awakened something in him and that he liked it. She was the first woman in five years whom he wanted to see again. And she made him hotter than hell. He didn't know where a relationship with Brooke Johnson would lead, but he was certainly going to find out.

CHAPTER 5

Jacob stared at the Capitol through the windows of his office in the J. Edgar Hoover Building on Pennsylvania Avenue. His desk was cluttered with reports that he needed to go over. Yet, he wasn't in the mood for them. Usually, he had no problem with his work. He even liked it. Marianne had left but a week ago. In the last year, her departures had left him feeling lazy, and he had difficulty concentrating. He attributed it to his having worked almost nonstop for the entire weekend, but the truth was the pint-size redhead got under his skin. He'd been uneasy since Sunday—since Marianne had flown back to Buffalo. She'd been reporting regularly for four years, yet something about this time was different. He couldn't put his finger on the cause, but the small redhead had held something back.

It was her eyes. Jacob was accustomed to reading what people meant by the way they moved their hands or shifted in their chairs. But the most expressive feature in all human nature was the eyes. Marianne's were large and brown. They twinkled when she smiled and filled with tears when she was sad. Jacob had seen many moods cross her face over the years, but this weekend's had no predecessor.

Jacob stood up, pushing the curtains aside and pulling the miniblinds to the top of the window. Absently, he toyed with the cord. Traffic below hummed its afternoon song as taxis and cars vied for strategic positions along the wide thoroughfare. Then, her call last night had unnerved him. It was possible that all the blood supplies in the area were exhausted, but he didn't buy that. Not after talking to Carl.

He looked at the white cord still in his hand as if it could answer his questions. Reports on his desk confirmed there was AB negative blood on the shelves of several hospitals in Buffalo, yet all their computers reported it as exhausted or outdated. Someone was manipulating the situation. Jacob had to find out who and how.

Maybe he should call Marianne. He checked his watch. She'd be at the restaurant by now. It was just past noon. She'd be too busy to talk, and Jacob didn't know what he wanted to ask.

Maybe tonight, he thought, maybe he could ask her what she hadn't told him before he dropped her at the airport. By tonight he'd have had more time to analyze the reports on the network. Maybe he would have something for her to watch out for. But more important, maybe he could find out what it was she wasn't telling him.

Dropping the cord, Jacob sat down and pulled the Jordan file in front of him. "Eyes Only" was stenciled across the manila folder. He opened it, reading the top page. A description of the hit man along with a 5" x 7" color photo. He was holding the photo when his office door was pushed inward.

"Jacob." Clarence Christopher strolled unannounced into his office. The director of the FBI was a man in his fifties with sparkling blue eyes and silver hair. He looked more like an aging screen star than the keeper of the national security of the United States. And he was Jacob's friend. "Are you free for lunch?"

"Of course," Jacob said, eying the director. Jacob often ate at his desk while he read the hundreds of pieces of paper that crossed it daily. "Is there something on your mind?" Jacob was straightforward.

"Yes, I thought I'd get your ideas over a meal."

Jacob quickly closed the files and locked them in his office safe, wondering what would bring his old friend to his office. Clarence Christopher and Jacob Winston went back to Jacob's days on the Chicago Police Force. It had been Clarence who brought him into the FBI after Cynthia was killed, but it was rare for him to show up without announcement.

Twenty minutes later, a taxi had whisked them through the cobblestone streets of Georgetown to O'Donnell's Restaurant on Wisconsin Avenue. Throughout the delicious meal of scallops in cream sauce and a tossed salad with a spicy mustard dressing, Clarence spoke of his family, the humid Washington weather, and the National Gallery's acquisition of a Rodin sculpture.

Jacob knew it wasn't his practice to discuss FBI business openly in restaurants. "Everywhere there are ears" had been a constant caution when he went through the training fifteen years ago. He also knew whatever the reason for the impromptu meal it had to be of national importance.

Jacob sat still but he was getting anxious. He wasn't used to holding back, and this small talk had gone on long enough. He wanted to know what Clarence wanted to tell him.

But he was kept waiting until the check was paid and they left the famous sea food house. Instead of calling or hailing a passing taxi, Clarence turned left and began walking.

"Do you remember the Alex Jordan case from five years ago?" Clarence asked when they reached the corner.

Jacob visibly tensed. "Yes," he nodded.

"There was a woman who uncovered the Crime Network."

"Robyn Richards," Jacob supplied.

"She testified at the trial. In fact, she was the prime witness against Jordan and his assassination network."

Jacob nodded again, not knowing where this was going.

"As I remember it, she went into the program."

"Correct," Jacob said, uncomfortable at Clarence's probing. "Is there a problem with Mrs. Richards?" Jacob had had many problems with Robyn over the years, but none of them had ever made their way to the director of the FBI.

"I'm not sure." Clarence stepped off the curb at the end of the street. "This morning I got a report that someone had been in the files."

"What files?" He hadn't had any such report.

"The Jordan case files."

Jacob knew he meant the deeply hidden, sealed files.

"I got no word of this. Do you think it was a hacker, who found his way in?"

"I don't think we can take that chance."

Jacob knew he wouldn't even if Clarence offered that option. He'd protected Robyn Richards for five years, and he wasn't about to stop until he was sure every member of the crime syndicate had been caught and put behind bars.

"Who do you think it was?"

"I read the Jordan files this morning. Apparently, Mrs. Richards went into the program, because there was a missing link to the network. I think the link has surfaced, but he's a shrewd operator. He was in and out of the files before we could catch him. He even managed to erase the phone number and overlay it with a number for the Washington Weather Bureau so we couldn't locate him."

"What do you want me to do?"

Clarence stopped, then quickly resumed walking. Jacob could tell he was concerned, so concerned he'd nearly forgotten protocol.

"I think you should discreetly find out if anything out of the ordinary has happened to Mrs. Richards in the past few months. We don't want to alarm her, but if someone is out there, she'll be the target."

Jacob forcibly controlled his breathing. His heart pounded in his chest. For five years, he'd known someone was going to find out that Brooke Johnson and Robyn Richards were the same woman. Yet, time after time, he allowed her to beat his arguments into the ground. And now that there was almost assurance, he knew he couldn't tell her he was actively investigating the Crime Network she'd uncovered. A network that had sent many of the FBI's most trusted agents to jail cells and had cost their leader his life.

And there was her daughter. Kari. If anyone wanted to force Robyn Richards, they could do it through the child.

"I'm just alerting you, Jacob," the director broke into his thoughts. "I'm putting a man on this. I don't want another fiasco like the one Mrs. Richards uncovered."

Jacob knew Robyn's wide-eyed idealism had caused her to stumble onto the plan. It had ballooned into an ugly scandal.

"The president raked me over the coals," Clarence continued, as he walked briskly in the humid air. "I'd never felt so naked as when I walked into the Oval Office that day. I don't intend to ever be in that position again." Jacob could hear the determination in his voice.

The credibility of the FBI had been shaken by Robyn's discovery. And five years later, it was still trying to live down the stigma of an international assassination bureau, with fingers stretching worldwide.

"Clarence, I know this is outside my department, but I'd like this one."

With the sun glinting off Clarence's uncovered head and his blue eyes squinting against the sun, he stopped in midstride and turned to Jacob. "I was hoping you'd want it, Jacob. This one is a can of worms if I ever saw one, and I need someone I can trust."

Jacob sighed. He'd never held anything back from Clarence. "There's been a new development," he told him. At Clarence's questioning look, Jacob related the details of Kari's accident and the dilemma of the blood supply.

"What's being done?"

"Marianne is keeping me informed. Blood arrived in time, and the little girl is expected to recover. And I'm planning to go and personally check out the situation."

Jacob purposely held back the information that Kari's own father was the person who donated the blood that saved her life.

The envelope slipped from Robyn's suddenly numb fingers. Her hand clutched her neck and its rapidly beating pulse. On the floor, partially hidden by the manila envelope, lay a black-and-white photo of Robyn Richards. It had been the sole content of the oversized envelope. Who sent this, Robyn wondered. She stepped onto the porch, looking up and down the quiet street. No one was about, only the soft morning breeze rustling the leaves on the trees.

Robyn stepped back, closing the door and snatching the paper off the floor. Was it Grant? Had he somehow recognized her? Her hand went to her mouth where he'd kissed her. Did he know instinctively that she was his wife? Did her reaction or her lack of reaction clue him into her real identity?

Questions flowed through her mind as she stared at the damning photo, especially the one question she feared most—had they found her? She didn't even know who *they* were. The reason she'd been inducted into protective custody was because a missing link existed in the Crime Network. An unknown threat still existed. Did they know who she was? Had Grant's visit been a signal that Robyn Richards was alive and hiding out as Brooke Johnson?

Robyn paced the room. Someone was suspicious, but did they know for sure. Was this a test? Something to rattle her into making a mistake. She had to do something, but what? She looked at the postmark. The envelope had been mailed from Washington, D.C. Should she call Jacob?

"Hello, Brooke."

Although her senses heightened, not even the flicker of an eyelash revealed surprise at Jacob's sudden intrusion. It had been two days since Grant flew back to Washington. She knew one of Jacob's men was bound to show up. She just didn't think it would be Jacob himself. "I thought you weren't coming back," she said dryly.

His blue eyes flashed. Robyn watched the imperceptible straightening of his shoulders; an indication that he was angry. Jacob stood six feet tall, but he appeared to be taller. His frame looked underfed, but she'd seen him training once and knew his strength and agility were concealed by his wiry appearance.

"Let's go for a walk," he told her, as if he were commanding troops.

Time hadn't changed Jacob. He was still looking over his shoulder expecting the bad guys to come bursting through the door. How he came to be in her dressing room at the back of Yesterdays she'd never know. As much as her logical mind told her he had to have come through the door, his usual method of appearing and disappearing could very well include materializing from thin air.

He took her arm and led her down the back stairs of the restaurant. The July night was warm when she stepped outside. Silently, they crossed the lawn, skipping the circular patio stones like kids playing hopscotch and passing the white gazebo crowded with flowers from today's wedding party. Moonlight shimmered on her sequined gown that clung suggestively to every curve of her lithe body. Earrings, dangling to the soft blush of her bare shoulders, sparkled like fireworks with each toss of her head.

Robyn looked at the staid countenance of the G-man as his height made it necessary for him to duck under the rose-draped lattice portico.

The grounds opened onto a small stream that wound its way through the property, creating pockets of picturesque settings.

Jacob swept the area with his eyes as if he had some kind of internal radar detector. He must have decided it was free of any bugs, microphones, plastic explosives, or other incendiary devices, for he turned to face her.

"Is it safe to talk now?" she teased, taking several steps toward the water.

"What are you up to?"

"Me?" She gave him a surprised look.

Jacob rounded on her. "Don't be flippant with me. You know damn well what I'm talking about."

"I'm not up to anything," she said calmly.

"What was he doing here?"

"Don't ask stupid questions." She spoke with anger. "If you know he was here, you know damn well why—my daughter was dying. She needed blood. If you remember, it's a rare type."

"And was that what made him spend the night at your house?"

Robyn's mouth fell open, then shut abruptly. "Is that what brought you out of retirement?" Her voice was savage but barely audible. "You think I slept with him."

"If you did or didn't is not the point."

"You're right, and it's also none of your business." She watched Jacob turn away and push his hands deeply into his pockets as he took several deep breaths in an attempt to regain some of the control that Robyn seemed to have taken away from him. When his shoulders settled back in the position of *G-man-ready-to-deal-with-difficult-female,* she told him the truth.

"Jacob, my thoughts were almost solely on Kari and her chances of survival. I won't lie and tell you I had no feelings for Grant, but I did *not* sleep with him." She thought she saw him relax a bit, as much as he ever relaxed in her presence. "My major concern was getting Kari the blood she needed."

"There were other sources," he said angrily.

"They were dry." Robyn stopped, sucking her breath in an angry hiss. "And why was that, Jacob? You promised me there would always be AB negative blood on hand for emergencies."

"I'm sorry. There was a mix-up."

"Mix-up? Kari could have died over a mix-up?"

"She wouldn't have died. Word got to us in time. We had a plane ready to fly out when news came you had called Grant Richards."

"Just for the record I didn't call Grant. I was surprised to find he was on his way to deliver the blood in person. And just how did you come by that tidbit of information?" Her voice dripped with sarcasm.

"You don't need to know, Robyn." He lapsed back to her given name. A clear signal he felt the area was clean.

"I'm so tired of that phrase. This is my life at stake here, as you've so often told me. Just who decides what I have a need to know?"

"I can't tell you that."

"Oh, Jacob, lighten up. Isn't there any human being inside that spy getup you wear?" She was sorry the moment she said it. "I didn't mean that, Jacob. It's just that you make me so . . ."

"Angry." He finished for her. "I know. You make me angry, too."

"Why are you here? It's been four years. You told me after the operation, we'd never have to see each other again. By now, I expected you to be bureau chief or something."

"That's not far from the truth. But I'm here to extract a promise from you."

"All right, Jacob, I'm ready. Hit me with it." She straightened her shoulders as if he were about to throw her a hard ball. She had to be ready to catch it no matter which side it curved toward.

The tall government agent walked to within a foot of her. "I want your promise, a reconfirmed promise, you'll play by the rules. You won't see him again."

"There was no blood available for Kari and he was my last hope. I only expected the doctors to fly the blood up. I promise you I didn't think there was the slightest possibility he'd come, too." She turned away. "You can't imagine what it did to me to have him so close and not to be able to tell him who I was and worse that the person whose life he saved was his own daughter."

"I do understand. I'm not completely inhuman, Robyn." Jacob's voice was softer than she thought it could be. And it was very close to her ear.

She turned back to him. "I said I was sorry, Jacob. I know you're a man with a job to do. And I know I'm not the most cooperative person you've ever had to deal with."

"Do I have your promise?"

She sighed. "You have my promise."

"Good, now you'd better get back in there. It's almost time for your song."

"How will you get back?"

"You don't . . ."

"Need to know." Robyn knew the answer. This time she smiled. "Jacob, will you do me a favor before you leave?"

"Of course."

"Smile for me."

"What?"

"All the time you spent with me, teaching me, arguing with me, and shaping me into Brooke Johnson, I've never seen you smile."

"I'll smile if you'll do me a favor, too."

"When have I ever refused you a favor?" Her smile was impish. As close as he'd ever come to a smile changed his features at her obvious comment. Then, he stepped back as if compliance needed room. Slowly, the skin of his lips curved back and upward, revealing clean, even teeth. "You ought to do it more often," Robyn said. "It changes your face completely." Quickly, the mask was refitted and back in place was the G-Man. "Now what's your favor?"

Without a word, Jacob began closing the distance that separated them. Robyn didn't know what to expect. When his arms encircled her waist, she was too surprised to react. His mouth took hers in a slow leisurely kiss. Behind it was no trace of the G-man character, no hard-line military attaché, not even a clumsy adolescent. The man kissing her was experienced and thorough. He held her lightly but securely as if he were afraid his strength could easily break her small rib cage. Hands roaming over the sequined gown brailled her body from her shoulder blades to her rounded bottom that he pulled quickly and surely against the length of himself. The protrusion pressing against her lower body left her in no doubt of why Jacob had come to find her. Reluctantly, he raised his head but didn't move his hands or step back to remove the imprint of his body on hers.

"If all goes well, Robyn, this is our last time together. But if you ever need me, I'll know and I'll be there." He released her, turned and walked away, his head high, and body at attention, advancing forward, with not even a backward glance.

Stunned, her eyes followed him as he crossed the creek and was swallowed up by the enveloping darkness of the night and the trees. Long after he was gone, she stood there. She found herself wondering if Jacob Winston was married. Did he have a family? Were there two, three children walking around with his face stamped on them? Inside her head, a metamorphosis was taking place. The cardboard spy was dissolving, an outercase eliminated, revealing a real person, with feelings, emotions, and hope. She felt sorry for him. That kiss told her he'd secretly been waiting for her. Hoping that with time and circumstances she'd fall out of love with Grant. But all the time he knew his job would never permit him to have any kind of relationship with her. She was a member of the elite society of protected witnesses. Involvement with her would be tantamount to a full-page ad in the *New York Times.*

As she retraced her footsteps over the moon-washed path, cut out like giant silver dollars against a background of dark grass, she remembered the photograph. She had planned to tell him about it, but his surprising kiss made her forget. She couldn't call him back. He'd said if she needed him he'd know and he'd be there.

Inside, the band played "A House Is Not a Home," reducing the noise of tonight's crowd to a whirling hum. It reminded her of the sound of blank space over an open telephone line. The lights were bright and happy. Robyn needed gaiety. She was caught in a no-win situation. Grant could never be part of her life. And she could never be part of Jacob's, no matter how much he wished it.

For the first time since she'd met him, she identified with him. He was no longer her enemy. She wished she could tell him.

"Where have you been?" Marianne greeted her as she walked into the dressing room. "Do you know you're on in five minutes."

Robyn had forgotten. "Thanks, Marianne. I'll be ready, but would you tell Mike I've changed my mind. I'm going to sing 'Secret Love' tonight."

Marianne's look of surprise wasn't lost on her. Robyn was a very decisive person. She had rehearsed tonight's show for three hours this afternoon. To change it without explanation was out of character, and Marianne recognized it.

"Why the sudden change?"

"No particular reason, just a mood change."

"Mood change? My mood would change, too, if that handsome man I saw at the hospital looked my way."

"Hurry and tell Mike," she said. It was rare for Marianne to pry into her life. Robyn was sure it was what had kept them friends for five years.

Robyn repaired her hair and reapplied the lipstick that Jacob had so expertly wiped off her mouth. With only seconds to spare, she took her place under the artificial setting of a moonlit garden, much like the one she'd vacated only minutes ago. As the orchestra began to play the introduction, she raised her head and remembered the smile Jacob had given her. Then, taking a deep breath, she began to sing.

Tonight, her voice was closer to her old voice. The tone was deeper. The words were rich and round as they floated on the small wisps of controlled air before spreading about the lounge. She kept the image of Jacob in her mind as she repeated the refrain.

Only Jacob couldn't tell anyone. She didn't know why he'd chosen to let her know. It didn't change anything—couldn't.

She ended the song slowly, thinking of the tall, khaki-coated man giving away his secret to the only person who had to keep it.

"Listen to that applause." Marianne's voice was choked as Robyn met her backstage after her third curtain call. "I've never heard you sing like that before."

"Marianne, you hear me every night."

"But tonight was—different." She hesitated as if the word didn't hold as much meaning as she meant to impart.

"Different good or different bad?" Robyn teased, deliberately misunderstanding Marianne's meaning.

"Good, of course."

"Thank you." Robyn smiled at the short redhead who reminded her of Little Orphan Annie with her mop of unruly curls and sprinkle of freckles.

Marianne followed as she moved toward the stairs. "I'm not being kind. There wasn't a person here tonight who wasn't moved by you—and that includes the staff."

Robyn entered the small dressing room. The lighted mirror was almost obscured by a huge vase of red roses.

"Who are you, Brooke?"

Thoughts of the flowers left her as she swung around to confront the restaurant manager. "What?"

"Brooke, I'm your friend, your partner. Yet, the woman who walked out on stage tonight bares little resemblance to the one I thought I knew."

"Nobody ever knows anyone completely—not even husband and wife."

"Is it him?"

Robyn didn't have to ask who she meant. Marianne had run into Will just before Grant came out. She'd burst into the waiting room, bubbling over with questions, one following rapidly on the heels of another.

"I told you he came because of Kari's blood type. I don't expect to ever see him again." The words fell like slow rain, washing away a chalk drawing on the sidewalk.

"Why not? He's male, attractive, and unmarried."

"We live in different worlds." It might as well be different planets, she added silently.

"How do you know that? You've been alone since your husband died. Don't you think five years is enough time to grieve?"

"I'm not grieving," she denied, pulling a red-and-black bustled gown with a slight train from the closet.

"What do you call it? You haven't been out with more than six men in the past two years."

"I'm very discriminating." Robyn threw flippantly over her shoulder.

"Discriminating, hell! You're turning yourself into a corpse."

Robyn swung around to face her friend. Every feature of her perfectly made-up face was in place.

"I'm sorry, Brooke, but you are burying yourself. First, in Kari, then in this restaurant. You won't leave any room for a man."

"I don't need one. Kari and I like our lives the way they are."

"Is that really true?" Marianne frowned. "You mean to tell me that Greek god physique with a smile brighter than sunshine, has no effect on your hormones? Honey, you are a corpse."

"Unzip me." Robyn turned her back. Grant had a definite impact on her. He was the reason she was held prisoner in this shell of an existence.

She'd exchanged her grasp at happiness for a defense system and the lives of ten men, among them her husband. With her eyes wide open she'd followed the one-way signs and passed uninhibited through the portal to this life. Eventually, it had been sealed. Behind her was a door with no handle and no key. She was trapped, irretrievably imprisoned in a new world. A world where she had to tell a practiced set of lies until they became truth and truth became a lie.

"If he does come back, Brooke, would you go out with him?" Marianne pulled the zipper down from the top of the gown. Robyn stepped out of it and hung it on a hanger.

Marianne went back to the bouquet of roses. She bowed her head to take in their fragrance. "What's his name anyway? It's probably not a good idea for me to address him as Mr. Tall, Dark, and Handsome."

"Grant Richards. He's an airline pilot."

Robyn waited for a response. When she got none, she continued. "Anyway, I won't be seeing Grant again. His routes don't come this way."

"Maybe."

Robyn snapped her belt closed. Marianne stood in front of the flower arrangement. A small white envelope extended from her hand like a bridge to the past.

Robyn's fingers closing over it completed the link between the past and the present. Pulling the card from its casing, she read it silently.

Seeing you, again—
is a very good idea.
Grant

She wanted to smile, but she knew Marianne was expecting a reaction, and she'd been taught too well to allow any of her personal feelings to sneak out through the cracks in the armor that she had carefully placed on her new life.

CHAPTER 6

As the week went by, Robyn's optimism waned until depression gripped her. Seeing Grant for a short while, then not being able to see him again, had cast her back into the role of grieving widow. The only bright spot in her day was Kari. She'd recovered quickly after the blood transfusion, but the doctors kept her in the hospital for a week while her other injuries healed.

"Mommy!" Kari wailed, running across the room and into Robyn's arms.

"Hello, darling." Robyn dropped to the floor, arms open to receive the ball of energy flying toward her. She planted a swift kiss on her cheek, noting the bandage on her arm, residual evidence of the accident. "I'm so glad to see you." She hugged the soft child, pushing her hair into place. "Here, look what I brought you."

Kari exuberantly ripped the white wrapping paper, decorated with teddy bears, away from the box. Inside, she found a white stuffed Care Bear. "Oh," she smiled. "Two more teddy bears."

"Two?" Robyn looked at her daughter, then around the room. She spotted the pink furry creature sitting on the guest chair. "Is that from Doctor Elliott?" she asked.

"Oh, no. That's from Uncle Grant." Kari left Robyn, still sitting on the floor, to go place the white bear next to the pink one. "He said I could call him that if it was all right with you."

"He was here." Robyn issued the inaudible statement to herself. Her heart began to pound.

"He went to get us something to drink. Is it all right, Mommy?" Kari asked.

"What, dear?" Robyn's disoriented attention focused.

"If I call him Uncle Grant?"

Robyn looked at Kari as if she hadn't heard the question. Her mind kept hearing *he went to get us something to drink.* "Kari, was Grant here—in the hospital?"

"Hi." Robyn's eyes followed her daughter's stare. Grant's unmistakable vitality blocked the door, a cup in each hand.

Don't react, don't let surprise register in your eyes, don't move your eyebrows. Breathe normally, make sure that when you speak your voice is normal. Jacob's voice seemed to whisper the repetitive instructions in her ear as he'd so often done.

"Here, Kari." He walked around Robyn and handed one of the cups to the little girl, then set the other one on the table. "Let me help you up."

Robyn had forgotten to move. He was having the same effect on her that he'd had when she found him asleep on her sofa. "I didn't expect to see you again."

"Well, I couldn't fly away on the day my newest friend goes home." He cast a friendly smile at Kari who returned it before continuing to play with her bears.

"I didn't know you two had become friends."

"Oh, yes, Mommy. Uncle Grant came to see me three times." She held up three fingers. "He's got the same kind of blood as me."

Robyn's eyes came back to Grant. "I must admit I did come to see Kari, but I hoped we'd run into each other again."

"Grant, I thought I made my feelings clear."

"Mommy, Uncle Grant's going to take us to Crystal Beach." Kari's excitement communicated itself to her. The child was oblivious to the tension mounting within her. Grant appeared amused at her discomfort.

"Not so fast, sweetie, Mommy has to agree first." He smiled at the child.

Robyn threw Grant a look that said they'd discuss this later.

"Can we go, Mommy?" Kari's small voice tugged at her heart.

"Kari, Doctor Elliott isn't going to let us go to the beach for a while," she said coming down to the child's level. "You're leaving the hospital, but you still have to get well."

"What about after I get well?" she persisted.

"How about we talk about it then?" Robyn smiled, opening her arms, knowing her daughter would immediately agree with her and run into them.

The nurse came in with the wheelchair then. "I get to sit in this," Kari said, leaving Robyn and running to the chair. She sat down and looked up at Grant. "Uncle Grant is going to push me," she announced. "He said he would go with us, Mommy."

Robyn's gaze joined her daughter's. Grant stared at her with a helpless expression on his face. She clenched her teeth and helplessly followed the small group as they left the hospital room.

Kari chatted between them as Robyn drove silently through the light traffic. Robyn admitted she was glad to see Grant. Seeing him standing in the doorway made her want to react. She wanted to jump into his arms, cover his face with kisses, and tell him she loved him. If she hadn't been conscious of Jacob's words guiding her, she was sure she'd have followed her impulses. And, now, she had to go through another good-bye scene.

"Mommy, are we going by the restaurant?" Kari had turned her attention to Robyn.

"No, darling, we're going home. Why, are you hungry?"

"Only a little."

"Good, Graffie is at home and he's making your favorite."

"Spaghetti, ooh, goodie." Kari's two favorite words bubbled from the small body sitting between her mother and father. Robyn could suddenly and clearly see her former image and Grant's clear good looks like a time exposure reflected on the miniature face smiling at her.

"Hey, watch out." Grant's husky voice, intoned with panic, broke her concentration.

Robyn's foot jammed the brake to the floor as she stopped the car just short of a busy intersection. "I'm sorry. Are you all right?" Grant nodded, but Robyn noticed Kari's hand grasp her arm in a harsh grip. Her eyes were wide and filled with fear. She remembered the accident that had placed her in the hospital. Robyn cautioned herself to pay attention and drive carefully. "It's all right, darling. Mommy will drive slower." Kari returned the smile Robyn gave her and relaxed her fingers.

"Here, Kari, you can hold onto me while Mommy drives." Grant took hold of the child's hand. A pang of jealousy sliced through Robyn at the ease with which her daughter released her arm and curled up in Grant's. Robyn berated herself. She'd never had to share her daughter before, and Kari and Grant seemed to get along so well. She had to allow them this time together. When he left tonight, they could never see each other again.

She turned her attention back to the road. The remainder of the journey was accomplished without incident.

"Graffie," Kari screamed as she came through the door.

Will opened his arms, and Kari ran into his arms as she had into her mother's. "I missed you, my little munchkin." He lifted her into the air and swung her around. Kari's tinkling voice drifted about the room.

"I missed you, too, Graffie. Mommy says we're having spaghetti."

"That's right. And it's all ready." He kissed the dark head moving toward the kitchen.

Robyn noticed the table was set for four. Will must have known Grant would be here. They all sat down to a delicious dinner after which Will excused himself, saying something about a TV mystery he wanted to see.

Robyn spent the next several hours with Kari and Grant. She read the child's favorite books and played a few cartoon tapes. Kari said she got to see a lot of new tapes while she was in the hospital. Grant joined right in as if he was part of the family. Finally, Robyn could see Kari was tiring.

"It's time to go to bed, Kari."

"How about some hot chocolate?" The child didn't argue that it was still daylight.

"Okay. You go get ready, and I'll make the chocolate."

"Will you come with me?" She invited Grant to her room. For the second time that day, jealousy tugged at Robyn's heart. Her daughter was usually reserved in her acceptance of strangers. Grant, in her eyes, must be different.

Robyn could hear the rhythmic beeps of a computer game while she made hot drinks in the kitchen. She smiled at Kari's animated laughter. To think that only two weeks ago she'd almost died. She pushed the thought away like removing a dark cloud as she poured hot chocolate for Kari and Grant, but made hot apple spiced tea for herself.

"Mommy, I beat him, I beat him," she shouted excitedly when Robyn entered the room carrying a tray.

Robyn looked sympathetically at Grant. "Don't worry she beats me, too."

"I can't believe a four-year-old has beat me at a computer game."

"Just how often do you and the Super Mario Brothers get together?" Robyn's eyebrows went up along with the curve of her lips.

"At least once a lifetime." He smiled, accepting the cup she offered.

Kari continued to jab the joystick back and forth, destroying the electronic space monsters that blocked her path. In less than a minute, she had topped her previous score.

"Okay, Kari, it's time to drink your chocolate and get into bed." The pink clad child frowned but accepted the cup.

"He's not bad, Mommy, but Graffie is better." Kari had a chocolate mustache that she licked in her childish way and completely circled her mouth with the brown liquid.

"Everybody's a critic." Grant set down his cup and tickled the Care Bears on her pajamas. Gales of high-pitched laughter flowed from the child.

"Come on, champ. Let's go to bed." Robyn turned the spread down on the bed and pulled back the sheet. Kari stepped out of Grant's grasp and went into the bathroom to brush her teeth.

"Goodnight, darling." Robyn whispered after she kissed the clean pink cheeks and settled her in the bed.

"Goodnight, Kari," Grant echoed.

Robyn felt good as she walked down the steps. She was glad Kari had gotten along so well with her father. But she knew in the next few minutes she was going to have to tell him she could never see him again.

"You look much more relaxed," Grant told her when she'd deposited the tray in the kitchen and returned to the living room.

"I am. I was extremely worried about Kari, but she's going to be fine."

"How about you?" Concern was evident in the softly spoken question.

"I'm fine, too." Grant had given her a perfect lead-in. Robyn sat down in one of the wing chairs. "Grant, why are you here?"

"I came to see you."

"I thought I told you it wasn't a good idea."

"But you didn't tell me why."

"You don't need to know." She didn't believe she'd said that.

"You're wrong, Brooke. I do need to know." Grant moved. He came closer, sitting on the coffee table facing her. "I need to know everything about you."

Robyn refused to drop her eyes. She looked directly into his dark black orbs. "There isn't a lot to tell. I'm plain, ordinary. I have a child, and I work. We live a perfectly ordinary life in this house."

"What about me? How do you feel about me?"

"I don't feel anything for you." She was amazed at how well she could lie and keep her face straight.

"Who taught you to do that?" he asked.

"Do what?" Maybe she wasn't as good as she thought. He'd thrown her a fastball. She didn't expect it.

"Tell such complete lies without blinking one beautiful eyelash." He outlined her eyes with his thumbs forcing her to close them.

"I'm not lying." She struggled to keep the shudder that passed through her from bubbling out.

"No?"

Robyn stood up, moving away from him. She waited until she got behind the sofa before speaking. "Grant, I'm very grateful for what you did for Kari, but I'm not going to have an affair with you."

Grant didn't answer her. He stood, too, and followed her around. Robyn backed away. She didn't know what he was going to do. Slowly, he stalked her until she backed herself up against the wall. He stopped. Barely three feet separated them. Grant looked deeply into her eyes. She could see the desire in his. In her own, she refused to let it show. Fire began a slow burn in the pit of her stomach and quickly spread throughout her being. Immeasurable seconds passed. Electricity snapped around the room. Her body ached for him. She knew she couldn't hold out much longer, when suddenly something propelled her from behind. Her arms were around his neck, pulling his mouth to meet hers in a ragged, life-threatening kiss. Grant took charge, burying his hands in her hair, trading one passionately wet kiss for another. Neither of them appeared to be in control. Need to touch, taste, possess each other led them on. Robyn was exhausted and tears filled her eyes when she finally pulled her mouth away and collapsed in his arms. She felt like crying, something she hadn't done in years. She wanted him, but he had to go. She'd promised Jacob she wouldn't see him again. She'd resolved her life without him, and now, here she was wrapped in his warm arms, loving him, loving the sight and feel of him holding her.

"You taste like—apple spiced tea."

This wasn't Robyn he was holding in his arms. This was Brooke. Grant knew it. It had been two weeks since she had sent him away. During that time, he'd tried to forget her. He'd only known her for a weekend, but for some unexplainable reason her image kept creeping into his thoughts. He admitted he liked having her in his arms, but he'd had many women in his arms, and only Robyn had left an impression until now. Three times he'd flown in to see Kari, hoping he'd run into Brooke. It wasn't until Kari told him she was leaving the hospital that he came back knowing if he stayed he had to see Brooke again.

And this time he'd hit the jackpot. She had made a move toward him, but even in doing so she had pushed him away. He liked the feel of her, the way her slight little body seemed to fit perfectly with his frame. Even though he held her, he knew she was pushing him away. Her mouth said "go away," but her body screamed for him to stay.

And he could go on holding her. She reminded him a little of Robyn. A twig of conscience pulled at him for the comparison. It had been years since he compared anyone to his wife. It was unfair to Brooke. It had to be the tea. Robyn liked herb teas. Most of the women he'd known since hadn't drunk tea at all. Brooke was refreshingly different.

Why she wanted to push him away he didn't know. He also knew he couldn't ask yet. She wasn't ready to answer that question. Why? Was her husband the man who had spoiled her for him? Had she had a bad marriage? Did he beat her? All he had were questions, and he couldn't ask any of them. Not yet, not to this beautiful woman. But in time. He'd come back often. No matter how much she objected. She stirred him, made him feel alive, and he suddenly, like a desperate man, wanted to be alive again. He wanted to feel, even hurt if he had to, but he'd conquer Brooke Johnson.

"I have to leave now. But I will be back." He still held her.

She tried to push herself away but he tightened his grip, holding her more securely against him.

"Please, don't come," she pleaded. "Just go and leave us alone."

"What is it, Brooke? Can't you tell me what's wrong?"

"No, I can't. Just go and not come back. There is so much you don't know, and I'll never be able to tell you. It's best if we just drop this association right now."

"After the way you kissed me. There's got to be more here than you're telling me."

"Grant, please. Don't ask me any questions." She couldn't keep the pleading quality out of her voice.

"I'm flying to Europe. I'll be back in a week, and I'll be here to take you to dinner at eight o'clock." He ignored her request. Releasing her slightly, he looked down into her face. It was glowing with the remembrance of recent kisses. For an uncontrollable moment, her mouth reminded him of Robyn's, swollen with spent passion. Rapidly, he pushed the thought from his mind. "Don't be late. I hate to be kept waiting."

With that, he smiled and dropped a swift kiss on her upturned mouth before pulling the door open and disappearing through it.

Robyn slid down the wall. Tears flowed from her eyes slowly. In a little less than ten days, she'd promised Jacob she wouldn't see Grant again, and already she'd broken her promise. She didn't know what to do. She wanted him desperately. Part of her rejoiced in knowing she would see him again, while the other part of her cried at the injustice of the system that had put her in this position.

"Mommy, are you all right?"

Robyn instinctively moved toward the small voice. Her hands wiped at the tears in her eyes. "Of course, darling. Mommy is fine. Are you all right?" Kari was standing halfway up the stairs. The bear Grant had given her hung from one hand as she wiped her eyes with the other.

"I woke up." Robyn smiled at the three-word explanation.

"Did you have a bad dream?" She sat down and pulled her daughter into her arms.

"No. Is Uncle Grant gone?" She asked, snuggling closer to Robyn.

"He had to go back to his airplane."

"Will he be back in time to go to the beach?"

She frowned. How was she going to explain to a four-year-old that they could never see him again? "Kari, he's a very busy man. He has to fly his plane a long way."

"But he promised. If it was all right with you. You like the beach don't you, Mommy?" Kari pumped her head up and down, giving the answer to the question she had asked.

"Of course, but we have to wait until you feel better and Doctor Elliott says it's okay."

Kari smiled the smile that would break men's hearts in future years. "Doctor Elliott likes the beach. He told me." Her head continued to bob up and down. "He'll say I can go."

"Well, we'll just have to wait and ask him. Now, back to bed young lady."

Robyn wished her problem could be solved as easily as a trip to the beach. That she could get her doctor's permission and everything would be fine. But her doctor had an office in Washington, D.C., and he only made house calls under extreme circumstances.

CHAPTER 7

Grant rarely got the chance to play in the air. But, today, the horizon had called to him as clearly as if it had a voice. He pulled back on the stick in his hand. The motion was light-years different than the computer controlled jets he usually piloted. His air service was a business, and for years, he'd put in twenty-four hour days to make it a success. But it had paid off. Today, he appreciated his work as he soared over the airfield in the World War I fighter plane he'd bought at a recent auction. The wind whirled through his hair as he executed a three-hundred-sixty-degree loop and hung upside down for a moment.

He grinned, slapping his thigh and letting out a whoop of laughter. This was flying. He felt like the Red Baron. Next time, he'd get a scarf to wear like the legendary German flier. There was just him and the wind. He controlled it with the stick in his hand. He pulled it back, and the rotating blades that controlled the single engine had the small double-wing plane climbing toward the heavens.

It was like the first time he'd flown—when he'd found the freedom of the sky. Everything he wanted, all of his love and feelings were there in the limitless horizon. After not belonging anywhere, not being wanted by the foster families he stayed with, the sky was his love. The families were kind, but he knew he was an outsider. At twelve, he went to stay with Aunt Priscilla. At first, their relationship was uneasy, but eventually, they began to tolerate each other. Now, he loved the old woman, and she loved him. But it wasn't until he met Will and took his first flight that he'd learned where he belonged. He hated to imagine what would have happened to him if he'd never learned to fly.

"Richards's Air calling 1701–Nancy."

Grant heard Adam Carpenter's voice crackle over the radio that his mechanic had insisted on adding when they restored the plane. Grant wanted to leave it out and be as authentic as possible, but Adam was a product of his time, the age of high definition television, air phones, and computers. He wasn't about to let Grant get out of communication distance with the ground.

Lifting the old-style handset, he depressed the speaker button and answered, "Go on, Adam. I'm here." Grant wasn't on a scheduled flight. He was playing and didn't answer in the customary fashion.

"I have a call for you."

"If it's not an emergency, take a message." Grant didn't want to be disturbed. Flying was his life, and today, he didn't want anything to interfere with the way he felt toward the sky and the plane.

"I think you'll want to speak to this little lady." There was a smile in Adam's voice. Grant immediately thought of Brooke. His grip on the stick tightened.

"Put her on," he said.

"Hi, Uncle Grant." Kari's high-pitched voice crackled over the radio phone.

Grant laughed at where his thoughts had been. "How's my favorite blood relative?" he asked.

"I'm fine. Graffie said I could call you."

"I'm so glad you did. What are you doing? Beating Graffie at Space Invaders or Super Mario?" These two games made up Grant's entire repertoire.

"No, Graffie's on his computer in the basement. I'm in the kitchen having a sandwich." Her small voice sounded as if she'd accomplished something big. Grant could imagine peanut butter and jelly smeared around her beautiful mouth.

"Will you make me a sandwich, too?"

"Of course, when are you coming to see me again?"

"I'll be there tomorrow," he said, feeling the anticipation of seeing Brooke again warm his loins.

"I'll make you lunch," Kari volunteered. "We can have oysters on the half shell as an appetizer." She faltered on the last word, but continued in her childlike voice, "followed by Crab Imperial and Mommy's special iced tea."

Grant laughed. The child was precious and definitely the daughter of a restaurant owner. Brooke had taught her a proper menu for lunch.

"Kari, I'm afraid I won't be able to make it for lunch, but I'd like a rain check." He couldn't keep the laughter out of his voice.

"All right, we'll have lunch another day."

"I promise, sweetheart."

"Good-bye, Uncle Grant."

"Good-bye, Kari."

Grant released the speaker button and replaced the handset. He was smiling at Kari's confidence. To think she could have died. He'd never even have met her if they didn't have the same blood type.

And he'd have never met her mother, Brooke. The smile left his face, and his brows knitted together. Brooke was an enigma. He was sure she wasn't a spy as Will had suggested, but she *was* hiding something. He didn't know what, but each time he'd been with her, he could feel there was something behind everything she said and did. And her constant refusal to see him wasn't hurting his ego, he joked to himself. It was as if she were afraid to continue seeing him. But why? Before that night in the hospital, they had never met.

He remembered that night. He'd thought she was Robyn. It was more than a thought, he knew she was Robyn. But how? Robyn was dead. And when she'd turned, his knees would have buckled if she hadn't been white as a sheet and looking nothing like his wife.

And, then, he'd taken her home. What happened on the sofa the next morning had started as a dream but hadn't ended that way. Yet, there were so many similarities between Brooke and Robyn: the way she moved, how she phrased her words, and even the lyrical way her hands stirred the air as if they were playing the piano.

Grant pulled hard on the stick in his hand. The plane climbed straight up until it looped over in a complete circle. It was how he felt. Brooke was driving him crazy, and his life was running from one circle to another, never finding a solution, just continuing along the same path.

Well, he'd change that tomorrow. He'd find out what it was she was hiding.

"I've decided not to see him again," Robyn pounded the dough for Yesterdays's famous dinner rolls. It was the third decision she'd made in as many days.

Marianne stood at the counter across from her. "You think you can hold to that?" she asked, throwing her a disdainful look while she dabbed white stars on a bunny cake.

"Of course," Robyn said, punching at the mass of dough in her bowl. In truth, Robyn wasn't sure of anything anymore. In just one day, Grant had upset the normal operation of her orderly life. She remembered how he'd upset her life that one day in Las Vegas when she'd met and married him within hours. She regretted her decision not to take him into the program with her, especially after she discovered her pregnancy.

Grant had been bounced from one foster home to another. He never developed a sense of belonging, never allowed himself to love anyone for fear they would leave him. Even Aunt Priscilla had told her he'd never opened up after he came to live with her. Flying was his freedom. Up there among the clouds and the wind was as close as he could get to the people who really loved him, and he'd never give up flying. He'd die if he couldn't fly.

Robyn knew firsthand what it was to give up something you loved. If it hadn't been for the microchip her decision might have been different. And it was only by chance she found it. Grant's uniform had needed pressing. The iron passed over a lump in the lining. She could find no rip and thought the uniform was flawed. Gently opening the fabric, she found the microchip. It was concealed inside a fake diamond. Anyone else would have thought it was an unset gem. Robyn noticed the flaw wasn't natural, but man-made.

Grant had told her the project was called Eagle, and it had national security implications. She immediately thought he was spying. He explained he wasn't but couldn't tell her anything more. When she found out her testimony would put her in the Witness Protection Program, she started digging for information on Project Eagle. Director Christopher found her one night and invited her to his office. He explained the position Grant held. He had been friends with one of the men who'd stolen a vital component of a defense system. Grant had been trying to get enough information to ensure the government would find the device. His position was unique, easy access in and out of the country, no association with any government agency, and a prior affiliation with the prime suspect.

Robyn had been stunned. What were the odds that her Grant could be working undercover for the government? The director could give her no definite time that he might complete this project, but that it was vitally important. When he was released from the Lebanese jail, they'd wanted him to continue his assignment. Afterwards, he could join her in the program, but there was no telling if that would be one month or one year.

Robyn had left his office with the weight of the free world on her shoulders. It was history now, Robyn shrugged. There was nothing she could do about it. She mentally shook her shoulders. Jacob *was* right. She couldn't be protected if she ignored the rules.

"When do you plan to let him know?" Marianne broke into her thoughts.

Robyn was jarred. Let who know? Then, she remembered her decision not to see Grant again.

"I thought I'd call his air service and leave a message." She expected to hear Marianne call her a coward, but the redhead remained silent, concentrating on dabbing the inner ear of the rabbit with dark pink icing.

"Marianne, you're awfully quiet. Why aren't you trying to talk me out of this?"

"It's your decision."

"What happened to all those speeches you gave me about dating? Not leaving any room in my life for a man?"

"Do you *want* me to talk you out of it?"

Robyn was silent for a long time. "I guess it's best if I stick by the decision I've made."

"Which one? Today's, yesterday's, or the one you might make tomorrow?" Marianne sounded unusually cynical.

"I thought you liked Grant, Marianne?"

"I like him as well as the next guy."

Robyn's head came up to look at her partner. "As well as the next guy," she repeated. "This, from the woman who referred to him as the man with the Greek god physique."

"You don't need me to talk you out of this. You're doing it yourself."

She *was* talking herself out of her decision. Robyn sat down. Her arms and face were coated with flour. Usually a neat cook, today she'd made a mess of the floor and herself.

"What would you do in my place?"

"I'm not in your place. And you haven't explained why you think going out with him will ruin your life."

Oh, Marianne, if only I could, Robyn wanted to say. So many times since she and Marianne had become partners, she had wanted to confide in her friend, but she'd remember one of Jacob's lectures and work out the problems for herself.

"Well, since you won't tell me, maybe you should stop killing that bread and go expend some of that energy through your feet." Marianne had finished the cake. She cleaned her hands and took the bowl of dough.

"You're right. If I practice, maybe it'll take my mind off Grant." She tried to smile as she cleaned the flour from her face and arms. Robyn paused next to the pink and white rabbit cake. "Who's this for?" she asked, licking some of the excess icing.

"Carrie Snodgrass. She feels about rabbits the way Kari does about bears."

Robyn smiled. "Will has just added to her collection."

"What did he make this time?"

"A trolley car full of bears. Kari loves it." Robyn smiled, and left Marianne in the aftermath of her mess.

In the lounge, the chorus line was busy working on a new routine. Sue-Ellen, the newest recruit, was having a hard time. Robyn slipped out of her warmup suit and joined the line. She wore a navy blue leotard with white footless stockings and beige pumps.

The music began, and she felt like Sue-Ellen. She kept missing the steps. Several times, the line stopped because of her mistakes. Then, she put her mind to it and finally found her footing. Every measure of energy she had, she channeled into the dance steps, giving no conscious part of her mind over to Grant.

"Take a break, everyone." Pete, the music director and choreographer, called.

Robyn grabbed a towel and patted her face. She hung it around her neck and left the stage. At the bar, she poured herself a glass of water and drank deeply.

"Brooke, do you want to dance the solo?" Pete asked, taking the seat next to her.

"No." Her brows went up as she faced him.

"I've seen more energy in your steps today than anytime in the recent past. What's going on?"

"I'm sorry. Am I causing a problem?"

"Of course not."

"I think you should let Sue-Ellen dance the solo."

"Sue-Ellen," he laughed. "She's falling all over her feet."

"She's just nervous. She needs a little confidence. And giving her the solo will do it."

"There you go being kind hearted again. But you know I love it. After all, where would I be if you hadn't been kind to me." Pete leaned forward and squeezed her hand. "Now, how about going through your song?"

Robyn smiled. She felt a lot better. "Fine," she nodded.

"Set up for the 'Time' number." Pete hollered to the stage crew. "I think we should try the dancing water with this."

"What do the sets look like?"

"There will be a huge moon, and the water will be backlit. On the stage will be you and the piano."

Robyn watched the movement on the stage. The grand piano was rolled into place, and the lights dimmed until the back wall was the only source of illumination. She went to her mark in the arm of the piano. Pete followed her to his seat at the keyboard. He raised his arm like a baton. Violins began the first notes of "One Moment in Time," and a spotlight highlighted her.

Robyn listened to the introduction, then took a breath and came in clear on the first note. Behind her, the water danced to the rise and fall of the piano and her voice. The words took on a secondary meaning as she went into the chorus. She knew where she stood at that moment in time, and it was up to her to decide where the rest of her life was going.

When the music ended and the house lights began to brighten the room, Robyn froze as the familiar form of Grant Richards stepped away from the bar and came toward the stage. He stopped near the four steps to the elevated platform. She was glad the piano was behind her. It provided support since her knees were suddenly weak.

"You're early," she said, coming to the end of the stage. Pete called the chorus back, and activity started behind her. "You're not due back for days. Why didn't you call?"

"If I'd called, you'd tell me not to come, right?"

Robyn leveled her gaze. "Yes," she said.

Grant spread his hands in answer and smiled.

Robyn didn't return it. "We have to talk." She walked to the barstool, retrieving her clothing, and then led Grant toward her dressing room. Before she reached the stairs, his hand took her arm and propelled her past the stairs and through the kitchen.

"Marianne, Brooke is leaving. She won't be back tonight."

"Yes, I will," she contradicted, as he hurried her about the counters laden with food for tonight's menu and through the door.

"Decision number four?" The redhead pushed her hands through her hair as she sat down on the chair behind her.

Washington National Airport was alive with activity. It was Friday. The sun hung low in the afternoon sky, and weekend travelers scurried to escape the city. Jacob leaned against the wall of windows in the waiting area of US Air. The tarmac was hot, and he could see the waves of heat rising off the black surface. A steady stream of planes entered and left the retractable jetways. Marianne was due in for her once a month report. Usually, she made her own way to the Watergate Hotel, and a car would pick her up on Saturday morning. For the rest of the weekend, they'd work in his office.

Today, he wanted to talk to her as soon as she arrived. He stood up straight moments later when he saw her short bob of curly red hair appear. He took a step forward then stopped when he noticed she wasn't alone. The man with her was tall and muscular, with straight black hair cut neatly above his shirt collar. He was dressed in a business suit instead of the jeans and T-shirts that were the uniforms of American travelers. Something around Jacob's heart tightened. He refused to acknowledge it as anything except disappointment at not being able to execute his plan.

The couple walked briskly toward the indoor runway that led to the baggage claim area, ticket counters, and taxis waiting outside. Jacob followed at a discreet distance. They both went to baggage claim. Jacob lifted a courtesy phone and had Marianne paged, leaving a message that a car was waiting for her. He watched as she found her bag, shook hands with the man, and made her way through the maze of people waiting at the carousel and its endless circle of luggage. He went outside and was there when the automatic doors opened and she came through them alone.

"Jacob," she greeted. "I didn't expect a car." Her smile was radiant.

"Let me have that." He took her suitcase and garment bag and led her to the government cars parked next to the entrance of the north terminal. "I wanted to talk to you," he said after he'd helped her inside, stored her luggage in the backseat, and slid into the driver's seat.

He started the car and reversed out of the space. He didn't go far before turning onto Boundary Drive and heading for Lady Bird Johnson Park. Puzzled, Marianne looked at him when he bypassed the entrance to the George Washington Parkway that would have been the route to the Watergate Hotel.

"Let's walk," Jacob said when he'd parked in the empty lot.

Marianne followed him down a path that led to a railing along the Potomac River. They were in the direct flight path of outgoing planes, and overhead, a huge jumbo jet thundered on its route toward an unknown destination.

Jacob rested his arms on the rail. He looked out over the water for so long, Marianne thought he had forgotten she was there. Jacob was different. What had made him come to the airport? He had never done that before. Not even the first time she came to report to him. The last time she'd been here she thought he acted slightly out of step, but this time he was totally out of character. Marianne wondered what had happened to change Jacob? She stepped closer to him, but he made no move to acknowledge her presence.

"Jacob," she called quietly. "Is something wrong?"

He didn't turn immediately but kept staring across the water. Then, he shifted and looked at her. Marianne had the feeling that he'd never seen her before and that he found it strange that she was standing before him. She reached for him, touching his sleeve.

"Are you all right?" she asked again.

He nodded covering her hand, then resumed his position at the rail.

Marianne let her hand stay where it was. She would have liked to explore the emotions rioting through her system, but she had an important report to give. With her free hand, she opened the large purse on her shoulder and pulled out a folded piece of paper.

"Have you ever seen this?" She handed it to Jacob.

He took it, letting go of her hand to open the fold. "Where did you get this?" He glanced at the photocopy of the picture of Robyn Richards.

"I found it in the safe at the restaurant, hidden behind some papers we keep there."

"Did Brooke say anything about this?"

"No," Marianne shook her head. "If she hadn't folded the envelope it was in, I'd never have noticed it." Marianne pointed to the bottom part of the photocopy where she'd copied the envelope and an enlargement of the postmark.

Jacob squinted in the bright sunlight. "This arrived before my visit. Why didn't she tell me about it?"

"I don't know. Since Kari's accident and Grant's arrival, she hasn't known which way to turn."

"But she must know someone has discovered who she is." He looked at the grainy photo. "That her life is in danger."

"Her life has been in danger for five years," Marianne hesitated. Jacob looked at her, waiting for her to continue. "She could think Grant sent it."

"Do you think she told him?"

"No," Marianne said without hesitation. "If she'd told him, she wouldn't be flip-flopping on whether to see him when he comes."

"She's still seeing him then?"

Marianne knew about Robyn's promise to Jacob. "Brooke doesn't invite him. He just shows up, and how can she refuse to go out with him? He's handsome, sure of himself, and he makes her feel like she's the only woman in the world." Marianne realized she was talking about herself as well as Robyn. "Beyond that, she's in love with him."

"'Wars have been lost and won over love,'" Jacob quoted some unknown poet. Marianne had no idea who. She knew how Robyn felt, wanting something she couldn't have.

"I'm going to have to act on this," Jacob said, his gaze moving from Marianne to the paper and back.

Marianne nodded. She knew he'd have to do something.

"Come on, I'll get you to your hotel."

He took her arm and led her back to the car. The drive to Watergate was made in silence. Traffic over the Fourteenth Street Bridge had more than the usual amount of snarl for a Friday. Jacob cursed under his breath as they inched along at five miles an hour. When they hit Constitution Avenue Marianne could see the flashing lights of police cars ahead. Jacob banked left and took the streets through downtown until they reached P Street. Since Rock Creek Park at this hour flowed West it was apparent they were taking a route through Georgetown.

Marianne turned her attention to the cobblestone streets. The silence bothered her. She wondered what Jacob was thinking, what he would do with the information she'd given him and how Robyn would react when she found out he knew. Over the years Robyn had not known anything about her reports to Jacob. Until Kari's accident there hadn't been much to say. Now she felt like a traitor.

"Jacob—," she began intent on asking him the question uppermost in her mind. She stopped suddenly, whipping her head around to stare at the back of a man walking up Wisconsin Avenue. His back was to her and crowds of tourist thronging the narrow pavement swallowed him up. She was sure—.

"What is it?" Jacob glanced over his shoulder quickly, then at her before giving his attention to negotiating the trolley tracks lining the broad avenue.

It couldn't be, Marianne thought. She thought she'd seen Will McAdams.

"Nothing," she finally said. Turning back she resettled her seat belt and stared at the shops and street vendors interspersed with a moving sea of people. Shaking her head she resolved the image as someone who looked like Will. After all, she'd only had a glimpse of him and she couldn't see much because of the people in her way. Will was probably fixing spaghetti for Kari. It was the child's favorite food and Marianne knew he watched her while Robyn ran the restaurant.

At the hotel she filled in the records card and smiled at the familiar clerk as she accepted her computer-coded key. Thoughts of Will had evaporated by the time the doors to the mirrored elevator opened. Jacob followed her, carrying her garment bag and suitcase. He'd just dropped them on the king-size bed and turned to leave when the first bomb exploded.

CHAPTER 8

Grant had finished checking in, and the green-and-white clad agent smiled and handed him the keys to his rental car. Heading for the automatic doors, he saw her. Marianne looked strained and pale as she awkwardly pulled her suitcase from the circling carousel with her left hand. She dropped it next to her feet as if the action hurt. He made his way toward her. She looked surprised and frightened when she saw him.

"Marianne, what happened to you?" he asked. When he picked up her suitcase and garment bag, Grant noticed the bandage on her arms. Her face looked as if she'd been in a tanning machine where the lights worked only on one side. And part of her lower jaw was covered by a gauze patch.

"I'm fine," she said by way of explanation. She offered a smile but it didn't seem to work. Her eyes misted, but she blinked the tears away.

"You don't look so good. I have a car. Let me give you a ride home." Grant didn't want to mention how badly she looked. He guided her to the area where the agent had told him he'd find the car and stored her suitcase and bag in the trunk. She dropped her head and looked close to tears.

"Can I help?" Grant offered.

"No," she answered with a long sigh and lay her head against the upholstery. It had been a long time since someone had tried to kill her. The first and only other time it had happened, she'd threatened to leave the service. She didn't want to be an undercover agent. It was then that she had been transferred to the program and had taken the assignment of protecting Robyn and Kari. The assignment had been easy up to yesterday. If Jacob hadn't come to pick her up, she would have gone back to that room and been killed. She shuddered.

"Are you cold," Grant asked. He reached for the air conditioning setting and raised the temperature of the digital display. Grant had reached Route 33 and was heading toward the restaurant.

"You'll have to pass the turnoff for Yesterdays and take the Parkside Avenue-Zoo exit," she directed.

Marianne sat quietly afterward. The car took ten minutes to reach the location, and at that point, she sat up and directed him past the park and onto the quiet tree-lined street where she lived. Her house was unlike Robyn's in that it was a tall but narrow Victorian. The paint, a soft blue trimmed in salmon pink, set it apart. It sat nestled among other Victorians of bright and muted colors.

Grant pulled into her driveway and got out. He went around and helped her out. She was wobbly at first, and for a moment, Grant was about to lift her and carry her up the five steps that led to the small front porch. She regained her balance and walked across the grass to grasp the handrail. Getting her suitcase, he followed her.

Inside, the rooms were dark since the windows were hung with heavy drapery. The furniture was sparse, giving the rooms an airiness when she threw every drape open.

"I'll be fine now," she told him.

Grant wasn't so sure. "What happened, Marianne?" he asked for the second time since leaving the airport. "You've obviously been in some sort of accident. I can keep a secret, if that's a concern, but you look like you need someone to talk to."

She hesitated, her chin shaking, as if she wanted to say something but was forcing herself to remain quiet. Her action reminded him of Brooke and her determined effort to control her words. "Would you like me to call Brooke?"

"No!" she shouted too loud and too quickly. "Don't call Brooke. She's much too busy right now." Her voice was lower.

"How about some tea?" he suggested. It was a trick Robyn used to use on him to make him tell her things he didn't want her to know. "A cup of tea will make you feel better."

In the kitchen, Grant filled the kettle sitting on the stove with water and searched the tea canister. It was filled with individual bags, but in the cabinet next to the sugar he found a box of loose apple spiced tea. Searching further, he found a tea ball in the drawer and used Robyn's recipe to make hot apple spiced tea. The aroma filled his senses and momentarily brought Robyn back to life. Then, he remembered the sad woman in the other room. He placed several spoons of sugar in the hot mixture and took two cups back to the living room.

Marianne was curled up on the window seat. Her arms were wrapped around her body tightly as if her life force would escape if she didn't hold it in. She stared vacant-eyed through the glass at the gray day. Grant could tell that her mind was miles away. Maybe she was back in her weekend. Something had happened there that had frightened her. He called her name. She didn't respond.

He set the two cups on the window ledge and took the seat next to her. "I'm not leaving until you tell me what happened."

She came back then. His voice drew her from the sound of the shattering glass and from Jacob holding onto her to prevent any harm from happening to her. Without his quick thinking, she shuddered to imagine where she would be now, dead or in the burn unit of George Washington Hospital Center.

"There was a fire," she told a half-truth. A bomb exploding in her hotel room had set it to burning. "My hotel room caught on fire. I barely escaped."

"Are you all right?" Grant's eyes went to the bandages.

"I wasn't burned badly." Her voice was monotone. "I was just scared, and my arms have a few blisters. The doctor said they won't scar." She swallowed a sob and lifted her chin.

"What started the fire?" he asked in a whispered tone.

"Electrical wiring," she lied. "It was a faulty switch in the room. Everyone escaped unharmed." Marianne sipped her tea. Life seemed to be returning. She felt better now that she was back on familiar ground. But if someone knew her exact hotel room in Washington, they also knew where she lived. Jacob had her house checked out. He'd been on the phone, barking orders since they'd left the hospital, and he'd taken her to his house in Rock Creek Park.

It was Jacob who had sent a message to Robyn telling her Marianne would be staying an extra day. He didn't explain anything, and Marianne knew Robyn wouldn't pry. The two of them had come to an unspoken understanding years ago, and neither of them interfered in the other's life. At least not until Grant had come to donate blood for Kari. Then, Robyn appeared to open up a little, giving Marianne glimpses of her feelings, but Marianne had been forced to keep her own feelings to herself.

Grant watched her. She was nervous and needed someone to help her. She drank the tea methodically. It must have been a trauma to find yourself in a burning room. Grant hadn't known any burn victims, but he'd seen films of plane crashes and had been required to take classes to handle emergency landings. The greatest hazard in force landing a plane was the likelihood of fire. Case studies of survivors had told him the trauma lasted long after the victims were safe. And Marianne had all the symptoms of delayed shock.

She finished her tea, and Grant coaxed her into going to bed. When she climbed the stairs, he used the phone to call Brooke. She was there in minutes.

"How is she?" Robyn asked the moment she came through the door.

"I'm not sure. She has bandages but doesn't appear to be in any physical pain. She looks like she needs someone."

"I'll go up."

Grant kissed her lightly on the mouth. "I'm going to the hotel. I'll call later."

Robyn nodded and headed up the heavily carpeted stairs. Marianne was lying on the bed fully dressed. She took one look at Robyn and burst into tears. Robyn ran to her, cradling her head in her arms and letting her cry. Her body shook in spasms. Robyn knew she had to let fear run its course. She spoke in a whispered voice, telling Marianne it was over. The fire was out, and there was nothing to hurt her now. After a long while, she stopped crying. Exhaustion made her sleep. Robyn covered her with a light blanket and went to the kitchen.

The tea Grant had made was sitting on the warming plate. Robyn poured herself a cup. She started for the pedestal table when the phone rang. Quickly, she snatched it from the wall, hoping the sound had not jarred Marianne from her much needed sleep.

"Hello," she answered.

At the other end, someone coughed then cleared his throat. "I'm sorry, I must have the wrong number." A muffled voice spoke into her ear. She was about to say something when the line went dead. Robyn looked at the phone before replacing it. There was something familiar about the voice, but it was disguised. Somehow she knew it.

She took her tea to the table and sat down. Her brows knitted together in thought, trying to focus on the sound she'd just heard. There had been something authoritative about it, almost military in nature. The only man she knew with a voice like that didn't know Marianne. That man was Jacob Winston.

She was all right. She was safe. Jacob told himself over and over. Marianne had stayed an extra day, but when he'd driven her to the airport, she was still pale and fearful. He'd had her house checked, and it was clean. But he didn't want her to return. He wanted her to stay with him where he could keep her safe, but she'd told him she couldn't do it. Her obligations were to Robyn and Kari, and there was no way he could do his job if he had to continually check on her.

Jacob knew she was right, but he didn't like the way she looked. Her vibrant personality had been changed by the bomb. The façade of control she tried to show was cracked, and he could see it. And he was sending her back alone. There was no one she could tell what had happened. They had gone over the story she was to tell to explain the bandages.

He'd squelched any mention in the news services, and the official version spoke of a faulty electrical switch that had been replaced that afternoon.

The truth was a small bomb had been placed over the door. He hadn't seen it until he'd turned to leave. And there it was, hanging inches from Marianne's head. It was amateurish, but the second blast that had been set off by the first had all the marks of a professional demolitions expert. Jacob had the room combed. His findings proved the professional theory. There wasn't enough left of the bomb to fill a thimble. But he knew it was a calling card. Alex Jordan has risen from the dead, and this time he was after him.

Well, his attention was fully focused. Marianne was an innocent. She had nothing to do with the Crime Network. This was meant to be a warning that they were close. Icy fingers skittered up Jacob's spine. It was personal now.

The private elevator to Clarence Christopher's office reminded Jacob of the Hoover years. Although J. Edgar Hoover died years before the first shovel of dirt to build the block size building bearing his name was ever turned, the elevator would have afforded the notorious director the cover of secrecy to hold his nocturnal meetings. As far as Jacob knew, Clarence had never held a meeting after dark. There were conferences that flowed over into darkness, but the clandestine reports of Hoover's era were not part of the Christopher culture.

Jacob stepped into the room. Clarence looked up from his massive desk.

"How is she?" he asked.

"A little pale, but Marianne's a strong woman. She'll be fine." Jacob remembered Cynthia, another strong woman. He'd never seen fear on her face as he'd seen on Marianne's when she couldn't breathe or felt the surge of protectiveness that came over him at the hospital when she'd put her arms around him.

"Has she returned, yet?"

Jacob took the chair opposite Clarence. "This morning. I put her on the plane myself." She insisted on returning against his wishes. He knew she was scared and returning alone was her way of dealing with it. He had called her this afternoon and Robyn answered. It was lucky he recognized her voice before he spoke. But Robyn was smart. He wasn't sure he'd fooled her.

Clarence picked up the pen in front of him and looked at it for a long time. "What have you found out about the explosion?"

"The bomb hanging over the door was crude and of no consequence. It was placed there as a decoy to prevent anyone from leaving the room. But the one behind the bar was the work of a professional. The plastic explosive was army-issue and experimental. It was designed to both explode and incinerate, leaving no trace of itself behind. It's cropped up in several terrorist attacks in recent years."

"Where do you suppose he got hold of it?"

"We're working on that. So far, the only place we've come up with is an out of the way air base in northern Canada."

"Canada?"

Jacob nodded. "We picked it up during the computer search that cross-referenced the blasting caps and the plastic explosive. Apparently, there's a research unit up there working on thermodynamics." Jacob knew that translated into bomb.

"Have they discovered any of their supply missing?"

"Not according to their records, but I have someone checking the physical inventory."

Clarence nodded his assent, then looked down at the report on his desk. "I've read your reports on activities in the last five years related to the Crime Network. Do you believe they are still in operation?"

"All the evidence points in that direction. Before Jordan was found, the targets were specific and expensive. The unit must have needed money to keep everyone in the elaborate lifestyles they were living. In the past five years, the actions have bordered on revenge. Each of those assassinated, we think, had an association with the other. Several members of the same army unit, three men who were roommates at college, and seven business partners. The list is short but there is a connection. I have the feeling we're looking for a small group of people or even a single man who's doing the hits."

"Any idea who or why?"

Jacob shook his head, frustration evident in the cast of his shoulders.

"What of Mrs. Richards?"

Sitting up straight, he looked directly at the FBI director. "She hasn't mentioned the photo Marianne brought. Someone could have discovered her identity, and then again it could be a false lead."

"You think her husband sent it?" Christopher asked.

"He could have." Jacob shrugged. "We haven't been able to prevent him from continually seeing her. We gave his service a greater work load, but he still manages to sporadically appear. There was a sale of surplus aircraft scheduled for next month. After last night's bombing, I had it moved to this week. He'll be too busy with it to have time to make trips to Buffalo."

Christopher nodded.

"Do you think he might be of use to us?" Clarence asked.

"As an unwilling pawn?" Jacob's brows went up.

"You don't like that idea? It's how we got Mrs. Richards to testify five years ago. And I know you don't approve of those kind of tactics, but sometimes it's the only way to get the job done."

"Maybe," Jacob said. "But if we'd just asked her she might have considered it her civic duty and helped without coercion."

"We didn't have time for that. Jordan was well connected. As it was, we had to protect her during the investigation.

"What about resettlement? We could give her a new identity; have her start over. This time her husband could go, too." Christopher suggested.

"That would be very hard on Kari, her daughter. She's four."

"What's your suggestion? She's either a target for some unknown assailant or uprooted." Christopher spread his hands. "It's your call."

Jacob didn't want to call this one. He remembered the first time he'd seen Robyn. She had looked like a frightened little bird about to be eaten by a giant cat. But she fought valiantly, if in vain. This time, she had to make the choice. It was her life. Too many people were running it without her knowledge.

Marianne was winning. She woke up without the burning pain that had plagued her arms and face. The room was dark, and she knew she'd been asleep a long time. Looking at the small clock with two white cherubs on it that Robyn had given her for Christmas two years ago, she found it was after eight o'clock. The crowd at Yesterdays would be spilling onto the porch. She should be there to help Robyn. A shaft of pain in her head as she tried to move warned her not to consider the possibility.

She raised herself up on her elbows. Pain shot up the back of her skull and threatened to blind her. The pain killers the doctor had given her were sitting on the night table. Suddenly, she remembered Robyn had been there. Robyn had given her the pills, and she'd fallen asleep. She reached for the lamp and turned it on. Her eyes squinted against the brightness that swept over the room.

Swinging around, she placed her feet on the floor. The pain in her head intensified to white hot. A wave of nausea threatened her, and she remained still until it passed. Gingerly, she stood up and went to the bathroom.

Robyn heard the movement from downstairs. She'd just finished making another cup of tea. Marianne would certainly be hungry by now. She poured a second cup and placed both cups on a claw-footed silver tray. She added a plate of the muffins that Grant had dropped by and climbed the stairs to the master bedroom.

Knocking lightly, she opened the door. Marianne was standing in the bathroom doorway, a paper cup in her hand. "Have you been here all day?" she asked, dropping the yellow flowered cup into the wastebasket.

"Most of it," Robyn nodded. "Grant came back to make sure you were all right. He told me what happened. I'm so glad you're going to be all right. But you should have called me. The message Pete took only said you would be a day late in returning. Nothing about an accident."

"I'm sorry," she apologized, knowing Jacob wouldn't volunteer any details that weren't absolutely necessary. "The hospital was busy with all the people coming in with minor burns and injuries."

Actually, she didn't remember much about the hospital. Just Jacob holding her.

"How do you feel now?" Robyn watched Marianne make her way back to the bed and sit down.

"I have an awful headache, but my arms don't hurt anymore." She looked at the bandages that were still on her arms. Underneath, her skin had first- and second-degree burns. Most of the covered area was red, and part of it was blistered. She knew it was time to change the dressing. Jacob had wrapped them for her this morning before he took her to the airport.

"Would you like me to change those?" Robyn appeared to read her mind.

"I brought some gauze back with me. It's in my suitcase."

Grant had left the case in the downstairs hall.

"I'll get it. Have some tea and muffins. You must be hungry, too. Would you like me to order you some food?"

Marianne shook her head. "The muffins look good."

"Grant brought them by before he left," she explained.

"He's gone, already." Usually, he stayed a few days when he came. She yawned. The pills she'd taken were making her drowsy.

"Something came up suddenly, and he had to go buy some planes. He didn't have time to explain it to me."

Robyn left to get Marianne's suitcase. Marianne understood Grant's departure. Jacob was manipulating his presence. The fire bombing had told them that danger was closing in. Grant had to be kept away from Robyn.

"You must have been a nurse in another life," Marianne said minutes later as Robyn cut the surgical tape and secured the last wrapping in place. She slid down in the bed.

"I don't think so, but I've bandaged my share of scraped knees," she smiled, thinking of Kari.

"Where is Kari?"

"She's with Will. The two of them have been inseparable since last weekend."

"What did they do?" she asked. Her question was more than gentle curiosity.

"Saturday, Will took her to the beach. She fell asleep in the sun and came home with a slight sunburn, but she was too tired and too happy to do anything but sleep. On Sunday, they went to a kiddie play at Studio Area. She can't stop talking about it."

Robyn smiled, and Marianne returned it. She remembered the man she'd thought was Will McAdams in Georgetown. Robyn's story had told her where he was. She had to be wrong. A man couldn't be in two places at one time.

"Who's managing the restaurant?" Marianne changed the subject.

"Would you believe Pete?" she laughed. "If we ever sell that place, we'll have to give it to him. He's playing king tonight."

"And who's playing queen?" It was Robyn's role.

"Sue-Ellen." Both women laughed. Marianne's eyes widened then held her stomach.

"Sue-Ellen!" She was the clumsiest dancer Marianne had ever seen. Yet, Robyn liked her. "Do you suppose she'll fall over the dessert cart or snag her dress on one of the tables?"

"She's not that clumsy," Robyn defended her.

"You know she's a runaway." Marianne put her hand over her mouth as she tried to stifle another yawn.

Robyn nodded. "But she's over twenty-one and answerable to no one."

"I can't see why you keep her around."

Robyn stopped a moment, then she said, "She reminds me of myself a few years ago."

"You could never have been that clumsy," Marianne stated.

"It's not that she's clumsy so much as lacking confidence. Given a little time, she'll begin to believe in herself."

Marianne didn't ask, but she thought Robyn was speaking about herself and not about Sue-Ellen. And she hadn't missed the slight hesitation Robyn had made before she had begun speaking. It was the first time Robyn had mentioned a past outside of the prepared one Jacob had ingrained in her when she entered the program.

"Give her a chance, Marianne."

"I promise, I will."

Robyn smiled at her friend who was obviously tired. "You should go back to sleep." She got up. Marianne didn't protest. Robyn found a pink gown in the top drawer and helped her into it. Within minutes, she was asleep.

Ladened with the silver tray, Robyn tiptoed down the stairs and into the kitchen. She thought about Sue-Ellen. And thinking of her brought her own past back, when she was Robyn Warren, dancing briefly in a chorus line, nervous and unsteady until the other dancers let her know she was one of them. Then, her steps became sure and easy.

And it had been like that when she'd been approached to testify in the

Alex Jordan trial. She was unsure and nervous. Grant being in Lebanon added to the pressure she was feeling. Then, the government came along and offered to get him out in exchange for her direct testimony. But to do so meant to suddenly and completely disappear from her friends. Even Susan didn't know where she had been sequestered.

When she'd arrived at the court, she was bombarded with flashbulbs popping in her face and an opposing attorney who was known worldwide for winning cases that had been considered open and shut. She, a twenty-five-year-old, was up against that. And she had needed someone to believe in her. That someone had been Jacob Winston.

Then, she didn't know he would also be the man who would coach her in the program and the man who would protect her life and that of her child.

CHAPTER 9

"Where are you taking me?" Robyn asked, as the sleek car sped through the afternoon traffic. Grant had shown up unexpectedly. His comings and goings were hard to predict, and no matter what Robyn did, she ended up at his side.

"Someplace I can talk to you without continually hearing you say you don't want to see me. When everytime I look at you, all I can see is a bedroom in your eyes."

"That's not true," she lied, looking away from him. She, however, knew whenever she looked at him, all she wanted to do was run into his arms and have him make love to her.

"Liar." His accusation was tempered by the smile on his face.

Robyn was silent. It had been two weeks since she had last seen him. Marianne's burns were almost healed, and she was back at work. Grant had called to say he'd bought some new airplanes and was busy getting them in operating order since his work load had also increased. Robyn didn't know if she was happy or sad. When he wasn't there, she missed him, but his presence meant danger.

They left the city behind and traveled up Route 33 to the airport. Grant guided the car into the airport driveway and proceeded to an area for small planes and helicopters.

Minutes later, they were seated in a helicopter flying over the city.

"When did you learn to fly helicopters?" She spoke into the headset Grant had given her. The noise prevented them from hearing each other without amplification.

"When I bought the air service, it came with helicopters."

"Is it the same as flying a plane?" Grant had taught her to fly a small plane years ago.

"It's quite different. There aren't nearly as many controls, but it is more difficult to fly."

"But you like it." She could see it in his face. It took her back to when they were first married. Flying had been his life, he'd told her. It was the only thing he loved that loved him back before he met her. He'd said he couldn't live without flying.

"I love it almost as much as I like breathing. I feel like I can do anything when I'm up here." He was proud.

"What would you have done if you weren't a pilot?" For some reason she needed to affirm her decision, to make sure her decision had been the only one that could have been made at the time.

"Not fly. I don't know. I was sixteen, still in high school, when I went on my first plane ride. It was then that I decided I had to fly, and since then it's been the only thing in my life." He paused a moment before adding. "I have to admit, if it weren't for flying, I'd probably have lost my mind when Robyn died."

"Look there's the Liberty Bank Building." Robyn, changing the subject, pointed to the twin statues at each end of the famous landmark. Further down Main Street, she could see the War Memorial Auditorium, and then Grant flew directly over Yesterdays.

"Have you ever been in a helicopter before?"

"Never, not even to sit in one."

"How do you like it?"

"It's wonderful." She offered a smile. "I didn't know you could get so close to things. I can actually recognize streets."

"Maybe one day you'd like to learn?" Grant asked.

Robyn sat back in her seat. "No, I don't think so. I do very little traveling, and I have no need for a helicopter."

"How about just for the fun of it? Someday, you could just soar off into the sky and leave everything behind you. Up here, it's just you and the sky."

Robyn had the sense he wasn't speaking to her anymore. He was in his own heaven. The sky was his world. The place where nothing else mattered, where he could go to solve his problems. A place to come to grips with anything the outside world threw at him. Even the death of his wife.

"Grant," she called to him tenderly. "This is not my world. It's your world. And I can't be a part of it."

"Why not? What happened to you that spoiled you for me? Were you beaten as a child? Where you so in love with your late husband, no other man can ever hold a candle to him?"

Robyn averted her glance, once again looking out at the blue of the sky and the clouds that contrived to make it a beautiful scene. She didn't want it to look like this. She'd rather the day be cloudy and wet instead of brilliantly alive. She felt like she was dying again. Everytime Grant flew into and out of her life, he took a little part of her with him. This time would be no different.

"Nothing traumatic happened to me," she lied. Death was always traumatic. "We don't travel the same paths. You're a pilot with government connections." Deep connections, she thought. "I'm just a restaurant owner with people to support. When you set me down again, we're not going to see each other so there's no need to make future plans."

"You're either very good, or you've been trained well," he observed.

"What do you mean?" Robyn asked.

"Your mouth says one thing but your body doesn't speak the same language."

"I mean what I say."

"Liar," he said again. Grant banked right, and Robyn noticed they were no longer over the city. Below them was nothing but green counterpanes of fields ready for harvesting. She'd only seen it once from this angle. Grant was right in his assessment of the flight. In the air, she felt like she was floating. She didn't need the metal casing around her. All she needed was the man sitting next to her, and he could take her to heights greater than any aircraft could.

"Does that stick control everything?" Robyn made another subject change as she pointed at the control Grant held.

"It controls the rotors, the blades on the top." He glanced up as if he could see through the roof. She followed his gaze.

"Are there elevators and ailerons and rudders to control?"

"You know how to fly!" A surprised smile curved his lips.

"No, I just took some ground lessons long ago."

"But you've never had the controls in your hands."

"No," not to a helicopter, she amended silently.

"How long ago did you take the ground course?"

"Before Kari was born."

"Did you want to fly then?"

"Yes."

"What changed your mind?"

"Nothing. I guess I'd still like to fly, but I'm no longer interested in taking lessons or flying planes. I had a fear then. I think I've conquered it."

"What scares you now?"

"Nothing." Robyn stole a glance at Grant. Had she said that too quickly? She was frightened. Afraid of a faceless, nameless person who knew her movements. She'd received the photo several weeks ago and done nothing about it, hiding it as if that would eliminate the problem.

Then Marianne's room caught fire. Did that happen because of her friendship? And yesterday the poison . . .

"There is something." Grant broke into her thoughts. "Something that terrifies you. I see it in your eyes. Something scares you so badly you don't want to confront it."

Fear knotted in her stomach. She pushed herself into the upholstered seat, her body tight to keep from trembling. She was losing her edge. Grant read her all too clearly. "Can we drop this? It's none of your business."

Grant set the helicopter down in a field and pulled a picnic basket from behind his seat. He ducked under the rotating blades and came around to open the door for her.

Robyn looked around, pushing all thoughts of yesterday out of her mind. They must be a long way from anywhere. "Is this legal? I mean, can you set a helicopter down anyplace you want?"

"Not in our country. We're in Canada."

"Canada?"

"I checked with the Canadian authorities before we left. That's why we had to answer those questions at the airport."

Robyn remembered the man asking her nationality, and how long they planned to visit. At the time, she was too caught up in her argument with Grant to recognize the questions were the same as those the customs officials asked when she crossed the Peace Bridge.

Grant spread a red blanket on the ground and proceeded to sit on it. "You may as well enjoy it. You'll notice we're quite a ways from anywhere. You can't run away. I have you at my mercy until I decide to fly you back to civilization."

Robyn wanted to be angry. She also wanted to drop down on the blanket and rummage in the basket with him. It was warmer since they'd landed, and her temperature rose just by being in his presence. She slipped the white jacket that matched her warmup suit off her arms and placed it on the edge of the blanket.

"We have Coke, iced tea, ginger ale." Grant offered her one of the aluminum cans.

"Ginger ale," Robyn took the canned beverage. She hated canned tea, preferring her own home-brewed concoction. She sat down as far away from him as the blanket allowed. "How long do you plan to keep me here?"

He sat up straight. "I didn't mean it to be a prison. If you'd like to leave, we'll go." He placed the can he held in his hand back in the basket, making ready to go.

"Grant," she said hesitantly. "I'd like to stay for a while."

He stopped, shifting his gaze to look directly into her eyes. Smoke clouded them. He didn't know how he was going to keep his hands off her if she looked at him like that. And he knew if he made a move in her direction, she'd freeze.

"Where are we?" she asked.

"Ontario, about thirty miles east of the beach Kari likes."

"Crystal Beach. It's really an amusement park." She took the sandwich he offered.

They ate in silence. He liked looking at her and didn't want to break the silence. She shifted several times, and he knew her back was uncomfortable with nothing to rest it against. Grant lounged against the back of a tree watching her. Then without him knowing it, he reached for her and pulled her against him. She fit into the cradle of his arms and didn't say a word. She turned her eyes to his, and he thought he'd lose himself in them.

"If you keep doing that I'll kiss you."

Robyn dropped her gaze and laid her head on his chest. She could hear his heart beating. It was going faster than normal, and she smiled at the obvious arousal she knew she caused in him. Settling comfortably, she watched the billowy clouds in the distant sky.

"Did you ever draw cloud pictures?" she asked.

"Everybody's done that. I used to paint them with bright colors."

Robyn laughed.

"Don't laugh. I was very good. With my fingertip, I had all the paint I needed, and I'd use vast amounts of red to draw smiles and big baggy pants. Tell me something you used to do?"

"I didn't paint the clouds. I used to let them form their own pictures, and then they'd talk to each other in foreign languages."

"Do you speak a foreign language?"

"No, but when I was ten I was going to learn every one I could—French, Spanish, and German." She shifted against him. He took her hand and brought it to his lips.

"I had a friend who could speak six languages. She'd been a service brat and lived all over the world. I envied her." She remembered Linda Sawyer fondly. The last she'd heard Linda married a captain in the air force, and they lived in Germany.

"What about you?" she asked Grant.

"Only enough to get me a good dinner and a hotel room with a shower in just about any country." The tinkle of Robyn's laughter had him fitting her closer into the crook of his arm. "When I flew for TransGlobal, I learned the rudimentary phrases."

"Do you miss flying for them?"

"Not anymore. I did at first, but I needed the air service. The time was right." If it hadn't been for Robyn's death, he might have never left. He'd been alone, devastated, and needed something to occupy his time and energy. During the long months in Beirut, when they tortured him and tried to get information he didn't have by inflicting pain on other crew members, thoughts of Robyn had kept him sane. At first, he was sure the hijacking had something to do with Project Eagle, but no one had questioned him about that. Then Robyn was gone—and with her, his will to live. Shortly after Eagle was safely put to bed, the air service deal began falling in place. He gave it everything. Night and day he'd worked until David and Susan thought he was killing himself.

Maybe, he really did want to die then, but it had passed, and now he wanted to go on living. He wanted to live with Brooke Johnson and discover all the mysteries that made her who she was.

"Tell me something else you used to do," Robyn broke into his thoughts.

"Well, when I was eight," he smiled, his eyes bright and dancing. "I had only seen the U.S. as a map. I thought the lines defining the boundaries of states were really there."

Robyn started laughing. He could feel her body shaking against his. She sat up and looked at him. Her laugh continued until she could barely control it. "When did you find out they weren't there?"

"When I met Will and he arranged my first flight." He joined her laughing. "I admit it's silly, but I believed it. Don't tell me you never believed anything silly."

"Me, of course not." She straightened her face. "I was a model child." She snickered. "I never believed anything silly." Her face cracked.

"Come on what was it?" He straightened, too. Sitting with his back fully against the tree.

"Promise you won't laugh."

"No," he said leaning toward her. "Give, what was it?"

"I thought the wind carved out Mount Rushmore."

Grant threw his head back and laughed. Robyn stared at him. Then, she laughed, too.

"And when did it dawn on you that it wasn't a natural occurrence?" He could hardly stop the tears coming down from the corners of his eyes. When he looked at Robyn she had tears in the corners of her eyes, too.

"I was in high school. Must have been a slow learner." She touched her head.

Grant caught her arm then and pulled her back against him. "Didn't you ever wonder why the wind," he stifled another laugh, "picked those particular men to carve into the side of a mountain?"

"Not until I saw an article in the newspaper when I was in high school. Then, it all sounded so silly. How could I ever have thought the wind could do such a thing?"

Grant laughed again. "You're wonderful, wonderful." He hugged her closer.

Grant's laughter died. Robyn looked up into his eyes. The playful whimsy that had been there was replaced by raw desire. She knew her own had to reflect the same burning rapture in their depths. Her skin was warm, but when his hands on her arms urged hers upward, fire burned into her.

"Grant, don't," she whimpered. "I'll be lost."

"I'm already lost." His mouth took hers. His kiss was scorching. Her lips opened to him, like a dry river seeking water. Thoughts of being Brooke Johnson intruded for only a second before she pushed them aside and became Robyn Richards. Her fingers tangled in the soft hair above his shirt collar. She pulled his mouth closer to hers, shifting her position as he pushed her gently back onto the blanket. Grant covered her with his body. She felt his arousal hard against her as his mouth left hers to travel down her neck and pause at the neckline of her leotard.

His hand came up to pull the fabric aside. The cool air pushed against her nipple. The pebble hardness of her breast thrust against the warmth of his palm as it traveled in circles. Robyn gasped at the excitement coursing through her body. Whimpers of delight escaped her mouth.

She smelled good, like flowers. Grant wanted to taste her. His tongue slid over her nipple, and he was rewarded as she arched closer to the pleasure he evoked. Her fingers slipped into his hair, and heat surged through him. He wanted her, wanted her now in this grassy meadow, under the shade of this tree. He wanted to know that she was his, to hear those sounds she made when he touched her in the right spots.

When his mouth found its way back to hers, passion gripped him in her strong clutches, and he ravished her mouth with as much force as she used to violated his. He pushed at her clothes, wanting to tear them from her body. He hadn't wanted to do that to anyone since . . .

Suddenly, Robyn was free. The weight on her had lifted, and cold air touched her where Grant's hands and body had been. She was disoriented and angry. Her breath came in short gasps. She pulled her clothes into place as she fought for control.

"What's wrong?" she finally asked. He stood several feet away staring into the distance, his back to her.

"It's time we left."

"Did I do anything wrong?" She walked behind him.

He turned to look at her. Robyn saw torture in his eyes and wanted to relieve it. "It's not you," he said. "It's me." His hand came up and gently touched her cheek. Robyn didn't move, although she wanted to lean into the gesture. She was sure he would pull away if she made any advancement.

Robyn and Grant were back in the air minutes later. He was a changed man, and she didn't know why. She didn't know if she'd done or said something wrong. One minute, he was crushing her to the ground—she warmed at the thought of his body stretched the length of hers—then, he was as closed and tight as a tin can.

How could he explain? For the second time, he'd had her in his arms and thoughts of his wife had intruded. Grant wasn't used to comparing women to Robyn. After her immediate death, when he tried to be a one-man love army, he compared everyone to Robyn. But he'd long since gotten past that, or so he thought. Then why? Why were thoughts of Robyn continually intruding whenever he saw Brooke or thought of her? Even in the dream, the two women kept merging into one and he couldn't tell them apart. But making love to one woman and imagining her to be someone else was something he would not do.

"Yesterdays, may I help you?" Robyn spoke automatically into the telephone while she watched Sue-Ellen continually miss her cue.

"I certainly hope so." The dark voice glided through her veins, elevating her blood pressure. Robyn's breath caught, and her heart started to pound. She wavered between depression and joy. Joy won. Clasping her palm over the mouthpiece, she allowed the tiny cry to escape as she turned away from the action on the stage to face the mirrored wall behind the bar.

"Are you still there?"

"Yes," she faltered. "I'm here." She hadn't heard from Grant for nearly a week, since that day they'd flown into Canada and had the impromptu picnic. She thought he was out of her life. He was so different after he kissed her. She didn't know what to think, and she refused to ask. Since she couldn't explain her own actions when he probed into her past, she couldn't ask him to explain.

The dull ache in her chest had become a hard pain and now hearing his voice made the ache even harder to contain.

"Where are you?" she asked.

"I'm still in D.C. but—" he paused. "I want to see you."

"Grant," she cut him off. "I've had a lot of time to think this week."

"Brooke, please don't say no so fast. Give it a chance? Give me a chance?"

"I can't, Grant."

"Why not? What's so wrong with me?"

"Grant there's nothing wrong with you." Words came hard. She wanted to ask him to fly in. She wanted to rush to the airport and be there when he came through the cabin door. She wanted nothing more than to fall into line with his plans, but somewhere out there was a loose end. Hiding within the protective walls of this program told her the Network was alive, and she knew someone was lying in wait for her. All she needed to do was to make a mistake. And around Grant, she'd be sure to slip up soon.

"I'll be there at six. We have reservations for eight."

"Grant . . ." The phone clicked in her ear. He wasn't listening to her. She replaced the receiver, looking at the black instrument as if it were the reason for her split decision.

She'd been so happy to hear his voice. Yet, every word drove daggers into her heart. She couldn't allow this relationship to develop. Somehow, she had to get that across.

She kept that thought uppermost in her mind as she slipped into her jogging suit and headed toward the kitchen.

"Marianne, I'm leaving and I might not be back tonight."

"Decision number nine?" Marianne asked. She looked up from the cake she was decorating.

"He called. I'm going to have to see him." Mixed emotions at the prospect vied for dominance, but confusion outweighed them all.

"But you intend to tell him this is the end." Marianne used the pastry bag in her hand to punctuate the point.

"That's my intention." Robyn's voice was decisive.

"Do you think it will work this time?"

"Marianne, before I came here something awful happened to me." Robyn noticed Marianne set down the pastry bag. Her full attention was directed toward Robyn.

"Come in here." Marianne led her into the office off the kitchen where they usually did the monthly accounts. The redhead closed the door and sat down next to Robyn in one of the two chairs stationed in front of the huge desk. "Now what happened?"

"Something I don't like to remember. Grant was indirectly involved. He doesn't know anything about it. Yet, if I continue seeing him, something may happen to him, and I can't be responsible for that."

"You love him that much?"

Tears fell from Robyn's eyes. "I love him." She had said it out loud and to another person. She loved him. She wanted him safe, away from her. The people looking for her had no statute of limitations on betrayal, and they could reach her through Grant. Worse, they could hurt Grant. She had to stop seeing him for his own safety.

Marianne was still thinking about Robyn and Grant when she let herself into her house after the restaurant closed. It was nearly three in the morning, and she was tired. She began her nightly ritual of showering and washing her hair before she went to bed. When she stepped out of the shower, the phone was ringing. It was unusual for anyone to call at this hour unless it was an emergency.

Draping the short towel around herself she padded into the carpeted room and lifted the receiver.

"Hello," she said.

"Hello."

Her knees immediately gave out and she sat down on the white comforter, ignoring the water dripping from her legs.

"Jacob!" she said in a surprised whisper. "Is anything wrong?"

"No, everything is all right."

Then why was he calling? He only phoned when there was something he needed to know, and she'd been feeding him his reports at the appointed times.

"How are your arms?"

"They're nearly healed. The scars are there, but they will fade."

There was silence on the other end of the line. Marianne was beginning to think something *was* wrong.

"Did you find anything more about the fire?"

"I have a report for you to read. It'll be here when you come again."

That would be another week. She was looking forward to seeing him. Their time together had been different since the fire. They spent most of it together, talking about everything. Jacob liked basketball and coached a team of young boys.

"I'll be there on Friday."

"I'll pick you up," he said.

Marianne was glad. He'd been there the last two times she'd arrived.

"And Marianne," he paused. "There's a party this weekend. It's an official function. I have a duty to attend. Would you go with me?"

Marianne was speechless. She forgot she had no clothes on until the towel slipped away and the cold air touched her skin. He wanted to take her to a party. Her heart began to pound, and it was difficult to speak, but she managed to say, "I'd love to."

"I'll see you then. Good-bye." He hung up.

She replaced the receiver, but didn't move. Jacob had asked her for a date.

Robyn looked around as the cold wind whipped her hair out of place and smacked her in the face with it. Grant was obviously going the wrong way, there was nothing this way but planes and the runway. She turned, taking his arm, intent on leading him back toward the terminal, but instead he swung her around, until she was again walking in the opposite direction. A wry smile split his face reflected in his dark eyes.

"We're going the right way," he shouted above the noise of airplane engines and helicopter blades.

"Where are you taking me?" Robyn stopped, her gown a cloud of white enshrouding them.

"Out to dinner," he smiled.

"Out to dinner, where?"

"You said I could pick the restaurant." He took her arm and pulled her into step with him.

"There's no restaurant this way." Robyn saw the small plane loom in front of her. The roar from the motors made her scream to be heard. The wind plastered her gown to her, pushing the fragile whisps of chiffon through her legs and making walking difficult. She had to take two steps to keep up with Grant's stride.

"We're going to Pier 7."

Robyn stopped, yanking her arm away. Pier 7 was in Washington, D.C. It sat on the Potomac River at the mouth of M Street in the fashionable southwest section of the city. She couldn't go there. She had missed D.C. in the five years since she'd left it. She couldn't go back. There were too many memories there pulling at her past.

"What's the matter?" he asked facing her.

"I can't go."

"Why not? Kari's with Will, Marianne's got things under control at the restaurant, you're free for the evening."

"But why D.C.? There are plenty of places to eat here. Why must we go four hundred miles for dinner?" Robyn pushed her hair back. The long curls, that had looked so perfect in her mirror, were tangled tendrils playing cat-and-mouse with the enhanced wind generated by the thrust of huge engines preparing to leave the airfield. Ceasing movement had given her gown time to release her legs only to veil them both in a billowing fog of white material.

"Come on, we can't talk in this wind." He shouted in her ear before once again taking her arm and leading her back into the terminal. The Cessna-110 sat outside, a looming enemy to Robyn's eyes.

"I thought I'd surprise you. Marianne and Will told me you hadn't been out of Buffalo for as long as they've known you. I thought this would be a nice surprise. I guess I'm a little out of practice when it comes to what women like."

Robyn felt small. She knew he was ignorant to the reasons she couldn't go to the Capital.

"We'll go someplace else. Where would you like to eat?"

It was against everything she knew she should do, but Robyn heard herself saying, "I know a nice restaurant on the Potomac River." She was rewarded with his smile.

"I promise to have you home before morning." He took her arm before she had time to change her mind, but instead of ushering her into the plane, he swung her toward the helicopter sitting several yards away. She felt like she had five years ago when he'd rushed into her life like a hurricane, and before she knew it, she was Mrs. Grant Richards. That couldn't happen this time. This time there was more at stake. There was Kari and the restaurant and the life she'd left behind.

Grant took the controls. Robyn heard the rotor blades begin their high-pitched whine as they started to turn above her head. The helicopter lifted off the ground. He took the stick and glided them through the air traffic until they were over downtown Buffalo. The glass and steel structures looked smaller from this vantage point. Lights flickered on and off in the buildings, and cars traveling along the roads inched by without confusion or congestion.

She pointed out the General Motors Building and Liberty Bank. Robyn smiled, and Grant dipped closer to the two statues holding lighted torches on the top of the hundred-year-old building. Further along, Main Street ended in the Niagara River. Grant abruptly banked right and headed north. Robyn looked at the compass.

"Where are we going?" she asked. "You've turned north."

"I thought of another restaurant. Do you have any objections to Toronto?"

"None," she smiled.

Fifteen minutes later they had covered the eighty miles and were en route to Captain John's Harbor Boat Restaurant. Robyn had never been to Toronto, but she'd heard a lot about it from Will and Marianne. Both had suggested she go there for a weekend and take Kari. Robyn never took the time to go.

Grant wondered what it was about Washington that made her almost frantic. He'd lived in Washington for fifteen years and loved the city. It had a beat unlike any other city he'd visited. Aside from congress and presidential parades, he loved the crowds. Every spring, the tourists came to town, eager to see Lincoln's bed, the Watergate Complex, and the cherry blossoms circling the tidal basin around the Jefferson Memorial.

Unlike most residents, he didn't mind the tourists getting lost in Rock Creek Park or holding up traffic during rush hour when certain streets suddenly reversed direction or became one-way.

Grant wanted to see Brooke there. He could almost picture her eyes wide and amazed at the national treasures bathed in white light. But for some reason going to D.C. terrified her.

"Why did you change your mind?" Robyn asked after Grant had landed the helicopter and rented a car. They were traveling up the Queen's Quay.

"It frightened you," he paused. "Do you want to tell me why?"

"I wasn't exactly frightened." She stole a glance at him.

"Why didn't you want to go?" Grant reached the restaurant and pulled the car into a parking space. "You were nearly frantic." He cut the engine and extinguished the lights. Around her, the car seemed to go dark. Grant made no move to leave the confines, and Robyn kept her place.

She held her breath for a moment, then got out of the car. Grant came around to stand in front of her. "It was a long time ago," she began. "Before Kari was born. Something happened while I was in D.C. It's just bad memories. Nothing important." She lifted her head and flashed him a smile. "And certainly nothing worth spoiling dinner over."

Grant took her arm and led her toward the restaurant. Whatever had happened there was significant. She'd chosen her words well. He could tell. But she wasn't ready to trust him with the information. He was convinced now, that whatever it was, it was the reason for the underlying sadness in her life.

Dinner proved better than he thought it was going to be when he first had seen the dark look in her eyes at the airfield. She'd been standing there waiting for him when he'd landed. The white dress that she wore gleamed against the dark tan of her arms. She looked like a portrait waiting for him. He liked the feeling she evoked.

She had smiled when he kissed her lightly, but there was no fire in her eyes like there had been on the blanket in Canada. She didn't know why he'd pulled back so abruptly. It was the sounds—Robyn's sounds. No matter what he did, he couldn't get Robyn out of his thoughts. Even when he held Brooke in his arms and began to make love to her, somehow his wife intruded.

Why? It hadn't happened in years. Why did she remind him so much of Robyn? Even now, he could tell she had something on her mind. Something she'd wanted to tell him since he saw her. He knew it was another one of her I-don't-want-to-see-you-again speeches. This time he was determined to get to the bottom of it.

"Grant, dance with me." His eyes focused on her. The fire was in them. They left the dining room and went into the bar. Several couples were already on the dance floor. The waiter led them to a table and brought her a drink. Grant had only tonic water with a lemon twist. He was flying, he explained.

They took up position on the wooden floor. She went easily into his arms. Robyn closed her eyes and let the music carry her away. She danced on a cloud high up in the air with Grant. Around them, the music tantalized and spun a fantasy world. She wanted it to go on and on, but she suddenly realized it couldn't. She pushed this thought aside. For the next few hours, she'd pretend she was back to being Robyn, and she'd enjoy the last night with her husband. They danced and danced. She was too wrapped up in being in Grant's arms. She whirled and whirled until finally they were the only people left in the restaurant.

Grant tipped the waiters generously as they left. He took her back to the airport, and they boarded the helicopter. The flight back was a blur. She could only stare at him. She was glad she didn't have to worry about working controls and coordinating the powerful machine through the air. Even though the trip was short, it was more than she was able to contend with tonight.

But when Grant parked the bird next to the hangar, the fantasy she'd been living vanished. The rotors turned slowly after Grant cut the power, their whine elongating into rhythmic puffs of air. When they finally stopped, the silence was deafening.

"Well, it's time for your speech," Grant gave her the lead-in.

"You know what I'm going to say?"

"Yes."

"Then, do I have to say it?" She looked through the glass windows toward the terminal. Everything was quiet. Lights from inside filtered through the windows in an attempt to brighten the night. She concentrated on the glow.

"You're going to have to tell me. I won't stop coming to see you unless there's a good reason."

"There is a good reason, but I can't tell you what it is."

"Why not?"

"Grant, I can't tell you." Frustrated anger crept into her voice.

"It has something to do with Washington, D.C., doesn't it?" he demanded.

"Please don't ask me any questions. I can't answer them." Anger filtered through her voice.

"Can't or won't?"

"It doesn't matter. The reason has little to do with you, and for all concerned, it would be best if we didn't see each other again."

"That's not good enough. Tell me the truth." It was a command.

"Grant, go home, find another woman, get married, but leave me alone."

"I can't." His voice dropped.

Robyn refused to look at him. "Can't or won't?" she screamed.

"Both," he shouted. "I can't and I won't. I'm in love with you."

CHAPTER 10

Marianne had a lighter step to her walk when she entered the terminal at Washington National Airport. Jacob would have a car waiting outside the terminal. And they had a date. Even the news of the poisoning incident didn't dampen her happiness. Her bags were the first off the flight, and she hurried to the exit. Quickly, her things were stored in the car, and they were speeding toward the nation's Capital.

"We've had another incident," Marianne began an hour later when they were seated side by side on top of a picnic table in Rock Creek Park. Jacob raised a taco to his mouth, and Marianne munched on a hamburger. "Two days ago, Brooke and I made one of our special chocolate desserts. Just as we finished, Pete's cat came into the kitchen. The cat has as bad a sweet tooth as I do and especially for chocolate. Brooke dished him the last of the icing we'd used. Not more than a teaspoon. In seconds, the cat was dead."

"Poison?" Jacob took a drink of his soda.

"Arsenic," Marianne confirmed.

"Did you call the authorities?"

"No, Brooke and I were the only ones who knew. I suggested it, but she wouldn't let me. We disposed of the dessert and had the cat autopsied. Brooke tried to cover it up, by claiming she'd picked up the wrong box. But we don't keep arsenic in the restaurant."

"Did you notice anyone strange hanging around."

"No one we don't already know. We have several people with records working at the restaurant, but I'd vouch for them. They're fiercely loyal to Brooke."

Jacob concurred. He'd had them checked out, and they were first time offenders, shoplifters, kids gone the wrong way. Robyn's trust in them was returned unquestioned.

"How's she taking this?"

"It's hard to tell. The shell around her is thick. She hasn't mentioned it since."

"What about the photograph."

"Still in the safe."

"Keep a close eye on her. I have a feeling something is going to happen soon, and I don't want her without help when it happens."

Robyn sat comfortably in the cabin of the Lear Jet. Outside, the plane cut through the air at more than four-hundred miles per hour, yet she felt very little motion. The "fasten your seat belt" sign had just been turned off. She loosened hers but kept the lock fully secured. Grant had explained to her years earlier, when he taught her to fly, the value of using a safety belt.

He had taken to dropping by unexpectedly and taking her flying. She loved it, and occasionally, he'd allow her to take the controls, complimenting her ability. Robyn had tired of trying to send him away when her heart wasn't in the task.

Since the night he'd taken her to dinner, he hadn't mentioned being in love and neither had she. She was too scared. This couldn't happen, she told herself. They had no future together, but she couldn't get him out of her life. She'd tried it once, and it hadn't worked. He was her other half—the part that made her alive, not just existing.

And she was glad he ignored her attempts to get rid of him. She loved his surprise drop-ins. Sometimes, days would pass without a word, then just as she was feeling low, he'd show up and take her on a picnic or out to lunch. She'd seen more movies in the past six weeks than she'd seen in five years. Once, they even went bowling, something she hadn't done since leaving college. But today was the first time he'd called to ask her out.

"Would you like something to drink?" Grant asked, moving from his seat to stand behind the bar facing her. His white shirt was in stark contrast to the black of his dinner jacket.

"Martini and Rossi," she replied, appraising how his tanned skin set her pulses running.

He poured the sparkling wine into two goblets and passed her one before lowering himself into the plush oversized chair at her left which swiveled to bring them face to face. Robyn raised her glass, feeling the tiny bubbles tickle her nose, as she sipped the chilled liquid. "Is this one of your planes?" she asked, the soothing blue-and-white color scheme making her feel comfortable.

"Do you like it?"

She could hear the pride in his voice. "It's beautiful. You must get a lot of requests for this kind of plane." Grant had shown her around before they took off. The plane seated twelve and was equipped with a private bedroom. The passenger seats were fully reclinable, and a low semi-circular sofa flanked the sunken bar. Tonight, they were alone except for the pilot and copilot locked away behind a door at the front of the air-craft.

"I've been fortunate," he answered. "The District of Columbia has a great need to fly people in and out on short notice. I've flown United Nations dignitaries, government officials, rock stars, and once, Princess Diana was my passenger."

"I'm impressed." Robyn smiled, releasing her seat belt and walking to another seat. She sat down and got up, repeating the procedure until she'd sat in all the seats. "To think," she said, lounging on the sofa, "I've sat in the same chairs as one of the most beautiful women in the world."

Grant laughed, a clear happy sound.

"Where did you take her?" She grinned feeling happier than she had in years.

"New York. She had a schedule to maintain and trouble developed with her own plane."

Grant picked up her wine glass and joined her on the sofa. Robyn accepted it, noticing his arm slide behind her along the back of the sofa. She sipped the liquid that added heat to the temperature rising in her blood. "Well," she began. "Now that we're traveling four-hundred miles per hour, and I'm dressed in my formal gown, as you requested." She smoothed the peach-colored chiffon that highlighted her dark skin. "May I ask where we're going?"

"We're going to a very special party."

"Great, I like parties." Lights registered in her eyes.

"It's an engagement party for an old friend."

As quickly as it had come, the light was dashed. Her body, that had been warming comfortably, was suddenly cold. David's face flashed into her memory. Her senses were alive and alert.

"Washington, D.C." she gasped. "Are we headed for Washington?"

"Yes." He took her hand. It was trembling and clammy with unexpected sweat. "It's only for a few hours, Brooke. I promise to have you safely back in Buffalo before breakfast."

"Why didn't you tell me?" she whispered, attempting to control her wildly beating heart.

"I've told my friends so much about you, they wanted to meet you."

There was nothing she could do about it now. Grant didn't know what he was doing. His subtle little trick could mean someone's life. She only hoped everything would work out, and no one would know she was in town. Somehow, Jacob always knew when she broke the rules. She was surprised he hadn't shown up again. Robyn had promised not to see Grant, yet in the past month, he'd been in and out of her life constantly.

"I'm sorry, Robyn. If it means that much to you, I'll have the plane turned around."

"What's your friend's name?" she asked cautiously.

"David Reid." Grant confirmed her silent fear.

Things would work out, she told herself. She was sure everything would be all right. It was just a few hours. She'd enjoy them. She was going to see David again.

"We used to fly together before I started my air service."

"Does he still fly?"

"He'll help me out in a pinch. But his flying is mostly for pleasure these days. He and Susan . . ."

"Susan?" Robyn interrupted at the mention of her old friend's name.

"Susan used to be my next door neighbor. She was my wife's best friend. She and David are engaged. Three years ago, David and Susan began a small business that has exploded." Grant spread his hands to demonstrate.

"What did they do?"

"They started a jewelry store."

"That's wonderful!" Robyn's exuberance was evident in her voice. She'd known Susan made her own jewelry. She'd done it since college. Many times, Robyn had encouraged her to sell it. She was pleased to hear Susan and David were to be married and that her friend had finally taken her advice and was making a living, selling the jewelry she designed.

Meeting them again was another story. If she'd known they were going to D.C., she'd never have boarded the plane. But she had to admit the idea excited her. For so long, she'd wanted to return to the Capital, but she knew better than to try. She told herself it was better to create new memories than to try and return to old haunts. She knew if she'd returned she'd end up in her old neighborhood, trying to get a glimpse of Susan or find out if Grant was still in their old house. The problem with her was she knew she couldn't stop herself if she started down that road. It was like being on a roller coaster and wanting to get off just before the momentum plunged the cars on the downward incline. So she avoided the temptation by not visiting D.C. Now, she was going to see them.

She was confident they wouldn't recognize her. If Grant didn't, surely David and Susan wouldn't know her. But they weren't the people she was concerned about. Jacob Winston was somewhere in D.C. Even if he wasn't, he always knew what was going on in her life. Up to now, she hadn't minded or even thought about it, but now she didn't want him knowing about this trip. She hoped luck was on her side, and by some miracle, Jacob's sources of information were investigating some other witness. She thrust thoughts of Jacob out of her mind. Tonight, she wanted to enjoy herself.

"You're doing it again." Grant's voice captured her attention.

"Doing what?" Her eyes opened in wide surprise.

"Going off on trips without benefit of transport."

"I'm sorry. It has nothing to do with the company." She smiled, hoping it would disarm him and lead him away from questioning her thoughts. "I was thinking of all the lovely pieces of jewelry I've stared at in store windows. One day maybe I'll get to visit one of Susan and David's stores." She tried to pronounce their names as if they were strange to her tongue. "What's the name of the store?"

"Trifles." Robyn knew the answer before he spoke. She and Susan came up with it one rainy Sunday when Grant was flying to England. After Vegas, Robyn tried to convince Susan she could make a living selling her own jewelry instead of continuing her boring job working in the commercial art department of the city's newspaper.

Robyn could picture the store. Even though Susan had shrugged her suggestion off, Robyn had insisted she sketch out a drawing of the store.

"Have they decided on a wedding date, yet?" She dragged her thoughts back to the present. She didn't want to be caught daydreaming again.

"Late August."

Robyn pictured herself dressed in a white gown, floating down the aisle as she took Grant's arm. It was the wedding every bride wanted, but for her, it never happened. She wasn't sad about missing the orange blossoms and a warm Saturday in June routine. She'd been completely happy with the justice of the peace in the Moonlight Wedding Chapel in Las Vegas.

"I've told them you'd come with me." Again, the deep voice snapped her dreams.

Grant caught her off guard. She couldn't go. She knew she couldn't. She was making this trip unannounced. There was no way she could have known he was taking her to D.C. when she boarded the plane. And in a few hours, she'd be safely back in Buffalo. But to make plans to return to the city where she had enemies sworn to kill her was dangerous. Yet, she was excited by the idea of spending time with Grant, and seeing Susan and David again.

"Grant, I can't. You know I have to take care of things at the restaurant."

"Marianne can handle the restaurant, and she told me you need a change."

Robyn rolled her eyes to the ceiling. Marianne was playing cupid. "I don't even know the bride and groom. I'm sure they won't miss me." Lie number three, she thought. "And that's Marianne's weekend away."

For as long as Robyn and Marianne had been friends, she went away on the third weekend of every month. Robyn never asked where she went. When her own life was such a mystery, how could she ask questions of another person. And Marianne never volunteered anything about her time away. The only indication was that on the Monday after she returned her moods were more somber, as if she'd had a fight and was trying to get over it, without involving anyone at the restaurant.

"It's not them I'm thinking of." Robyn returned her attention to Grant in time to see the wry smile play at the corners of his mouth. Heat, like the airplane, defied gravity, and spilled up her raw shoulders and neck to deepen her face.

"Honestly, Grant. The restaurant is very busy on Saturday nights. It's too much work for one person."

"What about tonight?" he asked, finishing the last of his wine.

"I'm not blind to Marianne's motives, Grant. Tonight, she's playing cupid. It's been a long time since I went out with anyone. She thinks that if I continue to see you, something will develop."

"Will it?" Fear made him ask, and he was holding his breath, waiting for her to answer. He looked directly at her. She returned his gaze, not wavering. Nothing in her eyes showed any emotion. Yet, he knew how he affected her. Since that first morning he'd kissed her, he longed to do it again. Yet, there was something about this woman. Some mystery he couldn't unravel, and she had yet to confide in him. He wanted her, but he wanted more than she was ready to give. He wanted her to trust him enough to tell him what it was that kept her pushing him away.

"It's impossible, Grant." He knew she would say it. She'd told him that before when she sent him away. But he hadn't been able to stay away. He was totally consumed by his love for her. She haunted him, and she didn't know it. He'd done nothing but think about her since he left. David and Susan's engagement party gave him another excuse to see her.

"Okay, it's impossible."

Robyn was nonplussed. She'd expected to argue with him, and he'd calmly accepted her decision. It didn't make her feel good. In fact, she hated how she felt. She wanted to run into his arms and tell him their relationship could go on eternally, but she was prevented. The wall around her was carefully in place, and nothing could pierce it. She sat quietly, sipping the last drops of wine from the heavy crystal goblet.

The house at 2430 Kalarama Road was alive with light, and a festive air penetrated the confines of the limousine that slowly made its way down the narrow street and delivered them to the circular driveway. Robyn gave her hand to the gloved chauffeur who provided support as she exited the car. She had learned as they left the plane and Grant showed her into the limo that he not only owned a charter service but also a fleet of limousines. He explained the need to get people to the airport in order to fly them to their destinations. The plush accommodations were as expensively decorated as the customized plane had been.

Tonight, she was getting the royal treatment. Grant took her arm and led her into the hall. Music greeted them as they stopped briefly to give her wrap to a uniformed maid. Her eyes were hungry for a glimpse of Susan, and she looked around trying to cover her excitement and keep anyone from noticing. Finally, she spotted Susan on the other side of the room. She was thinner. Her hair, that Robyn remembered as being shoulder length, was a short crop of curly ringlets. Her face was radiantly parted in a happy smile. David was by her side. He looked the same. Not even a gray hair had changed his appearance. But he looked more confident than she had remembered. From somewhere, the image of Don Quixote tilting at a windmill came into her consciousness. She could imagine David fighting for the woman by his side. They were talking to a couple whom Robyn didn't know.

In the back of her mind, guilt tugged at her thoughts. She shouldn't be here. She knew she was tempting fate. Tonight, she could make a fatal error. With a slight shrug, she pushed it to the back of her mind. Tonight, she was going to have a good time. Tonight, she wanted to be Robyn. For a few short hours, she wanted to slip back into the comfortable role of Robyn Warren-Richards and tell her husband she loved him. She wanted to rush to her friends and tell them that she'd missed them and spend the evening catching up on the past five years.

But Jacob's face loomed in front of her. The wall was back. Like a living part of her existence it stopped her. She couldn't go back. She had to be more on her guard than ever. These were people who knew her, knew everything about her. They were the ones most dangerous to her. She couldn't afford to let any word, any gesture from her past slip out and condemn her.

Squaring her shoulders, she walked toward them, Grant at her side. Susan looked up, smiled at Grant and came forward. David followed her. Susan hugged Grant, and David shook his hand. "This is Brooke Johnson." He introduced her.

"Hello," Susan smiled widely. "Grant has told us about you."

She gave him a questioning look. "I hope it was all good." She joked covering her embarrassment. "Congratulations, he tells me you're to be married."

Susan turned her gaze to the man she loved. Robyn's heart muscle tightened. She wanted to be able to openly look at the man she loved with the same unmasked emotion.

Robyn knew David had been married before. He told her it only proved he never wanted to be married again. She could see his meeting Susan had changed that. It was wonderful to be able to see them.

She felt like she were on the window side of a one-way mirror. She could look into their lives but they couldn't see hers. She smiled to herself.

"Would you like something to drink?" David asked them.

"Darling, I'd like a glass of wine." Susan responded, and Robyn nodded when Grant asked her. The two women watched as Grant and David headed for the bar.

"Will you be staying for the weekend?" Susan asked conversationally. She moved toward the edge of the room. Robyn walked with her until she stopped near a mahogany table. Above it was a large gold-framed mirror, ornate with cherubs, capturing the activity in the room.

"I'm afraid I have to get back." She watched as her friend's face seem to fall slightly. Robyn knew the expression. There was something on Susan's mind, and she was trying to hide it. For anyone else, it was unnoticeable, but they had known each other since college, and Robyn recognized it immediately. It couldn't be David, not after the way she'd looked at him. It had to be something else. "Is anything wrong?"

Susan smiled. "I'm sorry. Actually, it's none of my business. It's just that Grant has been alone so long, and then, you came into his life. We're . . ."

"I understand." Robyn took over. "You're his friends, and since his wife died, you've been his protectors. Suddenly, I show up, someone you don't know, who doesn't live here and can't be watched to tell if my intentions warrant approval?" She was rewarded by the look of surprise that replaced Susan's smile.

"If I didn't know better . . ." Susan began but appeared to stop speaking when she realized words were actually coming from her mouth.

"Excuse me." Robyn prompted, looking at the room from the mirror above her. Grant and David were talking quietly at the bar on the other side of the room.

"It's nothing, just that no one's read me so clearly since . . . well, in a long time." She corrected herself but Robyn knew she was about to say Robyn. "I'm surprised to find my thoughts so visible."

"I didn't mean to be unfriendly." Robyn wanted Susan to like her. In the back of her mind, she wished to tell her who she really was. Suddenly, the need to confide in someone was so strong she could barely contain the force that wanted to pull Susan into a room and pour her heart out to an understanding ear.

"I think I'm going to like you, Brooke."

Suddenly, her heart was full. Even if she had another face and a voice several notes higher than her former one, that invisible bond that reaches across time and keeps memory alive was shining in Robyn's eyes.

"I know I'm going to like you."

"I'm glad to hear that." Grant stood behind her. He set the glasses that he held on the table and placed his hands on Robyn's bare shoulders. Warmth washed over her, and she had to visibly keep herself from blushing. "Come, dance with me."

Robyn floated away, riding on her own cloud as Grant led her to the dance floor. The small band, hugging one wall of the large room, had just finished playing Billy Joel's "Piano Man." As she and Grant reached the temporary wooden floor, the band reached back in time and launched into Barry Manilow's "I Write the Songs." Her step faulted slightly before Grant turned her into his arms and glided her effortlessly around the floor. Robyn matched his steps, knowing the routine and following the feel of his lead as though their minds had merged and she knew what he would do before he did it.

Grant closed his eyes. She felt like Robyn as he held her in his arms. He lied to himself, saying it was because she was a dancer that she reminded him of Robyn. But he knew it wasn't true. In so many ways, she was like his wife. There was nothing he could see, and nothing she said, but there was something intangible about her that seem to bring Robyn into the picture.

He felt guilty about it sometimes. But there didn't seem to be anything he could do about it. He dreamed of Robyn, and his waking hours were filled with thoughts of how her hair had bounced when she'd moved her head or how her voice had sounded when she'd laughed. He smiled at the images he created. Robyn had been the only other person in his life who could make him block out everything and everyone else. He rationalized that this was the reason he couldn't stop comparing them.

The music stopped, but Robyn was too absorbed in being in Grant's arms to notice. It wasn't until someone bumped into her that she realized couples were leaving the dance floor. She and Grant made their way back to their drinks where she tried to cover her disorientation with the drink she raised to her lips. Susan and David were busy with other guests.

"Tell me what you think?" Grant asked.

"What I think about what?"

"Susan. You and she were having quite a conversation earlier."

"I think she's a wonderful person. I'm glad to see she's so happy." Robyn's eyes found Susan. She was laughing at something someone said to her. "Tell me how they met?" She brought her eyes back to Grant.

"Susan was our next door neighbor. When I was captured and taken to Beirut, David got her to help let Robyn know. They saw each other frequently at our house while Robyn waited for the state department to finish negotiations. After I came back and Robyn died, they started seeing each other."

"What's taken them so long to get married?" It had been five years since that day in her kitchen.

"I guess they were both being cautious. David had a bad marriage and so did Susan. This time, they wanted to be sure everything would work."

Robyn's gaze found Susan and David. They looked at each other as if each person's world centered on the other. "I'm sure it will work."

Dinner was announced then, and she found herself seated next to David. On her right was a thin, red-headed, woman who owned a fashionable dress shop in Georgetown. Robyn had a lovely time talking to her about styles, colors, and using fabric to decorate. She found out that the woman had a hobby of using the excess fabric from making her own designs to make doll clothes. She said she did it for her granddaughter, but the hobby turned into a business and now she sold the designs in a toy store on M Street.

"I'll have to visit it when I'm in Washington again." Robyn told her.

"And when might that be?" David captured her attention.

"I'm not sure." She turned to him. "I have a business to run in Buffalo."

"Grant tells me you own a restaurant, and you sing and dance there."

"I only sing one song, and I dance to fill in if one of the regulars is out. My role is managing."

"Who's minding the store tonight?" He raised a cup of coffee and drank.

"I have a partner. She's doing everything tonight, and I'm sure she's very busy." Robyn thought of Marianne coping with everything that could possibly go wrong. When they were both there, each had someone to depend on to handle things. Just the thought of not having to take care of everything made the operation run smoother.

"Susan and I are planning our honeymoon in Toronto. Maybe, we can drive down and have dinner one night."

"That would be wonderful." Excitement seemed to ooze from her. She'd love to see them again. And on safe territory. "I'll have the chef make your favorite foods."

David smiled at that. "Now, we'll have to come. And speaking of coming, can we count on seeing you at the wedding?"

Robyn took a deep breath. "I'm not sure. I do need to be at the restaurant."

"Can't you make arrangements? One day can't make that much difference."

"I'll let you know." Robyn knew she couldn't come. She had no right being here tonight.

"I'm sure Grant would want you with him."

"I promise, I'll try." She'd like nothing better than to attend her best friend's wedding. But the situation was impossible. Tonight's visit had been an unexpected one. But to plan to return to the city where men would kill her if they knew her identity . . . And where Jacob was only a few miles away.

David patted her hand and smiled, his arguments curtailed for the moment. Robyn spied Grant at the other end of the table. While she sat at David's right, Grant sat on Susan's right at the opposite end of the table. She wondered if they'd been placed that way for some strategic purpose. Grant was engaged in conversation and not looking at her. Then, the woman next to Robyn captured her attention and monopolized it through the rest of dinner.

After the meal, the dancing resumed and promised to go on late into the night. Robyn found herself at the bar with David by her side.

"Are you having a good time?"

"Yes," she answered truthfully. She was enjoying herself. She'd danced with Grant several times and talked to Susan. She felt like a ghost, able to see into the lives of her friends without them knowing who she really was.

"What's that smile for?" David asked, guiding her away from the bar. They walked into another part of the huge house where small groups of people nodded as they passed. Robyn recognized several of their mutual friends and former neighbors. David led her to the farthest corner of the crowded room. She knew he was about to feel her out.

"You're not going to ask me if my intentions are honorable?" she asked, lightly challenging him as she dropped into one of the maroon velvet chairs that dotted the room.

Throwing his head back and laughing loudly, David captured the attention of the room. For a brief moment, all eyes focused on them. He quieted and normal conversation resumed.

"You've been talking to Susan." It was a statement.

"We've decided to become friends," she smiled.

"I like you, Brooke Johnson. You're direct." Robyn dropped her head a moment before bringing her eyes back to his. "You're like Susan," David continued. "She, too, can't manage to stop saying what's on her mind."

"You love her a lot." Robyn didn't need to say it. She only had to look at them to see that they each were absorbed in the other.

"Fortunately, what comes out of her mouth is also what's in her heart and I love her—a lot." Robyn knew the small phrase came from his heart. It made her feel warm inside. She had liked David from the first, and Susan was her oldest friend. The two of them married would make her immensely happy.

Robyn raised her glass to him and toasted, "I wish you a lifetime of memories—created today, remembered today, created tomorrow, remembered forever." The look on David's face stopped her heart. How could she be so thoughtless? That was the toast he'd given to Grant and herself at their wedding dinner in Las Vegas. In the last five years, she'd been so cautious, now she was forgetting herself. She had to be careful. She promised herself it wouldn't happen again. In a few hours, she'd be safely back in Buffalo, away from everyone who'd been so important in the life she'd left.

"I gave that toast to Grant and Robyn. He must have told you."

She raised her glass, giving a noncommittal shake of her head and hoping her error would be covered.

He leaned closer to her as if the words he was about to say were for her ears only. "Grant is a changed man since he met you."

"What do you mean, a changed man?"

"More relaxed, smiles a lot." David leaned back in his chair. "The only change has been his frequent trips to see you."

"What was he like before?"

David's brows furrowed, and he sipped at his drink before answering. "I don't mean to sound like he was unhappy. He's told you about Robyn?"

Robyn nodded. "She died five years ago."

"After Robyn died, Grant burned the candle at both ends. He put everything into the air service. Sometimes, we didn't see him for weeks."

Robyn's heart contracted. Guilt over the pain she'd caused him washed over her like scalding water. Forcing herself not to shudder, she continued to listen.

"Finally, when the business began to prosper, we thought Grant would begin to take it easy."

"But he didn't?" Robyn asked.

"Not by a long shot. He wanted to fly every contract himself."

"That's not like Grant . . . I mean he doesn't seem like the type who wouldn't know how dangerous that could be. Couldn't you convince him?"

"We tried. Susan thought . . . well, I agreed . . ."

Robyn watched him fumble. She knew what he wanted to say. But she let him struggle a while before she helped him.

"You thought he needed a diversion, a woman, maybe."

"Exactly," David smiled, probably relieved she understood.

"Did it work?" she asked.

"Too well. He found a replacement for the energy he put into the business. About a year later, it stopped. He seemed like his old self."

"Did anything happen to cause the change?"

"I thought it was a resolution of Robyn's death. You see he never talked about her. Suddenly, he just began. I thought he exorcised all the demons keeping her alive. But it wasn't until a few weeks ago when he came back from Buffalo that I really think he began to let her go." The last sentence he spoke very slowly. Then, he paused as if he wanted the effect to sink into her.

Robyn's eyes bored into her friend. "Why are you telling me this? I'm a complete stranger."

"Grant's my friend. I want him to heal."

"Five years is a long time. You think that he's still grieving for Robyn?" Robyn asked herself that same question. Hadn't she found fault with every man to come into her life since she went into the program? Hadn't all her energy gone into the restaurant? Both of them were still grieving.

"I wouldn't want to see anything happen to cause him any additional pain."

"You think I would hurt him?" She moved to the edge of her seat.

"Not intentionally." David moved closer, taking her hands in his. "Please don't take this the wrong way," he hesitated. "You remind me of Robyn."

Robyn clinched her hands and immediately regretted it when she realized they were clasped in David's.

"You don't look like her, except for the hair. Your voice is different, but there's something about you that reminds me of her. And if Grant sees that, you could damage his healing process."

"What do you think I should do?" she asked.

"I have no solution, you could be the medicine he needs or . . ." He left the sentence hanging.

"Hey, you two have been hiding a long time." Susan came up behind Robyn. "And holding hands, too. What's going on?"

"I've just been trying to convince Robyn to come to our wedding."

"I'd consider it a personal favor if you'd come," Susan said.

"How can I refuse such an invitation." Robyn couldn't believe she'd let herself be talked into returning to Washington in three weeks. This was the last place on earth she should be.

"I've been looking all over for you." Grant joined the group. "Have they been ganging up on you?" He smiled at Robyn, and she returned it.

"No." Robyn looked at Susan before her gaze rested on David.

"Good, let's dance. Susan left me to Marsha Watson and I need someone to give me a sense of balance."

Grant took Robyn back to the dance floor. "Tell me the truth, were David and Susan giving you the third degree?"

"No, they're just concerned about you. And they wanted to invite me to the wedding."

"What did you say? You will come, won't you?" Grant circled the floor easily, and Robyn found it easy to combine her steps with his. "I know Susan will be the bride, but you'll be the prettiest woman there."

"I told them I'd come."

"Wonderful." Grant took the news by executing a series of turns that had her chiffon gown spinning about her legs.

The rest of the night seemed to pass in a blur. Grant stayed by her side, introducing her to his friends and keeping her busy on the dance floor. She smiled and laughed constantly and enjoyed being with him. It was like slicing a piece out of time. She was newly married and dancing the night away with the man of her dreams.

"Grant." David tapped Grant on the shoulder. "You might think this was planned, but you have a phone call. You can take it in the library."

Grant gave his friend a sarcastic look and ignored him. Again, he tapped. "I swear." A teasing smile pulled at his mouth. Robyn watched the exchange. Reluctantly, Grant left her, and David took his place.

David was not as tall as Grant, but was a good dancer. He swung her effortlessly about the dance floor, causing the chiffon skirt she wore to create a fabric cloud through which she moved. Memory made her match his steps. She couldn't remember the last time she had so much fun. When the music ended, she was excited and relaxed. Smiling and winded, David led her toward the bar.

"You dance well," David commented, after ordering another wine for them both.

Robyn smiled her thank you. She'd always enjoyed dancing with David. He usually gave her a good workout, and tonight was no different. His routine, however, was decidedly different. She realized when she went into his arms that she could not dance the way she remembered. And thankfully, she hadn't had to hold back her sure steps or fake the routine.

Grant's face was clouded when he re-entered the room. Robyn excused herself to go to him.

"Is something wrong?" she said, coming face-to-face with him.

"Come outside, I have to talk to you."

He took her hand, and she followed as they weaved through the crowd making their way to the terrace. There were couples meandering about, and Grant continued down to the lawn toward the back fence.

"What is it?" she asked, as a finger of fear slid down her spine.

"The decision will be totally yours. That was the airport calling. Apparently, there's been an emergency, and they need to use the plane."

Robyn let out the breath she was holding. "My God, Grant, you scared me. I expected something awful had happened."

"It'll mean you have to stay the night."

CHAPTER 11

Grant's condo was on the top floor of a pre-World War II building on Connecticut Avenue. Robyn stepped from the foyer into the spacious living room. It wasn't the typical male's apartment she'd expected. The room was color-coordinated as she figured was the rest of the apartment, indicating he'd hired a decorator.

Although it looked like something from *House Beautiful,* there was no life to the room. Paintings hung from the walls, detailed huge splashes of flowers that shocked the eye more than coordinated with the light-colored carpeting. The furniture was gray, upholstered with the same flower element, only a smaller version.

On the gleaming chrome and glass coffee table was a large vase with fresh flowers and several magazines. The flowers made her feel comfortable, and she smiled at them.

"My housekeeper, Mrs. Alexander, changes the flowers once a week," he explained, following her eyes.

Robyn nodded, her attention moving to the piano that sat in front of a wall of windows leading to a rooftop patio. She couldn't see the kitchen, but the dining area matched the living room. The tables continued the same glass and chrome scheme.

"It's a beautiful piano," she said, feeling breathless.

"I keep it tuned, but play it very little."

"You play?" The surprise showed in her voice. Grant hadn't played when they met.

"Not really. I hired a teacher once. He taught me only one song," he said.

Robyn returned her attention to him, "Just one."

He nodded.

"It must be something very special. Play it for me."

Grant dropped his keys in the bowl by the door. "I haven't played it in a long time," he said. "You'd laugh at me."

"I promise not to. In fact, if you want, I won't even look."

Grant sighed and went to sit at the keyboard. Robyn walked to the bar and found a bottle of champagne chilling in the small refrigerator. Her head was below bar-level when the first notes of Chopin's Nocturne in E-major filtered into the room. Numbness gripped her. Suddenly, she had no feeling in her fingers, and her knees turned to water. The bottle fell from her hand as she tried not to fall over in the confined space. Grasping the bar, she held on, trying to control her ragged breathing. Her arms had little strength, but she pulled herself up. Grant's back was to her. He sat erect, his fingers moving expertly across the keys. Music filled the room. Coming around, she collapsed on a barstool and listened to the haunting music. The Nocturne in E-major by Chopin was her favorite song.

In high school, she'd listened to a radio station, WNIA. Every night at midnight, they'd play Chopin's Nocturne in E-major. It was sign-off music for the station. Robyn would stay up, listening just to hear this song. Then, she'd fall peacefully to sleep.

She remembered the first time Mrs. Ross let her pick a recital piece. She'd chosen this song and worked hard to perfect it. And Grant had remembered enough to learn to play it. Tears gathered in her eyes.

When the last notes of the refrain died, water streamed over her cheeks like the fingers of time.

"You're crying," Grant came to her, taking her hands and closing her in his arms. "It wasn't that bad, was it?" he tried to joke.

Robyn was too choked up to speak. She tried opening and closing her mouth several times but found her throat closed by a clog of tears. Grant drew her closer. She buried her face in his shoulder and closed her eyes. Years melted away.

Few women were moved to tears by music, Grant thought, as he held the soft body in his arms. She smelled delicious. Right now, he wanted to lift her off her feet and carry her into the bedroom. But he just held her, allowing her to cry softly against him.

"I'm sorry," she finally said. "It's been a long time since I heard that song. And you play it beautifully."

"Why did it make you cry."

"Memories."

"Bad memories?"

Robyn shook her head. "No, they were wonderful memories. Why did you pick that particular song?"

He didn't want to tell her. He didn't want Robyn to intrude on them. But she was always there whenever he held Brooke, like he was doing now. He'd smell her hair and memories would flood through him. He'd kiss her neck, and it would be Robyn's neck. It wasn't fair, but he couldn't stop. When they were separated, she was always on his mind. Yet, when he was near her, he couldn't help the comparison.

Robyn stopped crying and pushed herself back. "Well, aren't you going to answer?"

"It's just something I liked?"

"Now, who's lying. No one hires a teacher for just one song unless it means a lot to them. It was her favorite, wasn't it?"

For someone so mysterious, she was extremely perceptive. He nodded. "Robyn loved it."

Grant stepped away then, going behind the bar and finding the discarded bottle of champagne. He opened it and poured two glasses. Robyn accepted one and sipped the bubbly liquid.

Her tears were dry now.

Robyn moved away from the bar. Carrying her glass, she opened the door to the patio. Night air and noise rushed into the room. Walking to the edge of the rooftop garden, she looked out. The length of Connecticut Avenue stretched before her. Even at this early hour of the morning, traffic brightened the famous thoroughfare.

"It's beautiful," she murmured.

"Yes, it's one of the reasons I bought it."

Robyn missed the city. She had loved living in Washington. The city had a life to it, a beat that seemed to mesh with the rhythm of her heart. She never thought she'd have to leave it. And although Buffalo had lots of snow in the winter and great summer sports, it lacked the opulence of Kalarama Road, the quaintness of Georgetown's cobblestone streets, and the frantic energy of Capital Hill.

She felt Grant behind her. He slipped his arms around her waist, and she stepped back. Her head fell against his shoulder. Grant's body hardened. Fire began a slow burn deep in her belly. Grant's hand came to cup her breasts as his mouth moved wetly across her uncovered shoulders. Where he touched her, small volcanoes erupted. She shuddered at the excitement that ran through her. Unconsciously, she moaned at the effect his touch had on her. She felt washed with a consuming heat, a heat that intensified and burned but didn't scorch.

His fingers flicked easily across the fabric of her gown, bringing her nipples to hard peaks. Robyn felt a scream rising. Her breath came in short gasps. Guttural sounds broke from her throat as Grant's hands burned her body. They left her breasts, that pushed and strained against the soft fabric of her dress, to cross her stomach and rub down her thighs. The heat between her legs doubled its intensity as his fingers beat a primal message to her.

Robyn's body felt light, almost liquid inside Grant's influence. Sounds coming from her grew louder as her need for him gained strength. She knew she couldn't take this pleasure-pain for any length of time.

The wind around them picked up, blowing her hair and lifting her gown in a puff of peach chiffon. But it was no match against the flames Grant ignited in her.

In one swift movement, she turned in his arms, seeking and finding the wetness of his hungry mouth. The passion between them had been held for too long, their need for each other kept at bay too long. Robyn poured everything into her kiss. It told him who she was. How much she loved him, had always loved him. How sorry she was for letting him go. She told him of their child and her years of loneliness. Nothing was left out as Grant's mouth fused with hers.

They were alone on a rooftop, but between them, they were alone in the universe. Grant found the zipper at the back of her dress and eased the metal fastening free. Robyn felt the cool breeze on her bare back for a moment before Grant's hands probed her sensitized skin. He lifted his head a second and looked into her eyes. There was no question there. Only a dark passion neither of them could deny. He stepped back just enough to let the dress separating them fall to their feet. His eyes devoured her breasts, making them thrust forward.

Bending, he lifted her and carried her through the apartment to the bedroom.

Slowly, he allowed her body to slip down his frame. Like two dancers in a private ballet he eased her down the long line of his thigh to the soft carpet. His eyes never left her face. It seemed to glow with a yellow-gold light. Tangling his hands in her hair, the velvet soft strands slipped through his fingers. He held her head and angled her mouth back to his.

Robyn felt his hard body next to her softer one. New levels of excitement rioted through her. She was burning with desire and could barely stand the intense moment of separation. She stood between his legs. His dark body pressed into hers. Her hands found the buttons on his shirt, and quickly, she peeled it away from his strong shoulders. Her fingers were frantic as they undressed him. When he stood before her naked, he took her hands in his and drew her back into his arms. His mouth took hers on a gasp of pleasure.

She didn't remember moving until she felt the bed against the back of her legs. Together they lay on it, Grant pulling her closer. Keeping her from leaving even the smallest space.

She touched him, running her hands against powerful shoulders, down subtle arms, across his muscular stomach and even lower. He felt like raw silk. She loved how he even made her palms sensitive whenever they came into contact with skin that rippled under her tutelage.

Grant's moans mingled with Robyn's until she didn't know from which one of them they came. Grant's mouth slid away from hers. He buried his face between her shoulder and neck for a moment. His body trembled against hers. Then, he rolled away and sat on the edge of the bed. For several moments, he looked at her, as if he were trying to memorize every dimension of her body. Robyn felt no embarrassment at his appraisal.

Grant reached across her to the drawer of the nightstand. Out came a foil covered pouch. "Here let me," she said, taking the silver disk from him. She left the bed and kneeling in front of him, pulled the covering away. The rubbery protector felt cool against her fingers. With her index fingers and a slowness borne of anticipation, she watched its length shorten as she gathered it. Keeping her fingers inside, she slipped it over his erection and rubbed the skin of her fingers against him. She felt the strain in him communicated through the motion of his throbbing maleness. Ever so slowly, she brushed her fingers up and down. Grant's hands grabbed her shoulders and squeezed. She dared to look at him. His eyes were closed, and his teeth were clamped on his lower lip as if he was holding back sound. With eminent slowness, she continued to pull the opaque rubber over his hardness, while her fingers reveled in the heat and throbbing energy of the instrument she covered. In a ritualistic finger dance, she made a ceremony of the protective covering. When she finally reached the fullness of his body, her hands went to his thighs. The thread of control that he held over himself was ready to snap. She felt the muscles of his legs bunch under her palms and heard the small cry of pleasure break from the big man sitting above her. She forced herself to maintain a steady pressure, to control the precision and speed with which she raked her thumbnails down his inner thighs. His hands tightened about her shoulders and found their way into her hair that fell down her back. It was exhilarating. When she reached his knees, she lowered her mouth and brushed her tongue over the surface.

Grant hooked his hands under her arms. He hauled her back onto the bed and rolled on top of her. He sought her mouth in an uncontrolled kiss that plunged his tongue deep into the well of her mouth. His legs tangled with hers, and his hands stroked her body drawing heat as they passed over her tip-hard breasts, stomach, and into the center of her being.

Finally, his knee separated her legs, and he hovered above her for a second. She knew he was forcing himself not to plunge into her. With expert direction, he lowered himself into her, but stopped as the heat of his body made contact with the throbbing need in her. A violent surge pushed through Robyn, and she moved forward, opening her body to swallow Grant inside her. But he kept her at bay. And just as she'd created a ceremony with her fingers, he made her groan as he pushed and retreated at the entrance but refused to take the full measure of her offering.

A scream from deep within her was rapidly working its way to the surface. Robyn didn't know if she could keep it from breaking. Pleasure spasms rioted through her. Grant continued his exercise. She squeezed her eyes shut and drew her hands into tight balls against his back.

"Grant," she called as she raised her knees and met his erection. This time he entered her fully. She felt her body close around his hardness, and then, response was out of control. Grant's easy strokes were quickly replaced by frantic movements. Their tango was a pristine dance, each knowing the other's wants and needs. Each pressing the right buttons, making the other cry out with delight as every pleasure point was erotically discovered and exploited.

Robyn couldn't help calling Grant's name. And hers broke from his lips more than once.

The climax was wild, savage, uncontrollable. Grant collapsed against her. She was unaware of his weight as she took long breaths. She felt good, unable to stifle the smile that lifted the corners of her mouth. Her arms tightened around him, and she pressed her lips against his sweat-soaked shoulder.

Grant reacted with a shudder. He turned on his back, pulling Robyn on top of him. Her hair tumbled in his face, and he brushed it away, hooking it behind her ears and holding her face between his hands.

"Even if your mouth doesn't say it, your body knows."

"Knows what?" She rested her elbows above his shoulders. A playful smile curved her lips. Her fingers stroked the scar above his eye.

"That I love you, and you love me." He cradled her head against him and held it, next to his heart.

They lay like that for a long time. Robyn felt happier than she had in years. Grant shifted, keeping her close to his side and gently running his hand up and down her arm. Robyn closed her eyes and reveled in the cocoon of love he weaved.

"Are you sleepy?" he asked. She felt his jaw move against her head.

"No," she answered.

"Good, tell me something about yourself?"

Robyn steeled herself, but didn't tense. She didn't know how to answer that question, and she had to be cautious about what she said. Lying here while the need to trust mingled with the aroma of passion; she wanted to tell him the truth. But did she dare? She thought she'd try lightness.

"Do you want to know when I had my teeth straightened, or how I went from being the skinniest kid in school to the one with the most zits?"

He chuckled as he drove his fingers into her hair. Then, he turned her face to his. In the semidarkness, it was difficult to see.

"Tell me about him?" Grant asked. The seriousness in his voice was unmistakable. "You don't talk about him much."

"I didn't think you'd want me to spend time talking about another man." Robyn tried to buy herself some time. She moved away, needing room if they were going to talk about Cameron Johnson.

Grant smiled and pulled her back into his embrace. "In most cases, that's true. I'm guess I'm just interested in everything about you and what made you the person you are."

Robyn stilled her reaction. How she'd like to answer all his questions, pour her heart out to him, satisfy the unknown questions she could see in his eyes. Tell him who she was, and plead for him to understand and forgive her for leaving him and taking his daughter with her.

Then, her eyes fell on the photograph of him standing next to *The Salt Box,* the plane he flew his first solo in. It was standing on his crowded desk in the corner of the room illuminated by a shaft of moonlight. No other photographs were present. Grant's happy grin poked into her guilt, and slowly, the air seeped out of it. She had made the correct decision. Even today, she couldn't take his love of flying away. It was the one thing in life he couldn't live without.

Grant touched her cheek, causing Robyn to shift her gaze from the hypnotic effect of his smile to the hypnotic effect of the real man beside her. "Tell me, Brooke Johnson, who is the real Brooke Johnson?" If it hadn't been for the mischievous grin he flashed her, she'd be concerned he knew more than she wanted him to know. Outwardly, her features responded, yet her calculatorlike brain went into action. "You don't talk very much about yourself, do you?" he continued.

"I'm not really that interesting," she hedged.

"I can argue that. You're the most mysterious woman I've ever met."

"Isn't mystery the definition of *woman?*" She attempted to redirect the conversation from herself to women in general.

"Every man likes some mystery about a woman. It keeps him interested. But you," he hesitated, searching for words to explain his meaning. "You make intrigue an art."

"What do you mean by that?" One part of her mind told her to steer clear of this avenue, while the other rushed hurriedly toward it.

"In the past month, I've told you about Lebanon, Robyn, and my charter service, yet, all I know about you is that you have a daughter with a rare blood type, you own a restaurant, and you're a widow."

"And you want me to fill in a few of the details." A ready smile traced her even teeth.

"No."

"No?" Her eyebrows went up.

"No, I want you to fill in *all* the details. I want to know everything about you." The eyes that searched hers were serious.

Robyn climbed out of the bed. She found his shirt and pulled it over her nakedness. "My husband's name was Cameron." She began the familiar tale she'd learned and relearned and relearned. "We met during spring vacation our junior year in college. We were married the day after graduation."

"And you lived happily ever after."

Robyn moved toward the curtained windows. She felt much like an actress playing a part. "Not exactly. We were so naive. We believed because we loved each other every problem could be solved."

"It didn't work out."

"It's not what you're thinking. We were so poor. We had no money at all. Getting jobs with no experience was impossible. Cameron joined the navy and had allotments sent to me. It made it easier for us both. When his ship was going to sail I went to San Diego for a week. We called it our honeymoon." She smiled exactly as she'd been cued to do. "On our last day there, he saw me off at the airport. On the bus back to the base, he died. Apparently, he had an embolism. The doctors said it was a blood clot too large to pass through a vessel in the brain."

"I'm sorry." Grant sat fully up in the bed.

"It's all right," she said turning to him. "I've come to terms with his death." She paused a moment. "Which is more than you've done." His gaze narrowed as he stared at her. "You keep Robyn alive. You and your friends."

Grant left the bed then, pulling his pants on and coming to stand in front of her. Robyn could hardly stand not putting her hands on his muscular chest and outlining the clearly defined sections of his torso.

"When David and I went to get the drinks, you and Susan were deeply engaged in conversation for a long time. And later, you disappeared with David. What did they say?"

"Susan was concerned that I could hurt you. And David told me about your life since you lost your wife."

"I see," he let the words out with a heavy breath of air.

"I apologize for their actions. They—"

"You don't have to apologize for them," she interrupted. "They're loyal, and they love you. They don't know anything about me except suddenly you're showing an interest in another woman, a woman they didn't pick and choose for you. I guess they want to make sure you're protected."

"I don't need their protection."

"Of course, you do. Everyone needs someone's protection. Before David met Susan, didn't you scrutinize every woman he saw?"

"Not exactly."

"Men are no different than women. We all want the one we love to like our friends. And have our friends like them. It's very important."

"I suppose you're right. I just never thought of it that way before."

"What about when you married Robyn. Weren't you pleased David liked her and she liked him?"

"I was more than pleased. David told me she was like the sister he'd never had. When she died, he was almost as broken up as I was. I guess that's why it seems she's still alive. Would you want your friends to forget you if you died?"

"I wouldn't want to be forgotten, but I'd want them to go on with their lives. I'd want them to live in the present, not the past."

"You think I'm living in the past, that I'm refusing to go on with my life because I never really let Robyn die?"

Robyn didn't know what answer she wanted to hear. "Is it true?"

"A month ago I'd have said, no. But since I walked into that waiting room, I'm no longer sure." He stepped around Robyn, giving his full attention to the street below for several long moments. Then he turned away. "You remind me of her."

The statement was short, but it hit her like a nuclear missile exploding in her brain. She could see her years of training and the false sense of security she'd made herself believe evaporate into a mushroom cloud of reality. David had seen the similarities in her, too, and Grant had confirmed his friend's fear that she could hurt him by being a constant reminder of his wife.

"It's not your voice, or the way you look," he continued. "In fact, it's nothing I can actually see. But in some way, when I'm with you . . ." He stopped. "I know that's an insult, and I apologize, but . . . it's true." The last was said quietly.

Robyn wasn't insulted. If she and his Robyn weren't the same woman, she would have been. But more important than being insulted, she knew the danger of her situation. She couldn't pull off this kind of charade. She wasn't a good enough actress. Sooner or later, she'd tell him who she was, or he'd guess.

She knew she had to stop. She'd known it since the beginning. And now that he was starting to recognize things in her that the identity of Brooke Johnson could not hide, she had to break off their relationship.

"Say something. Scream, shout, throw something. But don't subject me to your silence."

Robyn turned around and looked in his eyes. Desperation was reflected there. She didn't want to leave him, but it was inevitable. She would return home, and somehow, she'd make good on her promise to Jacob. She wouldn't see Grant again. But now. Just one more time.

"Take me back to bed," she said.

CHAPTER 12

She came easily into his arms. Her hands were like hot wax dripping along his shoulders as she caressed him. She seemed to revel in the feel of his skin, just as he came alive under her tutelage. He could feel his muscles bunch and relax at her touch as if they were under her orchestration. She pressed her mouth to his breast. Fires of emotion rocketed through him like a G-force, pressing his body against a stress factor too strong to ignore. He'd lifted her lithe body and carried her back to the bed. He slid her to the floor, her body tracing his on its journey. She was electrified. He felt jolt after jolt of energy pass through him as his tongue paused and rested in the contours of her sensually sculpted body. Standing her on the floor, he kissed her lightly, rubbing his lips gently, caressingly over hers. Heat emanated from her in vast waves. He knew she wanted him to deepen the kiss. Her hands were frantically working in his hair and across his shoulders. But he held back. He wanted to tease her, tease himself, make her want him so badly she'd be blind with urgency when he finally took her. He could barely stand not to devour her. Then, his hands went to the buttons on the shirt she wore, his shirt. He slowly undid them. Moon-drenched skin was exposed inch by inch.

He put his mouth to the exposure. Small whimpering sounds came from her as her fingernails dug into him. Lower and lower, he slid down her his hands memorizing her body and his tongue tasting her. The sound acted like an aphrodisiac, boiling his blood and driving him toward the edge. When all the buttons were released, he slipped the covering off her shoulders, and silently it fell to the floor. He stood back and looked at her, his eyes as hungry as his loins. She was beautiful. In the filtered-light of morning, she was the most beautiful woman he'd ever seen. She didn't appear aware of her nakedness. He discarded his pants, his erection hard and ready. He took her in his arms and lowered her to the silk sheets, joining her there.

He tangled his hands in her hair gently pulling her to him. He fit into the well of her body as if he had been constructed for no other reason. He took her mouth with a hunger that had worked its way from deep within his belly. Tongues and lips battled each other for dominance. He rolled over on her, extending his length, feeling her softness beneath him. Then, his hands ran over her body. She was warm and pliant, and with each touch of his fingertips, he drove her into a frenzy. Finally, he spread her legs and entered her. He knew it would be wonderful. She fit tightly around him, pulling him in and releasing him only to suck his body back to hers. He tried to be gentle, but she was too hot, too ready, and too out of control, writhing beneath him.

And, then, it happened. The soaring came suddenly and without preparation. She lifted her legs around him, and he scooped her buttocks in his hands, rocking her savagely. Fingernails grazed the sensitive skin of his back. He cried out at the fierce pleasure that tore through his body with widening radiation at the feel of her body taking him into it. He held on for as long as he could. The pleasure funnel spiralled upward with an ever widening vortex. He wanted the pleasure to continue forever, but finally, with one maddening cry, white heat tore through him and the night exploded. For the space of an eternity, she held him in that semiworld where life begins and ends. Then, he collapsed. His breathing was ragged as he took short gulps of air, trying to fill his lungs. His body was bathed in sweat, and his limbs felt as heavy as boulders.

What had she done to him? Never had he lost such complete control. Never had his bones turned to powder or his muscles held less substance than water. With his last ounce of energy he rolled his weight off Brooke. He cradled her in his arms and together they slept.

Grant's internal clock woke him. The summer sun shone through the curtains and brightened the room. Brooke was still imprisoned in his arms. He held her tenderly as if she were an endangered species. And indeed she was, at least to him.

He'd awakened in this room every morning for four years, but today it felt complete. This morning, Brooke was here, by his side. He smoothed the hair away from her face. She stirred, a dreamy smile lifting the corners of her mouth.

He wanted to kiss that mouth, wake her gently, slowly, ease her into the day, then make violent love to her until his name broke from her lips in shattering finality. He groaned as his body began to harden at the thoughts coursing through his mind. For a moment, he hesitated, then quietly left the bed. He dressed in the guest bathroom and headed up Connecticut Avenue at a leisurely pace. He smiled and whistled for the twenty minutes it took to reach Dupont Circle and the small Italian house of confections. The smell of sugar had his mouth watering the moment he opened the door. There were people ahead of him and suddenly he was impatient. He thought of Brooke waiting for him. It was unreasonable, but suddenly he was sorry he'd left her.

When it was his turn, he bought muffins. They were still warm from the oven and smelled delicious. Brooke would probably be asleep when he got back. He'd make coffee and crawl back in bed with her. They could eat, read the paper, drop crumbs on the sheets, and make love. He didn't care what they did as long as they did it together.

The doorman touched his hat and pulled the hydraulically operated glass door open when Grant returned to his condo. Grant smiled as he passed him. He took the first elevator. At the fifth floor, he got off. Everybody in the building must have decided to go out for pastries this morning, he thought. The small room was full of smiling faces, and every button was lighted. The smell of warm bread wafted through the confined space. He'd walk the last three flights. Holding the box in front of him, Grant took the steps two at a time. Waiting for the elevator to climb one floor at a time was too taxing while the woman he loved still wallowed leisurely beneath the white silk sheets of his bed. He was too excited to stay crowded in the elevator.

"Brooke," he called, pushing the door closed behind him. His smile was wide and welcoming.

Stopping midway through the living room, he turned around. His smile faded and was replaced with a frown. His heartbeat increased. Somehow, the apartment was different. Sterile was the word that came to mind. It had a hollow sound despite the gray carpet muffling his footsteps.

"Brooke?" he called again. No reply brought her voice or her person into view. Grant went into the kitchen, then to each of the bedrooms and the den. She wasn't in any of the rooms.

Dropping onto the piano bench, he tried to determine what had happened to the apartment. He got up and walked through the rooms again. Everything was as he had left it, almost. It was neat and clean—too neat and too clean. Brooke had cleaned the coffeepot and cup he'd left on the counter yesterday. The pot was back in its place on the stove, and the cup was neatly stored in the cabinet.

The bed had been made, and the living room furniture looked polished. He lifted the flower vase on the dining room table. No dust ring was present. Then, he went to the coffee table, repeating the procedure.

Again, no dust ring. It was as if the apartment had been sucked clean. Everything was in the exact place that he expected to find it, yet nothing was the same.

And where was Brooke? Somehow he knew she was gone for good. Why hadn't she left a note? Maybe she'd gone to Susan's. She seemed interested in the store when he'd told her about it. Grant reached for the phone and quickly dialed the number.

Susan hadn't seen her.

Where could she have gone? And why? Why did he know she wasn't coming back? The cleanliness of the apartment told him, she wasn't just out, she had wiped herself out of his life.

But how could she? After the night they had spent together, didn't she realize how much he loved her? She'd asked him to take her back to bed. And they had made love. She'd shown him how much of his life was missing. He wanted her more than he'd ever wanted another woman. She couldn't disappear from his life.

Robyn didn't know how she got there, but suddenly, she found herself in front of 1651 Gayle Street. She smiled at the pregnant woman working in the garden. Her old house looked happy. A young couple, probably having their first baby, lived there now. In the front yard, a young woman knelt, pulling weeds. Robyn was glad to see her taking care of the flower bed she had planted before her first anniversary. A moment earlier, a young man had left. He'd kissed his wife and reversed the Honda Civic out of the driveway with a happy smile and a wave to the woman on her knees.

Robyn wondered if they could be moles, planted by the men searching for her? She watched the pleasant looking woman for a while. Her body, in full bloom, had a glow that shown radiantly on her oval face. Robyn decided she was all right and took the chance of crossing the street and calling out to her.

"Hello," Robyn greeted, standing on the outside of the white picket fence that surrounded the carefully manicured lawn.

The woman turned, shielding her face against the morning sun.

"Good morning," she called, brushing the dirt from her knees as she approached Robyn.

"Do you know if Susan Collins will be back soon?"

"Susan Collins?" the woman repeated, her brow furrowing. "I'm afraid I don't know anyone by that name."

"She lives in the house next door." Robyn pointed to the white vinyl-sided ranch-style house with black shutters and window boxes spilling over with yellow and white mums.

"We haven't lived here very long, but Mike and Cara Evans live there."

"Oh," Robyn managed to sound sorry and look sincere. "I've been away a long time. I used to live here and Susan was my next door neighbor. I didn't realize she'd moved."

"You lived here?" The woman seemed surprised. "In our house?"

Robyn nodded. "It was a very long time ago. This is my first trip back."

"My husband's just gone to his office for a few hours. Why don't you come in and have some tea with me?"

"I couldn't."

"Of course, you can. I'm Jenny Bryant, and I love making tea." She pulled her gloves off and offered her hand.

Robyn smiled. "I'm Brooke Johnson." She took the soft hand.

"Brooke, what a wonderful name."

Robyn couldn't believe her luck. When she crossed the street, she had expected to talk briefly and leave. Being invited in was like grabbing the golden ring. Moments later, she found herself sitting in the spacious kitchen where she'd received the news of Grant's hijacking. The walls had been yellow then. Now, they were a Wedgwood-blue. The china cup and saucer holding the steaming cup of dark liquid was blue.

"I'm into names at the moment." Jenny rubbed her bulging stomach. "I like Brooke, but Brooke Bryant is to many B's."

She had to agree with that. "When is the baby due?" Robyn sipped her tea. It was bland to her taste. She always spiked hers with apple spice.

"Three more months. But I feel like a cow."

"You look wonderful. Enjoy the time. It's one of the best there is."

"You have children?"

"Only one. A daughter. Her name is Kari."

"How old is she?"

"Four. Have you decided on a name?" Robyn steered the conversation away from herself.

"Yes, I like Margaret Elizabeth if it's a girl and Warren Michael if it's a boy. My husband, William, likes Joann and William, Jr." Jenny frowned at her husband's choice of names.

Robyn envied them. It was something they could share. She had made the decisions alone. Grant wasn't with her, didn't even realize there was a child to name.

"William is an engineer," Jenny continued. "Unfortunately, he had to work today. I'm sure he would have liked to meet you. He has so many questions about the house."

"Maybe I can help answer some of them."

"Finish your tea, and I'll give you a tour. I'm sure you're dying to see what's happened to it since you left."

"You're right," Robyn confirmed as she obediently drained the cup.

Jenny led her through to the living room. It was nothing like she remembered. The plantation white walls were gone, replaced by a pale yellow that picked up the scheme in the multicolored sofa. On the walls hung several paintings which looked of the variety you find in any department store's glass and mirror section. They did coordinate the room and make it warm and cozy.

One of the walls in the dining room had been pulled out and in its place a glass door led out to the patio with brightly colored chairs surrounding an umbrella table. Robyn liked it. It gave the small room air and a sense of additional space. She had entertained Susan and David there often.

Grant's den which had built-in bookcases and a case for his collection of airplanes, was now filled with engineering books. Now, a drafting table sat in one corner, and the posters of airplanes that he'd hung on the walls had been replaced with photographs of bridges and tunnels.

Robyn's eyes misted over but she blinked them away. Jenny led her up the stairs and into the master bedroom. Here, everything was as she had left it that April morning five years ago. A gentle breeze floated through the windows, blowing the white sheers into the room.

It was then that she saw it. In a flash, she was across the room, lifting up the small carriage clock from the night table.

"Do you recognize it?" Jenny asked. "I found it wedged in a drawer of the desk downstairs. The desk was left with a drawer nearly sealed closed. When I finally got it open, I found the clock."

Robyn couldn't speak. It was the clock Grant had given her on their first anniversary. Tears misted her eyes, and she sat down on the queen-size bed.

"It's obviously yours," Jenny said, her voice quiet as if she knew the reverence Robyn placed on it.

"No-no." Robyn cleared her throat. "I just thought it was like one I used to have." Replacing the small gold-plated timepiece made her sorry she'd come. She had better leave.

After a second necessary to pull herself together, Robyn got up and straightened the coverlet. "It's time I was going. I have to meet someone, and I'm late now."

"I'm sorry. It was good visiting with you." Jenny walked her back to the front door. "If you're ever in town again, I do hope you'll visit me."

"I'd like that." Robyn smiled.

"Maybe next time, William will be here. He's working on a very important proposal. Something to do with building a dam in South America. Otherwise, he'd have been here today and could have asked about the tiny room in the basement."

"The darkroom. I used to develop a lot of film there."

"Oh, that's what it was. We thought it was an unfinished bathroom."

They reached the front door. "Thank you, Jenny. I enjoyed the tea and the tour. Good luck with the baby."

Robyn waved good-bye as she walked toward the car she'd parked a couple of blocks away. She envied the young couple. They loved her house and for that she was glad. She was also sad that she and Grant never got the chance to finish the things they'd planned when they had moved in.

Inside the car, Robyn inserted the key and turned the ignition. Then, she turned it off and leaned her head against the steering wheel. Suddenly, her hands were cold, but her body was burning. She liked what Jenny had done to the house. She could leave it now. She knew it was in good hands. Grant had left the memories behind, and now, she felt she could, too.

The only thing that haunted her was the clock. She'd wanted it. It was a piece of Grant, but it was also a part of another life. She didn't live that life any longer.

Robyn began to sit up. Suddenly, the door was yanked open, and something was pushed over her head. She fought whoever was attacking her. But the arms fighting back were stronger. She tried to scream, but an unknown hand came across her mouth, stuffing the fabric covering her head inside her mouth and cutting off her air. She kicked and fought blindly but was dragged from the automobile and pulled along the street. She couldn't tell how far she went, since all the while she tried to scream and hit out at the person forcing her to go someplace she had no intention of going.

The hand holding her mouth didn't move, but a knee kicked her in the back, edging her on until another hand pushed her head down, and she was catapulted into an unseen car. Immediately, the door snapped shut, and the car sped away, slamming her against the upholstery. She fought the confining fabric, which smelled of a strong detergent. At least it was clean she thought, realizing now that no one was trying to stop her from pulling the black bag from her head.

Finally, she was free of it.

"Jacob!" she screamed at the familiar face. She didn't know where the strength came from but she was fighting mad and began pummelling him with her fists. "I might have known you'd be behind a stupid stunt like this." Each word was punctuated by a blow.

Jacob grabbed her wrists and shook her. "Stop it!" he yelled. "What the hell do you think you're doing?"

For an immeasurable moment, they glared at each other. Then, he released her, dropping her wrists as if they had suddenly become hot. He straightened his tie, and the mask of G-Man slipped comfortably back into place.

"What do you want?" Robyn asked.

"I want to know what the hell you were doing in that house?" He didn't even try to hide his anger.

"Don't you know, Jacob?" Robyn straightened her borrowed dress, pulling the fabric that had ridden six inches over her knees back into place. "Aren't you privileged to everything that's happened to me for the past five years? Is there any moment of my life you don't touch?"

"Answer the question. Evasion will do no good."

"Damn it, Jacob, don't treat me like a child."

"Then stop acting like one," he shouted. "You have no right to be here at all. Coming back to this house. Didn't you think it would be watched? Did it occur to you that the residents could be planted there for just this kind of happening?"

"Of course, it occurred to me. But I met Jenny Bryant, and I saw her husband, William. Jacob, they're nice people. Jenny's going to have a baby, and her husband is an engineer."

"I know. He's bidding on an engineering project in Argentina." Veins popped out on Jacob's temples. "You just assured him of getting it."

"What?" Robyn turned to stare straight at him. "How? And if you tell me I don't need to know I swear I'll hit you." Robyn reached for her shoe. She needed something stronger than her hand.

"We keep tabs on this house, too. I believe the couple living there are exactly as they appear." Jacob sat back, straightening his tie. Robyn felt as if he were straightening his identity. "For that reason alone," he continued, "I'll make sure William Bryant gets that job, and in record time they will be relocated to Argentina."

"What about the baby? Will there be sufficient medical facilities for her?"

"She'll be fine." Jacob's voice was low. "You have my word on it."

Robyn looked into his eyes. He smiled at her and diffused her anger. "Do they really have to go before the baby?" She thought of all the doctors and sterile equipment that had been on hand in case of emergency when Kari was born. Would Jenny Bryant's baby have the same chance?

"You should never have come here." Jacob was nodding. "Now, we have to try and rectify any presence that could have an impact on your safety."

Robyn slumped in the corner of the luxurious car and sulked. Why couldn't she act like Jacob wanted her to? Why did she allow Grant to manipulate her life? Suddenly, his smiling face focused in front of her. It was that disarming smile that had her forgetting all of her promises and flying around the world with him, when she knew sooner or later Jacob would find out.

"Would it make any difference if I said I was sorry?" Robyn asked, not turning to look at the figure sitting stiffly beside her.

"Not much, but I would like to hear it."

"All right, Jacob, I'm sorry."

"Why did you lie to me?"

"I didn't lie to you. At least at the time, I wasn't lying. And I did do what you asked. I tried to resist him, Jacob." Robyn turned then and took hold of Jacob's arms. "I'm in love with him. Haven't you ever been in love with someone, Jacob? So in love you'd do anything for her?"

Damn, Robyn! I don't want to remember. Jacob looked at the misty eyes imploring him to forgive her. He knew he couldn't deny her request. Yes, he'd been in love before. Cynthia. He hadn't wanted to think about Cynthia, but Robyn made him remember. When he'd seen Robyn and known she had to be made over, the thought of stamping Cynthia's face on the scared woman was uppermost in his mind. He had resisted, knowing if he had tried, Clarence Darrow Christopher III would have pulled his hand.

Wrenching his thoughts back to the air-conditioned car, he answered softly, "I've been in love," he paused. "Robyn." He called her by her real name.

The tears Robyn had been holding spilled down her face, and she shrank into the corner of the luxury seat.

"Where are we going?" she asked, patting her cheeks and seeing the 14th Street Bridge outside the car window. The limousine was heading for northern Virginia.

"The airport."

Grant was at the airport. When she woke and found herself alone, she knew he'd gone to check on the plane. It was why she left. She wanted a quick tour before he returned. What would he think when he found she'd left without a word? Robyn whirled around just as Jacob pulled the familiar red, white, and blue airline envelope from his pocket.

"Your plane leaves in an hour. Marianne will pick you up when you arrive."

"Is she in on this, too, Jacob?"

"No," he answered directly. Robyn was so used to his evasions that she believed him.

"What about the clothes I left at Grant's apartment?"

"They're waiting at the airport."

"What's happened to his car? And this is Susan's dress." Susan had hastily packed her something to wear before she left last night. Robyn hadn't thought of anything but staying the night with Grant. While Susan had remembered practical things, reminding her how strange she'd look in a formal gown at ten o'clock in the morning.

"I'll see to it," Jacob told her in his usual noncommittal style.

"All the loose ends will be tied?" Robyn leaned forward. Her hair swung over her shoulders, separating her view from Jacob. She shifted in the seat and came back to stare directly at the man next to her. "Jacob, I promise to comply with all your conditions."

"Without exception?" One eyebrow went up, the only indication of his disbelief.

"With one exception."

"Go on."

"Susan and David are getting married the third weekend in August. I want to go to the wedding."

"No!"

"Jacob, she's my best friend. She asked me to her wedding. I want to go. Then, I promise, I'll do whatever you say."

"No, Brooke. You're asking the impossible. You should never have come here in the first place. You should not have made contact with any of them."

"But it's too late, Jacob, I've already passed that point. We've seen each other, talked to each other. They've invited me to the wedding, and I want to come. After that, I'll go back into hiding, and you'll never have cause to argue with me again. If you want me to move, I'll move. If you want Kari and I to change our names and disappear, we'll do it. I'll become the compliant female you always wanted me to be."

Jacob stared at Robyn. He found no comfort in her words. He'd tried to make her do what he wanted, but she never was the typical inductee. She was temperamental, feisty, alive, and wonderful—everything he'd ever wanted in a woman. Now, for a few hours at a friend's wedding, a friend who didn't even recognize her, she was willing to become a docile protectee.

"All right, you can go to the wedding."

"Thank you, Jacob." For the second time that day, she flung herself into his arms.

"Hold it, there are conditions." He pushed her away.

"Anything."

"You arrive shortly before the ceremony. Afterwards, you can spend only enough time at the reception to be considered socially acceptable. Then, you'll be flown back. Acceptable."

She heard the take-it-or-leave-it note in his voice. "Acceptable." She looked at her hands. "Is it all right if I bring Kari."

His heart went out to the baby he'd once held. Jacob hated to think of putting her in danger, but the child could be used as a barrier to keep the plan intact if anyone tried to change it. By anyone he meant Robyn. "Yes, bring Kari."

"Then, what, Jacob? Are we going to have to move, change our names and our faces again?"

Jacob ignored her question. "Why didn't you tell me about the poison or the photograph?"

Robyn lifted her head and directed her gaze at him. "How did . . ." She didn't complete the thought, knowing Jacob wouldn't answer.

"Has there been anything else I should know about?"

Robyn hesitated, refusing to drop her head. "My wings," she said quietly. "The day after the poison was found, a delivery was made to the restaurant. Inside the box were a pair of plastic wings. Grant had given them to me the night we got married. They were in my jewelry case when I . . . when we left for the airport." It was the day Grant came home. The television had been full of the reports about the hostages being released. Robyn had held the plastic wings in her hand. Then, she had dropped them in the box and closed it.

"How do you know they were yours? There must be thousands of those given out every year."

"The right side of the wing had a chip in it. Grant had offered to get me another one, but I wanted that one. On the back side of it, he had carved my initials and the date I flew solo." Robyn was quiet for a long while. "Jacob, I'm scared. He knows who I am."

"Brooke, we're aware of what's happening. We'll keep you safe. I promise."

Robyn stared at him. His face was open and honest, something he rarely showed to her or the world. What was going to happen to her? "Are we going to have to move, Jacob?" she asked again.

"Your plane is waiting."

The car had stopped, and the driver was holding the door open. Robyn looked out at the familiar terminal entrance to Washington National Airport. She took the driver's extended hand and slid out of the limousine. Jacob followed her. He led her straight through the terminal and to the departure gate, showing an I.D. as they bypassed the security machinery.

"Don't worry about anything, Brooke. We'll handle it." Jacob looked at her without the veil that always clouded his eyes. He was close enough to touch, yet the distance between them could have been miles.

"Grant. He'll be all right?" Tears gathered behind her eyes.

"I said we'd handle it."

"How?"

He took her arm and rushed her down the gangway. "You're holding up the plane."

At the entrance to the steel aircraft, she stopped. "Tell me? How are you going to stop Grant? He'll call or fly in."

"I'm expecting you to discourage that." The phrase was a definite threat, implying if she didn't—he would.

CHAPTER 13

Jacob needed a drink. He hadn't felt this gnawing hunger to drown his feelings in a bottle since *she* had died. Robyn had asked him if he'd ever been in love. Cynthia wasn't his first love, but she was the woman he'd wanted to marry.

It was dark in the nation's Capital. The streets outside his office window were wet from a light rain. Car lights were reflected on the street's damp surface, making a picture postcard of Pennsylvania Avenue.

He looked back at the desk. The computer screen beckoned. With several keystrokes, the monitor flickered, and she was there. It had been over nine years since he'd looked at Cynthia. Yet, there she was, hidden behind three levels of computer coding and several passwords. Tonight, Jacob needed her. He needed to remember. He hadn't been responsible for Cynthia's death. If she'd only done what he told her, she might be alive today. But she was too headstrong for that. She hadn't stayed hidden in the basement of the farmhouse where he left her, and she'd been killed.

Just like Robyn. She, too, wouldn't take direction. She defied him at every turn. Yet, he loved Robyn. But not the way he'd loved Cynthia. The two women were alike in temperament and beauty. Both of them got into his blood, and both refused to live the comfortable lives set up for them.

He had to admit he liked that in them. The majority of people he'd dealt with since becoming part of this program were too complacent, eager to get away and start an easy life at the government's expense.

Robyn hadn't been one of them. She'd given up everything and fought valiantly to carve out a life for herself. But she wasn't living. Jacob knew that. She was going through the motions, giving everything she had to enhance someone else's life, but not her own. She'd hired an alcoholic music director, giving him the chance to pull his life together. Some of the waiters had prison records or were former juvenile delinquents.

Jacob had them carefully screened. Currently, nothing about them posed a threat. Most of them were too young to have been involved with Alex Jordan or the Network. Need to intervene in her hiring practices hadn't been necessary, yet. And the latest one, an aspiring actress named Sue-Ellen. What he'd noticed happened with the people she helped was that they developed a fierce loyalty to her. He knew if anything were to jeopardize her, he could press these people into service, and without question, they'd rally to her aid.

Yesterdays had been a red wooden structure with ornate wrought-iron balustrades when Robyn bought it. Vinyl siding in light blue with white accents now supported the exterior frame. A single sign of rich red, deeply etched with gold lettering, denoted the name of the restaurant.

Robyn went up the walkway. She noticed everything tonight. The grass had been cut that morning, and the smell reminded her of fresh watermelon. She watched the wide expanse of it perfectly cutting out a circular driveway as it led to the front door. She rarely used this entrance, but tonight, instead of driving, she'd decided to walk the short distance from her house to Delaware Avenue. Arriving just before sunset, she could see the play of rays on the distant sky. It was red like spilled wine.

A couple, laughing as they passed her on their way to the door, brought her out of the suspended state she was in. Taking the last few steps to the canopied door, she entered. The old walls that had made the foyer narrow and dark had been removed. The area opened up on thick red carpeting that her feet sank into as she smiled at a group sitting on the comfortable chairs to her right. It was the usual meeting place for friends arriving at slightly separate times. From above, a huge chandelier brightly lighted the dark panelling and threw out arrays of prisms from the cut glass.

Upstairs were the small dining rooms and private party rooms. Robyn went toward her dressing room. The show wasn't due to start for an hour, but she liked to be prepared. At a moment's notice, she could be called upon to handle an emergency.

Tonight, she'd chosen a gown of black satin. It had a high neck and long sleeves. The gentle folds of the fabric fell about her legs like silk and ended at the black high heels she wore. From the left shoulder to the hem, glittery beads formed an exotic bird. The dress reminded her of flying. And, tonight, she felt like flying. She'd spent the last week depressed, going over and over in her mind what to do when Grant returned.

But he hadn't returned. He hadn't called. And she had survived seeing him, survived kissing him, even survived him making love to her. Although she had to admit, making love still reduced her to idiocy.

Marianne had been telling her for ages. It *was* time she stopped grieving over the past and went on with the future. Robyn had lectured Grant about keeping his dead wife alive. She was no better. For five years, she'd lived in the shadow of his memory, refusing to look forward. It was time she thought about her own life and what the future could bring. She would go out with other men. Somewhere out there was a man she could spend her life with and love, if not in the same way, enough to forget. She just had to find him.

"I know that look." Marianne stopped her on her way through the kitchen. Robyn looked at the desserts, her favorite.

"What look is that?" she asked, admiring the cake replica of the leaning tower of Pisa. The buttercream icing smelled deliciously of lemon. She remembered when she and Marianne were caterers working out of her kitchen. She had run out of white vanilla when she was making icing. As a substitute, Marianne had suggested they use lemon. The cake had smelled wonderful, and the guests loved it. Ever since then, she'd made it a part of her recipe.

"The look that says you've made up your mind. What is it this time? Do we change the drapes . . . remodel the lounge . . . or have you resolved never to see Grant Richards again?"

Marianne was remarkably perceptive. She wondered what other aspects of her life her friend knew about and had not exposed.

"I didn't have to decide anything about him. He's gone." She wanted to leave it at that, but Marianne had other plans.

"With or without a little help from you?"

"I don't know," she answered truthfully. He hadn't called since Jacob had taken control. She didn't know if he'd agreed to her plea not to see him again, if he'd been too angry when she didn't return, or if Jacob had *taken care of all the loose ends.*

"What happened when you went down there for the party? When I picked you up, you looked like someone had died." Uncharacteristically, Marianne pressed on.

"Nothing much happened. I told you an emergency came up, and he had to use the plane. I came back the next day."

"By commercial air." Something significant had happened. Jacob had called to tell her to pick up Robyn. She'd known her friend had left with Grant, but how she had ended up in D.C., Marianne could only speculate.

"He was busy, and I didn't want to leave you here alone."

"You're lying."

Robyn gasped. Marianne had never called her a liar before. The two women stared at each other over the leaning confection.

"Why did you say that?"

"Something happened. I could see it in the dark circles under your eyes. And I knew you'd been crying before you got off that plane."

"All right, I was crying. And Grant didn't send me home. I came alone, without his knowledge."

"Why?"

"Marianne, why are you asking? You don't even like Grant."

"I don't dislike Grant. I'm concerned about you. We've been friends a long time, and I hate to see you so unhappy."

"I'm not unhappy."

"You were certainly doing a good imitation of it until Kari had that blood transfusion. Then, you went from unhappy to miserable."

"Well Grant and I won't be seeing each other again. You were right the other night when you said it was time to stop grieving. It's time I got on with my life."

"Then why are you putting a barrier in front of Grant. He's the best looking man I've seen in years, and he came back to see you."

"He came to see Kari."

Marianne frowned. "Brooke, grown men don't travel four hundred miles to see a child unless it's his."

Robyn controlled her emotions, containing her reaction. "Marianne, you're confusing me. Are you saying you want me to see Grant? I thought your opinion of Grant was that he was just another guy."

"If he's what you want, he's not another guy to you."

"Then why did you say it? I can't keep up with you anymore. You're behind him, then you're against him."

"I'm for you, Brooke."

"It doesn't matter anyway, Marianne. He won't be back."

Robyn gave her a crooked smile and walked away. It was nearly time for her song. Marianne didn't know how to protect her friend. Since she'd been assigned, her job had been relatively easy. There were no complications or threats to Robyn's existence. There was also no life. The two of them ran the business and watched Kari grow.

Her own life was different, but just as unhappy. While Robyn gave everything to the restaurant and her daughter, Marianne had many dates, and there were several men in her life. It wasn't until Grant made an unscheduled appearance that Robyn began to live. It was also then that her life with Jacob had taken on a different flavor.

What were they to do? Robyn, for reasons that concerned her own life, could not go on seeing the man she loved. And her association, she refused to label it love, with Jacob was an added conflict that could jeopardize several lives. She shuddered to think of the hotel room and the explosion that nearly killed the two of them.

She needed to talk to someone about her problems, but there was no one. She couldn't tell Robyn, the person she protected, and, she couldn't tell Jacob, the man who protected them both.

Three weeks passed, and Robyn's life settled into a routine. She threw herself into Kari and the restaurant. It seemed Marianne was working out her own problem if the number of chocolate desserts could be counted. Each day, the ache in Robyn's heart dulled a little. Grant hadn't called, and she was sure he never would. She didn't know whether or how Jacob had contacted him, but she was sure he had a hand in his silence.

Susan and David's wedding was this weekend. She'd promised to attend but early in the week had decided not to go. How could she explain her actions to Grant? How could she look David and Susan in the eye after promising not to hurt their friend and doing just that? It would be best to avoid further contact with any of them. Yet, as the days passed, she found herself longing for one more glimpse into her past.

Pulling into her driveway for her afternoon with Kari, she found a strange car.

"Name's Hammil, Ma'am. Thomas Hammil." The man getting out of the blue Chevrolet extended his hand by way of introduction. Robyn took it. He gave her a quick, hard shake and dropped it. "I'm from the Bureau."

She knew without him telling her. He was from Jacob's office. She wondered if somewhere in Washington they had a factory where they molded these clones.

"Come inside." The tall blonde followed Robyn with the cadence of military training.

"The wedding's tomorrow, Ma'am. I'm here as your escort." The drawl was definitely Texan, she thought as Thomas came straight to the point.

"Jacob sent me an escort?"

"Yes, Ma'am. He's sorry he can't pull the duty himself."

"You can relax, Thomas, and call me Brooke."

"Thank you, Ma'am." Robyn didn't think he knew how to relax. He looked just as straight as before. "We have plane reservations for fifteen hundred hours, that's three o'clock this afternoon, Ma'am."

She hesitated slightly, turning away from Thomas Hammil. She knew what this was. It was a crossroads. One of those places where one decision changed your life. If she stayed here, she'd never see Grant again. If she went . . . she didn't know what lay ahead.

"Ma'am?" Hammil called.

Robyn turned back. "I'll be ready," she told him. "I just have to go next door and pick up, Kari. Would you like something to drink? Or eat?"

"No, Ma'am," he declined.

"Thomas, if we're going to spend the weekend together, don't you think you're going to have to relax a bit?"

"Sorry, Ma'am."

"I promise not to give Jacob a report on your behavior."

At that, he actually smiled.

"Then, if it's all right, Brooke, I would like a soda, if you have one."

Robyn remembered that people from the District of Columbia call pop, soda. It was one of the colloquiums Jacob insisted she learn, and for which he cautioned her never to mistake.

She handed Thomas Hammil a can of cola and filled a glass with ice. "I'll get Kari," she said, leaving him to walk the short distance to Will's house.

Kari met her exuberantly as she always did. She reminded Will of David and Susan's wedding. "I'll be gone overnight."

"I never heard you mention them before. And you're going to their wedding."

"They're friends of Grant's."

"Yes, I remember now."

"Will, are you all right? You never forget anything." She went to him and placed the back of her hand on his forehead as if he were Kari's age.

"Just getting old I guess." Will laughed, moving his head away from her touch. Robyn smiled but concern creased her brow. She loved the old man. In many ways, he was like her father. She wondered if he just didn't want them to go without him. Since he had moved next door, when Kari was just learning to crawl, they'd been friends.

"Will you need a ride to the airport?"

"I have a ride," she answered not bothering to explain the FBI agent waiting for her in her house. "Come on, Kari. You still have to pack your toys."

Kari was immediately ready. She'd been looking forward to going on the trip since Robyn had mentioned it to her.

"Will Uncle Grant be there?" Kari asked, as they walked across the connecting lawns.

"I think he's going to be in the wedding, darling."

"What's a wedding?"

"It's like a big party. First, a woman with a long white dress and a man in a suit swear to love each other for the rest of their lives, then everyone has a party and gives them gifts to start their life."

"Oh, like the picture on the mantel."

Robyn smiled. She stopped, going down to Kari's level. "Kari, that's me in the picture. I'm wearing the long white dress."

"It doesn't look like you," her childish voice said.

"I was a lot younger then."

"Was I a lot younger, too?"

Robyn hugged her with a laugh. "Yes, darling. You were a lot younger."

"What about my daddy?"

Robyn had answered that question before. Kari had asked about her father many times. She knew the same story Robyn had learned. Why did Robyn find it so difficult to lie to her daughter now?

"Kari, don't you know what happened to your daddy?" Her voice was serious.

Kari's youthful soprano was proud and sad. "He died before I was born."

"Yes, darling, he died."

Robyn stood up then, covering the distance that brought her to the kitchen door. She was about to take her daughter to see her real father, yet she had to tell her the figure of a man she'd never seen was her father.

Cameron Johnson, a man who happened to have the same rare blood type as Kari and who died in the service without parents or other relatives, was given to Robyn as her husband. This cardboard figure was Kari's father, while the flesh and blood man whose body had joined with Robyn's in love to produce a dark-eyed, dark-haired child could never know what he had done.

Inside, Robyn introduced Kari to Thomas Hammil and told her he was going to see they get to the wedding. While Kari went to pack her toys in her backpack, Robyn noticed Thomas had cleaned his glass, dried it, and replaced it in the appropriate cabinet. The can that had held his soda had been rinsed, crushed, and discarded in the appropriate recyclable container. It was as if he was erasing his presence from the house.

The fragrance of roses filled the church at Sixteenth and Gallatin Streets. It was a small intimate cathedral nestled off the busy northwest thoroughfare. The stone building had stood for over a hundred years and was covered in ivy as if an artist had sketched it out for a painting. Robyn sat near the back of the church on the right side. Thomas Hammil sat next to her on one side, while an excited Kari fidgeted on the other. Robyn and Kari had matching dresses of pink silk. Her hat was large and floppy. Thomas must have approved of the outfit for he made no comment.

The organ began, and Grant and David came from the vestibule in the front of the church. Robyn's heart lurched when she saw him. Suddenly, a restraining hand took her arm. Thomas Hammil was stronger than he looked. Robyn settled in her seat, but Kari was more vocal.

"Mommy, there's Uncle Grant." She pointed toward the front.

"Don't point, Kari." Robyn pushed her finger down. "I see him, dear."

"Does he know we're here?" she whispered.

"No, darling. Now, be quiet. The bridesmaids are about to come in."

Tears clouded Robyn's eyes when she saw several of her college friends float through the door. They shimmered down the aisle, a sea of golden yellow reflected through her tears. Baby's breath ringed their heads, and they carried baskets of silk flowers, picking up the yellow color scheme. When the organist played "The Wedding March," the congregation stood. Robyn helped Kari, lifting her onto the seat and holding her in the crook of her arm. While she waited for the bride to come through the door, she glanced at the front of the church. Grant's eyes caught and held hers. Anger shot daggers at her. She couldn't drop her gaze as a tremor ran the course of her body. Thomas Hammil came to her aid. He touched her elbow gently as Susan came through the door.

She was beautiful. Exactly the bride she should be. Her dress was covered in lace and pearls. The bodice fit snugly, dropping past her waist, then fanning out in layers of white lace and crystal pleating.

A fresh set of tears streamed over her cheeks. Susan smiled happily and began her slow procession toward her future husband. When all were settled in front, Thomas handed her his handkerchief. Robyn dried her eyes and hazarded a glance in Grant's direction. He had turned to face the minister.

The ceremony was short, and soon, the brightly clad women on the arms of black-tuxedoed men followed the bride and groom up the aisle. Kari waved at Grant as he passed. He lifted his hand to her but did not include Robyn in his welcome.

When the church was nearly empty, Robyn turned to Thomas. "Should we go to the reception now, or wait until after the bridal party has settled?"

"We can go now."

Robyn was not looking forward to coming face-to-face with Grant. The look he'd given her clearly told her that he was angry over her unorthodox exodus.

People gathered at the reception hall before the bride and groom arrived. Thomas found them a table and went to get Robyn and Kari drinks. He came back with a Coke for Kari, a piña colada for her, and something for himself that looked like a martini. They waited an hour before the bridal party finally arrived. Robyn did not join the well-wishers as the party came through the door, but Kari slipped out of her seat before Robyn could stop her and padded across the dance floor to be lifted into Grant's arms. His smile toward her was warm and genuine. He swung her around several times then kissed her on the cheek. Robyn sat stonelike, watching the gentle exchange.

After several minutes, he set her down, and she returned to the table.

"Uncle Grant's coming to see me, Mommy," she announced. Fear ran through Robyn. She'd made a bargain with Jacob, and this time she was going to keep it. Grant hadn't come to see them in the last few weeks. Why would he come now? Maybe Kari meant he was going to come to the table. Wasn't it customary to say hello to old friends, old enemies?

The reception line formed. Robyn rose and joined it, Thomas Hammil at her elbow. The first person in line was Marsha Jennings. They had been at college together. When Robyn and Susan lived next door to each other, they had often met Marsha for lunch. Marsha smiled, taking her hand. She suddenly froze, then fumbled as she looked from Robyn to Kari and back.

"Hello, I'm Brooke Johnson," she introduced herself. "This is my daughter, Kari. And this is Thomas Hammil." She turned slightly to include Thomas. And, hopefully, Marsha would think she was mistaken.

"How do you do?" She smiled down at Kari and shook hands with Thomas, then passed them along. When Robyn got to Susan, she was close to tears. How she would have liked to be a part of the ceremony, but it was enough to be present. She hugged her friend and whispered how lovely she thought the dress was. Then, she hugged David and congratulated him.

She placed her hand in Grant's. "What, no hug for me?" He held onto her hand, pulling on it slightly. Robyn had no choice, if she didn't want to snatch her hand away. She leaned forward, and he hugged her tightly, but briefly. His release didn't come until after he felt the tremor run through her.

Reaching down, he swung Kari into his arms. "Hi, precious. How's my blood doing? You're keeping it safe just in case I need it?"

"I'm keeping it safe," she chimed.

Robyn reached for her. But Grant dodged her grasp. "She's all right. She can stay." He'd won again. He knew she wouldn't fight over the child. The line behind her was long, and she was holding it up. Thomas edged her along, and she left Kari, returning to the table. She took a seat, her back to the raised dais where Grant and the bridal party would sit. She knew she couldn't take him glaring at her when they took their places. Moments later, the bridal party was led to the dais, and Kari was honored by being able to sit on Grant's lap for a while.

When Grant rose with a champagne glass in his hand, Robyn knew the toast. It was the one David had given them and she'd repeated the night of the engagement party. While the room saluted the bride and groom, Kari left the dais to return to her mother.

"I'm ready," she told the FBI man.

"Wait until after the first dance," a remarkably quiet Thomas whispered.

The wait was long. Robyn ate the meal but couldn't remember tasting anything but Grant's wrath against her back. Finally, the meal ended. David and Susan rose to lead the first dance. Other couples joined them, several stopping with words of congratulations. After the dance, Susan and David were immediately surrounded by people. Robyn waited, aware that Grant still sat on the dais. He talked quietly to the woman on his right. Several times, he smiled at what she said.

Robyn could stand it no more. She took Kari's hand and made her way to Susan and David. "It was a lovely wedding," she said with tears in her eyes. "I hate to have to leave so early, but Kari and I have an early flight."

"But—" Susan began.

"I do hope I'll get to see you again." Robyn cut her off. She hugged Susan and David in turn and found Thomas waiting for them by the door. The car was waiting. She and Kari were whisked away before anyone had a chance to stop them.

With the efficiency of a military maneuver, Thomas had her back in Buffalo and in her home before dinner had begun at Yesterdays. Kari was tired, and Robyn put her to bed early. Thomas excused himself and disappeared, leaving only the feeling that a ghost had been present.

Robyn was restless. Her thoughts scattered and unfocused. Why had Grant hugged her? What did he think, and why hadn't he called after she left? Even at the restaurant, there were no messages waiting when she called. She moved about the house like an automaton. Finally, she took a shower and dressed for bed. She tried reading a book, but after fifteen minutes she hadn't remembered a single word. Turning the light out, she tossed and turned for hours. At midnight, she got up. Maybe a hot drink would help. She'd make herself a cup of tea. It was soothing, and then, she'd be able to sleep. Leaving her bedroom, she opened Kari's door and checked on her. She was sleeping soundly. Pulling the door closed, Robyn crept down the stairs.

The doorbell rang just as she poured the boiling water into the tea pot. Robyn went to it. Through the sheer curtains covering the small panes that flanked both sides of the door, she saw Grant. She pulled the door in.

"What are you doing here?" she asked, backing away from the expression she saw on his face. He still wore the black tuxedo, but the bow tie was gone, and his ruffled shirt was open at the neck.

"I want to know why?" He came in the door, slamming it behind him. Robyn stepped backward. His expression was angry.

"What are you talking about?"

He reached for her. She sidestepped him. "I'm talking about three weeks ago. I'm talking about everything since I've met you. I'm talking about why you keep asking me to go away, and I'm talking about what happened when you hugged me this afternoon."

"Nothing happened." She turned away, putting the distance of the room between them.

"You're an awful liar," he sneered.

"Grant—," she began, but his raised hand stopped her.

"You don't have to answer everything," he shook his head as if in resignation. "Just tell me what happened to you? I came back, and you were gone. Everything about you was gone. Even the hairbrush showed no sign of your hair. If I hadn't been with you, I'd swear you'd never been there."

The picture of Thomas Hammil cleaning her kitchen suddenly loomed. "I had to go, Grant. I told you there was no future for us. I asked you to go away and leave me alone."

"Why? After the night we spent together. I love you, and you love me."

Their entwined bodies on his silk sheets crowded into her memory. "I don't love you," she said over the lump in her throat.

"You do."

"Grant, go away."

"Say you love me." He came toward her. There was no place for her to go.

"No." Robyn took refuge behind a chair.

He stalked her. She backed away, moving around the room. "Say it," he demanded.

"It won't make any difference," she pleaded. "There's no place in my life for you."

"Say it!" he shouted.

"Grant you'll wake Kari."

"Say it!" He reached for her as her back came up against the piano. Strong hands drove into her hair, taking fistfuls and twisting it until she was forced to move into the heated area that surrounded his body.

"I don't love you. I don't love you," she chanted, closing her eyes against stinging tears.

Grant pulled her closer. Her eyes flew open. She could see his mouth descending. She knew he was going to kiss her, and she knew she would tell him anything if he did. But she couldn't stop him. All she could do was wait, while his mouth hovered over hers.

"Darling, can't you find the champagne? I put it in the . . ." a deep male voice came from the dark stairwell.

Robyn and Grant separated as if they'd been pulled apart by giant magnets. Their two heads swiveled around toward the stairs.

"Jacob!"

CHAPTER 14

Robyn's gasp went unheard by Grant whose eyes were riveted to the partially dressed man at the top of the stairs. Jacob stood there, wearing a black kimono and nothing else. Her eyes were fastened to the man who stood in the light flooding from her bedroom. The front door slammed behind her. Looking around, she found Grant had gone. For a split second, she started after him.

"Brooke!" Jacob's voice halted her attempt.

She turned on him, her face red with anger. "What the hell are you doing here?"

Jacob closed the robe and went back through the door. Robyn raced up the stairs and followed him into her bedroom.

"He was a loose end."

"And you had to tie it? You couldn't trust me to do it?"

"I gave you the chance." Jacob picked up a pair of blue bikini briefs and stepped into them. "I heard what was going on downstairs. You couldn't control the situation."

"Jacob, it was none of your business."

He stopped, grasping her arm. She was sure he'd leave a bruise. "You are my business. You became my business five years ago when you stepped into a witness box."

He let her go. Robyn took two steps backward as he suddenly released her. Jacob continued to dress, putting on his pants and shirt as if he were alone.

"Don't I get a reprieve, Jacob? Is every facet of my life to be controlled by you or some unseen agent as long as I live? Did I give up the freedom of choice, of independent decision, when you walked into my life?"

"Damn you, woman." He turned, taking her upper arms and shaking her. "You're the worst nightmare I've ever had to contend with."

"Then drop me, Jacob. Leave me out there hanging alone. You've done your job. For five years, you've protected me. I'm the one who's changing the rules now. I'm the one putting myself in danger. Let me choose how I'd like to live the rest of my life. Because this shell of an existence is too much. I've coped with it too long. I've got cracks, Jacob. And each day they get wider. I want to stop. Let me?"

"I can't." This time he turned from her. His hands pushed deep into his pockets. "I can't do that, Brooke." He sighed. "If only I could."

"Why not, Jacob?" She went to him, taking his arm. The muscles tensing under her fingers surprised her. Jacob covered her hand with his own. His eyes were soft in the half-light. "The taxpayers can't be expected to take care of me forever." Her voice softened. She could take him angry, but his tenderness destroyed her.

He was silent, too silent. It was like the times after she'd testified. Signals would pass between him and someone else just before a bomb would drop. She could feel it. It passed through her. Robyn pushed herself back far enough to see his face.

"It's not over, is it, Jacob?" She was amazed at how calm she could be. Jacob shook his head—no placating comments about her not needing to know. Suddenly, she began to tremble. When she was telling him to leave, she'd be responsible for her own mortality, they'd been false words. The reality hit her. There was someone out there, tracking her, trying to kill her. Still, after all these years, someone wanted her dead.

Jacob grasped her trembling body and lowered her to a seat on the bed. "When the Network was uncovered, we knew at least one man or woman escaped our net. That's why we put you through the program."

"Who?" She looked into his eyes. His arms were still holding her as he knelt on the rug.

"We don't know. But in the past five years, discreet inquiries have been made about you."

"What kind of inquires?" Her heart beat with a fear she hadn't ever known.

"Computer files mostly, cross-referencing your name with people from your past." He couldn't tell her about Kari's accident. He could feel the terror rising in her.

"Grant—" she stopped. "What about Grant?"

"He's not as easy to track. He flies in and out of the country regularly. It's very difficult to protect him."

"But you've been trying." Her eyes were wide and glassy with unshed tears.

Jacob nodded. "We think something is going to happen soon. That's why I did what I did tonight. You've got to be careful. One word in the wrong place could get you all killed."

"Oh, Jacob, I'm so sorry. I tried to send him away."

"I know you did." He could hear the agony in her voice. "I know how much you love him." He ran a finger down her cheek. He understood how it was to love someone and not to be able to tell them, not to be able to make any plans together. He knew the gnawing feeling it left in your stomach when the situation was out of your control and totally manipulated by someone else. "Now get some sleep," he told her.

"I can't go to sleep," she protested.

"Try," Jacob said.

"Jacob, you can't really expect me to sleep now?" She was too agitated, wired. How could he expect her to sleep when her life was in danger?

"I'll get your tea." He was gone before she could accept or refuse. In minutes, he was back with a steaming cup of the apple spiced tea that she had gone to make. It now seemed hours ago.

She accepted the hot liquid and sipped it cautiously.

"Now, get in," he said, when she'd drained the small cup. Robyn got into bed, and Jacob pulled the covers up. He sat facing her. "You look like the scared little girl who was trying to appear brave, the first day I met you." He reached over and turned off the lamp. "Go to sleep. I'll be here for a while." He moved to the head of the bed and leaned her forward, making room for himself to sit down. Pulling her back, his fingers massaged her skin, relieving some of the tension bunching her neck muscles together. She was forced to relax.

"What was her name, Jacob?" The darkness seemed to disembody her voice.

"Whose name?"

"The woman you were in love with? The one you tried to pattern me after."

His fingers stopped momentarily, then continued their confident rhythm. "Cynthia." He sounded far away.

"Where is she now?"

"She died."

Robyn closed her eyes, forcing her breath to remain even. "How?" she asked.

"I was protecting her. She didn't follow orders." His answers were short but not cryptic.

"Why do I remind you of her. Do we look alike? I mean before."

"No, physically you're very different. But you are alike."

"You mean I won't follow orders either?" She dropped her head letting the magic in his fingers take some of the stress from her tired muscles.

"No, I mean you're a very strong woman. You won't let life beat you down. You fight for what you want. I didn't pattern you after her."

"I'm sorry, Jacob," she yawned. "How long ago did she die?"

"Nine years."

"I won't be like her, Jacob," she yawned again and turned in his arms, pillowing her head in his lap. "I'll follow orders." Robyn slept.

Jacob sat holding her in the darkness much longer than he needed to. He continued stroking her hair, loving the feel of the lustrous silk. It was her hair that was like Cynthia's. Although, hers was dark and rich, and Cynthia's had been the color of sunshine. Cynthia's face had a scar angled across her chin. Robyn's face was flawlessly clear. Yet, the two women had one thing in common, a vital spirit, and Jacob loved that in them.

He shifted Robyn to the pillow and moved to the chair across the room. He watched her until the dark of night reached its zenith. Then, taking the black kimono, he left the house as silently and unseen as he had entered it.

It wouldn't be long now. They had the blood bank computers, and soon, they would be able to trace the phone number that had manipulated the records. Hammil was covering the explosive since he was an expert himself. Each day, the circle closed a little tighter.

Thank God, Grant thought, as he shut down the engines of the cargo plane. If it hadn't been for the sudden spurt of government contracts, he didn't know if he could have gotten through the past three weeks.

He'd stormed out of Brooke's house with murder on his mind. When that guy came from her bedroom, wearing next to nothing, something snapped in him. There could be an explanation, but if there was, she would have called. In twenty-one days he'd heard nothing.

He'd also seen the man leaving her house in the early morning hours.

"Damn," he had cursed, remembering the scene as if it were unfolding before him now. He was still angry. If problems hadn't developed with the plane, and he'd been able to sleep, he wouldn't have been up to see the figure quietly steal out of Brooke's kitchen door.

But when he got to the airfield, he found he had a problem with the fuel pump. When that was fixed, something had gone wrong with the hydraulics that support the landing gear. On a ladder, he had gone at the problem. He had dropped the wrench he was using and had to climb down to pick it up.

Going back up the ladder, he had tried again to unhinge one of the joints. It wouldn't bulge. Hours had passed. He felt all his fingers had turned to thumbs, and he was no closer to solving the problem. His mind hadn't been working on the plane, it was dwelling on a six-foot figure with dark hair and a black kimono.

Frustration had egged him on. When the second wrench slipped from his grip, he finally had jumped down from the ladder and kicked the ladder. Pain had torn through his leg, but not enough to deaden his awareness. He then had taken on the metal hull with his bare hands. With clenched fists, he had beaten the ghostly image of the man in the black kimono, pummeling the painted hulk.

Several mechanics had had to wrestle him to the ground to prevent him from damaging the plane or himself. He had fought them, lost, not aware where he was. Finally, one of them calling his name, had gotten through. He had agreed to calm down, and they had released him.

It was then that he had called Will McAdams and had gone there for the night, leaving the repair to the mechanics. Why hadn't he slept in the plane? Why hadn't he gone to a hotel? Anywhere away from *her.* But the taxi had dropped his oil-stained frame only thirty paces from Brooke's door.

Will had looked at his swollen knuckles and, without question, had gone to get the first-aid kit. Grant had been a lot calmer after the fight with the airplane. But his hands had hurt like hell. Dried blood and lacerated skin so swollen that he couldn't close either hand, had been cleaned, medicated, and draped in gauze bandages. He had winced when Will applied the iodine. Nothing, however, had compared to the pain created by the vise grip squeezing his heart.

"Maybe I could get the story straight if you'd sit down and stop trying to wear away the carpet," Will had said, when Grant had finally showered and worn one of his old robes.

Grant had sat down. Then just as quickly had risen. He had taken his highball glass between both hands and had drained it.

"I wish I knew, Will. I came to work things out. But she's so damn mysterious. And then there was a man."

"A man? Who?"

"I don't know. I didn't get a good look at him. He came out of her bedroom, and the light was behind him. All I saw was a black kimono." Damn, Grant had thought, he still wanted to hit something. It had been as if some invisible force was conspiring against him, when all he wanted was to get as far away from Brooke Johnson as he could.

But there he had been, thirty feet from the woman who'd turned him into a raving lunatic. He hadn't made a lot of sense to Will. He hadn't known who the man was.

"She doesn't entertain a lot at home," Will had said. "Occasionally, Marianne comes by or one of Kari's friend's parents, but for the most part it's Brooke and Kari. I wonder who he could have been?"

"I have no idea," Grant had said. "She called him Jacob."

"Jacob." Will had repeated the name.

"Do you know him?" Grant had asked.

"No," he had shook his head. "Friday afternoon, when she left for the wedding, there was a strange car in the driveway. She said she had a ride to the airport. I thought one of the waiters was taking her. The same car returned earlier tonight but left after a short time."

Grant had poured himself another drink and immediately had swallowed it. He had snapped the glass onto the bar with an angry thud. As the night wore on, Will had gone to bed. Grant drank until he passed out. He couldn't remember what he'd said to Will or what Will had said to him when something had woken him. He had been in a chair in Will's den. His mouth had felt like cotton, and his head had been about to explode. A clock had ticked on the wall. It had been four o'clock. He had known sleep would not come again. Even the vast amount of alcohol he'd consumed wouldn't have dulled his senses enough for him to sleep.

He had gone to the kitchen for coffee. That was when he had seen the man leaving Brooke's. He had been tall, at least six feet, with dark hair. His face had been averted, and Grant couldn't have seen it, but he had moved with an assurance that made Grant sneer. Anger had rifled through him, and he had wanted to burst through the door and beat him to a pulp.

But he had remembered, Brooke had never said she loved him. He'd told her he was in love with her, but she'd never returned the sentiment. She was a beautiful woman. Why would he assume she spent her nights alone? There were probably many men in her life. Yet, Will said she rarely entertained at home. It didn't mean she didn't entertain elsewhere. Maybe this man was the exception.

Grant's head had been heavy, and the feeling around his heart had become more familiar each time he thought of Brooke and this man. He had watched him walk down the street. He didn't go to any of the parked cars but had disappeared around the corner. Who was he?

"Jacob! What are you doing here?" Marianne yanked the door open after finding him standing on her porch. His tie was gone, and his jacket was hooked on a finger over his back. "Do you know what time it is?" She finished tying the pink sash that held her robe closed.

The question seemed silly until Jacob glanced at his watch. His face was pale as if he were fighting off an infection. Marianne knew what the infection was—Robyn. Something must have gone seriously wrong. He'd come to her house before, but this was the first time he'd ever shown up at four o'clock in the morning.

"Come in?" she invited. She stood back, giving him entry. Jacob walked past her. He slung his jacket on the seat of the high-back chair that graced her foyer and went into the living room, a determined pace to his steps. Marianne sighed. He looked like a lost little boy.

Usually, they met in the kitchen, keeping everything businesslike, but tonight was different. Jacob needed someone, a friend or maybe only a compassionate ear to listen. She wondered if he'd approached Robyn; told her how he felt, and she rebuffed him. Marianne knew Robyn would be kind, but Jacob might not see it that way. Grant was definitely a factor with which to contend, even though he may have to be told to keep his distance for the safety of his family.

Jacob paced the narrow room like a big cat. His hands were thrust deep in his pockets. She watched him for several moments. He didn't seem to remember she was there as he fought a private battle.

"Can I get you something to drink?" she asked, quietly. He turned at the sound of her voice. Jacob wasn't much for alcohol. Carrot juice was about as heavy as he got. He was a man who needed to be in control. Alcohol would dull the senses. As far as she could remember, she'd never seen him drink anything more than an occasional glass of wine. But, by the look of him, two fingers of straight bourbon was exactly what he needed.

"No," he said, dropping onto the dark green sofa. Marianne went to the kitchen anyway and popped two cups of milk in the microwave. She made some hot chocolate. It was more for her than him, but it would give him something to hold onto and possibly soothe the feelings that were so visible he seemed to wear them on his sleeve. Hot chocolate was onc of her mother's remedies. Whenever she had a problem that made her silent and withdrawn, her mother would make two cups and sit down. Eventually, they'd begin to talk.

"Do you want to tell me about it?" she asked quietly, handing him the warm cup.

He shook his head, accepting it and looking at the marshmallows that garnished the top looking like miniature snowballs.

It was just like him, she thought as anger burned within her, to bury his feelings and never express them.

"What did you do tonight?" She wasn't sure he'd tell her. He paused for a long time, staring into the cup. Then, he took a drink and looked at the floating confection.

"I learned a very valuable lesson."

"What was that?" Marianne took a drink. The chocolate was delicious, but she had no taste for it tonight.

"I've learned in this life, there are only two ways to live, either you're a loner or you're on guard twenty-four hours a day."

"And you've resolved to live like that, never having friends or a family? Never having children of your own?"

Jacob stared at her as if the thought had never occurred to him.

"Don't you want to have children? You always ask about Kari. Do you know your voice changes then. There's a tender note in it that has nothing to do with your duty or her involvement in the program. Your eyes light up, and you smile."

His lips curved. "Kari's easy. I've loved her since the minute she was born. I was there, you know."

He had never told her that. "I didn't."

"I was Brooke's Lamaze coach. I saw Kari before she did." Jacob paused. "After her delivery, the doctor laid her in my arms. She was so pink and so tiny. I remember asking why she wasn't brown." Cradling an invisible baby, Jacob was quiet for a long time. "The nurse told me she'd eventually be the color that ringed her ears." Finally, he picked up the cup and drank some of the hot liquid.

Marianne knew the feeling. She had been a surrogate coach for one of the women at the embassy in Thailand on her first assignment. Her labor was premature, and her pains came too quickly to get her to a hospital. When she held the squirming little life in her arms, her heart was as full as an olympic-size pool.

"Don't you want to know that feeling again, with your own child?" she asked, immediately regretting the question as an image of herself and Jacob, clad in surgical green, holding their own child leaped into her mind.

Jacob did want to know that feeling, but not tonight. Tonight, he couldn't think about anything like that. Tonight, he was miserable.

"Marianne, I feel awful." There was a raw quality to the pain in his voice. "I don't know that I can forgive myself for what I did. Brooke certainly will hate me for the rest of my life."

"What did you do?" She refrained from leaving her seat and going to comfort him.

Quietly and without emotion, as if it had been drained from his body, he related the story of discovering Grant had left Washington and was on his way to see Robyn. He told her what he'd done in coming from her bedroom as if he were her lover. Laughter and horror warred within her—laughter that Jacob, with his stiff-as-a-board personality, would play such a role and horror that her friend had been so humiliated in front of the man she loved.

"I feel like a heel," he finished. "Like some rookie with no idea how to handle the situation. My choices weren't thought out or analyzed. They were—"

"Emotional," she finished for him.

The word was foreign to Jacob. Marianne could tell by the blank expression that took over his dark features. For too many years, he'd suppressed any and all feelings for people, living only for the job. She had been sure she was getting through to him on a different level. But whenever he could, he'd crawl back into his shell, and the world would pass by him like a battalion of retreating soldiers.

"How is she?" Marianne asked.

"I put Valium in her tea. She fell asleep immediately."

"Jacob, are you in love with her?" The question surprised Marianne. She hadn't intended to ask it. But it was out, and she couldn't take it back. She sat straight in her chair, her body poised for his answer, afraid of both yes and no.

Jacob didn't think he'd heard her right. Then, he remembered how well Marianne read him. No matter how often he refused to react to situations, she always could tell what he was thinking and feeling. He sat forward and looked her directly in the eye.

"I suppose that was very apparent."

"Only to me." She shook her head. "I'm sure most people don't know. I'd be surprised if Brooke knew, and she's very perceptive." Marianne had to force herself to breathe normally. The air in her lungs wanted to rush out as if they'd been punctured.

"I knew it was impossible," he told her. "I've always known, but I couldn't stop feeling the way I felt. As director of the program in which she is a participant, I couldn't possibly have any relationship with her."

Marianne stared at him as he studied his hands. It was true. A dagger stabbed into her heart. A white-hot heat tore through her, forcing her to clamp her teeth together to keep from screaming. She hung her head and placed the empty cup on the floor. Her fingers were shaking too much to hold it. Chocolate smears coating the sides looked like dirty snow. Jacob could have no relationship with a witness, just as she could have no relationship with him. Not because of Robyn or her love for him, but because of who he was and who she was. They both worked for the Witness Protection Program and had a certain fiduciary relationship to the participants. Any alliance between them was suspect. There was no written rule to keep them apart, but Clarence Christopher would frown on any attempt to exercise the practice.

Leaving her chair, she went to the sofa. She sat next to Jacob, their knees only inches apart. She took his hands. He looked at her, and she wanted to melt.

"I'm sorry," she whispered as if she was trying to soothe the wounds of a child. "Jacob, I'm your friend. I'll always be that." If she could have nothing else, she'd offer friendship.

"Thanks," he said, a twisted smile curving his lips.

She shivered slightly. He misinterpreted the action and pulled her toward him.

"You're cold," he said.

She wasn't, but to be in his arms was better than telling him the truth. Marianne let her head fall on his shoulder. "How did you come to work for the FBI?" she asked, no longer wanting to talk about Robyn or Jacob's love for her. She wanted to hold onto him just for the night, keep herself wrapped around him until the sun rose. For she knew in the light of the coming day, her life would change irrevocably.

"I was on the police force in Chicago. A case I was working went bad." She felt him stiffen and knew it was a subject he didn't speak of much, like so many of the subjects Jacob had buried. "Clarence asked me to join the government when I came off leave. It gave me a chance to change my life." There was a special relationship between Jacob and the director of the FBI. Marianne had even heard of it from some of the other agents with whom she'd trained. It was no secret. Jacob was envied but respected. He might have known Clarence Christopher, but he was solid in his performance.

Marianne snuggled against him. He slipped his arm around her shoulders. "Are you glad you went there?" She closed her eyes, imagining herself next to him on her bed upstairs.

Jacob hadn't thought of that before. Was he happy he'd gone to Washington after Cynthia died? Where would he be now if he hadn't taken the job? He wasn't used to thinking about what might have been. He only had time for what had happened to bring him to this point. And, usually, his mind was on someone else, never himself.

"I don't know," he finally answered. "I've never given it much thought." He yawned and slid down on the sofa. Marianne was practically lying across him, but she didn't move. She just kept her eyes closed.

"In Chicago," she said. "Before the FBI, there was a woman."

It was a statement. Jacob was used to Marianne knowing him. He even liked it that she did. "Cynthia," he didn't hesitate. He wanted her to know about Cynthia. "She died before I left."

"You were protecting her when she died."

It wasn't a question. Jacob didn't have to answer. He knew an answer was unnecessary. Marianne knew the truth. He slipped his fingers into her hair. His thumbs gently massaged her head. She stirred against him. Her hands passed over his legs and hugged his waist. And there she slept.

Jacob wasn't used to waking up next to anyone. His effort to turn over had brought him up against a soft, warm body. His eyes flew open, and in the draped-darkness of morning, he saw the wispy red curls rioting over her head. He smoothed them back, but they had a mind of their own. Marianne didn't move. He looked at her as she slept soundly.

He liked Marianne. She was an honest woman and a true friend. She'd never tell the things she knew about him, and with her, he could be open and honest. With her, there was no guard, no reason to hold his tongue or be careful of his words. He trusted her with his life.

CHAPTER 15

Friday night, the restaurant was crowded. It had been this way for weeks, and Robyn was thankful for the work. She had been too busy to dwell on the night Jacob had come from her bedroom and Grant had jumped to the conclusion that she was sleeping with him. Of course, that was exactly what Jacob had intended.

She wanted to call, explain, tell him the truth, but each time she picked up the phone, she thought of Kari and of Jacob telling her how both their lives were still in danger. Would this ever end?

Sue-Ellen passed her with a timid smile. She was helping out at one of the receptions. There had been a wedding in the afternoon, and two receptions were presently underway. For the first time in weeks, both Robyn and Marianne were on hand. For several months, either she had been gone, off with Grant, she amended, or Marianne had been away on one of her mysterious weekends. Robyn assumed she was seeing a married man. She never mentioned the trips, and of late, her returns didn't warrant a new chocolate dessert. She was glad Marianne was happy. She even envied her. While Robyn was unable to go from one relationship to another, Marianne appeared to bounce back without the slightest damage to her ego. There must be a new man in her life.

"Now, that's the first genuine smile I've seen on your face in weeks." The subject of her thoughts whispered from a point behind her.

"Well, we certainly cannot say the same of you." Robyn tempered her sarcasm with a broad grin. Marianne blushed. "Tell the cook I need some Alaskan crab legs and a two-pound lobster." Before Marianne had time to question her, she turned her attention to the couple standing near the end of the bar. "Susan, David," Robyn called. She rushed to hug them as if they were long lost friends she hadn't seen in years, instead of the three weeks since their wedding. "I'm so glad you came by. You look wonderful."

"So do you," Susan said. "Has Grant ever seen you in that outfit?"

Robyn's face fell slightly. She wore a black lace dress with a high bustle. "No," she answered quietly. "Why don't we sit over here." Robyn ordered a bottle of champagne, then led them to a table next to one of the windows.

"We didn't know the restaurant had a theme." David covered Susan's comment when they were seated.

"I think people like it," Robyn smiled, swallowing her pride. "They can look at it as a trip back in time or as a Halloween party. But to tell you the truth," she leaned closer, "I just love getting dressed up. In any case it seems to work."

"It's beautiful." Susan looked at the mirrors and photographs of the 1920s flappers above her head.

"I'll give you a tour before you leave," Robyn offered.

"I'd like that," David said.

The waiter arrived with the champagne. He went through the ritual of showing her the label with a flare of ceremony that made Yesterdays stand out from other establishments. Then, he poured the pale sparkling liquid into the three fluted champagne glasses and left the bottle in a stand next to the table. David lifted his glass and toasted the two women.

"You will be staying for dinner?" Robyn asked. Their presence had lifted her sagging spirits. And, if only she'd admit it to herself, she was starved for news of Grant. Spending the evening with them would be like getting a little of her old life back. And this wasn't breaking the rules. She had invited them before she'd promised Jacob anything.

"And the show," David said.

"We're not going back until tomorrow," Susan volunteered.

"You'll be my guests." Robyn lifted her glass and sipped the wine. "Anything special you'd like for dinner? I'll have the chef make it."

Both of them shook their heads. "We plan to order straight from the menu." Susan took David's arm and smiled at him. It was obvious these two were in love. Robyn had never seen her friend look so soft or David look so protective. They were still on their honeymoon. All the signs of being newlyweds were there. Robyn had seen a lot of newly married couples. In her garden, weddings were performed every weekend during the summer.

"How's Kari?" Susan asked. "We only got to see a little of her at the wedding. But she's a sweet little girl."

"She's fine." Robyn beamed. "She's home with her grandfather."

"She's certainly taken with Grant," David said.

"And he with her," Susan added.

Robyn dropped her eyes to her empty glass. She knew how much Kari liked Grant. She'd mentioned him several times in the past three weeks. But Robyn couldn't explain to a four-year-old that some relationships weren't always for the best. She told Kari that Grant was very busy and he couldn't come and see them.

"More champagne," David lifted the bottle and refilled their glasses.

"It was a lovely wedding," Robyn said moving the subject away from Grant.

"I'm sorry you had to leave before we had a chance to talk," Susan said.

"It was a big weekend here," Robyn provided an excuse. "We have weddings booked, and with the restaurant, both of us really need to be here." Robyn hoped they bought the story. She'd fallen back on the restaurant so often. Either Marianne or Robyn could run it alone if they had to. With the staff they had now, most problems were solved before they became a crisis.

"It is very busy," David looked at the number of people in the bar. It was crowded and the dining room was fully booked for the evening. Robyn was proud of the work she and Marianne had put into the business.

"How is the jewelry business? I'm told your designs are beautiful." She sidestepped mentioning Grant's name.

"Yes, it's how I spend the better part of the day." Susan looked pleased. "David is good with the public, but I like the background work."

"Well, women do like a good looking man telling them they look great in expensive stones." Robyn smiled at the man next to her best friend.

"You two talk about the store. I need to find a phone," David said.

"You can use my office." Robyn stopped one of the waiters and directed him to take David to her office. She looked after the man who slid his hand along his wife's neck before leaving the table. Turning back, she said, "You really look happy, Susan. I'm so glad for you."

"Thank you. I love David more than anyone else in the world."

"So tell me about the store. I want to know everything."

"I don't want to talk about the store. Tell me what happened," Susan began without preamble. "After the engagement party, Grant was frantic when you disappeared. Where did you go?"

"I came home. It was important that I get back."

"I know we haven't known each other long, but we agreed to be friends, I can tell you're not telling the whole truth."

Robyn's head snapped up.

"I promise not to tell David or Grant anything you say," she continued. "Speak freely. Did you two have a fight?"

"No."

"Then what happened? At the party, you two couldn't keep your eyes off each other. Then, suddenly, Grant wouldn't even mention your name. And everytime we mention his, you cringe. Now, he's off flying until he is too exhausted to do anything but sleep."

"Susan, he isn't doing anything dangerous, is he?"

"Grant knows the rules. He won't endanger himself or any passengers."

Robyn released the breath she'd held.

"You *are* in love with him. Don't deny it," Susan said when Robyn opened her mouth to protest.

"Yes, I'm in love with him," she admitted.

"Then what's standing in your way?"

"It's not that easy, Susan. There are things he doesn't know about me. Things I can't explain. Believe me, it's best if Grant and I don't see each other again."

"Brooke, there are few things in this world two people can't settle if they talk about it."

"Not this." Robyn was shaking her head. "It happened a long time ago."

"Nobody expects you to be a saint. Believe me Grant's not a saint either."

"It's not that. I can't go into it. Just leave it."

Susan sipped her champagne. "I don't believe you for a moment. I've never seen Grant so happy as he has been in the past few months. Then suddenly you two won't even say each other's name."

"Susan, drop it!" Susan's head came up abruptly. "I'm sorry. I didn't mean it, but please let's talk about something else. Tell me about the store?"

"We have two of them . . ." Susan began talking after a long silence, and although Robyn was interested, she couldn't keep her mind on what her friend was saying. Grant couldn't say her name, and she'd tried desperately to forget she'd ever seen him. But it was impossible. He was always in her thoughts.

"Well, it's all arranged," David said, slipping back into his seat.

"What's arranged?" Robyn asked.

"We'll stay at the Sheraton downtown and tomorrow visit Niagara Falls, then fly home tomorrow night."

"You can just flat out cancel the hotel," Robyn ordered. "You'll stay at my house. I have a guest room that's dying for visitors."

"But—"

"No buts," Robyn cut David off. "I won't go to Niagara Falls. It's good for honeymooners, but I'll see you get to the airport tomorrow night."

"That won't be—"

"That's a wonderful idea," Susan cut in.

Robyn lifted her champagne glass and toasted the couple. She sipped the dry wine. Her eyes went down when she lifted the glass to her mouth. Otherwise, she'd have seen the look that passed between her best friend and her new husband.

The day was unusually warm for the second week in September. Usually, the sky was overcast. The days began to get gray in anticipation of the harsh Buffalo winter. But this Saturday morning had dawned like a beautiful summer day, clear and warm.

Robyn and Kari had a wonderful breakfast of strawberry crepes and sausages with Susan and David. Will surprised them by coming in for coffee. Then, he and Kari joined the newlyweds for their trip to the falls.

Robyn was enjoying a brief rest in the late afternoon sun on her patio. Susan and David were due back by six. Their flight was scheduled to leave at eight, and Robyn wanted to take them to the airport.

That must be them now, she thought, hearing sounds inside the house. "I'm out here," Robyn called. Seconds passed, and Kari didn't come to find her. No one came out. "Kari," she called, standing up.

Suddenly, her hand went to her throat. She recognized the flight jacket and cap immediately. Grant stepped from the darkened kitchen to the sunlight of the patio. Her knees went weak, and her heart beat so loudly it drowned out all other sound. She caught hold of the back of the patio chair to support herself.

"What are you doing here?" she whispered.

He looked her up and down. She was wearing shorts and a T-shirt, but under Grant's gaze she felt naked.

"I went to the Sheraton. There was a message saying David and Susan were at this address, and the phone has been conveniently—busy," he spat the word.

"What?" Robyn hadn't been on the phone since she'd come in from the rehearsal. In fact, the phone hadn't rung either. She found the strength to move. Going into the kitchen, she lifted the receiver of the wall phone. Silence greeted her. The line was dead. The kind of dead you hear when a phone has been off the hook for a long time. It had passed the point where the recorded messages cease, and the high-pitched whine was long gone.

"There's a phone off the hook somewhere," she explained, replacing the receiver. "Excuse me." Going through the living room, she went upstairs. In the guest room, the phone was only slightly ajar as if it had not been properly replaced. She touched it slightly, and it fell into the cradle. A second later, she lifted it and was greeted with a dial tone.

Robyn replaced the receiver. For a moment, she wondered if Susan had done it on purpose, then rejected the idea. Suddenly, she remembered the way her friend had cut off David when he started to say something about going to the airport. He must have called Grant and said they were flying home with him.

She found Grant still in the kitchen when she came down the stairs. "Are you here to fly Susan and David back?"

Grant turned from the patio door to face her. The light silhouetted him. "David called me last night."

"They went to Niagara Falls. I expect them any moment now. David put their luggage by the front door." She sounded extremely polite as if the man standing a few feet away was not the man she'd spent a lifetime loving.

"I'll wait outside," he turned away as if he couldn't bear the sight of her.

"Would you like a drink?"

"I'm flying."

"Iced tea, orange juice, cola."

"Iced tea will be fine," he said and went through the door. Robyn's movements were stilted, and her thoughts were numb. She took down a glass and filled it with ice. Then, she poured tea into it from the pitcher in the refrigerator.

Outside, Grant sat on the edge of a lawn chair. When she handed him the glass, their fingers touched. She felt the electricity and snatched her hand back so fast she nearly dropped the glass. Grant placed it on the small table next to him.

Robyn walked to thc other side of the patio. "Would it matter if I said I was sorry."

"No!" The monosyllable exploded in the still air like an electric bulb bursting. He was on his feet, his back to her.

She came up behind him, wanting to reach out and touch him, but was afraid. A wall of granite separated her from him. "I am sorry, Grant."

"Who was he?" He turned on her. His hands grabbed her upper arms like steel shackles. "After the night we spent together and me finding you'd just disappeared. All you have to say is you're sorry?"

"I can't explain, Grant." She swallowed tears, wanting to cry but refusing to give in. He dropped his hands and presented her with his back again.

"I do want you to understand."

"Then, tell me." He swung around glaring at her. Robyn dropped her head like a four-year-old. "Make me understand how you could spend the night in my arms, making me feel like I was the only man in the world and then leave without a word."

"Oh, God, don't, Grant. I had to leave." She looked at him, spreading her hands, pleading for understanding.

"Why? What was so hellfire important here that you couldn't wait for me to bring you home?"

"Grant, please. I had no control of the . . ." she stopped.

"Go on. Who had control? The man at the top of the stairs in the black kimono?"

Robyn winced. "It happened a long time ago."

"What, Brooke. What happened a long time ago."

Robyn turned away. "I can't tell you."

"Can't? Or didn't you think of a good enough excuse yet? You've had weeks to do it."

"Please, Grant." She turned away from his dark anger. "Just trust me."

He took her arms and swung her around to face him. "Trust you, trust *you!*"

"Grant, I love you." Robyn felt the tremor run through his body. Then everything went still. "I love you," she repeated.

Grant's eyes bore into hers. There was fear there. She was afraid he wouldn't believe her. In his eyes was anger warring with some other emotion. His hands had tightened on her arms, and she felt like crying out but couldn't.

Then his mouth was on hers, and he was crushing her to him. "Why did you have to say that?" he asked against her lips. "Why do you have to be so beautiful?" His hands threaded through her hair as his mouth rained kisses over every peak and valley of her face. When his mouth came back to hers, it was druglike in its intensity. He plundered her mouth, his tongue dipping deeply into her vessel and extracting all the passionate emotion she had to give. He held her to himself, controlling the movement of her head, refusing to allow her to break contact even if she wanted to.

Robyn didn't want to stop. She wound her arms inside his jacket and around his waist, pulling his body into closer contact with hers. The shudder that quaked her body was both violent and explosive. At last, they collapsed against each other, each supporting the other. Robyn's legs were so weak she was sure she couldn't remain standing if he moved.

Grant clung to her, holding her tightly against him. Breath came in ragged gasps. Robyn's body was damp, and she could feel the moisture through the material of Grant's shirt.

"Grant," she said after a long while. "You have to go."

He was motionless for a long moment. Then, he pushed her away from him. His eyes were depths of deep hurt. Robyn didn't think she would be able to go on. She moved away from him, giving herself room to speak. She wanted to turn away so as not to have to look into the hurt that she knew her words would produce. But she kept her gaze steady. He must believe her.

"I can't tell you the whole truth. But please trust me when I say, lives are at stake. If you don't leave and never come back, it could be dangerous for me and Kari."

"Damn, Brooke." He took a step toward her and stopped. "You can't make a statement like that and stop. What the hell is going on here?"

"Grant, I can't tell you." She turned away. "I should never have given Doctor Elliott your name." She turned back. "Please, *please,*" she begged. "Leave us alone.

"How can you ask such a thing? You've just said you love me, and I love you."

"It isn't enough," she cried. "Grant, it happened five years ago. I can't tell you anything more. Just that your continued presence could cause people to find me whom I don't want to know I'm alive."

He came to her, taking her shoulders. Robyn stepped away, swinging around to face him. His touch was like a fire in her blood. It would be her undoing if she let him get close to her. "Are you in some kind of trouble?"

"Yes, the worst kind. And I've said more than I should. I know it's intriguing, and I know you want me to tell you everything, but I can't. It's too dangerous. All I ask is that you not come back."

Robyn heard a car door close. "Will must be back. Promise me you won't come back?"

"No!" His hand came out to grab her arm. Robyn moved away.

"You have to." Her voice was a whisper as if her guests were standing nearby. "Susan and David will be here in a moment. This is no joke, Grant. Don't come back!"

Robyn left him then. She went into the living room and through it to the foyer. When Susan and David came in with Will and Kari, she was composed enough to greet them as if nothing had happened. They talked for a brief while, promising to visit each other again and extracting a promise from Robyn to visit whenever she was in Washington. Grant joined them but remained quiet. Robyn almost fizzed under the stare he gave her. He lifted Kari into his arms and nuzzled her close. She laughed her usual high-pitched sound, and clasped her arms tightly around his neck when he held her.

When he set her on the floor, Grant took one of the suitcases sitting in the foyer and started for the car. David followed him.

Everyone hugged each other good-bye. Robyn had an excuse for the tears that curved down her cheeks. Robyn held Kari's hand as she waved good-bye. Grant reversed out of the driveway without a backward glance.

Will left shortly afterward, and Kari and Robyn went into the house. Kari happily chatted away about her day at Niagara Falls. She told Robyn about playing in the arcade and how she had beaten everybody on the Video Monster machine. After a long tirade, Kari said she was thirsty.

Robyn went to the kitchen to get her a drink. On the counter, she noticed the empty glass of tea she'd given Grant. The ice had melted, leaving an amber liquid graduated in intensity at the bottom of the glass. Next to it was a piece of paper.

Robyn went to the counter and lifted it. The paper fell from her fingers as if it were fire. It floated to the floor, crossing the fine line that kept the present and past separated. At her feet was the recipe for apple spiced iced tea:

2 Regular Tea Bags
1 Apple Spiced Tea Bag
Pinch of Baking Soda
Sugar
Pitcher of Cold Water

Drop tea bags in boiling water. Boil for three minutes. Add pinch of baking soda (as much as can be held between two fingers) and remove from heat. Pour hot liquid into pitcher of cold water. Sugar to taste. Serve over ice cubes. Makes 1/2 Gallon.

He knows.

CHAPTER 16

Grant's office was a tiny cubbyhole at the back of a private terminal at National Airport. As the air service had grown, he'd remained walled up in the small room with only a dinky window looking out over the planes. He never seemed to catch up on the paperwork. Adam Carpenter had urged him to hire an office manager. He was right. They needed someone to keep the records in order. Grant had time. For the past ten days, he'd had nothing but time.

He leaned his elbows on the desk and rested his head on the steeple of his hands. Ten days he thought, ten miserable days without Brooke. Since he'd flown away from her, he was still as confused. Was she or wasn't she? But how could she be? Robyn was dead. All he wanted was to be as far away from Brooke Johnson as was humanly possible. Yet, there were so many similarities. Beginning with the hair color and the eyes and the photographs of Kari. It was Robyn's style. She flew his plane with the same sureness he'd taught Robyn. She knew the fair winds signal and the song. His and Robyn's song had brought tears to Brooke's eyes. But the worst had been the times when they'd made love. The sounds were Robyn's sounds. Then the crowning blow—the tea, apple spiced tea. It wasn't unusual for people to drink it hot, but not iced! It was a recipe only Robyn had been able to duplicate. David and Susan had both tried making it. Even he had tried, but Robyn's tasted best. She had a patent on the formula. Just ten days ago when she'd left him alone on the patio and he'd lifted the innocent glass to his lips, he'd sampled that patent. It was all the damning evidence he needed.

He had been too angry to talk. David and Susan must have thought his rage was directed toward them for tricking him into coming to Brooke's house. As it was, he was too confused to speak. What could he say. *I just drank a glass of iced tea Robyn made.* Surely, they would think he'd lost his mind. And he wasn't sure he didn't agree with them.

They couldn't be the same. Why would Robyn leave him? How could her features be so drastically changed? And why? And, then, there was Kari. She had Brooke's hair color, but her other features were nothing like her mother's. If Brooke was Robyn then Kari was his daughter. She'd be the right age. He compared the happy child's features to Robyn's as if he held two photographs. He couldn't see her in Kari. But that was a minor point. Adults bear only a resemblance to themselves as children. There were too many unknowns, too much circumstance.

Brooke had told him life and death were related to their continued association. What was going on? All he knew was that she was scared. He could see that in her eyes. They had a fear he'd never seen before and one he couldn't erase no matter how much he tried.

Could she be alive? He doubted the truth as he knew it. David had told him the body was too badly burned for viewing. He wanted to spare Grant the ordeal of seeing the charred remains of the woman who had filled his life and whom he had lived for during the long months of his captivity. She'd been identified by dental charts. But he'd never seen her. Could they have made a mistake? His head snapped up as if a puppeteer had pulled his strings. A metal shelf holding books and an odd assortment of fighter plane replicas stood directly in front of him. He didn't see it. His mind was somewhere in the past.

If there had been a mistake, and Robyn was alive, why hadn't she called him? She'd told him his seeing her could put her and Kari in danger. What kind of danger? Who was after her and why?

He had to go back. He had to find out if Brooke Johnson and Robyn Richards were in fact the same woman. He stood quickly, galvanized for action. He came around the desk and pushed his arms into his jacket. Reaching for the door, his hand poised in air. What if she was?

"Who the hell are you?" Grant snarled, upon seeing a strange man step into the cabin of his aircraft. He was a man of action, and he'd made a decision to see Brooke again. The fates and his plane conspired against him. Maintenance was being done to the plane he needed. The others were scheduled, and Adam convinced him not to throw the schedule off unless the reason was paramount to the operation. Logic and Adam's expression penetrated his brain, and Grant agreed to wait for the mechanics to complete their work.

Several hours later, he got the final okay. Grant, who should have been able to calm himself during the wait, was as tightly wound as a spring and in no mood for a stowaway.

The man watching him hadn't answered his question. Reaching into his inside pocket, he took an identification folder out and dropped it on the wood-grain shelf separating two oversized seats. The leather pouch made a dull thud as it flopped onto the shelf. Grant stood in the front of the cabin near the door. He lifted the pouch and read the cards inside. Not tonight, he sighed, pushing his cap further back on his head. After everything else, he didn't need an impromptu inspection from the FBI.

"I already have security clearance for this aircraft and for flying government officials. I don't deal in drugs, contraband or illegal aliens. The FBI knows that, so why are you stowing out, away on my plane, Mr. . . . Winston?" he consulted the I.D.

"Jacob," he said from the bar where he'd begun, without permission, to mix drinks. *Jacob.* Grant froze. It was the last word he'd heard Brooke utter before he'd turned and slammed her door.

"I was there," Jacob confirmed Grant's unspoken suspicion. "My purpose was to get you out of her life." He finished mixing the drinks and offered one to Grant. "Scotch and water," he said. Grant made no move to accept it. Jacob set the glass down and retrieved his I.D.

"I don't want a drink. I'm flying out of here in a few minutes. What I want to know is why you're here and how soon you'll be gone?"

Jacob picked up his own drink, a whiskey and soda, no orange juice tonight. He needed courage for breaking the rules—even if it was Dutch. He took a seat facing Grant, propped his ankle over his knee and sipped the icy drink.

"I'm here to talk to you about your wife," he finally answered.

Tension grabbed hold of Grant at the mention of his Robyn. Grant took a seat. "What do you need to know about my wife. She's dead. She died five years ago in an accident. It's all in my records. And to tell you the truth, I'm in no mood to talk tonight."

"She told you then?"

"She?" What was he talking about? Told him what? Grant watched the FBI agent. Unease crept up his spine. He didn't know why.

Jacob knew what he was doing was against policy. It was a flagrant disregard for rules, and he lived by rules. But he'd made this decision. "I'm not very good at being gentle," he said. "So I guess I'm just going to have to give it to you straight."

Grant sat forward in the chair—waiting.

"The woman you're flying off to see, Brooke Johnson . . ." Jacob had a copy of Grant's flight plan.

"What does Brooke have to do with Robyn?" Grant seized the question before Jacob could continue. His hands were suddenly cold. He was going to confront Brooke with the similarities between her and his wife, and now this man had connected them, too.

"Brooke is Robyn."

The statement was spoken quietly, but to Grant's ears, it was like cannon fire. He felt like he'd been punched in the stomach and then had an elephant sit on him. He couldn't catch his breath, and he was paralyzed in his seat.

"Robyn . . . is . . . alive?" His voice croaked as he asked the question.

Jacob took Grant's hand, pressing the cold glass against Grant's palm. "Yes," he paused. "The accident five years ago was staged."

Grant threw the drink down his throat and swallowed it. The cool liquid stung his mouth, then radiated warmth as it coursed through his chest and into his stomach. Its heat relieved some of the pressure. Yet, Grant couldn't concentrate. He put his hand up and stopped Jacob when he tried to speak again. Then, he had to get up. He needed to relieve the pressure that was threatening to suffocate him. Yet, he was unsure of the strength of his legs. It couldn't be true. He clutched his chest, taking long gulps of air as he stumbled to the bar for support. The confined space seemed devoid of air. Going to the door, he sucked the oxygen into his lungs, but it wasn't enough. His hands and feet were suddenly freezing. He knew what it meant to have cold fear. He paced back and forth in an attempt to focus on something that would make sense of what he'd just heard. But nothing came, and he found himself covering the same strip of carpet time and again.

Suddenly, rage consumed him. He'd been right. He wanted to throw something. Anger at the absent Robyn filled him. His body seemed to coil and snap. Finding the glass still in his hand, he threw it at the bulkhead. The exercise acted as a catalyst, and suddenly, he was throwing everything that wasn't bolted down. Glasses, dishes, coffeepots, pillows, blankets, magazines—all went flying at the sturdy walls of the airship. And there was an animalistic sound. The sound of a wounded creature howling. It was almost a death cry.

Exhaustion caused him to collapse onto a seat. Jacob moved to sit next to him. He placed another drink in Grant's hand. He drained it.

"How?" Grant finally asked. His face was a pale ashy color, and Jacob thought he was going to pass out, but after several moments, he began to focus on reality.

"Five years ago she was a material witness in a federal case. When the case was over, she went into the Witness Protection Program."

"Five years ago?" Grant's brain refused to register. He could remember nothing.

"Before you were married, Robyn Warren worked for the FBI. She worked in an area she called the Assassination Bureau."

"She worked there after we were married, too. She said she liked what she did, especially working with the computer." He began to calm, but feeling didn't immediately return. His body was numb.

"In the process, she uncovered a group called the Crime Network. We don't know where they were based. But they only dealt on the highest levels. Robyn identified a mob hitman whose photograph she had seen. All previous reports said he was dead. But she saw him, and through her research she uncovered the plot to kill a man called Anthony Gianelli."

"Gianelli, I remember the name." Grant thought for a moment.

"When you were released from Lebanon, his trial was just ending. He was sentenced on the day you returned to Washington. Media attention for the release of the ten hostages pushed him off the front page."

"What did Robyn have to do with Gianelli?"

"Gianelli sponsored a modern day massacre. The plot was to assassinate massive numbers of racketeers in major cities across the United States at the same time. She uncovered the plot and the Network in time to prevent them from carrying it out. As it happened, her research also led her into the highest levels of government. In capturing Gianelli, records were uncovered which put many of his connections behind bars including some high ranking members of the FBI. Gianelli was tried and convicted, and the organization was uncovered. Their leader was also convicted, and the Network disbanded."

"Then why would her life still be in danger?"

Jacob left his seat. He poured himself another drink. "Did she tell you that?"

"She told me nothing, except not to see her again. And that her life and Kari's life could depend on it."

"We know someone or some group is looking for her."

"But if this guy, Gianelli, was put in jail, and it was his plot to massacre other families, why would anyone still be after Robyn?"

"It isn't the mob," Jacob said, returning to his seat. "It's the Crime Network."

"Didn't you say you disbanded the group?" Grant moved to the bar and made himself another drink, half of it disappearing in one gulp.

"We did what we could, but we knew her life would always be in danger. The number of departments she reached were many and varied. And there was always the possibility of parole or release. In the past five years, discreet inquiries have been made about Robyn Warren-Richards. Some references to Brooke Johnson have also been intercepted. But so far we haven't been able to find out who's doing it. But whoever he is, he knows the system."

"What does that mean?" He resumed his seat in front of Jacob.

"Everything is computerized these days. But the man accessing information can penetrate deeply into our files and those of some outside data banks. Robyn was one of the people who figured out how hackers were getting in to view sensitive data. Of course, the holes she found have been plugged, but a new one opens for every one we close."

"How are you controlling it?" Grant asked, taking a swallow of his drink.

"Robyn's file does not exist on any of the computers, but she does have a file. It's kept secured, accessible by very few individuals, and they must have top secret security clearance."

Grant was quiet for a long time. This man wasn't here telling him this for no reason. He wanted something. "What do you want from me?"

"Five years ago, Robyn made the decision to go into the program alone. Now, you have to make a decision. In order for us to continue protecting her, she and Kari must continue living their lives as they have in the past."

"Kari!" Grant stood but supported himself against the seat back in front of him. "She's my daughter?" He asked the question slowly as if each word took all of his breath.

Jacob nodded.

Grant dropped his head onto his arms and took several deep breaths.

"Robyn found out she was pregnant after she went into protective custody," Jacob explained.

"Damn her, *damn* her!" Grant shouted, hitting the cushioned chair. "Why the hell didn't she tell me? How could she take my child away and never let me know she was alive?"

The sound of Jacob's glass crashing into the mirror over the bar snapped up Grant's head. "Damn you!" Jacob took a menacing step toward Grant. "Robyn Richards gave up her existence so nine men could go home to their families. Nine men, whom she didn't know, could resume normal lives. She gave them back to mothers and wives who loved them. They don't even know her name or that she played any part in their release. And she gave you the right to do the one thing you would die without—fly."

"What are you talking about?" Grant interjected when Jacob stopped for breath.

"The government pressured her into testifying by using you as a pawn. You were a prisoner in Lebanon. They knew that, and you know the policy concerning terrorists."

"The United States government does not negotiate with terrorists," Grant quoted the same policy Robyn had quoted years earlier when David had told her about Grant's plane.

"Robyn Richards loves you so much she went through pregnancy alone. Then, the trauma of a new face and new identity. She settled in a town where she had no friends. She had to be careful of her words, look over her shoulder, and watch for double meanings in every stranger's conversation. All of this she did for nine unknown men. And her husband, a man whose past had been so unhappy, except when he was flying, that she couldn't take his love for the sky away from him. And you want to damn her."

Grant stared at the man before him. His eyes widened in understanding. Jacob Winston was in love with his wife.

"Robyn's in love with you," Jacob said.

"Then, why did she go alone? Didn't she know I'd choose her over flying? Didn't she realize she meant more to me than any airplane?"

"She understood. She also knew about Project Eagle."

Grant stared at Jacob not moving. Jacob read his reaction. Grant had shut down his responses as any good agent would do.

"I didn't tell her." Grant was adamant.

Jacob ignored the comment. "She knew when she made the decision."

Grant knew what Robyn would have done given the facts of his part in Project Eagle. He'd flown away that day with the chip concealed in his uniform. He was to meet his contact in France. It was set up, and it was a friendly reunion. When it was over and he found out the full magnitude of the system he'd saved, it was overwhelming. If someone had told Robyn only a fraction of what he was doing, she would have made no other decision.

"She did it out of love," Jacob told him. "The kind you read about, where one person sacrifices everything for the other. Most love is never tested the way yours and Robyn's has been. I admire her greatly for what she did."

"So what happens now?"

"There are two choices open. You can join her in the program. We'd have to give you all new identities, including Kari."

"Kari's only four. She wouldn't understand what would be happening to her."

"I agree," Jacob nodded. "You'd have to move to a new town and begin again."

"Or?" Grant prompted.

"Or we could relocate Brooke and Kari." Jacob held back the fact that they may have to do that anyway. The net closing in on Robyn was getting tighter, and so far, he had few clues as to who was trying to find her.

"What about this person trying to find Robyn . . . Brooke?" Grant was confused as to which name to use.

"There's always the chance something could alert him when the process takes place. But we'd take extra precautions."

"I see." Grant needed another drink. His capability to fly tonight was gone.

"Five years ago, Robyn had to make this decision alone, Grant. Now, it's your turn to decide whether you can go on living as you have since returning from Lebanon and let Robyn remain in her own life, or join her in the program."

"I either uproot her life or give up my wife and child." Grant dropped into the nearest seat. "It is a hell of a decision."

Jacob walked to the barstool opposite Grant. "It's the same decision she had to make."

"Let me think about this." Grant felt as if the world had fallen on him. He'd been in love twice in his life and with the same woman. Now, she was the last person on earth he had a right to see. For her own safety and that of his only child, he had to decide to live without them or have them make another change. What would this change do to Kari? Brooke had a business, a partner, a life she'd made for herself. He'd worked around the clock to get his service off the ground. She must have done the same. What would she think if he wanted her to give it all up and start over?

CHAPTER 17

Grant woke up, reaching for Brooke. An agonizing groan had him grabbing his pillow and hurtling it across the room when he opened his eyes to find the other side of the bed empty. How was he going to survive this grieving? It was worse than when he thought she was dead. To know she was alive and he was barred from seeing her, holding her, making love to her, was a sadistic decision. He couldn't live like this.

Swinging his feet to the floor, Grant hung his head in his hands. It throbbed with a blinding intensity. The sheets were twisted and tangled as if he'd battled demons in his sleep. The headache had been with him for over a week, since the night Jacob Winston had invaded his airship and opened his eyes to the real danger he could cause his wife. *His wife.* He couldn't really believe Robyn was still alive. For five years, he'd lived without her, finally coming to terms with her death. Finding out she was alive was like opening a wound. And Kari. He had a daughter, a child he wouldn't be able to see grow up. A wife and a child, all he'd ever wanted.

Yet, Jacob had given him no choice. For their safety, he had to leave them alone. Grant made his decision. He'd made several decisions, and each one was as quickly reversed as the first. Pushing himself up, he went to the bathroom. He swallowed two pain pills before turning on the shower. Cold water hit him, dousing the flames that the dreams of his wife brought and making him realize there was no place in her life for him and no place in his daughter's life for the father she didn't know she had.

Twenty minutes later, he was dressed and on his way to the airport. He was busier than he'd been in months. There was little time to think of Brooke or Kari during the day, but his nights were full of them.

"What have we got today, Adam?" he greeted the chief mechanic outside the hangar of Richards's Air Service. Grant's face sported a cheerful smile even if it was painted on.

"Emergency." Adam's clear face was set in austere lines. "I've been trying to reach you. You've got to get a beeper, Grant, or at least a car phone."

"What is it, Adam?" Grant cut off Adam's tirade on current technology.

"Frank's wife called. He's in the hospital—appendix."

"How is he?" Grant frowned.

"He'll be fine . . . but he won't be able to take his flight. I need you to deliver a group to the Niagara Falls Air Force Base."

Grant's eyebrows went up along with his pulse rate. Brooke's features surged into his memory. Niagara Falls was only a stone's throw from Buffalo. "Don't tell me the air force has run out of planes." Sarcasm edged his voice.

"Apparently, they have," Adam said. "This is a group of reporters following the president, who's decided to make a stop at the training facility in Niagara Falls."

"Isn't there anyone else who can make the run?" Grant didn't want the temptation of knowing he could turn around and find Brooke in his line of vision.

"I'm afraid not. It has to be someone with a high security clearance."

"What about Chuck?"

"Chuck's not due back until midnight."

Grant suddenly remembered Chuck was in Dallas at a training class.

"We've got contracts up to our kazoo and more coming in everyday," Adam reminded him. "Every pilot we have is busy. I don't know what's happening, but at this rate we're going to have to begin turning business away." Adam smiled at that. Grant returned it with genuine affection. He remembered when they'd joked about being so busy they could be discriminating about their contracts.

Adam had been with him since they both had left Trans-Global. He was the best mechanic Grant had ever seen, and he believed in the air service enough to work as hard as its owner to make it a success. Adam had no official title. He did everything and anything that needed doing.

"I guess it's you, buddy." He punched Grant's shoulder with a soft fist.

"I'll have to wait for them." The unconscious thought was spoken aloud.

"Yeah," Adam said. "They're due back tomorrow night. Frank had a reservation at the Hilton. Do you want me to change it?"

"No," Grant said. Adam knew about Grant's frequent flights to Buffalo. "I'll take care of it."

"Okay, buddy." His face went back to the chiseled mask.

Adam left him then. Grant knew his mechanic thought he wanted to spend his time closer to Brooke. He'd told him about her. Hell, he'd told everybody. He was so in love, thinking himself so lucky to find love twice only to have it ripped away like a severed arm. He hadn't imagined he'd have to forget ever seeing her again.

Grant stared across the field. Planes taxied in the distance. Waves of heat radiated from the outlying tarmac. The wind caught his hair. A fair wind, one that would be perfect for flying anywhere, except north by northwest.

"Hey, Grant," Adam called from the door. "I've filed your flight plan." He handed him the folded piece of paper. "The weather's a jewel today. You should have no trouble."

"Thanks." Grant took the papers, his mind four-hundred miles away. "When can I expect them?"

Adam consulted his watch. "You've got enough time for coffee."

As if on cue, a bus arrived with twenty men and women in various degrees of business and casual dress. They were loaded down with camera cases, suitcases, and garment bags. Several of them carried tripods over their shoulders. A vision of Robyn with her camera and tripod invaded his memory.

Adam and several men came out to take the luggage and stow it in the cargo hold. Grant went inside his office to get his flight bag. It was always packed and ready for a quick takeoff.

He disappeared into the plane and began the preflight checks. Jerry Asgarth, copilot, took the seat next to him after he'd made the final cabin count and closed and locked the outer door. Grant radioed the tower, and in minutes, they were airborne.

Fifty minutes later, he was on the ground. His grateful passengers smiled as they alighted into the sun of a crisp autumn morning. He toyed with the idea of flying back to Washington and returning in time to pick up his passengers tomorrow. The plane had to be refueled and checked before it would be ready to fly back. This would leave him with something he didn't want or need—time to kill. Unoccupied space in which to think of a dark-haired woman with lithe steps and a graceful body that fit his like a fine wine making a meal perfect.

Grant set off walking. He had no particular destination in mind when he started but found himself in the main terminal building facing a row of telephones. One was occupied by a uniformed airmen who hung up and left before Grant completed his internal struggle. He had no memory of lifting the receiver or dialing the restaurant, but suddenly Brooke's voice was in his ear and his courage deserted him.

"Brooke, this is Grant," he spoke over the lump in his throat. There was silence at the other end. "Are you there?"

"I'm here," she said, a strain evident in her voice. He knew she was holding back tears.

"I want to see you."

"Grant—"

"I know we have to be careful. I remember everything you said. And I promise this is the last time." He only wanted to say good-bye, he told himself. Brooke didn't answer. He was afraid she'd refuse. "Brooke, will you meet me somewhere?"

"Where are you?" she asked at the end of a silence difficult for them both.

"Niagara Falls, the air force base."

She didn't answer immediately. Grant could almost see her biting her lower lip and tapping her right foot. It was the outward display of her struggle with logic and emotion.

"Stay there, I'll pick you up," she finally answered.

Grant let go of the breath he was holding. "Do you know where it is?" he asked.

"I'll find it," she said with an assurance that told him she'd walk through fire to get here.

"How long?"

"An hour."

Robyn had just changed for rehearsal. Quickly, she slipped out of the leotard and back into her purple suede suit. She didn't want her last time with Grant to be in exercise clothes. Donning the matching coat, she set out to find him. Her feet nearly flew to the car, and within minutes, she was turning onto the New York State Thruway en route to Niagara Falls.

Grant walked to the main entrance and paced like an expectant father. Unsure from which direction she'd arrive, his head swiveled left and right as if he were watching a tennis match.

Robyn parked next to the grassy curb when she saw him. Getting out of the car, she stopped as he faced her. Without realizing it, she was flying toward him, her heels clicking against the asphalt, as she rushed into his arms.

"God! I missed you," Robyn breathed onto his neck. Tears gathered in her eyes.

"I missed you, too." Grant's arms were tight around her. He brought them up to her head and pushed it back far enough to fuse his mouth to hers. Robyn kissed him hard and long, giving herself up to the passion she felt. Ignoring the guards in the small station behind them and the wind pulling at their clothes, they continued in their enjoyment of each other until both of them needed breath.

"We'd better go," he whispered.

"Come on." Slipping his arm around her waist, he guided her to the illegally parked BMW. She slid into the warm interior, and he joined her. He slipped his arm around her neck for one more kiss before fastening his seat belt.

"Where are we going?" Grant asked when they turned away from the base road.

"Fort Niagara. It's a tourist attraction. In the summer, there are hordes of visitors, but after Labor Day the crowds thin considerably."

Grant sat in silence for the remainder of the ride. A shy smile creased the dimple in his right cheek. She didn't know. Jacob Winston hadn't told her, and he trusted him to keep her ignorant of his knowledge. He was satisfied just looking at her, knowing she was his wife. He could see the mannerisms that separately told him nothing, but the combination made her the woman he remembered.

Robyn took the curves with an assurance she didn't feel. Her insides were shaking as she passed the exit that led to the famous landmark and headed for the unpaved road through the woods. Grant had glanced at her but remained quiet. Even when she came to a halt in front of a log cabin and cut the engine, he made no comment. Opening his door, he came around the hood and opened hers.

"Thanks," he said as he took her hand, assisting her to her feet. "I only have until tomorrow. I didn't want my last hours with you to be in a room full of strangers."

Robyn blamed the tears that gathered in her eyes on the wind from the distant bay. Grant leaned forward and kissed her eyes, first one, then the other. The tenderness in his touch made a lump lodge in her throat. She resisted the sob that fought for life. Standing against the open car door, he continued his tender assault on her cheeks and finally her mouth. She leaned into him deepening the kiss until she was drugged with need of him.

"Let's go in," she said, a hoarseness lowering her voice by several notes.

Grant got his flight bag and followed her. The small cabin had two rooms downstairs, a general purpose living area and a kitchen. There was a loft and bathroom upstairs. The fireplace was lighted, bathing the room in warmth. The smell of coffee filled the air.

"How did you do this?" Grant asked, a surprised look on his face.

"Car phone," she smiled and closed the door. "Would you like some coffee? Something to eat?" Robyn didn't wait for an answer. She shed her coat and went to the efficiency kitchenette. When two cups were ready, she handed one to him. He took them both and placed them side by side on the counter.

His arms went around her waist, and he pulled her against him. Her hair smelled so good as he buried his face in the silky mass. "I tried not to call." Agony edged his whispered pledge. "I know it's not good for you or Kari . . ."

"Don't," Robyn told him. Her hands rubbed his back. "Don't worry. We're going to be fine."

He squeezed her tighter to him. She was the strongest woman he'd ever known. She'd survived for five years with the knowledge that he was alive, while he'd been safely protected behind the ignorance of her death. He could mourn and recover. She had to rely on her will to keep herself sane. Grant wasn't sure he was strong enough to handle the same kind of separation.

Robyn pushed herself back. Her eyes were dark and deep with love. He looked into them. They had less than twenty-four hours. He wanted to ask her a thousand questions, he wanted to find out everything old and everything new about her. Yet, there wasn't enough time. In a lifetime, there would be too little time for everything he wanted to know.

Slowly, he bent his head and kissed her. Her mouth was warm, her lips pliant. He tested them, teased, tugged at her lower lip, brushed his lips across hers. "I need you," he muttered against her mouth. "I'll die without you."

His mouth took her then, fully. Five years of longing and wanting poured through him as his tongue met and tangled with hers. He groaned at the whimpers she made, fitting her to him, carving her into his frame until not a sliver of air separated them. His tongue filled her mouth, and she strained toward him, giving and receiving in kind.

His hands were like bands around her, caressing her back and straying downward from the silk of her blouse to the resistance of her suede skirt. Robyn felt his arousal hot against the apex of her legs. She moved against him in an erotic maneuver. Grant joined her in the mating dance as his mouth continued to battle with hers.

When they had to separate for air, his passion-filled eyes bore into hers. Her feet left the floor as he lifted her. His mouth melded with hers as strong arms cradled her. Her fingers ran into the softness of his hair. She'd missed that hair, missed running her fingers through it, feeling its softness, and the smell of his shampoo.

Grant turned with her, carrying her to the narrow stairway that led to the loft. He stood her on her feet in the bright light flowing from the small window. His hands went to the buttons on her blouse. Robyn looked at them as they released the closure one crusading link at a time. When the last one slipped through his fingers, he eased the fabric off her shoulders. The garment fell to the floor. Grant bent, caressing her uncovered shoulders with his mouth. Her head went back, and her eyes closed as thrills rippled through her. His sienna-colored skin merged with the yellow-rose of hers, creating a glow as perfect as the sunrise.

Familiar fingers released the zipper on her skirt, and with the same silence, it joined the blouse at her feet. Robyn pushed Grant's jacket back, his arms releasing her for the moment it took to let it fall. She pressed her lips to the buttons of his shirt before slipping them through the tiny holes. Little by little, she exposed his skin, a study in dark chocolate. The belt bisecting him was freed, and soon, they were naked to each other.

Grant didn't immediately take her to bed, but let his eyes devour the shape of her breasts, the gentle sloping of her waist, and the crest of her hips as they extended into long legs. His hands traced her, pausing to revel in her reaction. It was a memory he would have to live with from this day forward. She was nearly the same. Her breasts were fuller. Kari accounted for that. Her waist and hips were the same curvaceous crescent moons he remembered.

Robyn felt no embarrassment in his open appraisal. It gave her time to feast on him, recall and refresh her memory of how he looked in the morning, how the sun played across his chest and tinged his hair-dusted legs with a reddish highlight. Robyn placed her palms over his flat nipples and stepped closer to him. Five years of sleepless nights spent longing for this moment were reflected in the eyes she lifted to him. Grant took her waist, a span so slim he could circle it with his hands.

His mouth touched hers, then quickly gorged it, exhausting himself in the satisfaction of holding her close. Any thoughts of taking this slow fled when her naked form welded to him. Heat generated as the electrical impulses in their blood synthesized into a lethal combination. Explosion was imminent, and Grant knew it.

He walked her backward to the bed and joined her there. The mattress was feather soft when Robyn's back made contact with it. It folded around the two lovers, pushing them close to each other, acting like the bread of a sandwich as it wrapped around them.

Grant slid over her, kissing her neck and working his way up the column to her ear. He paused for a heartbeat then his tongue traced the curved arc. Under him, she whimpered as spasms of sensation rocked her. With slow deliberation, he sponged the area purposely avoiding the inner cavity until her arms about him raked down his back. His own body was pained, but he forced himself to work slowly. She was driving him, forcing him to end the torture to them both, but somewhere in the recesses of his mind, he knew they needed this torment.

Robyn didn't know how much more she could take. Grant was hot and hard against her, and she longed for him to end this agony, but he appeared to want it prolonged. He was giving, and she wanted to take, take it now, end the pain in a quick burst, but she remembered this was to be the last time. Pulling herself up, she pushed him back and took position over him. Her hair fell in panels over his face. He smoothed it back, tugging slowly on her head as he brought her mouth down to his. Robyn's mind swam. Grant's hands caressed the curve of her back, and he used his palms to make carnal circles on her buttocks. Her body gripped, and she was tempted to plunge herself over his erection. She kissed his chest, stopping briefly to circle each of his flat nipples until they extended in hard pebbly peaks. Low guttural sounds came from his throat. They pushed her on until she came to his navel. His hands were buried in her hair. They squeezed unmercifully when her tongue dipped into the small spring. A well within him seemed to break, and he pulled her back to eye level.

Reversing positions, he spread her legs and entered her. The pleasure that rocketed through Robyn broke on a ragged gasp. She found his rhythm quickly and frantically complemented it as their hands, arms, and legs worked in tempestuous unison. Robyn held nothing back. Her love, her need of him, her belief in their past and future streamed from her like the dust of a shooting star. She loved this dark man, this man who had crossed time to find and love her. The exquisite pleasure of his touch drove her onward until she had to let the sound in her throat free. His name broke out on a bellowing ring.

Grant heard the wail and knew she was his. She was his like she would never be to another man. And he was hers. He wanted her forever but refused to think ahead of this moment. Brooke's body, clamped around his, drove all other thoughts from his mind except for the mounting hedonism that she evoked in him.

The end came in a blaze, like a star exploding in a fervor of expanding colors. Brooke writhed beneath him, her body alive with sensation as explosion after explosion rocked from one to the other. She squeezed him closer, trying to hold onto the moment a second longer. Grant swayed with her, giving, consuming, driven by instinct to go as far, as high as she wanted to go and beyond. With a wild cry, they collapsed in climactic resolution.

Breath came ragged and hard. Grant's chest rose and fell as he inhaled great gulps of air. He gathered Brooke's head in his hands. Her skin was moist, and her eyes were lazy with love. Tenderly, he kissed her, brushing his lips against hers. Then, he slipped off her, and together they slept.

This time when he awoke, she was there. He wasn't dreaming. Her hair was spread over the pillow contrasting darkly against the white sheets. Grant had never been one to believe in the metaphysical, but something had brought them together again, and he felt there was a solution to their problems. He had to find it. Leaving her and Kari was something he couldn't do. He knew that now, and he was willing to leave everything behind for her like a king abdicating his throne for the woman he loves. Grant's life would be worthless without her.

* * *

The last note ended, and the spotlight on Robyn went out. For a moment, there was silence, then the house lights came up, bathing the stage in a glare of white light. Rehearsal was over. She grabbed her towel and left the stage.

"Aren't you suppose to be away this weekend?" Robyn asked Marianne when she followed her into the dressing room.

"I won't be going this weekend." The short redhead seemed down. Robyn, in her own misery, noticed identical traits in Marianne.

"Did something happen?" Robyn glanced over her shoulder at her friend. She knew Marianne looked forward to these frequent jaunts. She had no idea where her partner went, but she was always high on the adventure before she left. When she returned, depression overtook her. Only chocolate sundaes helped her get over the experience.

"No," Marianne said. "I'll go again soon, but not this weekend."

"Anything you want to talk about?" Robyn asked. Marianne's head swiveled around to stare at her. "Sorry, I didn't mean to pry."

"It's not that. You've never even mentioned my weekends before."

"I have noticed how affected you are by them," Robyn recalled. "But you've never pried into my personal life either."

"Of course, I have. Wasn't I the one who told you to stop grieving and get on with your life?" A sad smile curved her lips. Marianne remembered what Jacob had told her about sending Grant away. Since then, Robyn had begun to retreat into her former shell.

Robyn smiled. "You did it in the nicest way." Marianne returned the smile.

"And you avoided the questions in an equal fashion," Marianne told her.

"Well, I suppose we're a couple of strange ones."

"Not exactly," Marianne returned. "I should have known it would take a man to finally crack that hard exterior of yours."

Robyn returned her stare. "Not today, Marianne, I'm not in the mood." She didn't want to talk about Grant. Her fragile hold on her emotions would have her in tears if she thought about him. Since having left the log cabin and kissing him at the entrance to the air force base, she'd responded like a robot to everything. She went through the motions of living without letting it touch her. Any contact would shatter the fragile wall she'd erected to protect herself from the pain of his leaving.

"You're only in one mood lately," Marianne's voice called her back "And that's cranky."

"It's the weather. October always make me feel a little sad."

"The weather hasn't put those dark circles under your eyes. You forget, Brooke, I've known you too many years. We've gone through four Octobers together. This is the first one I've ever known you to be any different than the even tempered, confident woman who was eager to begin a catering business."

"Okay, it's Grant." Robyn flopped down on the sofa. She pulled the towel from her neck and kicked off her dancing shoes. Her head fell back, and her eyes closed. She should be getting dressed to go home and be with Kari for the afternoon, but she had no energy. "He's gone, Marianne." The words were spoken quietly.

Marianne didn't move. "Why?" she asked quietly. "I thought you were falling in love with him."

"I am in love with him, but there are things I can't explain. Not to him, not to anyone."

"I understand," Marianne said. "We all have secrets only our hearts can share."

Robyn opened her eyes. There was a resigned note in Marianne's voice. "I wouldn't think that about you. You share everything."

"Nobody shares everything." Marianne's stare was direct. "There are things about me you don't know. Some of them you might even hate me for."

"I could never hate you," Robyn told her, knowing there were things she could never speak of to anyone.

The redhead smiled brightly. "I hope not. You're closer to me than a sister. I don't want anything to happen to our friendship."

"And it never will," Robyn told her.

Robyn sat forward. Marianne had taken a seat at the lighted dressing table. With the turn of events in her own life, she wasn't aware that Marianne might be going through her own brand of misery.

"Do you want to talk about something?" Robyn asked.

"Why don't we do something radical?" Marianne ignored her question, abruptly changing the subject. "Why don't we redecorate the lounge or build that photo-chapel we talked about? We have enough money."

"Is that a project to take my mind off Grant or to take yours off . . . him?"

"A little of both. It always helps me," Marianne said.

Robyn knew that. Whomever the man was that Marianne met, he pitched her into depression when their weekends ended. Robyn assumed he was married. Her method of helping Marianne over the rough spots was to involve her in a project to fill her mind and keep her from thinking of him. It usually worked. Now, Marianne was trying to do the same for her.

"Maybe the chapel isn't a bad idea. If we could get it ready by spring, we'd have more weddings than we could handle."

"Good, why don't we get some paper and pencils and sketch out what it should look like? You're always so good at doing that," Marianne said, moving to the desk, pulling sheets of paper in front of her and clearing a spot to work. She began drawing and chatting. Robyn listened but didn't hear much of what she said. She thought of Susan and the wet Sunday afternoon when they sketched out Trifles. What a good friend Marianne was, and how fortunate Robyn was to have found her when she placed the tiny ad so many years ago.

The two women complemented each other. Marianne was good with sculpting vegetables and arranging cold cuts into works of art, while Robyn took to confections. Candy, cakes, and cookies could be anything from the simplest sweets to the most elaborate designs.

Robyn gave Marianne a steady stare. "Marianne," she called. Her friend paused, turning to face her. "The man you see—"

"Which one?" Marianne asked. She saw several men, but Robyn knew Marianne needed no additional prompting on which man she meant. He was the only one she was serious about.

"The one whose name you've never spoken. He comes infrequently, but when he does, he leaves you drained."

"What . . . what are you talking about," Marianne faltered.

"I've always known."

"But you never said anything. Never mentioned—" Marianne looked away.

"I know, but lately . . ."she paused. "It's your business. Yet, whenever you've seen him, you're not the same. Is he . . . married?" Robyn whispered the dreaded question.

Jacob married. Her mind went back to him on the night he'd come from Robyn's. He'd admitted it was Robyn he loved. The times he'd held her and kissed her, their hours together over dinner or strolling through the streets of the Capital, she'd only been a substitute for her best friend.

"He's married to his work." Marianne dropped her gaze to the rich pile of the cream colored carpet.

"Is there another woman?"

Marianne raised her head and stared directly at Robyn. "Yes," she whispered.

The look she leveled at Robyn was so penetrating, Robyn wondered if she knew the woman, but decided not to ask. "What about the other woman? Is she married?"

Marianne's head bobbed up and down slowly as if she wasn't really sure how to answer the question. "He doesn't know I'm in love with him. He knows very little about me."

"Then, why does he come to see you?"

"I'm convenient. And there are times when it's necessary. We used to work together, and there are things I still do for him."

"Why, Marianne?" Robyn dropped to eye level. There were tears in

Marianne's eyes. "If he makes you so unhappy, why don't you stop seeing him. Tell him you won't do any more work for him?"

"I can't. For the same reason building that photo-chapel won't get Grant out of your system. It will help you deal with him not being here."

"We're a strange pair. Both of us crippled by men we can't get out of our systems." Robyn's laugh was mirthless. "Well, Marianne, we're a couple of survivors. We'll deal with the pain and the healing. In time, we'll laugh at this."

"Yes," Marianne smiled, fresh tears glistening in her eyes. "Now, let's go make something sinfully chocolate." A smile wavered through her tears.

"All right. I'll meet you in the kitchen. I want to call Will and tell him I'll be late." Marianne left as Robyn punched Will's number into the phone. The bell at the other end rang and rang, but Will did not pick up. Neither was there an answer at her house. He and Kari must have gone out for a snack.

In the kitchen, the two women went to work. "We'll call it 'Chocolate Thunder,' " Marianne said, grabbing a case of bittersweet chocolate from the storeroom.

"That's good. I like 'Chocolate Death.' It'll be the dessert of the day. We'll have Sue-Ellen make up some cards, and we'll set them on all the tables."

When they had a counter filled with supplies, Marianne looked at her. "Got any idea what we're making?" she asked.

Robyn laughed. The first genuine laugh she'd had in nearly a month. "How about a double chocolate cake, with chocolate icing. We'll make a hot chocolate syrup, layer the cake with slices of chocolate ice cream, pour the syrup over it, and top it with chocolate sprinkles. We'll serve it on those snow white plates in a pool of white chocolate."

"Yes," Marianne agreed. "That is 'Chocolate Death.' " Both women seemed in high spirits as they worked side by side. It was how they'd begun, before there was a Yesterdays, before Grant had walked into Robyn's life, and Marianne had fallen in love with her mystery man.

Marianne was stirring melted chocolate when Robyn went to use the phone.

"That's strange," Robyn turned after replacing the receiver of the kitchen phone. Marianne was lifting one of the chocolate cakes from the oven.

"What's strange?" she asked being careful of the hot pan.

"I've tried to call Will several times, and I get no answer."

"I saw him earlier."

"Where?" Robyn's brows rose. Will never came to the restaurant without telling her.

"He and Kari were walking about the grounds. It was during the photo session."

Because the weather had been so good, the wedding party scheduled for that afternoon had moved into the garden for pictures. Robyn had seen to all the arrangements before the afternoon rehearsal.

"Where were they going?"

"I don't know. They were walking toward the building. I thought they came inside to see you."

"It's probably nothing. Kari likes the restaurant. Will probably brought her for a visit and then took her for ice cream." Robyn trusted Will completely. He'd taken care of Kari since he moved in next to them. They couldn't ask for a better neighbor.

"Kari, be careful. I don't want you to fall and hurt yourself."

"I won't hurt myself, Uncle Grant. I'll be careful." Kari smiled as she balanced on the steps to the airplane.

Tears came to Grant's eyes. It was the first time he'd looked upon the dark-haired child with the knowledge that more than his transfused blood ran through her veins.

He sat down on the slatted bench outside the terminal office. Wind from the airplanes stirred the air, but it was pleasant sitting outdoors. Will sat next to him.

"Thanks for bringing her, Will. I've missed seeing her."

Grant's eye followed the little girl. One of the mechanics was telling her about the airplane. Grant was afraid to get too close to her. He didn't trust himself not to break down and cry in front of her. But from a distance, he could look at her black hair and see his own reflected there. Jacob's visit nearly a month ago had sparked memories. Memories he thought were safely buried. But he had found himself opening the storage closet in his condo as if he were opening a vein. Grief and happiness had mixed with laughter and tears as he poured over the photo albums Robyn had left behind.

Once he had opened the albums, he couldn't stop the memories. Floodgates had been pushed back, and the misery he'd hidden, buried within himself, he now had found alive and waiting on page after page of the albums. Under each photo was a caption. Her neat handwriting inscribed immortality just as her camera had captured a segment of time. *Silver bells, cockle shells, dandelions, and weeds are my only rows* was the humorous caption under a photo of the flower garden she'd planted in front of their house in northwest Washington. *Grant and David, pilot-to-pilot* was another. Every aspect of their short marriage had been recorded in the albums. Even during the period of his captivity in Lebanon, she'd kept up the photographs. Now, he knew she'd left him a record. Something to hold onto when she could no longer be there.

But these weren't the pictures he had been looking for. He had wanted to find his childhood photos. The ones when he was about four, Kari's age. He had found them in the bottom of a box. He was lucky they'd survived after so many foster homes. They'd arrived in the mail one day after he had gone to live with Aunt Priscilla. In another box, he found Robyn, smiling into the camera. He had taken them out and set them on the piano. There he saw it. Between them was the child they'd created. Kari was the best of both of them.

He wanted her, and he wanted her mother. Why should the only choices open to him exclude her from his life? Damn, it wasn't right. Robyn had been doing a job. It wasn't her fault she was good at it. So good, in fact, she had to give up her own identity and go into hiding for the remainder of her life. It was worse than being a prisoner. At least in prison, there was the chance of parole. Robyn had nothing. Nothing but the lives she'd given back to the ten men in exchange for her own.

"So what happened, Grant. I thought you and Brooke would be announcing your engagement any day." Will's voice snapped his dreams. "Then, suddenly, you disappear, and she looks like she won't live past noon."

Grant pulled his attention away from the child. "It got complicated, Will. There are things I can't tell you."

"She didn't turn out to really be a spy, did she?" Will grunted a laugh.

"No, she's not a spy. But you were right about her husband. He is cardboard. She was never really married to Cameron Johnson. He's just a convenient lie."

"I knew it." Will's fist punched the air, emphasizing that his intuition had been proven true.

"That's all I can tell you, Will. The rest is classified."

"Classified? Does she have something to do with the government?"

Grant shook his head. He'd already told Will more than he should. Jacob Winston had told him he was not allowed to tell anyone what he knew. But Will had been his friend since he was a child. And Will knew nothing about Brooke's former life.

"What about Kari? Is she really her daughter?"

Grant's gaze went back to his daughter. "Yes, she's really her daughter. And she was really born in Atlanta."

Will and Grant were quiet for a long time. Each seemed absorbed in the child. The mechanic still was showing her everything about the aircraft, and she, being so inquisitive, continued to ask the same question—why. Grant could hear Kari laughing.

"You and Brooke ought to make up. I'm sure Kari would love having you around all the time."

"If only we could," Grant wished. "If it were up to me, I'd drop everything and go with her. But it would hurt her more than help her. The only thing I can do is go back to Washington and forget we ever met."

"But how can you forget the child?"

"I'll never forget Kari."

"I know. I still think of . . ." Will swallowed hard. Grant knew he couldn't say his son's name. Grant knew the hurt must still be raw. "Sometimes it's hard to remember he's really dead."

"I'm sorry, Will. I didn't mean to bring up sad memories."

"Oh, it's not your fault. You had nothing to do with it. I blame myself. If I hadn't involved him, then he never would have been in the position . . ."

Grant squeezed the older man's shoulder. He knew exactly how he felt. Losing a child was not something you could get over. He'd never had any time with his own daughter. He didn't even have memories he could hold close in order to give himself any comfort. And to think it was an act of desperation that had brought him into contact with Brooke Johnson—his wife. He'd rushed to save a child, never imagining she was his own.

"Uncle Grant . . . Uncle Grant." Kari ran toward him. Her smile was wide, and she held something in her hand. She was dressed in a pink jacket with matching hat and gloves that dangled from her sleeves. Her hair, in two long braids, stretched down her back. Grant stood up, catching her as she flew into his arms. He swung her in a full circle before settling her on his arm and holding her to his chest.

"Uncle Grant, look what I've got." She opened her small palm to reveal a small airplane pin. It was the kind they gave children passengers.

"Why those are the most wonderful wings I've ever seen."

"They look like yours." Kari placed hers against Grant's jacket collar. "See?"

Grant looked at them. "Of course, they look like mine. Here, let me pin them on you." He set her on the ground and knelt at her level. Taking the plastic wings, he clipped them to her collar in the same place as his own.

"Why don't you two visit for a while?" Will said. "I need to make a phone call." Will smiled at the child.

"Graffie, do you like my wings?"

"They're wonderful, darling. One day maybe you'll be able to fly."

"I will fly, won't I, Uncle Grant? When I'm older, you'll teach me, won't you?" The high-pitched voice tugged at his heart.

"Kari will miss you when you're gone," Will said, giving Grant a level stare.

"I'll miss her, too."

Will smiled and turned toward the terminal building.

"Are you leaving, Uncle Grant?" Kari's mouth formed a pout not unlike her mother's. Grant wanted to kiss her.

"I have to go soon, sweetheart." He sat her on his knee, and they continued looking onto the airfield.

"Will you come back to see me? Mother said you were very busy, and you wouldn't be coming to see us anymore."

Grant took Kari's gloves and put them on her chilled hands. "Kari, Uncle Grant has to go away. It may not be possible for me to come and see you for a long time. Can you understand that?"

Kari's pout disintegrated into a frown. Her eyes filled with tears. "But I don't want you to go away. I want you to come and live with us."

Grant hugged the small body to his. He kissed the top of her head. "It's what I want, too, darling. But it's just not possible. But Uncle Grant will always be thinking of you. And, one day, you will learn to fly."

"Will you come back and teach me?" The suggestion brought her smile back.

Grant fingered the toy wings attached to her collar. "If it's possible, Kari. If it's possible."

The voice was raspy, old. Robyn felt as if it came to her from another life.

"Well, Mrs. Richards, it's been a long time. But I've finally found you."

Fear's cold finger scraped down Robyn's back. Her fingers clutched the phone so tightly color drained from her knuckles.

"I'm sorry you must have the wrong number. There's no one by the name of Richards here." The words were practiced, but Robyn never thought she'd ever have to say them. Her eyes quickly scanned the kitchen. Only Marianne was within earshot, and she had water running in the sink.

"I've made no mistake, *Mrs. Richards . . . Mrs. Robyn Richards.*" The way he said her name made her physically recoil. "I've waited a long time to find you, and now, I'm sure."

Robyn didn't know what to do. She couldn't acknowledge she was Robyn Richards. And, by denying it, she couldn't ask what he wanted.

"Who *is* this?" she stalled.

"I'm a parent just like you. Only you killed my son."

"I never killed anyone." She lowered her voice to a conspiratorial whisper. Marianne finished, and Robyn watched her head for the dining room.

"You have a daughter, Mrs. Richards."

Robyn's knees gave way, and she crumpled onto the chair next to the phone. Her face was as pale as the flour clinging to her hands. "Kari!" she whispered.

"Yes, Kari."

"What do you want?" Robyn fought for control over the shakes that took hold of her body.

"I want justice, Mrs. Richards."

"What are you talking about? I don't even know who you are?"

"But you knew my son . . ."

"Who was your son?" She was out of the chair.

"And I know your daughter," the man ignored her question. "She's a beautiful little girl. Where is she now, Mrs. Richards?"

His continually calling her Mrs. Richards was rubbing her raw. "Look, I don't know who you are, but you've got things wrong. I'm not Mrs. Richards, and I don't know your son."

"You'll never see her again." Each word was punctuated as if he were speaking to a child.

"Who is this?" she demanded. Restrained fear pierced her.

"I know," he said. "I know who you *really* are. You killed my son. And I've got your daughter. You'll never see her again."

"Who is this! Who is this!" She'd heard the click cutting off the connection. Still, she screamed into the phone. Dead silence answered her.

She dropped the phone. Her body was shaking, and she couldn't think straight. She had to do something, but what? Who could she call? What would she say? Who was on the phone? The police. Call the police, a voice in her consciousness spoke.

She didn't know how long she stood there unable to move or do anything. Marianne found her.

"Brooke, what is it!" She took her friend's hands and squeezed them. "Your hands are ice cold." Marianne replaced the phone, then pushed Robyn into a chair. "Who was on the phone?" she asked.

It took a while for her to be able to speak. Then the words came out slow and labored. "I don't know."

The phone rang again. Robyn jumped up. Her eyes widened in fear. If she'd had enough breath, she would have screamed, but her voice was cut short and a terrible pain lodged in her chest. Marianne picked up the phone.

"Jacob."

Robyn snatched the phone from her partner.

"Jacob!" she screamed into the receiver. "Kari's been kidnapped!"

CHAPTER 18

It had been too long a time since Jacob had a field assignment. Blood coursed through his veins like rushing wind. Adrenaline pumped through his system. He could smell the danger, taste the adventure. And it was thrilling. He maneuvered the rented Lincoln through the evening rush hour as people hurried toward their homes and uneventful evenings. His evening would prove to be quite different.

Jacob and Grant arrived at the same time. Marianne hadn't left Robyn's side. The redhead had managed to get Robyn home. Since arriving, the phone had not rung, but they'd found a note on the kitchen counter. Robyn's cheeks were the color of kindergarten paste, and she kept looking at the phone as if she could make it ring.

Seeing the two men come into the room together confused her even more. Before she had time to ask questions, Jacob broke the silence.

"Has any other contact been made?" he asked, taking command.

"We found a note," Marianne reported. "The restaurant will forward any calls."

"Where's the note?" Marianne gave the recipe card she'd found to Jacob. Grant's writing was on the opposite side. Robyn could see it as Jacob read.

He read the words Robyn knew by heart.

21 October

You will lose the one
you love above all others.
As I have lost.

Grant came to Robyn and took her in his arms. "Are you all right?" he asked.

"Grant, it's . . . it's Kari. Kari's been kidnapped." It was the final straw. Robyn dropped her head on his shoulder and burst into tears. Marianne and Jacob looked on.

"Can I talk to her alone?" Grant asked over Robyn's head. Jacob nodded. He led her into the kitchen.

"It's going to be all right, Brooke."

"You don't know that, Grant. There's so much you don't know. So much I can't tell you."

"I know you're my wife, and I've been in love with you since I saw you dance across a stage in Las Vegas seven years ago."

Robyn's eyes dried and came up to meet her husband's. "How?"

"Jacob. He's told me everything. The trial. Gianelli. The Witness Protection Program."

"And Kari?" she asked.

"She is our daughter."

"Oh Grant," she went into his arms. "Can you ever forgive me? I love you so much, I couldn't ask you to come with me."

"We'll talk about that later. Right now, we have to find Kari."

Robyn's smile was thin but confident. They returned to the living room. The activity had increased. Hammil was there along with two other men. They had cellular phones and laptop computers. Everyone seemed busy accessing data by phone or machine. Marianne and Jacob stood near the front hall. They were deep in conversation but stopped when Grant and Robyn reentered the room.

"Brooke, we've got to ask you some questions." Jacob came toward her.

"I'm all right." She lifted her chin in a gesture Jacob recognized. "What do you want to know?"

He started. The questions were fired one by one, and she answered them as she remembered. She repeated everything the man had said on the phone.

"Did you recognize the voice?"

"No, but I have the feeling I know who he is."

"Why?" Jacob asked.

"I don't know. Just that I've heard it someplace before." She put her hands on her temples and closed her eyes trying to pull the voice into focus.

"Where?"

"I don't know," she shouted, bringing her hands back to her sides.

"How long ago?"

"I don't know?"

"Jacob, stop badgering her," Grant interceded.

"It's okay, Grant," Robyn took his hand. "Jacob doesn't mean it the way it sounds." Grant's hand tightened on hers.

"Think, Brooke. Kari's life depends on you remembering."

"Don't you think I know that? She's my daughter," Robyn glared at him then felt guilty for it. Jacob was obviously concerned about her daughter, and this was his way of displaying it.

"Brooke, he said you killed his son," Marianne spoke.

"Yes, but he didn't tell me who his son was."

"There were only two men at the trial who are now dead," Jacob began. "Gianelli was found with his wrists slashed two days after being committed. And the Devil was executed."

"Who's the Devil?" Grant asked.

"He headed a very powerful organization called the Crime Network. For years, he was reported dead by eye witnesses. Then, he'd surface again after some magnificent kill. A man named Alex Jordan."

Grant was propelled from his position next to Robyn. He stood inches from Jacob. "Are you sure?"

"Absolutely," Jacob said.

All eyes focused on Grant. Sound stopped in the room. The computers stilled.

"Alex Jordan is Will's son."

Grant's voice was like rifle fire in a confined space.

"McAdams doesn't have a son. He's got four daughters . . ."

"Will never married Alex's mother, and for years, he didn't acknowledge Alex as his child," Grant interrupted. "Will's approval was the one thing Alex wanted above all else. He came during the summer, and because we were kind of in the same boat, we became friends." Robyn took his hand, knowing how he felt about losing his parents and belonging to no one. "Alex would do anything Will asked of him. Sometimes, Will was hard on him, not approving what he did when Alex wanted it so badly. There was an obvious love between them, but Will always pulled back, and Alex was forever trying to prove himself worthy of his father's respect. This afternoon Will couldn't even speak his name."

"You saw . . . Will this afternoon?" Robyn stammered. Her attention was on Grant, but she saw Jacob giving orders to Hammil and the younger man now going to the computer he'd brought with him.

"He brought Kari to the airfield. He called a couple of days ago and asked when I was going to be in town. I switched schedules with another pilot and flew in and out this afternoon. Jacob's call came almost the moment I landed."

"Will wouldn't take Kari." Robyn was shaking her head. "He loves her. She calls him Graffie for grandfather, and she loves him," she babbled on. "Will wouldn't do this. There has to be another explanation."

There had to be, Robyn thought, but as Jacob asked question after question, there appeared to be no other explanation. No one outside of that room knew about her. She had never told Will about her past. She had adhered as much as she could to Jacob's rules. The only man who knew slightly more had been Grant—and Jacob had been the one to tell him she was really Robyn Richards. So why would Will take Kari? What could he know? And how could he have found out?

The noise increased as the machinery was turned back on. The other agents were squawking into the phones, and several were punching on the small computer keyboards. Suddenly, it was deafening to Robyn. Grant's hand in hers was the only solid force in the room.

The night wore on. Robyn was tired of answering questions and coming to no conclusions. Where had he taken Kari? Where did they look? Why hadn't they called the police? Something had to be done. Someone had to find out what had caused Will to do this terrible thing, and someone had to save Kari. Suddenly, she knew. None of these people knew Will or Kari. It had to be her. She had to save her child.

"Jacob, I want my old job back," Robyn stepped forward, shouting above the noise.

"What!" His voice silenced the room. The fingers poised above the three laptop computers behind her stopped hitting the keys. The cellular phones, standard issue of the FBI, ceased their snappy whirling rings. None of the harsh voices of the strangers in her living room barked commands into the black plastic handsets.

Grant came up behind her, resting his hands on her upper arms. The gesture gave her strength.

"I want my old job back," she announced.

"Now!" Jacob looked at her as if the pressures of the past few hours had finally snapped her mind.

"Yes, now." Her voice was slightly impatient, but the gentle squeeze from Grant's hands calmed her.

Jacob raked a hand through the dark crop of curls that slipped onto his forehead like an errant cloud. He took a deep breath and for a moment, closed his eyes. "Would you mind telling me why you want to return to the FBI."

"I want to save my daughter's life."

"What does Kari have to do with your old job?"

"Kari doesn't, but somehow Will does," she paused a second. "It's back there, in Washington, locked in the computers of the Major Crimes Bureau. And I have to find it."

Jacob's coat and tie had long since been discarded. He had placed them neatly over the back of one of the wing chairs, but the constant sweep of men and equipment entering and leaving had caused them to fall in a heap on the floor. He stood before her with the collar of his white shirt unbuttoned and the hint of dark hair just below his collar bones. He looked at her with a steady gaze.

"It's been years, Brooke. Even if there was a connection, it would take days to find it."

"Not for me." She saw Jacob's eyes narrow.

"I know you were a computer wizard, but the technology has changed in the last five years. I'm not even sure they have the same equipment. You don't know the passwords to gain access. To say nothing of the security clearance required just to enter the building."

"Jacob, you can cut through the red tape and get me in."

He sighed heavily. The errant curls falling forward again. "I'll have a remote set up here." He turned to say something to one of the men behind him.

"No," Robyn stopped him with a hand on his arm.

"It's got to be in Washington. There are files there, access to other computers, and the response time here would be too slow."

She was trembling, afraid Jacob would argue against her going.

"Brooke, Kari is still here. We have no reason to believe McAdams has taken her out of the city. Why do you want to go to Washington?" Jacob took a step closer to her. Compassion entered his voice. "He could kill her at any moment."

"We've got two days, Jacob. He won't kill her until the twenty-first at midnight."

"How do you know that?"

Robyn's hand reached around in search of Grant's solid protection. She found it and held it tightly. "It's on the note," she said quietly.

Jacob's stride was determined as he went to the piano and picked up the damning piece of paper. It was dated October twenty-first. Two days from now. "This isn't proof, Brooke. He's deranged."

"You don't know that." Her eyes flashed. Will had been good to her and Kari. If it hadn't been for him, she didn't think she could have survived the demanding hours at the restaurant.

"All right, he could have just forgotten the date."

"He didn't forget." She knew the date, knew where she had seen it and what significance it had. "The twenty-first of October at midnight was when Alex Jordan had been administered a lethal injection at a federal penitentiary." She pushed aside the eye-for-an-eye thought. They couldn't let him inject Kari and kill her.

"I have to go, Jacob." Tears came to her eyes but she blinked them away. She was too keyed up now. If she let herself cry, she'd be hysterical in seconds.

"You really think there's something back there? Something we don't know here?" Jacob's gaze was that of a friend, not the official FBI agent who'd guided her into the program.

"Yes, I do," she answered calmly. He stared at her for a long moment. Then, the room seemed to galvanize into action.

"Give me a phone. I'll get us a plane." Hammil snapped a cellular unit in his hand like a nurse slapping a scalpel.

"I have a plane standing by," Grant dropped his hands. "I'll call the airport, and let them know we're on our way," he called over his shoulder as he went to her phone in the kitchen.

Jacob was already speaking into his unit. His comments were crisp and precise. "Get a jacket," Jacob said quietly. His voice was so tender she could almost believe she'd never heard its harsh tones directed at her.

Robyn ran up the steps quickly. She heard Jacob ordering Marianne to stay there and transfer calls. Robyn was in her room before he finished and didn't hear what calls needed transferring. Pulling a brown suede jacket with western fringe from its hanger, she pushed her arms through the sleeves. On her way to the door, she looked at herself in the mirror. Her face was pale and drawn, and there were dark circles under her eyes. Impulsively, she picked up her lipstick and coated her mouth with a rich red color. Then, using the same tube, she dotted her cheeks and rubbed the color into her skin. It highlighted her cheeks and softened her strained look. After pulling a brush through her hair, she left the room and hurried down the stairs.

Grant was waiting for her when she reached the bottom. He had his jacket on, but his face looked as tense as hers. The night had not been an easy one for him either. The room had been straightened. No sign, except the dark impression of footprints on the carpet, gave evidence that anyone had been there. Marianne and Jacob were in the kitchen. They separated when Robyn entered as if they'd been caught doing something wrong. Marianne turned to the sink and began cleaning coffee cups. Jacob's G-Man disguise settled over him like paint.

"What's that?" Robyn asked, the sound of an approaching helicopter taking her attention away from what her mind had registered.

"The chopper's here," Jacob explained. "This way." Robyn didn't blink as he led her toward the door. She stopped briefly to hug Marianne. Then, she followed the two men out into the dark night. Nothing Jacob did surprised her any longer. A helicopter on her back lawn was standard operating procedure for him. Robyn, Grant, and Jacob ducked and ran toward the giant machine sitting on the green grass like a squatting bird. She stepped on the ski and propelled herself into the small cabin. Grant and Jacob followed closely behind. Without a word, the pilot took off, and minutes later, she was high above the city.

It took less than five minutes to reach the airport. She was quickly ushered into Grant's plane. The moment Jacob stepped onboard the doors closed, and the plane began taxiing. After they were immediately cleared and were airborne, Robyn knew Jacob had pulled rank and cleared traffic.

At Washington International Airport, again, the sky was stacked with aircraft, but their clearance was immediate. Deplaning, she boarded a second helicopter which flew them directly to a heliport within the FBI complex. Robyn was seated behind her old computer at the Assassination Bureau, the tiny sign she'd printed years earlier was faded and torn, but taped to the top of a new monitor. An hour and a half after she had told Jacob she wanted her old job back, here she was.

None of them wore the visitors' badges required of every outsider entering the building. And how many rules had Jacob broken getting them into this facility? In addition, the room was clear. Every machine was inactive. It appeared as if everyone had left hours ago. Except for the heat against her hand when she touched the machine, she'd have thought there was no night operation. She knew Jacob's constant telephone conversations while they were on the plane were responsible for the empty area.

She turned on the computer. In seconds, the blinking cursor greeted her. Robyn typed in her access code and password. They took. She looked up at Jacob, her eyes wide but clear. Almost imperceptibly, he nodded. He'd had it reinstated. She wouldn't ask how he knew what her password had been. He'd only tell her she didn't need to know. But she was grateful.

"Is there anyone here who can help me?" she asked.

"What do you need?" Jacob asked.

"I need Will's files. And I'd like all the records, newspaper clippings, photographs, everything on Alex Jordan's hits. Anything even remotely attached to him. And I need the files on the Network." Somehow they were linked, and she had to find out how.

Jacob didn't waste time asking why she wanted the files. He picked up a phone and issued an order. Robyn knew an entire staff had just gone into action. She'd have what she needed in record time.

"Can I help?" Grant asked.

"Can you use a computer?" Robyn asked.

"I had a teacher once." He smiled and she remembered. He had taught her to fly, and she had taught him a few fundamentals about the computer. For a moment, tension in the room lightened.

"Jacob," she called. "Can he have access?"

"It's against regulations."

Robyn's gaze didn't waver. The strength of what he was doing for her and her child suddenly hit her. Jacob had put the entire U.S. government computer network at her disposal. He'd broken at least ninety of the one hundred regulations against unauthorized entry into the building. And she was asking for access for not one but two people who had no clearance, no authority, and no connection with the FBI. Robyn knew he could lose his job over this. And with what he was doing, very probably would.

"Please," she uttered the solitary word. She couldn't remember ever saying it to the man now facing her. But she didn't want to fight with Jacob anymore. She liked him. If he said no, she'd accept it.

Jacob stared at her for a long moment, then walked to the machine facing her and sat down. He typed something onto the screen. Less than a minute later, he stood. "Your code is FRIEND. The password is BROOKE." Robyn stared at him but he didn't look in her direction.

Grant took the seat Jacob vacated and typed onto the screen. Over his head, Jacob's eyes met Robyn's. She nodded a silent thank you. He walked past her without acknowledgment.

"Go through the menus to Military Service and access Will's records. Find out every place he's ever been stationed. Everything in the file," Robyn instructed. The moment between her and Jacob was gone. She realized he was probably the best friend she had or would ever have.

Jacob sat at the machine next to Grant. "What would you like me to look for?" he asked as he typed his own access code and password onto the screen.

"See what you can find out about Alex Jordan. Anyone he'd been associated with no matter how infrequently. What he liked and disliked. Look for the small details, too. Compile all the confirmed and unconfirmed assassinations linked to him. Create a file I can read."

Adrenaline was pumping through Robyn. She was back. It had been five years since she'd touched a computer keyboard, but it was like swimming, she didn't forget. Her fingers flew across the keys. Information came and went, and she took it all in as fast as the computer would display it.

Silently, they worked. The only sound in the room was the rhythmic tapping of the keyboards. Once or twice, she noticed the doors opening and in came the three men who had been at her house a few hours earlier. They were carrying boxes. Robyn knew they contained the data she had requested.

Someone pinned a badge on her. She barely looked at the man, too engrossed in absorbing the data flitting rapidly across the screen. If she had time, she'd laugh. Jacob couldn't resist being the man he was. He had to comply with regulations as much as possible.

Hours passed as green letters danced across the blue background. She sat for so long that her neck and back began to hurt. She ignored the pain and continued. When or how coffee showed up she didn't know. It was just beside her, and there were empty cups next to her computer. She didn't remember drinking it. Like in the hospital the day Grant came to give Kari the blood, she had no memory of food or drink.

Pushing her chair back, she relaxed a moment. Her head dropped back, and she gathered her hair in a hand-held ponytail for several seconds. Then, she stretched and yawned, her fingers flexed in the air above her head. Sitting up straight, she looked at the men about her. Everyone was engrossed in the work she'd assigned them.

Robyn got up. She joined Hammil who was stacking piles of paper from the storage boxes on a nearby table. Box by box, she emptied the contents and absorbed the information. She soaked up everything. When she finished, she was certain that the Network was comprised of a group of assassins. They were placed throughout the world, probably living normal lives. Some of them were married with families. When the call came through for services, contact was made, and a loving father or a Don Juan type playboy pulled the tools of his trade from mothballs and went into action.

She hadn't yet been able to determine who the leader of the group was, how large a network he commanded, or what connection he had with Will McAdams.

"How are you doing?" Robyn asked Grant.

"There doesn't seem to be anything here we could use. He was a model soldier. His file reads like a man campaigning for the Congressional Medal of Honor. There is nothing here but commendations and awards. From basic training through his retirement, he was at the top of his class or his field."

"What particularly did he excel in?" Robyn poured six cups of coffee into Styrofoam cups. There was no sugar or cream so she passed the revival liquid out to the tired looking men as Grant continued. She peered onto the screen of Grant's computer.

"He excelled in everything from grenades and high explosives to map and terrain reading. During the individual training, he scored highest on the ASVAB and went into intelligence. If you ask me, he was a model soldier."

"What's his I.Q.?" Jacob asked standing up from his machine and coming to stand behind Grant.

Grant scanned through the screens, "One hundred ninety-seven," he said with a low whistle. "The man's intelligent."

"Maybe a little too intelligent," Jacob said.

"I agree," Robyn concurred.

Grant craned his neck to see the two people behind him. "What does that mean?"

"I'm not sure," Jacob answered. "I wonder why a man of such superior intelligence would choose to spend his time making children's toys?"

"Will has always been fond of his girls. When we were young, he supported them in everything from sports to dating. It was only Alex who seemed to expect more than Will could give. His real family lives far away, and they don't visit often. Kari was probably the grandchild he longed for."

"Then why would he kidnap her?" Jacob asked.

"We don't know that he has." Robyn stopped the discussion. "The note doesn't have to be real."

"Face it Brooke. It's in his handwriting. And he's Alex Jordan's father." Jacob's voice was harsh.

She wasn't used to him jumping to conclusions. He was too logical, too much the calm, controlled, think-on-your-feet kind of guy. Jacob came to her, pushing two papers into her hand. Robyn read an account of Will's liaison with a Meredith Jordan before she married and became Meredith Van Buren. The second paper was a copy of Alex Jordan's birth certificate. Under father's name, the space was blank.

"There is another possibility," she added.

"Which is?" Jacob asked.

Robyn moved away from them. She stopped in front of the debris she'd left piled on the floor. "When you staged my kidnapping in Washington . . ."

"What!" Grant was on his feet.

"It's all right, Grant. Jacob was showing me what a dangerous game I was playing."

"Is that why you left so suddenly?"

She nodded. "It worked. He scared me into believing a Network gun lurked behind every pair of sunglasses. I was frantic, and I ran."

Grant covered the small distance between them and hugged her. She leaned against him for a moment, wanting to stay in the warmth of his arms, but Kari's face had her remembering why she was in this room.

"Jacob, suppose someone did find out who I was?"

"Impossible." His comment sounded like a quick snap of the teeth.

"Hear me out," she protested. "Suppose somehow my identity has been found out. Will was watching Kari. Suppose someone came in and kidnapped them both. To force us to think Will is the person who's got Kari, he forced him to write the note."

"Sorry, Ma'am." A voice from behind her arrested three pairs of eyes. Robyn recognized Hammil, the clean-cut agent who had been her escort for Susan's wedding. "We've had the handwritten note analyzed. It's definitely William McAdams handwriting. There are no indications of any stress-related impressions. When Mr. McAdams wrote the note, he was under no strain of anxiety."

"You can tell that from a piece of paper?" Grant asked incredulously.

"Sir," the young man began.

"That's enough, Hammil," Jacob cut the explanation off. The young man's face closed.

The door opened and a cloned agent, molded just like Hammil, stood there. He held his position in the doorway a moment before coming farther into the room.

He went straight to where Jacob stood and whispered something in his ear. Jacob nodded, and the unnamed man left the room. Robyn watched as Jacob picked up a phone.

"Put it through in here and have it traced," he said into the mouthpiece and indicated Robyn should pick up one of the other phones.

"Hello," she said.

"Hi, Mommy."

"Kari! Are you all right?" Relief and fear sliced through her as she heard Kari's voice.

"Mommy, I miss you. I'm fine. Are you coming to get me tonight?"

Jacob's signal told her to remain calm.

"Yes, oh yes, darling. Is Graffie with you?" Robyn's heart hammered in her chest. Grant took Robyn's hand and squeezed it.

Before the child could answer, the phone was taken from her and a gravelly voice said. "She's mine, now. You'll never see her again."

Blood drained from Robyn's face as the line went dead. She started to shake. Suddenly, the brightness in the room was blinding, and the two men across from her appeared to weave back and forth like drunks. Jacob's hand moved in slow motion as the phone left his ear and started an arc. She turned her head, feeling her hair swing around her head and hit her in the face as she looked at the black instrument in her hand. Brighter and brighter the room got until the light was so blinding, she had to close her eyes against it.

She tried to scream. She wanted to say something to Grant, but her mouth wouldn't open fast enough for sound to come through. Then, her knees gave under her, and she felt herself falling. Below her was a dark well. Her body was drawn toward it. She was going to fall into it, and she couldn't stop herself. Down she went, into the blackness of the abyss below. It felt cool, against her hot skin. Behind her was the blinding light, below her the coolness of the dark cave. She went into it gladly. It was comforting, taking her away from the pain of the light and the pain in her head. The coolness would make it go away. She embraced it.

She fell for a long time. There was no bottom to the well. She went further and farther into the coolness of the dark. Suddenly, something caught her. She fought against it. She wanted to keep going. She didn't want to be pulled back into the light. It was painful there. The dark was where she wanted to be. But whatever had her was strong. It caught and shackled her arms. She fought it, struggled against it until she was too tired to care. Then, the darkness swallowed her.

CHAPTER 19

Robyn fought her way back to consciousness. The acrid smell of ammonia assailed her nostrils, and she sat up, fighting the offending odor. One hand knocked the wet vial to the floor while her face turned to come into warm contact with Grant's chest.

She opened her eyes and pushed herself back. She was on the floor. Grant cradled her across his lap while Jacob knelt on her other side. The room was quiet and empty. She looked about for Hammil and the other men whose names Jacob had not given her. They were gone. Only the two men hovered above her.

"Grant, it was Will. He said he'd kill her."

"Jacob told us," Grant acknowledged.

Robyn remembered Jacob was on the other phone while the short conversation took place. She tried to sit. Both men's hands came out to stop her.

"I'm all right," she said, breaking the awkward moment. "Let me up."

They released her and she sat fully up, tucking her feet under her Indian-style. Both of the faces staring into hers looked as drained as she had looked hours earlier when she caught her reflection in the bedroom mirror.

"Do you think he's telling the truth?" she asked not knowing which man she expected to answer. Neither of them knew what Will was capable of doing. She'd been closer to him than either of them. She could hardly believe Will had tracked her for five years, moved next door, and infiltrated her life to discover if his suspicions were true. And, finally, he had. She'd trusted her child to him. He'd been so close and so loving to her and Kari. How could she believe he lived a double life?

"We'll find her," Jacob said finally. His stare was direct. "You thought there was something here that would give us a clue to what he would do."

Robyn and Grant got up. "Yes, what did you find out about Alex Jordan?" They helped her to her feet.

"Not much more than we knew five years ago." Jacob took the seat in front of the backlit computer screen. "He had very few associations. But he did seem to spend a lot of time in Sicily."

"Can we confirm where he was when the restaurant murders took place?"

"We can't say exactly." Jacob turned and met Robyn's eyes. "In Sicily, nine years ago, six American men were killed in a restaurant," Jacob explained to Grant. "The kill was impossible. No windows, door locked from the inside. The food was not poisoned. No marks on the bodies. Yet, they were all dead."

"How did it happen?" Grant asked.

"It's still unsolved," Robyn answered. She spoke almost to herself.

"What happened to the bodies?" Grant asked.

"What do you mean? They were identified by the next of kin and properly buried."

"Can you find the names of the dead and who claimed the bodies?"

"What are you getting at?" Robyn directed her attention to Grant.

"It's from a novel I read called *Lost Companions.*" Grant could tell he made no sense. "It's about a dinner party where everyone ends up dead."

"I understand." Jacob turned to the keyboard and rapidly began striking the keys. The screen flickered. "One of those men was not really dead."

Robyn knew he was connected to a modem and the computer was dialing into another data base. When the Interpol logo came up on the screen, she pulled a chair up. Grant followed suit, and they watched in quiet anticipation as Jacob combed his way through the maze of menus to reach his goal. The list of names came up. Nothing looked familiar to Robyn.

"How about military?" Robyn asked.

"They were all in the military at some point in their lives," Jacob volunteered. "None of them served together and interviews with the families could not produce any links."

"Can you pull up the names of the people who claimed the bodies?" Grant asked.

Jacob pressed several keys in rapid succession, and the list of the dead appeared on the screen. Along side of each name was the name of the next of kin.

"Does anything look familiar? Out of place?"

Both Robyn and Jacob shook their heads.

Jano, Sr., Keith	claimed by	Jano, Jr., Keith
Knight, Joseph	claimed by	Knight, Adam
Lance, David	claimed by	Holden, Jane
McBride, James	claimed by	McBride, Martin
Totten, Earl	claimed by	Totten, Robert
Williams, John	claimed by	Opal, Julia

She went through the names. They meant nothing. "There was a photo." Robyn left her chair and went to search one of the boxes on the floor. She leafed through it and found the black-and-white eight-by-ten glossy.

Three heads bowed over the picture of death.

"Do you know who belongs to the names?"

Robyn reached over and listed the names of the men sitting around the table. They looked as if they were all asleep.

"What day did this happen on?"

"May twenty-sixth," Jacob answered.

"Which was the first body claimed?"

"They were all released the same day, May thirtieth. A hearse arrived for each of the victims. Totten and McBride were the first to leave."

"It's got to be here." Grant whispered.

"You're losing me," Robyn prompted.

"If the assumption is correct, that one of these men was not dead, but only simulating death, then a doctor or a person posing as a doctor had to be in on the job."

"All right. Where does that take us?" Robyn asked.

"Three days is too long a time for a body to simulate death."

"Meaning," Jacob continued, "that the accomplice was part of the medical examiner's office."

"Or posed as part of the office."

"And that's how he escaped. Alex Jordan was either there or someone else was, and he claimed the body," Robyn concluded.

"No," Grant stopped her. "Will was the man there."

"How do you know?" Robyn reacted to his tone.

"I've seen this before." Grant took the photo and looked closer. He stood up, walking about the cluttered room with the picture in his hand. Two men sat on either side of the rectangular table. At the head were two others. Grant came back, straddled a chair and pointed to the man on the far side of the photo, directly right of the head. "This is Will McAdams."

"How can you be so sure?" Jacob asked.

"I knew I'd seen this before." His finger drew a circle encompassing the entire table. "It's in Kari's room. The toy table with the bears sitting around it. There are only five bears but six chairs. This is the missing one."

Robyn gasped. Grant was right. She'd walked by that toy tea party hundreds of times. Kari had moved the bears many times, yet the same chair was always empty. As if it was a message Will was trying to give her.

"Who is this man?" Grant put his finger on the position which had been empty in the toy representation.

"Earl Totten," Robyn and Jacob answered in unison.

"Then, Robert Totten is Alex Jordan," Grant spoke. "What did these men have in common with Will?"

"They were the old guard." It was Jacob's turn to explain. "McAdams wanted to set up Jordan as the leader of a worldwide syndicate of assassins. He proposed a new order, but the old chiefs refused to buy into his plan. He had them killed."

"How do you know that?" Robyn's hands went to her sides and her body froze. Jacob spoke as if he'd always known the men in the photo and of their connections to each other. She was convinced. He didn't need to tell her. "You knew then, didn't you?"

"I didn't know about McAdams's connection." Jacob didn't have to ask her when *then* was. Robyn could tell he'd been aware of the formation of the Crime Network. "When you discovered Alex Jordan's intent six years ago, we'd been aware of the Network's movements for some time. We didn't know who the leader was. He was very adept at eluding us. Now, I know it was because the father-son team swapped the leadership. An action which intentionally misled anyone who might try to infiltrate the organization."

"But it *was* infiltrated?" Robyn was still rigid.

"Yes, eight men had been recruited. They were the best. Some of the most spectacular assassinations were credited to them. When Gianelli ordered the destruction of organized crime, these men were sent. But you discovered the plot, and all eight of them were captured, tried, and remain imprisoned."

"How did Will find out about me?"

"He didn't know for sure, or he'd never have pulled his hand," Jacob explained. "He was in intelligence. He could have contacts and a network so deep, it would be impossible to discover. But still he was unsure."

"He's also proved to be extremely patient," Grant added.

"But how did he find me now? I swear I didn't reveal anything. What happened to confirm his suspicions?"

"I told him," Grant said. He stood up, facing the two pairs of astonished eyes. "Not in actual words. I didn't know for sure until Jacob told me the truth. Each time we met he was very interested in Brooke, even suggesting you might be a spy."

"What did you say," Jacob barked.

"When he came to the airfield to see me," Grant answered Jacob, but his eyes were trained on the pale face of the woman he loved. "Kari was with him. We talked and I told him you were never married to Cameron Johnson. He was a decoy, and your real life was a classified secret."

"Classified," Jacob snapped. "You used that word?"

Grant nodded, glancing at Jacob before returning his attention to Brooke. "Please, Brooke, don't be angry. I didn't know he had any connection with you."

Robyn was angry. How could he have been so thoughtless? How could he endanger the life of his own daughter? She stepped back, taking a long breath. It wasn't fair, she told herself. Grant didn't know what he was doing, and hadn't she mysteriously sidestepped issues that would make him curious enough to confide in a friend? Robyn's shoulders dropped as she let the anger fall away. Grant hadn't been trained like she was. He didn't know how one small sentence could change the course of her life.

"What are we going to do now?" She looked at Jacob. "We're running out of time, and we haven't come up with any method he might use on Kari."

"You think it will be another one of his spectacular kills?" Jacob asked.

Tears formed in her eyes. Both men moved toward her. Jacob stopped, and Grant cradled her against him. "He won't do that." Grant eyed Jacob above Robyn's head. His voice was soft. Robyn responded to it. Craning her head, she looked up at him. "He's here for Brooke, not Kari," Grant said.

"But he said I took his son, and he was going to take my child."

"He won't be able to do it."

"Go on," Jacob knew there was more.

"Will had four daughters and Alex. The girls have children. Children he's seen only a few times. He wouldn't tell me why, but he thinks it is an injustice that his daughters keep the children away from him. Kari is an innocent. It's you he wants." Grant looked down into her eyes.

"Then we have to go back," she said.

"Hold it." Jacob joined the small group in front of the computer terminals. "If you think I'm willing to trade you for Kari, I won't do it."

"It's not your decision, Jacob!" Robyn screamed. "Kari is my child, and I will decide how best to save her life. Not you. I've let you run my existence for five years, and I hate it. This time it's my choice." Her eyes reflected the anger now raging in her body that stepped out of Grant's arms and confronted him.

"All right," he agreed. "We do it your way."

Clarence Darrow Christopher III felt every one of his fifty-nine years. It was four o'clock in the morning. He should be home, in bed with his wife. Instead, he stood looking out of the window of his office at the Federal Bureau of Investigation. A light rain coated the streets of Washington. Street lamps reflected in pools of concentric circles.

What could Jacob be up to? Clarence really thought he knew the man. But in all the years they'd crossed channels between the CIA and FBI, this was the first time anything negative had been brought to his attention. Jacob was straight, bright, honest, a regulations-only man. If there was anyone who could handle the security of the United States, Clarence would have no reservations in recommending Jacob. Despite the incident with Cynthia, they didn't come any more reliable than Jacob Winston.

Yet, tonight, he had let all the years of hard work go right down the drain, the way the rain was going into the openings in the street. And for what? He didn't know. He'd read Robyn Warren-Richards's file. She had helped to put Alex Jordan away, and the United States taxpayers were thanking her for the effort. She was a beautiful woman, both before and after she entered the program. But that was no reason for Jacob to commit career suicide. Unless . . . He refused to complete the thought. Even Jacob wouldn't be that stupid.

Well, he had to do it. He might as well get it over with. Going to the phone, he pressed the button to summon one of the twenty-four hour secretaries who manned the station outside his office. Immediately, the door opened, and a woman of forty stood before him, a pad in her hand.

"Tell him I want to see him," he said with a sigh. Without a word she closed the door. Clarence dropped down into his chair. He glanced down at the folder of Brooke Johnson, open on his desk. He'd read it and there was nothing there that seemed to make sense out of what Jacob had done. He lifted the black-and-white glossy photo and looked into the sad eyes of a woman with dark hair framing her face. It must have been the eyes, he thought. I can see how a man could get lost in the silent vulnerability spoken there. But Jacob, he'd thought Jacob was a better man.

The phone rang. Jacob snatched it up. "Winston," he said.

"Mr. Christopher would like to see you in his office, Mr. Winston," an efficient voice said.

"I'll be right there," he answered and hung up without a salutation.

Robyn looked directly at him as did every other pair of eyes in the crowded room. Robyn couldn't remember when Hammil and the other agents returned. But the room was crowded again.

"Keep working," he said, as his body slowly left the chair. "I have to see Christopher."

Robyn took a step toward him and stopped. "Clarence Christopher?"

He nodded.

"Let me go with you?"

"No!" his voice snapped, then in a softer tone. "You have to stay here and finish what you're doing. If there's any chance at all of finding McAdams, it's got to be here."

Robyn nodded. She knew further argument would be fruitless. Jacob's face was relaxed but closed. He smiled at her and squeezed her arm before walking away.

Jacob closed the door behind him, turning left and walking to the private elevator at the end of the hall. He inserted his key into the security panel and waited for the car which would carry him to Clarence's office. He wasn't surprised to find the director of the bureau in residence at this hour. He'd known it would come to this when they stood in Robyn's living room and when he still had time to change his mind. Robyn thought Kari was in danger, and she was, but Robyn and Grant's lives were also in peril. And he wouldn't let William McAdams win. Not this time. This time he was protecting Robyn, and he wasn't going to let anything happen to her. She wasn't like Cynthia. Cynthia had done everything his way while Robyn challenged him at every turn. And Cynthia had died. And someone like McAdams had killed her.

They were going to find a link, whatever clue they could to determine where he'd taken Kari and what he planned for her. Jacob hoped Robyn was right, and the date on the note was a message of McAdams's plan. But even if it were, they were running out of time, and they were no closer to finding anything than they had been in her living room.

The door to the elevator slid silently open, and he stepped into the subdued lighting of the plush car. Well oiled cables raised him to the executive floor. Then, the doors slid back, and he stepped into Clarence's office.

"Come in, Jacob." Clarence stood with his back to him. He looked out of the window interested in the rain or the street below. Jacob stood in front of the recessed portal of carved doors, waiting.

He'd been in this office many times, but tonight he expected it would be his last. The overhead lights were out, and the room was illuminated by a lamp on Clarence's massive desk. Another lamp poured its yellow glow from a small end table next to the maroon leather sofa. Above the sofa, fifteen years of a man's life were reflected in several groupings of photographs. While most of them coupled Clarence with presidents, judges, and an occasional movie star, his face smiled from a fishing boat and from the background at a picnic.

"What does she know about you, Jacob?" Clarence left his position and came to sit behind his desk. Jacob lowered himself into the chair in front of it.

"Only what she needs to know, sir." The look Clarence leveled at him was not lost. Jacob had rarely referred to him as "sir," yet, tonight, it was warranted.

"Then, why, damn it? Why have you decided to throw your career into the Potomac and dive in after it?"

"Her child has been kidnapped," Jacob answered quietly. He saw the open folder on Clarence's desk. The contents of that folder had been sealed when she was placed in Buffalo. Clarence must have been extremely concerned to have it exhumed.

"Why aren't you letting the authorities handle this? It's out of our jurisdiction."

Jacob's body left the chair like a bullet. "Our jurisdiction?" He spit the word. "Where is the line for our jurisdiction, Clarence? Can you find where it lies today? Do you know where it will be tomorrow? When Alex Jordan was on trial, our jurisdiction extended to anything to get Robyn Richards to testify. We did everything whether it was within our authority of not. Then, it was all right. What about now, Clarence? She's downstairs, under who knows what kind of stress, trying to find some key, something to piece together an investigation we dropped five years ago, because it may provide a connection to save her daughter's life. And she's got less than two days to get it done. What do you think I should have done?"

"You should have followed the rules. Brooke Johnson should be living a quiet life without the need for constant care from us."

"Clarence, have you forgotten you gave me this assignment?" Jacob reminded the silver-haired man.

"No, I haven't forgotten, but I never thought I'd have you on my carpet at four o'clock in the morning."

"We owe it to her," Jacob said quietly.

"Jacob, what are you talking about. She got the same, better than the same, treatment as any of the members who ever went through the program."

"Did she, Clarence? We took from her. She gave us what we wanted. We put Alex Jordan away. But we took everything she had. We gave her nothing, but an empty shell to exist in until she's too old to care. She walked away from us with nothing, not even the husband she loved."

"Don't lay that at my door, Jacob." Clarence's hand came down hard on the desk, rattling the pencil cup and causing the phone to give a tiny chimelike ring. Clarence was on his feet coming around the desk. "She made that decision without our help."

"What kind of decision would you have made, Clarence, if you were in the same position? If you were a material witness in a federal case, and your government used the fact that your wife was being held in a foreign prison. And, as added incentive, they spring Project Eagle on you. The only attempt to free her rested with your testimony. Would you refuse to testify and leave her there? Or would you take her into the program with you where everything about her is different. Everything, Clarence. She'd be physically altered. The woman you married would cease to exist. A different woman would live in her place.

"And then, everything she liked to do would suddenly become taboo. She could no longer paint. Those hand-drawn Christmas cards she sends out each year would be forbidden. She could never again see any of her family. No more reunions or homecomings. No old college friends or people she worked with. Do you honestly want to tell me you'd opt for that kind of life for the woman you loved?"

"Jacob, we're not talking about what I would do. And that's all past decision now. The truth is we're not doing our jobs. We're no closer to finding who's after Brooke Johnson than we were months ago. For years, we've been running round-the-clock surveillance on her. Do you know how much this is costing the taxpayers?"

"No," Jacob lied. He knew exactly what the cost was.

"The past five years alone have run into the millions. And, if I project it out for the next thirty years, the cost is astronomical. When do you plan to close this? Do you plan to ever close it?"

Jacob remained silent. He knew as long as Robyn needed protecting he'd make sure she got it. Clarence stared at him for a long moment then sighed and went back to his position by the windows. Jacob also knew Clarence and that he was concerned about Jacob's feelings for Robyn. Alex Jordan had been a thorn since Robyn uncovered the Network. McKenzie Cranford had been deputy director, second only to Clarence, and he'd been at the top of the ring Robyn had discovered. Jacob knew Clarence's thoughts tonight were on the scene that had taken place five years ago.

"Unauthorized use of aircraft, unauthorized entry into a federal facility, unauthorized movement of secured files, unauthorized use of government equipment, unauthorized access to sensitive computer information including an investigation in progress." Clarence recited the broken rules as if they were charges against him. "What do you want me to do?" Clarence's voice was low. It held none of the anger of a few minutes ago.

Jacob looked at his friend. He'd turned to face him. Jacob saw the hastily donned shirt still wrinkled from the previous day, his feet pushed into brown leather slippers that had been Jacob's Christmas present to him last year. His hair was uncombed, and he looked older than Jacob had ever noticed before.

"I want you to trust me, Clarence." His voice was friendly, too.

Clarence was quiet for a long time. He and Jacob stared at each other. Finally, he walked back to his desk and sat down. He glanced at the file still lying open and picked up the photo of Robyn. Jacob watched him without words.

"Are you in love with her?" he asked, not looking up.

Jacob sat down. There were several things he could say in answer to that question. He could have told him she was still in love with her husband. He could say he was married to his work. He could lie and say, 'no.' But he met the eyes of the man across the desk directly and said, "Yes, I love her more than a sister, but less than a wife, if that's your point."

Clarence let out his breath slowly as if he were willing himself to control it.

"Does she know?" he asked.

"I've never told her. But I'm sure she knows." Jacob had only kissed Robyn once. But, in that kiss, he'd told her everything. After that, each time he saw her he could see her feelings in her eyes. He knew she loved her husband. None of the warm looks she directed at Grant ever came his way. Yes, he loved Robyn, but his allegiance lay with another woman.

Robyn was not the woman for him, but she was the one who had shown him what living was about. He would be hurt when all this was over, and she was gone from his life, but he could take the hurt. And he would go on. He would stop existing and begin living. The woman downstairs, so full of life despite the sadness in her eyes, had scratched and clawed to have a life. While he had existed from day to day, refusing to get involved because he felt guilty over Cynthia. He couldn't have saved Cynthia. He knew that now. No matter what he did. There were too many people against her. If the men in the helicopter hadn't gotten her, she still wouldn't have lived through the day. Jacob admitted it to himself. He'd done his best, and that's all he could ask of himself.

"Jacob." Clarence's voice pulled him back to the present. "Can I count on you to be objective?"

"Yes, sir." There was no hesitancy about his reply.

Clarence drummed his fingers on the manila folder. The circular seal, ragged on the ends, reminded Jacob of blood. It matched the words, Top Secret, spread across the jacket like a warning sign.

"All right, Jacob. I'll table it for now."

Jacob's body let out the breath he was holding. "Thank you, Clarence." He rose, going back to the private elevator. His hand held the security key, but before he slipped it in the slot, he turned. Clarence stood behind his desk facing him, his hands clasped behind him.

"Before I go, Clarence, I'd like you to know why I'm doing this. Robyn Richards made the highest sacrifice for her country short of dying. She gave up her right to be a human being. Because of her courage and forcefulness, ten men are happily home, living productive lives while she was shot-gunned into hiding. Not one of those men knew of her sacrifice. Not even the man she loved enough to leave. I only hope there'll be someone in my life who loves me as much as Robyn loved her husband. But even if it hadn't been for that, she uncovered a network which allowed us to crack one of the largest assassination rings ever organized. For that alone, she deserves the protection of the taxpayers for as long as necessary, even if necessary means the rest of her life." Jacob hesitated a moment, then turned and opened the elevator.

Clarence watched the doors close. He reached up and turned off the lamp on his desk, then sat down in the dark. When the call had come in tonight and he listened in horror as the details of Jacob's activities were described, he thought of retiring. He'd be sixty-two in three years, and someone else could take over this job. He didn't need the stress. He could stay home with his wife. They could go on a cruise. She'd wanted a vacation for years. But Jacob's comments had changed his mind. He had been right. Robyn Richards had sacrificed a lot, and she deserved better than the lot she'd been dealt.

But there was nothing he could do about that now. A major drug kingpin had been put out of commission and an assassin-for-hire ring had been taken off the streets.

He wasn't sure he could trust Jacob now. He'd admitted he was in love with the woman. And Jacob wasn't a man who loved lightly. Since Cynthia, he hadn't been involved seriously. Jacob had said he could be objective, but no man in love was capable of that.

Clarence Christopher reached across his desk and pushed the intercom button. "Get me Marianne Lincoln," he spoke into the quiet air.

CHAPTER 20

It was nearly daylight when Jacob came back. Robyn looked up as he opened the door. His face told her nothing. No indication that he'd spoken with the director of the FBI was revealed.

"If I ask, will you tell me?" she asked, as he resumed his seat in front of the computer screen.

"No," his voice sounding final.

"What's going to happen to you?"

"I don't know." His fingers went to work reestablishing contact with the central computer.

"What did he say?"

"Nothing that will help you find what McAdams intends for Kari."

"Jacob!"

"Drop it, Brooke. He didn't throw us out. So, for the time being, we've got the use of this room and the files. Let's try to get as much information as we can."

Robyn went back to her screen. She pounded on the keyboard. Jacob was the most closed-mouthed man she'd ever met. He could be so stubborn at times. His whole career could rest on this night, and he didn't want to discuss it. Didn't he think she cared what happened to him? Wasn't he aware of how much she appreciated all he'd done for her?

"Jacob?" Robyn got up and went to the desk where he sat. "I care, Jacob. I hope you always knew that."

"I know it, Brooke." He looked at her with one of the few unguarded stares she'd ever seen. His eyes were luminous and open. She could see his fears and wants in the tender expression that held hers. "It will be all right." He took her hand and squeezed it. "It will be all right."

Robyn leaned forward and kissed Jacob's cheek. "You're one of the truly remarkable men I've ever known," she told him. "I want Kari back more than anything in the world, but I don't want your career as her ransom."

"It won't be," he said quietly.

Robyn searched his face for any sign of insincerity. She found none.

"Let's find Kari," he said.

A swelling rose in her throat, and she had to swallow hard to remove it. Without another word, she went back to her machine. Grant touched her hand as she passed. Soon, she was back into the files. She scanned Alex Jordan's information. From the looks of him, she'd have more easily pictured him sitting behind the desk of a large corporation, not engineering the unsolvable crime.

She didn't know how long she worked, but when her head came up again, it was very bright in the room. The clock showed almost noon. Robyn got up from the color screen and stretched. With hands on her lower back, she walked around the machinery. Where was the clue? It had to be here. Yet, the sun was now shining high in the sky, and they were no closer to a solution than they had been eighteen hours earlier.

What had she missed? Would Will really kill Kari? She pulled the slats of the window blinds apart and looked down on the Pennsylvania Avenue traffic which spanned the wide thoroughfare oblivious to the people in the room above them. People who were tired of pouring over computer files and paper envelopes. Jacob's tie had long ago gone, and Grant's sleeves were rolled up to his elbows. Robyn's sweater had been discarded, and she'd combed her fingers through her hair so often all curl had long ago become limp tendrils of straight hair.

Grant came up behind her. "Tired?" he asked, massaging her shoulders.

"Extremely." She leaned forward as his fingers took some of the strain out of her shoulders. "There's got to be something here, but I can't seem to find it. My brain feels like mush."

"Why don't you take a few minutes to sleep? We'll keep digging," he suggested.

"I can't. If there's anything here, I'd be the one to recognize it. I've spent more time with Will than any of you." She went back to the boxes on the floor. Sitting down, she picked up a set of photographs. Leafing through them, she saw family photos of Will's early life. He was pictured with his children. Four blond girls smiled at her. Another picture had Will and Alex. The child must have been twelve. Then, she found one with Will and a woman who must have been his wife. Robyn had never seen Will's wife.

"Grant, what was Will's wife's name."

"Amanda." He joined her on the floor, glancing at the photograph. "She must have died shortly after that was taken."

"What did she die from?"

"She became interested in local politics. At a rally one evening, there was an assassination attempt. The candidate was missed, but several people near him were hit. Amanda was one of them. She held on for over a week. The bullet lodged in her chest close to her heart. But eventually she died."

"Oh, how awful." Robyn felt sorry for Will.

"Will was away when it happened. He was never quite the same without her. She was the one who got him interested in reading mysteries."

"He always has one in his pocket," Robyn smiled.

"Amanda used to write them."

"Oh, my God! Grant, that's it." The light bulb went on in her head. The switch was thrown and connection was made. "Did you ever read any of them?"

"Just one. *Dinner Companions,* the one that reminded me of the . . ." he stopped.

Jacob joined them. "Go on," he prompted.

"Were they published? Can we find them anywhere?" Robyn asked.

"They weren't published. But I saw them on the bookshelf in Will's library," Grant explained.

"There are eight of them," Robyn said. *"A Week of Knights, Cramped Quarters, A Case of the Nevers, Lost Moon . . ."*

"Yes," Grant confirmed. "Alex used to sneak and read them when she wasn't home."

"Do you know any of the plots?"

"A Week of Knights was about the death of seven men by a character dressed in knight's armor. It takes place in modern-day New York."

"The Stanfield killings," Jacob said. Robyn looked at him. "It's a series of seven killings attributed to Alex Jordan. Go on, Grant."

"Cramped Quarters takes place on a train. A nurse is killed on her way to visit her parents, who are involved in selling U.S. secrets to the highest bidder."

"Genia Novak." Robyn remembered from her research before the Jordan trial. "Genia Novak was a double agent selling secrets. Her death on a train was too spectacular to have any name connected with it except Alex Jordan."

"I don't know any others," Grant said.

"Jacob, what he's going to do to Kari is in one of those books. We have to go back."

Jacob picked up the phone and let the helicopter know they were ready. Grant did the same regarding the plane. With the same efficiency which got her to Washington, she found herself on her way back to Buffalo, New York. Now that she knew what she was looking for, her adrenaline was once again pumping. She couldn't sit still on the plane, and when they finally landed, Jacob ushered them into the helicopter which deposited her back in her yard before taking off again.

"Marianne, has he called?" Jacob asked coming into the kitchen.

"No, it's been quiet all night. Did you find anything at the FBI?"

"Yes, we know he's using the plots to his wife's books."

"What!"

"How are we going to get in there to get the books," Grant asked.

"With all the laws I've broken in the last twenty-four hours, what is breaking and entering?" Jacob asked.

"That won't be necessary," Robyn told him. "I have a key." She went to her purse and pulled her ring out. "Will gave it to me."

Jacob took it. "Stay here," he ordered. Robyn was too tired to argue. The two men went through the back door. Marianne took her arm and led her to the sofa in the other room. She left her a moment and returned with a cup of tea.

Robyn took two sips and put it down.

"You need some sleep," Marianne told her. "You look like you've been up for a week."

"Not yet, Marianne. I've got to find out what's in those books. And where Kari is."

"How are books going to do that?"

"His wife was a mystery writer. The Network used her plots for their kills. Jacob recognized three of them."

"You think he'll try that with Kari?"

"I'm not sure. Grant says he won't be able to do it. But he's killed so many other people . . . I just don't know." The night's strain was taking its toll. Robyn began to cry. "Oh, Marianne. He has my baby. He's going to kill my baby."

Marianne took hold of her. She rocked her back and forth, pushing her hair back. "Don't worry, Brooke. Jacob won't let that happen. He'll find out what Will's planning to do, and he'll stop him. Kari will be all right."

She continued rocking Robyn as if she were a child and not a thirty-year-old woman. This was how Grant and Jacob found them. Marianne signaled for them to be quiet. "She'll be fine. She just needs to rest," Marianne whispered over Robyn's head.

"Brooke," Jacob squatted in front of her. "I want you to go to bed."

"No!" Robyn's head came up. "I have to read the books."

"You'll be no good if you don't get some rest."

"No!"

"I insist—"

"Jacob," Grant stopped him. "Let her read them. It will take her less time. Then, she can go to bed."

Robyn looked at Grant. She didn't say anything. It wasn't necessary. He knew her, all her secrets. There was nothing they didn't share, and she silently thanked him for his understanding.

Confusion showed on Marianne and Jacob's faces. "Brooke has a photographic memory. She can read the books in minutes and tell us the plot."

The silence in the kitchen grew louder after Grant's comment. Robyn could almost hear accusation, incredulousness, disbelief, and astonishment directed toward her. This was her secret. Few people knew of it. Since she left the Assassination Bureau, she'd had no real need to purposely use it.

"Don't look at me like that," she demanded. "I haven't changed. I'm still the same person you knew two minutes ago."

"That's why you wanted your old job back," Jacob said. "You went through those files so fast, and you remembered everything you saw. It explains so much; how you could put the Crime Network together and conclude what their movements were going to be. Why didn't anyone know?"

"I didn't tell them. I learned early how people treat you when they find out. They think you're a freak," she paused. "Now, let me read the books."

Grant set the leather-bound books he'd brought back on the table in front of her. "Take your time," he told her, dropping into the space beside her.

Robyn opened the first book. Will must have had them bound. They were type written and the letter 'e' didn't close properly. She began to read, turning the pages more rapidly than any of the other three people in the room could read. She ignored the loud silence and the anticipation of the people around her. Finishing, she quickly outlined the plot, and Jacob confirmed the case adjunct to it. Robyn repeated the procedure five times. Jacob accounted for all but one of the plots.

The book's title was *Trolley Ride to Murder.* The plot had a passenger of a trolley killed and the police baffled by his connection to the prime minister of Great Britain.

"What could that have to do with being here in Buffalo? The only trolley we have is the one downtown, and it only runs through the shopping district on Main Street. Anywhere else the tracks have been taken up or paved over." Robyn looked from face to face, each one as blank as the other. "As for a public figure, Kari doesn't know any and neither do I."

"What about five years ago when you first came here?" Marianne asked. "Did you have any associations before you went into the program?"

"No-no," Robyn bowed her head, holding it in her hands as she shook. "I can't think of a single . . ." She stopped in mid-sentence, her eyes darting to Marianne.

"What is it?" Grant asked. "Have you thought of someone?"

Robyn stood up. She walked to the fireplace. The photo of Cameron Johnson stood steadfast and unchanged in its place. But all was not well. Her mind was tired and fuzzy, but she had heard correctly. Robyn was used to being careful of her words, even when she was upset. And she didn't think she could get any more upset than she was now. But Marianne had mentioned the program.

"How did you know that?" Robyn asked. Her eyes bore into Marianne as if she could look into her mind.

"Know what?" Marianne's face screwed into a perplexed look.

"I never said anything about a program, and it wasn't mentioned before we left or since we returned. Yet, you know I'm part of one. How?"

Marianne looked from Robyn to Jacob.

Robyn closed her eyes and let her head fall back. Her shoulders dropped in a gesture of defeat. "Oh, no," she cried, turning her back on the room. She hung her hands on the mantel, gathering her anger, fighting for control. "She works for you." It was a statement, and Robyn directed it at Jacob. She faced him, her body in tense control. "You've had her spying on me for five years." Then, she swung her gaze back to Marianne. "It's him, isn't it? He's the secret admirer I thought you sneaked away to see every month? When all the time you were going to give him a report on me—who I was seeing, what I was doing." Robyn was angry with the two people who'd affected her life more than anyone else in the past five years. "I wondered how you knew so much about what was happening to me." She threw her attention back to Jacob. "How you could seemingly materialize from thin air, when it was Marianne, giving you clues to my movements."

Grant watched the exchange without a word. He hadn't noticed the words Marianne had said. Jacob had told him about Robyn, and he assumed, sometime in the past five years, Robyn had confided in her friend.

"Brooke—" Jacob began.

"Jacob!" Marianne interrupted, the note of command in her voice was stronger than Robyn had ever heard it. "I want to explain this to Brooke." She raised her hand to her forehead. "Please, leave us alone."

The room cleared quickly. Robyn paced the sequestered space, her arms folded in front of her.

"I know you're upset, Brooke."

"Upset!" Robyn exploded. "Why should I be upset. I find out my daughter's been kidnapped by the man I considered my father, a man I trusted has betrayed me and my best friend . . . my best friend . . ." She couldn't continue. Tears were streaming down her face. She buried her head in her hands as she plopped down on a wing chair.

"Brooke, it hasn't been like that." Marianne sat on the lower table in front of her. "I am your best friend. Jacob didn't send me here to spy on you. He sent me to protect you, and up until yesterday, I was doing a pretty good job."

"But you reported everything to him."

"What was I suppose to do? I knew there were people out there looking for you. I didn't know who. And I had to report to Jacob. It was my job." Marianne pulled Robyn's hands from her face. "We only thought of your safety." She handed Robyn a tissue to dry her face. "For a long time, there was little to report. Jacob was only a sympathetic ear. He was there when I needed someone to complain to. He was there to help when things were getting out of hand. I'm sorry. I know you must hate me, but I only did what I thought was right, and I haven't hurt anyone."

Robyn blinked a fresh batch of tears. Robyn had given up control of her life when she went into protective custody. She'd fought for a small amount and thought she'd won a few battles. But she'd been manipulated and ruled by those she had called friends.

Grant's appearance, Kari's kidnapping, Marianne, and Jacob—how much more could go wrong? Robyn turned back to Marianne.

"I haven't changed either," the redhead said. "When I answered your ad, I was sent by Jacob, but it didn't take long before this became more than a job," she paused, her eyes pleading with Robyn. "Brooke, I love Kari, and you're as close as any of my sisters. You've got to believe me."

"I do, Marianne," she said calmly. "I don't hate you." Robyn's anger dissipated. She knew Marianne only had her interests in mind. Jacob had jeopardized his career to help her find Kari, and even if no one around her was who they appeared to be, they had her interests at heart.

Marianne *was* like her sister. She was glad the truth had been uncovered. "How can I hate someone who can turn ham slices into those cute little faces with olives for eyes?" she asked. A hesitant smile made Marianne giggle. A bubble of laughter broke from Robyn. She covered her mouth and tried to stop but couldn't. Suddenly, both women were laughing heartily.

Robyn felt the tension of the past twenty-four hours falling away. The release was wonderful. Tears were streaming from her eyes as her laughter continued. She couldn't stop. Finally, with hands at her sides holding the pain in, she took a sobering breath. Dragging gulps of air into her lungs, she calmed herself.

Grant poked his head through the door. Marianne waved him back.

"They're going to think we've lost our minds," Marianne said, giggles still erupting.

"Let them, it's time Jacob had something to worry about," Robyn told her.

"What about Grant? Hasn't he worried enough?"

"Yes, he has." Robyn calmed herself, wiping her happy tears away. "Jacob—he's the man who makes you moody after your weekends with him."

Marianne was quiet.

"He's not married, Marianne. You told me that. So what's the problem?"

"There's another woman."

"You know who she is?" Robyn felt this from their other conversation. Marianne stared at her. She continued until Robyn felt uncomfortable. Suddenly, light dawned. "Me!" she exclaimed. "You're wrong."

"Jacob's been in love with you since he first saw you. You have to know that. After the night in the garden when you sang "Secret Love," I thought you were in love with him, too."

"Jacob's not in love with me." Their voices had lowered to conspiratorial levels. "He was in love with a woman named Cynthia. I remind him of her."

"He told me."

"Does he know how you feel about him?"

"No," she shook her head.

"Are you sure?"

Marianne looked her straight in the eye.

"Jacob's not good at expressing his feelings," Robyn continued. "He's probably erected an invisible barrier to keep you from seeing how he really feels."

Marianne leaned forward. She remembered the night Jacob had come to her. She'd thought of herself as a substitute for Robyn. Could she have been wrong? Could Jacob have been thinking only of her?

"How can I find out?" she asked.

"With Jacob you have to be direct. Ask him, although that doesn't guarantee you an answer." Robyn knew first-hand how closed-mouthed Jacob could be.

Marianne thought about that. "I will," she said. "When this is over and Kari is safe, I'll ask him. Now, come on." Marianne stood up, pulling her friend with her. "Let's find out where there's a trolley car around here."

They went into the kitchen. The chaos of the FBI room was duplicated around her counter. Quiet overtook the room when the two women joined the group.

"Are you all right?" Grant came to her.

"I'm fine." She hugged him, knowing how lucky she was to have a man who loved her as much as she loved him. She couldn't keep herself from watching Jacob to see if he looked at Marianne with the same tenderness in his eyes as Grant had for her. All she saw was the wall she knew he had in place. "Have you discovered anything?"

"Nothing," Jacob said. "We've checked the old city maps to find out where trolley tracks used to run. We've also searched for trolley museums in the area, trolley cars being used as restaurants, or tourist attractions. We've come up with nothing."

Robyn's hand suddenly closed over Grant's. Her eyes sought Marianne's. "Crystal Beach," they said in unison. "He's taken her to the beach," Robyn went on.

"When Will first moved here, he worked at the amusement park," Marianne told the group. "It's got a trolley car from San Francisco."

"It's the Trolley Whip, the giant roller coaster." Robyn's voice had the dry dragging sound of a person gasping for air.

Grant put his arm around her. "He won't hurt Kari."

She turned to face him. "No, he wants me. He's been planning this for years, and it's me he wants. Kari is his way of making sure he gets me."

"What do you want to do?" Jacob asked.

"I don't know." In Washington, she was adamant about making the decision herself, now she didn't know how to handle the situation. "Crystal Beach is in Canada."

"I have no jurisdiction there," he said. She heard defeat in his voice.

Robyn looked at the clock on the mantel. It was six o'clock. A mere six hours before Will's promised execution. "The park is closed. We can't even get into it." Tears clogged her throat. She made an effort to swallow them.

"We can get in," Marianne said. "We know the manager at the park. He's a regular at Yesterdays." Robyn's nod confirmed Marianne's comment.

"Call him," Jacob ordered. "I'll get us some authority."

"How?" Robyn asked.

"Clarence Christopher."

"Do you think he'll help?" Robyn could hear Grant's heart beating fast as he held her. She was glad he was here. She needed him, needed his strength more than she'd ever thought.

"I don't know. I can ask."

"What did he say when you went up there, Jacob?" Robyn knew the FBI director hadn't been in his office in the middle of the night without good reason.

Jacob didn't answer. He gave her a look which told her the discussion between him and Clarence Christopher was a subject she need not bring up again.

The sun had long since dropped behind the horizon of Lake Erie's western shore when the two cars pulled up at the park's main entrance.

Another two were at separate locations. Jacob insisted they go in without sirens blaring. Grant held onto Robyn's hand, while Jacob and Marianne followed.

The park manager met them, and they slipped into the darkened area. Robyn scanned every corner for some sign of Kari. It was eerie being in a closed park. Sound echoed with every footstep, magnified by the quietness. She kept looking over her shoulder for someone following her. Robyn had only seen Crystal Beach when lights extended far into the sky, outlining the rides in gay colors. Crowds of people with cotton candy or stuffed animals walked before her. Tonight, the ghostly silence enveloped her.

"Where do you think they are?" Robyn whispered to Grant.

"I don't know. The roller coaster is over there." He pointed to the grimly outlined structure.

Robyn could see the giant thrill machine. It reminded her of a huge dragon. Its fires were dampened for the moment, but with a little effort, it could spring to life and breathe death to the ground.

"I want the lights turned on." Robyn heard Jacob. "At my signal." The park manager started to leave. "Call the fire department, too," Jacob called to the man's retreating back. "And get the rescue squad," he amended. The gray-haired man nodded, and Jacob took the lead, directing them to the base of the roller coaster.

"I'm sorry, Brooke, but if Kari's hurt we'll need help."

She tried to smile. "Thanks, Jacob."

"They've been here," Marianne pointed to empty wrappers from McDonald's. Fresh catsup oozed from the discarded paper.

"All right," Jacob commanded. "Spread out. Hammil, Price, go check the other side." He pointed toward the lower end of the roller coaster.

"It's so nice of you to come, Mrs. Richards." A laughing voice boomed from the darkness. All eyes shifted up, looking for the source of the grating sound. Robyn could see nothing. Her heart thudded against her chest. Suddenly, the lights came on with blinding intensity. Her hands came up, blocking the stabs of illumination. Still, she saw nothing.

Jacob's hand grabbed her arm and pulled her out of the light. Marianne had Grant. They crouched behind a closed concession stand.

"Did you see Kari?" Grant whispered.

"No," Jacob answered.

"Hiding won't help you, Mrs. Richards." The disembodied voice bounced off the stationary thrill machines. "You didn't fly all this way to hide, did you?"

"How's he able to track our movements so closely?" Marianne whispered.

"A good question," Jacob answered. "One I've asked myself since last night when he called Brooke at the headquarters building."

Marianne looked at Robyn. "I don't know how he knew we were there," Robyn explained.

"Come out, Mrs. Richards," Will called to her.

"Why does he keep calling you that?" Grant asked.

"At Alex's trial, it was how they referred to me. The defense attorney made a habit of ending each question with my name. I think they were trying to make the subtle point that you were a hostage, and I was willing to say anything to have you freed."

"Did they know about the agreement she'd made?" Grant directed his question to Jacob.

"With the levels Brooke uncovered, it's possible they knew. The newspapers hinted at it, but it was never brought up in court."

"Jacob, I want to talk to him," Robyn said, looking over her shoulder.

"Brooke, if you have any idea of trying to exchange yourself . . ."

"No," she interrupted. "I know him better than you. Maybe I'll be able to talk him out of this."

"Let her try," Grant said. "Kari's probably scared to death. It'll make her feel better if she hears her mother's voice. If we can get her back without anything more happening, it's worth a try."

Robyn saw the look pass between Jacob and Marianne. Marianne nodded. Then, Jacob looked at Robyn. "All right," he agreed, reluctance in his voice. "But I warn you. Don't try to change the script. We're not going to let him get both of you."

Robyn nodded. She stood up, but remained concealed behind the barricade. Grant stood next to her. She took his hand.

"Go on," Grant said. "I'm right here."

"Will," she called. Her voice was shaky. "Will, it's Brooke." Silence met her. "Will, is Kari all right?"

Again silence.

"Will, please answer me." There was desperation in her voice.

"You killed my son." A thundering voice came back. "And I'm going to take your daughter."

Robyn had never heard hatred in Will's voice. It was there now. A hatred fueled by years of searching and looking for the woman who'd given testimony against his son. The woman who'd uncovered the Crime Network and then disappeared behind the protective custody of the United States government.

"Will, Kari is your granddaughter." Robyn forced herself to remain calm. "Didn't you tell me your own daughters didn't visit? And Kari was closer than any of your grandchildren? Will, you can't hurt Kari."

"I can, and I will. At midnight. The same time Alex died."

Robyn trembled. Grant squeezed her hand and put his arm about her shoulders. "Will, what do you want?"

"I want my son back."

"Killing Kari won't bring Alex back."

"No, but it will make up for living next to you, waiting for a chink in that rock-hard armor of yours to crack."

"Will, it's me you want . . ."

Jacob grabbed her shoulders, wrenching her away from Grant. "No!" His eyes glared into hers. "Just keep him talking. The longer he talks the better chance we have."

Robyn dropped her eyes and nodded.

"Keep her here," he said to Marianne, then slipped out into the darkness and disappeared.

She took a deep breath. "Will, I can't bring Alex back. I didn't kill him."

"He was my son."

Robyn heard the cry in his voice.

"I know, Will," she shouted. "You loved him, and he loved you."

"You took him away. You killed him."

"I had a job to do, Will." Robyn thought she'd appeal to his sense of duty. "I had orders, like you." She paused. "Will, is Kari all right?" Robyn persisted, more quietly than before but loud enough to carry to him.

Jacob came back then. The park manager and one of the nameless agents arrived at the same time. "She's up there. He has her tied to one of the cars. If he lets it go," he paused, looking directly in Robyn's eyes. "It will crash into the cars below. The cars have been welded together, and there's a bomb attached to them. She'll be killed."

Robyn gasped, stepping back as if the words were fists that beat at her. Grant turned her into his arms. "He won't do it, darling. He won't hurt her."

"You don't know that. He thinks I killed his son. He wants my daughter in exchange, and he has her. There's nothing we can do to stop him."

"The fire department and ambulances are here," the park manager whispered.

"Thank you," Jacob spoke in hushed tones. "Could you let them know the situation and have them quietly take up position?"

The manager nodded. "The police are also here."

"Good," Jacob said. "Let them know there's a bomb under the roller coaster, and we need a bomb squad. Show them where it is when they arrive."

"Will treated Alex badly, but he loved him," Jacob heard Grant saying. "I want you to keep talking to him. Remind him she's his granddaughter. I'm sure he loves her, and it's difficult to kill someone you love." Grant kissed her and started to move in the same direction Jacob had.

"Where are you going?" Jacob asked.

"I'm not sure. But my plan is to see what I can do to save my daughter."

He was determined. If Jacob had any intention of stopping him, he was in for a fight.

Jacob looked at him a long time. "I'll go with you," he said, then turned to Marianne. "Keep her here." He pointed to the ground.

"I will," she said.

"We'll take the route around the back of the *Tilt 'o Whirl,* then split and approach from both sides."

The men left. Marianne took hold of Robyn. "Talk to him," she said.

"Will, Kari loves you. And I know—I know you love her," she stammered. "Will, can I talk to her?"

The silence that met her lengthened. Robyn fought her tears. She took a deep breath and reined in her fear.

"Will, please! She's only a little girl."

Marianne held onto Robyn for what seemed like hours before they heard the tiny, frightened voice.

"Mommy," Kari called.

Robyn instinctively moved toward the sound, but Marianne blocked her efforts.

"Kari, are you all right?" She struggled to keep the fear in her heart out of her voice.

"Mommy, I'm scared. Can you come and get me down." There were tears in her voice, and again, Robyn tried to move toward her.

"Tell her Graffie will help her," Marianne stopped her.

"Mommy can't reach you, honey. Graffie is there. Graffie will help you."

"Graffie said I'm going down by myself. Mommy, I'm scared." Robyn could hear giant-size sobs coming from her daughter. "Mommy, help me, help me."

"I will, Kari. I will." Tears streamed down her face. Kari sounded so afraid. Her voice was so tiny in the huge space. "What am I going to do, Marianne. I have to go out there. You have to let me. If he takes me, he'll let her go."

"No!" Marianne was adamant. "You heard what Jacob said."

"She's not Jacob's child, she's mine."

Marianne didn't say anything for a moment. When she spoke, her voice was gentle. "I know she's your child, Brooke, but we don't know much about Will's state of mind right now. If you go out there, you'll be a target. And we could well lose both you and Kari. As long as we can keep him talking, it will give Jacob and Grant a chance to do something. Trust them, Brooke."

"All right," she agreed. Then to Will, she asked, "What can I do, Will? What will it take for you to give me back my daughter?"

"You can't have her. She's mine now," he answered.

"But there must be something. Alex has been dead for five years. I've seen you with Kari. She makes you smile. You look forward to seeing her each day. You can't be willing to kill her without a second thought."

"What have you got to exchange?"

Robyn hesitated. This was the opening she'd sought. Instinctively, she knew Will wanted it, too. He wanted to see her in pain, see fear on her face and in her eyes. She knew he wanted to extract everything from her that he felt she'd taken from his son.

"You're not going, Brooke," Marianne repeated Jacob's words.

"What do you want?" Robyn asked the old man.

"What I want you can't give me."

"No one can bring Alex back."

"Then I want you, Robyn Richards. I want you in place of Kari."

"No, Will." The two women heard Grant's voice. It sounded open and free as if he was standing in full view of the park. "You took her away from me once. I won't let you do it again."

"I never took anything from you." Indecision crept into his voice.

"You took Brooke away from me when you set up Alex and forced her to do her civic duty. Isn't that what you taught Alex and me? Always do your duty. Obey orders. Aren't those your words?"

"Alex did what he was told. And she killed him." Will pointed at the ground.

"I won't give her to you," Grant said. "She's mine."

"All right," Will agreed. "I have the child. I don't need the mother."

"Yes, you do," Robyn took a step closer to the light that cut geometric patterns on the ground. "It was me who testified against Alex. Kari wasn't born then. She's entirely innocent in this, and if you want an exchange, it's me you'll get." At that point, she pushed past Marianne's restraining hands and stepped into the light. Marianne followed her. "I'm here, Will." She took a step forward, Marianne at her side. "Let Kari go."

"Go back, Brooke," Grant called. He looked up at the scaffolding. "Will, I'm coming up."

"Don't do that. I'll let the car go," he warned.

"I'm coming up." Grant grasped the painted metal structure and swung his body into one of the X-shaped supports. A shot rang out. Robyn screamed, and Marianne pulled her out of the line of fire. The bullet hit the ground next to Grant, chipping the asphalt and ricocheting blacktop about his body. "I'm not kidding, Grant. I don't want to hurt you, but I will."

"Kari's my daughter, too. I want to spend time getting to know her. I want to hold her in my arms and praise her when she tries things. I want to love her like you loved Alex." Grant swung another foot into the structure.

"Don't do it, Grant," he warned. "I'll let this car go."

Several seconds passed as Grant continued his climb. Robyn got up and went closer to the huge machine. She didn't know where he came from, but Hammil was on one side of her and Marianne on the other. Two other men walked in front of and behind her, forming a human shield.

The sound of the metal wheels of the car against the track was like the scream Robyn let out when she recognized the source. The car started toward the packed vehicles on the ground level. Robyn's eyes riveted to the plunging car. She squeezed Marianne's hands until she cried out in pain, and Marianne pried her fingers loose. Unable to turn away, she watched her child plunge toward death. But the impact she expected didn't come. Turning her head, she saw the grouping at the bottom, rigged to have the top car crash into them, move along the rails as if the park were open and crowds of people were waiting for their chance to go to the top of the loop. Three of Jacob's men appeared. Two pulled the brake stick back while, hidden between the floorboards of the giant death machine, a third did something she couldn't see. The car stopped safely on a cushion of air.

Robyn tried to get through the crowd around her. She wanted to run to the car and get her child.

"She's not in it," Marianne's voice penetrated her thoughts. Robyn's eyes went back to Will. Kari's legs dangled dangerously over the side of the edifice.

"Oh, dear God," she prayed. They all watched Grant as if he were a human fly scaling the wall. Without knowing it, the group inched closer to a small fence which in summer separated park visitors from the spaghetti of cables needed to run the monster machine. Robyn found herself pressed like a sandwich between Hammil and Marianne. They forced her behind another barrier.

More men stole into the park. Like thieves they came under the structure, spreading foam along the ground. Robyn blinked and clamped a hand over her mouth to stifle the sobs she felt coming to the surface.

"Graffie, I'm scared." Grant heard Kari's voice. "I want my mommy." Tears soaked her face making tiny streams of the dirt that covered it.

"I know, sweetheart. Graffie knows. Your mommy is down there." He pointed to the small group.

"Can I go to her?" she hiccuped.

"Soon, Kari. Soon."

"Why did you try to hurt Uncle Grant?"

Will looked at Grant. "Take one more step, Grant, and I'll drop her." Will's voice was menacing.

Grant stopped, glancing down. He saw Robyn push her way to the front of the congregation.

"No!" she screamed. "Will, don't hurt her. She's a child. She hasn't had time to do anything to anyone. It's me you want. I'm here. Take me. Let Kari go."

Grant took another step. Will's eyes returned to him. Grant was very near the top. With another step, his head would be level with Will's feet. He could see Jacob climbing on Will's blind side.

"I warned you," he said savagely and held the child by her arms out over the ground. "One more step, and she's history." Kari squirmed in his grasp.

"Kari, don't," Grant yelled, then lowering his voice he spoke softly to the child. "Be very still, Kari. Graffie won't hurt you."

Kari responded to his voice, and Grant returned his attention to the man he'd looked on as a hero. "Will, she's your granddaughter."

"Not anymore. She's hers."

"Graffie, I'm scared." Kari wiggled her legs, trying to get back to Will's arms. "Graffie, don't drop me." Kari turned wide eyes at her grandfather. Only the innocence of children could look like that, Will mused. She'd been with him for two days, and she still trusted him not to hurt her. He wanted to press her close to him and hug her small body. But there was the woman below. He forced himself to think of Robyn. She had destroyed his world and taken his son. He would take her daughter.

Will McAdams looked at the child and quickly closed his eyes. Kari continued wiggling.

"Graffie, don't hurt me. Mommy needs me. What would she do if I'm not there? When I was sick, she was so sad. She cried all the time."

Will hesitated. He looked at the struggling child, but he saw Alex. Alex as a baby reaching for him.

"Graffie, I want my mommy," she cried.

Kari's legs began to swing. She attempted to reach safety.

"Kari, don't do that," Will shouted. His arms were beginning to tire. Kari stopped at hearing the tone of his voice. She started to cry.

"Graffie, help me. I'm scared."

Will looked at her. Indecision gripped him. He'd planned this for over a year. He'd waited, methodically following every step, careful to say nothing, betray nothing until he was positive. And now he was.

Grant vaulted over the top. "Listen to her, Will. Don't make another mistake. Don't hurt Kari for something you couldn't give to Alex."

"Graffie, please," Kari cried. "I want my mommy."

She was Alex again. He couldn't keep them separate. He was holding Kari, then Alex would be there. His tiny arms reaching for him, wanting him to pick him up and carry him. But he wouldn't. He didn't want his son to be dependent on anyone. He pushed the child away until Alex no longer came to him. He wanted his mommy.

"I want my mommy," Kari's frightened voice reached him. Tears clouded his eyes, and he started to pull her back.

Grant took a step closer. He was close to reaching Will.

"No!" a voice screamed as if in agony. A shot followed it. Grant heard the collective cry from the ground as he watched Will stumble to his knees. Blood spread over his shoulder and down his right arm. Kari went over the edge. He could hear her scream.

Robyn clamped her fist in her mouth. Behind her there was a scuffle, but her feet found forward motion. She rushed to the scaffolding, jumping the fence to catch her child.

Will struggled to pull Kari up. Grant hurled from toehold to toehold, trying to reach her before Will's strength gave out. Jacob climbed as fast as he could. Each person was trying to reach the child before she fell.

Marianne got to Robyn and pushed her out of the way. She was prepared to take Kari's weight plus the G-force she'd create by her free fall. A second shot rang out. Marianne screamed, spinning around.

Will's last ounce of strength was tapped as death took him. Kari's fingers slipped free. She fell. The fire department rushed the crash net past the fence, one officer throwing Marianne out of the way. She felt her collarbone snap as she crashed against the support brace. Kari hit the crash net held by six strong men.

Robyn raced to it, pushing aside the big men and reaching for her daughter. "Kari! Kari!" she cried. "Are you all right?"

Tears smeared her face as she reached for her mother. "Mommy," she called. "Mommy, I'm scared." Robyn hugged her, running her hands over her back, arms, and legs, making sure she had not been hurt. She rocked back and forth as relief flooded through her.

"Is everything all right?" Jacob asked from the top.

"How's Kari?" Grant shouted.

"We've got a man down," one of the fire fighters shouted back. "She's been shot!"

"She!" Jacob's voice was a shrill cry.

Robyn whipped around to find Marianne on the ground, her face contorted in pain as blood coated her left arm. Still holding Kari, she went to her.

"Marianne," she called.

"Is Kari all right?" she asked, her hand on her shoulder.

The child continued to cling to her. "Yes, she's fine." Robyn turned to the firemen. "Get that ambulance in here," she demanded.

Jacob's feet reached the ground, and he sprinted across to the small crowd that surrounded Marianne.

He knelt beside her. "The shot," she whispered, one hand holding her broken bone, her face twisted in pain. "It came from Hammil."

"Be quiet," he told her. "I saw Hammil. Where's that damn ambulance?" Two ambulances with red flashing lights screeched to a halt just outside the ring of people surrounding Marianne. Several police cars followed it. Men in white coats got out of each of them and came forward. Two went to Marianne, and two came to Kari. She was welded to Robyn and fought when they tried to separate her. Robyn looked over her shoulder as the paramedics led her away from Marianne and the men working on her. Grant joined them. Together, they took Kari to one of the ambulances.

Marianne's smile was painful. Paramedics hovered over her, checking for other injuries. They had her on a collapsible gurney by the time Jacob managed to reach her again. Robyn looked over her shoulder at the scene of her friend and those with her.

"Are you all right?" Jacob asked her.

"I'm fine," she said.

Robyn knew she was lying. She was in a great deal of pain. Robyn smiled, still clutching Kari to her, as the ambulance sped away with her and Grant.

"Jacob's in love with Marianne," she told him, looking back through the park entrance.

"I know." He put his arm around Robyn and Kari and held them to his side. "I'm glad. For a while, I thought he was in love with you."

Robyn's head fell on his shoulder. She kissed the top of Kari's head. The child had fallen asleep. The past two days and her fear that Will would drop her had taken its toll. She was tired, but even in sleep her arms remained clamped to Robyn.

Grant held them. His family. Everything was going to be all right. He was certain things would work out. He'd make it work out. He wasn't going to be separated from his wife and child again. Neither Jacob nor the government would keep them apart, but he didn't think that would be a problem.

"I love you," he said, hugging Robyn and Kari closer to him. He kissed her and pushed her head back on his shoulder. Holding them for the moment was all he needed. They were safe, and that was enough.

Jacob's face was drawn and tired after two days of nonstop activity. He'd sat in the hospital waiting room until Marianne was out of surgery. The nurse came to tell him she would be all right and wouldn't wake for hours, but he insisted on staying. Finally, they took pity on him and let him wait beside her bed. She slept peacefully as he watched her, holding her soft hand until he, too, fell asleep with his head on the starched sheet.

Marianne woke in the early hours of the morning. The room was dark except for a soft light above her head. She recognized Jacob immediately. He held her hand loosely. She pulled it free and slipped her fingers into his soft curls. The movement woke him, and he sat up.

"What are you doing here?" she asked, her mouth parched.

"How do you feel?" he asked, ignoring her question.

"I'm thirsty."

He stood up and got her water from the pitcher beside the bed. Then, sitting on the white sheets that covered her, he held her head while she drank through the plastic straw.

"What time is it?" she asked, when he leaned her back against the pillows.

Checking his watch, he said, "Five o'clock."

"You should be asleep," she said. "You look so tired." Her hand reached for his face. He took it in his hand and kissed it.

Marianne bit her lip at the emotions his touch caused.

"How's your shoulder?"

She had a burning pain that threatened to sever it from her body. "I don't feel it much," she lied.

"Should I call a nurse?" His eyes were dark with concern.

"No," she shook her head, biting the misery back. She didn't want him to go. "How's Kari and Brooke?"

"They're fine. Kari was treated for shock and released. They stayed until you were out of surgery. I sent them home then."

"But you stayed." Her eyes were wide when they found his. "Why?" She had to be direct with Jacob. He wouldn't come out and tell her what he felt, and she had to know.

"I couldn't leave."

"Why not? You needed to rest. Kari was safe. My life was not in danger. You could have gone. Why didn't you?" She knew she shouldn't push, but she was past caring. If Jacob was still in love with Robyn, she'd go on with her life and forget him.

"Don't you know?" he almost smiled. "You're so good at reading my feelings."

"I don't want to read them," she looked away. "I want to hear them."

"I love you, Marianne." His voice was so quiet, even in the silent room, she was afraid she hadn't heard him. Slowly, her face turned back to him. He looked scared as if he expected her to reject him.

"What did you say?" She needed confirmation.

"I said I couldn't leave because I'm in love with you." He sat on the bed and reached around her. He leaned forward and kissed her surprised mouth. "I don't know how it happened. I never thought of being in love with you, but for months I haven't been able to get you out of my mind."

Marianne tried to reach for him, but pain shot through her shoulder. She squeezed her eyes closed and waited it out.

"You are in pain." He hugged her until she relaxed. When he released her, there were tears in the corners of her eyes. "I'm going to call the doctor."

"No!" she stopped him. "Not yet. They'll give me something to make me sleep. I don't want to sleep yet."

He wiped the tears away with the pads of his thumbs. "I don't want you in pain. I was so scared when I saw you on the ground. I thought Hammil had . . ." he looked away, refusing to complete the thought.

"Don't think about it." She caressed his cheek. "It's over, and everything is going to be fine."

Jacob looked at her. "You need to go back to sleep."

"I don't feel like sleeping," she told him. He'd confessed that he loved her. She wanted to talk to him, tell him everything about herself, her family and find out everything about his. She hugged him tighter, content to be in his arms. Then, she remembered the night he'd come to her house. "Jacob?" she began, knowing she had to ask the question.

"Yes," he answered still holding her close.

"That night at my house."

"I remember." She could feel him smiling against her neck.

"You told me you were in love with Brooke."

The gentle nibbling stopped. He sat up straight and stared at her. "I was," he said. Feeling her retreat, he took her hand. "For years," he explained. "I thought I was in love with her, but I wasn't. I'm not quite sure what I feel for Brooke. She's a strong woman, and I have a great deal of respect for her, but she doesn't make my blood boil. I suppose we were together for so long, she was constantly on my mind, but you filled my dreams, making me crazy for you."

"I thought you wanted Brooke, and I was a poor substitute."

Jacob folded her close to him. "You'd never be a substitute."

"I've loved you for years," she told him.

"Oh, my God!" he hugged her. "What a fool I've been. I intend to tell you everyday for the rest of your life. I love you, Marianne."

"I love you, Jacob." She raised her arm around his shoulder and met his mouth as it slid over hers.

CHAPTER 21

Jacob came through the door of his office and took a seat behind the large desk. Robyn and Grant looked at him from the two chairs directly in front of it. His stare was direct, but not chiseled. He looked . . . *happier,* Robyn thought. He even smiled at her.

"Is it over, Jacob?" she asked.

"It's over. Hammil told us everything. He met McAdams while on assignment in the Caribbean. Several years ago, Hammil's father died suddenly. He left very little insurance, and his mother was sick with cancer. Hammil poured all of his money into her treatments. By the time she died, he was heavily in debt. McAdams found that out and manipulated him, getting him to supply bits of information in exchange for money."

"Where did Will get the money?" Robyn asked. "He lived a very meager life, comfortable but not showy."

"He'd amassed it from the Crime Network and hid it in Caribbean banks. McAdams had plans of reviving the Network and using Hammil as his inside man."

"But didn't Hammil eventually pay off his debts?" Grant wanted to know.

"Not entirely. Most of the medical expenses were paid, but there were massive debts left by his father's failed businesses. Some of his ventures were financed by sources that were less than legal, shall we say."

"How were they going to set up another Crime Network?" Grant asked.

"McAdams had done it before. He knew everything that had to be done, and he was an extremely patient man. When we searched Hammil's apartment, we found files on several key people in the FBI. Most of the records centered on people having financial difficulty. The same method McAdams had used to rope Hammil would be employed to gain whatever information he needed."

"Why did Hammil shoot him?"

"He was at the end of indentureship. With Kari and you out of the way, McAdams had promised to give him all the documents he'd collected regarding his practices here. He'd be free to do his job without the threat of a sword hanging over his head. When McAdams pulled Kari back, Hammil saw his last chance for freedom evaporate."

"I can't believe it's over," Robyn said.

"You're free to go," Jacob stared at her.

"What does that mean," Grant asked.

"Exactly what it says," Jacob returned. "There's no reason to keep Brooke in protective custody. We're sure McAdams and Hammil acted as a team. You're free to become a family again. Go where you like, live where you like, no restrictions." Jacob spread his hands and leaned back in his chair.

Robyn took a breath. She got up and walked to the window. Outside, traffic buzzed along the street. It had been six weeks since that night at Crystal Beach. It was winter in Washington. Around the tidal basin were clusters of plowed snow. The Japanese cherry trees stood as a bare, black contrast against the white marble monument and distant sky.

Freedom, what a beautiful word. If she wanted to, she could run through the trees with no more resistance against her than the wind blowing her hair. She'd become so used to being careful, to actually be free of the invisible jail was both frightening and exhilarating.

"I can't help feeling sorry for Will," Robyn spoke to the window.

"Don't feel sorry for him," Jacob said. "That old man engineered the deaths of at least two dozen men. If he'd lived, who knows what damage he and Hammil could have caused."

"I hear what you're saying, Jacob, but to me he was a loving father. To my daughter he was the grandfather she needed. Kari and I never could have survived without his kind nurturing."

"I know how she feels," Grant said. "Will was the perfect father figure to me, but to his own son, he was unyielding. Like Brooke, he was there when I needed him."

"It's hard to believe the man who killed a room full of men in a restaurant is the same person who stayed up nights when Kari had ear infections, who went to nursery school with her, and cooked her favorite food."

Robyn didn't ask Jacob how he knew that. He knew everything about her. Some of it became clear when she found out Marianne really worked for him. Her reports told him when she was sliding off center. It was only at the furthest tangents that Jacob appeared to materialize.

"Brooke, there's another freedom you have," Jacob interrupted her thoughts. "You can go back to being Robyn Richards if you like. We'll correct everything."

Robyn turned to look at Grant. "Robyn Richards died in an automobile accident five years ago," she quoted. "She was en route to Dulles Airport to welcome her husband, a returning Lebanonese prisoner, home."

Grant left his seat and came to take her hands. He followed with the rest of the story, "Grant Richards met Brooke Johnson in a hospital in Buffalo, New York. He immediately fell in love with her and can't possibly live without her."

"And they lived happily ever after." A voice came from the doorway.

"Marianne!" Robyn and Grant said at the same time. "When did you get here?" Robyn asked, coming to hug her.

"This morning," she answered. "Jacob picked me up."

"You will have to get married again," Jacob told Grant when everyone was seated. "When Brooke went into the program all previous records were annulled to give you free and legal rights to remarry."

Grant looked at her. "This time we can do it right, with orange blossoms and a warm weekend in June."

"Maybe we can make it a double," Marianne stilled the room with her comment. She got up and went to perch on the arm of Jacob's chair. He slipped his arm around her to the gaping surprise of the two other people in the room.

"Marianne! That's wonderful." Tears sprang to Robyn's eyes, and she left her seat to hug her friend once again.

Grant got up and shook hands with Jacob. "Congratulations," he said with a smile.

"Where is Kari?" Marianne asked. "I expected to see her here."

"She's with David and Susan," Grant replied. "They were thrilled to find Robyn alive, and they've practically adopted Kari. I think this afternoon they're taking her to see the pandas at the zoo."

"Well, partner," Robyn began. "Now, that we're getting married what are we going to do with the restaurant?"

"Everything is under control. We find we have a staff fully capable of handling things when both of us are away," Marianne smiled.

"I guess Pete has taken the reins and is king of all he surveys."

"I believe that's a true statement." Marianne's head bobbed up and down.

"Do you think we should sell it to him?"

"You'd sell the restaurant?" she asked in surprise.

"I thought you were being reassigned." Robyn asked her. She knew after everything with Will was cleared up, Marianne would no longer have an assignment to protect her and Kari.

"Marianne isn't being reassigned, Brooke." Jacob slipped his arm around her again. "She's being furloughed, permanently."

"I find I like making broccoli flowers, shaping cheese and butter into topiary art, and my confections are always a surprise, not to mention the ultimate chocolate dessert."

Robyn's eyes found Grant's. "I haven't thought about this, but maybe we could let Pete and Sue-Ellen manage Yesterdays in Buffalo, and we can open a branch here."

"That sounds great. Then we wouldn't have to dissolve the partnership," Marianne said. She came around the desk and grabbed Robyn's hands. The two women were ready to sit down and discuss expanding their partnership in Jacob's office. Grant knew that. "We could use . . ."

"I hate to break this up." He stopped Marianne looking at his watch. "But if we're going to meet David and Susan, we'd better leave. You know Washington traffic." If he didn't get Brooke out of Jacob's office, she and Marianne would spend the day planning.

Robyn got up and hugged Grant. "Isn't it wonderful? Washington traffic? And I can go out in it and not wonder if there's someone out there looking for me." She released him and went to Jacob. "Thank you for everything," she said and hugged him. "Marianne, I'll see you soon." Grant caught her hand and led her through the door.

Jacob lifted Robyn Richards's folder from his desk drawer. He took the contents and placed them in a fresh manila folder. *Top Secret* was printed across the cover. Sealing it with red tape he stamped CLOSED across it.

Marianne put her arms around him from the back of his chair. "I'm so glad everything worked out," she said.

"Me, too." Jacob stood, turning her into his arms and lifted her chin. "I love you very much." She opened her mouth to return the sentiment, but he stifled it with a kiss that had her purring like a contented cat.

Robyn awoke cradled in Grant's arms. She felt as if she were glowing, that a light actually radiated from her. But she knew it was only a feeling. The sun must be setting, for the light filtering through the curtains was dim.

After she and Grant left Jacob's office, they went to his condo and spent the afternoon making love. She felt whole, complete as if her soul had been drifting free, without form, for the last five years until Grant found it and restored it to life.

Turning her head, she gazed at him sleeping next to her, his features relaxed. A well of sudden emotion burst forward, giving her no time to stop it or even dampen it down, before it racked her with a force that pierced her core. Suddenly, tears were running silently down her face.

She'd felt fate had dealt her a blow, but now that everything was clear and she was free to do as she pleased, she knew the fates looked upon her with favor.

Without disturbing Grant, she lifted his arm and crept out of bed. His shirt lay on the floor where he'd discarded it. She picked it up and slipped her arms into it as she left the bedroom and padded to the living room. The room looked different now. When she'd been here before, this had been Grant's apartment. This was where she would have remembered him when she allowed herself the luxury of thinking about him. But now she could think of herself in relation to this space.

Outside, darkness blanketed the city like a shroud. In the distance she could see lights dotted against the evening sky. Her eyes fell on the piano. She went to it. The piano had changed, too. Before it held a large vase of flowers, now there were picture frames with Kari and herself. The two photographs added life to the room.

Robyn fingered the keys making a tinkling noise. Then, she sat down. The seat was cool through the thin shirt.

Grant stood in the bedroom doorway as Brooke's hands hovered above the keys. He knew what she'd play before her fingers touched the keys. Quietly, the strands of Chopin's Nocturne in F-major began. He knew it was only a matter of time before she was no longer able to resist sitting down. Since the night at the park when Kari had been calmed, she'd been here several times and each time she seemed drawn to the piano, but she hadn't played it. She played the song with the same intensity she made love. It started slow, ever so slowly, like her fingers on his back. Then, she began the build, a steady drive that climbed and climbed up toward the edge of the world, climbed toward the crescendo of light that drew them into the vortex of expanding emotion. Her fingers shimmered across the keys, bringing the music to life and releasing the rhythms of love until it forced them to cry out in a shattering light that burst into color and carried them over the edge. Then, lingeringly, she prolonged the end, slowing the pace until his heartbeat returned to normal, and the last note of the song died in the reverberating silence of the darkened room.

He loved her. He didn't know how much he'd missed her until he saw her sitting at the piano, wearing his shirt, her hands on the keys. When Jacob explained the reason she pushed him away and was forever saying good-bye, he thought he'd die knowing she was alive and not knowing where she was or how to get in touch with her.

He went to her. Robyn looked up as he came toward her. She took his hand. "I want to talk to you," she said. She got up, and he followed her to the sofa. He draped his arm around her shoulders and pulled her close. "In all these weeks, Grant," she began tentatively. "You've never asked me why I went alone."

"I guessed you'd tell me when you were ready."

She squeezed his hand. She needed something to hold, an anchor. "It wasn't because I didn't love you more than anything else in the world." Bending, she kissed his knuckles. "Part of it was the flying. The other part was Project Eagle.

"Clarence Christopher explained your part in regaining possession of a vital part of a defense system. More than your life and those of the nine other men was at stake. Without that system, he explained, millions could die."

"Brooke, don't you know nothing is more important to me than you? Nothing was *ever* more important than you."

"I know that, darling. I thought I was doing what was best for both of us. According to Christopher, we had to have that system part returned. And flying was your life."

"I . . ."

"No-no," she stopped him. "I thought of having you come into the program later, after the defense system job was complete, but there was no guarantee as to when that would be. By then, you'd have done your grieving, and I was so completely changed . . . it didn't seem fair."

"You don't know the kind of hell I've lived without you."

"At the time, I thought it was better for you," she apologized.

"I can live without the sky, without everything except you. Without you, I'm nothing. Promise me you won't ever make that kind of decision again?"

Robyn's eyes were blank as she looked at him. How could she do that? She loved him too much still to take everything he lived for away from him.

"Brooke," Grant insisted. "You are my life and now Kari is, too. Without the two of you, there is nothing." He pulled her against him. "Promise me, darling. Promise me it's for better or worse?"

"For better or worse," she promised.

Grant kissed her, and for a long time, there was silence in the room.

"There is just one more thing, Brooke Johnson." Grant spoke into her hair.

"What's that?" She could feel him smiling against her.

"I'd like to propose."

Robyn sat up. "All right, propose." She switched the light on.

"Right now?"

"Right now." A smile tilted her mouth.

"You don't want to be dressed in a flowing gown, with moonlight and roses?"

"No, Kari can have that."

"Will you marry me?" he asked, gathering her to himself.

Robyn placed her hand on his chest, stopping the forward motion. "You don't mind that I'm not going back to being Robyn?"

"Not in the least. I've gotten used to you being Brooke, and I'm one of the few men in history who can be a bigamist—legally." He grinned at her.

"I love you, Grant."

"I love you more than I thought it possible," he ran his hand down her cheek. "Will you marry me?"

"Yes," she said, leaning forward and placing her mouth against his. Grant kissed her hard. His hands removed the shirt from her shoulders, and he carried her back to bed.

White Diamonds

To my grandmother, Sallie Farrow Hailstock, who never learned to read or write but taught me more about life and love than anyone.

ACKNOWLEDGMENTS

I am especially indebted to David Anderson, an on-line buddy, who took the time to research some information on helicopters and to answer my hundred and one questions on how they operate and fly.

To Diana and Garikai Campbell, two Ph.D. candidates in algebraic numbers theory at Rutgers University, who put the world of mathematics into understandable terms.

A special thanks to Jinny Beckler, Director of the Plainsboro, N.J., Public Library, for her and her staff's untiring efforts to find obscure pieces of information each time I walk through the door or call the reference department.

CHAPTER 1

"Blood!"

Sandra Rutledge's eyes opened wide as she stared at the red stain dripping through her fingers. The white snow, reflecting from the ground, made the color stand out brighter.

The man in the car lay slumped over in the driver's seat. She had tried to pull him up when she felt the stickiness on her hand. She hadn't even seen his face. What could he be doing on this road? It was the only one that led to her parents' Pocono Mountain cabin.

Her mother's first order would have been to check the extent of his wounds, but Melissa Rutledge was a doctor and her daughter wasn't. So Sandra pulled him upright to find out who he was.

She gasped when his pale face came into view. Wyatt Randolph! The junior senator from Pennsylvania. His face had been plastered all over the news for a week. Stories of his disappearance had topped every newscast. Speculation ranging from his being in a sanitarium to on a covert operation in a foreign country had played over different news stations. Sandra now knew none of them were true.

What on earth could he be doing here? Why was he bleeding? And who had beaten him up? She frowned at the bruises discoloring half of his face. One eye was swollen, with blue veins visible against his dark, pale skin.

"Damn," she cursed. What would her mother do now? Sandra thought for a moment, then pressed her hand to his throat. She felt a pulse. Her breath came out with relief at the weak but steady thump against her fingers. *Stop the bleeding.* The thought came from nowhere. She tried to find the source, but his position in the car hindered her. She had to get him back to the cabin. At least there she'd be able to see what she was looking for. Not that she'd know what to do then, but at least they wouldn't freeze to death in the wind. She reinforced her decision by telling herself she couldn't undress him here, with snow flying in her face and the north wind whipping at them. She pulled his legs out of the car and placed his feet on the ground. Polished black shoes sank into the snow. He wasn't even properly dressed for this kind of weather, she thought. Where were his parka and boots? Again she wondered what he could be doing up here. The weather forecast called for twenty inches of snow before morning. Any fool would know better than to try these roads in a car without four-wheel drive during a snowstorm.

She heard a groan as she called on all her strength to get him out of the driver's seat. Good. That meant he was still alive. His weight leaned against her, almost crushed her. One hundred and twenty pounds could hardly carry him. She dragged him across the short expanse to the snowmobile and placed him on the seat. It had to be a good mile back to the cabin. Sandra was good on a snowmobile, but she'd never tried to balance an unconscious senator while she drove one.

She took a deep breath, calculating the distance between their position on the road and the cabin on the distant hill. Despite the wind and cold, she was sweating although her hands were raw. She took a moment to put on her fur-lined gloves. Mounting herself behind Senator Randolph, she turned the key in the tiny vehicle and set off for the cabin. "I can do this," she said out loud, hoping the words would make the actions truth. Wyatt Randolph's body wobbled like a puppet from side to side, forcing her to compensate quickly for his shifts. The snow pattern behind her looked as though a drunk had weaved a crooked line to her door.

How she got him into the cabin she'd never know, but she did have him on the table of her mother's surgery. Melissa Rutledge often came here to work and relax. She wrote many of her papers at this cabin. She also found out that as a doctor she was often needed for some emergency. What had started as a small den had grown into a full surgery. This is where Wyatt Randolph lay.

Now what? Sandra asked herself. She checked his eyes, lifting the lids to make sure . . . of what—that his eyeballs were still there? She'd seen it done countless times, but had no idea why anyone did it. She was the daughter of a famous surgeon, a woman whose medical skills included the successful transplantation of human hearts. Melissa Rutledge led a team of experts whose mastery was world renowned, yet she, Sandra, didn't know how to change a bandage.

She did know there was more blood on the senator's belly than had been there before. Either she had made the wound worse by moving him or the heat in the cabin was warming him. The bruises on his face were superficial. She didn't think there would be any permanent damage to his eye, despite the fact that he looked like a monster from an old black-and-white movie. Whoever beat him had only damaged one side of his face. The other half was unmarred. Carefully, she began opening items of clothing to reach the source of the blood. Her protected fingers worked quickly to unbutton his coat and shirt. When she should have found skin, she discovered a band around his waist.

It was a crude attempt at a money belt. Blood soaked it. She frowned, skewing her nose at the amount covering the cloth. In this storm he should have picked a different road on which to get stranded, one where there was a doctor!

Sandra glanced at his face. He was helpless, unconscious. A paleness clung to him like a death shroud. She was his only hope. Sandra went back to work, taking a pair of bandage scissors and cutting the bound cotton in two places. She lifted it away and stared at the gaping wound. Blood oozed from it. Even her untrained eyes knew he'd been stabbed and that he needed stitches.

Absorbed by the thought that she was going to have to administer to this wound, she let go of one side of the cloth she held. Suddenly, she jumped at the noise and stepped away from the shards of glass pecking her legs as they fell from the bloody cloth and danced about her feet.

Sandra gasped, dropping the cloth. Diamonds, huge, cut stones, stained the white floor, skittering about like bloody jumping beans before momentum ceased and they came to rest. Her mind whirled with questions as her eyes darted back and forth between the floor and the man on the table. What was he doing with all these diamonds? An unnamed fear rose in her throat but she pushed it down. She didn't have time for that now. At the moment she had a man who needed her complete attention.

Ripping off the rubber gloves, she dropped them in the medical wastebasket and, without lifting the receiver of the speaker phone, she punched her mother's phone number at George Washington University Hospital in Washington, DC. She waited while the secretary connected her, praying silently that Dr. Rutledge was available and not in surgery.

Sandra knew surgeons could assist in operations in all parts of the world by satellite hookup. Here, in the remote Pocono Mountains, they didn't have that kind of equipment and she was no doctor, yet the man lying on the table behind her would bleed to death if she didn't get help for him. This was the best she could do. Sandra let out a relieved breath when her mother's strong voice came over the line. She was going to have to walk her through the steps that would save the life of a United States senator. Then Sandra could wonder about the diamonds on the floor.

Twenty-four inches and more on the way . . . Sandra turned at the crackled sound of the radio weatherman's voice. She hugged herself as a sudden chill shook her. In all her years of growing up in Budd Lake, New Jersey, snow had been a natural result of winter. Yet today was the first time she'd felt stranded and faced with several feet of the white puffy flakes.

The last time she'd been here John had been alive. The grass was green, sloping like an emerald rug away from the cabin. They'd played like children, laughing, running, and rolling down the hill, then ending their day making love in the large bed upstairs. It had been a happy summer. Summer had turned to fall and then winter. Three winters. Would the pain ever go away completely?

Sandra turned away from the window and stretched. Snow continued to pile up outside the cabin as it had all night and all day. The sun, low in the sky, dropped quickly behind the mountains. In moments the light was gone and the solitary cabin was draped in total darkness. She lit several lamps, suddenly needing the light for no apparent reason.

She'd been up here alone many times and had never felt remotely uneasy, yet tonight she was afraid. Upstairs a man who'd been stabbed lay in her sister Annie's bed. Wyatt Randolph had become both famous and notorious in the last week. Sandra didn't know which of the many newscasts detailing his background she should believe. In her experience, what the newscasters said was rarely the real story. Yesterday, her life had coincided with the senator's, and that fact didn't make her comfortable, even if she discounted the millions of dollars in precious stones he'd had with him.

Reviewing the facts in her mind as she often did aloud in class for her students, she thought: he's a US senator with access to all manner of information not available to the public; he could be a member of a powerful sub-committee, although as a junior senator he would have little power; he'd been missing for over a week and apparently no one knew where he was, at least no one who'd come forward. Unease made her shiver, but she continued her mental assessment of the facts. He'd been stabbed. Quickly, she turned about, looking in every direction as if someone else was in the room and could hear her thoughts and knew that the senator was here. Running her hands up and down her arms, she tried to dispel the coldness that seeped through to her bones. Someone had deliberately tried to kill him. *He could have fallen on a knife,* she thought, rejecting the theory before it had time to form. And he'd come here. Why? They didn't know each other. Her father, the senior senator from New Jersey, was not here and her mother was so closely followed by the media that it would be easy to find her if it were Melissa he was seeking. He had to be looking for her father. But why then hadn't Wyatt gone to his office or called?

Sandra had the phone in her hand and was dialing before she could decide what she would say when her father answered. She checked her watch. It was after eight o'clock, but she knew he would still be in. His secretary, Michael Waring, spoke crisply in her ear after the first ring. He told her that her father was unavailable and could not be reached. She knew better than to try to badger an answer out of him, but this was an emergency. She wouldn't politely accept that he was away and say goodbye.

"Where is he?" she asked.

"He can't be reached at the moment."

"This is an emergency. I need to talk to him."

"I'll ask him to call you when he returns."

"Are you expecting him tonight?" Often the two of them worked late, and since her mother had left town, her father had no reason to go home early.

"He didn't say."

Sandra's frustration level increased. Why was Michael being so mysterious? He'd never been that way before. "Please ask him to call me when he returns, no matter what the time," she added.

"I will."

Sandra replaced the receiver and quickly lifted it again. She tried the Georgetown house. The maid told her the senator had gone away last week and had not returned.

This was not unusual for her father. But why hadn't Michael said something? Senator Rutledge often went on fact-finding missions, some of them publicized, others not. Yet, this time she feared something was grossly different. Her hands grew clammy and she brushed them down her long sweater.

"Stop scaring yourself," she told the empty room. There was a perfectly logical explanation. It was like mathematics, everything fit together and worked in a logical order. All she had to do was wait for the senator to regain consciousness and ask him her questions.

Remembering the man in the bed upstairs, she looked at the ceiling. Sandra had been called upon twice today to use Herculean strength to save his life. She was more than a little afraid of what she had done. Suppose infection set in, suppose he began to bleed again? What if a fever developed? Suppose he needed a *real* doctor? What could she do? Her mother had been bound for the airport when Sandra's call had stopped her. It wasn't likely Sandra would be able to repeat what she'd done earlier.

Melissa Rutledge had used her calm professional voice to take away the panic Sandra felt at having to check the senator's body and then close his wound. She'd done exactly what she was told, even reconnecting the automatic chair apparatus to the stairs they hadn't used since Sandra's grandmother passed away six years ago, to get Wyatt Randolph to a comfortable bed on the second floor of the house.

He'd been little help in his semiconscious state, and Sandra had used all her available strength to get him to one of the three bedrooms. When she'd finally laid him down and pulled the quilt over his prone frame, she remembered her mother's last instruction, to call Brian, the forest ranger at the Pocono station. She knew she should report the stab wound, but Wyatt Randolph was a United States senator. Shouldn't she give him a chance to explain before he found himself confronted by a roomful of police? Her logic didn't make sense and she knew it. He'd been stabbed. He carried a cache of diamonds clearly worth enough to start a revolution, but something made her want to talk to him before she reported him to the police.

Sandra knelt on the sofa, her finger playing with the bright stones lying on the small table that held a lamp, several books, and a candy jar filled with leftover Christmas candy.

She'd cleaned the blood away until they shone, yet they were flawed. She could see the flaws with her naked eye. It didn't mean they weren't worth a fortune. The diamonds were another reason she should report to the authorities. Gunshots and stab wounds were required by law to be reported. Her mother had told her that just before she hung up. She felt guilty that she hadn't followed Melissa's instructions. They had a good relationship and Sandra never lied to her. Yet today, when she'd asked who the man was, Sandra told her his eye was swollen so badly and his face so bruised that he'd be hard to recognize even if she knew who he was. Technically the truth, she rationalized, but she'd recognized Wyatt Randolph the moment she'd pulled his slumped body up in the car.

Sandra chewed on her lip remembering her decision not to call Brian until she could at least talk to the senator. Maybe she'd been wrong. She should have called the police. The snow had continued until it was impossible to reach the small house now. If the senator died it would be her fault.

Again she looked at the stones, fifteen of them. They'd make a beautiful necklace, she thought with a wry smile. What was he doing with them? she wondered. Why did he have them banded about his waist and who had tried to kill him?

The radio crackled static. Sandra jumped as she turned and stared at it. The cup of coffee shook in her hand and she set it on the table. Why was she so nervous? Wyatt—He was Wyatt now. She'd checked on him several times during the night. He did develop a fever and she'd spent part of the night sponging his face and chest, keeping him cool. After such intimate contact she no longer thought of him as Senator Randolph. He had only been in her house one day and he was already upsetting her normal routine. She hadn't thought anything about studying for her orals since she'd seen the blinking lights of his car in the distance and wondered who could be on the road in such bad weather.

"K7950 calling K5895. Princess, are you there?"

Sandra's spirits lifted at the absurd tag Officer Brian Court used when he called her on the shortwave radio. He called frequently when she was staying at the cabin under the pretext of checking to make sure everything was all right. Sandra knew he had a crush on her, but that was all it was. Going to the unit, she flipped the switch to TALK and spoke into the microphone. "K5895, the Ivory Tower: Good morning, Brian." She smiled into the instrument, ignoring the rules of ham operators. Brian had called the Randolph cabin the Ivory Tower because it was so far up the mountain. When she was younger he'd dubbed her sister Annie the princess of the tower and referred to her as the other princess.

Sandra didn't mind. Brian acted like most men did when they saw her beautiful sister. He still called them both princess. "I'm fine," Sandra lied. She'd put twenty stitches into Wyatt Randolph and a nervousness she couldn't define settled on her since she'd found him in the road yesterday, but she kept this from Brian.

"Just checking. We had a might of snow last night."

"The weathermen were right on the money this time. Twenty-four inches," Sandra confirmed. Thank God, she finished silently. She'd gone out after getting Wyatt to bed and cleared a path back to his car. Then she'd driven the distance back to the cabin and walked to his car. It had taken her an hour to get it back to the cabin. Without four-wheel drive it was virtually impossible to climb the mountain road, or what passed as a road. Her mother and father had wanted absolute privacy when they built the cabin. It sat near the top of the mountain with few avenues of access other than the air and a four-wheel drive vehicle.

"Drifts must be up to your porch." Brian's voice jarred her back to the present.

"And then some," she told him. Sandra had stepped onto the porch at first light. The blowing snow of last night completely covered the path leading to the spot where Wyatt's car had been. The five steps that led to the cabin's wide porch were obliterated.

"You sure you don't need me to fly up there and bring you down?"

"I'm sure, Brian." She held the strain in her voice. She didn't want any visitors until Wyatt was conscious. "Besides," she remembered. "You and Starfighter can't occupy the same space."

She bit her lower lip. She didn't think the senator would want to find a representative of the law, even if it were only a forest ranger, when he opened his eyes. Her conscience tugged at her for a moment. She knew her mother was right and she should report to Brian that Senator Randolph had been stabbed and was comfortably asleep in Annie's bed. Yet, something made her hold back the information. Why was he on that road? Of all the places in the world he could choose to go, why did he pick the road leading to her family cabin? It had to concern her father. Yet, Sandra didn't discount her sister, Annie.

Annie had always been a wild one, and millions of dollars in diamonds could be part of a scenario that had her name on it. On the other hand, Wyatt Randolph was a senator and so was her father. She shivered at the thought that somehow the two of them had something in common. Either way, she had to find out the truth before she let Brian or the police know about him.

"How are you fixed for food and water?" Brian's voice had a serious note in it when it pulled her back to the shortwave. She knew he was concerned about her. She also knew he was a fine ranger. Her mother said he often called to check on her when she was here writing one of the many medical articles she published each year. Her trips were generally taken during summer weather. Why Sandra had chosen to prepare her defense during the winter, even she questioned now. She'd told herself the timing was right. Her exam was scheduled for the end of April. The cabin was deserted. She'd have absolute quiet to concentrate, no hikers dropping by unexpectedly, and she wanted to prove she could withstand the memories of John and this place without falling to pieces.

"Princess?" Brian called her back to the present.

"No problem," she continued. "All services are still working." The electricity and water had been unaffected by the sudden cold and mountainous snowfall.

"I don't like you being up there all alone."

"Brian, I'm not alone." She had a US senator in residence. Granted he was unconscious, but he was there. "You're at the end of the radio and I've got a Jeep with a snow plow if I really need to get down the mountain."

"That Jeep won't be much good in this kind of weather. It would take you hours to plow that road, *if* you could do it."

How well she knew that. Brian's voice told her he had doubts of her ability. Sandra's chin raised an inch. She had plowed that road, at least as far back as the senator's car. It had front-wheel drive, but had been hard to move. The car now sat safely in the car shed next to the Jeep. The night's snowfall had completely covered any trace of her handiwork.

"I also have Starfighter," she told him.

"Yeah," Brian laughed. "Thank God for that."

Sandra suddenly looked up. She heard a thump upstairs and knew Wyatt must have awakened. Her heart thudded as if Brian could see through the handset.

"Brian, honestly, I'm fine. If I need anything you'll be the first person I call."

"You make sure I am," he paused.

"Have there been any new developments on 'the ground' I should know about?" Again she used his designation for the distance between the ranger station and her cabin. She hoped he'd tell her the latest news about the man she was harboring.

"Other than the weather, Senator Wyatt is still commanding the front page."

"Anything new on his whereabouts?"

"Only speculation. One paper even has him in our neck of the woods. In order for that to happen he'd have to be a polar bear."

A nervousness gripped Sandra that made her hands shake. She grabbed the microphone with both hands. Thank God they didn't have the computer hookup that transmitted delayed still photographs. "He does represent this state." Sandra tried to make her voice sound normal, but the sound came out unusually high. "Coming here doesn't seem unreasonable."

"He's never been here before that I know of. Not even when your father comes up. If he's found in these parts I'd have to believe the stories that he's at least one egg short of a full dozen."

Sandra wasn't sure of that yet. Wyatt Randolph was still unconscious. She looked up again as if she could see through the beamed ceiling. At the moment she only knew that Senator Randolph *was* in the area and that he could have died trying to get there. She had yet to determine why he didn't seek medical help but instead had driven up a mountain in a snowstorm, a stab wound in his side, to reach her parents' cabin with a cache of diamonds tied around his waist.

He had to be looking for her father, the senior senator from New Jersey and chairman of the powerful defense subcommittee. Were they working on something together? Had he asked him to meet him here?

"I have to go, Sandra," Brian said. She heard the static of another call coming in over the open airwaves. "Remember to call me if you need anything."

"One more thing, Brian." Sandra's heart beat fast. She didn't want Brian to become suspicious, but she needed to ask him a question. "There haven't been any . . . strangers in the area, have there?" She bit her lower lip, hoping Brian didn't hear the hesitation.

"Princess, are you sure you're all right up there?"

"I promise you I'm fine. It's just that with all the snow, I feel a little isolated." That was the truth. "I wondered if there were any climbers or polar bear buffs in the area, just in case someone knocks on my door."

"We've been all over this area, and with the falling snow, only a fool with a death wish would be out in it. As far up the mountain as you are, they'd never reach you before they froze to death."

How little he knew, Sandra thought. Wyatt Randolph must have been very determined to get as far as he got and without the aerial surveillance of the forest rangers finding him.

"It's good to know," she said. "At least I can sleep well."

"Princess, you sure about staying up there? I can have a chopper there in no time."

"Brian, don't think about me. I'm sure you have plenty to do rescuing tourists and weekend skiers."

"Ain't that the truth. Last night we took two skiers to the hospital suffering from exposure and frostbite. They'll be fine."

"Who were they?"

"A couple of college kids," he said. "Don't worry, they weren't from Rutgers. I think they came from somewhere south of here, Morgan or Howard. So they weren't here trying to get you to change their grades."

Sandra laughed with Brian, glad to hear there was nothing more to add to her increasing feeling of paranoia.

"Well, Princess, I have to go now. Duty calls. K7950 signing off."

"Thanks, Brian, and I will call you if I need anything. K5895, Out."

He didn't know how true that was. The uneasiness that had settled over her since she found Wyatt bleeding in the snow had not left with the light of day. Someone wanted him dead, and if they'd tried to kill him once, she didn't think they'd stop until they'd completed the job. He was here for whatever reason. Whoever was looking for him was probably not far behind. What would she do when they caught up with him? Hopefully, Brian would be close enough to summon.

Sandra heard the thump again as she switched the microphone off. She ran up the stairs and into the room where she'd left Wyatt. He was sprawled diagonally across the twin bed, his bare feet on the floor as if he'd tried to get up and fallen back against the pillows. For a moment she stared at his legs, powerful, athletically muscular. Her stomach clinched. Sandra moved into the room and checked him. He was asleep, his breathing even. Perspiration lay on his forehead, but he was cool to the touch. Raising his shirt, she saw the stitches were holding and no additional blood had seeped through the dressing. Lifting his legs, she swung them back onto the bed and covered him with the sheet and quilt.

Next to the bed she'd placed a bowl of water and a cloth. She wrung out the cloth. He was so far across the mattress she had to balance herself on one knee and lean over him to dab the perspiration from his brow. He was a handsome man, she thought. Not as good-looking as the newspaper pictures showed, but in those his face wasn't swollen and bruised. His skin was dark and smooth like milk chocolate. Strangely enough, she liked touching it. She continued sponging his face after it was no longer necessary. The swelling around his eye was smaller this morning, and it didn't appear so veined as it had the night before.

She stared at him. Half of his face was unmarred. That half was gorgeous. She could only imagine what he would look like without the disfigurement. Her mouth suddenly went dry. She swallowed, trying to wet her throat. The stubble on his face showed he'd gone several days without a shave. It in no way detracted from the strength of his features. She could see why his constituency had voted him to office. Without knowing his platform, she thought he had an honest look. She wondered why they had never met at the many political functions she'd attended in support of her father.

He had brown eyes; indeed she'd looked into them earlier. As if he could read her thoughts, Wyatt Randolph's eyes opened and he stared directly into hers. Sandra, caught off guard and feeling as if she'd been discovered doing something wrong, was paralyzed. For a moment they stared at each other. Then Wyatt's eyes closed and he went back to sleep.

Sandra let go of her breath and sat back on the coverlet. What had happened to her? The man only looked at her and he wasn't even fully awake, yet her heart was pounding and she felt as if she couldn't take enough air into her lungs. Quickly, she scrambled off the bed and stepped away from him. Wyatt didn't move, didn't even know she was in the room. Sandra felt gripped by some indefinable aura that bound her to him. Why? she wondered, but got no answer.

She left the room, closing the door and taking a deep breath. It wasn't possible. She knew nothing about him outside of what the papers had printed over the last week. Until he woke up, she was going to have to wait to find out his reason for disappearing. Hopefully, when that happened she'd have better control of herself.

Wyatt groaned and opened his eyes. He couldn't see anything, just a large, hazy blur. He blinked several times. Finally he could make out the bedpost at the foot of the small bed. In the corner a bureau materialized, then a dresser with a mirror. The door in the center of one wall stood half open. He could only see the rough surface of a wall outside of it.

"Ohhh," he moaned. Every part of him hurt. He raised his hand to his aching head. Unintentionally he hit his eye. Agony shot into his head. His entire body clinched. As the pain subsided, he gingerly felt the swelling about his eye. His hand touched a gauze bandage near his brow.

Memory surged into his consciousness. Had they caught him? Why wasn't he dead? He tried to sit up. Pain shot through his side, sapping him of energy, forcing him back against the pillows. Sweat poured off him and he opened his mouth to take in gulps of air. Where was he? Trying to calm himself, he breathed deeply, his chest heaving as he gritted his teeth and waited out the pain.

Light flowed through the windows. Bright light. He concentrated on that instead of the paralyzing agony in his side. It must be late afternoon. He didn't recognize the room and he wasn't tied to the bed, so he must have been found by someone who hadn't called the police or the FBI. It could be Senator Rutledge's men who were holding him.

Wincing, he pushed himself up, feeling his left side. They'd stabbed him, tried to kill him. And it was his fault. Why had he gone into that alley? When he spotted the man following him, why hadn't he gone for the car or the subway? The alley was darker than the street, and he thought he could hide. He'd been wrong. Wyatt had turned at the last minute, feeling something was wrong. The man was coming toward him, fast. They struggled, fought, traded blow for blow. He saw the knife too late to dodge it. Luckily, he'd rolled away and come up with the gun—Chip's gun. The guy had run, and Wyatt had taken a breath. He got to the car and started driving. How he got here he didn't know.

He remembered the snow, blinding snow, and then he passed out. Someone must had found him, someone who'd dressed his stab wound. Who? It felt tight under the bandage. He wondered if whoever had found him was friendly. He hoped so, for he was in no condition to escape a capture. And he *was* still alive.

Where was he? He listened for a sound, any indication that he wasn't alone. He heard nothing. Had whoever found him left him alone?

He swung his feet to the carpeted floor and hung his head as dizziness accosted him. It cleared in a moment and he tried to stand. The effort washed him in perspiration. Clamping his teeth together, he shifted his weight to his good side and squeezed his eyes shut. The pain in his head vied for dominance over that in his side. Still, Wyatt forced himself up. A minor victory, he told himself as he spread his feet and let go of the bedpost several agonizing moments later. He could stand. Pushing his shirt aside, he placed his hand over the dressing and tried to force the burning pain concentrated there away. The dressing was clean. He wondered who had tended him—and why?

Listening again, he heard nothing. He limped quietly toward a closed door inside the room. Opening it only wide enough to see inside, he found a bathroom. Pushing it further, he found it empty and connected to another room. The second room looked much like the one he'd awakened in except it had a queen-size bed and more female frills to it. Closing both doors, he used the facility but didn't want to alert anyone to his presence by flushing the toilet. He checked his face in the mirror and frowned at the broken and discolored skin he saw. He looked as if he'd been in a fight, and God knows he had.

Carefully stripping the dressing off his side, he looked at the neat row of thread that held his skin together. Again he wondered who had done this.

Returning to the bedroom, he limped to the window. Maybe his car was outside. If he did need to run, he didn't want to do it on foot.

"God!" he breathed. He'd never seen so much snow. He'd grown up in Philadelphia. With the subways and elevated trains, snow generally melted quickly after falling. During his junior year at Morgan State University, he and several fraternity brothers had taken a trip to Switzerland to ski. Some of the Florida brothers had never seen snow before. He'd at least seen it, but what was outside this window could rival the Alps.

He wondered if the entire house was surrounded by as much snow as what he could see from the windows in this room. There would be no escaping if he was being held by the men who'd tried to kill him. But if he were, why hadn't they killed him? They had to have found . . .

His hands went to his waist. Where was it? He jerked his shirt aside. Suddenly he weaved back and forth, grabbing the windowsill to still the room and make the whirling halt. The band was gone. His gaze darted around the room. His watch and wallet lay on the nightstand. His pants hung from a wooden butler in the corner and his shoes sat in front of it. He was wearing his shirt and shorts. Nowhere did he see the band or the stones.

He couldn't have lost them. One man had died for those diamonds. He was almost the second, but somehow he'd escaped his assassins and made it here—wherever here was.

What was he going to do now? He needed to know where he was and how many people were in the house. He needed to know if they were friend or foe, and if they were foe what more they wanted from him.

The first thing he needed to do was get dressed. He found the thought difficult to execute. The pain in his side took more out of him than he cared to admit. Sweat popped out on his brow, dizziness overtook him several times, and thoughts of giving up and going back to the comfortable bed had to be forcibly removed.

After the last week, Wyatt knew the benefits of having the element of surprise on his side. He had to leave this bedroom, before whoever was holding him came back. There was only one door. He hoped there was no guard standing outside it. Quietly, he peeped through the opening. The hall looked deserted. He opened it wider and slipped out. He pressed himself against the wall, straining to hear. Not even a floorboard creaked. The stairs were several feet away.

He made his way toward them, the effort requiring every ounce of strength. Then he heard someone move. A chair scraped across a floor. He froze still, sure whoever it was knew of his movements. He listened intently. No one started up the stairs. Sweat beaded on his forehead and rolled into his eyes. He wiped it away with his sleeve. How many were there? he wondered. The sound had not repeated and he could hear nothing more. That could mean only one person was in the house, or it could mean, if there were others, they weren't talking. At the top of the steps he peered down. He saw nothing.

Then she walked by. He jumped back, flattening his back against the rough wooden wall, grinding his teeth together to keep the pain inside. His hands were sweaty and his head felt as if he were carrying the Congressional Record on it. His hand went to the sore spot on his side. Who was she? Was she alone? He'd seen her only briefly as she passed. She had dark hair pulled into a ponytail, and she was wearing black pants and a ski sweater.

He wondered if he could still ski. If he had any chance of escaping it would have to be over the snow. He remembered trying to get up the road and knew that was no longer a way out. He hadn't been on a pair of skis in at least a decade, and with the pain in his side, he wouldn't last more than a few feet before he'd need to shift his weight onto the side that certainly wouldn't support him.

He didn't like the situation. He was trapped. His only choice was to go down the steps and find out how bad it was. They hadn't killed him yet, and they did have the stones. What else could they want?

CHAPTER 2

Everett Davis Horton removed his wire-rimmed glasses and massaged the bridge of his nose. He stared through the windows of the upstairs sitting room. Lights beamed at him. No matter what direction he chose, he couldn't see much more than the beams of the thousand-watt bulbs that illuminated the White House. If he looked over them he could make out the sky and faint shadows of buildings in the distance. Life here was certainly a fishbowl, constantly in view of the nation.

They stared at him, scrutinized everything he said and did. They had the advantage. He couldn't see quite as well as they could and there were things that had to be hidden, things that if brought into the light would cause widespread fear and chaos; things like the nearness of global destruction. Former presidents had battled to fund star wars projects, class M submarines, and stealth missiles. His claim to history would be as the President who had lost Project Eagle, a defense system so vital it could change the course of world power. The man who'd designed it was dead and the man who had the key element couldn't be found.

Behind him lay the debris of his meeting. He turned from the window and sat down on the sofa. Stale coffee, half-eaten sandwiches, and burned cigarettes were the only remnants of his advisors, cabinet members, and secretaries. They advised, administered, and argued, yet none of them had a shred of information that would bring them a step closer to finding out what had happened to Senator Randolph. The senator held the fate of his presidency in his hands, not to mention the world, and the man didn't even know it.

Well, he might as well go to bed. There was nothing more he could do tonight. Until someone found Wyatt Randolph and the computer system he had, all they could do was wait and hope . . . hope the newspapers didn't find out about it, and hope no other government got to him first.

Everett pushed himself out of the chair and walked across the carpet. His feet made only a whisper of sound. He doused the lights and opened the door. Before him stood the imposing hallway that led to his bedroom. The staff had lowered the lighting for the night. Since John Adams had become the first occupant of the national mansion, lights had never been completely off inside the White House. He strolled down the hall that the ghosts of former Presidents had walked. Every term had had its problems; Teapot Dome lived long after Warren Harding died, Kennedy's problems with J. Edgar Hoover was the subject of documentaries, and Andrew Jackson's ribald inauguration party was touted out every four years. He felt these were minor infractions compared to shutting down world communications.

Wait until he told Casey in the morning. Quietly he opened the bedroom door and slipped inside. Casey had been asleep for hours and he didn't want to wake her. The President's wife had as many obligations as the President.

"Wishing we'd never left Texas?" she asked.

"I thought you were asleep." Everett turned toward the bed.

Casey Horton leaned over and pressed the button on the bedside lamp. She squinted as she pushed herself up.

"You might as well tell me about it tonight."

"Casey, I can't tell you everything. You need a security clearance to know what happened tonight."

"What's the highest clearance?"

"Ten."

"Well, my level is twelve. I know everything about the President and I'll go to *The Washington Post* and spill all. Now tell me."

Everett laughed, the simple act releasing the tension that had coiled inside him. He'd loved this woman for thirty years. She knew everything about him and commanded respect even from his advisors. He'd have appointed her to a cabinet position if it wouldn't have thrown protocol into a frenzy.

"Not tonight, Casey. I'm talked out. When the sun rises, I'll tell you everything."

Casey pushed the covers aside and got out of bed. She wore a white, clinging gown that showed off her body. At forty-nine she still looked like the woman he'd met in college, thin and firm even after giving birth to two children.

The sun would be up in a few hours. He was dead tired, but suddenly he wanted his wife. He met her, hugged her close, and kissed her shoulder. He smelled the perfume she always wore. Their schedules kept them apart so often that he cherished time when they were together. When he'd decided to run for a small office in their Texas town, he never imagined it would end at the White House. Casey always reminded him of that when he felt this way.

He pulled her soft body closer, feeling his own arousal. He turned her face to his and found her mouth.

"Do you think the country would approve of your actions now with the world in crisis?" she asked in a sexy voice that was breathy against his skin and throaty to his ear.

"I'm sure half of them would approve," he said, reaching down to lift her from the floor and carry her to the bed.

"Which half?"

"What are you doing out of bed?" Sandra pushed her books aside and stood up. He'd startled her. She hadn't heard him moving about upstairs or descending the steps. He'd moved like a thief stealing in the darkness, and that was most likely what he was, senator or no senator.

He didn't answer her immediately but looked her up and down as if he were surprised at her statement. His gaze darted around the room, checking every doorway as if he were looking for someone.

"We're alone," she told him, thinking better of her statement only after she'd said it. She went toward him. "You really should stay in bed. The stitches might come loose and I don't think I can redo them."

He checked over his shoulder and looked toward the kitchen. There was a kind of caged fear in him, she noticed. Fear took hold of her. What horror had she let herself in for? Why hadn't she told Brian he was here? Why hadn't she done what was expected of her? She'd always done so before.

His hand went to his side. Sandra's gaze followed it expecting to see blood seeping through the whiteness of his shirt.

"You—"

"I'm not a doctor," she told him. "It was either me or bleed to death. I didn't think you'd mind if I made the choice." She felt the need to explain.

"You *saved* my life?"

He asked it as a question. Sandra nodded. "I did my best."

"Where . . . am I?" His hesitation told her he was far from able to be out of bed.

"You're in my cabin at the top of the Pocono Mountains."

"Who are you?"

Sandra still thought he was the best-looking man she'd seen in a long time, but he looked as if he couldn't hold his position much longer.

"You really ought to go back to bed," she said.

"Who are you?" he asked a little more forcefully.

"My name is Sandra Rutledge."

"You're related to him?" His good eye widened in surprise as one hand gripped the newel post for support and the other went to his swollen eye. "What?" he paused.

Sandra could see he was in obvious pain.

"Sister? Niece? In-law?" he pressed on.

"What are you talking about?"

He was weaving as if his knees wouldn't hold him up for long. Sandra knew he'd fall soon. Quickly she looked for the stair-seat. It was at the top of the steps where she'd left it when she got him to Annie's room. She took a step forward, instinctively ready to catch him, although she doubted she'd be able to support his bulk.

"How are you related to him?"

His words stopped her forward motion. "Who?" she asked, confused at his apparent train of thought.

Both hands gripped the newel post. "Senator Bradford Campbell Rutledge." He said it as if he were announcing the next candidate for President of the United States.

"He's my father."

"Father?" he whispered. "Senator Rutledge has a daughter?"

He'd asked it as a question, although Sandra didn't know if he was actually speaking to her. She answered anyway. "He does. There are two of us. I have a sister."

She wondered why he didn't know that. She and Annie had been part of every campaign her father had participated in for as long as she could remember. They'd been posed and positioned, told where to stand and how to smile to best show off the perfect American family. Wyatt Randolph was the junior senator from Pennsylvania. Maybe he hadn't taken note of the neighboring state of New Jersey or maybe he hadn't taken much interest in Washington politics until he'd campaigned for the Senate.

"What are you doing here?" The question broke into her thoughts. "I'm looking for him."

Suddenly her back went up. Something about the vehemence in his voice. Just who was interrogating whom? This was her domain, yet his attitude made her feel as if she were an intruder.

"Excuse me."

"Where is Senator Rutledge? This is his cabin. I expected him to be here." It was as close to a shout as he could get.

"Well, you've been misinformed."

His hand went to his head. Sandra moved in. He recoiled as though he expected her to attack him. His hold on consciousness must be from sheer will, because his weaving was getting worse. Sandra wondered how he could keep the force in his voice. Her anger left her. The man was obviously sick and in pain. She should have more compassion.

"You need to sit down," she told him. He must have agreed with her, for he looked at the step behind him. "Let me help you."

She didn't get the chance. At her first step his legs buckled. She reached for him, spreading her own legs to balance his greater weight. He staggered forward as her arms encircled his waist. She zigzagged backward a few steps before they both crashed to the floor, Sandra pinned under him like a butterfly. Lying inert, she tried to regain the breath Wyatt Randolph's bulk had knocked out of her.

He lay on top of her heavy and unconscious. She touched his shoulders, intending to push him away, but contact with his heated skin changed her. Suddenly she was aware of him not as her patient but as a man—a vibrant, strong, and virile man. Sandra felt his warmth seep into her where she touched him. How he managed to stand for so long, she didn't know. He was over six feet tall and she fit under his arm like a natural extension. *Why did she think that?* She'd seen him before. His face had been on the news. She'd watched his story every day for the past week. Yet, in all the Washington parties and politically mandatory events she'd attended, the two of them had never been together in the same room. Until now. She forced herself to breathe in, but the effort drew the clean smell of the soap she'd used to sponge him, the indefinable scent that was unique to him, and a breath of the outdoors. His nearness and his warm body enhanced her awareness of him. Heat pooled in her stomach hot as a self-cleaning oven. Sandra felt his form from breasts to hips. His head lay against her shoulder and his legs settled in the V of her hips. Sandra gritted her teeth and tried to force herself from under him. The effort aroused her. Her female body recognized the signs of sexual awareness.

It's been too long, Sandra, she thought. Too long since she'd been with a man. Even now, while Wyatt Randolph lay unconscious, she felt a need she'd hadn't felt since John died.

Her battle to free herself ended. Lying still, she waited for the state of normalcy to return, but it didn't. The longer she lay under him, the more she wanted to stroke his arms, his back, run her hands over him. She only felt more and more the need to stay where she was. His weight impeded her breathing, yet she didn't mind carrying it. Halting her thoughts, she heaved him aside and skittered out from under him.

Putting the distance of the room between them, she curled her arms around her legs and rocked back and forth, staring at the static figure lying on the braided rug. Dropping her head onto her knees, she denied what was happening to her. It must have something to do with all the thoughts of John she'd had since Wyatt arrived. She missed John, and finding herself spread-eagle under a man had to make her body instinctively react. There was nothing to be concerned about. She was a warm-blooded female who hadn't had a man around in a long time. It was perfectly normal to react as she had. After twenty minutes of telling herself this, she almost believed it.

Slowly Sandra unraveled her long legs and got up. She couldn't sit and watch Wyatt all morning. He might be really hurt and all her work would have gone to waste. Steeling her emotions, she turned him over, purposely avoiding his face and looking at his side. She held her breath at the sight of the muscles of his stomach and concentrated on the stitches. He'd removed the bandage, but thankfully the binding was holding.

"Wyatt," she whispered. "Wake up." He didn't move. Running to the bathroom, she wet a cloth and rushed back to the figure on the floor. Patting his forehead and cheeks with the cold cloth and calling his name softly, she tried to wake him.

After a few moments of coaxing, the darkest chocolate eyes opened and focused on her. She clamped her teeth down on her inner lip to buy herself enough time to speak coherently. "Can you sit up?" she finally asked.

He nodded. Sandra slipped her arm under his head and helped him rise into a sitting position. She noticed his wince as he moved forward. Helping him to his feet, they made it across the room and he sank onto the sofa, his head falling back against the upholstered back. Sandra dropped down on the other end before her knees gave way and she fell.

How could this be? She was a rational thirty-two-year-old professor. She'd had relationships with men before. But she'd never reacted like this to a man. Why was her body turning into warm syrup when she touched him? She didn't even know him. Why did she have these feelings when his face was swollen and disfigured—and when she thought he was involved in a major crime?

He sat on the sofa holding his head. She watched him labor with the pain for a moment, feeling at a loss for a way to help him ease it. When he began to relax, she felt better, too. As if she were going through his pain with him.

"If you'd relax the pain wouldn't be so intense," she told him.

"How long have I been here?" He ignored her words.

Sandra suddenly had the feeling he was headstrong and difficult. She thought it better to answer his questions, since she had her own set that needed answering. "The snow fell for three days. You showed up in the thick of it."

"Three days!" He tried to sit up straight, but fell back against the sofa. "Has anyone been here? Looking for me?"

Sandra kept the panic that reared inside her out of her voice. "Not yet. No one can get up the mountain." She paused to take a deep breath. "Is someone chasing you?"

"I don't know. I thought I'd lost them, but in the last week . . ."

He stopped. Instinctively Sandra looked over her shoulder. There was no one behind her and she knew they were alone, but she felt even more afraid now. *Relax,* she told herself. *You're safe and Brian is only a call away.* When she looked at Wyatt again, his eyes were closed and he appeared calm. Sandra breathed a little easier. For a long moment she looked at him. His swollen eye had gone down a lot in the past three days, and she'd fed him water with ibuprofen in it. It should have helped his pain and the inflammation. Another week in bed would do wonders for him.

Suddenly, she found herself shaking. She didn't want him here for another week. In that time Brian would be certain to come up the hill to check, despite her constant assurances that she was fine. Whoever was looking for him could find him in that time, and she had no desire to be in the middle of people who wanted him dead.

She didn't want him dead. She didn't know why. She didn't know much about anything she felt since she'd pulled him out of the car and brought him here. When she'd touched him she didn't want to stop. As his face had begun its return to normal, she looked at his profile, staring at his sensual lips and wondering what they'd feel like on hers, before she forced her thoughts back to the logic of mathematics. That's what she should be doing now instead of staring at him.

"Where . . . where are they?" he asked without moving. Sandra was startled. She didn't have to ask what he meant.

"I put them away."

"Where?"

"You don't need them now."

"Where . . . are . . . they?" His voice was forced. He tried to raise himself, but couldn't.

"You must be hungry." Sandra seized the first thought that came into her head. "Wait here, I'll heat you something to eat."

Not giving him time to protest, she left the room and escaped to the kitchen. There she breathed freely for the first time since she'd touched him.

What was wrong with her? She thought earlier when he'd awakened and she was leaning over him that it was a fluke, but now her reaction to his proximity was stronger than anything she'd ever felt toward any man. Why? Slamming her thoughts closed, she refused to even entertain the idea of an association with Wyatt Randolph.

Mechanically, she fixed a tray with a tossed salad, beef stew, rolls, a slice of apple pie, and a large glass of iced tea.

She took as long in the kitchen as she could. When she had no further reason to remain there, and when she felt her heartbeat was substantially back to normal, she reentered the living room.

Wyatt lay where she'd left him. His eyes were closed. She set the tray on the table next to her books and went to him. He was asleep. For a long moment she just looked. *Why?* she wondered. *What is it about you that makes me want to protect you?* She'd found at least ten million dollars in diamonds in a bloody band, yet the man laying before her had the most honest face she'd ever seen. Even his bruises didn't take away from the strong jawline and sensuous mouth.

Sandra wet her dry lips. Quickly, she stepped back. She wanted to kiss him. Why? Her eyes widened in surprise and her hand went to her lips as if the deed had been done. Sandra moved back so she wouldn't bend down and put thought to action.

Turning away, she went back to the table and removed the tray. In the kitchen she restored the food and wondered why each time she came into contact with the man in the other room her emotions surfaced to skin-level.

Night had fallen when Wyatt awoke. The back of the sofa restricted his movement. It was just as well since the small movement brought the pain to life. Sandra sat at the table in the dining area of the room. He'd barely looked around before. There was another sofa with a low wooden table in front. From his vantage point, nearly eye-level with it, it appeared to be the size of a dining-room table, polished and uncluttered. Two winged chairs covered in blue chintz fabric sat on the opposite side of the table and a fire burned warm in the hearth before him. He didn't remember it being there when he fell asleep.

She must have put the blanket over him, for he noticed it now. It smelled sweet, like a perfume, and had a decidedly female aroma. He knew it had to be hers, and it wasn't at all unpleasant. Without rising, he saw her sitting at the table on the other side of the room. The table was covered with open books. Some of them lay on top of others and a calculator stood close to her right hand. An unconscious finger pushed her glasses up her nose and smoothed her hair back. A laptop computer held her concentration.

Wyatt was reminded of his law school days. Nights poring over law books, learning, memorizing, referencing and cross-referencing case after case for his constitutional law class. Con Law. Little did he know that class would have the most influence on his future—if he had a future.

He hadn't had time in the last week to think things through. Since the package had arrived on the heels of finding out Chip was dead, he'd been running. Keeping only one step ahead of the killers and not knowing where to go and what to do next, he'd hidden. Then he'd found the connection between Senator Rutledge and the stones and he knew he had to get to him, had to convince him to turn himself in, that selling out his country was not the answer.

He hadn't counted on finding a daughter, and a beautiful daughter at that. He pulled the blanket closer to his nose. She didn't see him, didn't know he was awake yet. He studied her as she studied her books. The light above her head shone off her hair. It was brown but had a reddish sheen to it. She'd pulled it free of the ponytail she wore earlier and it hung loosely about her shoulders.

Her eyes were light brown and compelling. He'd hate to have her opposing him in a courtroom. Not only did she command attention, but juries believed people who looked them straight in the eye as she had done to him. He liked her. A smile came to his face. It had been a while since he could say that about anyone. Every woman he met wanted something from him—an appointment or an introduction to someone, a job in the government, or the promise of a favor.

He didn't often meet women who had nothing to do with the government. Technically, Sandra Rutledge had a connection, too: her father. His smile turned to a scowl when he thought of the majority senator. He was involved with those diamonds up to his nose and Wyatt would prove it. Again he looked at Sandra. Regret surfaced. He'd truly like to get to know her, but when he explained his reasons for looking for her father, the only emotion she'd have for him would be hate.

"What are you studying?" he asked quietly.

She jumped as he knew she would. Her hand snatched the glasses away from her face as if she didn't want to be seen in them. It was quiet enough to hear the wind blowing outside.

"You're awake." She got up and came toward him. He watched her walk. Her gait was short, but strong and sure, and her hips swung under the hip-length sweater.

"I got you up the stairs once," she explained. "I didn't have the strength to do it again."

He didn't mind sleeping on the sofa. It had allowed him to see her in an unguarded moment. Her eyes were hooded now and her defenses in place. Wyatt had read people's expressions all his life. As a trial lawyer he'd used his ability to determine the meaning of body language, and Sandra Rutledge's body told him she was nervous. Why?

He remembered the gems. How long had he slept? Had anyone called looking for him? He noticed a phone on a small table next to her. Had it rung while he slept? Did anyone get through the snow? Was he safe?

His heart began to beat faster. It had been running nonstop for the past week. Each time he thought of the diamonds and the men trying to get them, his heart pounded with a cold fear. He was no spy or government agent. He was a plain lawyer who'd planned to spend his career in corporate law, wearing clean shirts and eight-hundred-dollar suits. He'd planned to deal with estates and wills, maybe a few tax cases; being a criminal lawyer hadn't been his idea, and running for the senate was the last thing he expected to do. Taking the job in legal aid had been to gain experience, but he'd gotten caught, snagged into defending the common man, people who needed him, who had nowhere else to turn. He found he liked it.

"What did you do with them?" he asked quietly.

Sandra sat down on the low table. He didn't need body language to tell him she was disconcerted by the stones. Anyone would be, even a jeweler.

"The diamonds?" she finally asked.

"Where are they?"

She hesitated, deciding. Wyatt could tell her curiosity was getting the better of her. She wanted to know about them, more than she wanted to keep them a secret from him.

"I washed the blood off—"

"With water!" He tried to sit up but only got as far as his elbows.

Sandra leaned back as if he could reach her. When she saw he couldn't, she relaxed. "There are many jewelry cleaners on the market. I've tried several of them to clean my rings." She held up her hands, each finger naked of any adornment. "However, the best way to clean diamonds is to use ammonia and water. You can drop them in a solution and let them stand for twenty minutes. The brilliance of the stones and even the setting will gleam in normal light."

"Tell me you didn't."

"I didn't," she said, and smiled. It was the first genuine smile he'd seen since his arrival. "We don't have any ammonia. I used a dry cloth to clean your blood away. The residue I brushed away with an old toothbrush." She paused. "I examined them."

"And you found," he prompted.

"I found them to be the most unusual stones I'd ever seen."

"It that all?"

She nodded. "Is there more?"

Of course there was more. A man had died over those unusual stones, and right now both their lives could be in danger. "Where did you put them?" he asked, ignoring her question.

"In a safe place."

"There is no safe place. I need to know where they are." He was getting irritated, but the pain of the knife wound reminded him of his limitations.

"Are you a thief?"

The question threw him. "No," he grunted more than laughed. "I'm not a thief."

She stared directly at him, her features fixed. Wyatt knew she didn't believe him. She didn't fear him, either, at least not at the moment. She was safe. In his condition he couldn't overpower her. Even as slender as she appeared, she could incapacitate him with a touch to the tender flesh she'd sewn back together.

"How much are they worth?" she asked. "I estimated ten, twelve million dollars."

"You can't possibly know their worth." Or their cost, he added silently.

CHAPTER 3

The vast concrete gardens of the Watergate Hotel calmed Jordon Ames. The day's shoot hadn't been easy and he needed to unwind. The Kennedy Center sat in the distance, its marble facade lighted like a huge pedestal waiting for an ancient king. Already crowds were gathering for tonight's performance. One he thankfully would not be attending. He would have a leisurely dinner, good conversation, and, if he was lucky, a good night's sleep, but that all depended on Suzanne.

The woman never walked into a room. She made entrances. The air of money, old money, surrounded her like a cloak. Her chin tilted slightly higher than the rest of the world. Most people thought she was a snob. Yet, he knew better.

She paused on the top of the two steps that led to the sunken dining room and leisurely surveyed the area. The hesitation was just long enough for every eye in the room to turn to her. Jordon Ames lifted his third martini and drained the glass. He could watch her all day and never tire of the face that launched ships, lips that puckered for lipstick ads, or eyes that sparkled for mascara. Jordon frequently watched Suzanne Wright, a name she'd chosen the day she started modeling. Called Suzanne by everyone who knew her now, she used to be plain Annie—Annie Boatwright. She had left the backwater town in rural Georgia and through some stroke of luck become the adopted daughter of Senator and Mrs. Bradford Rutledge. Her life with them had been privileged, but Jordon knew Annie still harbored a deep-seated fear that life would one day plunge her back to the poverty-stricken one she'd escaped.

Her face was her fortune. She'd taken New York by storm when she walked into the first modeling agency she'd tried. Jordon remembered meeting her that day, struck almost dumb by the raw beauty of her skin tone and the natural way she carried herself.

Since that time everything about her had changed except that exquisitely delicate look she used to get whatever she wanted.

Jordon knew this, yet he still watched her. He watched her through his camera lens and it loved her—almost as much as he did. Her skin was smooth and dark. She was the darkest woman he'd ever seen, but the smoothness of the color forced, almost commanded notice. Even if she hadn't been as beautiful as an Egyptian queen, she'd have demanded attention.

Jordon got up and went toward her. She noticed him before he reached the step where she stood. Her face transformed into a smile. How often had he seen that? She could smile when she didn't mean it. When the product called for a smile, it was there waiting. When tears were necessary, they fell from her brown eyes like large marbles.

"Jordon," she purred, descending the two steps as if she were royalty. He offered his arm and she took it.

He led her to their table. "Well, Annie . . ." he said as he pulled out a chair for her. He was one of the few people she didn't throw an angry look at for dipping into her past. Jordon took his own seat and twirled the empty martini glass. "How does it feel to have Washington, DC at your feet? You can have any job you want. The most photographed woman in the world. Second only to Princess Di."

Suzanne, instead of tossing her hair and giving him her most disconcerting smile, dropped her head just as he saw the pain come into her eyes.

"What's wrong?" he asked, immediately sorry that he'd hurt her. He never wanted to hurt her. He only wanted her to look at him and see *him*. Not the photographer, but the man who loved her. The man who wanted to give her the things money couldn't buy.

"Nothing's wrong," she snapped. "Order me a drink."

Jordon called the waiter and ordered a cup of coffee for himself and a white wine for Annie. He'd seen her in all kinds of moods, but tonight's was different than any he'd recognized before. He wondered what had happened. Had she met someone new or lost someone old? He was certain the root of the cause was a man.

"I'm sorry, Jordon," Suzanne apologized. "I don't want to fight tonight, and least of all with you." She paused a long time before taking a breath and saying, "It's just that I don't like Washington."

Jordon knew that. She'd never told him why, but when the assignment came through for a major ad campaign using the historical landmarks as a backdrop, Annie immediately refused the job. It had taken him days to persuade her to take it, and then she wouldn't tell him the real reason she didn't want to come to the capital.

"Sandra called a few minutes before I left the room."

Jordon knew Sandra was Annie's stepsister. The girls had once been close, and despite what Annie said, he believed it was Annie who had erected the barriers between herself and her sister.

"Is everything all right?"

"Sure."

When their drinks arrived, Suzanne immediately took a swallow.

"She knew I was in town."

The implication of how she knew was left hanging. He hadn't told her. In fact, he had only seen Sandra Rutledge once and that was at a campaign fund-raiser for her father several years ago. She'd been in the distant background and had left as soon as she could. He had gotten the impression she was camera shy.

"She wanted to know if I'd seen or heard from Dad. I hadn't."

"You didn't invite her down? How long has it been since you two have seen each other?"

"Not long enough." Suzanne raised her wineglass and stared through the golden-colored liquid. "Not long enough."

All families have difficulties, Jordon thought. He and his own father had fought constantly while he was a teenager, but as time had passed they'd become close. Jordon wanted her to open up to him, let his be the shoulder she cried on. Usually he was. She'd talk to him like he assumed two women would talk, but Annie had few women friends and she seemed completely oblivious to his true feelings for her.

"Suzanne . . . Suzanne Rutledge!" someone suddenly called.

They both looked up. The man was tall and well-built. He looked as if he worked out daily. Jordon could easily see him posing for an ad selling a muscle-building protein mix. He had a full head of dark hair with only a sliver of gray running through it and no evidence of a receding hairline. His bone structure was good. He would easily get through another ten years without a face-lift.

Suzanne's face lit up when she saw him, and Jordon's stomach instantly clinched.

"Lance." In a second she was on her feet and in his arms.

Jordon wished he had another martini.

"It's so good to see you. Sit down."

"Only for a moment. I'm having dinner with Senator Walsh and he's a stickler for protocol."

Suzanne followed the glance Lance threw over his shoulder. Jordon did, too.

"Jordon, this is Lance Desque, undersecretary of defense and clearly the most influential man in Washington. Lance, meet Jordon Ames, my photographer."

The two men shook hands.

"She exaggerates," Lance said. "Suzanne and I have known each other forever, Jordon?" He ended the sentence with a question mark; silently asking if the use of first names was politically correct. Jordon nodded.

"I've known Suzanne since her father first came to Washington. He was in the House then."

He paused and smiled at Suzanne. Jordon thought his smile was greased with oil. Suzanne didn't appear to share his opinion.

"Shortly after that he built the mountain cabin, right, Suzanne? Then you were just little Annie."

Jordon thought she would correct his use of her childhood name. He felt privileged thinking himself the only person she allowed to call her that. Yet, she nodded without batting even one of her naturally long eyelashes.

"Been up there recently? I hear the snow this winter has provided the best skiing weather they've had in years."

"I don't get up there often," Suzanne said. Jordon noticed her voice was tight.

"How about your father? He still ski as much as he used to?"

"Yeah, Dad still loves winter sports." Jordon wondered about the tone in Annie's voice. Then she changed the subject. "What are you doing these days? Are you still running the show over at the DOD?"

He glanced at Jordon. "My title makes me a minor executive," he explained. "I'm only a glorified gofer and I know it."

"Gofers don't often have dinner with senators or Presidents, do they?" It was a dig and beneath him, but Jordon didn't care. He didn't like Lance Desque. There was something about him that reminded him of a bandit from the Old West.

"In Washington, Jordon, everyone is a gofer for someone. Tonight it's for the senator from Illinois." Quickly, he turned his attention back to Suzanne. "Will you be in Washington long, Suzanne?"

"A couple of weeks."

"Good." He smiled the oily smile. "We'll have to get together and mull over old times."

"I'd like that."

"Are you staying here?"

Suzanne nodded.

"Why don't we have lunch. Do you have any free time?"

"How about Thursday at The Charter Club . . . one o'clock?"

"Thursday it is." Lance glanced over his shoulder again. "I'd better go now or Senator Walsh will lecture me for the rest of the night on proper procedure in a Washington restaurant and I'll never get him to agree to sponsor a proposal I have in mind."

He stood, shook Jordon's hand, then bent down and kissed Suzanne on the cheek.

Jordon wanted to grab him by his expensive suit and toss him through the smoke-glass window, especially when he noticed Annie's gaze follow him all the way across the room to join the table with several other people.

He wondered if the next man Annie cried over would be Lance Desque?

"Aren't you going to eat?" she asked. Wyatt had been staring at the darkness for five minutes. Sandra watched him without speaking, wondering what he was thinking and when he would either tell her or begin to eat his food before it cooled. He'd done neither. The diamonds lay on the polished wooden surface just above the quilted placemat.

She'd expected him to grab the stones and hide them again, but he'd hardly glanced at them. He was listening to something, but to what she had no idea. She could hear nothing more than the singing of the wind outside. His thoughts were miles away. She wondered how far and to what extent.

"Don't you feel like a prisoner here?" Wyatt asked as he turned to face her. She wondered if he'd heard her question.

"Not often," she told him. She'd never felt that way at the cabin before, but she did now. Since she'd been a child she felt confined to a restricted space. Before cameras, in campaign offices, someone was always watching. Here in the cabin she had felt free until he arrived.

Her thoughts darted to him whenever he wasn't actually in her presence. *It's just been too long,* she told herself. She'd been too wrapped up in class schedules, teaching, and working on her degree to think much about men. After John died she thought her life was over, but being pinned under Wyatt had added a new dimension to her perspective.

He looked down at the steak and potatoes she'd prepared as if only now remembering them. He attacked the food as if he hadn't had anything to eat in years.

"You shouldn't eat so fast," she told him. "After not eating for three days it's bad for your digestion." Sandra had hesitated about serving him the food. She'd thought of having only chicken broth and Jell-o, but remembering his shoulders and muscular legs, she decided against it. Still, she made him a light soup, added small portions to his plate, and ended with the gelatin dessert. "How long has it been since you had a decent meal?"

"I don't remember; two or three days maybe . . . before I got here. I do know it's been even longer since I've had a home-cooked meal."

He smiled then and Sandra's heart turned over.

"How did you do this so fast?" He indicated the food on the table.

"Microwave."

"Even the rolls?" He picked up a piece of warm bread and lathered it with melting butter. "Mine always come out soggy or as rubbery as elastic bands. Then they harden into golf balls."

"There's a toaster oven." She told him. "With school, some nights I barely get anything to eat unless I stop at The Ledge." Seeing him frown, Sandra explained. "That's the student center. The food is almost all grease or sugar-filled."

"You're a student?"

She nodded. "I'm a teacher at Rutgers University in New Brunswick. Right now I'm off, preparing to defend my dissertation."

"You're a Ph.D. candidate? What's your specialty?"

"Mathematics."

"Isn't that like saying I study law?"

Sandra smiled, trying to put what she did in terms a layman could understand. "My specific area comes under the algebraic number theory. It's called elliptic curves and involves curves on a plane that have special properties."

"What kind of properties?"

Without an in-depth knowledge of mathematics she knew he wouldn't understand her. "The kind that can be defined by an equation you wouldn't understand. Do you really want to know?"

He frowned. "I was horrible at math," he groaned, taking a drink of his iced tea.

Sandra smiled. His was a common reaction by people outside her profession. "You were probably good at something else," she said softly, at once realizing the sexual innuendo of her words.

The tea glass, on its way to his mouth, stopped midway and their eyes locked. Heat flashed through her. Sandra couldn't drag her gaze away.

Wyatt broke contact first. He turned his head and emptied the glass of tea.

"Can I get you some more?" she offered, confused and needing to escape his presence until she could get her emotions back under control.

"No." He shook his head, not at all uncomfortable with the moment. "Who in your family is from the South?"

"My mother grew up in Tennessee. I suppose iced tea in the middle of January is a dead giveaway."

He nodded with a smile. Sandra noticed his even, white teeth. She'd thought his mouth was sensual while he slept; now she could hardly keep from leaning toward him and placing her lips on his.

"I grew up in Philadelphia," he explained. "Both my parents and grandparents were also born and raised there. Iced tea before Memorial Day or after Labor Day is near sacrilege."

Sandra laughed. She liked laughing with him. She could go on making small talk, but it was time. She needed some answers.

She stared at the window. It was dark outside. Brian had called for his second check-in while Wyatt slept on the sofa. For the second time she concealed Wyatt's presence. According to Brian, there were no new developments concerning Senator Randolph's disappearance. He'd ruled out any rumor that the senator could be in the area. Brian also gave her the latest weather report. The snow had stopped, but by the looks of things no one could get up the mountain. There had been a couple of inquiries from people who wanted to ski the new snow.

"Amateurs," Brian had called them. An experienced skier would know this kind of powder was too soft to ski in. The weight of their bodies would cause them to sink up to their waists.

"You look lost in thought," Wyatt said, providing her with the perfect opening.

"I was thinking about you," she told him. She expected him to smile, but he didn't. Instead, a frown crossed his face. "Why are you here?" she asked.

He didn't answer immediately. She wondered what he was thinking. Was he trying to formulate a lie to tell her? She'd had students who used the same technique when asked questions. If they had no ready answer, they hesitated trying to make one up.

"I didn't expect to find you," he finally said. "I wanted to speak to your father."

"Why?"

"It's personal."

"Who stabbed you?"

The abrupt subject change got a reaction. His head whipped around and he stared at her. After a long moment, he answered. "I don't know."

Sandra dropped her eyes to her near-empty plate. Shards of lettuce merged with Russian dressing formed a pink-and-green sea. She pushed it away.

"You don't believe me?"

"No," she answered quietly. "You get yourself stabbed deep enough to bleed to death, but instead of getting medical assistance, you trek up a mountain in the middle of a snowstorm looking for my father. If you'd asked for my mother it would make more sense. At least she's a doctor."

He suddenly placed her. Senator Rutledge's wife was a famous heart surgeon. Dr. Melissa Rutledge. He remembered seeing her name under a photograph in a Washington paper. She'd been with her two daughters, one a New York model and the other . . . Wyatt stared at Sandra. She was the other daughter.

He got up and went to the window, his hand on his left side. Leaning against the wall, he pulled the curtain aside. Outside, the snow lay like a glittering blanket under the full moon. He'd seen postcards that looked like this scene. In the past he'd thought a photographer had set it, placed lights at strategic places and filmed the scene. Yet, here there were no photographers' lamps. Only natural beauty had created the shining moon and thick flakes of snow. It was beautiful.

At this distance he could easily forget the world at the bottom of the mountain: It was a perfect place to escape to. Forget life in the city and stay here, he thought, where there was only a beautiful brown-skinned woman and peace; where his heart only pounded because of his attraction to her.

He sighed heavily and sat down in the chair next to the window. Sandra remained at the table. She hadn't said a word since he'd gone to the window. He couldn't help but think how much he liked looking at her. Why did she have to be Senator Rutledge's daughter? Why couldn't she have been anyone else but the daughter of a traitor?

She wanted answers. What would she say when he told her the man who had tried to kill him had been sent by her father? he wondered.

"Project Eagle," he finally said.

She stared at him without comment. He could tell it meant nothing to her.

"Ever heard of it?"

She shook her head. Leaving the table, Wyatt watched her long-legged stride as she came and stood in front of him. Then she dropped down and sat Indian-style on the floor. With the Aztec pattern on her sweater and the sheen of burnished curls hanging over her shoulders, she could have been an Indian princess. Too bad she wasn't, he thought. He wasn't looking forward to telling her why he'd come here.

"What is Project Eagle?" she asked.

Wyatt didn't speak immediately. He'd run for more than a week. He'd been caught, stabbed, and nearly bled to death. He could have died. Sandra Rutledge had saved his life, but she was Senator Rutledge's daughter. He wanted to trust her. She deserved an explanation for what she'd inadvertently become involved in. She was part of it now, even if she didn't know it.

"Two weeks ago I'd never heard of it," he began. "Then one morning I open the mail and find what I think are millions of dollars worth of diamonds."

They both glanced at the loose stones lying on the table. Since she'd given them to him, he hadn't touched them. They reminded him of Chip and he didn't want to have anything to do with them, but he knew Chip wanted him to uncover the truth or he'd never have sent the stones.

"Who sent them to you?" she asked.

"A friend." He stopped as emotion clenched his heart. He and Chip had been friends since childhood. He thought they'd grow into old age together, but now he'd been denied that, and he wouldn't allow the people who'd taken his life to go unpunished. "We grew up together in Philadelphia."

A hundred childhood memories of Chip and him flowed through his brain like a movie reel; riding the El on summer nights to go downtown and hang out; running up the steps of the Philadelphia Museum of Art and acting out the final moment of *Rocky,* or hiding out in the gardens of the Rodin Museum and taking Polaroids next to the green statues. He was thankful for those times together. They'd spent college semesters, summer vacations, and Christmas holidays in and out of each others' houses. When they left college he'd gone to law school and Chip had taken a job in a government computer lab. Never seeing him again was something he didn't think he'd have to deal with until they were very old men.

"Who is he?" Sandra's voice brought him out of his daydream.

"He was my best friend. We'd known each other since we were children. Two weeks ago he was . . . died," he finished.

Sandra leaned forward, placing her hand on his knee. "I'm sorry." She felt the tremor run through him when her hand touched him. She wanted to remove it, but that would call attention to the gesture. She let it be.

Wyatt leaned forward and took her hand. It was soft and slender, with long, unpolished fingernails. He needed the contact. When he told her about Chip he needed an anchor, and she was the closest he could get. "His name was Edward Jackson, Jr., but everyone who knew him called him Chip. His family had always called him that, although most people thought it was because he was a computer wizard. I don't mean just *good.*" He felt the need to explain. "I mean a real wizard. He'd always been that way. He excelled in math, and no problem eluded him for long."

Wyatt remembered Chip's perseverance when he was involved in a problem. He'd keep at it, relentlessly, until he'd picked every concept apart and mastered it. Wyatt often envied his friend this ability. It wasn't until he'd been given his first indigent client that Wyatt knew the feelings Chip derived when he solved some abstract problem.

"Chip worked for the Defense Department. He was working on something top secret. The only thing I know about it is the name Project Eagle, and those stones have something to do with it."

"How did Chip die?"

Wyatt swallowed and closed his eyes. He let go of her hand and sat back in the chair. The horror of what he'd seen when he got to Chip's house was more than he wanted to remember. He'd been tortured. Wyatt hardly recognized the body when he identified it. "He died of stab wounds," he said supplying the minimum of truth.

"By the same man who stabbed you?"

Wyatt stared directly at her. She sat bathed in light, apparently not realizing they were discussing something as final as his mortality.

"I believe so."

"What do those stones have to do with this Project Eagle?"

"I don't know. They arrived in an envelope with only the words written on the outside. When I began asking about them, people tried to kill me."

"You said Chip worked for the Defense Department. My father is chairman of the congressional defense subcommittee. Do you think he knows what Project Eagle is?"

Wyatt gritted his teeth. "Yes." He spoke the single word, watching her with a steady gaze for any sign of change. He got none. Whatever Bradford Campbell Rutledge had done, his daughter was unaware of it.

"Why did you think he was here?"

"He wasn't in his office. The only information I could get from his secretary was that he wasn't in the city. At his house, the maid said he was away and she didn't know when he'd return. I knew about this place and how secluded it was reported to be. I thought it was the next logical step. Finding you was a surprise."

Her head came up at that. She had the most expressive eyes, very light brown, much like the cat-eye marbles he'd had as a child. He couldn't help staring into them.

"A lucky surprise," he went on. "I would have died on the road."

She opened her mouth, then closed it quickly as if she wanted to say something, but thought better of it.

"Wyatt?" she asked a moment later. "What connected Project Eagle to my father?"

He knew she'd put two and two together soon. He dreaded having to tell her. The lights in her eyes would dim, and forever she'd look at him as the enemy.

When he got the envelope he'd called the senator. Wyatt didn't know much about defense, but Chip had worked there and Senator Rutledge was chairman of the subcommittee. He'd called and left a message. He mentioned Project Eagle. That had been a mistake. That same day he'd been involved in a car accident. He narrowly escaped, but the other car and its sole occupant had died. After that he'd been followed. He had managed to lose the man following him and had hidden for a week, all the while trying to reach the senator. He'd finally decided to try to find the Rutledge's cabin when he'd been attacked.

"Wyatt, please answer me," Sandra said.

"I think you'd better have a really good look at those stones."

Sandra glanced over her shoulder and back at him. His gaze was steady. Unfamiliar fear slid up her spine, and she got to her feet. Hesitantly, she went to the table. The remnants of their meal sat before her in pools of leftover food. Before Wyatt's plate lay the loose diamonds. They were large, several carats each, some larger than others. She picked up one of them and stared at it. Then she lifted it to the light and squinted to see what was inside. She could make out something more than a natural flaw, but she couldn't see what it was.

Remembering her mother's medical surgery, she grabbed the stones and headed for it.

"Hey!" Wyatt called from behind her.

Sandra didn't stop. She went through to the room her mother had insisted be part of the construction. It was originally a den, but had been converted into a country doctor's office. It had all the equipment Melissa Rutledge would need for light emergencies which happened more often than expected in these hills.

By the time Wyatt's aching side brought him to the door, she had one stone under the powerful magnification of the microscope. Sandra leaned back in the chair. It rolled several inches before she put her foot on the metal rail and stopped the motion.

"They're fake," she said.

"Fake!" Wyatt pushed her aside and stared into the microscope. "Someone is trying to kill me for fake stones?"

"I thought you knew they were fake."

"I knew there was something inside them, but I thought they were real." He looked up at her, then back into the microscope. "What's in there? It doesn't make any sense."

"They're microchips," Sandra explained. "And by the size of them, you can't buy these at your local computer store." She looked at him for an explanation.

"Where could you buy them?" He straightened, staring at her.

Sandra hesitated for a moment. Then she looked directly at him. "If I had to guess, I'd say these are not for sale."

"Why is that?"

"Most computer chips are just over an inch in length. Even the simms that go inside today's machines are about as long as your fingernail." Both of them stared at his short, manicured nails. "These are less than half that size. They're strictly government issue—and a secret issue at that." She waited for the information to sink in.

"How do you know that?" Wyatt asked.

"When I was in college my father got me a summer job working in the government printing office. I found out the government catalogs everything. There's a part number for everything from the smallest component to an entire system. The numbering system is unique to the government. And one of them is on this chip."

Wyatt looked into the microscope. The number was small and barely discernible, but could be seen.

"Why would anyone put microchips inside diamonds?"

Sandra knew he spoke more to himself than to her. Why, indeed? she wondered.

"Why did your friend send these to you? Why not someone else, someone in the military?"

"I don't know." Wyatt pulled himself up on the gurney where he'd lain a few days earlier. He looked tired. Sandra realized it was his first day out of bed and that he really should be back there now. Yet, she wanted to know what he thought about her father.

"Do you know what Chip was working on?"

Wyatt shook his head. "His projects were frequently secret. Many times he'd be sequestered on some mountain or other. I never knew where and how long he'd be out of the public eye. Over the years I'd learned not to ask about his work. Whenever I called him I'd leave messages, and when he was in town he'd return them."

Sandra slid herself forward and stared into the eyepiece. Metal prongs stared up at her. She had the magnification level at 150X. What were these for? she wondered. Looking up, she picked up one of the other stones she'd laid next to the machine. She turned it over and over in her hand, running her finger over the facets. One side was smooth, while the other was rough. Why?

Going back to the microscope, she turned the stone over and looked at it again. There was something there. Pushing her hair back, she reached for the focusing knob and turned it. The blur lessened but didn't bring it to crystal clarity. On the surface of the stone was a definite symbol. She squinted, trying to focus. She thought she recognized it as a scientific notation, but she didn't know what it meant.

"Did Chip have a connection with something scientific?" Sandra removed one stone and replaced it with a different one.

"Why?" Wyatt came to stand behind her.

"There are symbols on these." She replaced the stone again. When she'd seen the third symbol, she rolled the chair back to allow Wyatt access.

"I haven't the slightest idea what they mean," he said with a sigh.

"Neither do I," she said. "But they have to mean something. I can't accept that they've been put there for decoration."

Sandra was sure they were some kind of instruction, maybe necessary to a specific configuration. She was speculating, knowing she didn't have enough information to form any kind of hypothesis, let alone a theory. She wasn't going to find anything more tonight. She needed to talk to Jeff Taylor, her own computer whiz kid.

Wyatt's eyes were nearly closed when she looked at him. She should suggest he go to bed, and she would, right after she asked one more question.

"Wyatt, I've looked at the stones. I've found the symbols and the chips inside. Now, what do these have to do with my father?"

She watched him swallow heavily. "I think Project Eagle is either part of or the whole top-level computer system being developed by the Defense Department."

Sandra stared at him. She waited for more, but Wyatt didn't seem to be forthcoming. "So," she prompted.

Wyatt didn't want to tell her. For a while longer he watched the play of light in her eyes. He hadn't met a woman in a long time who affected him the way she did, but she was Senator Rutledge's daughter, a woman he'd never know. His teeth clenched.

"I think your father wants to sell it to the highest bidder."

CHAPTER 4

Sandra stared at Wyatt over breakfast the next morning. He'd been too tired the night before, she told herself. He didn't know what he was saying. He had to be reacting to the stab wound in his side. Maybe she'd fed him too much medication. She didn't know. She only knew that after she left him she couldn't sleep.

This morning she was calmer, although her mind whirled with questions. Wyatt hadn't said more than good morning, but he looked a lot better. Somehow it angered her that she'd tossed and turned and he'd rested well.

"Would you repeat what you said last night?" she asked, hoping he didn't remember, that he'd been too upset by the stones and his friend's death to think rationally.

"You father is trying to have me killed so he can get the stones and sell them to a foreign government," he said.

Sandra sat still, stunned. He might think she hadn't heard him. She didn't care. Whatever she thought he might say, this was not it. Her father was no traitor.

"You have to be mistaken," she said, her voice calm and controlled, as if she was ordering a ham sandwich on white bread. She got up, brushing past him and folding her hands over herself. She paced the small dining area.

"I'm not mistaken." Wyatt followed her, turning her around and forcing her to look into his face. His gaze was steady. Sandra knew he was serious, but he was wrong. She snatched her arm free.

"You're accusing my father of . . . of—"

"Treason," Wyatt completed the sentence.

The word stung her. *Treason.* She'd learned it in school, connected to people like Benedict Arnold and Judas Iscarius, but not her father. He had to be wrong. Bradford Campbell Rutledge was the most honest man in America. He truly believed he could make a difference, that his work in the Senate was the best place for him to exercise change. Doing anything to endanger the safety of the United States just wasn't in him.

"On what information do you base this accusation?" Sandra found her anger rising, but she took a deep breath to try to control it.

"For starters, your father is a member of a very powerful senate defense committee. He's privileged to many secret documents and finances that are not accounted for or controlled."

Sandra frowned, wondering where he was going.

"When I got the stones and the note, he was the first person I confided in, and since that time I've been followed, beaten, stabbed, and nearly frozen to death. My house has been ransacked and I haven't had a moment's peace. All because I mentioned Project Eagle to your father. What would you think in my situation?"

"That's all circumstantial."

"I assure you the knife in my gut was far from circumstantial."

"I'm not talking about a knife," she exploded. "You know my father didn't stab you."

"No, but whoever did was sent by Senator Rutledge."

He'd said her father's name as if it tasted of dirt. Sandra didn't like it. He was making no sense and she felt as if she needed to know what had happened to lead him to this conclusion. She knew part of her was attracted to him, and she couldn't be attracted to a man who thought her father tried to have him killed.

"You said you didn't know exactly what Project Eagle was, so why do you think it's important enough to kill over?"

"One man is already dead."

"We don't know that his death is related. Yes, he sent you the stones, but his death could have another explanation."

"Like what?"

Sandra swallowed. She searched her brain for a reason, but she had none. She didn't know Chip Jackson, didn't know his personality or if he had something in his past that would get him killed. She didn't know Wyatt Randolph's, either. He had been stabbed and could have died, so he had a right to be upset, but he hadn't convinced her that her father had anything to do with Project Eagle, Chip's death, or Wyatt's condition.

"I never met Chip," she began. "I don't know what kind of life he led, but he could have had enemies. His death and the diamonds could be totally unrelated."

"And Kwanzaa doesn't follow Christmas."

Sandra continued to hold on to her temper, but she realized she was on a short fuse. "I have a good mind to throw you out of here." She took a menacing step forward. "You come up here in a car that's designed to get stuck in snow. Then I find you, save your stinking life, and you repay me by accusing my father of treason."

"Calm down," he told her. He took a step forward, but when Sandra recoiled, he stopped.

"I will not calm down. I should have left you freezing to death in that car. Then I'd be obliviously studying for my exam and know nothing about you, Chip, or Project Eagle."

She scooped the stones from the table and put them into the small box where she'd stored them. Closing the lid, she determinedly walked to Wyatt and stuffed them in his shirt pocket. "Now get out of here. I never want to—"

"Quiet!" Wyatt shouted above her shrill voice.

"Don't tell me to—"

He grabbed her arms. In one fluid movement he swung her around, clamped a hand over her mouth, and used the other hand to pull her body against the solid wall of his.

Her free arms proved a weapon he hadn't counted on. With her elbow she wrenched it into his gut, forcing the air from his lungs and connecting with the one tender spot in his side that sent pain signals to his whole body. Surprised, he released her, his hand reaching toward his side. Taking advantage of his shifting weight, she flipped him over. His body sprawled on the braided rug. Stunned momentarily and unmindful of the pain in his side, he shook his head to clear it, then grabbed her leg and pulled her down to the floor with him. She struggled, but his superior strength won out and he reversed positions until he was lying on top of her. She squirmed under him.

"Listen," he whispered in her ear.

Sandra went still. The unmistakable sound of an engine broke through the silence. Wyatt moved his hand.

"Are you expecting anybody?"

"No," she told him, wrenching around and looking over her head toward the window. "Brian would have called first and—"

"Who's Brian?"

"A forest ranger." She returned her gaze to him. "He calls a couple of times every day—on the shortwave."

"Would he come to check on you?" The urgency in his voice must have frightened her. He felt a shiver run through her body.

"Not as long as I let him know I'm all right."

"Go call him." It was a distinct order. "Find out if he's up here."

He rolled off her.

Sandra hesitated, then sat up.

"Stay down," he ordered again, his voice a stage whisper, his arm forcing her back to the floor.

"Wyatt, what's going on?"

"Stay away from the windows." Another order, but no answer to her question.

"If you're trying to scare me, it's working."

Wyatt squeezed her shoulder in an assuring gesture. His eyes had a sadness in them telling her he knew he'd involved her in whatever had gotten him stabbed and he was sorry for it. Emotions raged inside her. Suppose he was telling the truth and the men who tried to kill him were outside. She was anything but assured. Why did he have to intrude in her life? Why was she attracted to him and how could he think her father could possibly sell American secrets to the highest bidder?

"He didn't do it, Wyatt," she whispered. Her voice cracked.

Wyatt's head turned slowly and he stared into her eyes. He didn't speak for a long moment. "Stay away from the windows," he repeated.

Sandra raised herself up on her knees and crawled toward the radio room.

He left her side to press his back to the wall next to the living-room window like an actor from a spy movie.

"Go," he told her, peering through the curtain.

Sandra's knees were weak, but she found they supported her as she moved.

Sandra threw the switch, grabbed the earphones and mike and held one in each hand.

"K5895 calling K7950. Brian are you there? Over."

The familiar crackle startled her, telling her how raw Wyatt had made her nerves with his spy tactics.

"K5895, go ahead. Over."

"This is Sandra Rutledge at the top of the mountain. I'm looking for Brian Court."

"Hi, Sandy . . . I'm—Ms. Rutledge, this is Olson Andrews." Sandra knew Olson's father must be close-by. He'd called her Sandy ever since her family had first come to the mountain and met them. Their families had become close friends. But Olson's dad was a stickler for the rules and Olson only called her Ms. Rutledge when someone could hear him. "Brian is off today and tomorrow. Is there something I can help you with? Over."

She suddenly remembered Brian telling her he'd be away helping his sister move.

"Olson," she began, controlling her voice. She didn't want to panic if there was no need. All she knew was she heard an engine and Wyatt had gone into severe-caution mode.

"I was wondering if they'd cleared the roads yet?"

"Only the trails, ma'am, and access to them."

She knew business came first. Skiing was a revenue-producing sport for the winter and all catering went there first. It was one of the reasons her mother had bought Starfighter. In an emergency she had to have immediate access off this mountain.

"I'm afraid it'll be a few more days before we can reach you, unless this is an emergency. Over."

Wyatt came in at that moment. Her gaze went to his face. His features had paled to a dull gray. All tenderness and compassion had left it. Harsh angles showed in the ruthless square of his jaw.

"Do you need immediate assistance? Over."

She looked to Wyatt for the answer. His silent gaze told her he was concerned.

"Olson, I have Senator Wyatt Randolph with me. He's been stabbed—" Wyatt snatched the mike away. The button she'd been holding to speak snapped up and opened the channel to listen.

"Christ! Sandy, did I hear you right?"

The unmistakable sound of Olson Andrews, Sr., boomed into the room, reverberating off the walls as if he had brought his bulk in person.

"You heard right," Wyatt said. "We need assistance immediately, unless you have a trawler on its way here."

Sandra could feel Wyatt next to her. Everything about him had changed. He was alert, and a strength exuded from him like a lion ready to do battle. Somehow she pushed the fear gathering around her heart away and pressed the speaker button.

"Uncle Olson, we're taking Starfighter. Clear the area. Out."

She didn't wait for the weather report or wind conditions. Instinctively she knew time was limited. They had to get out and get out now! Using as little effort as possible and taking no time to explain, Sandra threw open the closet and took out John's jacket and boots. She didn't give herself time to ask why she'd never thrown them away.

"Put these on." She pushed them into Wyatt's chest.

He didn't argue or waste time asking where they were going. He'd seen her ride out on the small snowmobile. It wasn't much of a chance, but it was the only one they had.

Wyatt trudged through the thick snow. He was out of shape after being confined for more than a week. His side ached and the brightness blinded him. Used to working out every day, his inactivity showed in his laboring efforts to keep up with Sandra. Even with his heart beating fast, he wondered what Sandra did to keep in shape. She seemed to have no problem with the deep snow. Even carrying the backpack which contained her laptop, notes, and a few books she'd been studying, she easily slipped through the whiteness.

"We had better hurry," she threw over her shoulder.

I'm trying, he thought but didn't say. His side split and pain burned up his chest to his armpits. Within sight was the building where she'd parked the snowmobile and his car. He wondered why it wasn't closer to the house. Why hadn't they attached the garage? The place was built within the last twenty years. Attached garages weren't a novelty then. Yet, this shed was several hundred yards from the house.

Sandra slid a door to the side and disappeared inside. He followed as fast as he could. Behind him the sound of the engine was getting closer. It trudged along slowly. Wyatt wondered what kind of vehicle it could be. It didn't sound like a car engine. He couldn't tell how many rpm he heard at this distance. It could be a snowmobile. For some reason it sounded like a—tank. He rejected the idea. What would a tank be doing in the Pocono Mountains?

He entered the building where Sandra had gone. What he saw made the possibility of a tank not so farfetched. In front of him was a helicopter. Looking like a giant bug in the darkened cavern, Wyatt stood frozen in place.

"Damn," he cursed. "And I was thinking about a snowmobile." Relief spread through him. They had an avenue of escape. It had been there and she'd known about it all along.

The helicopter was equipped with both wheels and skids. Sandra was already in the cockpit placing earphones over her ears.

"Can you fly this thing?" he shouted above the noise created by her turning on gauges and flipping switches. His heart began to pound again. Maybe they wouldn't be able to escape. Checking over his shoulder he expected men to suddenly burst through the door, guns drawn, and begin shooting. "Can you fly this thing?" he repeated, this time with more urgency in his voice.

"Better than I can perform medical procedures. Get in."

"Are you sure?" Wyatt hesitated. He wasn't sure he wanted to die in a helicopter accident in the snow-covered mountains of Pennsylvania. "That snow trawler is getting closer."

"It's a piece of cake, Wyatt." She glared at him. "This is an Enstrom F-28C. It has a supercharged Lycoming HIO-360 piston engine that generates over 200 horsepower. The engine operates on 100 octane gasoline and it's blue. Feel better?"

"Only if you tell me you can fly it."

"I start the engine, engage the rotor clutch, bring the throttle up to takeoff power of 2900 rpm's, pull the collective until the skid is approximately three to five feet off the ground, use the tail rotor pedals to rotate into the wind, push the cyclic to lower the nose slightly and accelerate to a climb speed of sixty knots. And then I fly. Any questions?"

"None," he said. He couldn't hear the engine of the other vehicle above the chopping sound of the one he was in, but he was sure they, whoever they were, were getting closer.

Swinging himself into the seat next to her, he slid the glass door closed. She pulled a stick forward and the air-car eased forward. It rolled onto the snow. Wyatt was sure it would sink into the soft powder, but she worked the controls and he felt the heavy machine settle. He knew she had changed from wheels to skis.

"There they are." He pointed to three men trying valiantly to negotiate the elements and get to the helicopter.

Sandra looked in their direction. "They have guns!" she exclaimed as a shot rang out. It missed them, but startled Sandra. She pulled the stick forward, and the chopper lifted off the ground. A flurry of snow churned below them like an explosion of feathers. The men on the ground shot blindly through the cloud. Wyatt raised his hand, warding off possible injury. Sandra raised the metal bird on an angle, then banked right, directly over the men chasing them.

Wyatt felt the air pressure change as she ascended. As soon as she cleared the trees she headed south. He could see the men on the ground scurrying back to the trawler. One of them raised his fist to the sky. He squinted but recognized no one. Who were they? They probably scared Sandra to death.

"K9051, calling K7950. Over." Sandra adjusted the mouthpiece connected to her headset as she spoke.

"Sandy, what's going on?" She'd called Olson Andrews her uncle ever since she was a little girl.

"We're in Starfighter and heading for the station. Several men with guns got out of a trawler and shot at us."

"Are you hurt?" His voice boomed into her ears. She looked at Wyatt. He'd put his earphones on and was listening to the conversation. He shook his head.

"We're fine."

"Good."

She could hear the relief in his voice.

"You come on in. Pad F is free."

Before she could answer, Wyatt stopped her. "What's the range on this helicopter?"

She checked the fuel gauge. It was full. "Five or six hundred miles, why?"

"We can't go to the ranger station. They would have left men there."

"You don't know that."

"They couldn't have just found this place. They came in a snow trawler, not your standard snow vehicle for Pennsylvania. They were determined to find me. Sandra, they're not stupid. If they got that far, they certainly covered their bases."

She opened the channel. "Uncle Olson, are you alone?"

"No, there are other men on duty, but no one is in the room at the moment. What's on your mind?"

"Mr. Andrews, this is Wyatt Randolph. Are there any strangers at the station?"

"There've been people all over for days, what with the good weather and all the snow we've had. A stranger wouldn't be noticed."

"What about people asking for directions to Senator Rutledge's cabin?"

"A few days ago, before the roads were cleared, a couple of guys asked about skiing in that area, but left when we told them there were no trails that way."

Wyatt cut the transmission again. "We can't go there," he told her again. "Believe me, Sandra, I've been running from these guys long enough to know they'd leave someone behind. Go somewhere else."

"Sandy!" She heard her name screamed into her ears. "What are you doing? You've just passed over us."

"What do I tell him?" she asked Wyatt.

He hesitated for a moment, thinking. "Don't tell him anything. Cut the speaker."

"I can't—"

Wyatt yanked the earphones and speaker from her. The sound of the rotors vibrating deafened her. She had to use her hands to control the aircraft and couldn't let go to fight him. Then she remembered *she* had control. She could turn and sit down on Pad F or she could keep going. However, men *had* chased them and fired shots as they escaped from the cabin. It wasn't too far a reach to believe what he said about there being men at the ranger station. Pad F was out in the open. If they did sit down and someone was waiting, they'd have no cover and no time to take off again.

Giving him the benefit of the doubt, she quickly adjusted the controls and laid in a course for the nation's capital. If he was telling the truth, she wanted verification, and where better to get it than from her own father? They could go to Washington and all this would be cleared up in a matter of minutes. At least her father's part would be cleared up. She didn't know what it would take to get rid of the men shooting at them.

CHAPTER 5

The lights of the capital dazzled like fiery points in the distance ahead. Sandra watched them come closer as she angled the aircraft forward. She rarely got to see the monuments from this angle, bathed in light and Lilliputian size. Usually she entered the capital from the Baltimore-Washington Parkway, a heavily trafficked route where she was more concerned about negotiating the converging lanes and the many vehicles on the road than checking out the scenery.

Careful not to stray into restricted airspace, she headed for Washington National Airport in nearby Virginia. Wyatt had been deep in thought since he realized she wasn't heading for the ranger station. She didn't disturb him but flew silently for the hour trip to the District.

Suddenly he sat up straight and asked, "What are we doing here?"

"My parents live here," she offered as explanation.

"Coming here is like taking out an ad. I can't go anywhere in this town where I won't be recognized."

"Then it seems like the best place to hide. Who would expect you to return home?"

"Those same guys who found me at the cabin will have my house watched. Just how do you think we can survive here?"

She wondered if he knew he'd included her in his plans. She wasn't sure she wanted to be part of them, but she didn't have a choice until this business about her father being a traitor was laid to rest.

"We won't go to your house. We'll go someplace else."

"Where? We can't walk up to the senator's house. I'd be dead before I cleared the first flagstone."

"You've been to the house before?" Sandra's eyebrows raised. The courtyard to her family's Georgetown address was inlaid with pink and green flagstones.

"Only once, and I didn't get out of the car."

He stopped abruptly and Sandra was afraid to ask him why. He looked agitated. It could be due to a real fear that there were people on the ground who wanted to kill him, but it could also be that he'd been lying all along. Sandra had to find out which was the truth.

Why would he lie? she wondered. Lying usually meant a person had something to gain. In her role as instructor of mathematics, she heard plenty of student lies; everything from oversleeping to the death of a family member. What would Wyatt have to gain? She had no answer for that. She'd only known him a little over a week, and looking objectively at the circumstances of his arrival and the story he'd told her, she wasn't sure where the truth lay. Yet, she knew the part about her father had to have another explanation and she was determined to prove it.

As she approached the airport she reached for the switch to talk to the control tower. Wyatt's larger hand covered hers.

"What are you planning to tell them?"

"That I need landing instructions."

"And when we get to the ground?"

"Wyatt, they don't know you're with me."

"What about that ranger? He didn't radio ahead?"

"He didn't know where we were headed."

"He might have guessed. You are a senator's daughter. Where else would you go except back to the nest?"

"I don't live with my father. For all Uncle Olson knows I could have flown to Johnson Hall."

"It might have been better if we had gone there—wherever there is."

"Johnson Hall is the name of the building that houses the corporate headquarters of the mega-health care company, Johnson and Johnson. They have a heliport in New Brunswick. The building was constructed in the style of the university with an angular roof and cupola. It sits directly across the street from the main campus where I teach." She paused a moment, glancing at him to check his reaction. "They don't allow private landings except for their executives."

"All right," he conceded. "I suppose if they knew I was at your father's cabin, they also know about you."

Sandra shuddered. She remembered the men with the guns and being shot at. The idea that someone might be watching her house in New Brunswick scared her.

"There are a few rules I insist on when we land." Wyatt's voice pulled her out of the shock.

"I'm listening."

"First, you get out alone. Tell no one, *no one,* I'm here or that you have seen me."

Sandra nodded agreement.

"Then get a taxi and go to the Commodore Hotel. I'll meet you there."

Sandra hovered above the heliport, dropping altitude on an easy cushion of air. National Airport was busy for both planes and helicopters. No one took any notice of them.

Wyatt suddenly popped his seat belt and climbed behind her seat. He wouldn't be seen by anyone coming toward them when they reached the ground. Sandra touched down inside the brightly painted circle on the ground. She reached for the switches to begin shutting down the engine when Wyatt stopped her.

"Wait," he said.

"In there." He pointed to a gray-painted hangar not far from where she'd set down. A small sign reading Richard's Aviation hung on the outside wall.

She looked at him. "It's highly unusual," she said.

"I don't care."

Sandra taxied the helicopter into the hangar. She gathered her backpack and prepared to open the door.

"One more thing," he said, his hand on her left arm. "Take these." He threw a small box into her lap.

"You're giving me the stones?"

"Not all of them. Just enough for insurance."

"Insurance?"

"You don't really believe everything I've said. In case anything happens to me, I won't have all the stones, and whatever their purpose, all of them are necessary to accomplish it."

"I'm to be your safety net?"

"Not exactly. If I don't survive, you're the next target."

Wyatt could see her walking away from him. Her hips swayed from side to side. He couldn't help the sexual excitement that rushed to his loins as he watched. She didn't turn back and glance over her shoulder. He'd expected that she would. Maybe she'd bought into his story and thought looking back could alert anyone watching that she expected something else to take place. Disappointment tightened in his gut. In a moment he pushed it aside.

She swung the backpack onto her right shoulder and struck an easy gait. Her footsteps echoed in the cavernous hollow. The heavy parka she wore covered her from neck to knees. Her legs were protected by ski pants and she had on knee-length boots, yet he knew the body concealed under all that clothing. He'd held it against him and knew her softness and her smell.

He felt like a heel putting her in danger, but it had to be done. He told himself he had to be sensible, logical. If he were to survive he had to cover all the bases, and Sandra Rutledge believed staunchly in her father. He didn't know what she would do when confronted with the truth. If he'd given her all the stones, she could have turned them over to the man responsible for sabotaging Project Eagle. Yet, if his ability to judge character held, she would at least examine the options before making a decision. He was counting on that.

Wyatt had made her a target nonetheless. She'd gotten out of the helicopter in plain view. If someone had seen her they would have no problem in capturing her and finding out everything they needed to know. It was a risk, but he had to take it. He didn't want her hurt, and if there was anything he could do to prevent it, he would.

She'd been gone five minutes. Wyatt checked the exterior grounds for anyone who might be within sight. Scanning the area like a human periscope, he saw no one. He let himself out of the cockpit and skirted the ground until he reached the wall of the huge building. Quietly he listened for voices, any sign of life. Since he'd been on the run, his life had depended on his powers of sight and hearing. He could hear a pin drop during a hurricane or a gun cocking in the horn-honking cacophony of rush hour traffic.

Rejecting the obvious avenue of escape, he looked about for another exit. There were no windows, only giant doors at both ends of the building.

Deciding to take the one opposite from Sandra's choice, he worked his way around the hollowed room and blended into the shadows near the slate-colored wall. He skimmed the edge and peered outside. It was bright, as cloudless an afternoon sky as any pilot could ask for. Visibility was probably endless. Activity went on everywhere. If he stepped outside, anyone could see him. Sandra had walked about freely and no one stopped her. Maybe if he followed her lead, acting as if he belonged here and knew what he was doing, no one would take notice of him, either.

Looking behind him, he took stock of the hangar. The helicopter was the only occupant. Around the room were different machines used to diagnose mechanical problems in the equipment, an old luggage cart without the Jeep to drive it, cans of oil and dirty rags, and someone's baseball cap. He took the cap and pulled it down over his head. A pair of overalls lay on the luggage cart with the name "Adam" stitched onto the breast pocket. Wyatt slipped into them. They covered most of him, leaving his boots and about five inches of his pant legs showing above them. Reaching down, he stuffed his pants into the boots. He didn't think he'd pass the *GQ* male-model test in this outfit, but he hoped it was good enough to pass as a mechanic.

It was the best he could do. With an I-belong-here-and-know-what-I'm-doing attitude, he strolled casually out of the hangar and walked toward the arrivals building. If he got to the building, he'd discard the "borrowed" clothes in the first men's room he came to, but he'd keep the hat, then jump into a cab.

He made it, almost.

"Hey, mister." A kid of about eleven stood behind him. Wyatt stopped, thinking it was better to find out what the kid wanted than to ignore him and have him begin making loud comments to his back. He remembered being eleven well and knew how he and his friends used to act. The last thing he needed was to draw attention to himself.

"Are you lost?" Wyatt asked, hoping it was something as innocuous as that, and pointing him in the direction of the information booth.

"Aren't you that senator I saw on TV?"

So much for his chameleon act. Maybe he should have kept the mechanics clothes, not just the baseball cap. Wyatt checked his surroundings hoping no one had heard the boy. He might have been an intelligent kid, a good kid, but at the moment Wyatt wanted to muzzle him.

"Yeah, Senator Rut—Rut—something."

"Rutledge," Wyatt whispered, trying to keep the surprise out of his voice.

"Yeah, that's the one." A wide smile split his face revealing teeth that seemed too big for his mouth. "Can I have your autograph?"

Wyatt almost laughed with relief. "Of course. Do you have something I can write on?"

"I only have this." He shoved a copy of *Sports Illustrated for Kids* and a pen at him.

Wyatt smiled and took the magazine. He clicked the pen and signed Senator Rutledge's name in a script so unreadable no one would have a clue what it actually read. He handed the book and pen back to the boy.

"Gee, thanks, mister. Wait until I show my friends." With that, he was off, looking in one direction while he ran in the other. Wyatt could see he was going to collide with someone in the busy terminal and waited long enough to see it happen. The unlucky victim was a harried traveler carrying bags and cases. Everything went haywire, but the kid was unhurt.

Wyatt turned and went on. He felt luckier, freer, his shoulders not so bent with the weight of the burden he carried. Outside again, he walked to the curb, pulling the baseball cap further down to hide his face. He opened the door of the first cab that pulled up, stopping short when he saw the interior was occupied. His gaze met the boots first, knee-length black boots joined ski pants, and recognition registered in his brain.

"Hello, sweetheart," Sandra said, reaching toward him and nodding her head at the taxi driver.

"I was detained," he told her as he got in and took her in his arms for a staged kiss. Wyatt kept his face away from the cabdriver. He knew this was Sandra's reason for kissing him.

It was a quick embrace; the pressing together of unresponsive flesh. Wyatt told himself that's all it was and all it was supposed to be, but in the second that Sandra's arms loosened, he looked down at her and some spark between them ignited. For an eon they looked deep into each other's eyes. Her breath mingled with his. He could taste her without touching the warm sweetness of her mouth. He knew he shouldn't. This was the moment to pull back, to turn to the driver and give him a destination. This was not the time to think about how good she looked this close, how sweet she smelled, and how his body longed for hers.

The groan in his throat died as his lips closed the small space separating them and pressed against hers. Nothing about her was the same. No longer did unresponsive flesh touch him. Her mouth was searing, sweet as chocolate syrup, and wonderful. He knew it could take him places, knew this woman could change his world, but he couldn't let that happen. He couldn't let her.

She pushed him away. He could see her eyes pleading with him. They were deep with an unknown mystery; something far and hidden that held a secret only she knew and was unable or unwilling to reveal. Wyatt understood. He wondered if his own eyes told her what he was feeling. His gaze dropped to her lips. They were slightly parted, dark and swollen, from his kisses. He wanted to kiss her again, wanted to understand the depths of her being and ask all the questions that crowded his mind and begged for answers. He would have asked them, too, except that the taxi driver interrupted him.

"Where to?" Wyatt turned to find the widely grinning driver staring at them.

"The White House," Wyatt said.

They got out on the corner of 15th Street and Pennsylvania Avenue near the Treasury Department. No longer could cars enter the two block area which ran directly in front of the President's residence. Tourists milled about in the asphalt garden. The pleasant January afternoon brought out more people than a rainy, wintry day would have. Sandra wished it had been raining. At least they'd have reason to conceal their faces.

Cameras snapped as couples posed before the wrought-iron gates to capture evidence of their visit to Washington. Wyatt adjusted the baseball cap and kept his back to the area.

"What are we doing here?" Sandra asked. "This place is teeming with tourists. If you didn't want to be recognized, why didn't we go to the Capitol and hang out in your office?" The facetiousness in her voice was apparent.

"I couldn't think of anyplace else. My house has already been ransacked and your father's house isn't a place I want to approach without scoping it out first."

He spoke like an army officer planning strategy for some war.

"Well, at least I can call."

Sandra pulled her backpack off and fished inside it for a quarter. Finding a phone near Riggs National Bank, she dialed her parents' Washington residence. Wyatt leaned against the side of the building, his head down, his face completely concealed from anyone passing by.

Moments later, Sandra depressed the receiver button. "He's not home and not expected until very late," she explained, then asked if Wyatt had a quarter. Wyatt gave her the coin and she dialed the Senate Office Building. "He's not there, either."

"We've got to get off the street," Wyatt said, apparently not surprised she couldn't locate her father. "We're going to need a place where we're not likely to be recognized."

"I'm not sure we can do that with all the press coverage you've received but, come on, I have an idea."

"This is your idea?" Wyatt asked ten minutes later as the taxi dropped them on 4th Street in northwest Washington near the reservoir. "We're going to hide in the dorms?"

Behind them stood the Howard University Quadrangle, a configuration of five dormitories enclosing a large courtyard that hid a flowering magnolia tree. Sandra had spent her freshman year in Truth Hall.

"The dorm is not our destination." Sandra turned and faced the hill that led to the main campus of the one hundred and thirty-year-old institution of higher education. They crossed the street and went through the iron gates. Students passed them hurrying to classes or getting out of the cold. No one took any special notice of who they were.

Sandra remembered her days here. Time hadn't stood still, but she could almost hear Marjorie Lanley, her roommate, using their sorority signal to call her from the opposite side of the campus.

Founders Library sat on her left, and the School of Home Economics on the right. Past the Home Ec Building the main campus opened up into an expanse of walkways and winter-brown grass. The School of Religion stood directly in front of her, while Douglass Hall stood next to it. Directly across from the famous columned classroom building was the New Building. It had a name but no one used it. Though the building had been completed in the early sixties, this name endured. In the basement was the computer center. There she knew she'd find Jefferson Taylor, III, a forty-year-old, five-foot-tall, gray-haired man with eyes as sharp as a cat. She'd see Jeff later. Now they had to find someplace to hide.

"Where are we going?" Wyatt asked as they passed Crampton Auditorium and headed onto Georgia Avenue.

"I hope you don't mind walking a bit."

"I don't mind walking, but I'd like to know where we're going."

"Trust me, Wyatt. If I wanted to turn you in I could have called the cops from the helicopter."

They walked over to 16th Street and up to the 4000 block. On Shepherd Street, Sandra turned, and two blocks later entered a house on Crestwood Drive.

"Who lives here?" Wyatt asked.

"No one," she said, dropping the backpack by the door. "It's my house." She pulled the white sheet from a chair and threw it in the corner. "My grandmother left it to my sister and me when she died. Annie never uses it, so it's closed most of the year."

Sandra continued removing the sheets. Finally, she adjusted the thermostat and went through to the kitchen. "Why don't I make us come coffee. And why don't you make a fire in the living room. It'll be a while before it warms up in here."

"Will you stop with the Donna Reed act?" Wyatt sounded irritated.

Sandra had heard his irritation before and she knew it wouldn't last long. She hadn't been here since last summer and only then to make sure there was no trouble with the place. She kept the electricity and gas on, although it got minimal use. Today she was glad she'd never had it completely shut off. Sandra pulled the refrigerator door open, frowning when she found nothing there but clean shelves and bottles of mineral water.

Wyatt sighed and headed for the fireplace.

There was no milk, but she found non-dairy creamer in the cabinet. In a moment she had the machine dripping. There was little else in the refrigerator, but the freezer had remnants of last summer's stock. Wyatt had a roaring blaze in the hearth going when Sandra returned with a tray. She set it on the table and poured cups for them.

"We have to decide what we're going to do," she began.

"We? You're not part of this."

"Look, Wyatt Randolph." Sandra set her cup on the table and leaned toward him. "Might I remind you that you've already involved me. The moment you told me about those stones, I became part of this . . ." She didn't know how to end the sentence.

Wyatt looked away from her.

"You implicated my father in the worst imaginable crime short of murder. If you think I'm going to let you go off alone and make my father the scapegoat of some plot, you can think again."

"What do you propose to do?"

"I don't know." She stood up and walked to the fire. The heat was warm against her arms and legs. Suddenly, she whipped around. "But you haven't done anything, either. You ran for a week, then you got stabbed and nearly died. You ran to me and they found you. How long do you think you can keep running? You've got to have a plan or the next time you won't make it." She paused. "They'll kill you."

He heard the crack in her voice when she said "kill." She cared about him. He'd been angry with her, but the anger went when he realized there was as much fear in her voice as there was bravado.

"I have a plan. I need to talk to your father."

"Good idea," she agreed. "He could clear this up in no time."

The look he gave her told her he didn't believe it would.

"Suppose," he said. "Just for a moment, consider that I might be telling the truth."

Sandra hesitated. He couldn't be right but she went along with him. "All right. 'If you are telling the truth, and I don't believe for one minute you are, my father is the last person you should go to."

"What would be your suggestion in that case?"

She thought a moment. "Have those stones analyzed by someone who knows about computer chips. Find out what they can do and if they are the reason Chip was killed. If you're going to die, at least know the real reason."

Wyatt admired her. She was intelligent, loyal, and honest. He wanted her on his side, but her father stood between them. After this was over, if he lived, she'd never see him again. No matter what he felt for her, and she stirred more feelings in him than any woman ever had, they had no future.

"I would like to take them to someone, but the only people I know work for the Defense Department and I don't think it would be a good idea for me to walk in unannounced."

"Then let's take them to someone I know."

Wyatt glared at her. Had she planned this? Was he wrong about her? She could be setting him up. In no time he rejected the thought. If she wanted to set him up she'd had plenty of opportunity and she hadn't taken any of them. He had to trust her. There was no one else, and she was right, he couldn't run forever. His time was limited and whoever was looking for him had more resources than he did.

"Whom do you have in mind?"

"A professor I had in undergraduate school. He's here at Howard."

"Is that why we went there?"

She nodded. "After we started across campus I thought it would be better to discuss it with you first."

Wyatt almost hugged her. Obviously, she wasn't used to discussing her decisions with anyone. In his capacity as a US senator, he was constantly bouncing ideas off other senators, asking the opinion of advisors and counselors.

"Who is he?"

"He's a wizard," she smiled. "He knows everything there is to know about computers. I guess he's a little like Chip. He eats, sleeps, and dreams in cyberspace."

"Can he be trusted?"

"I've never had a top-secret project, but I'd say yes, he can be trusted."

"We'll go in the morning." Wyatt stood up and went to her. "Smile, Sandra, they haven't got us yet."

She didn't smile, but looked up at him. "There's one more thing you should know."

Wyatt braced himself. "What is it?"

"He used to work for the Defense Department."

CHAPTER 6

Casadia Androcles Horton had been called Casey all her life. She would be fifty years old in less than a week. The White House staff had been alerted that a huge party was planned for the occasion. Casey loved parties, had loved them since she was a child on her grandfather's ranch. People came from miles to attend one of his barbecues. Her coming-out party had been attended by the governor of the state along with several minor politicians. Also in attendance was a young law student named Everett Horton.

From that night to this one he'd never failed to inspire admiration in her and in the country which he now led as its President. She watched him and the men in the room. Everett was tired. His entire career rested on the problem of the missing system component. He hadn't slept well since this business began. She knew he wouldn't rest until it was over.

"What have we got, gentlemen?" Everett asked. His voice was strong, authoritative and sure. Five men sat on the sofas in the study. Melanie West occupied the wingback chair that faced the fireplace and the desk where Casey sat.

"Mr. President," Clarence Christopher, head of the Federal Bureau of Investigation, began. "We know he's with Senator Rutledge's younger daughter, Sandra. They left the mountain cabin and returned to Washington yesterday. Dr. Rutledge's helicopter was discovered at Washington National in an unauthorized hangar. From there we don't know where they went. Other than trying to reach her father, both at his residence and at his office, we know they haven't contacted anyone else connected with the defense system."

Casey listened without comment. She would have her say later directly to the President and without the opinions of the men in this room. When it came to the calm, orderly management of their respective agencies, they were competent, but in this kind of emergency, they were next to useless. Clarence was the best of the lot. He was also discreet. She trusted him and would believe anything he said and did.

". . . fired on as they escaped in the helicopter." Tyler Kirkus, Secretary of Defense, was speaking when she came back to the conversation. "We found bullet holes in the helicopter and one of the forest rangers told us Ms. Rutledge reported ground fire as she took off."

The discussion went on for two hours, each man talking but no one saying anything useful. Casey was glad to see them go when they finally filed out of the second-floor study.

"In all this subterfuge, Everett, the missing link is Brad Rutledge. Where is he and why hasn't anyone seen him the last week?" Everett's closest friend and advisor, Melanie West, asked the question. She'd been with him from the first, and Casey had long since ceased being jealous of her. Casey knew Melanie and her husband. She and Everett had sat with Caleb West at the cesarian births of both his daughter and son, and Casey had earnestly cried when both children married and moved away.

Everett kissed Melanie on the cheek and closed the door behind her. He sighed and turned back to the room. He came to Casey, reached for her hands, and she placed hers in his and stood. They hugged each other. She loved Everett Horton more than life itself.

"What did you think of them?" Everett asked.

"You know what I think of them. Except for Clarence and Melanie, you could fire the lot and not notice a loss."

Everett stepped back but kept his arm around her waist. Together they walked to the sofa and sat down.

"I need a drink," he said.

"I'll call—"

"No," he stopped her. "Don't call the staff. We keep them working enough without asking for more."

"Everett, they're pleased to serve you."

"I'll just have an orange juice." He started to get up.

"I'll get it for you." Casey knew how much weight his shoulders carried. She also knew he didn't expect her to serve him. He had as much concern for her as he did for the hour and the White House staff. She poured his orange juice into a wine goblet instead of a juice glass and handed it to him as she resumed her seat.

"Clarence said Sandra and Wyatt hadn't tried to contact anyone who would know about the system except her father."

Everett shook his head and gave his full attention to his wife. "They're obviously being cautious. There's nothing that can be done if they don't make a mistake, and so far they seem to be keeping those to a minimum."

"Maybe we shouldn't concentrate so much on them. What about people who aren't connected with the system?"

"Like who?"

"Well, if it were me, and I knew all my sources inside the agencies would lead to a possible death, I'd try to find someone who could help me who isn't connected with the government."

Everett leaned back. He looked like a light bulb of comprehension had gone off in his brain. "You think he'll use the senator's daughter as a source."

"I would." She took the glass he drank from and finished the juice. "We need to find out everything we can about Sandra Rutledge, and there will be our lead."

Sandra pushed the antenna down on the cellular phone. She bit her lower lip. Wyatt wasn't going to like what she had to tell him. Uncle Olson had been upset when she suddenly broke communications and flew off to an unknown destination. She knew he would be. He was volatile at times, but only because he was concerned about her. He wouldn't have told anyone about Wyatt until he'd talked to her, but the FBI had shown up and he was obligated to tell them about the shootout and the escape.

By now they'd discovered the helicopter and knew they were somewhere in the District. Wyatt hadn't awakened yet. He'd been dead tired after yesterday's ordeal. During their long walk she'd noticed him favoring his left side. He must have been in pain but he said nothing. Even after they arrived he didn't complain, but he did remain seated unless it was absolutely necessary that he move.

She made coffee and popped some of the muffins she'd run out and bought this morning at the bakery on Mt. Pleasant into the oven. It had been years since she stayed here with her grandmother. Few people recognized her and she felt quite safe in going the short distance. Her only concern would be the neighbors. Lights would notify them someone was in the house.

Placing the coffee on a tray, along with the muffins and *The Washington Post,* she was relieved there was no mention of her name in the story that featured Senator Wyatt Randolph's disappearance.

She knocked lightly on the door and opened it. Wyatt wasn't in the bed. He stood in front of the large window at the head of the room. The curtain dropped from his hand when she entered.

She'd been up since six. Wyatt wondered if she'd slept as badly as he had. He'd watched the car come out of the garage and circle the small cul-de-sac as it traveled to the end of the street and disappeared. He didn't know where she'd gone, but she'd returned within half an hour. During her absence he'd explored the rooms of her grandmother's house, finding photographs of both her and her sister, he assumed, in various poses and ages. She was no longer dressed in the ski outfit she'd left the mountain wearing. Maybe she was wearing her grandmother's clothes. Although he doubted her grandmother could ever have fit them as nicely as they outlined Sandra's curves. The bouncing ponytail was also gone. Her hair framed her face and curved to her shoulders. She stirred his sexual juices in a way he didn't want.

"Good morning," she said cheerfully.

"Where have you been?" he replied.

"I guess that means you didn't sleep well."

She set the tray on the end of the rumpled bed and started to pour cups of coffee. She was playing Donna Reed again, but this was not a situation that Donna Reed would ever find herself in. Wyatt didn't understand his anger. In three strides he came up beside her and wrenched her hands free of the coffee.

"Where have you been?" he repeated.

"Only to the bakery. We needed more to eat than refrigerated coffee."

His action had brought her body into close contact with his. She was looking directly at him. He could smell the soap she'd used in her morning shower. Clean and intoxicating. He stared into her eyes wondering what was happening to him. He thought she'd left him, run out, leaving him stranded and alone. The relief he felt when he saw the old Pontiac turn into the street was so weakening he'd had to sit down.

Now he had her, only a kiss away, and he couldn't deny the fact that he was glad she'd come back, couldn't deny that he liked holding her, that he'd liked it yesterday when she'd kissed him in the taxi and that he wanted to kiss her again.

"Wyatt," she said, her voice low and tight. "Let me go."

The moment snapped like a wet spider's web. Wyatt raised his hands and moved back. Sandra continued to stare at him for a long moment, then turned back and resumed preparation of their coffee.

He took his cup and went back to the window. There was little to see from here except Rock Creek Park sloping away from the end of the yard. His stomach was in such a hard knot he thought the coffee would hit it and evaporate into a steam that would incinerate him.

"Wyatt."

Sandra spoke his name in a whisper. He turned. She'd taken a seat on the edge of the bed. The light skimmed her hair. Wyatt blinked.

"I talked to Uncle Olson this morning."

She went on to explain her conversation. Both the FBI and Senator

Rutledge's men were looking for them. It was no longer only him. They knew about her. He didn't know whether the senator would sacrifice his own daughter for whatever the system they had meant, but it was too late to send her away. Whether he wanted a partner or not and whether he liked the way she made him feel or not, she was tied to him.

He should have been upset. He knew if he got into a mess it was better not to think about anyone except himself, but he'd been alone for so long and never even realized it until he'd found her in that cabin.

"What are you thinking?" she asked quietly.

Wyatt set his cup on the nightstand. Near the bed was a royal-blue velvet Queen Anne chair. Wyatt pulled it close to the bed and sat in front of Sandra.

"We have to get out of here." He took her hands in his. They were small in his large ones. "If your uncle told the FBI that you're with me, your life is being processed through every computer network inside the government. They already know everything about you—where you've been, who your friends are, and who their friends are. They'll know about this house and they'll come here."

She shuddered, pulling her hands back. He held them until she relaxed.

"They're the FBI. Aren't they on our side?"

"I don't know yet," he answered honestly.

He didn't know who was friendly and who wasn't. Until he did, the best thing was to proceed with caution. "We need to get out of here."

"All right." She stood up so abruptly, Wyatt had to move back. "There's only one more thing I need to do before we leave." She started for the door. He got up to follow her. "Stay here," she stopped him. "Take off your clothes and lie down on the bed."

Sandra signed the register card at the Best Western Motel on New York Avenue as Martha Dandridge. She smiled at the irony of using Martha Washington's maiden name.

"Here's your key, Mrs. Dandridge." The uniformed desk clerk smiled as she handed her the computer card. "It's around back, end of the second row of buildings. Enjoy your stay."

Sandra accepted the key to Room 178 and bent to pick up her suitcase.

"Oh, Mrs. Dandridge," the desk clerk called her. "Your receipt." The woman extended a small slip of paper. Sandra wasn't used to checking into motels, and the times she had, she'd always paid by credit card. Today she'd paid in cash. She looked like a tourist coming to the capital for a few days. A camera hung over her shoulder, and she carried a bag with new clothes for both her and Wyatt. He'd agreed to meet her at the room as soon as she called him with the number.

She found the room and went inside. It was standard motel decor, two double beds, a long dresser with a mirror, a round table suitable for making notes after a business meeting, and a bathroom with a double sink and mirror outside.

She dropped the camera on the bed near the wall and set her suitcase on the floor. Taking her key and purse, she left the room and found a pay phone near the closed pool area. She called Wyatt, who was waiting at another pay phone not far away.

He was there in minutes. Sandra swung open the door and helped him to the bed. "We can stay here for a few days, then we'll have to move again," he said, as she helped him out of his coat.

"Don't worry about moving now." She found the bottle of Tylenol she'd bought when she'd picked up the suitcase and clothes. Tearing the paper away from the hotel room glasses, she filled one with water and gave it to him.

"What's this?"

"It'll help the pain," she told him. Even though she wasn't a doctor, she knew it was too soon for him to be running about the city after being stabbed. She'd removed the stitches this morning before they restored her grandmother's house to its unoccupied state and hailed a taxi on 16th Street.

"Rest now."

"I can't rest." He sat up, wincing. "We have to see your professor friend."

"We've got time." She took the glass and pushed him down. "Rest a while. We'll see him at the end of the day."

Within minutes he was sleeping peacefully. Sandra removed his boots. John's boots. Wyatt had worn them since they'd fled the cabin in a hail of gunfire. It seemed a lifetime had passed since then, yet it was only twenty-four hours. She'd only known him for a week. Could a person fall in love in that short amount of time?

She watched Wyatt for a long while. When she'd met John, her attraction hadn't been instant. It had taken a while. They had grown comfortable with each other. They had met frequently and almost drifted into love. Her wedding day had been the happiest day of her life. Together they had envisioned an idyllic life, but two years of trying to conceive sent them to the doctor's office, where they found out John had leukemia. Only six months had elapsed from the day the doctors uttered the dreaded death sentence to the day she had stood by his open grave.

She was alone then, having trouble filling her days and even more filling her nights. Sandra didn't want to return to the Washington scene, although her parents wanted her to come back and stay with them. She resumed her job at the university and plodded through the semester. Then Sandra decided to enroll in the doctoral program and immersed herself in studying and teaching. She filled both her days and nights so as not to allow herself time to think about John and the future they had lost.

Then Wyatt fell, bleeding, into her lap. Just his presence changed her. She had loved John, but it was a different kind of love. Wyatt made her heart pound, and his presence in a room seemed to dominate it. He stood out in a crowd with the strength of personality. Her attraction had been instant. Sandra shuddered to think that they might never have met if his search for her father hadn't led him to her door. She trembled that she might never have known what it was like to feel wonderfully alive.

Sandra moved to the bed where he lay. The bruises on his face had nearly faded. The swelling was completely gone and his handsome features were becoming defined. Wyatt lay on his side. She pulled a blanket over him. He shifted but didn't waken. She ran her hand down his cheek and over his chin. The roughness of his unshaven face rasped against her hand. Sandra sat down. She didn't know how, but they were going to have to get over this. She was falling for this guy, but how could she love a man who'd implicate her father in anything as horrible as treason? There had to be another explanation. She hoped Jeff would be able to shed some light on the situation. In the meantime she'd try to reach her father again.

The Senate office buildings sat to the left of the Capitol Building on Constitution Avenue. It could be reached through a maze of tunnels or the underground subway that traveled between the Capitol and several of the government complexes. Senator Rutledge had a suite of offices on the third floor. From his windows he could see the huge rotunda with the bronze statue of Freedom on its cupola.

Michael Waring had served in many capacities for the senator. Presently he was his aide, secretary, administrative assistant and general problem solver. Today and for the past week he hadn't seen or talked to the senator. He'd dodged questions as to his availability, canceled meetings that had been scheduled for months on the pretext of an unforeseen emergency, and concealed the fact that Bradford Rutledge's whereabouts were as remote a secret as the location of Senator Wyatt Randolph.

He'd accepted the abuse of disgruntled congressmen and constituents who happened to be in the city on vacation, but the hardest people to appease were the senator's family. Yesterday Sandra had called. She called often, and Brad never failed to talk to her. Then Suzanne, the black sheep of the family, demanding information as if she were some important government official. Finally, Dr. Rutledge, with her warm voice had been perturbed that she'd missed him before she left the city and hadn't been able to reach him since.

None of them, however, had posed as much of a problem as the caller he now had on the phone. "Mrs. Horton, I assure you I will give the senator your message as soon as he returns."

A call from Casey Horton was like getting a call from the President himself. He sat straighter in his chair and spoke clearly as if he were acknowledging an order. She'd stepped outside of the Washington chain of command and called the senator directly. Whatever Brad had gotten into, it was big.

"Thank you, Michael," Mrs. Horton said. "Give my regards to Rose and ask her to call me for lunch one day next week. I haven't seen her since the literacy reception last fall."

"I will do that, Mrs. Horton. She'll be pleased."

Michael replaced the phone with a smile. She was a truly gracious lady, and he was proud to call her a friend of the country. She had a terrific memory for details. He was sure she remembered everyone she'd ever met, including the names and birthdays of all their spouses and children. His wife would be glad she'd asked about her, and ecstatic that she wanted to have lunch with her.

Michael lifted the phone and punched in the number of his wife's office. Her happy voice helped lift his spirits. His first marriage had been a disaster, but in the last nine years of having Rose Gordon-Waring as his wife he had never tired of going home to her and finding her waiting. They had no children of their own, but at forty he still had hopes that she would conceive one of these days. He related the news of Casey Horton's invitation and as usual received an enthusiastic reply. Rose had met Mrs. Horton more than once, but had never been asked to a formal luncheon before. She said she'd call her this afternoon.

As Michael replaced the phone, his mind worked over why the President's wife suddenly wanted to eat with Rose. Was she trying to pump her for information that Michael had withheld? Was she acting with the President's full knowledge and consent? Was there something going on that involved the senator that he didn't know about? Senator Rutledge hadn't made a move without him since he was a junior congressman. He felt as if he were a wayward child being disinherited.

The ringing of the phone cut into his thoughts. The senator's private number again. Only the family and the President called on this number.

"Senator Rutledge's Office, Michael Waring speaking. May I help you?"

"Michael, it's Sandra. I'd like to speak to my father."

"I'm sorry, Sandra, but the senator is not in at the moment."

"Where can he be reached?"

"I'm afraid I can't give out that information."

"Michael, it's me, for God's sake. For the past two days all you've told me is you can't give out that information."

Michael pulled at the collar of his shirt. He was a neat man. He liked being pressed and looking as cool as if he'd stepped off the pages of a fashion magazine. Generally, his job afforded him the opportunity, but this week of hedging was getting to him.

"You're his secretary, Michael. Where is he?"

"He's away, Sandra. That's all I can tell you."

It was all he knew. If he knew more he would tell her. He knew how much the senator loved his family. He could remember when the girls were only children. Suzanne had changed her name and was a supermodel traveling all over the world and Sandra was about to complete her doctorate in mathematics.

"Well, when he does return tell him I have some very valuable information concerning a certain missing junior senator from the state of Pennsylvania."

Michael was suddenly on his feet. "What! Where are you?" Everyone in the country was looking for Senator Randolph. What could Sandra possibly know about him? She had to be lying. She was trying to get a rise out of him and he'd let it work.

"Find him, Michael. I need to talk to him."

Her tone had been serious. She hadn't said good-bye or given any salutation, just the click in his ear when she hung up. This was unlike Sandra. Did she truly know something about the senator or was this a ruse for him to get her father to return her call?

He swung around and stared through the window. The Capitol loomed in the bright January afternoon sun. All around him were the spoils of the rich. Dark cherry wood paneled the walls of his office. Built-in bookcases made him mindful of a lawyer's library. The lamp on his desk had a gold shine to it and had cost more than his first car. It matched the gold-tone accessories that Rose had given him when the senator was elected to office. He wielded a lot of power in his position, earning an income phenomenal for a poor boy from the streets of Camden, New Jersey. He had a wonderful wife and a large, rambling house in the Virginia countryside. Everything he could ask of life had been given to him.

Today he hated this job.

The phone on Clarence Christopher's desk rang. It wasn't the ring of Alexander Graham Bell's telephone but the new sound that had come into being when communications suddenly meant more than the simple picking up of the black instrument and talking.

The phone on his desk was a virtual station in itself. He could call any department he wanted with a three-digit code. He could call the president by pressing only one number or hold a conference call with a roomful of people thousands of miles away.

For the most part he liked the technology. He only wished he were young enough to be able to get his hands into the nitty-gritty of it.

"Christopher," he said.

"It's Agent Norman, sir. We have her on the line."

"I'll be right there."

Clarence left his office by way of the private elevator. In moments he was walking through the door of the communications room. He'd personally authorized the wiretap on Senator Rutledge's house and office. The waiting had nearly killed him. Finally, his daughter had called. He could only hope Waring had kept her on the line long enough for them to get a fix on her location.

"What?" he asked, coming into the room. The temperature there was controlled to suit the machinery rather than the people.

"Sorry, sir."

Agent Melvin Norman truly looked sorry. He replayed the tape of the conversation between Sandra Rutledge and Michael Waring.

"We'll have it analyzed for background noise and see if there's anything that can help us determine where the call originated."

"Thank you, Mel." Clarence was disappointed. He didn't have a thing to report to the President, and the two fugitives were making the FBI look as if it couldn't find its way out of a paper bag. "Keep me informed."

Clarence left the control room and headed back to his office. They were after the senator and Ms. Rutledge because they held the defense system, but someone else was after the senator. Someone else knew about the system and probably wanted it themselves. Clarence knew the President's primary interest was getting that system back. He would follow his instructions to thc letter, but it was time he looked into the real reason Edward Jackson had been killed.

Wyatt Randolph was a fine man. There seemed no reason he would not bring the stones to the government, yet something or someone had changed his mind. Clarence wanted to know who that was. When he found out, he would have the man who killed Jackson, and Wyatt Randolph would have no reason to stay out in the cold.

Washington, DC, had grown up around the federal influence since George Washington had mapped out the tract of land he thought should house the new nation. Small wooden houses had been built close to the influential, if young, government. When the city burned due to poor fire conditions and the abundance of wooden structures, a law was enacted requiring the use of inflammable building materials.

Bricks were more expensive than timber, so the houses were built attached to each other. This both contributed to savings on heating the household and the swelling population of the nation's capital.

Jefferson Taylor, III, lived in one of the renovated brick buildings on W Street in the northwest section of the city. The house was within walking distance of Howard University. Jeff liked living here. It afforded him the use of the university computers without the need to drive across town in the middle of the night as was often the case when he got involved in a problem.

Tonight he was involved in encrypting a file so the code couldn't be broken. He'd done it thousands of times for a company that wanted to have an edge on the market. They paid him tons of money in consulting fees for this service. The average hacker on the street couldn't break the code, but the company wasn't trying to keep them out. It was security against other manufacturers.

They'd asked him to come and work for them, but he'd refused. The work paid the bills and gave him the security of knowing his old age would be comfortable. It also afforded him the time to teach at the university. He liked standing in front of his classes and trying to get through to brains that only had hormones on their minds. Sometimes he did get through. The rush of actually penetrating a young mind was as much an aphrodisiac as sex to him. Of course, he'd never tell anyone that. He didn't want them thinking he was strange or anything, at least no stranger than an absentminded professor.

He'd been working on a new algorithm. This one was longer and more complicated than any he'd ever worked on for the Defense Department. Even the fly-boys in Intelligence wouldn't be able to break this one. Jeff worked vigorously. He heard nothing and nothing penetrated his mind other than the mathematically complex structure he was building.

He didn't know how long the doorbell had been ringing when he finally heard it. He was expecting guests and wanted to get to the door before they left. Hitting the Save key, he got up and jogged to the front door.

"I don't think he's here. We should have called first," Wyatt said as they stood in the yellow wash of light over the front door. It was eight o'clock and pitch-black outside. Wyatt, always thankful for the early darkness, was still inclined to check over his shoulder for assailants who might materialize out of the shadows.

As they turned to leave, the door swung inward. "Dr. Rutledge . . . Senator Randolph, come in. I've been expecting you."

Sandra and Wyatt looked at each other, both surprised by his comment.

"Come, Sandra, you always were one of my very best students." Jeff took her arm and prodded her through the entrance. Wyatt followed. "Take off your coats. Sit down."

He shuffled excitedly about the entrance like a man who rarely received guests but enjoyed having them. Wyatt and Sandra gave him their coats and went into the crowded living room. Jeff smiled at them and walked into the kitchen. Wyatt thought he'd stepped back into the

Victorian Age. Dark furniture set on dark rugs. Heavy damask drapery hung at the long windows. Books lined the built-in shelves in haphazard disarray.

Wyatt loved it. He could be comfortable here. Jeff entered a moment later laden with the weight of a silver tray. Wyatt took it and waited while the shorter man removed some of the outdated magazines and books from the coffee table.

"Jeff, you were expecting us?" Sandra frowned.

"I had visitors this afternoon," he said as he poured tea in the china cups. "They were from the DOD. Wanted to know if I'd seen or heard from you recently. All I could tell them was I thought you were up in the mountains getting ready to become 'Doctor' Rutledge."

"I was, but something's come up." She glanced at Wyatt. Jeff, too, looked at Wyatt. "I need your help."

Wyatt suddenly got up. He went to the window and checked outside. If Jeff had had visitors today, the place might be watched. He had an uneasy feeling about being here.

"Is there a way out of here other than the front door?" Wyatt asked.

"There's a back door . . . and a cellar exit. Why?"

"I think we'd better get out of here."

As he said the words, a sudden banging on the front door paralyzed them. Jeff was the first to move. "Follow me," he said. They grabbed coats on the way to the cellar door, then quietly and quickly they went through the darkened passage. Sandra reached for and found Wyatt's hand. Above them they heard a crash, then the ripping of wood. The heavy front door had been forced. All three stopped and stared at the dark ceiling.

"Keep moving," Jeff ordered.

Holding on to Wyatt's hand, Sandra followed the troll-size professor. She could hear footsteps above her head and recognized the muffled sound of authoritative voices. She wondered who had come. Was it the police, someone from the government, or the men who'd tried to kill them?

Fear made her heart pound, and her breath come in short gasps. At the outside door Jeff stopped. Sandra stopped her advance just short of running into him. She wondered about Wyatt and his injured side. He'd been favoring it for more than a day. If they had to run, he wouldn't make it.

Jeff peered out of the door. "They don't seem to be back here," he whispered. "I have a car in the garage across the yard. It opens on the alley so you'll have a good chance of getting away. The keys are here." He handed them to Sandra.

"What about you?" she asked.

"I'll stay here. There isn't time to discuss it." He stopped her from arguing.

He was right. The upstairs door to the cellar opened.

"Go." He pulled the door open to let her pass. "Nice meeting you, Senator," he said with a smile that told him he enjoyed the game.

Sandra heard the comment as Wyatt slipped through the door and Jeff pushed it back into place. Wasting no more time, they ran across the wet grass and into the rear door of the detached garage. Sandra got in and slipped the key into the ignition. Above her head she found a garage-door opener. "Thank you, Jeff," she said to no one. She pushed the button and the doors automatically rose. When they were high enough to clear the car, she started the engine and slipped out, pushing the button again to bring the door down.

"They're behind us," Wyatt said. She adjusted the rearview mirror for her greater height and brought the blue and red flashing lights into focus.

"I've never tried to outrun the police before."

"I think tonight is the night to begin."

Sandra raced down the alley. Behind her was a flood of revolving lights. She only hoped another police car didn't appear at the mouth of the alley and cut off her escape route.

"Oh, my God!" Sandra instinctively braked.

Wyatt turned in time to see the police car block the exit. "Don't slow down," he ordered. "There's an opening coming up on the right, three houses from the end," Wyatt navigated. "Turn there. It'll be tight, but it will take us out onto the street."

Sandra followed the directions. To the car at the end of the alley, she looked like she was going to ram it. Both doors opened and uniformed officers ran for safety. With no margin of safety Sandra swung the small vehicle as wide as the narrow alley allowed and turned into an even narrower corridor. She had the feeling of traveling through a tunnel. Behind her she heard the squeal of tires as the fast-moving cars were taken by surprise. Unable to make the turn, they crashed headlong into each other.

She hoped no one was hurt, but had no time to ponder the thought. From here there would be no escape if the avenue in front of her was cut. She pressed her foot to the floor and the car shot forward at an immense speed. The small decline at the end of the alley sent a hail of sparks shooting about the car as metal and street made contact. The tires bounced on the pavement. She struggled to keep control of the two-ton missile. Sandra swung it south and headed toward Fourth Street. At this time of night there wouldn't be much traffic, and as long as she didn't hit one of the college students she'd have a clear path to outwit the police.

"Oh, no!" she wailed. "Where are they coming from?" The entire force of police appeared to be behind her. She raced past the Quadrangle, swinging around a couple crossing the street at the light. The reservoir reflected the lights of the Student Center across from it. She accelerated further, edging the car ahead, passing the other vehicles in front of her, checking both directions, but running every traffic light between her and freedom.

Wyatt sat still next to her. His hands were braced against the dashboard, his head constantly whipping back and forth checking the police cars behind them and the road ahead.

"Take the next right," he shouted.

"It's the hospital center. They'll box me in."

"I know. Take it."

She hit the brake and turned into the driveway. As predicted, several cars followed her while the others went to the only other entrance.

"What do I do now?"

"Go to the back. They're doing construction. I saw something."

She followed his direction, seeing the construction trailers dead ahead. Two ribbons of colored lights ran parallel on the two roads leading to the end. Wyatt kept watch. Instinctively, she knew he was timing the sequence.

"Make a left," he said. "Go straight over the ramp."

Sandra clamped her teeth together. In front of her were two slats of wood propped up on cans. The width between them would accommodate the small car. The tire spread of the police cars was too wide. If Wyatt's plan worked they'd be airborne, while the police cars would crash into each other. If the traction held, she'd cross the grass and slip into the parking lot of the Veterans Administration Hospital. No police cars had gone to that lot. If she got back to Irving Street before they regrouped, she could disappear into the northeast.

She hit the wood doing fifty. The car cut the air like a rocket. For a moment she was on a ride. Time slowed down and there was no sound. Only the easy travel through unrestricted space.

Then she hit the ground. The tires dug into soft earth and stuck. The engine died. Sandra took a moment to stare through the back glass. Flames poured from the cars that had run into each other, brightening the sky with an artificial light. White-clad doctors and nurses ran from Children's Hospital toward the wreckage.

"Start the engine." Wyatt's practical voice jarred her fascination with the melee behind them. She turned the key and the powerful engine roared. Throwing the gearshift into drive, she spun the tires.

"Back up."

Wyatt's command and the executing action came at the same time. The car lurched out of the mud, but she'd lost her edge. One of the police cars had already entered the parking lot and would meet her before she could get away.

"Time to play chicken," Wyatt told her.

Sandra inched the car around the mud and headed for the lot, gaining speed as she went. She skimmed the car coming toward her by inches. Another car turned into the opposite lane.

"Head straight for it."

"We're going to hit him." Sandra's voice was strained as she pointed the car straight at the one in front of her. Playing chicken wasn't her game. She started to turn the wheel.

"Don't!" Wyatt shouted, and she straightened the car. "He'll back down."

Sandra hoped he was right. Her gaze was pasted on the oncoming car. She bit her lip and forced her eyes to remain open when she wanted to close them.

"Keep it steady," Wyatt said in a calm voice.

She took his direction and kept her speed even as the car ate up miles. With a mere car length between them, the police car swerved to the right and she continued on a straight course. Wyatt let out a breath. She glanced in the mirror. The car hit the curb and flipped into the air. It came down on its roof in front of an approaching car, which rammed into it. Sandra stopped at the sign at the end of the driveway and turned to look behind her.

Assured that there were no other cars approaching, she turned onto Irving Street and followed all the rules of the road back to Professor Taylor's house.

CHAPTER 7

"Are you out of your mind?" Bradford Rutledge shouted in the soundproof room. Three men stood in front of him. They stared straight ahead like soldiers, but they weren't attached to the military. "Six men critically wounded, five more with second- and third-degree burns, two with broken bones, fifteen blue and whites damaged beyond repair, three civilian vehicles burned, *and* you could have killed my daughter." He paced the director's office he'd borrowed, holding the report of last night's events in his hand. "Just who authorized you to call in the DC police?" He slammed his fist against the circular conference table in the corner of the room. The polished wood surface pedestal skittered across the floor at the force of his pounding. "And with half the arsenal of DC's finest thrown at them, two amateurs got away." He threw the report across the room. Papers flew about like toy airplanes. "I've a mind to have the lot of you fired."

He turned back to them and faced the only other occupant of the room, Lance Desque, undersecretary of defense. "Lance, I thought you would have the good sense to stop this."

"Senator—"

"Get out of here," he shouted to the other three men. As if they'd gotten a sudden release from an angry father, the men left the room.

"Senator," Lance started. "By the time word reached us, the pursuit was practically over." He stopped, waiting, then continued. "It was never confirmed that the senator and your daughter were actually in the car."

"Then why are their names so prominent in this report?" He gestured to the litter of paper scattered over the floor.

"We could only assume since they had been to see the professor that it was the two of them who entered his house and then left by an underground route."

"Yet no one actually saw them, and Professor Taylor denied they had ever been there."

Lance nodded.

Brad Rutledge had worked with Lance Desque for over ten years. The man was a genius at diplomacy. He'd often wondered why he hadn't advanced through the ranks faster. Finding out about the disaster from Lance didn't sit well with him. That Sandra had been at the center of it had him raving like a mad man. What was Sandra doing with Wyatt Randolph? She was supposed to be at the cabin. He'd deliberately left her alone so she could study. Not only did the degree mean a lot to her, but she needed to confront John's death and that was the best place for her to do it.

Finding out she had been in a high-speed chase through the streets of the District had nearly given him heart failure.

"Have you learned anything more?" Brad asked, his voice calmer.

"I'm afraid not. Your daughter and the senator seem to be very resourceful."

Brad smiled. "I always thought Sandy could be resourceful if the circumstances ever called for it."

"She seems to be doing all right now, sir."

Brad had to agree with him.

"Soon, however, she and the senator will have to run out of cash and use a credit card. Then we'll find them."

The paper trail, Brad thought. It was the downfall of many a criminal but Sandra was no criminal. She was over her head in dealing with Senator Randolph. The sooner he found her and got her away from him the better off she would be.

Lance was discreet. He would find her and bring her to him. He'd explain, let her know that Senator Randolph wasn't the man she thought he was. He only hoped Lance would get to her before Wyatt Randolph got her killed.

Clarence Christopher crossed the lobby of the Federal Bureau of Investigation. He usually took the elevator from the garage to his office on the top floor. This morning he wanted to walk the halls, see the displays that the public saw when they went on the forty-five-minute tour. He wanted to smile at the staff who conducted the tours and see the great seal of the agency that J. Edgar Hoover had made into a strong symbol of respect.

Taking this tour would delay his arrival at his own office where he expected a message to be waiting for him from Everett Horton.

Clarence's phone had rung at midnight. The report arrived thirty minutes later by special messenger. He shook his head as he read. And for what? he thought. After the destruction that left the parking lot of Children's Hospital looking like a Middle Eastern war zone, Senator Randolph was still at large.

What was he going to tell Everett? That they had found out the couple had been to the Crestwood Drive house and they had missed catching them there? It sounded like an excuse, and he hated excuses. He stopped on the second floor and looked at the gun collection. Fifty thousand guns had been confiscated from various illegal sources, yet Wyatt Randolph and Sandra Rutledge had eluded a large contingent of DC police without firing a single shot.

Working his way around, he passed the first tour group of the day. The guide stopped and introduced him, and he answered a few questions before the guide led them away and he went toward the elevators. He had a private elevator, but today he took the general one.

It was crowded when the doors opened. Several people were speaking in low voices. When he stepped inside all conversation ceased. That was the one thing he hated about this job. Most people stopped talking around him as if it were some unwritten law.

He spoke and smiled as the doors opened and people got off to go to their respective positions. Finally, he was alone. The doors opened on the top floor and he went directly to his office.

"Has the President called yet?" he asked his secretary.

"No, sir."

Clarence had been expecting his call since the report arrived last night.

"Get him for me."

Gone were the days when Everett Horton could lounge in bed on Sunday morning and leisurely read the newspaper. When he and Casey were first married and he was working sixty hours a week as a lawyer, Sunday was their only day to relax and spend totally together. God, he missed those days.

Six newspapers arrived precisely at seven o'clock each morning with his breakfast tray. By seven-thirty he'd eaten his meal, read the news, and was ready to begin his day. *The Washington Post* lay at the foot of the king-size bed Everett and Casey Horton had brought to the White House when they moved in almost three years ago to the day. There were only two items he'd insisted on taking with him. One was his bed, the other his pillow. *A man should be able to sleep in his own bed,* he'd told Casey, and she'd agreed with him. Everything else waited for them in the Texas house he planned to return to when his term of office ended. From the aerial photographs showing billowing smoke and a full-color blazing fire, that term might be four years shorter than he'd anticipated.

Somehow the wire services had gotten hold of it and the same photo made front-page news in the *Miami Herald, The New York Times, The St. Louis Post-Dispatch, The Philadelphia Inquirer, The Atlanta Constitution,* and *The Los Angeles Times.* The story that followed gave detailed accounts of the high-speed chase through the streets of the District in pursuit of Senator Randolph and the daughter of the chairman of the powerful defense subcommittee.

He swung his feet over the side of the bed and stood up. He stretched and bent over to touch his toes. The small gesture made him feel better. Then the phone rang.

Wyatt could hear Sandra's sobs muffled through the closed bathroom door. Last night when they'd come in she'd been punch-drunk. The ordeal of running from the police and surviving moment after moment of near misses with death had given her a heady feeling. She'd climbed the walls in giddy triumph, wavering between hysteria and tears. Nothing he could do calmed her until he'd put her under the cold water of the shower. She'd fought both him and the water, until exhaustion claimed her and she clung limply to him. He held her, letting the cool water cascade over their fully clad bodies.

He talked quietly to her, then left her alone to complete her shower. When she came back to the room her hair was slick to her head and her face was clean of makeup. Her skin shone like black pearls. He wanted to touch it, feel the smoothness under his hand. Her eyes were large and glassy and stared straight ahead. The short gown that covered only part of her said more about what was under it than if she'd been naked. Wyatt's body reacted instantly to the total package. He shifted in his chair at the uncomfortable tightness in his pants. Moving was out of the question. If he got up there was only one place he would head. When Sandra was settled in the bed and asleep, he went into the bathroom and took his own cold shower and thanked God the room had two beds.

With morning came the aftereffects. She'd switched on the television as soon as she rose. The news photos of the crash scene played like a memory. She'd sank onto the foot of the bed. Her hand covered her mouth and her eyes grew by degree until they were as large as saucers. The news account of the tragedy had the effect of changing a faded memory to trauma impact. She rushed into the bathroom and slammed the door. The fact that people had been hurt in those fires and crashes that occurred in the wake of her skill as a driver hit her hard. She turned on the water to muffle the sound, but he knew she was crying. The urge to go to her was overwhelming. Wyatt left his bed and headed for the door, but stopped short of opening it. Despite water running in the sink, he could hear her sobbing.

"Sandra?" he called to her. Through the door he heard her sniff. "Sandra, are you all right?"

She didn't immediately answer. He could almost see her trying to control the tears and sobs that would come through in her voice if she spoke. The image choked him.

"I'm fine," she finally answered.

"Open the door," he said.

Seconds passed before the lock clicked and the door opened a crack. She made pretense that everything was fine by pushing her hair back. The gesture was designed to distract his attention from her swollen eyes.

"It's all right," he told her. "Last night you were fighting for your life. Today reality sets in. You're grieving over the consequences. It's daylight and everything is brilliantly visible."

"How come you're not in tears?"

Wyatt pushed the door fully open. He reached for her and pulled her into his arms. "We all grieve differently," he told her.

He hadn't meant to take her in her arms, but just like the brilliant visibility of morning, it seemed the right thing to do. He squeezed her closer. She felt good, smelling of toothpaste and soap. Her arms pulled him, too. They stood there. He didn't want to let her go. He didn't want anything to invade this moment.

He forgot she was Senator Rutledge's daughter. She was a woman he wanted to know better. He kissed her neck. A tremor ran through her. He felt it. The reaction gave him courage to continue. He kissed her ear and her cheek until he worked his way to her mouth. He covered it with his own. Every part of him reacted to her nearness. He swept his tongue past her teeth and tasted her. She was vitally alive and she made him feel alive, too. Suddenly, he knew how a dying man felt when he grasped a straw, trying desperately to cling to life. Fitting her further into his body, he deepened the kiss, devouring her mouth, running his hands over her back. She'd been what he was waiting for. In all his years and the few women he'd had relationships with, none compared to the fire she ignited in him.

Sandra's mouth matched his in its aggressive plunder. Then he felt the change in her. She ground her body suggestively against him. He hardened in response. There was no doubt he wanted her and no doubt she was willing. Wyatt was close to insanity when Sandra rubbed one of her legs against his. Before the last vestige of reason left him, he grabbed her arms and yanked them from his neck. He slid his mouth from her but kept her in the circle of his arms.

It was the hardest thing he'd ever had to do, but in her present state of mind he would be little more than taking advantage of the situation.

"We'd better get dressed, Sandra," he whispered in her ear. His voice was thick with emotion. "We promised to meet Jeff for breakfast."

Sandra couldn't have been more ashamed of herself if she'd deliberately set out to seduce Wyatt. What was she thinking? That was the problem. She wasn't thinking. When he'd kissed her, emotion took over. Feelings she didn't know existed burst full-grown inside her. Wyatt only wanted to comfort her, but she'd changed that. Finding herself in his arms, she'd lost her sanity and done what came naturally. That in itself should have told her something was different. She'd never lost such complete control. She'd wanted Wyatt to make love to her.

Thank God he had better command of his emotions than she did or they wouldn't be staring at the Tidal Basin. Sandra knew it was better that they remember what was at stake here, but the lines between what was right and wrong were blurring where Wyatt Randolph was concerned. He leaned against the railing. The Jefferson Memorial stood bright in the cold morning light.

Wyatt rubbed his hands together trying to produce heat in the cold air. The park police had driven by once but had taken no notice of them. The city was coming to life and it wasn't unusual to find people pointing cameras at the marble monuments. That wasn't their purpose in being here.

He dwelled for a moment on that purpose. Since he'd met Sandra he'd been at her mercy. Now they were waiting for her friend, a man he didn't know, to come and possibly help them.

"Why are you doing this?" Wyatt asked, continuing his train of thought as if she had heard his thoughts.

"Doing what?" she asked.

"Why are you helping me? You're obviously loyal to your father. Why should I trust you?"

"Isn't it a little late to be asking that?"

"Maybe, but so far I still have the stones and I can leave this park before anything else happens."

Sandra frowned at him. She probably wondered what had brought on this conversation. He didn't even know if her loyalty was the reason. After this morning he wasn't sure of his feelings, and he didn't want to lower his guard and suddenly find himself cornered.

"There isn't any reason you should trust me," Sandra said, her voice slightly angry. "I don't believe my father had anything to do with your project."

"What do you believe?" He wanted her to tell him she believed in him. It was suddenly important.

"I'm not sure," she said. "I believe my father had nothing to do with the death of your friend or the attempt on your life, but . . ." she stopped.

"Go on," Wyatt prompted. "But . . ."

"But I have to know."

"Will you be willing to work with me to find out the truth?"

Sandra hesitated. Wasn't the truth right? Why didn't she answer immediately? Had Wyatt shaken her faith in her father? Suppose he was right? He couldn't be, she told herself, but there was only one way to find out. She had to join forces with him. One of them would win and the other would lose. Sandra hated the odds.

She nodded finally. "If you're right, everything my father ever stood for would be a lie." She stared in the distance for a moment. "If you're wrong, you would have maligned an honest man. You know what that can do in a town like this."

In either case she would lose, but it wasn't so much her father she was concerned about. It was herself. She'd lose him.

"I'll do it," she heard herself saying. "On one condition."

"Which is?"

"You don't hold anything back from me. Whatever you find out, you tell me. Right or wrong, I want to know."

"That goes both ways," he reminded her.

Sandra stared at him for a long moment. Wyatt was so handsome. She wished they'd met under different circumstances, but it was too late for that wish.

On the path near the water, Jeff walked leisurely toward them. He had a brown bag in his hand. Sandra scanned the area for any police. An occasional jogger had passed them, and after last night she was suspicious of everyone. Jeff walked like a man without a care in the world.

"Any problems this morning?" he asked as he came to a stop in front of them. Somehow, she felt Jeff enjoyed this game of spies and counterspies.

"No," Wyatt answered, then glanced at Sandra. She wondered if he was thinking of what had happened between them this morning. A heat wave racked through her.

"There were at least two cars guarding my house," Jeff laughed. "They're still there. They think I'm in bed, but I skipped over the roofs and left through Ellen Magfly's. She lives down the block and she's kind of . . . let's just say she didn't mind." Opening the brown bag, he pulled out cups of coffee and handed one to each of them. "Now tell me what it is that's causing so much destruction among the DC Police Force."

Wyatt had liked Jefferson Taylor when he'd talked with him in his house the previous evening. After he'd helped them escape, his trust had been further built. During the night he wondered if Jeff was real. Could he be part of a plot to get his trust? He didn't know him and the only person who recommended him was Sandra, and she had an ulterior motive for working against him. Despite the fact he couldn't get her warm body out of his mind, he needed to think clearly because anything else could get him killed.

"Sandra tells me you used to work for the government."

"Computer specialist," he said. "I worked in the Intelligence area, decoding transmissions that had been intercepted from the former Soviet Union. When communism failed, I returned to the academic world."

"Do you maintain your ties with the government?"

"Some of them. A man needs friends sometimes."

How well Wyatt knew that. Since the stones had appeared in his mailbox he'd wondered if he had any friends left.

"In fact I have a dinner engagement with one of them tomorrow night." Jeff's voice brought Wyatt back to the present.

Wyatt knew he had to make a decision. They'd come this far, and without someone who knew about computer chips, he and Sandra were doomed to running until they got caught and killed.

"Have you ever heard of Project Eagle?"

Jeff sipped from his paper cup. He started to walk, and Wyatt and Sandra fell into step. Finally, he shook his head.

"I don't know what it is," Wyatt said. "But my life became worthless right after I mentioned it."

"Who'd you mention it to?"

Wyatt looked at Sandra.

"My father," she said flatly.

Jeff stopped. His gaze bounced between the two of them.

"Wyatt thinks Project Eagle is some kind of system that my father wants to sell to a foreign government," she continued.

Jeff whistled. "Treasonous undertaking." He turned to Wyatt. "I certainly hope you can back that up. With the popularity of Senator Rutledge you'll have a hard time making a comment like that stick."

"I know. I have more to lose than the senator, and his daughter here is set on proving him as squeaky clean as his profile claims, and me as black as Jesse James." After this morning, though, he wasn't quite sure of that. She dropped her gaze preventing him from confirming his words by looking into her eyes.

Wyatt gave his attention back to Jeff and explained everything he knew about the stones and the concealed chips. When he finished, he pulled out the small box containing the huge stones and poured them into his hand.

Jeff took one and rolled it between his thumb and forefinger. He felt each of the facets, then held it up to the light. After careful perusal, he took another one and followed the same procedure. When he was holding the third stone up to the light, he asked. "Will you let me keep these for a while?"

"How long?"

"A couple of days." Jeff continued to examine the stones. One by one he went through the same procedure.

Wyatt looked at Sandra for some sign. She nodded.

"A couple of days," he agreed.

"I can't tell you much until I get a good look at the chips inside these."

"Any idea why someone saw fit to put them inside fake diamonds?"

"Not a clue," he said, bringing his gaze back to Wyatt. "But in a couple of days I should at least have a theory."

"Thanks, Jeff," Sandra said. "I knew you'd help us."

Jeff smiled. "Did she ever tell you she was one of my best students?" He resumed walking.

Wyatt shook his head.

"Logic, 101 . . . she was head and shoulders above the rest of the class. I wanted her to stay here and teach, but she chose some tiny college up in the wilderness of New Jersey." He bastardized the pronunciation of the state name and screwed his face as he said it.

"Jeff," Sandra warned. "Rutgers is not some tiny college. It's the state university. And New Brunswick is not a wilderness as well you know, since you were born and reared there."

Jeff smiled again. He hugged Sandra, taking the bite out of his words.

"I'll see you in a couple of days. Now you better get out of here before the park police drive by and recognize one of us."

Wyatt shook hands with Jeff. "Be careful," he said. "Someone is trying to kill me over what those stones represent."

Jeff nodded and left them. Wyatt adjusted the baseball cap, casually taking Sandra's arm. Together they headed toward the street.

He'd made the first step and now he needed to go one more. This time he didn't want Sandra with him. He knew he'd just promised he'd tell her everything and he would—after it was over. He needed to get some inside information, and that could be dangerous. Last night they'd been running from the police. He was sure they'd had orders to take him into custody, but knew nothing about what secrets he held, secrets he didn't even know. He hoped Jefferson Taylor would be able to throw some light on what those secrets were.

He still needed to talk to the guys in the department. He had been their friend, but he was no longer sure who his friends were. He might not come out of this, and if he walked into a trap he didn't want her going in with him.

"Sandra, I think it's time we moved to another motel," Wyatt began, leading into a conversation that would give them reason to split up for a while.

Sandra had thought the same thing.

"How are we fixed for money?"

Wyatt liked the way she included him in the "we."

"Not a lot," he said. "I have enough for another couple of days. After that we're going to have to go to a cash machine."

"I have some," Sandra revealed. "I'd planned to spend the rest of the winter at the cabin. I left most of my money when we escaped, but I have enough for about a week." She didn't know how much more they'd need or how long this episode would last. They both would know better after Jeff had a chance to look at the stones.

"Why don't we follow the same method we devised before?"

It was cloak and dagger and she knew it, but after the narrow escape they'd had last night she was inclined to go along with Wyatt. She also wanted to call her father again, and she needed help she didn't want to tell Wyatt about, despite her promise. She was going to have to call Annie. No matter what her sister felt about her, they were sisters and she needed her now more than she'd ever needed her. Annie had to help her.

CHAPTER 8

Suzanne tilted her head back as she'd been directed. The tassels on the Japanese headdress swung like pendulums next to her ear. She'd been at this for hours and she hated it. The dress was too tight, the headgear weighed a ton, and if she leaned any further back she'd fall over.

"That's fine," Jordon called. He was all business today. The attack-Annie mode of a couple of days ago had all but vanished. Attack-Annie, that's what she thought of him when he constantly brought up her family. He knew she wanted to forget that she had ever had anything to do with her senator stepfather and her perfect professor sister. She had nothing against her mother, but their schedules kept them apart, so there was little conflict.

"Got it, honey. Why don't we try a couple over by the columns?"

Suzanne shivered as she slipped her arms into her coat. The weather had been mild so far, but it was January. Jordon was having fun. The day was overcast, and he loved this kind of light. He reveled in what he could do with the sky and the way it bounced light off the white marble stones. She didn't understand this shoot. If they were all made up in this pasty-colored makeup, dressed in kimonos and wooden flip-flops, why hadn't they done this shoot in Japan? American women would never dress in this kind of clothing. The female workforce called for business suits and low-heeled shoes, clothes that were smart, chic, and functional. She couldn't see any functionality to a garment in which she had to first kneel before she could sit. And the only good thing about the headdress was that it promoted good posture. If she didn't stand up straight she'd pitch over. She couldn't see secretaries filing with this on their heads.

"You could look a little happier," Jordon told her as they moved from inside the domed structure housing Thomas Jefferson and his legacy to the American people to the new location.

Suzanne put voice to her questions. "Jordon, why didn't they use Japanese landmarks? These photos can't be designed for an American magazine."

"I just shoot 'em, ma'am," he mimicked a western twang. "I don't decide what people do with 'em."

"Be serious."

"You like Japan, don't you?" The question was rhetorical, since he didn't give her time to answer it. "I can't see why. You tower over most of the people in that country. You hate the food, and by the look on your face you couldn't care less about the clothes."

"Am I not giving you what you asked for?" She angered so easily these days.

"It's not what *I'm* asking for. It's that there's no life to you. I know how you photograph. What you're doing today is only technically correct. If I were interviewing new models, I wouldn't choose you. You're not *in* the shoot. When you're into it, I get fantastic pictures, and when you hate it—"

"It's obvious," she finished for him. He'd told her that before. This time she couldn't identify the reason for her bad mood. It must be this city. In Washington, at any turn, she could run into one of them. Here, they were just too close. It wasn't Jordon's fault. This was her job and she was good at it. She would do it well now.

"All right, Jordon. You have my word. When you get set up, I'll be there, totally." The faster she satisfied him, the faster they could complete this job and get back to New York.

She walked down several steps, looking at the bridge in the distance. Kneeling, she sat down on the marble steps, drawing her knees up and hugging them. She rested her chin on her knees and waited. Jordon's crew was efficient, but he left her to supervise them. It wouldn't take them long to move and get ready for the next take. Suzanne checked the sky. A startling mixture of blue-gray and violet streaked across the horizon. The distant Virginia landscape appeared to be mountainous. At times Jordon had used the clouds to give the illusion of mountains. That's what her life had been for as long as she could remember—an illusion.

She remembered when she and Sandra had experimented with their new cameras. They must have been fourteen and fifteen. Suddenly she frowned, remembering Sandra's pictures. They were perfect. Her sister had probably calculated the probability of light leaving the sun and traveling to earth, along with any infraction it might go through before finally bouncing off the subject and striking the film. As it was, Sandra's photos looked like postcards and Suzanne's had fingers or leaves or miscellaneous heads blocking the subject.

She was no good at taking pictures, but she was good at posing for them. She'd used some of the shots Sandra had taken in her portfolio when she went to New York.

"Hello, Suzanne."

She looked up and blinked. Suzanne blinked again. She had to be dreaming. There wasn't enough sun to blind her, so she *was* looking at her sister. What was she doing here? How had she found her? What did she want?

"You never call me Suzanne." She went to get up, then remembered the restrictions of the costume. Sandra instinctively put out her hand. Suzanne looked at it, then decided to accept the assistance. She got up, towering over Sandra. At least her height gave her a sense of control.

"I need a favor and I didn't want to anger you."

"Does this have anything to do with my noticing your name in the headlines of *The Washington Post* this morning?" She was rewarded by seeing her sister flinch. "Ah, sore point, huh? You're lucky no one was killed. Otherwise they could have you up on murder charges." She laughed. "Who would have ever thought you would be the one running from the law?"

"Annie, please don't judge me."

"It's Annie now. I thought I was Suzanne."

"Can't we get over the anger, Annie? We're sisters. Even if you try to ignore that, it doesn't change the fact."

For a moment the catch in Sandra's voice got to her. She hated it. Suddenly, she was whisked back in time, back to the cabin. John was alive and everyone was anticipating the summer wedding he and Sandra were soon to have. It was then that Suzanne had discovered the secret. She hated Sandra.

"Annie, we're ready."

"I'll be right there," she called over her shoulder. Jordon stood staring at them. "I have to go back to work. What is it you want?" she asked Sandra bluntly.

"I need some money. I can't go to the bank and get it myself. It would start a paper trail."

"In your predicament you can't afford that."

"You know how to transfer funds. Send them around the world so the maze is so complex no one can figure out the origin."

"I'm sure that mathematical brain of yours can also do this. You could probably leave the damning information inside Fort Knox to really screw up the government." Suzanne couldn't resist the dig.

"It wouldn't look legitimate if I did it."

"How much money are we talking about?"

"Not much, about five thousand."

"That's enough for two tickets to Brazil. Of course you wouldn't have anything to live on once you got there, but then, they don't have extradition, so you and the senator would be safe."

"I'm not planning to leave the country, Annie. We just need some money to sustain us until everything is cleared up."

"You think there is a way of clearing this up?"

"Of course there is."

How typical of Sandra. Every problem had a solution. All she had to do was work at it hard enough and sooner or later she could unravel it.

"Will you do it, Annie?"

She loved that pleading note in Sandra's voice. This time she needed her. She'd love to stick it to her, but what did it matter. She didn't have a chance of eluding the police for long. She wasn't as resourceful as Annie. She'd never been.

"Sure," Suzanne threw at her with a shrug of her shoulder.

"You will?" Sandra smiled. Relief showed in her eyes. She was so transparent. That's the reason she never got away with anything. Sandra just couldn't do anything but tell the truth.

"You and Wyatt Randolph must have been grown from the same bean pod."

"What do you mean?"

"You're so honest. Everyone knows he's a Boy Scout. His having anything to do with a top-secret defense project is ludicrous."

"How did you know about that?"

She didn't know about it, but Sandra didn't know that. Lance had met her at the door of the restaurant last night. She'd been waiting for Jordon to get the car. They decided to drive to Georgetown for a while. Lance mentioned a secret system, and if Sandra contacted her, she should let him know.

"Grow up, Sandra," Suzanne said. "You think you're the only person who ever talks to anyone. Even though I hate this city I still have friends here . . . and they talk."

"What have they said about Wyatt?"

"They haven't told me whether you're sleeping with him. Are you?"

Sandra's eyes opened wide. "I don't think that's any of your business."

Suzanne laughed out loud. She wanted to throw her head back, but remembered the headdress just in time. "Be careful, sister dear," she warned as her laughter cut off as quickly as it started. "You don't want to anger me, remember?"

"Annie, will you get me the money? You can go into Grandma's account. That way it wouldn't raise any notice."

Suzanne sighed. She didn't care about the money. She hadn't played the world financial markets in a while. It might be fun to set a trap, then close it in a fog of electronic chaos. It would be more fun to tangle Sandra and Senator Randolph in a maze of unexplainable transactions. A grin stole across her face.

"Where do you want it delivered?" she asked.

"It can't be delivered. I'll have to meet you somewhere."

"Where?"

"I don't know. I'll call your hotel tonight and we'll arrange it." She turned to leave, then quickly turned back. "Thanks, Annie. I'll never forget this." She smiled and was gone.

Suzanne watched her walk down the steps of the Jefferson Memorial. Sandra was scared. Suzanne felt a tightening around her heart. The sensation must be new to her sister. She was positive Sandra had never been scared before. She didn't know what real fear was like. When she and Wyatt Randolph were caught, even having a senator for a father couldn't get her out of the trouble she was in. There was just one person who might be able to save Sandra and her lover—little Annie Boatwright. It wouldn't take more than a phone call from Suzanne to the right ear, but Sandra didn't know that.

The Pentagon was the world's largest office building when it was completed in 1943. The five concentric pentagons, or "rings," as they are called, cover thirty-four acres with floor space to accommodate twenty-five thousand military and civilian employees. Adjacent to thc building, just off the busy highway leading into northern Virginia are the parking lots. With parking for ten thousand cars, minibuses run the thousands of employees and visitors back and forth to the many entrances of the famous facility.

Wyatt stared at the massive stone structure, deftly avoiding the minibuses. He wondered how he was going to get inside. He forced his steps to be casual, as if he was early for work and enjoyed the exercise of a leisurely walk. The Pentagon operated on a twenty-four-hour-a-day schedule, though not with a full complement of employees. Enough people were coming and going so Wyatt felt sure he wouldn't be conspicuous.

He wore the uniform and bars of a second lieutenant. When he got to the door he'd ask to speak to one of his friends—Colonel Sam Parker. He'd called Sam and was expected.

He neared one of the minibus stops. Then he saw it. By chance and luck he saw the silver clip of an identification badge lying on the ground in front of him. This scheme just might work, he told himself as he leaned down and picked up Colonel Efrem Riddenhouse's security badge. The colonel would be sorely reprimanded when he appeared for work in the morning without the proper identification. Examining the badge, Wyatt's knees suddenly grew weak at his good fortune. Efrem Riddenhouse must be a forgetful man. He'd written his identification code on the back of the badge.

During any other time Wyatt would have been glad to drop the tag off at the information desk where it could be returned. This was just too helpful a find, for he could gain access to the building without anyone knowing.

He thought of Sandra. She was probably wondering where he was, but it couldn't be helped. It was past time for her to call the phone booth they'd agreed upon. He had what he needed. He couldn't stop to go back into Washington now and he couldn't wait until tomorrow. He stared at the ID in his hand. This ticket was good for only one night, and he had to redeem it while he had the chance. Sandra would have to understand.

Before he went into the building he'd need a colonel's uniform. Buying the khakis at the Army-Navy store had been a good idea. He had a handful of bars and leaves in his pocket. He didn't expect to need a major's decoration, but he was prepared for anything all the way to a four-star general.

Checking his watch, he removed the bars and pinned the leaves into his collar. He had about an hour to get to the phone booth before she called again. He wasn't going to make it. She had a cellular unit. If he got inside and found a phone, he'd call her. That was the best he could do.

The real test was in front of him. The next minibus was headed his way. It was too close for him to walk away from its approach. He would have to board it and hope he wouldn't be stopped before he found out what secrets Chip had on his computer.

Wyatt's heart pounded and sweat broke out on his forehead. He checked his uniform, making sure his jacket was open and the leaves of his uniform visible. The entry doors to the Pentagon looked miles away. He could be stopped before he even made it that far. The driver could ask who he was, require identification to board the bus, look with special attention at the photograph of bald, red-faced Efrem Riddenhouse and notice his own face and the badge didn't match. A hundred disasters ran through his mind.

Stiffening his back, he moved forward. Men were still out to kill him for the diamonds and he needed to know why. Sandra had said it. *If you're going to die, at least know the reason why.* Her voice came to him, light and musical. He wished it was for her that he had to keep going, but her father was behind this. Proving it to her would mean anything between the two of them would die before it could live. He already wanted her more than he ever wanted any other woman. In time she would come to accept her father's part and go on with her own life. He knew she had the strength to overcome that, but she would never forgive him. He'd tear her comfortable world apart, and because of him she would be an innocent victim in the fallout that inevitably would occur.

"Colonel," the civilian driver nodded. Wyatt kept his head down but the man had barely looked at him as he stepped into the bus and took a seat. He only saw the leaves on his collar. Taking a seat away from the driver's line of vision, Wyatt sighed with relief. He was on his way. The first step had been taken. Wyatt had been to Chip's office several times. He remembered a maze of corridors and hoped he could repeat the trip alone. He'd have to enter the code and then run the ID card through a machine. If that went well he'd be in. There would be no going back once he entered the building. Either he got what he was looking for or soldiers with rifles would have him cornered and he'd be led away in handcuffs. He almost laughed. That was if everything went *well.* If it didn't, he only hoped he'd have the chance to be led away cuffed. His second alternative involved blood, toe tags, and body bags.

"What's going on?" Sandra muttered as she replaced the receiver after her fifth call. Every hotel and motel in the city seemed to be full for the night. She'd already checked out of the place where they'd spent the last night and the desk clerk had mentioned they were expecting a tour bus at any moment. This was January, not April when the cherry blossom festival brought thousands of tourists to the city. Why were there so many people occupying hotel rooms?

Sandra sat at the train station on North Capital Street. It was convenient and private. Union Station had been restored in recent years, and it was a hub of activity for the capital. It still had the old wooden telephone booths where a person could sit in privacy and talk. The forty-watt bulb over her head provided illumination for the thick Chesapeake and Potomac Telephone directory that rested on the small shelf. An array of coins lay under the mirrored surface of the phone. Using her finger she ran it down the list and picked another motel. She dialed the number and waited for someone to answer.

"I'm sorry, we are completely booked for tonight and the rest of the week," she was told after inquiring about a room. "We might be able to book you if you call after six tomorrow."

What were they going to do? It was getting late and Wyatt hadn't answered when she'd call the appointed number. They'd been separated for three hours, the longest they had been apart since she found him bleeding in the snow. Suppose he'd been caught. Was he in jail? Was he dead? She shivered.

Going to see Annie alone had been a mistake. Although they needed the money if they were to continue, she should have had Wyatt go with her. At least she'd know where he was and if he was all right. She dialed the memorized number he should have answered, but only the relentless ringing continued in her ear. Wyatt was missing.

"Damn." She slammed the phone down. "Wyatt, where are you?" She admitted she missed him. Before he'd come into her life she'd been doing little more than existing. Even now, when her life was in so much turmoil, she felt more alive than she had since John's death.

Wyatt was all right, she told herself. He'd survived for a week before he met her. But he'd been caught and nearly killed. If he'd only call her or go to the phone where she could reach him! Something had to be wrong.

Sandra sat staring at her fingernails. They were short and unpainted. She peeled at the skin about her index finger wondering what her next move should be. Grabbing a coin, she dropped it in the slot and dialed her father.

"Michael, this is Sandra." She tried to keep the rising panic out of her voice. "Have you found my father?"

"Just a moment, Ms. Rutledge," he said formally.

Sandra chewed her lower lip, pressing the black instrument closer to her ear as the seconds stretched out.

"Sandy, are you all right?"

"Dad!" She almost cried at the familiarity of his voice. "I'm fine. I'm fine. I need to talk to you."

A minor hesitation preceded his reply, "Of course. Are you sure *you're* all right?"

"I've been with Wyatt Randolph. He's said some terrible things about you and I need you to clear them up."

"Where are you?"

Sandra looked through the glass of the phone booth. The cavernous structure reached three stories into the sky. A glass skylight arched upward like a bubble umbrella. Suddenly, she wasn't sure of her own father. Had Wyatt undermined her this badly? Outside the booth she heard the garbled announcement of a train arriving. She covered the mouthpiece until it ended.

"I'm downtown, not far from you," she told him. "Can you meet me somewhere?"

He cleared his throat. Sandra knew that gesture. He used it as well as he used the pregnant pause to buy himself a few seconds while he decided what to say. "I'm on my way out right now. Why don't I call you later and we can meet?"

For a moment she didn't think she'd heard him correctly. He'd rarely refused her requests to talk. No matter what was happening, he'd told her he would always be her father first, a senator second.

"Sandy, where are you staying?"

"I don't exactly know."

"What does that mean?" Concern crept into his voice.

"Don't worry, Dad. I'm not sleeping on the streets." She didn't know *where* she would be sleeping. Revealing that information would only cause him unnecessary stress, and she didn't want to do that. He was still her father.

"Are you with Senator Wyatt?"

"Not at the moment."

"You do know where he is?"

Sandra remembered the call to the pay phone. "I haven't seen him in a while."

"Sandy, you have to get away from him."

"Why?"

"I can't explain it now."

"Then meet me somewhere."

Again she heard the hesitation. "All right. There's something I must do first. Then we'll have dinner."

"Good."

"Do you have your cellular unit?"

She glanced at her purse. The red light pulsed indicating it was on. She'd hoped Wyatt would remember she had it and call her. "Yes."

"Good. I'll call you when I'm free and we'll meet."

"All right," she said. "Dad, can you make it soon? I don't think we can keep running too much longer."

"It's nearly over, honey."

His voice was low and warm, the way she remembered it being when she'd been a gangly teenager and needed to talk to someone. Wyatt had to be wrong. Her father would call. They would meet and everything would be cleared up. She hung up with a smile. She'd tell Wyatt and soon this horrible business would be behind them. She could return to her studies and Wyatt could go back to representing the people of Pennsylvania.

Sandra frowned. Why did she find the prospect of returning to her everyday routine unappealing?

Agent Melvin Normal followed the secretary into the inner sanctum of Director Christopher's private office. He'd been with the bureau for six years. This was his first time on the top floor.

Clarence Christopher's office was large, but not gigantic. Photos on the wall showed him smiling with various men and women. Normal recognized past Presidents, a few bureau directors, and even a Hollywood movie star.

"Agent Norman," the director acknowledged his presence.

"Sir, Ms. Rutledge is in a phone booth at Union Station. Agents have been dispatched to pick her up."

Christopher shook his head, but otherwise indicated no emotion.

"She spoke to Senator Rutledge in his office. He's to call her back on a cellular unit."

"Find the number and have it located."

"We're already on it, sir."

Star Wars! Worse than Star Wars. Wyatt couldn't believe his eyes. He'd have sworn this kind of thing had died with the Reagan/Bush administrations. When communism failed, it was no longer necessary, but it seemed as if Chip hadn't realized it.

Wyatt hadn't been sure what he would find when he entered Chip's office. It had been two weeks since Chip died. Would someone else already occupy the office? Would everything be moved and his trip be wasted? He found the computer still connected, but everything else had been packed. The walls were bare of plaques and photographs Wyatt remembered seeing on his last visit.

Three boxes sat on the floor next to a file cabinet. He could see Chip's degree sticking out of one of them. He wondered why they were still there. Why hadn't his sister come to get them? He turned away, not wanting to think about his friend.

Wyatt sat at Chip's computer. He'd stolen into his office and turned on the machine. The color monitor beamed his notes over the microcircuitry, offering the only light in the room. He'd found Project Eagle as a password-protected directory.

Wyatt thought he'd discover the password quickly. He and Chip had known each other forever, but it took him much longer than he expected. Finally, he found it. Opening the directory, he discovered only one file was readable. The others were encrypted. Gibberish flowed like lightning across the pentium-powered screen. The idea of copying the files came on the heels of seeing the tape backup drive open and empty. Chip was meticulous about making sure he didn't lose data due to a hard-disk crash. He was, however, tied into a network. That would be backed up nightly and he'd have no need— Wyatt didn't complete the thought. If Chip had no need to back his own files, why did he have a backup drive? Why was it open and what had been inside it? Someone else had been here, Wyatt thought; been here and taken what Wyatt was looking for.

There must be other tapes, he thought. Pulling the drawers open, he found only a few paper clips and an array of disks scattered in the bottom.

"Thank God!" he prayed. Wyatt began copying the directory. It took twenty-seven disks and over an hour to complete. His palms sweated as the machine continued to require another disk. Pacing the room, his heart pounded as if he could force the process to complete faster than the drive could handle it. The sun kept sinking, darkening the room except for the light produced by the monitor. Wyatt wondered what time the guards began rounds. Would someone come in and find him? Computer piracy would be added to the lists of crimes he'd committed by just being here. And he still had to get out. He'd wanted to leave with the crowd during rush hour, but he hadn't finished.

He also hadn't called Sandra. Chip appeared to have high-tech equipment, including his phone. The Pentagon probably had the best phone system in the world. Chip's phone had several extensions on it. Wyatt recognized words like CAMP, FLASH, and FORWARD from his own phone back in the Senate office building. He knew when he picked up the receiver his secretary and several of his aides knew he was on the phone. He couldn't take the chance that someone might notice the light from an extension of one Chip Jackson, recently deceased.

Finally, the prompt appeared without the message to insert another disk. He was done. Wyatt banded the disks in two piles and stuffed them in the pockets of the jacket. Suddenly, he wished for the ski jacket Sandra had given him when they escaped the mountain.

Before turning the machine off he checked for other references to Project Eagle. He found none. Flipping the switch, the screen went black. The only light seeping into the room came through the vertically slated blinds. Wyatt checked the outside, finding nothing but the incessant traffic on Route 1 whizzing by at speeds in excess of the legal fifty-five miles per hour.

His time was up. He had to get out now. When he turned back to the room he could see everything outlined in the dimness; the desk, the computer, the boxes on the floor. He lifted Chip's degree which had hung on the side wall next to a book case a few weeks ago. *The trustees of Morgan State University certify that Edward Jackson has satisfactory completed . . .* He knew the words by heart. The two of them had been ecstatic about graduation. They were going to conquer the world. Now Chip was dead and he was a fugitive from both the law and some unknown assailant.

Wyatt slipped the frame back in the box and straightened. He looked at the wall, seeing more in his mind than through his eyes, the place where citations for community service work had shared space with certificates from continuing education programming and computer software classes. Turning away from the memories, Wyatt started for the door. The anteroom remained empty as it had been when he arrived. He cracked the door to the hall and peeped out. The hallway was clear. He prayed his thanks and stepped onto the polished floor.

He walked down the hall, forcing his steps to be unhurried. He made it through the first security checkpoint. The disks didn't register under the metal detectors, and he passed through. The activity in the second ring was busy and hurried. People passed him as they scurried to whatever emergency was at hand. Wyatt hoped it wasn't him. Continuing, he made it through to the first and final ring. The exit door was in sight. Just a few steps away and he'd be out, clear of the building and out of imminent danger.

Ten feet from freedom a colonel stepped in front of him. He stopped, his feet spread apart, his arms behind his back. He rocked slightly back and forth. "Senator Randolph, welcome to the Pentagon."

When Sam Parker had blocked his exit, Wyatt thought his life was over. His stomach sank. He swallowed hard over the lump clogging his throat and waited, waited for men to grab each of his arms and restrain him. Instead, Sam stepped forward and pumped his hand as if they were old friends who hadn't seen each other in a long time. Together they left the building and walked to Sam's car, parked in the first lot.

"You've got to be the craziest man on earth," Sam told him as they left the parking area and joined the traffic. "What did you think you were doing, breaking into a government building?"

"I didn't break in." Wyatt checked the sandstone-colored building they'd just left. "I thought you'd turn me in," he said, returning his gaze to Sam.

"You're lucky I saw you before someone else did."

Wyatt wasn't sure. He and Sam had known each through Chip. The three of them had spent a lot of time together, but he wasn't sure how things stood now that Chip was dead. He'd called him, but Wyatt didn't know if his agreement was fully trustworthy. When he found the security badge he'd decided to go it alone.

Sam worked in the same area as Chip had, computerized defense systems. That was about as much as Wyatt knew.

"Chip was my friend, too, and I want to know who killed him," Sam said.

Wyatt checked Sam's expression closely. He didn't know if he was telling the truth or not. "What has the Pentagon said about it?"

"They issued the standard condolence statement and said the investigation was under the jurisdiction of the police department."

"They dropped it?"

"Not altogether. Officially the department isn't saying a thing, but behind the scenes I hear snatches of conversation, see an occasional memo. Except for trying to find you, nothing is open. Of course, the grapevine says Chip sent you something. Only a few of us actually know what it was."

So Sam knew about the stones. Is that why he'd helped him get out of the Pentagon? Was he trying to get them back?

"You want to know if it's true?"

"I already know it's true," he laughed. "If you didn't have them, you wouldn't have taken such a big risk to get into Chip's office."

"How did you know I was there?"

"Where else would you go?"

"What are you going to do now?"

"Relax, Wyatt." He glanced at him. "I'm on your side. If I wanted to turn you in, I could have done it when you phoned."

"Why didn't you?" Wyatt asked suspiciously. "You're a career soldier. What you've done could get you court-martialed, drummed out of the service with no pension and no benefits." Wyatt didn't mention it could also get him killed. "Why would you want to put all those things on the line to help me?"

"Because Chip is . . . was my friend, too," he repeated, "and I don't like what I think they're going to do to him."

"What is that?"

Sam sighed heavily. He turned the car onto the Beltway and headed toward Maryland. Wyatt waited, his patience slipping away.

"They're setting him up to be the scapegoat . . . and you, too. You're a wildcard. They hadn't counted on Chip taking the stones or sending them to you. I also think my involvement is also on the line."

"How are you involved?" Wyatt asked.

"Chip and I were working on the same project. We were at different points and didn't know about the other. We're only allowed to discuss our work with someone who knows about it. For weeks we didn't see each other, although we worked in the same building. By chance we met at the end of the lunch hour one day and I happened to mention that the Eagle was driving me crazy. I was more than a little surprised to find out he knew what I meant. We talked later, away from the Pentagon, and found out we were working on the same thing, but mine was a device to sabotage foreign communications, while his was a linking mechanism to use the combined power of separately orbiting satellites."

"That's what the stones do?"

Sam stared at him. "You don't know? Chip didn't tell you what you're holding?"

"No."

Sam pulled into the driveway of his house and cut the motor. He didn't move to open the door, but turned to look Wyatt directly in the face.

"Project Eagle is a communications device that can eavesdrop on anything from a single phone to the entire world."

CHAPTER 9

"Dad?" Sandra grabbed the ringing phone and shouted into the receiver. She'd been waiting all afternoon for him to call. Wyatt hadn't answered any of her attempts and she was so angry she could eat nails.

"You called your father?" Wyatt's voice was reprimanding.

"Wyatt! Where are you? I've been out of my mind with worry."

"So out of your mind you called your father?" he shouted.

Her anger intensified. He'd been missing all day. She didn't know if he was alive or dead and he was shouting at her. "What did you expect me to do? You weren't where you were supposed to be. I called that number over and over and not once did you answer it."

She heard him take a long breath. It was calming also to her. "I talked to my father this afternoon."

"What did the senator have to say?"

Sandra heard the dark censure in Wyatt's question.

"Not much. We agreed to meet later for dinner."

"You didn't tell him where you were?"

"No, at the time I didn't have anyplace to tell him. I just found a room. He's going to call me later."

"How?"

"On the cell phone—"

"Listen to me, Sandra. You're in immediate danger. I want you to get out of there, now!"

"Wyatt, you're not making any sense. Do you know how long it took me to find this room? I'm not—"

"Sandra!" he shouted. "Get out of there, now! Go to the Lincoln Memorial. I'll meet you there."

"Wyatt, why—"

"I'll explain later. Turn off the phone and go. Promise me you'll do what I ask?"

Sandra paused. She wasn't used to following orders. What was wrong with Wyatt?

"Promise me?"

"All right," she conceded. "I'll come."

"Now, Sandra. Time is not on your side."

"All right, I'll do it, *now.* I don't understand, but I'll do it."

Sandra switched the phone to Off and grabbed her backpack. Hiking it on to her back she took the canvas bag she hadn't unpacked and started for the door. She peeped through the curtain and saw nothing. If it had been Wyatt's plan to frighten her, he'd done a good job. She opened the door and went out. Taking a route away from the registration desk, she had reached the end of the motel complex when she turned. Two men with guns drawn flanked the door of her room.

Clamping her hand over her mouth, she stopped the shriek that struggled to escape. Her other hand went to her stomach, which flopped as if she'd gone over the top of a roller coaster. Sandra crouched against the building. Her knees threatened to buckle. Who were they? Who'd sent them? They kicked the door in and rushed inside, one going high, the other flipping over inside. The force of their movement gave her feet the ability to move. She quickly hailed a cab and instructed the driver to take her to the Lincoln Memorial.

By the time she arrived, there was little skin left around her index finger and drops of blood beaded on her hand. She ran up the hundred marble stairs and rushed inside the hushed quiet of the temple honoring the sixteenth President of the United States. Her head whipped from side to side as she scanned the cavernous room. Wyatt wasn't there.

Sandra was close to tears. Her life had been turned upside down. There was no one she could trust, not even her father. That bothered her more than Wyatt's disappearance. He was the only person she'd told about the phone other than Wyatt. Yet, he hadn't come to her. Men with guns had come. Sandra trembled. She needed something familiar, somewhere she could relax and put things in order. She went to stand between two of the thirty-six columns representing the states that comprised the United States when Lincoln was President. The Colorado marble was cold to her touch, but she needed the coldness to stabilize herself, help her to calm down. Men with guns had been after her. What would they have done if Wyatt hadn't insisted she leave the room? Would she be dead now? Would they try to force Wyatt's location from her or would they assume she knew where the stones were and try to extract that information?

She shivered in the cold dimness of late afternoon. Her shoulders began to shake with the beginnings of hysteria when strong arms caught her and turned her around.

"Wyatt!"

She went into his arms and clung to him. The solid feel of his chest against her cheek calmed the hysteria. She pressed herself closer to him forgetting the words he'd said about her father's involvement, only needing the strength he offered and she readily took.

"They came, Wyatt. Men with guns."

"Shh," he whispered. "You're safe. I won't let anything happen to you."

"How did they know?"

"The phone," he explained. "It's only a radio signal. When you told your father to call you on it, you sent out a signal. It wouldn't take long to identify the source and find you."

She tried to pull away, but Wyatt kept her in place. "They can't be that precise? It's a cheap phone. We're not talking about state-of-the-art equipment here. How could they find the exact motel room I was in?"

"The Defense Department has the best equipment in the world."

"But why me? Why would anyone think that I warranted a trace so important—" She stopped. "It's wasn't me, was it? They were looking for you and the diamonds?"

Wyatt nodded and cradled her head against his shoulder. Moments later, he led her away and to a waiting car. Sandra got inside and let her head loll against the upholstery. When the car was in motion she opened her eyes. She recognized them crossing Memorial Bridge, connecting the Lincoln Memorial in Washington to Arlington National Cemetery in Virginia. Wyatt headed toward Alexandria. Then she noticed Wyatt's clothes. The cap of an army colonel sat on his head. She straightened in the seat as if she were coming to attention. Her eyes widened as she took in the collar inside the jacket, then the tan-colored cloth of his pants.

"Why are you dressed like that?"

"Don't you like it?" he joked, offering her his profile. "I thought women liked men in uniform."

She took a second to notice that he did look wonderful, but impersonating an officer was a punishable offense. "Don't joke," she told him. "Where did you get that uniform?"

"I bought it at the Army-Navy store."

"Why?"

"I went to Chip's office in the Pentagon."

Sandra's mouth dropped open.

"How did you get in? Their security has security at that place." She'd been in the Pentagon. Lance Desque had once given her a tour while her father attended some meeting. "Suppose you'd been caught? Do you know what they would have done to you?"

Wyatt put his hand on her arm. "It's all right. I got in and I got out without incident."

She didn't believe that for a moment. "Are you sure? Even when you don't know you're being observed, you are." Lance had shown her all the security devices they used to monitor the building. If you've been in the Pentagon, they know it."

Wyatt pondered this for a moment. He did think it strange that he'd been able to spend so much time in Chip's office and not be discovered, but he thought it was due to Chip's death. The office hadn't been locked and anyone who knew Chip would be able to figure out his password and would know his habits. Wyatt suddenly felt exposed.

"Where did you get this car?" Sandra looked about as if this was the first time she noticed the plush interior of the Chrysler LeBaron. They were passing Crystal City, a huge complex of hotels, shopping centers, and office buildings. It was near enough to the capital to provide spectacular views of the national monuments.

On the heels of his discovery about Chip's office, Wyatt didn't want to tell her about meeting Sam Parker in the hallway or that this was Sam's car.

He felt uneasy again, like he was being watched or followed. Wyatt checked the rearview mirror, but saw nothing more than a progression of taxis en route to the airport. Other cars swung from lane to lane in a traffic dance that ran nonstop through the nation's highway system. On impulse Wyatt swung into National Airport and parked.

"Come on." He was already getting out of the car. Sandra quickly followed him. Reaching for her hand, they moved quickly and purposefully toward the terminal as if they were late to catch a flight. Sandra suddenly remembered their clothes. She'd left them on the backseat. Wyatt restrained Sandra, whose pull on his arm slowed them and showed her fear.

"I left the suitcase."

He saw the shoulder straps of her backpack securing it to her right arm. The canvas bag was conspicuously absent.

"Leave it," Wyatt decided. Their near-running steps slowed to a walk. Running would draw attention to them.

As a cautionary move, Wyatt led her into the terminal. They went through the glass doors and proceeded through the building before exiting a door in another terminal and getting into a taxi. He gave the driver an Alexandria address, and the car raced from the curb. Sandra was jostled against Wyatt as the driver jockeyed for position among the many cabs leaving the busy airport.

Wyatt put his arm around her shoulders and hugged her to him. Behind them, in the parking lot where Wyatt had left the car, the bomb exploded.

Suzanne admitted the room-service waitress into her suite. The woman set the breakfast of scrambled eggs, toast, croissants, cereal and milk, Canadian bacon, fresh fruit, and hot coffee on the dining-room table. She loved breakfast. Jordon never commented on what she ate. As long as she got into the size six gowns she was fine.

She signed the bill, and the woman turned with a smile. Jordon came in as she pushed the food tray into the hall.

"Good morning." He took a seat and immediately opened the silver covers, inhaling as if food was the best thing on earth. Suzanne thought he did it to irritate her. So often she had to refuse foods, but not today and not breakfast.

She rifled through the mail next to the fresh flowers the hotel changed every day.

"Why do they keep inviting me?" she asked, holding an invitation to an embassy party. The agency handled her mail. Bills were sent to her accountant and anything important they sent to her wherever she was.

"You *are* the daughter of a US senator, not to mention all the dignitaries you've met and friends you've made in your travels," Jordon answered. "You'd be upset if they didn't," he added absently. He poured a cup of coffee and drank it black. "Who's it from?"

"There are three new ones today." She dropped one and looked at the embossed emblem on the invitation. "One from Egypt, I haven't been there in years."

"Ah, but you're remembered, my dear."

Suzanne threw him a cutting glance. "The other two are from the Japanese Embassy and the Embassy of the Republic of China."

"You might want to consider the Chinese one. It could be useful if we have to go there for a shoot. And of course, it's only polite to attend the Japanese one since you are wearing their clothes."

Suzanne deliberated over adding marmalade to her toast. She was eating it dry and wanted the sweetness, but decided to save the calories for something else. "I'll think about it," she said.

"You usually like these parties." Jordon eyed her suspiciously. Suzanne kept her gaze on her plate. "What's different about these?"

"Nothing," she said, bringing her gaze to him. "I just want to get this assignment over with and get back to New York."

Jordon didn't reply. He stared at her, his eyes so piercing that Suzanne felt as if he were delving into her mind. Another of his habits which she detested.

"She's beautiful," Jordon began changing the subject, his stare never leaving her face. "High cheekbones, lovely eyes, and skin that looks like nature sculpted it. We'd need to do something about her hair, but I couldn't resist looking at the two of you through the lens of my camera. Who is she?"

Suzanne stopped with the toast halfway to her mouth. "Jordon, you didn't take our picture?"

"Would that be a problem?" Jordon folded his arms on the dining-room table where the waitress had laid their breakfast. He stared directly at her. Suzanne smiled at him, changing her mind and adding the marmalade to her toast.

"You know you need permission to use photographs of strangers."

"I never said I wanted to use it. I just want to know who she is."

"Her name is Sandra Rutledge. She's making news with Senator Wyatt Randolph by leaving a path of destruction wherever she goes." Suzanne pushed the newspaper toward Jordon. The story of the car bomb at National Airport was the lead story on the front page. The car was identified as belonging to Colonel Sam Parker who reported it stolen from his home yesterday. Several cars had been burned in the lot, but no one was hurt.

Sandra still had that going for her. So far she and the senator hadn't killed anyone, but on the path they were headed, it wouldn't be long.

"Sandra is your sister." Jordon made it a statement.

"She is."

"What do you think of this?" Jordon slapped the paper.

"Nothing. It's Sandra's life for as long as it lasts."

"She's in trouble, Annie. Can you really be that cold?"

Suzanne's eyes flashed at him. "Jordon, you don't understand."

"What is there to understand? Did she come to ask for your help yesterday?"

Suzanne nodded.

"And you refused her?"

"Jordon, hold on to your blood pressure. She wanted money and I told her I'd get it."

Suzanne grinned. She had the five thousand dollars safely hidden in the dresser drawer. She'd had a ball driving around the beltway and stopping at shopping centers to hook her laptop up to pay phones and begin her worldwide network of wiring funds from bank to bank. Finally, after enough transactions that would have an expert unraveling them for a month, she'd walked into Riggs National Bank and withdrawn the cash.

"Annie, tell me what happened between the two of you."

She got up. Her white gown trailed behind her as she walked away. She knew how to walk. She'd practiced putting one size-seven-foot in front of the other on every major runway in the world.

"How much longer do you think we're going to be here?" She changed the subject.

"You're not going to answer the question?"

"Which question was that?"

"Don't be obtuse, Annie. What happened between you and your sister that makes you get money for her, but won't let the two of you stay in the same city?"

"Jordon, stay out of it. It has nothing to do with you or anything that you should get involved with."

"Well, let me tell you something, Annie. It affects everything you say and do." He got up and walked toward her. Suzanne was surprised by the vehemence of his voice. She'd known Jordon since she took her first modeling job, yet she'd never seen this side of him. '"If you don't let go of this anger, it's going to eat you up until there's nothing left."

"Jordon, what is wrong with you?" She frowned.

"Wrong with me? I'll show you what's wrong with me."

His hands grabbed her arms and pulled her against him. Without warning his hand threaded into her hair and his mouth took hers. Suzanne had no time to stop him. His mouth was wet and warm and she found herself reacting to him. She turned toward him, fitting herself into his body as passion flared between them. All thoughts of Sandra were wiped from her mind as Jordon deepened the kiss. Her arms tightened, pulling him closer. He felt wonderful, and she wanted him to continue kissing her. His tongue swept within her mouth. Suzanne thought she would incinerate from the heat being produced by the two of them. Inside her a deep hunger broke free and surfaced. Her kiss answered his as she molded and wound herself against the length of him. Jordon's mouth devoured her and she'd never felt more like surrendering in her life. Then he lifted her and carried her to the bedroom.

"You lied to me!" Sam Parker shouted. He slammed a copy of *The Washington Post* on to the polished sheen of the conference room table. "They could have been killed. Innocent people could have been killed." He paced the room like a caged tiger.

"Sam, calm down, everything is under control."

"How can you say that?" He pointed to the paper. "Do you see what it says here? They've been accused of being terrorists and trying to blow up the airport."

"Nobody got hurt."

"Much to your disappointment. If you'd had your way, Wyatt would be charred meat this morning." Sam took a breath. "And I would have helped you do it."

"Sam, why don't you go back to work and forget about this?"

"Forget that I betrayed a friend, that I was party to the death of a man I respect? Forget that I came to you when he called me and agreed to your plan, forget it could have cost him his life? I don't think so."

Sam Parker slammed the door on his way out of the conference room.

"He's going to be a problem," one of the two men left in the room said.

"I agree."

"We'll have to get rid of him."

"Leave it to me. I'll do what's necessary."

"What about the sister? I hear she's in town."

"She's staying at the Holiday Inn near the Capitol."

"Anybody watching her?"

"I've got a man stationed there, but I don't expect anything. The two sisters haven't been friends for the last few years. I'd be surprised if we found the senator's daughter and her sister together."

"Nevertheless, make sure someone keeps track of her."

"Honey, wake up," Wyatt crooned into Sandra's ear. He cradled her against him, grabbing at her arms as she fought demons in the air. "Wake up, you're having a bad dream." He pushed her hair away from her face and kissed her on the cheek. Her face was clammy with sweat, but she shivered. "Wake up, Sandra."

Her eyes flew open. "Wyatt," she whispered in a breathy voice that sounded as if she'd just run a mile.

"I'm here, dear." Wyatt hugged her close, as if she were a small child. "You're all right. It was just a dream."

"It was horrible." Her arms ran around his waist. "You were in the car. I was running toward you. The car blew up." Tears clouded her voice. "Flames leapt at me. I could feel my arms burning." She rubbed her arms, convincing herself they were still there and it had only been a dream.

"Shh, it's all right. You're safe. You're with me." He kissed her forehead.

"Hold me," she pleaded as her arms tightened about him. "Don't let me go."

He held her until her arms slacked and she went back to sleep. Then he laid her back in the bed and crawled in next to her. She needed the rest. At any other time she'd have been the only thing on his mind, but Sam Parker's betrayal held dominance over his consciousness. He'd been awake all night thinking of the man he'd trusted and the near-disaster that would have fallen on them. If Sandra hadn't told him about the security in the Pentagon, both of them would be statistics this morning.

Randolph and Rutledge Killed in Car Bombing, he envisioned the headline if they had in fact died. Wyatt berated himself. He'd convinced Sandra not to trust her own father and then he'd let himself fall into the trap of trusting an old friend. It wouldn't happen again. Until he got to the bottom of Project Eagle they were on their own.

Sandra shifted, throwing her arm over him. He caressed it gently. Her breathing became even and she settled into a comfortable sleep. Wyatt watched her relaxed features and hoped he could keep her safe until she was no longer a target. He couldn't let her go. There was no place she would be safe until this ended.

The rain woke her. Sandra opened her eyes to the dimly lit room. The heavy curtains that blocked the windows only let slivers of light into the room. She could hear the water pelting against the outside glass.

Wyatt lay beside her. His arm around her waist cradled her against him. His body was warm against her bottom. She hadn't awakened next to a man since John died. She liked the security of knowing he was there, and she liked waking up in his arms. Turning over, she faced him. His head was higher on the pillow than hers and she had to keep herself from reaching up and kissing him awake.

Why couldn't they be just two people getting to know each other and falling in love? Why did they have to be on the run, trusting no one and wanted for a list of crimes that increased each time they stepped outdoors? Sandra shivered slightly and Wyatt scooped her closer to him. She had no place to put her arms except around him.

She stiffened slightly, knowing she shouldn't enjoy the feel of his strong arms, but he was asleep and it couldn't hurt. She ran her gaze over his dark arms. Her fingers danced lightly over his skin. It was smooth to her touch. She liked the feel of his muscles as they quivered and relaxed. Shifting her head on his shoulder, she stopped short of running her hand over his chest. Wyatt only had the uniform now. He was near-naked next to her. The thought was arousing. She could feel an ache in the pit of her stomach and her nipples were hard and erect against his chest. She knew better than to let anything get out of control. He was still trying to prove her father guilty of treason, and despite what had happened, she was convinced there had to be a logical explanation for her father's apparent collusion in a plot against both her and Wyatt. Even with that between them she was still attracted to him. She knew he found her attractive, too. After the way he kissed her, she could be in no doubt. Sandra settled next to him and closed her eyes.

Behind her eyes the image of Wyatt formed. Sandra had thought she'd never replace John with another man, and while she hadn't replaced John, she had relegated him to a safe place in her heart. He had been her husband. She'd loved him with all her heart, thought they would have a family and grow old together. The cruelty of the illness that took their future had long since been resolved. Wyatt could be thanked for giving her back the will to live. Now that her life appeared so close to ending, she found she wanted to live. She didn't just want to fill her days with so much work that she had no time to think. She wanted to have a purpose and . . . Wyatt? Did she want Wyatt in her life?

Sandra frowned at the impact of her thoughts. If the two of them survived to expose Project Eagle, her father could be involved in it as Wyatt suggested. What would that do to them? Could she fall in love with a man who ruined her family?

Her hand on Wyatt's arm stilled. He reached up and took her fingers. Sandra lifted her head and found his eyes staring into hers.

"What's wrong," he asked.

She looked away. "I-I . . ." She couldn't tell him. She went to move away from him, but Wyatt's arms pulled her into contact with his warm body. Her head came up and she looked into his eyes. He was too good-looking and the situation was too intimate.

"Sandra, I know yesterday was traumatic, but time will take care of that. We'll get over it. Don't worry. I'm not going to let anything happen to you."

He'd misunderstood her expression. She'd forgotten the car bomb and her inability to sleep comfortably the previous night. It was why Wyatt shared her bed, why she'd awakened in his arms, with nothing more than a T-shirt on, and why she was more miserable than she'd ever been.

"Look at me," Wyatt said.

She hesitated before raising her head.

"I understand," she said, deliberately allowing him to believe he'd touched on the reason for her pained expression.

She felt so good. Wyatt had warned himself not to get into this situation. Last night she'd fallen asleep on his shoulder and he'd held her through the night. Now he didn't want to let go. He wanted to hold on to her for the rest of the day, forget that there was anything they should do or be cautious about.

Wyatt wrapped his arms around her, tightening them. Her face came up close to his. He knew better. He'd told himself to let this one pass, to keep everything simple and leave the sexual part out of it, but right now with her this close, with her body touching his, he couldn't. Her fingers were light, as if she didn't want them to feel his skin, but they couldn't help it. He couldn't help it, either.

Something other than the two of them had entered their relationship. Something that knew them better than they knew themselves but each refused to acknowledge. Wyatt lifted her chin closer to him. His heart slammed into his chest when his lips touched hers. He pushed back, surprised at the impact of the simple contact.

Sandra's eyes were wide and expectant. Her hand came up and caressed his cheek and his mouth covered hers. He leaned forward rolling her into the mattress as his mouth took on a life of its own. His tongue slipped between her teeth and the nectar was his undoing. Her mouth was hot and his entire body took in her heat, combining it with his own. Why they didn't burn the sheets off the bed he'd never know.

Her legs wrapped around his. The smooth surface of her shaved thighs met the roughness of his and the friction drove him crazy with need. His hands reached under the hem of her extra large T-shirt, the only garment she was wearing. Slowly he let the fire burn in his palms as they traveled over her, caressing the flat plane of her stomach, then moving to the rounded globes of her breasts. She moaned a low, guttural, primal sound when he touched them.

Wyatt's mouth left Sandra's to seek, taste, and touch her neck and arms in a direct map to her breasts. He could hardly contain himself when he reached the darkened nipples. Her hands buried in his short hair as her head thrashed back and forth on the pillow in a sexual frenzy. Wyatt wanted to satisfy her. He wanted to swing his body over hers and enter her, but he wasn't ready yet. He was enjoying the feel of her thighs and arms as her fingers kneaded and massaged the skin at his shoulders and neck. His tongue laved and sucked at her breasts as his arousal intensified, the night sounds that escaped her throat pushing him forward to the breaking point.

"Wyatt?" she moaned, her fingers scratching at his shoulders.

Wyatt pulled the T-shirt over her head and stopped to gaze at her in the half-light. She was beautiful, her body like a vessel of expensive wine. He devoured it, kissing her belly, her breasts, her arms until he made his way to her mouth, which was hot and ready for him.

He slipped his hand between her legs. The same pulsating warmth pushed his erection harder. Control slipped rapidly and the something between them grew to unlimited proportions. This time Wyatt swung his leg across Sandra.

"Protection, Wyatt," Sandra whispered, her voice urgent and breathless.

Wyatt stopped. For a single moment he hung suspended above her. Then he collapsed.

"What's the matter?

He didn't answer immediately. His arms gathered her to him and he held her. He couldn't tell if the trembles that passed between them originated with him or with her.

"Wyatt?" Sandra prompted.

"I don't have any," he said.

She, too, went still beneath him. Then she was shaking. He raised his head thinking something was wrong—and it was. Sandra was laughing.

What started as a silly smile on her part became uncontrollable mirth. She threw her head back and laughed out loud, letting the tension of the week's run, the near-death situations, and the police chases exorcise themselves through uncensored laughter.

"We'd better get dressed and go to meet Jeff," Wyatt said when her stretch of frivolity ended.

While Wyatt took his shower, which she hoped was cold, Sandra regained her composure and took the laptop computer from her backpack and popped one of the disks he'd left on the table in the drive. She tried to concentrate on the screen but images of Wyatt's naked body in the shower behind her kept interfering with her concentration. She should be glad they didn't have a condom. She should be able to concentrate on the problem, to be logical and methodical about the situation, but all she could remember was how good he felt lying on top of her, how good his mouth felt against hers, and how alive she felt right now.

The shower stopped. Sandra jumped up as if he could hear her thoughts. Self-consciousness overtook her. Her shirt was too short and her legs too exposed, and the image of water flowing over Wyatt had her ready for him.

"Damn!" she cursed. Why didn't either of them have a condom?

Sandra showered and dressed in yesterday's clothes and tried to concentrate. She went back to the disks, taking a different one and slipping it into the drive. She had several word processing programs on the hard drive. None of them would read these disks. Then she went to an internal editing program. The encrypted files spanned the entire width of the screen and scrolled about at lightning speed. He'd risked his life to get these and they were unreadable!

She knew what an encryption algorithm was. In a pinch she could even write one, but she had no idea where to begin to find out what was hidden here.

Now they had two mysteries. First the riddle of the stones had to be unraveled and now these files. She had no doubt that one would enhance the other, but finding someone who could read them would be a problem. They could ask Jeff, but if they were as complex as she assumed they were, it would take him at least a month to figure them out.

As much as she wanted to believe she and Wyatt had a future together—and after their episode in the bed she was sure she wanted one—she knew it wouldn't span a period long enough for Jeff to make a difference.

Popping the drive door open, she took out the disk and replaced it. The screen directory showed the same unreadable information. She was about to take the disk out when something struck her as strange. Looking closer at the screen, she found one file that wasn't encrypted. It was in Japanese. Now, what could that mean?

At ten-thirty they left the hotel for Jeff's. Returning to his house or even the lab could be dangerous, so they'd arranged to meet at an address in the northeast. The taxi let them out on Fort Totten and Buchanan and they walked the last mile, clinging to each other like two lovers strolling in the rain. It was Wyatt's idea, but Sandra agreed to it just to be able to touch him.

Before they'd gone a block, they were soaked to the skin. She tried not to shiver, taking the need for caution from some inner radar that communicated itself to her. They approached the apartment complex on Hawaii Avenue from the farthest distance to the designated address.

Cars whizzed past them spraying water and making them even wetter, their clothes heavy and difficult to walk in. Wyatt took the worst of it. Sandra's fingers were stiff and cramped, but she continued walking without complaint. They ducked into the apartment complex and circled the courtyard before climbing the front stairs and immediately exiting on the other side.

Sure there was no one following them, they found apartment 3J and knocked on the metal door. The door creaked open like some horror movie sequence designed to scare the audience. Sandra's heart leapt to her throat. She gripped Wyatt's hand in a bonecrushing squeeze.

Wyatt put his finger to his mouth to keep her from saying anything. She couldn't speak if she had to! He edged the door open wider and they looked inside. The lights were all on. They could see nothing. The television played softly in a corner.

Wyatt took the first step inside. Sandra pulled him back. "Maybe we should go."

"You stay here. I'll go in," he told her. He pushed her out of the doorway and stepped inside. Sandra followed, crouching. She'd seen the two men who'd gone into the motel room seconds after she'd left it. They had had guns. She and Wyatt were unarmed.

She shadowed Wyatt's movements and was behind him when they discovered Jeff lying on the floor, blood soaking into the cream-colored carpeting.

"Jeff!" she shouted, and pushed past Wyatt. In a flash she was next to him and lifting his head. Wyatt pressed his hand to the man's neck, searching for a pulse.

"He's alive," he announced.

"Jeff?" Sandra called.

Jeff's eyes fluttered open. "Sandra, you came."

"Jeff, what happened?"

"I . . . didn't . . . tell . . ." His voice was weak and he coughed between each word.

"Call an ambulance!" she ordered Wyatt. Jeff grabbed her arm. His grip was weak. She took his hand and squeezed it. Tears clouded her eyes.

"No . . . time," he coughed.

"Jeff, did they take the stones?" Wyatt asked.

He shook his head, a crooked smile on his face.

"Where are they?" Sandra asked.

"Ninety-five," he said through his cough.

He was slipping fast. Sandra doubted he'd be able to tell them where the stones were.

"Ninety-five, what?" Wyatt asked. She could hear the control in his voice.

"Ro— 95 . . . 147 . . ." Blood seeped out of his mouth. Sandra pressed her hand against her stomach, fighting her own bile.

"What does that mean?" she asked. "Jeff, what is Row? Jeff?"

Wyatt put his hand on her shoulder. "He's dead, Sandra."

"He's not dead." She glared at Wyatt. "He can't be dead. He can't be dead." Tears fell freely from her eyes. "He can't be . . ."

Wyatt came around behind her. "We have to get out of here." He took Sandra's shoulders but she shrugged him off. "Sandra, you can't help him. We have to go." He pulled her to her feet and led her to the door.

Sandra looked back. "He was my friend."

"I know, honey." Wyatt's voice was sympathetic as he closed the door and led her away. They retraced their steps back to Fort Totten. No taxis appeared on the heavily traveled road, so they walked. Oblivious to the rain pelting her face and head, Sandra walked in a daze. Salty tears mingled with the rainwater as they got farther and farther away.

At Buchanan Street they turned toward North Capital and were lucky enough to find an empty cab.

"Holiday Inn on Third Street in Southwest," Sandra instructed the driver.

Travis Green walked under the train trestle near the Holiday Inn. He'd been stationed here to watch for Senator Randolph. It was broad daylight and raining. Travis found it difficult to be unobtrusive in this area. There was a lot of road traffic and no place to park except in underground lots. A car on the street would be noticed by the many patroling police cars.

Pedestrian traffic wouldn't be as conspicuous during the lunch hour, but at this time of day his continuous walking made him more the hunted than the hunter.

Across the street he'd seen another man. He was obviously watching the place or Travis Green was no government agent. That was the problem with this town, everyone watched everyone else. Between the two of them, they couldn't keep the place properly in view. Cars drove in and out of the off-street entryway. It was impossible to see inside each one or to tell if they went to the garage or turned back onto the one-way street at the side of the building.

Whoever designed this building didn't do it for unobstructed observation. It was time he went inside. He'd use the men's room in the restaurant and get a cup of coffee. He hoped there were different people in the coffee shop this time. He'd been in twice already and he didn't want to be recognized.

A taxi turned left at the light while he waited on the opposite corner. It disappeared into the hotel driveway. He crossed the street, checking for the other man observing the comings and goings of the building's traffic. He was still there—watching. Travis had a mind to go over and ask him who he was looking for. He didn't like not having all the facts of a job. If he'd been sent to stake out this building, why was someone else given the same assignment and why wasn't he told?

As the cab pulled away from the curb, Wyatt whispered in her ear. "Are you all right?"

Sandra nodded.

Wyatt pulled her against him, encircling his arm around her shaking shoulders. Her muffled cries joined the water already soaking him. He knew better than to believe she was all right. He also knew how she felt. He'd had the same numb feeling when he found out Chip was dead. Now, two people had died over the stones and he had no idea where they were. Row 95147 didn't mean anything to him. He was sure it was also a mystery to Sandra, but now wasn't the time to bring that up. She needed a period of mourning. But it would have to be short. When they got checked in and were alone he could talk to her. Meanwhile, he'd just hold her close.

Wyatt paid the driver with the last of his cash when the taxi stopped under the off-street entryway. Before they entered, Wyatt stopped. "Do you want to get the room and I'll meet you there?"

"We're not checking in."

She bypassed the lobby entrance and went to the tower entrance. Pulling the glass doors open, she went inside. Wyatt followed her. She walked as if she knew where she was going. They passed the restaurant, which looked empty, then Sandra punched the button for the elevator. Inside she hit the button for the top floor, and when it required a passcode, she entered it to Wyatt's surprise.

"Where are we going?" he asked when the doors slid closed and the small car began its ascent.

"Among other places, to get a change of clothes."

The ride was short. Since the Washington Monument was completed in the 1860's, no building in the city could be built taller than the

Capitol. Few of them had more than eight floors. The elevator opened and Sandra turned left on her way out. She went directly to Suite 8008 and knocked authoritatively on the door.

"Whose suite is this?"

The door swung inward. "My sister's," Sandra said. "Wyatt, this is my sister Annie. Or Suzanne as she's also called."

"You two look like something the river threw back. Where have you been?" Annie asked.

"Can we come in?"

She stepped back and they filed in.

"Don't stop there," Annie said. "You're dripping all over the carpet. You." She pointed at Sandra. "Use the bathroom over there." Wyatt followed her line of vision. "Senator." He brought his attention back to her. "There's another bathroom through there."

Wyatt started in the direction she pointed. Before he closed the door he heard her pick up the phone.

"Jordon, you'd better come over here." She paused. "And bring a change of clothes, everything from the skin out."

CHAPTER 10

Colonel Samuel Parker had felt uneasy since leaving the briefing meeting this morning. He kept looking over his shoulder, scanning the rearview mirror when he drove. He had the feeling he was being followed, but never saw anyone or anything.

Instinctively, he knew someone was there. He shouldn't have told them. Normally he was a cautious man. He'd lived his life being cautious. The Army had taught him that. He didn't volunteer for assignments and he didn't offer information unless it was asked for. When he'd been approached to talk to Wyatt, on the heels of a phone call from the senator, he'd agreed. That had been his mistake. He was livid when he found out the car had a bomb on board and that he had been a party to attempted murder. He was an officer and he would never willingly lead a friend into a trap. They must have known that when they asked him to aid Wyatt in finding the component.

They couldn't arrest him. He didn't have the component with him and they needed to know where it was. Wyatt was operating in the dark and he didn't know it. He'd been asked to assist them, help Wyatt get out of the Pentagon and loan him a car so he'd have transportation. They were only going to put a tracking device in the car.

"Some tracking device," he muttered.

When Wyatt led them to the component everything would be over, they told him. Wyatt wouldn't even be charged with anything. They'd even make sure the woman he was with would also go free. Sam knew that woman wasn't just anybody. She was the daughter of the powerful Senate subcommittee chairman.

Parker had been smart enough to get that in writing. He'd secured the document in his safe at his home. He'd checked on it last night before he went to bed and this morning when he got up. It was still there. Sam Parker was a cautious man. He'd made copies of the document and put one in a new safety-deposit box, a box he had only opened two days earlier. As an added safety he'd scanned the document into the computer and encrypted the file in the Project Eagle Directory. As Wyatt spent his hour making a copy of that directory, he'd taken the document out of the building.

His day was over and it was time to go home. The hairs on his neck stood up and the uncomfortable feeling settled over him like a shroud. They'd tried to kill a US senator and the daughter of a US senator. He was only a colonel, but he was under no illusion that they wouldn't snuff him, too.

He couldn't outrun them. Wyatt had eluded them for the past three weeks. He'd waltzed right through Pentagon Security, although he'd been made the moment he entered Jackson's office. Wyatt was more resourceful than he was. He wouldn't last a day on the run. So, since he couldn't run, he'd have to do something else. He strapped his laptop over his shoulder and picked up his briefcase.

Parker adhered to the energy-saving notice on the wall above his light switch and turned off the ceiling lights. At this time of day the buses to the parking lot would be crowded. Since it continued to pour, they would be packed as tight as sardines. Parker felt uneasy about boarding anything packed so tight he could be stabbed and not even fall. He decided to walk to his car.

Checking over his shoulder, he opened the black regulation umbrella and started across the parking lot. He found his car easily, but wondered if it was bombed, too. The thought stopped him. While he worked, had some unseen person rigged his ignition with a bomb? He continued. He couldn't walk from here. His raincoat was soaked when he reached the new LeSabre. The car was only three months old and he'd hate to see it blown to bits. The explosion wouldn't do much for him, either.

Parker checked his memory as he came within range of the electronic security system. He pushed the button on the hand keypad, ready to turn and duck in the event of an explosion. Nothing happened. Few car bombers set bombs to explode as the doors were opened. The exploding impact could push the intended victim away and they'd only be hurt instead of killed. The preferable methods were to use the spark of ignition, have the car in motion and reach a certain speed, or when the brakes were applied after a certain speed. The car he'd loaned Wyatt had a simple timing mechanism. At a certain time it exploded. Gingerly he opened the door. A sigh of relief escaped him when nothing catastrophic happened. He inspected the drive shaft and the concealed wiring below for any sign of tampering. Everything appeared exactly as it should be. Standing back, he used his umbrella tip to push the electronic button that released the hood. The lock popped free. With the umbrella still in his hand, he repeated the gesture to open the trunk.

"Anything wrong?"

He jerked at the shouted question. Attack was on his mind. Only the briefcase and computer saved him from decking one of the secretaries.

"No, nothing is wrong."

She smiled warily and got into her car. Sam waited for her to leave. As soon as she was gone he checked the underside of the car. Finding nothing suspicious, he went to the back of the car.

Checking the trunk first, opened to its full height, he only found his spare tire under the gray carpeting and his tools for changing a flat tire. He threw his briefcase and laptop carrying case inside and, after looking at the lock mechanism, reached to pull the trunk closed.

The thought of tires made him take the tire iron and pull each hubcap free. Nothing was out of the ordinary. Under the hood he found the same okay state. He breathed his relief and got inside. The engine roared to life at the turning of the key and then purred like a satisfied cat.

Pulling out of the parking space, Parker joined the queue of cars waiting to enter Route 1. Tonight he wouldn't be heading home. He had an entirely different destination in mind.

Sandra felt refreshed after the shower. Her eyes looked tired and she had dark circles under them, but she felt better. Annie had come in and taken her wet clothes. In their place were dry ones. Sandra pulled the dress over her head. It was a long-sleeved denim, with a scooped neck and gathers just under her breasts. She and Annie were both high-waisted and had long legs, but Annie's dress reached her ankles. Staring at herself in the mist-frosted mirror, she remembered the two of them sharing clothes as teenagers. Annie had even left her a string of white pearls. She smiled and draped them around her neck.

When Sandra returned to the living room the table had been laid with food. The flowers which had been in the center of the shining glass rectangle had been moved to the end and stood near a newspaper and a pile of envelopes. Sandra was suddenly famished. Wyatt came in moments after she arrived. He'd shaved. His face was clean and she saw the clear lines that defined his character. She had an overwhelming need to rush into his arms and pray that everything would be over soon and they could just hold on to each other for comfort and . . . love? Did she really want his love?

She didn't have time to decide. A noise behind them caused her to shift her attention. Wyatt stepped up and took her hand. It was a small gesture but one she needed, and she was grateful he'd heard her silent message.

Like her, Wyatt also was wearing dry clothes. A baggy navy-blue sweater hung on his frame as if it had been worn for many years. Poking out of the collar was a white shirt. Jeans clad his long, muscular legs. They stopped at his ankles, but thick blue socks and black sneakers concealed their ill fit. If his face hadn't looked so haggard she would have noticed how handsome he was, but instead she understood that life running from one possible catastrophe to another was taking a toll on him. She wondered what she looked like. She'd washed her hair and pulled it, still wet, into a ponytail. She wasn't wearing a speck of makeup, and Annie's dress hung on her like a gunnysack.

Annie, on the other hand, looked like the fashion model that she was. She had smiled from countless magazine covers around the world. Everything about her was perfect, from the white stand-up collar on her hip-length sweater, its gold sequins catching the light and glittering, to the matching lamé stirrup pants that tapered down her legs like a second skin. Sandra didn't think she could feel any worse, but at that moment Wyatt smiled at her and her spirits lifted.

Seated at the table, Sandra recognized the man who'd called to Annie during their conversation on the steps of the Jefferson Memorial. He was dressed much the same as Wyatt and she knew the clothes Wyatt wore must be his.

"This is Jordon Ames, my photographer," Annie introduced him. "Jordan, my sister, Sandra, and you probably recognize Senator Randolph."

The two men shook hands. "Feel free to keep the clothes," Jordon said with a smile. He was the only person in the room who appeared relaxed.

They sat down and Sandra took a canned cola from the selection of beverages on the table. Popping the top, she poured herself a glass and drank half of it in one long swallow. Wyatt took the coffee Jordon offered. Sandra liked Jordon. He acted more the host than Annie did the hostess. She wondered if the question Annie had asked her about sleeping with Wyatt applied to Jordon and herself. She smiled slightly, hoping it did. The two sisters had been estranged for years, but Sandra felt Annie really needed to be understood. She also needed happiness in her life, and Jordon looked at her as if he'd like nothing better than to make her happy. Unfortunately, she didn't see the same gleam in her sister's eyes.

"Eat," Jordon said. He took the basket of rolls and passed it to Wyatt. Neither Wyatt nor Sandra waited for any additional encouragement. They devoured their medium-cooked steaks, baked potatoes, and mixed vegetables. She and Wyatt had been living off raw fruits and vegetables, grocery-store salad bars, and fast food.

Jordon observed the people in the room. One of his favorite occupations was people watching. Annie and Sandra were the back and front of a mirror, Annie dark, Sandra fair. He could see Sandra was logical and thoughtful, while her sister was impulsive and volatile. Both women had equally expressive eyes, which were the most naked part of their body. While Annie's were usually shaded, Sandra's were bright and alive despite the dark circles under them. Jordon wished he had his camera.

When he'd seen them together he was sure Annie was the beautiful one, but today he found Sandra's looks compelling. Her beauty was more classic, the kind that made a man look at her once but remember her long into the night.

He moved his attention to Wyatt Randolph. He could see it in his eyes. He wondered if the senator even knew how much the college professor had captivated him.

Again he wished for his camera. The diffused light from the rain-streaked sky would give Sandra's no-makeup and no-hairstyle features a softer edge. He also wanted the beauty of both the sisters, side by side, captured on film so he could study it and see why Annie had the power to make his blood boil, yet her mirrored opposite sister possessed the more commanding beauty.

"Jeff's dead," Sandra said flatly.

"Jeff Taylor?" Annie's reaction was exactly what Sandra had expected it would be. Shock registered on her face before it turned to horror. Sandra didn't understand it, but Jeff was a friend to both of them. Usually Annie detested her friends, but in Jeff's case she'd made an exception. Annie's face went ashen. Sandra wanted to go to her but knew better. This was the most she'd seen of her sister since before John died. If she made a wrong move or an off-handed comment she knew Annie would explode.

"He was helping us," Wyatt continued, his voice low and compassionate. "We'd agreed to meet this morning. When we got there," he paused, "we were too late."

"Annie, we couldn't call the police." She stopped, remembering Jeff's labored speech and the blood all around him. She squeezed her eyelids shut trying to blot out the image. After a few seconds she opened them. "Someone needs to go there and . . . see to things."

"I'll do it," she agreed readily.

Sandra gave her the Hawaii Avenue address and Annie wrote it on a napkin.

"What are your plans now?" Jordon asked. "You can't keep running." He glanced at the newspaper next to the pile of envelopes that looked like invitations. "From the looks of things, you're not going to make it much longer."

Wyatt stared at the two of them. He'd never seen Jordon or Sandra's sister before today and his natural instinct was not to trust anyone. Jordon was right. At the rate they were going, there would be nowhere to run by the end of the week. They had the files on Project Eagle, but no way of deciphering them. They no longer had the stones, just a cryptic message given to them by a dying man that was as encoded as the computer disks.

Now he sat with two more people who wanted to know what they were up to. Wyatt wasn't about to tell them.

"To keep you safe," he said. "It's better if we don't tell you anything."

Jordon looked from face to face.

"Everyone we've told is either dead or being hunted. I don't think it's wise to add anyone else to the list."

"Then what are you going to do?"

Wyatt waited again. He needed to find Sam Parker so he could wring his neck, he needed to find the stones and to find out what was on the computer disks that he'd been allowed to copy.

"I'm not sure." Wyatt looked at Sandra. Her eyes were tired and scared. She needed more rest. He wanted to leave her behind, know she was in safe hands, but he didn't think there was anyplace that was really safe for her now. Guilt settled over him. Why hadn't he learned whether the senator was actually at the cabin before he'd started for it? She'd be safely studying for her oral exam and he'd . . . He stopped the thought. He'd be dead. He'd have bled to death in that alley or some such other place, but Sandra would not be part of his life and she'd be safe.

Suzanne got up and went to the end table next to the overstuffed sofa. She pulled a drawer open and extracted an envelope. Coming back to the table, she dropped it in front of her sister. Sandra didn't move to pick it up.

"What's that?" Jordon asked before Wyatt had the chance.

"Money," Suzanne said. Wyatt had the feeling it was a trump card, and she'd waited for the precise moment to play it. "A lot of money. Enough to get the two of you out of the country until this thing blows over."

"This isn't going to blow over, Annie," Sandra charged. "People are trying to kill us. Wyatt's been stabbed. Men tried to shoot down Starfighter. The police are chasing us all over the District. Jeff's dead and Dad is somehow mixed up in this." Tears ran unchecked down her cheeks. "We're not talking about a traffic ticket here. We're talking about national security, and if we don't find out what the hell's going on, Wyatt and I won't live out the week." She kicked the chair back and stood up. Several feet from the table she turned away, her shoulders shaking with grief. Wyatt put his hands on her arms and turned her around. He wrapped her in his embrace and held her close.

He never felt so helpless as he did allowing her to cry against his shoulder. Just as he'd done during the night, he let her lay against him until the sobbing stopped. Suzanne passed him a tissue and he gave it to her.

"We'd better go now," Wyatt said when he turned back to Suzanne and Jordon. They were standing near them, but with sufficient distance as to feel inadequate and helpless, too. "Thank you for the food and the clothes, but it's best if we don't stay in one place too long."

"You can't take her out like this," Jordon said. "She's dead on her feet. Why don't the two of you go to my suite and rest. You can leave later, maybe after dark."

Wyatt weighed the proposition. He looked at Sandra. Slumped against him, she looked small and tired. She did need the rest, but he decided against it. Anyone who knew them, knew their families, and if they were looking for Sandra they might think she'd seek her sister out. Wyatt was surprised to find the two women had already been in contact with each other.

They did need money. He'd used all the cash he had in the last few days. How they could continue to survive without creating a traceable credit card trail had been on his mind. Obviously, it had been on Sandra's, too, since she'd approached her sister for cash.

"Thank you, but I think we'd better go."

At that moment someone knocked on the door. Sandra pressed herself closer to Wyatt.

"It's only the bellman," Suzanne said. "He's returning your clothes."

Jordon went to the door and accepted the laundry, signing the receipt but not allowing the man to enter the suite.

"Sandra, what did you mean when you said Dad is involved?" Annie asked when Jordon returned, laying the cellophane-covered clothes over the back of a nearby chair.

By mutual consent the four of them moved to sit on the facing sofas. Wyatt had his arm around Sandra on one sofa, while Annie and Jordon sat close but separated on the facing seat.

"I'm not sure." She felt the warning pressure of Wyatt's hand on her shoulder. "I talked to him yesterday." A tremor ran through her. She was sure Wyatt felt it. "He was . . . different." Sandra didn't want to tell Annie about their father. She knew about the feud between them and she didn't want to add fuel to the fire.

"How . . . different?"

"Annie, I won't give you ammunition to use against him."

"I'm not asking for ammunition. I don't even talk to the man." Her voice was high-handed as if discussing the man who'd taken her into his house and loved her as his daughter was distasteful.

"When I've had time to talk to him and find out the truth, I might be willing to tell you everything, but I really think the two of you should work out whatever differences you have."

Annie closed up like a vault. Sandra knew if they talked the rest of the night nothing more would be said. She was glad for once. For the first time in years, she didn't want to talk about their father. She had doubts. Had Wyatt done this to her? Had yesterday really meant anything or had she written more into it than was there?

She wanted to talk to her father, wanted to ask him why strangers with guns had shown up at the motel, why he hadn't called her as promised, and was he really involved in Project Eagle.

"Annie, why don't you have her call the man you introduced me to the other evening?"

"Lance?" Suzanne's voice interrupted her thoughts.

"Who?" She hadn't heard her sister. She had been concerned about her father.

"You remember Lance Desque." She eyed Wyatt. "You must know him, too. I saw him a few days ago."

"Of course I remember Lance," Sandra said.

Wyatt nodded. "I've met him once or twice."

"I'm sure he knows as much if not more about defense as the joint chiefs."

Lance might not be a bad idea. Sandra wondered why she hadn't thought of him before. He'd worked with her father for years. If there was a way to get at the truth and she couldn't reach Bradford Rutledge, then Lance Desque was the next best thing.

"I can call him. Does he still work in the Pentagon?"

"Why don't you have lunch with him?" Jordon suggested. He looked at Suzanne then back to Sandra. "He invited Annie to lunch. Why don't you go in her place? He won't expect you, so you'll be relatively safe."

Sandra gazed at her sister who was staring at Jordon as if he'd grown an extra head.

"That might not be a good idea," Wyatt interjected. "An open restaurant is much too public a place. People we don't even know could recognize us and call the police."

"Well, Annie can't make it anyway. We have to shoot tomorrow since we lost today."

Annie still hadn't said anything. Sandra's state of shock wasn't paralyzing enough to miss the jealousy in Jordon's comments. *He* didn't want Annie to have lunch with Lance. Finding a substitute would solve both their problems.

"We'll have to think about it," Sandra said. "I will call him and find out if he can help us."

"If you decide to go, it's The Charter Club at one." Jordon gave the information.

"We'd better go," Wyatt said. They all stood. Wyatt pulled their coats from the plastic covering. Sandra was grateful they were dry. She looked through the windows and found the rain had stopped.

Wyatt and Jordon moved toward the door. They spoke softly, and Sandra couldn't hear what they were saying. Then Annie called her.

She turned back and looked at her sister. Annie had a smirk on her face, but Sandra ignored it. She was afraid for her sister.

"Annie, be careful," she whispered. "I've had the feeling that I'm being followed and I don't want anyone to hurt you."

"Don't worry about me. I can take care of myself."

Sandra tried to smile but failed. "I know you can," she said. "You were always good at getting yourself out of situations." Sandra still wanted to warn her to be careful. "Just check that you're not followed when you go out. If possible, go out with someone." She glanced toward Jordon. Instinctively she liked him. "Watch out if any accidents start to happen, anyone suddenly gets hurt and needs to be replaced on the shoot. Any strangers that show up, be leery of them."

"Sandra, you're inventing ghosts," she told her, laughing her concerns off.

"I hope so." Sandra gave her a long look and started for the door.

"Don't forget this," Suzanne said. She picked up the thick envelope and slid it across the table. Sandra reached for it. Her hand stopped the forward motion, but knocked the neat stack of mail to the floor. She bent down and picked up the invitations. She recognized several embassy emblems on the expensive paper; Thailand, Japan, Republic of South Africa, England.

"I don't know why I'm telling you this," Suzanne said when she straightened. "I hate you."

"Annie—"

"Don't interrupt." She held up her hand. "You're in this deep, so deep that you don't know if you'll ever get out of it. But . . ." She paused. Sandra knew it was for affect. "But if you end up with your back against the wall, call Grant Richards."

The name sounded familiar. "Who is he?"

"Don't worry who he is and don't call him unless you're desperate."

"How can I find him?"

"He's listed in the phone book. His wife's name is Brooke. You'll like her. She's good with computers."

Suzanne also grabbed a small leather bag no larger than a briefcase. She stuffed the dry clothes in it and handed it to her sister. They were moving toward the men at the door when the telephone rang.

Sandra jumped at the sudden noise. As Annie picked up the receiver, Sandra joined Wyatt and Jordon.

The strange air of hostility that took over the room like a tangible hand as Annie spoke into the receiver then stopped caused conversation to cease. They all turned to look at her. She held the phone stiffly in her hand and her face was as ashen as it was when Sandra told her Jeff was dead.

"It's for you." She pushed the phone through the air toward Sandra as if it was thick and heavy enough to cut. "It's Dad."

Suzanne stood looking through the windows at the ground below. Taxis pulled in and out of the sheltered canopy. She couldn't tell if Sandra and Wyatt were in one of them or if they'd walked away from the hotel and taken a taxi on Independence Avenue.

She followed several yellow cabs as they moved like toys on the wet road below. Suzanne couldn't believe he'd called here. Her father. Sandra's father. He hadn't even asked how she was doing, only if Sandra was there and was she all right. Why was it always Sandra? Why couldn't he for once give her a little of his love?

"So," Jordon said, drawing out the word in a drawl. "You don't really hate your sister."

"What makes you think that?" Suzanne stepped away from the window and faced him.

"Why did you give her the money?"

Suzanne tossed her head. "It wasn't my money. All I did was go get it."

Jordon came toward her. He stopped about two feet away. Suzanne didn't like the way he looked at her, as if he was looking into her mind. "Let me get this straight." He paused. "You go out of your way to get money to help a person you couldn't care less about if she died."

"I never said I wanted her dead." She walked away from him, from those piercingly knowledgeable eyes. Sometimes she hated Jordon, hated the fact that with him she couldn't completely hide behind the mask she erected for the world. Jordon stripped it and she had no power to prevent him from doing so.

"The pearls were a nice gesture, too. If they run out of money they can sell them."

Annie sank into the plush dining-room chair. The debris of the meal they'd eaten was scattered over the table. Annie spied the newspapers. She shuddered at today's story. She thought about how she'd feel if Sandra did die. She felt nothing, only a numbness that sapped her arms and legs of their strength.

"What was it, Annie?" Jordon dropped down next to her and took her hand. "Tell me. I promise not to judge you and not to repeat anything you tell me, but I need to know why you're so estranged from everyone who loves you and why you won't let anyone love you."

"Loves me? He doesn't love me. He's never loved me. Only *her.*"

* * *

The Capital Beltway spans a circle around Washington, DC. It traverses southeastern Maryland and northern Virginia, crossing the Potomac River in two spots, but never touches the ten-square-mile tract that houses the US government. Sam Parker left the Pentagon and entered Route 395. He bypassed the city of Alexandria and picked up the beltway. For the last hour and a half he'd driven full circle around the capital keeping a keen eye on the rearview mirror.

He'd driven the fifty-five miles an hour legal limit, careful to not waver from the constant speed as other cars weaved in and out of lanes in a rush that both defined and produced the rhythm and pace that made the capital a unique city. Nearly convinced that he wasn't being followed, Sam took Interchange 30 at Silver Spring. He drove through the streets turning one corner after another to make sure he was not being pursued, before finally heading for his destination—Wyatt Randolph's town house in Georgetown.

Whoever had done this place was good, Sam thought as he looked around. This was no merely professional job, but a government-authorized military bugging. Few men could do this kind of work. Few people could ever afford this kind of surveillance. Wyatt Randolph had needed the best. Sam was better.

Before he'd been confined to a computer desk, he'd been in Intelligence. He could string a site that would throw pictures sharp as a laser disc to a satellite thousands of miles above the earth and print them on a home computer. God, he'd like to talk to the guy who'd strung this. For several moments Sam admired the handiwork, the quiet instruments recording, registering, and transmitting every move made in the space below. Anyone living on the three lower floors wouldn't hear anything more than the steady operation of a refrigerator motor. In fact, the entire setup was synchronized with the refrigerator. Even if the motor wasn't running no one could discern the low hum of these state-of-the-art devices. Wyatt should be proud.

Sam sighed quietly. He'd better get what he needed and be gone. Being found here wouldn't be good for his health.

"Don't argue with me, Wyatt. I have to do this."

"You don't have to do anything." Wyatt grabbed her shoulders and forced her to look at him. "You could be walking into a trap and you won't even know it."

Sandra wrenched herself free. "Like you did when you went to the Pentagon and neglected to tell me anything about it. At least I'm telling you where I'm going."

Wyatt took a deep breath. "I'm sorry about that. It couldn't be helped. I sincerely thought I could find something to help us in Chip's office."

"Well I feel the same. The man is my father, Wyatt." She raised her hands to stop him from saying anything. "I know what you think of him, but I don't believe it."

"Even after what's already happened to you? What do you want . . . him to stand up and say 'I'm a traitor'?"

"If that's what it takes, yes." She calmed herself, lowering her voice before she spoke again. "Wyatt, he won't hurt me. He's my father. He won't lead me into a trap."

Wyatt took her into his arms and caressed her back. "I just want to be there." He wanted to believe her, but he was scared. She scared him the way she made him feel. He wanted to be there to protect her if he could. He squeezed her closer. She smelled like scented soap, probably from the shower in her sister's suite.

"I'll go tomorrow night and find out what he wants. Maybe we can have everything cleared up by this time tomorrow."

"Maybe," he agreed, but didn't feel any confidence in the hope. He kissed her quickly on the mouth and went back to holding her close. What was Brad up to? Why was he meeting his daughter at the Quantico FBI facility? What was wrong with a restaurant in the District, where she could get up and grab a taxi if the need arose? He didn't like this at all. It smelled rotten, but he couldn't convince Sandra there was any reason she should refuse to meet her father.

Sandra hugged Wyatt. She knew some of what he said was right, but Brad Rutledge was her father. In the past two weeks she'd only heard about him from Wyatt. She had to give him time to tell her the truth, or at least his version of the truth. Then it was up to her to decide which of them she'd choose to believe.

She closed her eyes against Wyatt. She wanted him in her life. She also wanted her father. The way things stood now, she was bound to lose one of them tomorrow night.

"Sandra?" Wyatt pushed her back and looked into her eyes. "No matter what happens tomorrow, we have to find those stones. Maybe we should try to find out what Jeff was trying to tell us."

She smiled and released him. They'd found a small hotel room in Arlington, Virginia, and for the better part of the day, when they weren't arguing over her father's phone call and invitation to dinner, they were trying to find something that would tell them what 95147 meant.

"What about part of a phone number?"

"There are many possibilities. He couldn't have begun with an area code. There is no 951 area code, which would mean it would have to be a local number."

"The 9 could be the number you dial to get an outside line."

"In that case the area code would be 514. There is no 514. Five one six is on Long Island and 519 is in the Midwest, but so far the phone company hasn't assigned 514."

Wyatt cocked his head, wondering how she knew that.

"I've always been able to remember numbers." Sandra grinned. Her father had thought it uncanny when she was a child and could add columns of numbers in her head.

"All right, it could be part of a phone number, but not a local one. The metropolitan area doesn't have any 951 exchanges."

"What about zip codes?" Sandra asked.

"95147." Wyatt thought about it. "It would have to be out west. Any idea where?"

Sandra shook her head. She grabbed the phone book and looked up the number of the closest post office. "San Jose, California," she said, as she hung up the phone.

"Do you think there's a connection?"

"I don't know what to think. Jeff wasn't the kind of person to talk in clues. He liked the direct approach. The easiest route was always the most efficient, he used to say."

"Then whatever or wherever 95147 is, we should be able to find the diamonds."

Sandra nodded.

"You're a numbers person, Sandra." The tension showed in Wyatt's voice. "Think! What could they mean?"

She tried. 95147 could be anything. San Jose was too far away to have any connection. "Safety-deposit box number, post office box number, shipping numbers, receipt number, bill of lading, part of a credit card, the possibilities are endless. Without more information, we're dead in the water."

" 'Dead' being the operative word."

"I didn't mean that."

Wyatt sat down at the circular table. Her backpack with books she hadn't looked at since they left the mountain sat there. He let his head fall back against the upholstery of the wing-backed chair and sighed. Long and slow, it had the sound of defeat in it.

She came to him and began massaging his shoulders. "Wyatt, we're not beat yet."

"We're awfully close. We have nothing. We don't even know who's looking for us. So far we've run from the District police, a man I thought I could trust bombed the car we were riding in, we've lost the stones, and another man is dead. I spent over an hour copying gibberish onto twenty-seven disks. We've got a number that could mean one of a thousand things. We're sitting pretty, that's for sure."

CHAPTER 11

The Washington Post was established in 1877 as a four-page arm of the Democratic Party. Since then it has gone through financial difficulties, been a conservative paper, a chronicler of the sensational and the world of society, merged with its competition and evolved into one of the best papers in the United States. Residents of Washington, northern Virginia, and southeastern Maryland wake up to the Post each morning.

Wyatt Randolph loved the *Post.* It rivaled his state's *Philadelphia Inquirer,* but as a news reporter, it equaled *The New York Times.* For the past few mornings Wyatt had dreaded reading accounts of his life sprawled across the thirty-six ounces of printers ink used to produce the two-and-a-quarter pound paper. This morning he expected to read the story of the death of Jefferson Taylor III. He knew he and Sandra would be implicated if not accused of a direct connection to his murder. He wasn't disappointed. Their names came up in the first paragraph. Sandra's photo, a grainy gray that did no justice to her beautiful dark features, sat next to his. Everett Horton and his reception for the Japanese ambassador had been pushed to the bottom section of the paper. Wyatt gave the story a cursory scan. He didn't read the rest of the front page.

Wyatt didn't like being a celebrity. He'd rather read about someone else than have his own life put there for the world to review. What must his family think? He admitted he hadn't had much time to think about them lately. He was too busy trying to save his own life. He needed to call his parents, find out if anyone had questioned them. Were they being followed? He needed to let them know he was all right. He knew his mother would worry, but he wanted to hear her voice.

He looked over at Sandra. She slept soundly in the other bed. After they'd left her sister's, they'd found a room and checked in. Sandra had been exhausted but restless. By the time darkness fell she was too tired to argue about going to sleep. Wyatt had been awake most of the night. Just as the sun tinged the horizon he'd gone out and bought a paper from the newsstand on the corner near a bus stop. Few people stood there at this early hour and he'd waited until the bus had come and gone before approaching the plastic-covered stand. Returning to the room, he'd sat on the bed and skimmed the news.

He and Sandra hadn't come any closer to finding out what the number Jeff had uttered meant. Neither had he been able to talk her out of meeting her father tonight for dinner. He'd even mentioned going with her, but both of them knew that was a bad idea.

Wyatt turned the page of the daily journal checking to see if the noise aroused Sandra. It didn't. When he turned back to the paper, he nearly lost his grip at what was printed there. His heart thudded against his rib cage. Page three was a full-page ad. In the middle of the white space was what most people would see as a huge computer chip. Wyatt recognized it as a tie tack. Chip had it made, and he'd given it to him one Christmas. In the middle of the original chip, Wyatt Scott Randolph, his full name, had been engraved in gold lettering. As he looked at the paper chip no company logo took up that space. In the center the word CALL was written in capital letters. It jumped out at Wyatt like a four-letter word.

Around the edge of the black center with silver prongs sticking down like metal teeth, Wyatt saw his own name. Not his given name, not his family name, but the storybook name that Edward "Chip" Jackson and only a few other people knew—Earp and Scott. Most people thought he was named after Wyatt Earp and Randolph Scott because his mother, Endora Randolph, a teacher in the Philadelphia school system, was a fan of old western movies. Wyatt's name really came from a black Indian who helped carve the West. Chip knew the true story, but Chip was dead. He couldn't have placed the ad.

Then who did and why? What were they trying to say? Call? Call who? He couldn't call Chip.

Wyatt tried to apply logic. Sandra would have done this. She would analyze it and find the inner meaning. He thought it was a cruel joke. Chip was dead. No one but Chip could have sent him a message like this. Was he supposed to call . . . Chip?

Weather in the District is changeable. Yesterday's rains had given way to a bright sunny morning. The coldness that had chilled Wyatt to the bone twenty-four hours ago had been pushed out to sea. Behind it came a warm breeze that held the promise of spring. Wyatt walked casually with his arm around Sandra's waist. They were close enough to appear to share the same grief and far enough apart to look like they dreaded walking through a graveyard.

In Sandra's case that might have been true. She'd been quiet this morning, agreeing to his decision to visit Chip's grave with little comment. He wondered what was on her mind, but decided not to ask. She'd tell him in due time and he didn't want to bring up her father and the dinner she was scheduled to attend this evening.

Wyatt glanced behind them. He searched the area as if he was a human radar detector. No one else seemed to want to spend the beauty of the morning in a cemetery. They were alone.

Wyatt felt different here. The place commanded silence, reverence. His tennis shoes made a suction sound on the paved passageway, much like rubber sticking to the ground and being pulled free. He walked softer, reducing the sound, as if the noise could disturb the dead.

The cemetery was large and Chip's grave was near the rear. When it came into view Wyatt slowed his steps. Sandra instinctively adjusted her gait to match his. His senses piqued, came alive. Some sixth sense told him to be ready, for what he didn't know, but he wanted to be able to reverse direction and run if the situation turned deadly. Seeing nothing, they continued.

Wyatt had attended Chip's funeral. Only three weeks ago he'd stood here in the cold while a group of black-draped mourners said their final farewell to a man whose life should have spanned another fifty years. Wyatt hadn't any idea then how his life would change the Monday following Chip's burial. The diamonds would be delivered and his mere mention of Project Eagle would set into motion the machinery that brought him to this place now.

The grass, which looked like a winter carpet over most of the ground, dropped short of Chip's grave. There was no headstone. It couldn't be set until later. The only marking was the mound of fresh earth working its way back to the surface of the ground. By summer the grass covering it would be as well manicured as the rest of the place.

Wyatt took Sandra's arm and walked to the head of the grave. They said nothing. Wyatt looked down. The red earth stared at him, mute silent. Then he looked about the place. No police came flooding through the gates, sirens blaring, lights flashing. In fact, he was beginning to feel the trip had been worthless. Then he saw *him.*

Dropping Sandra's arm, he lunged across the soft earth. Lowering his head, he hurled himself, not with the finesse of a veteran running back, but with the rage of a bull seeing red. Wyatt had never played football. He preferred the fast-paced movement of a full court press, but when he saw the khaki-colored pants and green raincoat of the man who stepped from behind the nearby tree, rational thought took a vacation, leaving him with only the instinct to seek revenge. Wyatt's fist slammed into the man's stomach. He heard a grunt as the air whooshed out of his lungs and he doubled over in pain. Wyatt grabbed his chin and pulled him up, then punched him squarely in the face. He stumbled backward and fell into the wet ground.

"Wyatt, stop!" Sandra rushed to him, grabbing his arm. "What are you doing?"

He unconsciously pushed her aside, only half noticing her stumble over the red earth before gaining her balance. His breath came in ragged puffs. He started for the man struggling to get to his feet. Wyatt tore at his arm, wrenching him upward only to knock him down again. He wasn't fighting back. Wyatt didn't care. He was going for him again, intent on beating him to death. He must have seen the murderous glint in Wyatt's eye because he scooted back when he saw Wyatt coming. "Wait!" he shouted, raising a warding-off hand.

"Wyatt, no!" Sandra cried.

Wyatt didn't know if it was the panic in her voice or her hands clutching his arms that stopped him from trying to kill Colonel Sam Parker.

"I didn't know, Randolph. I promise you I had nothing to do with the bomb." He stopped to take a deep breath. "They set me up, Randolph."

"Who are they?" Wyatt took an angry step forward. Sandra hung on his arm and Sam pushed himself further up in the mound of soft dirt.

"I don't know. I only talked to Colonel Whitfield. He said to let you get into Chip's office and give you all the time you needed. He said you had something the department needed that was too secret for him to tell me about, but they didn't want more than for you to lead them to it. Then you and the senator's daughter . . ." he glanced at Sandra. "He said nothing would happen to you and you wouldn't be charged with anything."

"And you believed him?"

"I had no reason not to." Sam started to get up, checking to see that Wyatt didn't make any negative moves. Wyatt stood his ground, glaring at him as if he still wanted to break him in pieces. Sam got to his feet, brushing the excess dirt and mud from his clothes. Some of the dust came off, but he looked as if he'd been in a fight. "He's always been straight with me. When I heard about the car bomb I was as surprised as you."

"I'm sure that's not the truth, but I would have been dead and there would have been no way you could apologize."

Sam hung his head. "I'm sorry, Randolph. I didn't know."

"What are you doing here now?" Sandra asked. When she'd found out who he was she wanted to pound his face in the dirt, too. "Why did you send Wyatt a message?" Sandra tried to be rational.

"They're after me. They know I didn't have anything to do with Randolph and you or the car bomb. Whatever you have, Randolph, they want it and they want it bad enough to kill you to get it."

Wyatt didn't have to be reminded of that. He kept his hand from going to the healing puncture wound in his side. He could still feel the four inches of cold steel that had nearly killed him.

"Why did you come to us? Every arm of the law and people outside of it are looking for us. It seems to me you'd want to stay as far away as possible." Sandra's logic was flawless.

"I came because you haven't got a chance alone." He glared at her, his voice forceful and strong. That quality left it with his next statement. "I haven't got a chance without you, either. We've got to work together, combine our information and try to find a way out. We're nothing without each other."

"We've managed without you so far. When you stepped in somebody tried to kill us."

He nodded at Sandra as if acknowledging her argument. "I was working with Chip on a different aspect of Project Eagle. I have information you need. Until all the pieces are back in place we'll be hunted by our own government—and foreign governments, too—to get what we have."

Wyatt only knew part of what they had. Sam might know, but then, he might be lying. If he accepted him, trusted him, he could be walking into a trap and taking Sandra with him. In this bizarre nightmare he'd learned no one was trustworthy. Everyone wanted something and they would go to extreme lengths to get it.

What did Sam want from him? The two of them had met over a defense budget two years ago. Since then, Wyatt, along with Sam and Chip, had spent a lot of time together. He'd have sworn the man was honest, but the flames coming from the Chrysler LeBaron were charred in his memory.

"Why should I trust you?" Wyatt asked. "This could be another setup. You've burned me once."

"I'm telling the truth, Wyatt. I can't give you anything more than my word."

Wyatt weighed that and didn't find it convincing enough. He knew the government wanted the stones. Sam could be an emissary to find out where they were. Wyatt knew they were important, that people were being killed because of their existence. He was beginning to learn just how important.

"Why would I come here, Randolph? Why would I seek you out, knowing you'd assume I'd been directly involved in trying to kill you if I had been part of the conspiracy?"

"Because it didn't work and you want another chance."

"Okay, that could be true, but it isn't. The truth is, I'm scared to death. I know they'll come after me next."

Sandra suddenly looked around. Wyatt could feel the fear coursing through her. The thought that if someone was looking for Sam, he'd have led them straight to Wyatt and Sandra hit them both at the same time. No one veered down on them. Yet, if Sam wasn't telling the truth, they'd never make it out of the cemetery alive. He almost laughed at the irony.

"I'm alone," Sam said, picking up on their body language. "If we could just go somewhere and talk, I'll tell you everything I know."

"It could be another trap," Sandra warned.

Wyatt recognized words he'd said to her about trusting her father. His instinct told him Sam was telling the truth. His reason told him Sam had given him a car with a bomb in it. He was confused about which choice to make. He didn't know if the information he'd taken from Chip's office was of any use. He didn't know if Sam could decipher it if he trusted him to come along or even if he'd do it for them. What did they have to give Sam?

Wyatt scrutinized Sam. He was scared and nervous and looked as if he'd been on the run for weeks, too. Sandra's hand was resting on his arm. Wyatt wrapped his around it and looked down at her.

"We have to trust him," he whispered.

"What? He tried to have us killed."

"I don't think so."

"I think whoever tried to kill us used Sam. I believe the real enemy goes a lot higher than Sam Parker."

Sandra pulled her hand free. "You think it's my father."

"Welcome to the White House." Casey Everett greeted him as if he were her first visitor as First Lady. She greeted everyone who came to the White House in this manner, no matter how many times they passed through the entrances. At first Lance had felt important. He was finally a VIP, but later he knew she did it to humble people, to let them know that within these sheltered walls they represented the people of the United States and she would not allow them to forget their obligations. Casey would have made a wonderful queen if the United States had followed the British form of monarchy. She was made to stand above the crowd and wave at state functions, but she was also a governing queen. She was as keen as any scholar and always remembered the trust she'd been charged with.

In his own ironic way, Lance approved of Casey. She was older than most of the women he favored, but she looked a lot younger. The public loved her and Lance admitted to himself that Everett Horton was a lucky man. Lance needed a woman like Casey on his side. There was no limit to what he could do with someone as smart, popular, and good-looking as Casadia Horton.

"Good afternoon, Mrs. Horton. Is the President waiting?"

"He just went in." She began walking toward the dining room. "He'll be glad to know you're so prompt."

Lance nodded, knowing that was another of Casey Horton's cons. She disguised her insults in compliments. If he'd been even a second late, she'd have lectured him on the many duties of the presidency and how Everett needed to stick to a very tight schedule.

The White House was a monstrous place, but Lance loved it. He didn't feel awed by the-twenty-foot ceilings, he felt powerful. Inside these walls what the President said and did became law, national policy, affected millions of lives. With the brush of a pen he could send relief to an underdeveloped nation or repeal the social welfare laws.

Of course Congress provided some checks and balances, but this was the most powerful position on earth and Lance wanted it. If he managed in his present course, he'd have the country behind him in a couple of years. By the next election the entire world would know his name and he'd occupy the Oval Office.

"Lance, thanks for coming." Everett extended his hand and Lance took it. "You know Tyler and Melanie." Lance shook hands with the Secretary of Defense and Melanie West.

"Mr. Secretary," he acknowledged. "Mrs. West."

"Let's sit down."

Lance didn't have to see Everett signal the White House staff. They were a trained group and knew precisely the right moment to begin serving the lunch that began with oysters and ended with a circle of vanilla ice cream on a chilled plate that had been sculpted with raspberry sauce and cream. Each plate had a unique design as if the chef was moonlighting as an artist.

"Well, Lance." Everett pushed his chair back and crossed his long legs. "Can you update us on what's been happening in the saga of our wayward senator?"

There was mild laughter from the two women and two men looking in his direction. President Horton didn't stand on ceremony when it came to asking for information. Instead of directing his questions to Tyler Kirkus, he went straight to the man who should know. He was just as apt to call the corner grocer and ask for a delivery of ice cream than to leave instructions for the cook to do it.

That was probably what the country liked in Everett Horton. He was one of them, a man on the street, a neighbor who could be trusted to keep his word. So far, Everett Horton had accomplished all his campaign promises. His ratings couldn't be higher. He was sitting on the pinnacle of the pyramid and with this defense component he could topple quickly and no one would remember anything else except the scandal it could create.

Lance put his spoon down and adjusted his suit jacket as he sat forward in his chair. The movement was coordinated. He liked presenting a positive face, as if anything he said would be the absolute truth. "Senator and Ms. Rutledge have apparently disappeared from the face of the earth." He paused to allow the words to sink in. "We'd tracked them through Colonel Parker until his automobile was abandoned at National Airport. A taxi driver remembers taking a couple to a motel in Alexandria, but a search proved negative. Since that time we haven't been able to find them."

"What about Jeff Taylor?"

"I'm sorry about him, Mr. President. I know he was a friend of yours."

"I want to know who killed him."

We're not the police, he said silently. "The DC Police Department is working to find that out, sir."

"They think Wyatt Randolph and Sandra Rutledge are responsible," Horton said.

"Quite frankly, Mr. President, all evidence points in that direction," Lance replied.

"That's what makes it so unusual, Lance." Melanie West spoke in her quiet nonassuming manner, a style he knew could cut as sharply as any rapier. "We know Jeff had been a friend of the Rutledges' for years. It was no surprise when she went to him with the stolen parts. For her to be involved in his death goes against the grain."

"If I might play the devil's advocate for a moment, Mrs. West," Lance said, keeping his voice even and as politically correct as he could. "Jeff examines the parts and finds out only the Defense Department would have access to something as complex as the stones. He tells the senator and Ms. Rutledge what they have is bigger than they are and he should call someone in the DOD. They disagree. He then becomes a loose end."

"And they kill him?" Melanie West asked, her ridiculous hat cocked to the side of her head.

"It could happen," Lance answered with a shrug.

"That's a crock of bologna if I ever heard any," Horton shouted. "Jeff Taylor was my friend, but the man was no saint. If he'd found out what Randolph had, he'd want to know more about it. He certainly wouldn't go running to the DOD waving a white flag and telling them how he wanted to make sure their property was returned to the rightful owners. That's something Wyatt Randolph would do without a second thought."

"But he hasn't," Casey reminded them. "Care to comment on that?"

Lance deliberated for the shortest amount of time. He didn't want it to appear that he was hesitating. He could only tell them as much truth as he knew.

"Since the stones were . . . lost, Randolph's found his apartment ransacked. He's been followed and chased by the police. He borrowed a car from a friend which subsequently exploded. If I were in his position, sir, I'd be leery of walking into the DOD."

"He did go there, I'm told." Everett Horton surprised him. "He went to the Pentagon and spent over an hour in Mr. Jackson's office."

"That was my idea, sir," Tyler Kirkus spoke up. "I assumed if we let him in and let him take what he needed, he would lead us to the stones."

"But that backfired," Melanie West stated.

Kirkus nodded.

"We have no idea where the senator is now, gentlemen. I need to know that." Horton's voice brooked no argument. "My entire career rests on finding the stones Mr. Randolph is holding. Do you understand that?"

Lance understood perfectly. If Horton's career was to veer out of orbit he wasn't going to let it take him alone. Lance knew he would be one of the stars sucked up in the vacuum created by the fall of the presidency.

"I understand," he said, echoing Tyler Kirkus's comment.

"I want to know where he is by this time tomorrow."

Lance stood, accepting that as his cue that the interview was over. "Thank you for a lovely lunch, Mr. President." He nodded to the First Lady and the President's trusted advisor, then stared at Tyler Kirkus. Tyler stood and joined him. The two men were at the door when Horton stopped them.

"Tyler, one more question."

"Mr. President," he said. Lance watched him stiffen. Tyler Kirkus had perspiration on his upper lip. It was a sure sign his blood pressure was rising.

"What did Senator Randolph do for an hour at the Pentagon?"

Tyler cleared his throat. "He searched through the system Jackson had been working on when he died."

"Those files are encrypted. He couldn't possibly have read them without knowing the codes to unlock them."

"Right, sir."

"Good." Horton looked toward the window. "We don't need anything else going wrong."

Lance and Kirkus exchanged a knowing glance. "Mr. President," Kirkus said. "Senator Randolph made copies of the files."

Everett Horton got to his feet slowly. Lance felt he was going to explode. He noticed Casey looking at him with a warning glint in her eye.

"Let me get this straight, gentlemen. You let him walk into the Pentagon, spend an hour in duplicating classified files and leave without stopping him?"

"Sir, we never expected to lose track of him. We thought the situation was covered."

Horton walked toward them. He was a big man and seemed to grow taller as he approached. "It appears you're dealing with a very resourceful man who's a loose cannon out there. He's got both the key and the lock now. All he needs is the door to have enough to topple this administration. I want him found. I want the stones found and restored or I'll have more than your petty jobs. I'll have your hides."

Lance had dealt with Horton before. The man did not make idle threats. He also didn't like information kept from him. He never wanted to have to go to the American public with an excuse that he didn't know something was going on in his administration. Lance knew it was best to let him have everything he knew. If he held back on an important piece of information, Horton would be ruthless with his threat.

"Sir," he began. "Colonel Parker didn't report for work this morning."

Horton frowned as if he didn't recognize the name.

"Sam Parker, Mr. President." Tyler Kirkus took up the explanation. "We think he's with the senator."

"Why should that bother us?"

"Colonel Parker worked with Jackson. He knows all the algorithms to break the codes protecting the files that Senator Randolph copied."

Horton linked his hands together behind his back and rocked on his heels. "The key, the lock, and the door."

Sandra paced the ten feet of free space. She felt like a pawn in some poorly written spy thriller. The bare surroundings of the warehouse where Wyatt had led them were cold, and damp. A small space heater sat in the corner and Wyatt had turned it on. It whined in the quiet air and the visible coils turned a bright red. Sandra hovered near it.

"Sorry," Wyatt apologized. "I know the owner here. The place is empty and it's the best I could do."

Sandra nodded with a weak smile and dragged a chair close to the localized heat.

"All right, Sam." Wyatt swung around to look at the colonel. "Spill it."

"You think Project Eagle is another Star Wars. It's much more than that. Project Eagle is a communications defense system. In its fully functional state it links control of several orbiting satellites. Any one of them can pinpoint a single telephone in a single apartment anywhere on the planet and render it unusable. And not only telephones, any communication device."

"It's that powerful?" Sandra got to her feet and joined Wyatt. She slipped her hand around his arm anchoring herself to reality.

"More than that, Ms. Rutledge." Sam shifted to include her in his area of concern. He stood at parade rest with his hands clasped in front of him. "The Eagle's span can cut off any form of communications within a point as small as one unit or as large as the entire globe."

"Every government in the world would want this."

"They do and you have it."

Sandra's fingers closed tighter around Wyatt's arm. The problem was they didn't have it. They'd given it to Jeff Taylor, and he was dead now.

"At least you have a vital part of it," Sam went on.

"The satellites are in place and the software to control it is on the computer system at the Pentagon," Wyatt stated as if he had been part of the project since its inception.

"Not quite," Sam corrected him. "The system isn't only at the Pentagon, it's at another, secret site. I don't even know where it is, but Jackson knew. He had to be part of the installation team."

"If there's more than one copy, why is everyone looking for Wyatt?"

Sam hesitated too long. Sandra began to shiver. Wyatt felt it and put his hand over hers. The effort helped but didn't stop the chill that penetrated to her marrow.

"I don't know for sure, but my theory is that there are other people who want the system. Like you said, every government on earth would want the kind of power Project Eagle would give them. They're willing to kill for it."

"Two men are already dead," Wyatt reminded them.

"If they find us, there will be three more."

"Is my father involved in this?" Sandra had to ask.

Again Sam hesitated. "Senator Rutledge spearheaded the project. He got the funding and sat on the advisor panel, working closely with the military. As far as I know, he was present at every demonstration of the system and its capabilities."

Wyatt looked down at her.

"It doesn't mean anything," she told him. "He's probably spearheaded many projects. This doesn't mean he's behind the men trying to kill you."

"No," Wyatt agreed, but his voice was unconvincing. Sandra pulled her hand away. She took a deep breath to calm herself and faced the colonel. Thank God she'd be seeing her father in a few hours. She couldn't believe he was involved. No matter what Wyatt believed.

"Colonel, why did Chip encase the component in man-made diamonds?" Sandra turned away from Wyatt.

"I don't know. My nearest guess is that it was the only way he could get them out of the building. The security detectors are state of the art. Surrounded by that material they were camouflaged sufficiently to get them out."

"Do you think he found out someone was trying to steal the parts?"

Sam looked over his shoulder as if someone else might hear. "I'm not supposed to know this, but what can it hurt," he said almost to himself. "I believe the system has been stolen."

"What do you mean?" Wyatt asked.

"I only heard part of a conversation, but it involved Jackson, Senator Rutledge, and some high-level military types. Several of the joint chiefs were there. It made me think the software portion of the system was missing. They were grilling Jackson as to how such a thing could have happened. Two days later Jackson was dead and the components were missing. Thank God he sent them to you."

"We don't have them," Wyatt said flatly.

"What!" Sam looked from one of them to the other. "You're serious. What happened to them?"

"We gave them to Jeff Taylor. He must have found out something about them, but he died without telling us what it was or where he'd left them. For all we know whoever killed him has them now."

"I don't think so."

"Why not?" Wyatt asked.

"When I left the Pentagon there were several high-level meetings going on. Everett Horton's name even came up."

"President Horton and Jeff were friends."

"You didn't tell me that," Wyatt said.

"I'd forgotten. We never talked about the President."

"Was Taylor dead when you found him?" Colonel Parker pulled the discussion back to the immediate problem.

"No," Wyatt said. "He lived for a couple of minutes after we got there."

"Did he say anything that could help in finding out where he left the stones?"

"Nothing we could decipher," Sandra answered.

"What was it?"

"He gave us a number, 95147."

"What does it mean?"

"We haven't a clue. We tried phone numbers, shipping number, zip codes, nothing fits."

"Maybe it isn't one number, but two or three."

"What are you getting at?" Wyatt asked.

"Longitude and latitude, map routes, an address."

"We've gone through this, Sam," Wyatt glanced at Sandra. We haven't come up with anything that makes any sense. The location of those stones died with Jeff Taylor."

"We better hope they didn't."

Sandra's head came up suddenly.

"If they did," Sam explained, "our lives are worth about as much as one of those fake diamonds."

CHAPTER 12

My third toothbrush in a week, Sandra thought as she rinsed the white bristles and pink handle. They'd stayed in four hotels in the last seven days. Sandra was beginning to hate hotel rooms. Wrapped in a thin white towel, she pulled the blow dryer from the wall hook and brushed it through her straightened hair. When she met her father later she didn't want him to see how badly life on the road was affecting her.

She'd bought a dress at a shop not far from the hotel. They were having a one-day sale and the place was mobbed. No one had time to notice her what with the women grabbing for bargains. The long-sleeved, scooped-necked dress hung behind the door.

The dryer clicked and hummed as if it would short-out at any moment. It also drowned out any sound coming from the next room. Wyatt sat beyond the closed door. Until she'd gone to take a shower he'd been relentless in trying to convince her not to keep this appointment. She'd given him every argument she could think of, but she had to go, had to give her father the benefit of the doubt. She didn't believe he'd let her walk into a trap.

Switching the dryer to a higher setting, she used the brush to curl the ends of her hair. Then sweeping up the thick mass, she anchored it with a pearl clamp and whipped the ends along the side of her face. She dressed quickly in the royal-blue dress and added gold earrings and Annie's necklace as her only adornments.

Taking a last look in the small mirror, she pulled the door open expecting Wyatt to start again.

Wyatt glanced up from the laptop screen. Whatever he'd been planning to say went out of his head. He'd only seen her in a ponytail or with her hair pulled down straight to her shoulders. It wasn't just the upswept style that took him by surprise; *all* of her took him by surprise! The hairstyle emphasized her eyes and framed her coppertone, oval face. The dress claimed her curves for its own. She was gorgeous.

Wyatt didn't want her to leave him. He cleared his throat trying to say something but found he could do nothing but stare.

Time hung between them like an invisible hand holding them in place. He could go on looking at her forever. He hoped he'd have forever. Tonight, possibly this moment, was the last time they'd see each other. Wyatt's stomach muscles clenched. He'd become used to her. He liked listening to her quiet breathing while she slept and finding her there when he awoke. He liked the way she smiled and smelled when he held her. He wanted her more than he'd ever wanted a woman and she was the one he'd never have.

In his heart he didn't think Bradford Rutledge was trying to hurt Sandra. In Brad's mind he was rescuing her. Getting her away from Wyatt was the first step. Like kidnapping a child from an occult camp, Senator Rutledge was luring Sandra to his form of freedom.

It was for the best. Her father would protect her. He could do what Wyatt couldn't. He'd put her in danger the moment they met and he could see no way of getting out of the situation. Eventually he had to be found. When that happened he wanted to know that Sandra was safe.

Wyatt got up. "What time do you have to leave?"

Sandra checked her watch. "I have a few minutes."

Neither of them moved. The awkward moment stretched on. Wyatt didn't know what to say. He let his gaze take in her shining hair and the perfect symmetry of her features. His stare roamed over her curves, memorizing each turn until he could cup his hand just so and achieve the same angle. He'd need to recall this in the dark stretches of night that were his future.

"What are you doing?" she finally asked, snapping his thoughts and bringing him back to the present.

He glanced at the computer he'd set up on the circular table. "I thought I'd look at the files I copied."

"Why?" She moved around to look at the screen. "I thought they were encrypted."

"They are. I just need confirmation that what Sam said is the truth."

The screen had gibberish on it. He could read nothing. "The files might have been planted. One of them is in Japanese. Why else would they let me take them out?"

"If you think they're planted why are you wasting your time?"

He hadn't been wasting his time. He'd been trying to keep his mind busy so he wouldn't think about her leaving. She was beautiful and intelligent, she reacted well under pressure, she was staunchly loyal, and she didn't want anything from him. Her agenda was on the table. She only wanted to prove her father to be the man she thought he was. Wouldn't he have done the same thing for his father if a strange woman had come to him with the story he told her?

"What did you think of Sam's story?"

Sandra took the chair across from the computer. Wyatt sat down in front of it. "I think it's pretty fantastic." She paused and glanced away for a moment. "Quite frankly, it scared me to death. A device that sensitive, I'm not sure anyone should have it. It's like eavesdropping on a global scale. Even if only part of it is true, we have got to find those stones."

"I agree, but we haven't a clue where Jeff hid them or what 95147 means." Wyatt stared at her. "The only thing I remember is that he was having dinner with a friend."

"That's right." Sandra stood up as if an idea forced her to her feet. "That's what we have to do."

Wyatt waited for further explanation.

She walked across the room. "We have to find out everything Jeff did in the days before he died. That will tell us who he talked to and where he went. The stones have got to be in one of those places."

"That's right," Wyatt agreed. He hesitated a long time before he made the decision to tell her. "Sandra, *we* aren't going to do it."

"Why not?" She looked confused. "Have you got a better plan?"

"I've decided this is the perfect opportunity for us to split up."

"What!" She swung around to face him. The blue dress swirled out like a parachute opening.

"You're going to see your father. This is your opportunity to get out of this. He'll take care of you."

"What about you?" Her heart pounded at the thought of his being alone.

"I'm not your problem."

Sandra's expression suddenly changed. Her shoulders dropped and she stared directly at him.

"What are you planning to do?"

"Nothing," he said honestly. She raised an eyebrow indicating she didn't believe him. "I swear," he said.

"Then why are you trying to get rid of me?"

"I'm trying to protect you," he said. "All along you've told me your father had nothing to do with the stones. I agree. When you go to him, you'll be out of this."

"And you'll be alone." She took a step and stopped. "You'll be here with no help and no backup until someone finds and kills you." She stopped to take a breath. "What are you trying to do?"

Wyatt went to her, holding her shoulders. "I'm trying to save you, Sandra. Don't you know the people looking for me won't care that you're innocent? They'll ride over you to get to me and I don't even have the parts they're seeking."

She shrugged away his hands. "Let me tell you something, Wyatt Randolph. I'm in this until the end. You began this adventure by accusing my father of treason and I'm not going to let you off the hook until you admit he had nothing to do with Project Eagle, fake diamonds, or anything else." Emotion made her voice heavy.

"I don't want to prove Brad Rutledge had anything to do with this. I want to take advantage of an opportunity, one we're not likely to get again."

"Without discussing it with me. Just who do you think you are?"

"Sandra, think of it analytically. You've been chased by cops, shot at by people we don't even know; we're hunted by our own government and maybe some foreign powers who think we have access to a defense system. You can end it now, tonight. You can be safe."

"Well, maybe I don't want to be safe." She walked away from him. "Maybe my life has been too safe, too planned," she shouted. "Too damned boring. Maybe I need the excitement."

The words came as a surprise. She had buried herself, and it had nothing to do with John or his death. She'd run from her father's constant front-page coverage and from her mother's limelight, hiding herself in the safe world of elliptic curves. Theorems didn't flash cameras or thrust microphones in her face. Number theories didn't force her to think and act with the speed of light. And she liked the fast-paced world Wyatt had shown her. She didn't like being shot at or running from the law, but there was something about living for the moment that thrilled her and she wanted to hold on to that feeling.

She could still teach her students, but she wanted more out of life than just being a college professor and going from one chalk-dusty classroom to another.

Sandra stopped pacing in front of the window. Her arms were wrapped around her as if she were holding something in. Wyatt went to her, turning her around and into his arms. He pulled her close to him, smelling the sample shampoo that had been in the bathroom.

"I only want to know that you'll be safe." He lifted her chin and kissed her mouth tenderly. "I'm in love with you."

Sandra pressed the accelerator and the speedometer inched closer to seventy. Why couldn't they have met in a restaurant closer to Washington? It was dark and cold. Wind and rain batted against the small rented car.

Wyatt had said he loved her. She'd hadn't let herself explore her feelings for him. Until she'd talked to her father and cleared this mess up, she didn't want to deal with her emotions where Wyatt Randolph was concerned.

He was trying to protect her. He couldn't survive for long alone. The thought made her shudder. She wanted him alive.

Pushing aside any further thoughts, she decided to concentrate on something else—Sam and the stones. She didn't trust Sam Parker enough to accept the use of his car. His story had been fantastic, and she still wasn't prepared to believe it all. She was glad Wyatt agreed with her; neither of them trusted him fully.

They'd left the warehouse and gone in opposite directions. They didn't know where he would be and they refused to tell him where their hotel was located. He'd given them a phone number. Wyatt promised to call when they'd had time to think about what he'd told them.

Sandra looked at the phone that came with the rental car. Annie and her friend Jordon had rented the car together, although his name was on the papers in the glove compartment. The miles flew by in green markers as she sped south on Route 95 toward Richmond.

A system that could not only knock out communications but listen in on private conversations anywhere in the world. Her heart pounded at the thought. Planes would fall out of the sky, space travel depended on communications with the ground, control of televisions, even the news media was transmitted over satellite links—and those were just the small uses. Nuclear warheads could be launched with communication codes, computer networks shut down or activated. Chip Jackson had created a doomsday machine and sent it to Wyatt.

She checked the rearview mirror. It was too dark to identify the car behind her, but she was sure it had been the same car she'd noticed since she'd left the District. Sandra shuddered again. Could it be Sam Parker? Had he told them the truth or did he just want to find the stones? Was someone tailing her? Initially Wyatt hadn't wanted her to go alone, and right now she saw the merit in his concern.

She was headed to the FBI training facility at Quantico. Pressing the accelerator, she eyed the needle as it passed seventy. The car behind her maintained distance. She slowed. It slowed.

Her heart jumped into her throat and fear sent a shiver down her spine. She was in this one alone . . . and she didn't like it. Exactly as she'd tried to explain to Wyatt. If she left him, he'd have no backup. No one to help him out of situations. She glanced at the phone. Who could she call? Wyatt had no transportation, her father hadn't given her a number, she didn't trust Sam enough to use the number he'd supplied. He could be driving the car behind her.

Gripping the steering wheel as if her life depended on it, she continued for several more miles. Cars and trucks joined the parade, some passing her, spewing excess water and reducing visibility, some leaving the highway at various exits, but the single car kept a steady pace as if it was connected by a tractor beam. The rain intensified, plopping large drops of water against the windscreen. Sandra was forced to slow down. She didn't want to cause her own accident. Glancing in the mirror, she saw the car behind her slow to maintain the same distance.

She tried to decide what she should do. Should she get off the highway, continue to Quantico, or pull into the next state police station? Her options were limited. She wasn't familiar with this part of Virginia. Getting off could put her on a dead-end road and she didn't want that kind of end. Going to the police would mean turning herself and Wyatt over without any leverage, since they didn't know where the stones were. Her only option was to continue to Quantico. She was heading for the FBI facility. If she'd get any protection at all, it would be there.

By the time she neared Quantico the road junctioned. The car following her turned to take that route. Sandra let her breath out. She felt as if she'd been holding it for miles. The relief was almost delirious.

When she pulled into the parking lot next to the main training building, she had her nerves under control. She parked under a bright light as Wyatt had instructed her. If anyone tampered with the car they would be in plain sight and under surveillance by the many concealed cameras positioned about the grounds.

Before she pushed the door open she dialed Wyatt at the hotel. The phone rang several times, but no one answered. She wondered where he'd gone. He hadn't mentioned anything to her about leaving. Fear attacked her and she took deep breaths to calm herself. Like the missing stones, she could do nothing about Wyatt at the moment.

The first flakes of snow hit her in the face as she exited the car and set the alarm. Large, fluffy, and beautiful, ice crystals caught in her hair and on her coat, but she didn't want to see them. She wanted a pleasant, uncomplicated ride back and snow would hinder her progress.

She checked the perimeter, looking for the cameras but seeing none. She knew they were there, knew that someone concealed inside the huge whitewashed building had observed her since she turned into the road leading to the training facility.

She saw her father as she pushed the heavy glass doors that led into the reception area. The seal of the Federal Bureau of Investigation took up the entire wall behind the reception station.

"Sandra!" he called, straightening up from a conversation with the desk clerk and coming to her.

Sandra stared at him for a moment. Before her was the man whose arms were always open to her, the man who'd held her hand when she visited Santa Claus, who'd lifted her into his arms when the monstrous figure of Mickey Mouse waved his giant hand at her. This man was not sinister or evil. He was her father. Sandra took a step forward, then ran into his arms.

"Dad!" she cried. "It's so good to see you." Tears misted in her eyes and clouded her vision. The words seemed so inadequate for what she meant. He'd been her friend, mentor, and confidant for as long as she could remember. In the past week she'd missed not having him to talk to and explain the horrible things that had happened to her and Wyatt.

"Hello, Ms. Rutledge," the desk clerk said. She recognized him but didn't remember his name. "I was sorry to hear about Mr. Taylor."

"Thank you," she said, swallowing the lump that lodged in her throat each time someone mentioned Jeff. She felt responsible for his death. If she hadn't asked him to look at the stones he might be alive today.

"He was here only the day before he died. He had dinner with Mr. Desque."

"Lance—"

"Come on, honey," her father interrupted. "We'll go somewhere and talk."

He took the identification badge from the desk clerk and, hugging her about the shoulders, led her away. He led her though a maze of hallways and doors. On the second floor he opened a door that led into an apartment. Overstuffed sofas faced each other floating in the large room defined by glass tables and lamps. A small dining area had been set up at the end of room. A dinner table with candles and flowers waited for them. The room was light and comfortable. The walls had matching pictures of a garden in full summer bloom. Somehow Sandra knew they were soundproof.

"Why are we having dinner here?" Sandra asked when she'd taken her coat off and laid it over a chair near the door.

"I'm working here for the time being and I need to be up early in the morning. I thought it would be convenient."

Convenient and isolated, she thought. It wasn't unheard of for members of Congress to assist with FBI training. Brad Rutledge had been on the training staff for several years before seeking his first seat in Congress.

He crossed to the dining area and held the chair out for her. It was a deep maroon velvet with a firm, cushioned bottom. Sandra wondered where they'd come from and why they were in a training facility.

"Did you have a difficult drive?"

"No," she said, deciding not to tell him about the car she thought was tailing her.

"Good," he smiled. "Now, what would you like to eat? You can order anything your heart desires."

"I'm really not that hungry. I have some questions and I'd like to get them answered."

"You look thin."

She'd hoped he wouldn't notice her weight loss, but parents notice everything, her mother had once told her. She supposed it was only natural.

"I had the chef prepare your favorite foods. Why don't I ask them to serve us?"

Sandra nodded. She tried to relax as her father picked up the phone and spoke into it without dialing a number. Several moments later the door opened and in came a white-clad waiter with rolls and water and a small tossed salad with fresh Russian dressing. Sandra found she was hungrier than she thought. The salad was followed by lobster tails, broiled to perfection, a baked potato so flaky it melted in her mouth, and broccoli that had to have been fresh off the farm. She refused dessert but accepted the cup of flavored coffee.

When her father leaned back in his chair she figured she'd waited long enough. It was time for some answers.

"Dad, are you guilty of treason?"

Bradford Campbell Rutledge let out a whoop of laughter that benefitted the soundproof room.

"What has Randolph been filling your ears with?"

"He's told me about Project Eagle and he thinks you're the ring leader trying to find the components and sell them to the highest bidder."

"Sandra, you know I would never do a thing like that," he said soberly.

She'd always believed her father was above reproach, but life had taught her that everyone had a price.

"Are you involved, in any way, with Project Eagle?"

He hesitated. She tensed, knowing the gesture. Why was he playing a game with her? Why didn't he just tell her the truth?

"I'm chairman of the defense subcommittee. I'm privileged to a lot of projects. Eagle is only one of them."

"What would you do if I told you I have the missing parts and I could give them to you?"

He leaned forward. "Give them to me, Sandra." His voice was low, as if they were conspiring to do something. "I'm the only one who can get them to the right people."

"The right people! People who can eavesdrop on the world. Suppose they don't like what they hear? Are they going to react?" Anger made her speech rushed. "Will people suddenly disappear without cause? Dad, this is a Big Brother machine." She took a deep breath and calmed herself, then continued in a voice both quiet and deadly. "You've always hated the thought of too much interference by government. It's one of the ideals you campaigned with. People voted for you because they thought you'd keep control of all the computer networks and centralized identification systems. Now you're involved in a system that can tap into any home in the world." She spread her arms, encompassing the room. "Project Eagle can obliterate the ability of people to talk to each other in whole sections of countries. Why did you let such a system be built? We thought you were looking out for the people."

"Sandra, I can't discuss this with you. It's classified information."

"Well, declassify it. I'm already owner of the one vital part that allows everything else to work. Without it, all you have is a massive paperweight."

"You can't keep it, Sandra." He paused again. "I didn't want to tell you this, but Senator Randolph is the traitor. He wants the parts to sell to a foreign power. Right now the Japanese are interested, although the Iranians and several of the republics in the new Russia are making noises."

"I don't believe you!" Sandra stood up so fast the chair fell over behind her. She gave it only the slightest glance before glaring at her father. "Wyatt would never do that. He's trying desperately to find a solution to the ownership of the parts."

She said she didn't believe him, but was it true? Could Wyatt's reason for trying to keep her away from her father have been because she'd learn the truth? What was the truth? She no longer knew if she could recognize it.

Wyatt had said he loved her. And she loved him, too. Oh, God! She wanted to cry. She couldn't be in love with a traitor.

"Sandra, he's lying. You can't believe anything he says. Look how he grew up. He's been poor all his life. His mother teaches school and his father is a carpenter."

"Both very respected professions."

"Do you know the kind of money he could command if he sells that part? The amount of power he could garner? He's never even *seen* as much money as selling the component will bring him."

"Then why hasn't he already sold it? Why did he show up at the cabin looking for you with a hole in his side and blood spurting out like Niagara Falls?"

"I don't know. When he first talked to me—"

"Wyatt said he never talked to you," she interrupted. "He left you a message."

"That's right, he wanted to talk to me. Later we did talk. He's misguided, Sandra. He thinks I'm the cause of his misery. He wants me to go public with the news that Project Eagle exists, that no one is safe from its span."

"No one is." Sandra was confused. She didn't know who to believe. Her brain told her what her father said about Wyatt couldn't be true. He'd never lied to her. Some of what he said made sense. The amount of money a government would pay for the system would be enough to cause anyone to think of selling it.

"What about you, Dad? Was the amount of money so great you couldn't resist? Is Wyatt the one telling the truth?"

Brad Rutledge looked at his daughter as if she were the enemy. "How dare you accuse me of such a thing." He got to his feet like a sleeping giant coming to life. "I am your father." He stamped each word out as if he were working a teletype machine.

"Yes, you are!" she shouted. "And as my father it was your job to teach me and to live up to the ideals you tried to instill in me. Yet, tonight you've denied, evaded, and sidestepped every question I've asked you. You've told me . . . nothing." She stopped suddenly. A light bulb ignited in her brain. The room was soundless. Their anger hung between them. "You didn't bring me here to get information from me, or even to make sure I was safe. You wanted me away from Wyatt."

"Sandra, I did—"

"What have you done to him?" She remembered trying to reach him on the car phone.

"As far as I know, Sandra, he's safe. I promise you."

"I don't know if I can believe you anymore." She backed away from him. She had to get out of here. Something was awfully wrong and she didn't understand.

"Sandra, don't go like this." She stopped, but more at the shrill sound of the phone ringing than his words. They both looked at the white instrument as if it could speak.

After a moment Brad Rutledge walked over and lifted the receiver. Sandra listened to the one-sided conversation.

"Yes, sir . . . no, sir . . . she's here, sir . . . yes, sir." Without a salutation he hung up.

"Who was that?" she asked.

"The President of the United States."

Sandra rolled her eyes. "Oh, God, is he part of this, too?"

CHAPTER 13

Wyatt strapped on the backpack and bent to tie his sneakers. With Sandra gone he had time to do some snooping. They'd agreed the best way to find the stones would be to discover what Jeff had done in the days before his death. He couldn't stand being in that room knowing she was leaving and might not come back.

It could be a trap, like he'd told her. It could also be the best thing that had happened to her since she got involved with him. He had to do something to keep his mind off Sandra and what was happening to her.

9-5-1-4-7. The number ran through Wyatt's mind like an unrelenting song. What could Jeff have meant? He'd told them he hadn't given away the location of the stones. Not even he and Sandra knew where Jeff had hidden them. The most likely place was either his house or his office. He hadn't died in either place, but both could be under observation by the local authorities or some other far more threatening agency. He'd have to be careful. Blend in and at the first sign of trouble, forget the whole thing.

Wyatt jogged in the drizzling rain. Anyone seeing him would think he was a student training for the track team. He was too thin for football, but still young and agile enough to pass as a student. The fact that he exercised regularly was on his side. He only hoped his period of inactivity and the tender ache in his side didn't show to a scrutinizing eye. Luck was with him when he saw a couple of guys with Howard University Athletics Department written on their jackets jogging in his direction. They passed him without a nod. He hung back as if he were with them but not as well-conditioned and able to keep to such a fast pace.

He passed Jeff's house without a glance. The windows were dark, giving the place an empty, unlived-in look. When Wyatt reached the alley that had eluded the police and allowed him and Sandra to escape a week earlier, he checked his surroundings and quickly turned into it. He stopped, pressing his back against the wall of the first house. His breath congealed in the cold air as he watched and waited for anyone to follow him. Assured he was not being tailed, he continued his jogging until he reached Jeff's backyard.

Peering through the window of the garage, he found the sports car in place. No lights shone on the back of the house and he found it easy work to jimmy the lock and get inside. From the backpack he pulled a flashlight and began his search. The place had the definite stamp of police on it. It wasn't likely they'd left anything for him to find. He was hoping to find the stones, but he only expected to locate a date book or some type of calendar. He moved slowly from the living room and dining room through the kitchen, opening drawers, checking inside canisters and ice trays. He found nothing. Upstairs was the same. Jeff's computer equipment occupied one bedroom. Most of what was on it was the same gibberish as was on the disks in his backpack. He did find a few games and a file of letters to his sister in Baltimore, but nothing to help him with the disappearance of the stones. On impulse he looked in the computer address file for his sister's phone number and address. Neither had 95147 in any part of it. The basement and the attic proved the same fruitless effort.

Wyatt let himself out as he'd come in. Snow had begun to fall while he was inside. He wasn't sure if he'd look suspicious jogging in the snow, so he walked to the campus. Cars passed on the major thoroughfare and students rushed toward their dorms. He fit in and no one noticed him. The closer he got to the campus, the more students were on the street. Several classes must have ended recently.

He stopped at the light on 4th Avenue across from the wrought-iron gates leading to the main campus. Two students joined him as they waited for the light to turn green.

"We wondered how long it would take before you came, Senator Randolph."

Wyatt jumped at the voice and the mention of his name. He jerked around to find two men on either side of him and one directly in front. Wyatt didn't recognize any of them. The one in front spoke. "Would you come with us, please. There are several questions we'd like to ask you."

"Damn!" Sandra cried. The car skidded across the road as she sped out of the FBI compound. Her father and several agents had chased her as she traversed the hallways to find an exit and get back to her car.

Tears blurred her eyes and snow impeded her travel, but she defied caution and tore up the winding road. Behind her, cars scrambled to stop her. The surprise exit gave her the minutes she needed to get away. If she could make it out of the small town and back to the highway she would get lost in the traffic.

"That's what they expected," she said out loud. They would expect that she'd head for the highway. If they were smart there would be cars blocking that direction. She didn't know the country. She could get lost if she tried a different path. Well, she'd just have to get lost. Wyatt had been right. It was a trap. She wouldn't do what was expected. This time she would do something unexpected. She abruptly turned into the small town. Thankfully, other people had been on the roads. They were deserted, but their tracks in the snow covered the four directions. Sandra turned left and followed a narrow winding road. Checking behind her, she found no lights reflected in her mirror. She kept going, hoping this would lead somewhere. A Virginia state road sign stood on the right, but it was covered by the blowing snow. The route number was partially visible. She read a three but it could just as easily be an eight. The rest of the number was obliterated. She didn't know where she was or where it would lead. Pushing ahead, she slowed and followed the road. When it ended she turned right, hoping that was north. The road wasn't well traveled and the car slipped and slid over the icy ground like a kid on his first pair of skates. At this rate she'd never make it back to Washington. If she was lucky she wouldn't pitch into one of the ditches and if she wasn't she'd be caught by one of her father's men. Then she saw the sign for a motel.

Feeling a little like Janet Leigh in *Psycho,* she pulled into the parking lot. Registration was cautious for both her and the desk clerk, a fifty-something-year-old woman with dirty blond hair wearing a flowered house dress. Sandra kept her face averted, using the pretext of brushing snow out of her hair and the woman stayed behind a glass window with only a tiny opening in which to pass money and keys.

"Sorry, honey," the clerk said. "It's the last one in the back. We got a sign up on the highway and tonight everyone is looking for somewhere to sleep."

"I appreciate it," Sandra said.

"Thank God you came." She handed Sandra a key. "Now I can turn the sign on and go watch TV. My favorite show is on in a couple of minutes." Sandra noticed the pink neon Vacancy sign change to No Vacancy. She turned to leave.

"Honey," the woman called. Sandra turned back, but kept her face hidden. "That last cabin's got a shed next to it. If you want to keep the snow off your car, you can use it."

"God takes care of babies and fools." She repeated the cliché as she drove to the cabin. The shed more than protected her car; it concealed it. Lawn mowers and shovels were stored against the walls. Sandra pulled inside and cut the engine. She left the car and closed the barn-style doors. Then, using the key, she went into the room. It was adequate, clean but freezing. She found the thermostat and turned it to the highest position. There was a television, a Gideon Bible, with a crumbled bus schedule poking out of it, but no phone.

She toyed with the idea of going back to the car, but she didn't want to be out if anyone came by. The heating unit hissed and rumbled as the heat went through the ice-cold coils. Sandra huddled on the bed wondering where Wyatt could be.

Several times she checked the windows wondering if she had been followed. The desk clerk would certainly remember a single woman arriving around this time. From her room she couldn't see the entrance. If people came looking for her, she was at the worst place to execute an escape.

An hour later the room was warm and no one had found her. She let her shoulders relax and thought of the things her father had said about Wyatt.

He had to be wrong. Wyatt would never do anything like what he'd claimed. Who should she believe? They both accused each other of the same heinous crime. Wyatt had had the diamonds for a week before he stumbled into her at the cabin. If he'd wanted to sell them, he'd had every opportunity. Unless he was planning to meet someone in the mountains. Their cabin didn't *have* to be the destination he was seeking. He could have been lost in the snow and turned onto the road leading to her parents' cabin by accident. The room he was in had pictures of her and Annie with their parents. He would have recognized the senator and knew someone had to be related to him.

Where was Wyatt? He knew she'd call. Why had he gone out? *Had* he gone out, or had someone found their hiding place? She paced the room, feeling as if it was a cage. She tried to relax, knowing she needed to sleep, but too much was keeping her awake: her father's comments, Wyatt's disappearance, and the thought of FBI agents bursting through the door.

She turned on the television. The color picture played everything in green, all stations and all programs. An old movie she recognized but whose title she couldn't remember was playing. She watched it for only a moment before thoughts of Wyatt invaded her mind. Pulling the bedspread free, she wrapped herself in it and stared at the green pictures. Her eyes drooped and eventually she slept.

She awoke with a start. The old movie was gone. In its place was another one. She recognized a young Sidney Poitier. Lamplight seeped in through the sides of the room-darkening shades. Then she remembered the events of the night. She'd kicked the spread away in her sleep. The temperature in the room must be in the nineties. She checked her watch. Two o'clock in the morning. Wyatt would surely have returned by now.

Picking up the car keys, she left the room and went back to the shed. Her heart pounded in her ears. She needed to know what had happened, *if* something had happened. Looking at the car phone, she suddenly wanted to call. Sandra snatched it up, then quickly put it back. Her location had been found once due to a phone. She was afraid of it happening again.

Biting her lower lip, she decided to take the chance. She'd be quick. All she needed to know was that he was all right. She dialed the motel. This time the desk clerk told her the guests had checked out and the room was free. Sandra was speechless. It couldn't be. Wyatt wouldn't check out. She hung up. Something was wrong, very wrong. She had to go back. Now!

The red sports car had gone no more than thirty feet when she saw the first patrol car. It was unmarked but with the distinctive features of law enforcement. Sandra turned at the first intersection and came to a halt along the shoulder. She'd cut the engine and the lights. The warm temperature immediately dissipated and she felt the cold begin to seep into the interior. She'd never make it in this car. It had been identified and every cop and agent between here and the District would be looking for it. She had to ditch the car and get back another way.

Remembering the bus schedule that had been in the Bible, she wished she'd taken it. But this was a small rural town; the bus would have to come into the center of town. She could go back the way she'd come, which had been at the crossroads of town. How long she'd have to wait she didn't know. Starting the engine, she drove slowly toward town. Using the phone a second time, she tried the motel again. She gave the same information to a different desk clerk. Mrs. Marta Ainsworth, the name she'd registered under, had checked out.

Along the side of the road, before coming into the center of town, Sandra spied a crop of trees. Parking the car, she used snow and branches to conceal it. Jordon and Annie would probably give her hell for leaving it, but she had to find Wyatt.

Brushing the snow from her hands and coat, she walked the short distance into town. Her shoes took the worst of it and her feet were freezing when she walked into the only lighted building. The sleepy clerk who doubled as ticket seller and general store manager told her the bus was late but due any minute. She waited only half an hour before the silver-and-red Trailways bus pulled up in front of the store. Three people got off and Sandra got on.

The driver explained to the clerk, who appeared to care more about getting his sleep than listening to the explanation, that he was trying to get back on schedule and would not be waiting the usual twenty minutes. Sandra was glad to hear this. When she saw passengers getting off, she knew they could be bound for only one place. Soon they would be picked up by the very people she was trying to avoid.

The bus sped along Route 95 heading toward Washington. Sandra pushed up the armrest between the two seats and tucked her feet under her dress and coat. Her toes were wet and stiff with cold. She leaned against the window watching the miles pass and the wintry scenes blur.

What was she going to do when she reached Washington? She didn't know the first place to try to look for Wyatt. He'd said he couldn't go to his house. She didn't expect to find him there. Maybe she could find a phone number and call to see if anyone would answer.

She looked up as they passed mile marker one-fifty. Jeff had come here, she remembered. The man at the desk said he'd had dinner with Lance Desque? How did Lance fit into this saga? Maybe when she reached the city she could call Lance. Jordon and Annie had suggested she go to Lance. He'd been one of the last people to see Jeff before he died. Maybe Wyatt had gone to Annie. She could hardly wait for the bus to get to DC. Mile marker one forty-seven. God, it would be another hour. Suddenly, it hit her, one forty-seven. Jeff hadn't said 9-5-1-4-7, he'd said 95-147. Route 95, mile marker 147. She turned to look behind her. The bus sped forward. All she saw was a bed of rocks. If someone was threatening Jeff and he knew it, he'd hide them in a place where no one would be likely to look.

An hour later the bus parked at the station and Sandra resisted the urge to sprint off the huge people carrier. She waited her turn, then went straight to the phones. She tried Annie, knowing her hotel room was probably bugged by now. She didn't say who she was, only that she was trying to find someone. When Annie began berating her, she cut into the conversation. Seconds later, Jordon took the phone and accepted her cautious questions. Neither he nor Annie had heard from Wyatt.

Sandra left the bus station and walked several blocks until she found another public phone. She was tired and scared and anxious. She looked for a number for Wyatt's Georgetown house, but found none. She called Michael at her father's office but got nowhere. Behind her a woman came who wanted to use the phone and Sandra left.

She'd developed a headache and was near frantic when she walked down the steps to the basement of a department store and found a phone. She dialed the number Sam Parker had given them. No one had heard from Wyatt. It was as if he didn't exist.

She left the department store in a daze. Her shoes were damp but her feet were no longer wet. She wouldn't have felt the cold anyway. She was thinking about Wyatt. She hadn't wanted to confront her feelings, hadn't told him she loved him. Now she might not get the chance. She was sure he'd been caught by now. Hadn't that been her father's objective in getting her to go all the way to Quantico, so he could have Wyatt apprehended?

Sandra felt alone, and numb as she continued up and down the streets. People passed her, cars sprayed water as they rushed to and fro. Sandra didn't notice. Her mind was on Wyatt. Was he dead? How, in the millions of people who lived and worked in the capital, could she find one man? Tears rolled down her cheeks. Streaks caked and froze in the cold. She brushed them away with her hands, but didn't feel the cold. She felt nothing. Only the loneliness of never seeing the man she loved again.

Why had she been so stupid? Why hadn't she told him she loved him when she had the chance? Where was he?

Lance Desque was a creature of habit. At precisely twelve-thirty every weekday afternoon, Sandra knew she could find him at The Charter Club. He had a standing table reserved each day. He'd sampled each of the entrees and decided on the five best the house had to offer. Each day he ordered one of them.

Sandra entered the fashionable restaurant and went straight to the ladies' room. After restoring her face and clothes to a presentable state, she reentered the restaurant as if she were returning to her own table. She found Lance with no problem. He was seated where he could be seen by those in power who also frequented the establishment. For Sandra this might not be the best location, but it was the only one available.

Slipping into the chair across from him, she kept her back to the room. Lance's soup spoon stopped on its way to his mouth.

"Sandra!" he whispered, checking about them with a discreet turn of his head to make sure no one noticed her. The soup spilled and he put the spoon on the plate under his bowl. "What are you doing here?"

"I need to talk to you."

"This is not the place or time. If you plan to maintain your present state of freedom, you should never have come here."

"Lance, I need your help. If we can't talk here, then let's go someplace where we can."

Lance cut his eyes to her and then canceled his meal and quickly signed the check for his soup. As he led her out of the restaurant, Sandra kept her face toward him and away from any prying eyes. She climbed into the waiting limousine and Lance rolled the screen up even before his startled driver had seen him and rushed to the car.

Lance picked up the phone and spoke into it. "Drive anywhere," he said.

The car pulled away from the curb. Sandra noticed it crawl into the afternoon traffic and hunt its way up Pennsylvania Avenue toward the Capitol Building.

"Sandra, I am so glad to see you. What can I do to help you? Do you need anything . . . money?" He reached for his wallet.

"Thank you, Lance." She put her hand on his arm and shook her head. "I'm fine."

"Then what can I help you with?" Lance asked.

She shifted into the butter-soft leather. "I had dinner with my father last night."

"Yes."

"We ate in one of the training apartments at Quantico."

Lance waited. Sandra wanted him to volunteer something, anything, but she'd forgotten how cautious he could be, how he calculated every move and every question before replying.

"The desk clerk told me you had dinner with Jeff Taylor the day before he died."

Lance cleared his throat. "Yes, I did."

"Lance, that means you're one of the last people to see him alive. Did he say anything?"

"Nothing that I can remember. We talked about old times at the department, what he was doing now in academia, nothing that could help find his killer."

"Did he mention Project Eagle?"

Lance stiffened almost imperceptibly. If she hadn't been looking for a reaction, she wouldn't have seen it.

"No, he didn't. And you shouldn't know about it, either."

"Well, I do."

"What has Randolph told you?"

"I don't want to talk about Wyatt now."

"Do you know what Project Eagle is capable of doing?"

She thought about that before answering. Lance had been a friend of the family for years. She should be able to trust him, but Wyatt had cautioned her against trusting anyone, and until she found out better, that seemed to be the best course of action.

"I know enough," she answered, not committing herself one way or another.

"Do you know where the stolen parts are?"

Sweat popped out on Lance's brow. She couldn't remember ever seeing him sweat. "Yes," she told him with confidence in her voice.

"Turn them over to me and I'll see that you're exonerated in this. You can go back to your mountain and finish studying for that degree. Forget all about Project Eagle and concentrate on what's important in your life."

"You don't think Project Eagle is important to everyone?"

"Of course it is." He recovered from his blunder with polished ease.

"There are people working with this system, experts who know how to best put it to use. Sandra, believe me, these people have the best interest of everyone in mind."

She doubted that. She doubted that anyone could have another person's interest at heart when they were dealing with something as monumental as the power that could be had with this system.

"Where are the stones, Sandra? Do you have them with you?"

"No," she said, suddenly wondering if she'd said yes, would Lance have searched her in the back of the limousine.

"We can go and get them now, and by nightfall your life will be back on track."

"What about Senator Randolph?"

"I can't promise anything, but I'll do my best."

Lance smiled, but his words sounded suspiciously like he would do nothing. She didn't even know where Wyatt was. She wanted Lance to help her, but he seemed more interested in getting information from her than giving any. In his defense, he did work for the department that had lost the final part of the system. Regaining it would put a major feather in his cap. It would also increase his popularity and probably get him a Cabinet post in the next administration.

But Lance had higher ambitions than that. Why had she never noticed them before?

"Is something wrong?" he asked.

"Lance, I don't believe you."

"Sandra, I wouldn't lie to you." He took her shoulders and turned her toward him. "He's a dead man, Sandra. You're away from him now. Why don't you tell me everything and let me take over from here. If you ally yourself to him you could get killed."

She shuddered. "Lance, who's trying to kill Wyatt?"

"I don't know."

How could he lie with such a straight face? "This project would have to come under your direct supervision. You have to know what's going on."

"It's out of my control, but if you tell me where the stones are, I will use my influence with the secretary and make sure nothing hurts you and your father."

That's good, she thought. Now he was using psychological pressure. Making her feel that she'd bring shame to her family. Hadn't her father already done that? Lance didn't know what had transpired between her and her father last night; how her father had known about the project all along and how he was probably behind the plot to kill Wyatt.

"I'll think about it," she said.

Lance let her shoulders go. "There isn't much time, Sandra. You have to make a decision now. There's no telling what the FBI will do. They have to be getting close to you and Wyatt or homing in on where you've hidden the stones."

Her head snapped up. "You know Jeff had the stones."

"That's only a matter of deductive reasoning. You and Wyatt were chased from Jeff's house."

"That was only alleged. None of the police officers could say with any certainty that they actually saw us driving the car."

"But it was you?" He smiled with all the finesse he was known for.

Sandra ignored the question. Checking where they were, she saw the Washington Monument in the background and the Tidal Basin in the distance.

"Several days later, Jeff is found dead and you show up at my lunch table. I don't think I need much more to convince me." He paused a moment. "So tell me, Sandra. Where have you hidden the stones?"

Sandra smiled. He wanted the stones bad. And why not? They would mean greater visibility for him and certainly a promotion. For her, they were a bargaining point. But she was bargaining with something she didn't have.

"If I were to give you the stones, Lance, what would you do with them?"

"I don't understand."

"You said you'd take them back to the Defense Department, to the people better able to put them to use than Senator Randolph or myself."

"I would," he agreed.

Sandra sighed. "I can't give you the stones, Lance."

She saw him recoil. It was as close to a reaction as Lance had ever let another human being see.

"Why not? You can't stay out there with them. There are too many people who want them. The Japanese can't wait to get their hands on them. Any government would kill, *kill,* Sandra, to have what you've got. Do you know what you're doing?" He stopped, took a breath and straightened his tie. "Unless you're planning to sell them yourselves."

Sandra stared at him as if she'd never seen him before.

"Is that what Senator Randolph has convinced you to do? To take the stones and sell them? That's what he wants, you know."

"God! I don't have to listen to this." She rapped on the darkened window. "Let me out of here."

"No." He reached over her. "Think about what you're doing, Sandra. Randolph has obviously filled your head with a lot of nonsense. You're a logical person. Think about what will happen to you when you get out of this car. You're a hunted woman. There's no way you can survive without my help."

"You'll save me and sacrifice Wyatt. I don't like that solution. The chips were sent to Wyatt. He should be the one making the decision to turn them over."

Lance straightened in his seat. Realization dawned in his face. "You're in love with him."

She didn't deny it. She wanted to know where he was, but Lance was going to be no help. He was only interested in getting the stones.

"Sandra, he kidnapped you. And you fall for him?"

"He didn't kidnap me."

In the condition she found him, he could have done nothing to her. He couldn't even help himself. She wondered if he could help himself now. Where was he and why had he left the hotel? Checked out of the hotel, the clerk had said. Wyatt had promised he'd be there when she got back. Was he lying? Was he truly the way her father and Lance painted him? She'd spent the better part of the last three weeks in his company and she had a different opinion. Of course, she was looking through the eyes of love. There was a lot of money involved, millions of dollars. Was it enough for a man to compromise his principles?

"Lance, I don't have the stones. I promise to talk to Wyatt about them." *As soon as I find him,* she added to herself.

Sandra knew Lance thought she'd lead him to the stones. After she'd hopped out of his limo she'd darted into a metro station, crossed the street underground and exited on the opposite side. Walking up several streets and taking a bus going north on Independence, she wondered what she should do now.

Cars darted up and down the streets. The lunch hour was nearly over, but Washington never seemed to be completely free of foot traffic. Keeping her head down so people passing couldn't get a good view of her face, she walked toward the Capitol.

Fear suddenly seized her. She was alone. Lance was looking for her, the police were looking for her, even her father was looking for her. She didn't know what to do any longer. Where was Wyatt? She needed him. She wanted to feel his arms around her again, feel his kiss and tell him she loved him.

She found herself standing on a corner. The traffic light turned green and she stood there. Where was there to go? She had no clue. Turning around, she spotted a phone, went to it, and picked up the receiver. Who was she going to call? She put it back and stared at it.

She'd talked to the hotel more than once. Wyatt simply wasn't there and he wasn't going to be there if she tried again. He didn't know where she was, either. If he tried the car phone she was a hundred miles away. She couldn't hear it ring.

There was one phone call she could make. Annie had told her, if she got backed into a corner to call somebody. What was the name? Sandra grasped the receiver but didn't lift the handset. Think, she told herself. What was his name? Richman? Richie? Roberts? "No," she said to herself. "Grant . . . that was the first name." She looked down for a phone book. Nothing. Annie had said he was listed in the phone book. Behind her was a federal building. Sandra walked through the door. She no longer cared about being recognized. Along the far wall was a bank of phone booths. She went into the first one and closed the glass door. The heavy Chesapeake and Potomac directory came up and she went to the R's.

Richards, it came to her. His name was Grant Richards. She found the listing. Dialing the number, she asked to speak to him.

"Mr. Richards, this is Sandra Rutledge."

"Are you all right?" he asked.

"Yes," she swallowed.

"Suzanne told me you might call. Do you need help?"

Sandra needed help, but she didn't know Grant Richards and she and Annie hadn't been on the best terms in years. His name sounded familiar, but she couldn't remember where she'd seen or heard it.

"You're wondering if you can trust me?" he said.

"Frankly, yes," she told him. "Annie . . . Suzanne doesn't usually do favors for me."

"I know," he said.

Sandra was surprised. Did he really know? Did he have any idea what was between her sister and herself?

"If it's any help to you I had a minor part in Project Eagle. At one time I had the computer chips."

"You're my last hope. I can't find Senator Randolph. I think he's been . . ." She couldn't say it.

"Where are you, Sandra? I promise there will be no police or anyone connected with the law."

She didn't care anymore. She was tired of running, tired of looking over her shoulder, and without Wyatt she just didn't care.

"I'm in a federal building at the corner of Fourth and Independence Southwest."

"Stay there. A car will pick you up in ten minutes."

"All right," she said, defeated.

Sandra left the building, nodding to the guard as if they saw each other every day. As Grant had promised, ten minutes later a stretch limousine pulled up at the curb. The driver, clad in a black suit and a flat-top hat, got out and opened the door for her. "Ms. Rutledge?" he said.

Sandra hesitated only a moment before entering the soft leather interior. The car was occupied, but not by anyone who could be Grant

Richards; rather by a pregnant woman with long black hair that must have curled to her waist. She smiled and rubbed her protruding belly.

"Brooke Richards," she said, offering her hand. "You don't have to tell me who you are."

The car pulled away from the curb. Sandra glanced at the window but saw only her own reflection. The windows were completely black. The divider between the two passengers and the driver was also black. She felt claustrophobic but said nothing.

"Are you involved in this, too?"

"No." She shook her head. "I only help out when needed, and Grant thought I could do more for you than he could."

"Do you know what happened to Wyatt . . . Senator Randolph?"

"I'm afraid not. I only want to assure you that you're safe."

"Where are you taking me?"

"I won't be going with you. The driver is taking me to my restaurant. He has instructions to take you to another location."

"Where is that?"

"I'm not privileged to that information, but don't worry, you're in good hands. Nothing will happen to you while you're with him."

Sandra was anything but reassured. The black windows bothered her. She had no idea which direction they were going in.

"Look," she began. "I've been shot at and chased by too many people to name. Now I'm in a car with windows you can't see through and a pregnant woman telling me to trust her? Give me one good reason why I should?"

"Because you don't have anybody else to trust."

Sandra fell back against the upholstery. It wasn't a good reason, but it was the truth. She had no other place to turn. Wherever she was going had to be better than continuing to run through the streets of Washington.

Sandra checked her watch when the car stopped. She'd been riding for half an hour. The door opened and Brooke took her hand. "Good luck," she said. "Call us if you need us."

The driver helped her out of the car. He closed the door as Sandra tried to glimpse something that might tell her where they were. Moments later the car started up again and they were off. She clocked the time against her watch. They drove for twenty minutes. Outside, she heard the unmistakable roar of helicopter rotors beating the air. A cold burst of air invaded the compartment when the door opened.

She got out. A man extended his hand. "Grant Richards," he said. "You just met my wife."

Sandra took his hand.

"I'm your pilot."

"Can you tell me where you're taking me?"

"To a safe house," he smiled.

He led her to the helicopter which also had black glass in the windows which wouldn't permit her to see where they were going. As far as she could tell, he was the only other person on board. Again she clocked the distance. It took them forty minutes before they set down. Assuming this helicopter was at least as powerful as her mother's Starfighter, she clocked the distance at about a hundred miles.

But a hundred miles in which direction? Was she in Maryland or Virginia? Had the helicopter crossed into Pennsylvania or gone farther on to West Virginia? Why couldn't she relax? Both the Richardses had assured her she was safe. She hadn't been safe in so long, yet when Wyatt was close she felt less afraid. Would she ever see him again?

The door opened and the wind was colder. When she got out there was little to define the area. She was in the middle of nowhere. All she could see was mountains. Another stretch limousine sat next to the helicopter pad. Grant opened the door and followed her inside.

This drive was short and the windows weren't camouflaged. The car stopped in front of a large white house. The grounds, though covered with snow, had been cleared. It must look wonderful in summer. White columns defined a huge porch, and Sandra wondered what it had looked like last month decorated for Christmas.

Grant helped her out and walked her to the door. He opened it with a key and stood back extending the key to her.

"This is where I leave you."

Sandra took the key. "Before you go, I'd like to ask you something."

He said nothing, but gave her his attention.

"Annie . . . Suzanne, my sister. How does she fit into all this?"

"I'm afraid she'll have to explain that to you."

Sandra wasn't satisfied, but she didn't think she could get him to tell her anything more about her sister. So much didn't make sense. "Is there anyone else here?" Sandra asked him.

Grant smiled and left her. She watched him leave, then went inside and closed the door. She remembered then where she'd heard his name. At the airport when she and Wyatt arrived. She'd left the helicopter in a hangar with a sign that said Richards Air. *Was he that Richards?* she wondered.

She looked around. *Where am I now?* she wondered. What will happen here and where was Wyatt? She stood in a large foyer. Taking several steps, she moved into the main entrance hall, a circular-shaped room with a domed ceiling that ended in a small skylight. A long chord hung from it holding a massive chandelier. After the hotel rooms she and Wyatt had occupied this was heaven. At least it would be if she knew where Wyatt had gone.

Thoughts of Wyatt clouded her short-lived cheer. Anger rushed to defend her volatile emotions. When she found him, she'd kill him for what he'd put her through. They'd argued that she should stay with her father. Would he have checked out so she would be forced to take his advice? Was he sacrificing himself for her?

The anger left her. Suppose he hadn't checked out on his own. Suppose he'd been caught? He could be hurt. He wouldn't do this to her without discussing it. The only explanation had to be that he'd been caught. Where did they take him? How would she find him?

"Wyatt," she whispered. Would she ever see him again? Would she ever get the chance to tell him she loved him?

Anger loomed again. "Wyatt, where are you?" she screamed.

"Up here," he said.

CHAPTER 14

"Wyatt!" Sandra cried, swinging around and looking toward the sound. He stood at the top of the stairs. Tears sprang to her eyes and she seemed rooted to the spot. She never expected to see him again. She'd told herself he was dead and that the next time she heard of him it would be an account of someone finding his body.

She couldn't move. The only part of her that functioned, other than her pounding heart, was her tear ducts. Rivers of water poured from them. Wyatt ran down the stairs and pulled her into his arms.

"Where did you go?" she hiccuped. "I called and called."

Wyatt didn't answer. He couldn't. He was too glad to see her. The lump in his throat and the one squeezing his heart made speaking a useless effort. He kissed the tears from her eyes. A hunger deep in his body roared to life, tensing his stomach muscles and heating the air around them. He admitted he hadn't had much time for women in his career, but this one was different. He wanted, really wanted to make time for her. His mouth kissed her face from her forehead to her cheeks and neck. He didn't seem to be able to stop himself. At the corner of her mouth he felt the wetness of her lips. Her mouth turned toward his, but he raised his head, looking deep into her eyes. Their brown depths seemed to melt and swim before him.

She completely captivated him, like a gypsy witch with a potion that was meant only for him. He drank willingly of the liquid and wanted more, much more.

He stared at her lips. They trembled ever so slightly, making his insides turn to pulverized jelly. For an eon he hovered above them before he could keep himself in check no longer. His mouth covered hers, and the explosion that had been building in him detonated like an atom bomb. His mouth devoured hers, his tongue sweeping inside her mouth finding all the sweetness he knew was there. His hands went into her hair and released the clamp that held it in place. He felt its silkiness as it cascaded over his hands.

Time between them seemed to slow down. He could feel the slightest sensations related to her, the way her hair felt as the tips touched his fingers, the smell of her skin, the soft sounds that gurgled in her throat. His hands moved to her shoulders and he pushed the coat aside. It slipped down her arms and came to rest at her feet. He felt the pearls at her neck and raked the back of his hands down her smooth arms. Taking her waist in between the span of his large hands, he fit her closer to his aroused body. He shuddered as she moved against him. He didn't think he'd ever be able to let her go.

In a movement as natural as breathing he lifted her into his arms and carried her up the winding staircase. Standing before the king-size bed in the master bedroom, he lowered her to the floor.

Sandra slid down his body, feeling every deliciously hard inch of him. He stared at her as if she were a queen. She never thought she could feel like this again.

She was breathless under his stare. His hand went behind her back and found the zipper of her dress. He didn't immediately pull it down but waited. She opened her mouth to breathe. Her body was hot, her nipples already erect and he hadn't even touched them. No one had ever made her feel like this. Slowly the zipper began a downward movement. She felt the air touch her skin. It was cool and helped to damp down the flames Wyatt created in her. But it was no match, for with each inch of freedom the furnace inside her intensified. She arched her back, leaning into him.

"Wyatt," she groaned. The zipper had reached the curve over her buttocks. Wyatt let his hand rest there. He urged her forward. Her hips ground into the hard strength of his erection. A pleasurable sound defying description escaped her throat. Sandra floated away from the dress. It pooled around her in a circle of royal blue. She wore only a blue bra and panties, high heels, and white pearls. Wyatt moved his gaze from her face to her feet, taking in every sensual inch of her. Sandra felt no shame in her nudity. She wanted him to see her, wanted him to touch her and make her his.

Wyatt leaned forward and kissed her tenderly on the mouth. Their mouths barely touched, yet the intimacy was overwhelming. Her hands with less finesse than his fumbled with the buttons on his shirt. She freed one of them, then another. Her knuckles brushed against his skin. It was hot like fire, but a fire she wanted to touch. She let her fingers splay against him when his shirt fell to the floor in a love match with her dress. His heart pounded under her fingertips. Its rhythm matched the thundering pound of her own heart.

She released the belt hook at his waist and unzipped his trousers. Her hands brushed against his hardness and she trembled. He was big. Anticipation flowed between her legs. Her eyes closed as her hand massaged him. He groaned a loud guttural sound. "Sandra," he moaned.

In a flash he pulled her to him and kissed her hard. His mouth grazed hers. His hands were like ropes of fire as they massaged her back, moving with ease across her skin. With the flick of his fingers he dispensed with her bra. Her full breasts were freed of their lace confinement. They stood erect, anticipating his touch to blossom to full life.

Wyatt edged her back until the bedcovers pressed against her legs. He pressed her down, then made a ritual of drawing her panties over her hips and down her long legs until her only item of clothing was the single strand of white pearls. She thought she'd incinerate with the heat he created inside her. She burned for him, wanted him now. Dispensing with his own clothes, he joined her on the bed. Sandra reached for his broad shoulders and folded him close to her. She shivered suddenly.

"Anything wrong?" he asked, moving to look at her.

"Only that I thought this would never happen."

"Believe me, honey. It's going to happen."

Sandra let her gaze run over his face. He was beautiful. If she'd never noticed it before, she knew it now. She ran her hands around his head and pulled his mouth to hers. She brushed his lips from side to side, then slipped her tongue between his lips. Wyatt opened his mouth letting her have access. He tasted good, a taste different from any other man on earth, a taste as intoxicating as liquor. Wyatt's hands touched her breasts. She quivered as his smooth palms found her nipples and moved over them. The pebbly-hard nubs sent sensations through her that fanned out inside her like ripples of pleasure. She arched closer to the exquisite rapture.

Her eyes shut as she tried to hold on to the pleasure he created. Then he shifted, hovering above her. She felt his hard erection against her already wet sex. His mouth kissed her breasts one at a time. As he took his mouth away to find another spot, her back arched, reaching toward him as if she didn't want him to move. He kissed her belly, her arms, every part of her. Sandra tried to keep control of herself, but she found it a losing battle. Wyatt made her feel like no other man ever had. Finally, he kneed her legs apart. She heard him tear the foil packet and watched him cover himself to protect them both.

"It's going to happen, baby," he said, his voice heavy with emotion as he penetrated her. In one easy movement he was inside, filling her, making her eyes water with the pleasure that raced through her like fire trails. Wyatt set the rhythm and Sandra matched it. She'd never felt so at one with a human being in her life. It was as if he drew breath and she exhaled. She'd felt it, known it since he'd come to the cabin, since she'd begun this great adventure. She and Wyatt were made for each other. He'd taught her things about herself, things she didn't know and would never have known without him. He rocked the foundation of her sheltered world and now he'd taken her to heights beyond any fantasy she could create.

Wyatt groaned with each powerful thrust. He'd known she'd be like this, known that making love to her would be a revelation for him. He felt encased in rapture. Sandra wrapped her legs around him, pulling him into her, deeper and deeper as if there was no end to the connection between them. Wyatt wanted to scream, cry, he wanted to release a lifetime of love and affection on Sandra. She made him feel things he hadn't known existed. Her hands touched him and his skin turned to molten rock. As she whimpered her pleasure, sensations rocketed through him. If he had to die he wanted to do it now, while she held him in the throes of a consuming passion, while he experienced the ultimate in human exchange. With his body he pledged himself to her, gave freely his heart and his love until together they collapsed in mutual satisfaction.

Sandra had never been so fulfilled. She ran her hands over Wyatt's back. It was smooth and warm. The intimacy only heightened her love for him. She knew she wanted to spend the rest of her life with Wyatt Randolph. Despite his life in front of the camera, despite the cloud hanging over him, she knew she'd be incomplete without him.

"I love you, Wyatt," she said.

She felt him stiffen. He raised his head and stared into her eyes. "Do you mean that?"

"More than I've ever meant anything in my life. I love you."

Wyatt gathered her close to him and kissed her. A long and tender kiss. Then he pulled her into his body and rested his head above hers. A tear fell from his eye and rolled down his cheek.

Wyatt watched her. He'd been doing that since they were forced together in the close confines of motel rooms. This morning was different. This was the morning after she told him she was in love with him. This was the first day of their life together. Yesterday he'd made love to her for the first time. And through the night they'd made love again. He didn't seem to be able to get enough of her. He didn't think he ever would. Sandra Rutledge. He rolled her name around in his mind. If someone had told him that Chip's little package would lead to the woman of his dreams he wouldn't have believed them. He was too used to women who wanted something from him. Sandra had asked for nothing. All she'd done was help him, watch his back, and be loyal to him. He couldn't ask for a better partner.

Bending forward, he kissed her on the side of the head. She stirred, reaching for him. He cradled her close, observing the contrast of their skin tones and wondering what their future children would look like.

Anise Kingsley had been housekeeper at the guest house through five administrations. She was the soul of discretion, made a point of learning the cultures of every foreign dignitary who'd slept within the covered walls. Everett Horton didn't know how the country would run without people like her.

"Good morning, Mrs. Kingsley," Everett spoke into the receiver from his bedroom.

"Good morning, sir."

"Are they awake yet?"

"No, sir. I think they had a very late night."

"I have a busy schedule. I need to talk to them by noon. Do you think they'll be up by then?" He knew the answer. Mrs. Kingsley would have them dressed and polished as if they were children and they'd never know they'd been manipulated. Everett wished he had her skills.

"I'll take them some tea, sir."

"Thank you, Mrs. Kingsley."

She replaced the receiver and added a small flower vase with a single rose in it. She smiled. Lovers, she thought. Few of them ever spent the night here. Usually the place was filled with feuding nationals, each refusing to budge on his particular point, and the President in the middle, acting as mediator. She'd seen many presidents, but found this new one more able to get work done than the other four she'd met.

With the tray in hand, she climbed the wide staircase and set it on the mahogany server outside the master suite. Gently, she knocked on the door.

Sandra climbed closer to Wyatt, fear in her eyes. He tightened his arms about her. "Come in," he said.

A small woman in her fifties opened the door and brought a tray to the bed.

"Good morning," she said. "Glad to see you're awake." Her face held a smile that twinkled in her eyes as she introduced herself. Sandra liked her. "I've brought your breakfast," she announced.

She moved to set the bed tray down. Sandra and Wyatt shifted toward each other. Sandra grabbed the sheet she'd nearly let go of when she moved. When they were sitting up against the pillows, she set the silver tray on the bed between them.

"Clothes have been provided for you in the closet and drawers," she said without censure. "If there's anything you need just call me." She indicated the phone next to the bed. "It has a code for housekeeper. The President has to go back to Washington this afternoon. He'd like to see you at noon."

She turned to leave.

"Mrs. Kingsley?" Sandra stopped her. "President? Clothes? Where are we?"

The older woman stood up to her full height which couldn't be more than five feet. The gesture was more pride than haughtiness. "You're in the guest house, Ms. Rutledge. At Camp David."

Sandra found everything she needed as Mrs. Kingsley had promised. The clothes fit perfectly. They should. They'd been brought from her house in New Jersey.

Sandra held up a skirt and sweater in recognition, and Wyatt did the same with his garments. "Obviously the President has enough clout to get what he wants," he commented.

"What do you think he wants with us?"

"What everybody else wants. He wants us to give him the stones." Sandra was quiet. "Too bad all we'll be able to tell him is that we've lost them."

"Wyatt," Sandra called his name softly. "What do you think we should do if we really had the stones? I mean . . . I know Chip was your friend, but what he built is a dangerous weapon. We can only imagine the implications of any one government having access to a device as deadly as Project Eagle."

"I thought a lot about that in the past few days. If any government should have access to the system I'd want it to be ours."

"But it's our choice, Wyatt. It's as if we're the only two people on earth. We hold the future of the world in our hands."

Sandra looked at Wyatt's hands. They were strong and sure, and she remembered them holding her through the night.

"I believe that's why Chip sent the stones to you. He knew, when the time came, you'd make the right decision of what to do with them."

Sandra stood before the mirror brushing her hair. Wyatt stood next to her, fixing his own. She wanted to have a future with him. Was it possible? She was the only person alive who knew where the stones were. At least she thought she knew. She looked at it as Eve must have looked when she offered Adam the forbidden fruit. She had the secret. She could change the course of power on earth. The weight of that knowledge was overwhelming. She didn't want it. She wanted to tell Wyatt, share what she knew with him, but until she was sure of the President's purpose she'd keep her information to herself.

The car was outside waiting for them by the time they were dressed and ready. The same driver appeared to open the car door and drive them a short distance to the main house. Mrs. Horton greeted them at the door.

"Welcome to Camp David," she said. "I'm Casadia Horton. I'd like you to call me Casey."

She introduced herself as if she wasn't the most known face in America. Separate from the President, she was a wonderful champion of the American people. She went into disaster areas, homeless shelters, and hospitals and had no qualms about getting her hands dirty if she could help someone.

Sandra smiled and kept hold of Wyatt's arm. "Senator Randolph, it's good to see you again."

Wyatt took the hand she offered. "This is Sandra Rutledge." Sandra also shook hands with her. Her hands were soft and warm, heightening the contrast with Sandra's cold one.

"I know introductions aren't necessary. I've been following the account of your life in the papers. I feel as if I know you."

"Good afternoon." Sandra could think of nothing to say. She'd have liked it better if the nature of her newspaper coverage wasn't due to infamy. Casey turned, walking toward the other end of the house. She and Wyatt followed. Sandra had thought the guest house beautiful. This one was almost palatial. They were led into a large dining room with Wedgwood-blue walls and white molding. The drapes were white and the china held the Seal of the United States on each piece. Sandra wondered if there was a subtle message in them.

"Welcome, Senator, Sandra. I may call you Sandra?" Everett Horton asked.

"Of course, Everett," she said.

He laughed boisterously. "I'm going to like her," he told Casey. "I've always admired your father," he said to Sandra. "It's a pleasure to find the same wit and humor in his daughter."

Not only were the President and First Lady present but the director of the FBI, the Secretary of Defense, and the ever-present Melanie West. She wondered why her father wasn't among the honored guests. Sandra had the feeling a long meeting had preceded their entrance. Clarence Christopher had a briefcase of files he was returning to order when the door was opened. Sandra wondered how large a file he had on her. His gaze met hers as she turned back to the room. She was sure he could tell what she'd been thinking. He only offered her a nod.

The comedy of manners was required in polite society. Sandra knew that better than anyone. They each took a seat at the dinner table. She and Wyatt were next to each other, and she was thankful for that. Etiquette stated people unacquainted with each other should be dinner partners to ensure that something was learned about a new person.

No one mentioned Project Eagle and she knew nothing would be said until the meal had been eaten and cleared away. When the remnants of dessert and a good coffee were the only items left on the white linen tablecloth, Everett Horton would ask his questions. She would tell him lies.

Wyatt hardly knew what he ate. The conversation on winter vacations versus summer vacations was getting on his nerves. Not one of them was really interested in vacations. They all wanted to know about Project Eagle.

"Everett!" Wyatt called, taking the same boldness as Sandra had. "You've brought us here for more than our opinion on skiing in the Pocono Mountains."

"You're quite right, Senator." Horton took a sip of his coffee. He then leaned forward with his arms folded on the white tablecloth. "I'm going to cut straight to the chase. Do you have the computer chips Edward Jackson developed?"

Wyatt didn't immediately respond. He'd expected this question. Wyatt weighed the options of answering yes or no. He was facing the President of the United States and several of his most important advisors. He should be able to trust this assembly of government heavyweights, but he wasn't sure. If they knew enough about him to get clothes from his house, why didn't they know that he and Sandra had lost the stones when Jeff Taylor died?

"No, sir," Wyatt replied. "We gave the stones to Jeff Taylor. He didn't have them when we found him."

"So you were there," FBI Director Clarence Christopher said.

"We were there," Sandra spoke up. "We arrived just before he died."

"Did you get to talk to him?"

"Only for a moment. He said he didn't tell his attackers where he'd hidden the stones. He died before he could tell us."

"I'm sorry, Sandra," Horton said. "Jeff was my friend, too."

"Was that all he said before he died?" Christopher asked. She knew he was qualified for his position, and from his questions she could tell he could be relentless.

"He gave us a number," Wyatt answered.

"What kind of number?"

Wyatt explained all they knew of Jeff's death. Sandra listened, adding nothing to his story. "Since then we've been trying to piece together his last days and determine where he could have hidden them. So far no luck."

"Not exactly," Sandra contradicted. "He had dinner with Lance Desque the night before he died."

No one reacted to the name. Through some strange psychic connection she knew Christopher had made a mental note to talk to Lance.

"What are you going to do to us?" Wyatt wanted to know.

Everett stood up and adjusted his clothes. "Gentlemen," he said, as if giving a cue. Like actors, everyone except Casey left the room. "Sandra, you've been very quiet. What do you think of Project Eagle?"

She stood up, feeling too much at a disadvantage to sit and speak to the President. "Before I give my opinion, I'd like to ask what yours is."

"Fair question." He came to stand in front of her. She wanted to move away but stood her ground. The vast ceiling and images of former heads of state who had been in this room weighed heavily against her. "Project Eagle didn't begin as a communications defense system. Jackson started the programming on a personal basis and the Defense Department found out about it. I can't tell you how, probably something as innocent as lunch conversation."

Sandra thought of the innocuous discussion they'd just had.

"Soon his personal project became a defense project and funds and personnel were allocated to work with him. Colonel Sam Parker, whom you've met, was one of the people."

"How operational is this defense system?" Sandra asked.

"The stones are the only missing link."

She shuddered. They were ready to use it.

"My opinion of Project Eagle is it should never have been started. It should be melted down, all files burned, and no one ever discuss such a massive listening device ever again."

Sandra was relieved to hear that. Her body language must have told him so. He raised his hands, palms out.

"Don't jump to conclusions. That was the opinion of Everett Horton, citizen of the US, not that of Everett Horton, President."

"But, Mr. President, you have the power to stop this now. You are Commander of the Armed Forces. You have the power to—"

"You don't have to teach me civics," he interrupted. "I had the power until recently."

"What happened?" Wyatt joined Sandra, who was facing the President.

"We've discovered certain discrepancies in military inventory."

"There's more than one system, and the other has been stolen, probably piece by piece."

Everett smiled at Sandra. "Bingo," he confirmed. "We discovered the theft about the same time we found out Mr. Jackson had taken matters into his own hands and sent the chips to you, Senator."

"Who killed him?" Wyatt asked.

"I don't know."

"So, what do you want us to do?" Sandra asked.

"I want you to work with us."

"Everett," Sandra said. "My opinion of the defense system mirrors yours. I don't think the world needs a doomsday machine."

"I don't, either. We also didn't need a Cold War or a Bay of Pigs, we didn't need reconnaissance satellites and nuclear submarines, but the fact is we have them and they serve to keep America safe," Horton said, speaking like a military commander.

"Each one of those items defends America from foreign aggression. Not one of them will invade the privacy of individuals, not one of them can eavesdrop on private conversations from the safety of a Pentagon office or sweep sections of the globe and stop every form of electronic transfer of information. The implications of this device reach far beyond the scope of any world leader." She stopped short of saying that included him.

Wyatt put his arm around her waist and pulled her close.

"The fact is, Sandra and Wyatt, we're no longer in a position to dismantle the system. We know the parts that have been stolen have been assembled and are waiting for the final, crucial parts that you had. In order to find out where the stolen parts have been placed so we can retrieve them, we need to activate the Pentagon system."

His speech was met by silence. Everyone seemed to retreat into their own thoughts.

"Wyatt . . . Sandra," Casey, who hadn't spoken since the others left the room, called them back. "You might want to think about this and talk to the President later. Why don't you go out for a while and talk about it. We have to fly back to Washington this afternoon."

"Casey's birthday party is this evening," Everett said, placing his hands on his wife's shoulders. "If you'd like to attend, we can arrange it."

Wyatt looked at Sandra. Neither of them spoke. She needed time to think about what the President had said. She needed to talk to Wyatt. In the past few days she felt as if her mind was being overloaded with information and she needed to let it sink into her brain so she could sort through it, find the right methods of dealing with it.

"You don't have to decide now," the President said. "I'm sure we've given you plenty to think about. Just let Mrs. Kingsley know if you decide to come. She'll take care of everything."

"Thank you, sir."

Sandra and Wyatt shook hands with the President and First Lady. At the door Sandra turned back.

"Mr. President," she said. Everett turned to her. He suddenly looked taller and straighter. "How involved is my father in all this subterfuge?"

Everett didn't hesitate. He pushed his hands into the pockets of his pants and rocked on his heels. "Up to his proverbial eyeballs."

Sandra muttered something and left the room. A military aide escorted them back to the front door where the car waited.

"What do you think?" Everett asked his wife. He'd joined her at the table.

Casey poured herself another cup of coffee. "I think Sandra Rutledge has very passionate beliefs. She's a solid citizen and she has the American public's best interest at heart. She'd make a wonderful president." She patted her husband's hand. "I also think she's lying through her teeth."

CHAPTER 15

Wyatt took Sandra's hand as they watched the presidential helicopter lift off and head for the White House. Wyatt hadn't bargained for this when he'd decided to run for office. Never had he known he'd be called upon to make a decision that could effect the lives of the entire world. He knew his constituency and he was prepared to fight for his small section of the country and to look out for the entire nation, but he never assumed this kind of weight went with the job.

Sandra had been preoccupied since they left the President. He was sure the knowledge that her father was involved in the situation was something she was trying to deal with. He hadn't even asked her how her dinner with him went. Last night seemed years ago in light of the importance of this morning. It should be the only thing on his mind. He wanted it to be the only thing on his mind. He wanted to be allowed to delve into the feelings Sandra created in him, revel in the euphoria he felt at the thought of making love to her. He shouldn't be forced to put aside his remembered rapture to concentrate on the world and what could happen to it if he and Sandra didn't find the stones and turn them over to the Defense Department.

They walked in the gardens surrounding the guest house. Sprawling land faced them in all directions. Wyatt knew somewhere out here was an underground defense station, a safe haven for the President and other government officials in the event of some catastrophe. He was sure they were under surveillance. He wondered if what they said could be heard. For a moment, last night flashed in his memory. Had anyone been listening in as he made love to Sandra? He rejected the idea. Too many foreign dignitaries had slept in that house. What could we have possibly learned if Project Eagle had been functioning then?

On one side, much of the negotiation could be reduced to the real issues and the politics eliminated, but on the other side, the farreaching effect was that countries could be blackmailed because their secrets could be discovered or their devices made inoperable. It was a dangerous system. No one country needed that much power.

"Do you want to go to the party?" Sandra asked, calling him back from the brink of world destruction.

He stopped walking and linked his arms around her back. "If you'd like to go, I'll be your date."

Sandra laughed. He hadn't seen her laugh in days. A permanent sadness had settled over her. Sadness was probably on his face, too, but he didn't have to look at himself. He noticed it on her and he much preferred a smile.

"I've never been to a White House party."

He'd rather take her back to bed and not get up for days, but if she wanted to attend Casadia Horton's fiftieth birthday party he'd certainly take her. He dropped his head to kiss her. God, she was the most wonderful woman in the world. He only intended a simple kiss, but when had anything ever been simple where she was concerned? She was complex and beautiful and his mouth hungered over hers. Her lips parted and his tongue swept inside like a cyclone finding an open door.

Her arms climbed over his shoulders and she went up on her toes, pressing herself against him in a way that, despite their coats, was most arousing. If anyone was watching them they were certainly putting on a good show. Wyatt didn't care. He only knew that he was happy.

When he slid his mouth from hers she clung to him. Her cheek against his was warm and soft. He wanted her out of her coat and out of the skirt and sweater she wore beneath it. He wanted nothing between them, as there had been yesterday and all of last night. It was time they went back.

"I know this isn't the right time," Sandra said against his ear. "Times couldn't be worse. I don't know if we'll ever get out of this, but I've never been happier."

She'd voiced what Wyatt felt. He pulled back to look at her. Her face glowed. She smiled.

"I love you, Wyatt."

"I love you, too. I'll always love you."

He turned her toward the guest house. With arms twined around each other, they walked back as carefree as lovers on a holiday.

"We haven't talked much about the President's proposal. I guess we'll have to say something to him before the night is over."

Sandra stopped him at the back entrance. She didn't say anything. Wyatt wondered where her mind had taken her. Since she'd arrived she hadn't said a word about her father or what he'd told her. The fact that she'd returned told him nothing. He knew she was confused about the two of them. They both loved her and they both had different stories about the stones. She had to sort through the maze of information alone and decide who was telling the truth and who was lying.

Wyatt wanted to help, but he couldn't. This was a decision she'd have to make on her own. He did want to know what Senator Rutledge had said.

"Sandra, what happened at dinner?" he asked.

She told him everything, leaving out nothing. She told him about her father's accusation that he, Wyatt, was the person trying to sell the stones. She told him about the motel and hiding the car, about her bus trip to the District and calling Grant Richards. The only thing she didn't tell him was that she knew where the stones were.

When she finished her story, Wyatt led her inside and asked Mrs. Kingsley to get them some hot tea. They went to the library and Wyatt added wood to the already blazing fire. Sandra sat on the end of the cushioned sofa near the warmth. When Mrs. Kingsley had come and gone and she had her hands wrapped around a cup of strong black tea, she completed her story.

"Wyatt, I know where the stones are hidden." He sat across from her on one of the winged chairs. He stared at her. "At least . . . I think I know."

"Where are they?"

"When Jeff died he didn't say 95147. He said Ro 95-147."

Wyatt looked confused. "What difference does that make."

"It's two numbers not one. He was saying *route.* Route 95, mile-marker 147. I saw it last night on the bus coming back from Quantico. There's rock bed there.

"Jeff had dinner with Lance near Quantico. It rained, and if he knew people were following him, he'd want to get rid of the stones. I drove to Quantico in the snow last night and there isn't much in that area. I don't know that he had the stones with him. They could be in his house."

"I checked there." Wyatt explained his nocturnal escapade up to being caught and flown here.

"That must mean they're at his office or he had to have them with him when he met Lance. If he needed a place to hide them where no one was likely to look, that rock bed would be the perfect place."

"We've got to go there."

Sandra shivered. "Wyatt, what do we do when we find them? Do we give them back to the government?"

"We'll decide that if we find them."

* * *

The party was in full swing when the helicopter let them off on the grounds of the White House. Sandra hadn't thought of arriving like this. She might have been invited to a party with her father, but she assumed she'd get out of a car at the famous portico door, not out of a helicopter.

Their intention when leaving Camp David was to pretend to go to the party so they could get a ride back into the city. Both Sandra and Wyatt had assumed they would return by car, but the helicopter had come back for them and landed on the White House lawn. They had to go in.

Wyatt looked magnificent in his tuxedo, and the red and silver sequined gown she'd found hanging in the closet fit as if it had been made for her. The only thing out of place was the backpack.

She expected they'd be the talk of the party and knew that if Casey Horton wanted her fiftieth birthday to be a memorable occasion she was certain to get her wish. The ballroom was decorated with balloons and streamers and a large sign wishing the First Lady a happy birthday.

"Ready for the lion's den?" Wyatt whispered in her ear as they stood at the entrance to the reception room.

"I guess we have to go forward," she whispered back.

Unlike most receptions, the President and Mrs. Horton did not stand at the entrance, but were in the middle of the room. She and Wyatt were going to have to run the gauntlet to get to them. He took her hand and they started across the room. Like the parting of the Red Sea, the crowd backed away. An audible hush settled over the room. Nothing could be heard except the band playing a soft show tune in the background.

"Welcome," Casey said when they reached her. "You've gone through the worst. From this point on it'll be a breeze."

"I hope so," Wyatt whispered in a voice only the four of them could hear.

"I'll start it off. Sandra, would you dance with me?" Everett asked.

Sandra looked at Casey. It was her birthday and this was the first dance.

"Don't worry, Sandra," Casey assured her. "We're a very untraditional First Family."

Everett led her to the middle of the dance floor and took her in his arms. Sandra noticed Wyatt and Casey dancing, making them the only two couples on the floor. Everett waved his hand and eventually couples joined them.

" 'Fugitive Kicks up her Heels at First Lady's Birthday Bash,' " Sandra said.

Everett laughed.

"Don't laugh," Sandra chastised, "That will be the headline in the morning's *Post.*"

"Don't worry about the reporters. They're just jealous I got to you before you could tell them the story."

"Are there any here?"

"Oh, yes, there are reporters permanently assigned to the White House."

"I'll bet by now they're burning up the telephone lines."

"That's all they'll burn. I've given orders to keep them away from you and Wyatt if you showed up. I suppose they're fighting mad."

His eyes danced with a mischievous twinkle.

" 'President Protects Fugitives; Keeps Reporters Off-limits.' " She gave another headline. "They'll accuse you of aiding us."

"What do you think they'll do if I sign an executive pardon?"

The dance ended and he was called away to other guests. Wyatt appeared at her side. The music started up and Wyatt turned her into his arms just as a crowd converged on them. Several people called them by name, but Wyatt danced her away holding her tighter and more intimately than the President had.

"How are you doing?"

"We should have skipped the party," she returned.

"We would have if Everett had sent a car for us and not the helicopter that landed on the East Lawn. We're the center of attention."

"I guess slipping away unnoticed is out of the question."

"Completely," Wyatt agreed. "At least for the time being. Maybe later we can go for a walk . . . through the East Gate."

"Do you know somebody at the East Gate?"

"Not yet." Wyatt checked his watch. "I will in about an hour."

Sandra laughed for the crowd watching them. "What happens in an hour? It won't be midnight."

"Sam Parker is picking us up."

They were late in meeting Sam by nearly an hour. The colonel, dressed in civilian clothes and short-tempered from having to sit for so long out in the open, spun the car around on Fourteenth Street and headed for the bridge to Virginia.

Getting away from the crowd all wanting to know if Wyatt and Sandra were guilty of the accusations printed in the papers hadn't been easy. They evaded most of the questions and spoke briefly to Everett and Casey before leaving. Wyatt told him they were still considering his offer and would let him know in the morning. They escaped before he could stop them.

On the north side of the Interstate 95 just short of mile marker 147 was a bed of gray and white rocks slightly larger than Sandra's hand. Sam left them on the road adjacent to the highway, only a few hundred yards from the rock bed, still angry and still hot-tempered. "Maybe we should have stayed at the party," Sandra said as she used Wyatt as a post to remove one shoe and clear it of dirt and small stones. Thankfully, the snow of the night before had melted in the day's heat, but the ground was mushy and wet. She was ruining another pair of shoes.

When she replaced her shoe, Wyatt slid a few feet with her directly behind him. They reached the bank of rock. From the highway the stones had looked like a small plot. Up close they covered a good eight-foot square. Cars whizzed past them creating a wind that blew her hair back and made her eyes water.

"See anything?" Wyatt asked.

"We'll probably have to turn over these stones." Sandra kneeled and started to move the first one. Wyatt grabbed her hand.

"Wait," he said. "Let's see if we can find anything that looks as if it's been moved."

Sandra scanned the area. Every rock looked the same, as if they had gone undisturbed since the highway was landscaped. She hoped her logic was good and that Jeff had decided to stash the chips before someone caught him.

"See anything?" she asked.

"They all look the same to me," Wyatt agreed.

"Let's start turning them over."

"I'll start at the top."

"Thanks," she said. The ground at the bottom was flatter and she'd have more stability. Sandra methodically began turning each rock over and looking under it. She broke three nails by the time she reached the seventh row. Cars constantly flowed up the highway at speeds exceeding the maximum limit. If anyone saw them in the beam of a headlight they continued on their journey without stopping to investigate. Sandra hoped they would find the stones soon. Some do-gooder would eventually pass and let the police know of their presence by way of cellular phone and they'd have a slew of new charges tallied up against them.

Sandra continued. She finished another row and found nothing. Cold, tired, and sweating, she pulled her coat closer, turning the collar up, and sat down on the freezing bed of stones. Wyatt came and sat next to her. The uneven surface felt strange to her backside. Shifting, she tried to find a more comfortable position.

"We're nearly done," he said.

"I don't think there's anything here," she admitted. "I'm sorry I dragged you here for nothing."

He put his arm around her and she leaned against him. "It was a long shot, but we didn't have any other lead. This is the first sensible thing that's come along since Jeff died."

"Yeah, but it was a useless effort."

"I suppose Sam is getting tired of waiting, too. We promised to call him as soon as we knew something."

Sam had driven them the hundred-plus miles and dropped them off in the clearing where Sandra had hidden the rented Jaguar. The car was still concealed and the two of them took it to their present site. At least they had a ride back to Washington after this useless trip.

Wyatt picked up one of the gray stones behind him, turned it over and replaced it. Then he took another and another to the same task. Sandra shivered. He pulled her closer.

"Ouch!" she said.

"Did I hurt you?"

"No, the rocks under me are unsteady. I'm slipping."

"Let's get the last three rows done and we can go."

Wyatt got up and reached for her hand. Sandra took it and he helped her to her feet. As she tried to take her first step, her heel caught between two rocks and she pitched forward. Wyatt's strong arms grabbed for her, but she overbalanced, crashing into him and tumbling them both backward into the wet ground.

They came up a mass of arms and legs tangled inside her dress.

"Wyatt, are you hurt?"

"No, I'm wet."

"My foot caught."

Wyatt lay back with her on top of him. He pulled her close, and despite the uncomfortable position, she wanted to stay where she was. Images of them making love came to her. Wyatt stared at her and she saw desire in his eyes. They ignited a fire inside her that burned to her toes. Warmth flooded through her system. They had better get out of here, she thought or the travelers on Route 95 would really get a show.

Sliding to her side, she dislodged the rock that had tripped her.

Nothing was under it. Quickly they finished looking through the rest of the grouping and found nothing.

"I guess that's that." Sandra felt defeated.

"It's got to mean something," Wyatt told her. "We just haven't found out what it is yet."

They started up the incline on their way back to the car. At the top Sandra stopped next to a tree to free her shoes of the debris they'd collected during the walk. Wyatt waited for her. Sandra noticed his gaze swing from the tree where she stood to others in the area. When he'd swept the flashlight back and forth several times, she said, "What?"

"Look at this tree." He shone the light at the base of the tree. Sandra followed his direction. Nothing seemed unusual. Then he swung it to another tree. Again she saw nothing out of the ordinary. When he flashed it the third time she noticed the base of the tree was ringed with rocks.

"Rocks," she said.

"The same rocks as we've just seen."

Wyatt went to them and began turning them as they'd done to the bed next to the highway.

"Wyatt?" Sandra called.

He didn't look at her, but continued his task.

"Wyatt!" she called again.

He glanced up at her quickly. Her hand reached for him but her gaze was trained on the junction of the two major branches above her head.

Wyatt rose. Sandra pointed upward. "What's that?"

He switched the light to the point in question. Above their heads was a small plastic sandwich bag. A thumbtack held it to the tree so it wouldn't fall down. The "Y" effect of the tree protected it from both the elements and the wind.

Wyatt reached up. The juncture was higher than he could reach. He turned to Sandra. "How would you like to go for a ride?"

She looked at him, then looked up. She nodded. Wyatt squatted down and grasped her below her knees. As he stood she was lifted the several needed feet to reach the plastic bag. She yanked it free.

"I have it!"

Wyatt lowered her to the ground. She opened the seal the minute she was steady. Inside was a plastic disk holder. She opened that to find a small piece of paper.

Wyatt shone the light on it. Three words were written across it in Jeff's handwriting. "Truth . . . Logical . . . Method." Wyatt read them. "Another meaningless clue," he complained. "I'm tired of being on this scavenger hunt."

Sandra stared at the words. "They mean something to me."

"What?"

"Let's get back to the car. I'm freezing." She shivered confirming her words.

The heat didn't take long to make the interior of the small car warm. Sandra could feel herself thawing after the thirty minutes of freezing wind she'd endured. Wyatt drove, passing the motel where she'd spent part of a night and entered the highway a mile south of the rock bed they'd turned over.

"When I was a freshman at Howard University I stayed in Truth Hall," she began. "It was named for Sojourner Truth or a traveler seeking freedom and truth. My mentor, or resident assistant, was a woman called Marjorie Lanley," she explained. "Marjorie became my roommate during my sophomore year when I pledged the sorority for which she was already a sister."

"That must have been grueling," Wyatt observed.

Sandra remembered those six weeks. They were some of the worst of her life, but afterward she and Marjorie became the best of friends.

"While I pledged, Marjorie gave me that as my Line Name." She pointed to the paper. "I had to answer as Ms. Logical Method more times than I care to remember."

"I suppose you were famous for coming up with a logical method of getting the work they required of your line done."

She cut her eyes to him and Wyatt smothered the laugh she knew was kept off his face by the strongest of controls.

"What could Jeff have meant by returning you to a nostalgic past?"

"I don't know." She picked up the car phone. "I'll start by calling the dormitory." She dialed the number.

"You remember the telephone number? It must be . . ." He mentally calculated the number of years since she was a freshman at Howard.

"Ten years," she supplied. "What's your ID number?" She shot the question to him.

"326165," he answered without thinking.

"How long has it been?" The question was rhetorical. "You remember that. I remember a lot of numbers."

The office phone rang in her ears. On the fifth ring a recorded message began. She hung up. "A machine," she explained.

"What is Marjorie doing these days?"

"She's the Dean of Students at Howard."

"I suggest we pay a visit to Marjorie Lanley."

CHAPTER 16

"You couldn't have missed them by more than five minutes," Michael Waring reported to Senator Rutledge. Brad looked about the room hoping to find his daughter. She'd left so abruptly after their dinner that he hadn't been able to explain things to her fully and now it was time he did so. She must have been scared to death with everyone chasing her. He'd made one mistake and compounded it several times over.

He knew President Horton had taken matters into his own hands, but discovering he'd invited Sandra and Senator Randolph to Casey's birthday party was a complete surprise.

"Good evening, Senator."

He turned to find himself facing Everett Horton. Casey held his arm and both of them smiled as if they were being photographed.

"We're glad you could join us."

"Happy birthday, Casey," he said, and leaned forward to kiss her cheek. "I hear my daughter and the senator were in attendance tonight."

"Yes," Casey said. "They made quite a stir. I don't believe we've had as much fun in the White House since Andrew Jackson was inaugurated."

Brad wasn't impressed by that. He didn't care that Sandra was becoming a national hero in all the news services, that people across the country were behind her flight with Randolph, even that Casey Horton had admiration in her voice when she spoke of her. Sandra was in trouble and he wanted to help her. He wanted to get her away from Senator Randolph because he was a target and he didn't want to lose his child in the crossfire.

"Do you know where they went?"

"They didn't tell us," the President said. "I spoke to them this morning at Camp David."

Brad held his features still. They'd been to Camp David. Few people were ever invited to go there with Everett Horton, who considered his vacations purely private. Brad wondered what he'd asked them and what they'd told him.

"I asked them to work with us."

He stared at President Everett. The man's face could rarely be read and Brad found himself at a decided disadvantage. Most people he could see through, but Everett and Casey Horton must be made of lead, for if they didn't want you to see something it simply wasn't there.

"I expect to hear from them tomorrow." Horton was speaking when Brad came back to the present.

"Could we go somewhere and talk, sir?" He glanced at Casey.

Brad knew it was poor form to take the President away from a reception. But he was sure Casey would understand, and this wasn't an international function.

He was right about Casey. "Go on, Everett," she urged her husband. "I'm sure I can handle this crowd." Casey smiled and Horton kissed her on the cheek, then led Brad toward another room.

Passing Lance Desque, who came through the entrance as they crossed it, Horton invited him to join them. Lance turned to his date, a buxom blonde who had to be ten years younger than Sandra. Lance loved attending White House functions and he never came alone. A beautiful woman was his trademark and the younger the better.

Lance was ambitious. Everyone on The Hill knew it. He liked his women smart and young, but he also knew the right one to choose when career moves were at stake. Project Eagle was definitely a career move for him. Brad had to admit, it would also benefit him.

Next to the main ballroom was a smaller room where important conferences could be held if need arose. Rarely under the Horton administration had this been done, but the White House staff was required to keep it ready. A fire burned in the fireplace and refreshments were laid out on a small table. President Horton took a seat at the circular table that held four chairs. Brad and Lance sat in two of the others.

"Have you located the missing parts?"

"No, sir." Lance answered before the senator had time to respond.

"Lance," Horton said as he put his elbows on the table and made a steeple of his fingers. "If we don't have the stones, what do you think will be the worst that could happen?"

"Off the record, sir."

Horton shook his head. "If it happens, it certainly won't be off the record."

"Sir, we have a major piece of government property which has been stolen and it's our duty to recover it."

Horton waved his hand, stopping him. "What is the worst, Lance?"

Lance looked at his hands, then up at the President. "The worst, sir, is the story will break in the papers. Foreign governments will be outraged that the United States could develop such a weapon. The world press would make us the worst of the bad guys. Our reputation in other nations will fall into a hole so low climbing out might be impossible. Behind the scenes every government in the world will be searching for the parts.

"Blame will have to be placed. Sir, you're at the top of the star and it will begin with you. The press will dredge up every lousy piece of news that's ever been recorded and use it against you. You'll be branded a dictator, called the man who wanted it all, or, worse, accused of trying to make the United States your kingdom. Every program you've had anything to do with will be deemed unnecessary. The polls won't have enough negative signs to put in front of the number to record how low your popularity level will fall. From there the blame will trickle down. The fingers will be deep and far-reaching. Of course, Senator Randolph and Ms. Rutledge will be as notorious as Bonnie and Clyde, and everyone associated with them will fall."

When Lance finished, only the crackle of the fire could be heard in the room.

"There's no silver lining in that scenario," Horton said.

"The situation doesn't have a silver lining, sir."

Everett Horton prided himself on being a good judge of character and he had a bad feeling about Lance Desque. He was sure the picture he'd just painted would no doubt happen if the stones were not recovered. The other thing he was sure of was Lance Desque. The man wanted his job. He wanted it so bad that he'd be willing to throw him to the wolves if he could save his own skin. And Everett had no illusion that Lance Desque would come out of this with his skin as clear and tanned as if he'd been on a Florida beach.

Brad, his daughter, Senator Randolph, Casey, and himself would be tried by the American press and found guilty of being war-mongers.

"Brad, do you agree with that?" Horton asked.

"Not entirely, sir. We will be hurt, but if we don't leak the story to anyone, then it could die a natural death."

Everett thought little of that happening. No matter what they tried to hide—and past administrations had done just that—the press always found out. Everett had no doubt it would happen. He couldn't go under the illusion that nothing would find its way to the corps of press people who occupied space in the White House.

"We might be able to weather this, sir," Brad Rutledge said. "If we drop the investigation now we may be lucky if nothing happens until the next election is over."

"You're dreaming, Brad," Horton said. He couldn't believe the senator would even consider such a thing. "The next presidential election is a year away. Your own term comes up for reelection at the same time. If we did give up the search, a year is enough time for whoever has stolen Project Eagle to find or develop their computer module. In a year we could be sitting here without communications. We have got to find those stones. Our existence is in question."

"Everett." Casey stood in the doorway. "Are you almost done? We have guests."

"I'll be right there," he told her. She smiled and closed the door.

"I'd like to have a meeting with you two in my office tomorrow at two. I'm sure I'll have Senator Randolph and your daughter's answer by that time."

Everett stood up.

"Sir," Lance said. "I'm confused. What answer from Senator Randolph?"

"Yes, Mr. Desque. You weren't here earlier. Senator Randolph and Ms. Rutledge are my guests. They attended the party briefly. I've asked them to bring the stones directly to me when they find them."

"Sir, is that wise?"

"I thought it was." He turned to face the undersecretary of defense. "Obviously, you have another opinion."

"Sir, we know an entire system has been stolen. We can only assume it's been assembled at some location. The last link is the arrangement of chips. Should it be known that they are to be delivered to you, you'll be setting yourself up as a target. Forgive my saying it, but I don't think the country needs a state funeral at this time."

"Why, thank you, Lance," he smiled. "I didn't think you cared."

"My, my, my. Look who's coming to dinner. And I see you've dressed." Marjorie Lanley completely blocked the doorway of her 16th Street home in the Flower Section of Northwest Washington.

It had been eleven-thirty when Sandra reached her, but it was nearly one o'clock before she and Wyatt parked the car in front of her house. They'd driven around several times, checking for anyone who might be watching. The other houses on the street were dark and sleepy looking. Marjorie's house sat in the middle of the block. It had been years since they'd seen each other and except for a Christmas card each year they rarely talked. She didn't think anyone could link her with Marjorie.

Marjorie was two inches taller than Sandra. When they'd last seen each other she couldn't have weighed more than a hundred and twenty pounds.

"Marjorie!" Sandra sounded surprised. She stepped toward the obviously pregnant woman and pressed her hands on her stomach. "When did this happen?"

Marjorie looked past her friend to Wyatt standing on her doorstep. "Come in, Senator. Sandra seems to have lost everything over the prospect of a baby."

"Marjorie," Sandra stopped her. "Are we welcome? You know we're wanted by the police."

"How can anybody in DC not know?" she asked, her eyebrows raised. "You make the news every day. Of course you're welcome. If you weren't I'd have told you over the phone. Now, get in here!" She grabbed Sandra's hand and pulled her forward.

Sandra was relieved. She'd been afraid that her old friend would not want to link her name with Sandra's, since knowing her could mean being investigated and questioned by the DOD.

Marjorie led them to a lovely room done in soft colors of rose and beige. "I must say, Sandra, I am a little surprised at your actions." A man watching television stood up as they came in. "This is my husband, Earl Morrison," Marjorie introduced. "Earl, my college roommate and the missing senator."

"Don't mind her," Earl said, switching off the television and shaking hands with them. He was a big man, looked like he'd played football for a pro team sometime in the past. "The pregnancy has affected her sense of humor."

They all laughed. "Sit down," Marjorie said.

Sandra took a seat on the sofa. Wyatt sat next to her. Marjorie sat on a straight-back chair that didn't go with any of the furniture. Sandra knew it was the chair that had been brought in for her back.

"Let me get you something to drink," Earl offered.

When he'd left the room, Sandra said, "I didn't know you were married."

"That's what happens when you bury yourself up in New Jersey. Not even news gets in up there."

"That's not true," Sandra said, a wide smile on her face.

"Earl and I met two years ago at a NABE, National Association of Black Educators' Convention. I'm at Howard and he's at American University. We fell in love, got married, and in another month we'll be a trio."

"Marjorie, that's wonderful."

"Congratulations," Wyatt echoed.

Earl returned and passed out glasses of wine. Marjorie's contained sparkling cider.

"I've been expecting you, Sandra."

She and Wyatt exchanged a glance. "Why?"

"Because of the package."

"What package?" Wyatt asked.

"It came a few days ago. It's all dressed up like a little treasure chest. A note arrived with it saying to hold it and that you would be by to pick it up."

"May I have it?" Sandra asked.

"Sure." Marjorie pulled up her bulky body and left the room. She came back with a small jewel-encrusted case.

"It's Jeff's," she whispered to Wyatt.

"I've been dying to find out what's inside," Marjorie said. "In another day or two I don't know if I could have held out any longer."

Sandra looked to Wyatt for guidance. Should she open the box? She didn't want to have to explain if she found fifteen ten-carat stones inside.

Sandra tried the lid. "It's locked," she said, trying desperately to keep the relief out of her voice.

"I'll bet I have a key," Marjorie smiled. "It's not that expensive a case. I've seen several like it in the stores. I'll bet my luggage keys will fit it." She was on her feet and rushing from the room before Sandra could stop her. She returned faster than any woman in her final trimester should be allowed to travel.

"Try this."

Sandra took the thin key with a square head and inserted it in the lock. "It doesn't fit."

When Marjorie opened her hand, three other kinds of small keys lay there. Sandra tried them. The second one turned and she heard a slight click. The chest was open. She pulled the key out and laid it on her lap. Slowly, she lifted the top. Silently she thanked God the chest didn't open to a 180-degree angle. Only Wyatt, sitting next to her, could see to the bottom of it. The stones lay there, white against a black velvet background. She felt him take in a breath, but could discern no physical movement.

Sandra reached inside. At the back of the chest was a computer disk. She wondered what was on it. Had Jeff left them a message? She pulled it free, being careful not to disturb the stones.

"Who's it from?" Earl asked. "It arrived by messenger, but no one could tell us who sent it."

"It has something to do with the reason you two are running." Marjorie stated the truth.

"Yes, it does," Wyatt told her. "The less you know the better for you. You're a family. We won't make our problems yours."

"Sandra, is there anything I can do?" Marjorie asked.

She shook her head.

"The least we can do is let you look at what's on the disk," Earl offered. He stood as if ready to lead them to an office.

Closing the chest, they stood and followed him. He turned on the machinery and left them in private.

"What's on it?" Marjorie asked the moment they returned to the room.

"It's encrypted," Sandra told her, glad she could speak the truth. "All we could see were hearts, flowers, and other ASCII symbols filling the screen."

"I know a person who might be able to break an encryption code." Earl reached for his wife. "Brooke Richards works for the university. She's phenomenal with those kinds of things, but she, too, is away on maternity leave."

Lance slammed the door. He'd taken his date home and left her there alone, much to her surprise. His, too. Everett had ruined his evening with news that he had been in direct contact with Randolph and Rutledge's daughter. This was clearly his, not Horton's, investigation and he did not take kindly to anyone interfering, and that included the President of the United States.

Pulling at the tie of his immaculate suit, he took the stairs two at a time. He went into his bedroom. He would find the stones. *He* and not Everett Horton. Horton was a poor President, despite the popularity of the polls. What did polls know? They were as fickle as the wind. One day they were for you and the next they'd crucify you.

Well, they would crucify Horton. Casey, too. He was sorry about that, but it couldn't be helped. Horton had lost it. The battle lines had been drawn and fought and there was no way he could win. Even if he managed to keep it quiet, keep the news out of the papers, there were too many people who knew about it. Too many people who'd been involved in the theft, the coverup, and the search. Senator Randolph and Senator Rutledge's daughter couldn't have played better roles if they'd had a script.

Lance put his tie on the rack in the closet and proceeded to undress. He stripped to his shorts and walked to the adjoining room which he'd converted to a gym.

Standing in the middle of the mirrored hall, he surveyed the iron-and-steel equipment. Taking a deep breath, he began his routine of stretching before picking one of the many machines to work his biceps into hard-as-steel muscles.

Twenty minutes later, he felt better, in fact, he felt great. If Everett continued on his present course, Lance would get his office years before he planned.

Wyatt woke to the wind. He was still alive. The smell of coffee wafted through the air; flavored coffee, irish cream, he guessed. He'd slept badly. Despite Sandra next to him and the comfortable guest bed that Marjorie insisted they use, thoughts of what to do now that they actually had possession of the stones commanded his conscious attention.

He'd heard Earl leave about seven-thirty. The house had been quiet since then, but now Marjorie was moving around downstairs. He could hear her muted sounds as she went about her morning routine. He leaned over, looking at Sandra sleeping.

His breath caught at how beautiful she was in the morning sunlight. He smoothed back her hair and studied her features. Her dark-brown skin contrasted with the bedding. The sun streaming through the windows highlighted her rich brandy skin. Her hair, loose from the clamp, was thick and lustrous. He threaded his fingers through it.

Wyatt continued playing in her hair as he glanced through the window. The bare branches of trees waved in the morning wind. It was strong, bantering against the windows and trying helplessly to get inside. Sandra was warm under the blankets.

He hated to wake her, but it was time for them to go. He knew how she felt about the stones. He agreed with her for the most part. Chip should never have developed such a dangerous system, but the fact remained it existed. And since it existed and was in more hands than a few, he had to decide what to tell the President and what to do with the actual stones.

He picked up the chest and opened the box. The computer disk sat securely in place. He stared at it, willing it to give up its encrypted secret. White diamonds, he thought, fingering the stones. They were beautiful. He could see them set into a necklace gracing Sandra's beautiful neck. Too bad they weren't what they appeared to be.

What would he do if he were in Everett Horton's shoes? The entire country looked to him for direction. The world regarded him as a wise leader. Project Eagle represented power, true and absolute. According to his high school history teachers, absolute power had destroyed many lives and many leaders. Eventually the masses would rise up and overthrow the dictator making their lives miserable.

With a weapon like Project Eagle, would there be a method of overthrowing the user? How much secrecy would surround such a device? How long would it be before world leaders fought each other for possession of the device? It was too dangerous.

Wyatt picked up one of the stones and held it up to the light. It was brilliant, near perfect to the naked eye. He searched it, trying to find a compromise to the two arguments that would change the course of world power. Wasn't that what the President did? He represented the interest of *all* the people, not just one group. Where was the compromise here? Who stood to gain and who stood to lose?

Wyatt never had a problem so urgent and so necessary than the one he studied embedded inside a white diamond.

The President had said they needed to activate the system in order to find out where the other one had been assembled. If they didn't a[illegible]ely find it, whoever had stolen it would have all the time in the worl[illegible]evelop the one final piece. With the number of computer hackers, experts, and advancements in technology out there, a working system could probably be operational before the end of the year. The danger with that option was that the owners of the new system would be some other government. Whatever their agenda might be, it would certainly be intensified with a weapon as powerful as Project Eagle.

He dropped the stone into the chest and closed it. Letting his head roll back, he stared at the sky. The sunlight warmed his face and felt good on his skin. Activating the system was just as dangerous. It was natural to test it, make sure it would do what it had been designed to do. Once that was seen and used, the probability of it being moth-balled was about as remote as bottling sunshine.

There had to be another solution. Maybe when they got the disk read, something would come to him. It had to. He was a novice congressman, not the President or some elder statesman with years of experience. He wasn't Thomas Jefferson who could visualize the future and know what needed to be done. Chip had handed him an awesome legacy. He'd put the world's most basic right in his hands: the right to free speech. It was up to him to protect that right and make sure it endured today and into the future. Could he do it?

Sandra had been staring at Wyatt for some time. She could tell he was grappling with a problem. She knew what it was and knew its gravity. It had disturbed her sleep since Sam Parker had explained Project Eagle's capabilities.

When he'd first come to her, his body torn, his face bruised, she'd been afraid that she'd do something to make his injuries worse. Now, without the discoloring bruises and with barely a noticeable twinge in his side, she trembled for another reason. Just looking at him made her weak. Her thoughts turned to John. They were alike and different. They were both leaders, decisive and caring about the needs of other people. They were both strong men, but where John had an openly compassionate face, Wyatt often hid his behind a facade. Only when he'd made love to her did she feel he was completely open; everything he thought and felt was clearly revealed in his face and body then.

She reached over and rubbed her fingers against his beard-roughened skin.

"Did I wake you?" he asked, taking her hand.

"No," she said, finding her voice husky and thick. She pulled herself up on one elbow and looked down at him. Her hair fell like ragged pencil points. Wyatt stared at her. His eyes moved all over her face, then his fingers threaded through her hair and he pulled her to him. Their mouths touched, tasted, molded. She ran her hand along his chest. Pearly buttons trapped her seeking fingers and she released them one by one. Her hands went inside the fabric to find hot skin waiting. He was smooth. Her fingers roved unhampered until she came to the definable muscles of his chest. Her thumb padded over his flat nipple and she could feel the tremor run through him like liquid lightning. Its speed caught her, too, as her blood began a song as old as time. His mouth took hers deeply, his tongue inside tasting, draining her of its sweet nectar. She freely gave and took what he offered.

Her heartbeat accelerated as the lightning erupted around her. Wyatt levered himself up and pushed her back onto the mattress. His hands moved over her, finding and bringing to life every erotic spot on her body. She moaned her pleasures at each new point of contact. He pushed the short but voluminous nightgown Marjorie had provided over her head and exposed her maple-warm sweetness to the morning light and his desirous eyes. He drank her in before his head bent and took one hardened chocolate-covered strawberry into his mouth.

Sandra arched toward him as rapture streaked inside her. Her body turned to syrup and melted under Wyatt's exquisite torture. She knew then, knew as his hands massaged her flesh and brought every inch of her to life, that she hadn't been alive before she'd met him. The moment he'd opened his eyes and she looked into their depths, she'd known they would end here, locked together in each other's arms, showing each other what life meant, the reason man and woman walked the earth.

"Wyatt!" she cried his name as his wet tongue licked her stomach and fire burned her. He was undoing her, taking her apart piece by piece, and she was helpless to stop him. She didn't want to stop him. She wanted everything he was doing to her. She gasped for breath as he kissed her thighs and the apex of her legs. Her heart beat wildly at the spot where he pressed his mouth. Sandra knew he could feel it. She could hear the rush of blood singing through her system.

Reaching for him, Wyatt took her hands and worked his way back in an arousingly slow journey that ended at her mouth. His hands still touched her everywhere. He drew small circles over her belly. They widened into ripples until they reached the point of her body that throbbed for him. His fingers entered her. She gasped at the pleasure his touch gave her. The pad of his thumb sought and found the spot on her that drove her insane. She cried his name over and over as he moved with a designed rhythm that took her to the brink of madness.

Only then did he remove his hand and enter her. With patience and superhuman control, he walked his way into her, creeping along inch by glorious inch. Her mouth opened and a low moan escaped. An ecstasy that she'd never known racked her body, shredding her control into ribbons of pleasure.

Her legs wrapped around him. Wyatt groaned. She was going to kill him, he thought. His arms went around her. Telling himself to take his time, he savored every hot inch of her. Finally, cupping her cheeks in his hands, he ground her hips into his. Her fingernails jabbed into his flesh as her tight body caught and held him. The slight pain pushed him forward as the rhythm of centuries joined them. Her hands roamed over his back in a frenzy that drove him deeper and deeper into her. He couldn't stop now if he wanted to. He wanted her as he'd never wanted another woman. He wanted to make her his so completely that she'd remember their lovemaking for the rest of her life. He wanted her to know this was more than sex; he wanted her to know he was committed to her and only her.

His heart pounded, threatened to burst in his chest. He filled her over and over again. Each time he knew would be his last. He was going to die inside her. Her body spoke to him, telling him of a need he'd never known was there. Deep and wanting. She could fulfill it. Only she had the secret formula that could make him whole, give him life. He had to have it. He was weak and powerful at the same time, driving himself at her demand. And she demanded!

"Wyatt!" she cried. "Wyatt." Her head beat the pillow as it flopped from side to side. Wyatt's control snapped with her words. His body took hers, hard and fast. She took every powerful thrust, returning each one with a power greater than the sum or her parts.

Suddenly, he was no longer part of the room. They'd transformed into light and energy. He and Sandra had found that place all lovers sought. That place where souls burned together. Like two planets, cracked away from the sun and flung into space, they whirled fiery and spinning. Coming together, combining, burning, the heat of their pulsating bodies intensifying, they incinerated, transformed into pure energy.

He felt the grip that told him he was nearing the point where the madness would take over, where life began, where the most deliriously rapturous sensation man could know would occur. It was harder, tighter, more intense than he could ever remember. Wyatt expected to explode, waited for it, welcomed the release, anticipated the wonderful sensations Sandra would make him feel. Yet, he didn't burst. Together they seemed to implode, pulling everything with them. There was a calmness, quiet, as if time and sensation had stopped for a space of a millisecond. Then it came. The big bang. Like creation, the world, his world, he and Sandra were part of the nuclear blast that came together in the void and forged a shining new world.

CHAPTER 17

Sandra drove the Porsche fast. Porsches were designed for speed and today she felt like giving the small automobile its full head. She sped up and down the rolling Maryland hillside en route to Grant and Brooke Richards' house. Wyatt said nothing. He didn't ask her to slow down or point out that they could ill afford to be stopped by a local policeman trying to make quota for the month.

She was alive and happy, and after making love with Wyatt this morning, she refused to let anything dim her view of the world. The drive from Marjorie's took over an hour, but the sky was clear and the roads deserted. It was her kind of day. She could drive forever on a day like this one.

She found the turnoff as Brooke had described it and turned onto a winding road. For several miles it twisted and turned passing restored farmhouses and huge tracks of undeveloped land. Behind walls of wrought-iron or stone Sandra continued until she reached the farthest point, where the road gave way to the natural beauty of the land. The house was situated at the end. A modest country French farmhouse that had been restored.

Sandra parked and got out. The wind was crisp and cold. She held her hair to keep it from smacking her in the face. There was a natural barrier of evergreen trees along one side of the house. The other side was free to the wind and Sandra saw a landing strip in the flat plane below her.

"Hi." Brooke Richards came out onto the porch, holding her engorged belly. The wind blew her hair in all directions. "You'd better get out of this wind."

Quickly, they raced across the yard and joined her. Inside, it was warm and cozy. She had cups of hot coffee waiting in the sunken living room which had hardwood floors that gleamed brightly in the sunlight streaming through the many windows. Area rugs cut the space into definable groupings and gave the expanse an intimate atmosphere.

"I was surprised you called, Sandra," she said. "From what Grant told me I was sure you'd have everything you needed."

"I'm sorry we disturbed you." Sandra wondered if her husband had told her where he'd taken her. Did Brooke know that she and Wyatt had been guests of the President? That they had been whisked to Camp David and been treated as honored guests?

"I'm glad for your company." She rubbed her belly. "I'm not used to being home all day. It's good to have visitors."

"When is your baby due?"

"Not for another couple of months." Her hands moved across her stomach again. Sandra had seen many pregnant women do that. Marjorie did it. She wondered what it felt like to be pregnant and why the women constantly touched themselves that way.

"Is this your first," she heard Wyatt ask.

"My second . . . and third," she said. "I'm having twins. I have a daughter, Kari. She's in school now."

For a moment Sandra envied her. She and John had tried to have children. That's when they discovered John had leukemia. She never thought she'd get over his death, but she'd met Wyatt and couldn't imagine life without him.

"What can I help you with?" Brooke asked, bringing her attention back to the information they needed.

"We need a disk read." Sandra got straight to the point. "As I mentioned on the phone, it's encrypted."

"That shouldn't be too hard," the long-haired woman told her. "Why don't we go into my office."

She moved toward the back of the house. In a room with a window that looked out on the airstrip was a series of computers and shelves of books. Sandra looked at the titles. Everything from food preparation to quantum mechanics.

"Do you teach?" Wyatt asked her as she turned on the equipment and waited for it to boot up.

"No," she laughed. "I used to work for the FBI."

Wyatt stiffened.

"That was years ago. Then I started a chain of restaurants. My partner manages them now."

Now Sandra understood the cooking books.

"I'm a consultant at the university on certain government projects," she finished.

Sandra realized she hadn't really said anything. She wondered what Wyatt thought. Sandra trusted her. She'd trusted her in the limousine that night when she'd come to her rescue.

"Let me have the disk."

Wyatt had it. He slipped it from his pocket and handed it to her. Wyatt had been cautious this time. Sandra had the original in her backpack, along with the chest of diamonds. Wyatt had made a copy on Marjorie's computer before they thanked her and promised to return the borrowed clothes they now wore.

"Where did you get this?" Brooke asked in a whisper. A frowned creased her brow.

"A friend sent it to me," Sandra hedged.

"This is good, very good." Pride at a fellow colleague's ability showed in her voice. "Whose work is this?"

Wyatt looked at Sandra over Brooke's head. "Jeff Taylor," he answered.

She swung around on the office chair. "I'm sorry," she said to them. "I heard about his death. I never met him. He'd left the government about the time I started consulting. People spoke of him with great pride."

"Do you think he made the code so complex, we won't be able to discover what his message says?"

She swung back to the screen. "It does look complicated, but I'll see what I can do. Why don't you two make yourselves comfortable. This might take some time."

"How about a walk?" Sandra suggested and she followed him, putting her coat back on and leaving Brooke seated at the console screen. She was already into the work, oblivious of them. There was nothing they could do anyway.

They didn't go any farther than the porch. The wind whipped at them as it had done last night when they were digging around the rocks on Route 95. Wyatt put his arm around her and pulled her close.

"I've been thinking a lot about President Horton's request that we work with him. I want to know what you think about it."

Everett's question had been at the top of her mind, too. She hadn't come to a decision yet. "I think we need another alternative," Sandra said. "I've been racking my brain trying to come up with something that will be workable and not harm anyone now or in the future, but I can't think of a thing. This might be a problem which has no solution and certainly no winner."

Wyatt turned her face to him and kissed her forehead. She'd come to the same conclusion he had. God, he loved her. He couldn't imagine what he'd have done if he'd never found her. If nothing good came out of this mess over Project Eagle, at least he'd met the woman of his dreams. He couldn't ask for a better partner.

"I think we'd better let him know we've agreed to his plan," Wyatt said.

"But we haven't," Sandra corrected.

"He won't know that. We need to play his game, let him think he's making the rules. At least until we can find another alternative."

"I'll ask Brooke if we can use her phone."

Brooke had been cloistered in her office most of the day. Sandra and Wyatt had paced the floor, looked through all the windows and speculated on what Jeff could have given them until finally they lapsed into silence. Only the incessant wind could be heard in the quiet house.

A maid had prepared a light meal at lunchtime and taken a tray into Brooke. Wyatt and Sandra had eaten silently, and finally he'd fallen asleep on the sofa. Sandra knew how little sleeping he'd done the night before. She pulled off his shoes and covered him with an afghan from the back of the sofa. Then she put another log in the fireplace and sat reading a magazine.

She couldn't remember a word of what she read. Finally, she put it aside and stared at Wyatt. She wondered all sorts of things about him: what was it like where he grew up; were his parents still alive; did he have brothers and sisters? They had been on the run virtually since they met. They'd had no time to exchange the facts of background or tell stories of their pasts. Now she was in love with him.

It felt like the first time. He was her first thought in the morning and her last at night. She loved sleeping in the warmth of his arms and finding herself cradled like a baby when she awoke. She liked the newness of discovering things about his body, where he was ticklish and what turned him on. She liked the feel of his skin and the smell that was only his. She liked the way he could make her hot by only looking at her and that she could become aroused just thinking of him.

Their morning in bed had been a powerful experience for her. She thought their first time was the best it would ever get, but each time something new and exciting happened to let her know that Wyatt Randolph would surprise her every day of her life. She wanted those surprises, longed for them. She wanted to anticipate what he could do and how she could help him. She didn't mind being in the limelight if it bathed the two of them. He was a good senator. He believed he could make a difference, and if he believed he could do it, then she believed too.

"Sandra?" The voice calling her was so soft she almost didn't think it came from outside her head. She was staring at Wyatt. "Sandra?" It came again. Suddenly, she realized Brooke was standing in the doorway. She stood up quickly but didn't wake Wyatt.

Going to the office, both women went inside and closed the door.

"Have you found out what's on it?"

She nodded.

Sandra tried to read her face, but saw no change of expression.

"It's a schematic." Brooke sat down at the computer screen and pulled the image up.

Sandra looked at it, but only saw a convergence of lines.

"There are fifteen diamonds," Brooke said.

"How did you know that?" Neither Sandra nor Wyatt had mentioned anything about the stones.

"The message on the disks talks about them. There are fifteen. They have to have a particular and specific arrangement in order for the system to work." She glanced at Sandra. "Jeff didn't mention what the system does, so I don't know."

"It's a communications system," she said, feeling compelled to say something. She couldn't give her a full explanation, but this was as close to the truth as she would go.

"The stones have specific shapes." She pulled one stone up on the screen. It grew larger and larger. "Even though the sides might look the same, they are minutely different. These differences allow light to pass through and be refracted. The refraction along with the computer system activates the system."

"So that's why," Sandra said. *That's the real reason the chips are encased in stones. It has to do with light bouncing off the cut surfaces. Fifteen diamonds all with different cuts. It would take years to re-create what Chip Jackson had done. Even with two systems ready and waiting for the stones, only one set of stones in the world would work. And he's sent them to Wyatt.*

"Why what?" Brooke asked.

"Nothing important," she said. "Is there anything else?"

"Yes," she said. She pulled the connecting lines back onto the screen. Then she superimposed the jewels over the lines at specific points. What Sandra saw on the screen reminded her of a necklace.

"It's beautiful," Sandra whispered.

"Beautiful and deadly." Brooke pointed to the screen. "Each of the stones has a symbol on one side. Seven of them have it on the right, seven on the left, and the fifteenth stone has it on the bottom tip. The symbols are both mathematic and musical. You need an electron microscope to see them."

"What are these symbols?" Sandra thought she recognized some of them when she'd first seen them.

Brooke pulled them up on the screen. As she'd done with overlaying the stones on the lines, next to each stone appeared a symbol. The mathematical symbols went down the left and the musical notations down the right.

"They seem to have no order. Did Jeff say they have a meaning?"

"I couldn't find that anywhere."

Sandra looked at them. Did Chip use them for something special, or merely identification? On the left she saw the mathematical symbols for pi, delta, summation, function, square root, greater than and equal. On the right the musical symbol for a whole rest topped the first stone, followed by the G clef, F clef, pianoforte, a quarter note, the time signature for a waltz, and the staff. The symbol for the final fifteenth stone was infinity.

"Do you think they mean anything?"

"In programming nothing is done for cosmetic reasons. Everything has a purpose or it would be a waste of the programmer's time to put in unnecessary information. These symbols could be for identification only. Whatever the program, it doesn't necessarily have to have anything to do with the symbol."

"Then why didn't he just number them one through fifteen?"

Brooke shrugged. "You got me there."

"Math and music?" Sandra walked to the windows and looked at the bare branches blowing in the high winds. "I don't know about the music, but the math symbols are incomplete. For example, function alone doesn't mean anything. It needs to be a function of something. And square root? Square root of what?"

"The musical symbols don't give much, either. All of these symbols would be used in various pieces of music. The three-quarter-time signature indicates a waltz, but there are hundreds, thousands of waltzes."

"Do you think the light refraction has to bounce off these symbols?"

Brooke hunched her shoulders. "They are on the stones and the light isn't going to know if its a facet or a symbol. I can't even offer an educated guess to their purpose."

Brooke suddenly looked through the window over Sandra's shoulder. "There's my daughter's bus. I have to go meet her."

"Sure," Sandra said, seeing the yellow school bus making a complete turn in the circular space outside the stone wall. Sandra was glad they hadn't blocked it.

"One more thing. I said the jewels were deadly."

"Yes."

"The fifteenth stone is necessary to the system, but it serves a dual purpose."

"What is it? Of the other stones, that one is larger than any of the others."

"That one," Brooke cautioned, "is a bomb."

"Absolutely not!" Grant stared at his wife. He stepped back from the embrace of a moment ago and wondered what could be going on in her head. Very likely, a hormonal imbalance.

"Grant, I can do it."

"Have you lost your mind? You're carrying twins, sweetheart. If you're not thinking of yourself, think of them."

Her dark eyes pleaded with him and he melted in the love he saw reflected there. Usually he denied her nothing, but he'd lost her once. It had been five years before he found her again. No way was he letting her work with a bomb.

"They can call the bomb squad. *You* are not doing it. What do you know about bombs anyway?"

"It isn't the bomb as much as programming it to do something else."

"And suppose something goes wrong? Robyn . . . B." He slipped back into the use of her real name when he was truly angry. "I'd die without you. You know that."

He put his arms around her engorged body. Brooke only had two more months to full term. He'd missed the birth of his daughter, Kari. Brooke had been Robyn then, and in the Witness Protection Program. When he'd found her, hiding behind an alias, he'd sworn he'd protect her and never let her out of his sight. When the twins made their entrance, he didn't want to be anywhere but at her side.

They had had a rocky couple of years while the federal Witness Protection Program put their lives back in place. Since it had settled into a normal routine he didn't want it disturbed. His own connection as a pilot with the government on a part-time basis and Brooke's consulting on government projects was enough excitement.

"Grant, look at them." She pulled him around until he could see Wyatt and Sandra through the office door. They were standing by the fireplace in the next room. Wyatt had his arm around Sandra. Grant could see how much in love they were. They were both in love and in danger. He remembered his own life just two years ago when he'd flown into Brooke's life and couldn't stop himself from seeing her again and again. Despite the danger she was in and the threats to her life, she'd risked everything for him.

He knew the couple he was looking at would do the same thing. Brooke was soft-hearted. She'd always been like that. She hired people at her restaurant who needed a second chance. She was always willing to give them that chance to turn their lives around. She was asking that for Senator Randolph and Sandra Rutledge.

Grant had read the accounts in the newspaper and he knew from personal experience that there was more to the story between the couple in his family room, a lot more. He ran his fingers under Brooke's hair and massaged her neck. She leaned into him.

"They need us, Grant. We have to help them."

Grant sighed and gave in.

* * *

Wyatt hugged Sandra to him. He could feel the warmth of the fireplace behind her, but the heat she generated in him was no match for a mere fire. They'd been there long enough. Brooke Richards had helped them with the information on the disk. It was time for them to go. He'd become too used to moving around to stay any longer. Grant and Brooke Richards and their daughter Kari were a wonderful family. He no longer wanted to disrupt their lives.

"It's time we left," he said into her hair. It smelled like shampoo, and he could have gone on smelling it all night.

"What are we going to do now?"

"I suppose we should report to the President what we've found."

"I think he already knows how the system works. He probably knows the significance of the symbols."

"I'm not sure. For some reason I feel Chip was riding solo by the end of the project. When he decided he didn't want to be part of a system this enormously powerful, he'd have deliberately built traps in it."

Sandra had told him everything Brooke found on the disk, including the secret of the fifteenth stone.

The bomb needed a trigger mechanism and there didn't appear to be one, according to anything Jeff had left on the disk. Sandra assumed the trigger had to be on the connector board. If she was right activation of the system would cause it to self-destruct. But there were two systems. Did both of them have the same trigger? Had the stolen system been taken before Chip made the decision to set the trap?

Chip was the only person who knew the answer to that and he couldn't answer. Her guess was, only one of them had it, and she didn't know which one. For Chip it wouldn't have mattered. If the one system was destroyed, the other would be inoperable. It needed these stones and these only. The opportunity for another programmer to develop the fifteen exact stones would take a millennium. She wondered if he'd thought that some other enterprising systems analyst could configure the system to accept another set of stones.

Grant and Brooke came in. Sandra and Wyatt separated.

"Sandra, I talked to Grant and we agree I can take a further look at that last stone."

Sandra knew exactly what she meant. She could either try to disarm the stone or reconfigure it.

"Absolutely not!" Sandra and Wyatt said in unison.

"Mr. President," Lance acknowledged as he walked into the Oval Office. The room was full of people and he felt as if he was late for a meeting. He hated being late. Why hadn't he been invited to attend when the meeting was convened?

"Lance, you know everybody here." Horton looked at him. He nodded. The room was full of advisors, the FBI director, secretary of defense, Melanie West, Senator Rutledge, and several other members of Congress. Even the Vice President was in attendance. Lance took a seat next to Senator Rutledge.

He didn't like this. He felt his blood rush in his head and forced himself to relax. He didn't want anyone to see him sweat. Didn't want them to know that he was not in complete control.

"Lance, let me bring you up to date," Everett sat down and stretched his long legs in front of him. The man didn't look like a President. He was overly tall and clumsy. The only thing he had going for him was charisma and Casey Horton. The First Lady was absent from this congregation, and Lance wondered where she was. The two of them ran the country as a team, unfortunately leaving the Vice President out.

When he was elected, he'd refused to be kept out of policy making decisions. He'd already felt Senator Whittaker out. The man was another extremely popular personality. If he played his cards right he'd be on the ticket for the next election.

"We've discovered someone hacked into the DOD computers last night," Everett was saying when Lance looked up.

"Was there a violation of any sensitive information?"

"Any time there's a break-in, there's that possibility, but the hacker wasn't interested in taking anything, just using it."

"I don't understand, sir."

"The hacker wanted to use the encryption-decoding data banks."

Lance forced his features to remain in place. There were only a few people in the country who had enough savvy to hack into the DOD. Their names were known to the FBI's computer theft division. They were also known to him. There were few of them in the Washington, DC, area and only a couple whom Senator Randolph would be able to locate.

"Were they successful, sir?"

"Very. We let them take everything they wanted and we kept track of the data."

Lance hated Horton. He wanted to make him sweat. He liked seeing him squirm. Why didn't he just come out and tell him what they'd found out? Why were they doing this asinine dance? Lance smiled. Horton wasn't as smart as he thought. He already knew about Mrs. Brooke Richards's invasion into an unauthorized area of the DOD computers. The report had been put on his desk almost as she'd gone in. He granted her his respect. She was good. Better than good, she was one of the best. She'd bypassed most of the bells and whistles that would have caught nine out of ten of the others on the list. He knew everything she knew.

The urge to take Horton down a peg by revealing he already knew the facts of Horton's explanation was so strong he almost couldn't resist making a fool of the President in front of an audience. But he held his tongue, thinking better of it. Let him think he had command. It was a false illusion and soon everyone would know it. He had time.

Lance knew where Randolph was. He'd have him in a matter of hours. Then Horton's world would fall apart brick by brick and Lance would stand as the level headed-leader. The television cameras would roll with his decisions. He'd stand as a pillar of strength as everyone around him scrambled to blame someone else for the mess Horton had created.

"I talked to the senator this morning."

Lance's head came up with a snap.

"He has the stones. He's coming in."

This was a change. Randolph couldn't turn himself in. Not to Horton. That wasn't part of Lance's plan. He wouldn't allow Horton to tear down everything he'd planned. He needed to get to Randolph first.

Jordon looked through the lens of his Leica. It was a battered old camera. He'd bought it used from a retiring photographer when he was a younger man getting started in photography. It had been around the world more than once and served him well.

He had many cameras, newer models, but he loved this one better than any of the newer ones. Today he was playing, not really intending to take a picture, just looking through the lens. The woman on the other end of his viewfinder was Annie. She lazed on the bed where they'd made love. The room was full of them. Her hair was mussed from his hands threading through it. She had no clothes on under the satin sheets, that made her look more sexy than if she'd been naked to his view.

Only her right shoulder and part of her left leg could be seen. Against the white satin her darkness was near black. Jordon opened the aperture wide and increased the shutter speed. Everything around her would be blurred. Only her perfect form at the center of the shot would appear sharply defined when he developed the film. He pressed the shutter button with a reverence that surprised himself.

The shutter sound made her lift her head. The sheet slipped down her back as she turned, exposing one full, ripe breast. The film automatically moved through the camera and Jordon took another shot. He took several as she moved. He wasn't doing this for the contract or any contract he would ever get. The shots would be worthy, probably would pay more money than he'd ever received from a contract before, but they were for his private collection.

"Jordon, stop," Suzanne said. "You know I don't do nude photos."

He set the camera down and went to her. Taking her in his arms, he said, "You should." Then he kissed her. "For my eyes only." Ignition as hot as plastic explosives shot through him as his mouth found and covered hers. They made love fast. The tempo catching and pushing them into a feverish frenzy. Like high school kids who couldn't keep their hands off each other, Jordon lost even a fraction of control whenever she touched him. He wondered if he'd ever get used to her enough to make love to her slowly, to savor the emotions she kindled in him like nitro exploding.

When their hearts had returned to a normal beat, Jordon gathered her to him and held her. Her smooth legs matched the length of his under the white cover.

"What do you plan to do when this is over?" he asked her.

"What is over? I have at least five new contracts waiting for me. And you well know it."

"I'm not talking about contracts. I'm talking about your sister and Randolph." Suzanne tried to move away, but Jordon held her tighter. "Don't do it, Annie. Each time I bring up your sister, you retreat into another world. I want to know about her."

"There's nothing to know."

She stared up at him. Her eyes were bright, flaring with hurt and anger. Jordon kissed her. He didn't want to make her hurt, but he knew she couldn't spend the rest of her life holding the anger she felt toward her family. He wanted to help her. He wanted her to trust him, to tell him everything about herself. He wanted to be the man she turned to in the night with her body and in the day with her triumphs and her problems. He also wanted to go to her when he had those same needs.

For better, for worse, in sickness and in health, till death do us part. The words seemed to flow into his mind like images forming on nitrate-treated paper. He wanted to marry Annie, make her happy. He knew she could make him happier than any other woman in the world. He wanted that chance.

Jordon didn't ask again. He looked at her without comment. Her eyes clouded and she suddenly hugged him.

"Jordon, hold me."

He put his arms around her and pulled her to his side. Tears fell on his chest, hot and scalding. He swallowed the lump in his throat and waited.

"He's my father," she began. "My *real* father."

Jordon didn't push her. He wanted to ask who she meant, but he didn't. He waited, holding her and stroking her hair.

"They say he adopted me, found me in a backwater town and gave me a better life, but he didn't find me. He knew I was there. He's my real father."

"Senator Rutledge?"

"Yes," she sneered. "The great, powerful, and popular Senator Rutledge has a bastard daughter."

Jordon lifted her chin and looked her straight in the face. She was serious. "Annie, are you sure?"

"Of course I'm sure."

"You know politicians these days. In order to run for office they have to be squeaky clean. Something like an . . . illegitimate child would give the media, not to mention the senator's political opponents, enough fuel to kill any election bid he'd care to make. How is it they never found out?"

"You don't believe me," she accused, turning away and wrapping her arms around her knees. Jordon stared at her bare back and naked buttocks. Taking the sheet, he covered her and pulled her against him.

"How long have you known?"

"Four years. I found out just before Sandra got married."

Jason expressed surprise at Annie's comment. Annie explained the circumstances, then took a deep breath and went on. "Sandra had to get all the legal papers ready to get a marriage license. She was in such a frenzy and I was helping her. Sandra was still living here then. I went to get the papers for her and that's when I found my own birth certificate. My real one. Not the one that was produced when I was adopted. That one has Melissa and Bradford Rutledge as my mother and father. The one my biological mother received when I was born had her name on it, Catherine Boatwright, and under Father was typed in clear legible English, Bradford Campbell Rutledge."

"He knew you were his real daughter and he never said anything?"

"He left her, used her, and when I was born he never even came to see me. He left us in that swamp to live or die. He didn't care. He was a senator. His career was taking off, soaring. He couldn't afford a bastard daughter from some backwater town pulling him down." She stopped and took a breath. "I confronted him with what I'd found. We had a really bad argument. I left and I've never seen him since."

"Yet, he called here. He knew you were here."

"He knew *she* was here," Suzanne sneered. "Sandra, the precious one, the legitimate one, the one with all the best things in life. He didn't call me. He wanted to know why his precious little princess was making the front page of *The Washington Post.* He wanted to protect her, not ask if I was sick or dying."

She climbed off the bed, pulling on a robe. Grabbing the sashes, she tied a tight knot around her waist.

"He wouldn't care if naked pictures of me appeared on the morning news, but let Sandra's name be linked with anything that could malign her puritan reputation and in comes her father, like a white knight, ready to do battle."

"Then why did you help her?"

"I didn't."

Jordon stood up. He didn't pull any clothes on. His body was lean and hard, though nothing he'd choose to photograph if he needed a strong male, but he liked the way Annie looked at him when he was undressed. Even if he didn't consider himself in a class with muscle-bound hunks, she made him feel like he was.

"I know you helped her," he said quietly. "You got her the money."

"It was her money."

"But you used those banking skills of yours to cover any possible trail. When she came here you took them in and got them food and clothes. You even gave her the pearl necklace." He stopped, raising his hands to prevent her from speaking. "You gave it to her in case she ran out of money and needed to get more. The truth is, if anything happens to her, you'll feel guilty. She's not guilty of anything your father did and you know it."

Suzanne moved to turn away, but Jordon took her arms and stopped her.

"Look at me," he commanded. "She was a little girl. It wasn't her fault that her father treated you badly. You know it and you had to help her. No matter what you think about your father, Sandra didn't do anything to you. She loves you and you love her."

Suzanne looked at him for a long time before dropping her eyes and putting her arms around him. Why couldn't she deny his words? Why did he, of all the people she knew, have to be the one person who could see through her motives? Why did Sandra's plight have to become hers? When she'd seen the first newspaper account of her sister, the instinct to help, to protect, to set the record straight was too strong to deny. When Sandra showed up at the photo shoot that day, she wanted to hug her, to tell her everything would be all right, to ask her if there was anything she could do. But she wouldn't let herself.

Tears ran down her face. Jordon's arms tightened around her, pulling her into contact with him, making her feel secure and wanted. She loved him.

When had that happened?

Jordon listened to the water in the shower. He cracked the door open and heard Annie singing gently under the spray of the water. He closed the door and went into the living room. Picking up the phone, he glanced back toward the bedroom door.

He dialed the private number and waited for it to be answered.

"Christopher." The voice came over the line, clear and strong.

"Clarence, good morning."

"Jordon? What are you doing calling this line? Is this another one of your pranks?"

Jordon laughed. He liked the director of the FBI. When he wasn't under the pressures of his job, he had a wonderful sense of humor. Jordon had met him several years earlier when he'd been called to photograph the new director.

Portraits of executives were an unusual assignment. He'd thought the request clearly unusual, but he'd gone out of curiosity.

"No prank, Clarence. I have some information that I'd like checked out."

"What do you think this is, your personal data bank?"

Jordon chuckled. "You must be having a really bad day," he teased. Jordon checked his watch. "It's not even noon yet."

"I am having a bad day. It's been bad for weeks now, and I'm extremely busy. So could you please clear this line. I have an appointment with the President in twenty minutes."

"Senator Randolph is the subject, I take it."

"I don't think our business is any of yours."

"It might just be. I've seen the senator."

Silence greeted him as if Clarence was letting what he heard sink into his brain. "Jordon, I want to know everything you know. Be in my office at two o'clock."

"I'll be there, but I want something from you."

"This is not a negotiation."

"I want you to check out Suzanne Wright. You know her as Anne Rutledge."

"Bradford Rutledge's daughter? Why? It's the other daughter we're trying to find."

"I need the information."

"For what? Does this have to do with department business or are you using the agency for your personal research?"

"A little of both," he admitted. "Her real name is Annie Boatwright. Senator Rutledge adopted her when she was ten years old. She's from a rural Georgia town."

"What are you expecting us to find?"

"She says Rutledge is her real father, her biological father."

Christopher's silence told him more than he wanted to hear.

"Clarence, I know what you're thinking and that's not why I called. Promise me you won't do anything with what you find until I've had a chance to review it."

"I don't work for you, Jordon." Christopher's voice was authoritative, but Jordon knew him as a man of honor. He would first give him what he asked. "Remember, be here at two."

CHAPTER 18

Wyatt put his hand to his head and closed his eyes. He'd left Sandra at the jeweler's and walked around the corner while the stones were being set. He didn't want to leave, but he'd been too restless to sit there silently while the man worked. This running had gone on long enough. He was tired. He and Sandra had what everyone wanted. He could end the stealing around, depending on friends for support, help, and even clothes and shoes. He looked at the pants he was wearing. They belonged to Marjorie's husband, a man he'd only seen once in his life. The shoes were his. He'd had the dress shoes since the night they'd gone to Casey Horton's party and ended up digging stones along the highway in Virginia. Red dirt clung to the sides and inside the stitches. He wanted to go home, sleep in his own bed, get up in the morning and go to a job, ride the metro, take vacations, do the things ordinary citizens did. But he couldn't. He couldn't because of what he had, what he knew.

Lafayette Park sat across from the White House. Lady Bird Johnson had beautified it when her husband Lyndon Johnson was President. None of the fountains were on, and the flowers lay dormant under the snow waiting for spring. Wyatt sat on the cold bench, a solitary figure, in the darkness of early evening. Across the park and the deserted street was the most famous house in America, a place where the President of the United States lived.

He'd told the President he'd call him the moment he had something to report. News that they actually had possession of the stones should make his day. Yet, Wyatt was reluctant to place the call.

He stared at the White House. Lights blinked in many of the windows. He wondered which room Everett Horton was in and what would go through his mind if Wyatt walked through the gates and turned the stones over to him.

What would Sandra think if he did that? He'd become used to discussing everything with her. She was as involved in this as he. He couldn't make any decisions without her approval and he knew she wouldn't give them over without conditions. Conditions they were sure would be met. He needed to talk to her. She was practical, logical, and passionate. He loved her passion, not only in bed, although he loved that, too, but her passion for what was right and wrong. An idea was forming in his mind and he wanted to talk to her about it. He thought he had a solution that could get them out this, but it was dangerous.

He stood up to leave, then stopped abruptly when he noticed Sandra standing several feet from him. She stared at the house across the street. She seemed mesmerized by the lighted structure that symbolized the country's authority figure.

Wyatt liked Everett Horton. He'd even voted for him, and in the next election he'd probably vote for him again.

Sandra stood still, unconcerned about the coldness of the air. Wyatt wondered what she was thinking. He wondered if she was as tired as he was and only wanted to be rid of Project Eagle and all its implications.

He went toward her. She made no move, no indication that she was aware of his presence, until she spoke.

"We aren't going to the White House, are we?" She'd been quiet for most of the drive back to Washington. At the jewelry store she'd said little, other than giving instructions for the setting of the stones. Now, with her vision trained on the White House, she spoke quietly, but Wyatt knew she was as alert as a spy stalking his prey.

"Not yet," he answered. He turned, following her gaze. Across the street he could see the guards at the Pennsylvania Avenue gate. The gate was closed. No cars, not even authorized visitors, could check in at that point. Yet, the guards maintained their posts. Wyatt wondered if anyone ever walked through those gates. "I know what President Horton said sounds right," he began. "But I have a nagging feeling in the pit of my stomach that turning these stones over will mean I'll be the one dropping the next atomic bomb, and I don't want that recorded as my history."

Sandra turned to him and smiled. Wyatt joined her, lifting his hand to run his knuckles down her cheek. She caught and held it close to her face. Her eyes were sad as if she'd been struggling with a problem and was unable to find a viable solution. Wyatt pulled her close and let his arms circle her.

"What do you plan to do?" she asked against his chest.

"We're going to do exactly what Horton suggested doing. We're going to activate Project Eagle and let the eagle fly."

Sandra turned her head, watching the light dance off the earrings that glittered in her ears. She fingered the chain around her neck which held the large stones, including the fifteenth stone. It had been Brooke's idea that the best way to keep the stones in order was to set them. She'd even recommended the jeweler. Sandra couldn't have asked for a better looking fake.

Of course, the idea of wearing a bomb around her neck took some of the glitter away from the stones, but she loved the feel of them as they brushed her skin. Wyatt had explained his plan on the walk back to the jeweler's. She admitted it was dangerous, but with a little luck they just might pull it off.

"They're beautiful pieces," the jeweler said. His name was Greg, and Brooke had told her he and Grant had known each other for years. "Few people would even be able to tell the stones weren't real diamonds."

Sandra nodded. She remembered when she'd first seen them, tumbling about on the floor of her mother's examining room. They were covered in Wyatt's blood and had none of the brilliance they now possessed.

Suddenly, she had an idea. Turning away from the mirror, she asked, "Do you think you could make a duplicate of these?"

"I could duplicate the stones, but certainly not the cargo," he said.

Brooke had sworn he was trustworthy. "I'd like a matching set, and I need it flawed. To the naked eye I want people to think there's something inside."

"Why?" he asked. "Most women want perfect fakes."

She reached up, removed the earrings and unhooked the precious stone hanging around her neck. Staring at them, she said, "I need them for a very specific purpose."

He hunched his shoulders as if he realized she wouldn't tell him the real reason. "They'll be ready by this time tomorrow."

"I appreciate your help."

Sandra and Wyatt left the jewelry store and went to Sandra's sister's hotel. She knew Annie wasn't going to take kindly to finding her on her doorstep again, but in order for Wyatt's plan to work, they needed to find out who had the most to gain from getting the stones.

Using the same cautionary moves they'd employed before, they avoided the men watching the place and got inside. Taking a deep breath, Sandra knocked on the door. Annie opened it a moment later. She was dressed in a Japanese kimono. Her face had been completely made over with pasty white makeup that completely covered her dark skin. Black eyebrow pencil defined her eyebrows and her lips were unnaturally red. Her wig was jet black and on her head was an ancient Japanese headdress.

Sandra knew she hated the white makeup. One Halloween when they were planning to be clowns Annie had suddenly bolted when it was time to smear her face with the white color.

Sandra was surprised to find her still in costume. At six feet tall her height should have made her look silly in the outfit, but Annie's carriage was too good, too professional to make her look anything but wonderful.

"What is this, a convention?" she cried when she saw the two of them. Sandra and Wyatt filed into the room.

"You'll excuse us, Senator," she said, as she pulled Sandra into the bedroom and closed the door.

"Why are you here, *again?*" she asked. Annie pulled the wig and headdress off in one movement. She sat them on the dresser with all the care of broken glass.

"Annie, I need your help."

She opened a jar of cold cream and slammed the top on the dresser. "You know." She wagged her finger in front of Sandra's face. "I am not the Salvation Army. Why do you keep coming here? What do you want from me?"

Something had happened and happened recently. Sandra wondered what. Annie was angry with her. She wasn't just taking her anger out on her. She'd shown up at the wrong moment, and whatever set Annie off had a direct connection.

Annie soaped her face with the cream. She was using way too much but Sandra didn't think this was the time to tell her.

"Annie, sit down," she said, as gently as she could.

Annie glared at her. Her eyes filled with unshed tears. Finally, she sat on the makeup bench. Sandra pulled a tissue from the box and began removing the white makeup from her sister's face. She didn't talk to her, didn't ask what was wrong. She knew her sister wouldn't tell her even if she wanted to. But at this moment Annie needed someone. All her life she'd tried to prove how much she didn't need anyone, but Sandra knew better. She found out when she met Wyatt how much people needed each other.

Sandra wondered where Jordon was. He was in love with her sister. Could he be the problem? Was Annie fighting the fact that she was in love with him, that he was the one man she really needed and wanted, but had she sworn she would never allow any weakness—including love—make her subservient? Didn't she know that in love there was no subservience? That in love there was a combined strength that made each partner stronger for having the support and trust of the other. Could Annie trust Jordon?

Sandra got most of the makeup off Suzanne's face. She went into the bathroom for a wet cloth. As she cleaned the cream from her face and hair and applied a light moisturizer she asked, "Where's Jordon?"

"I don't know."

"Did you have a late shoot?"

Annie nodded and closed her eyes. Sandra hadn't done her sister's makeup for years. She didn't want to destroy the moment of sisterhood that existed, but she knew it wouldn't last.

"Are the tears for him?"

Annie abruptly turned away. "I wasn't crying, and if I were I wouldn't do it over a man." She rubbed the cream into her skin a little harder than necessary.

"He might be worth it, Annie. I think he's in love with you."

"What would you know about it?"

"Not a lot, I admit. But I have eyes and I can see the way he looks at you. If you can't see it, you must be blind."

Annie didn't answer. She went on with her face. Holding a brown eyebrow pencil she enhanced eyebrows that were already perfect.

"Are you blocking his advances, Annie?"

She threw the pencil down and turned to her sister. Sandra took an involuntary step back. "What business is it of yours?"

"None," she said. "You've always told me how you didn't need anyone. How you'd never be like me, never be dependent on anyone. But love isn't like that, Annie. Love can provide mutual strength rather than a giving up of control."

"Is that what you came here to tell me?"

"No."

"Then stay out of my personal life. It's none of your business. I don't need or want your help or advice."

Sandra knew the subject was closed. She turned around and crossed the room, giving Annie space and herself a moment to let her heart rebound from the sting of her sister's words.

"Annie, you might not need my help, but I need yours."

She grunted more than laughed as she used the foam applicator to apply a gold tone to her eyelids. Staring at her through the mirror, she asked, "What makes you think I'll help you . . . again."

Sandra met her gaze in the mirror. "I can't possibly explain the importance of what is going on, but believe me, what we're dealing with has life and death hanging in the balance."

Annie stopped and stared directly at her. Then she rolled her eyes. "Sandra, you're being melodramatic."

"I'm not prone to melodrama or exaggeration and you know it. I promise you this is the truth."

"All right," she agreed. "You don't know how to lie, either, so there must be at least an element of truth in the statement. "If I do what you want, will you get out of here and never come back?"

Sandra's head snapped up and she stared at her sister. "Annie, you can't mean that; never come back? You're not just talking about here." She pointed to the room. "You mean wherever you are?"

"I don't want to see you again." She spoke distinctly as if she were speaking to a child.

Tears clouded Sandra's eyes and she turned away. In the few years since she and Annie had been estranged she always thought they would get over their problem. They would need each other, remember they were family and want to spend time together. She'd never known how deep Annie's hate for her was.

Brushing the tears away with the back of her hand, she turned back to face her sister and nodded. If Annie hated her that much, Sandra wouldn't impose on her. Annie's words had cut deep, but she'd survive them. She wanted a relationship with her sister. She wanted a solution to the problem Annie had, but it seemed now that she'd lose her sister forever.

"All right, what do you want me to do?"

"I need you to use your knowledge of banking to find out if any of these people have money problems or if they have huge bank accounts." Sandra opened her purse and handed her the list she'd written. "Anything you can find out about them will be helpful."

Annie's eyes widened in surprise. She looked up at Sandra. "You have lost your mind. Do you know what I'm going to have to do to get information on these people?"

Sandra hadn't a clue. She knew it wasn't going to be easy, but she also knew her sister was one of the few people who could get the data and get it fast.

Annie sighed. "When do you need it?"

"As fast as possible. Tomorrow, if we can have it."

Annie gave her a long and thorough going-over. Sandra felt as if she'd been put under a microscope.

She dropped the list on the dresser next to her case of mahogany powder and went back to making up her face.

Sandra wondered if she'd been dismissed. She felt as if she had. Turning around, she went to the door and took one last look at her sister. With her hand on the doorknob, she turned back.

"Annie." She waited for her sister to look at her. "Since you don't want to see me again, would you tell me what it was I did that made you hate me so?"

Annie stood up. Wearing the kimono and her own makeup, she looked ridiculously out of place. "Ask your father," she replied.

* * *

Wyatt read the invitation to an embassy party from the Imperial Republic of Japan that lay open on the table next to the sofa where he sat. The moment Sandra came through the bedroom door he could see she was shaken. He'd determined the two sisters weren't the best of friends when he was here before, but this time Sandra looked pale, as if she'd just received the news someone had died.

He got up and went to her. She stared blankly in front of her, but lifted her head to his face as he approached. He took her shoulders and pulled her close. A moment later, he raised her chin to look into her eyes.

"Oh, Wyatt!" she wailed as she burst into tears.

Wyatt gathered her close and held her. Her arms climbed around his neck and she squeezed as tight as she could. Tears racked her body with a thundering intensity.

Anger walled up inside him like a raging bull. He didn't want her to cry. What had her sister said?

"Sandra, honey. It's all right. If she won't help us, we'll find someone who will. Stop crying."

She hiccupped trying to get control, but fresh tears replaced the ones he tried to wipe away.

"Sandra, what did she say to make you cry like this?"

When she didn't answer, Wyatt pushed her aside and started for the bedroom door. He'd tear her sister limb from limb for making Sandra cry. She'd only asked a simple question. She could have said she wouldn't do it and let it be. But she'd done more. Sandra wouldn't cry like this if she hadn't.

"No!" Sandra held on to his jacket as he tried to move. "Let's get out of here."

Only the pleading in her eyes made him forget her sister and take her around the waist and steer her out the door. By the time they'd reached the car in the garage the last remnants of tears tracked down her face like rutted tires.

Wyatt opened the door and helped her inside. He went around the hood and opened the driver's door. The interior light came on and went off as he got inside.

"What happened in there?"

She told him Annie's harsh words; her condition for helping them. Sandra sniffed, fighting a new batch of tears.

"What happened to make her dislike you?"

"I don't know. Whatever it was, it happened just before I got married." She staved off an emotional outburst and continued. "We grew up together, were the best of friends until I married John. I can't remember precisely when it started, but I know it was about that time. I couldn't figure out what I'd done, but suddenly Annie and I were arguing all the time. She was arguing with everyone, except Mother. For a while I thought it was John. That somehow Annie had a thing for him, that she was jealous, but that wasn't it. Then I thought she was upset that we would no longer have the relationship we'd had in the past, but when I tried to talk to her she shut me out."

"What happened then," Wyatt asked.

"Annie took off for New York and later Europe. She didn't come to the wedding, and since then has refused to see any of us. She doesn't attend any family functions and she hates us."

Her tears started anew and Wyatt pulled her to him and held her. It was all he had the strength to do. He wanted to comfort her, but she'd kicked him in the stomach. He took deep breaths trying to control the shudders that ran through him as Sandra's shoulders rose and fell with her tears.

She's married. She has a husband. The words rang in his head like the sound of a tinny piano in a lonely wooden-floored bar. Why hadn't she told him? He'd fallen in love with a married woman. Where was her husband? Why was there no mention of him?

"Sandra." Her name came out a strangled whisper, passing over the lump that clogged his throat. "You never mentioned you were married."

CHAPTER 19

Sandra explained everything to Wyatt during the drive to meet Sam Parker. She told him how she'd met John in college and dated him. After graduation, John had taken a job in Europe and stayed there for years. When he returned, they met again at a Christmas party given by a mutual friend. They fell in love and married. She told him about their attempts to have children, John's leukemia, and his subsequent death.

Wyatt drove without speaking. He listened to Sandra. She spoke nervously, but continued in detail. She felt as if she had to explain. He'd made her feel like that. He shouldn't have, but he didn't stop her. He wanted to know about her life. He wanted to know everything from the moment she took her first breath to the next one she was about to take.

They'd been constantly together, but in that time they'd been trying to save each other's lives. Little things like family and husbands didn't seem to come up in the discussion.

"I've never been married," Wyatt said when she lapsed into silence. "I have been in love. Her name was April. We met during a lawyers' conference in Dallas. She was a lot like you, intelligent and beautiful."

He stole a glance at her hoping for a smile. Her face remained interested but aloof.

"Our courtship was fast and volatile. In less than six weeks I knew I wanted to be with her for the rest of my life. I asked her to marry me."

Wyatt swallowed, remembering the hurt as if it had happened to another person. He'd thought he was going to feel that until he died, but it was gone.

"What happened?" Sandra prompted.

"She was already married."

He heard the small intake of breath that came from her. For a moment he thought it was happening to him all over again. He didn't know if he could survive if Sandra wasn't his. He wanted her more than he ever wanted April.

"I'm sorry, Wyatt."

Irrationally, Sandra hated the woman who had hurt Wyatt. She knew there was nothing she could do about it. If he hadn't left her, he might not be with her today, and despite their difficulties, she wouldn't give up even one day with him.

When they reached the place where they'd agreed to meet Sam, Wyatt got out of the car and came around to her side. Helping her out, he took her in his arms and kissed her. Sandra wrapped her arms around him. The kiss was so tender and sweet, it nearly brought more tears to her eyes. Wyatt's tenderness made her melt in his arms as his kiss deepened. She clung to him, returning the passion he produced in her kind for kind.

She never wanted to let him go, never wanted him to hurt or feel that there was anything the two of them couldn't work out. She was free. He was free. And she was in love with him. She told him so with her mouth, her body, her hands. She branded his mouth with her love, with a promise that was as binding as it was blinding. When they pulled apart, she slumped against him, wondering how she'd managed to live before she met him.

Her love for John was safe and warm and in a special compartment of her heart. She wouldn't forget their time together or wish it had never happened. Wyatt wouldn't want her to. She discovered she had a heart large enough for both John and Wyatt.

Lance studied the report on his desk. So they had been to Mrs. Richards'. She'd decoded the information on the stones. He didn't have to take three guesses to figure out what they'd found. They probably knew about the configuration, found the symbols, but they couldn't know about the last one. Even if they did, what could they do with it? Nothing. They were amateurs playing with professionals. The net was closing and soon they'd be caught like fish.

Sandra should have taken his offer when he gave it. She could have walked away scot-free, but she chose to band together with Wyatt Randolph. He might be a Boy Scout, but that didn't mean he could get away with what he'd done and been accused of doing. Lance would make sure of that. It was Lance's turn to pitch, and everything that could be thrown at Wyatt Randolph would be.

If Lance had learned nothing else since coming to Washington, he'd learned how to play the game. He was a master at it and he could see his reward just ahead. He was close to it, so close it was almost in his hand. Senator Randolph. He smiled. Senator Randolph would be the person who handed him the brass ring.

Lance closed the report and locked it in his safe. It was time to go get the distinguished senator from the state of Pennsylvania.

Colonel Sam Parker's hideout would rival any of America's castles. Set in the sprawling countryside of Reston, Virginia, it was a twenty-thousand-square-foot country home. From the look of it, someone had disassembled an English manor house and rebuilt it on a thousand-acre tract in the shadow of the nation's capital. Entrance to the estate was through a wrought-iron gate mounted with closed-circuit cameras. A three-mile leisurely drive on a narrow paved road led to the door of the gray stone house. He should feel secure here, but he didn't.

His access was legitimate and above board. The house was owned by Wagner Van Zee. Wag owned an electronics company that had been in on the ground level when personal computers were first being born. His parts supply company had grown to be a major contributor to the industry. Sam could shoot himself every time he thought of Wag's efforts to get him to join in his budding company. Sam had opted for the service and it had led him here, AWOL and hiding from the very people he'd worked with.

"Wow!" Wyatt whistled, getting out of the car. Sam ran down the front steps and shook hands with him. He nodded at Sandra Rutledge.

"We should all go into hiding in a place like this." Wyatt looked around the house and grounds.

"It belongs to a buddy of mine," Sam explained. "We went to school together."

Inside, Sandra found the furnishings elegant enough to grace any museum.

"He's away in Europe and 'loaned' me the use of this," Sam scanned the huge room, "whenever I needed it."

He watched Sandra as she looked around nervously. "Sam, places like this have their own security staff. This house alone would take a staff of fifty to maintain it."

"Fifty-three, actually," he said. "Since it's winter and unoccupied, it gets by with a skeleton crew of seven. They're loyal and completely trustworthy." Before Wag left, he'd told them Sam was an eccentric writer working on a book and needed peace and quiet. They were to disturb him as little as possible and to do anything he asked. So far he'd had no problems.

"Where are they now?" Wyatt asked.

"I gave them the day off. They won't be back before nightfall."

"That's good," Sandra muttered. He knew he wasn't supposed to hear her, but his sense of hearing had always been keen. She didn't trust him. He couldn't blame her, but he wanted her to know he was doing nothing to hurt her or Wyatt. His own life was in danger, he'd thrown away his career, and there was nothing left for him but to work with Wyatt and Sandra and hope against hope that somehow there was a solution to this crisis. He hadn't known how much he believed in the Constitution until its basic rights and freedoms came into jeopardy. Now he was willing to do anything to help restore it to the place it had been intended. Wyatt and Sandra wanted the same thing. They only had each other.

Sam gave them a tour of the house on the way to the office. Wyatt was clearly impressed when they entered Wagner Van Zee's home office. The place could be the corporate headquarters of a major industrial company. The room was huge. A conference table sat in front of a large window. Fresh flowers graced a crystal bowl in the center of it. The desk took up so much room he'd wondered on first seeing it if it had been built inside the room. Computers, telephones, even a small television were built into the work-center.

Taking the chair behind the desk, Sam went right to work. "I take it you've discovered the secret of the fifteenth stone." The look that passed between Randolph and Sandra told him he'd guessed right. "If you hadn't, there would be no need for you to call me," he explained. "I know you don't quite trust me." He let his gaze settle on Randolph, then move piercingly to Sandra. "I'm not the enemy. I want what you want. So let me help. It's why you came here."

Wyatt looked at Sandra. He'd looked around the grounds as they drove up the long driveway. If Sam had wanted to turn them in to the military, this was the perfect place. They had the stones with them, the iron gate had locked them in as if this country-club setting were a prison. The deserted place had no telephone lines to prevent anything, even helicopters, from landing right next to the house. There would be no escape if Sam was playing for the other side.

Sandra must have felt the same way. She returned Sam's stare without the trace of a flicker. She got up and walked around the desk. Standing close to Sam, she had the advantage with him seated.

"We don't have much time," she said. "We've got to end this running. If we don't, the government only has to wait for us to make a mistake, run out of money, or be identified by some good citizen who happens to see us in a convenience store."

Sam stared quietly at her.

"Wyatt has a plan and we need you to help execute it. When it's done there's no guarantee than any of us will get off scot-free, but at least we'll be alive and no longer a target for some unknown assassin."

Sam stood up. His demeanor portrayed him every bit the colonel, sure, confident and alert. "I have nothing to lose, Sandra," he said. "My career ended the moment I left the Pentagon and never returned. I never knew how much I wanted that menial job until it was no longer mine, but I would like my dignity intact. Whatever I can do, I'm willing."

Wyatt watched the two of them. The tension was almost palpable. He stood, but to them he wasn't even in the room. Sandra searched Sam's face for any sign of insincerity. She gave no indication that she agreed or disagreed with Sam, but a moment later she opened the backpack that was their constant companion and pulled out the jewelry case.

Sam gasped when she opened the velvet case and he saw the fifteen stones, brightly polished and connected by a delicate, braided gold chain. He recognized the configuration: two strands equal in length holding several stones. The others, including the one solitary and deadly fifteenth stone, was connected to a chain. He wondered how they'd found out so much in only a few days.

"Did Taylor tell you this?" He took the case from her hands and turned toward the lighted windows.

"He left us a disk. The configuration and information were on it."

"Sam," Wyatt began. "You worked with Chip on this system. Can you take that fifteenth stone and defuse it?"

Sam turned back to them. "This stone," he looked down at it. "This was the most important part of the configuration. The system cannot be activated without the stone. It was the fail-safe chip. If it were set in the wrong configuration, the program would execute the explosion routine. Conversely, the chip itself is expecting to find certain instructions. If these are not found, then the connector links will cause the explosion. It's a bit complicated, but the answer to your questions is, tampering with the chip will cause it to detonate."

A tremor ran through Wyatt. Thank God they hadn't let Brooke Richards try to do anything with it. He shuddered at the mental picture of her and her family being blown to bits before his very eyes. His knees weakened and he sat down.

"What about changing it?" Sandra suggested.

"What do you mean?" Sam asked.

"If we can't remove it, is it possible to have the chip issue an instruction other than detonation?"

Wyatt sat up. He hoped Sam was about to say yes, but he was already shaking his head.

"Jackson had been working on something like that. He'd only mentioned it to me the day before he died."

"Do you know how he planned to get it done?"

"He showed me the programs, but I didn't have time to study them before I had to go to a staff meeting. By the time I thought about it again, Jackson had been found dead and the stones were missing."

Sandra dropped down in a chair. "Well, I guess that's that."

"Not quite," Sam said, taking a seat himself. Wyatt and Sandra stared at him, waiting for him to continue. "Where are the disks you copied from Jackson's computer?"

"In the backpack." Wyatt looked at the navy-blue LL Bean bag they'd been carrying ever since they escaped the mountain in Pennsylvania. Sandra had had little time to work on her thesis, yet she kept the bag close to her.

"The plans are in there," Sam said.

"They're still encrypted," Sandra pointed out.

"Not to me," Sam smiled.

Wyatt and Sandra both came forward in their chairs as if they were puppets and someone had just pulled their strings. When he'd devised this plan, he didn't think it could possibly work, but as he got nearer and nearer to the end his confidence built. Now all they had to do was slip undetected into a government military installation, find Project Eagle, set the stones and activate the program, then locate the second machine, get access to it and deactivate it. Impossible. The word flashed in his mind like a danger sign.

Large red pulsating capital letters.

"Good news or bad?" Casey asked Everett as soon as they were out of earshot of anyone near them. They walked through the White House toward the upstairs study. There he could have privacy and speak freely.

Everett smiled at her. "Didn't you see us shaking hands in front of the White House press corps? The President of the United States and the Prime Minister of Japan both smiled and said the negotiations were going well."

"Yes," she said drily, preceding her husband into the study. "I did see that, and I'll see it again and again on the nightly news and probably plastered on the front page of the *Post* in the morning."

"The truth is, I'm getting nowhere, Casey. The man is a rock. I have the impression that he doesn't have all his cards on the table, that there is something else they want and they're stalling for time until they get it."

"What could that be?"

"I don't know. Are there any other dignitaries due to arrive from Japan?"

"Not to my knowledge. I'll have it checked," she said.

"Any word from our wayward senator?" Everett asked with another sigh. He dropped down onto the sofa and slipped his feet out of his shoes.

"As a matter of fact, there is."

"There is." Everett stopped in the act of reaching for his shoes to place them out of the way. "Good news or bad?"

"He didn't say. Apparently, the junior senator wants to speak to the Commander in Chief of the Armed Forces."

"Oh, God!" Everett said. "I'm not going to like this."

The number of miles they had driven in the last few days could rival the Daytona 500. Sandra and Wyatt were back in the car racing toward the capital. Sandra was glad they weren't in her home state where they'd have many toll roads to travel and more opportunities for people to recognize them.

Sam had the stones and was busy trying to accomplish what Chip had begun. He'd ask them to leave the house. If anything went wrong and the bomb detonated, the beautiful stone building would be a small pile of rubble. They'd walked in the gardens, explored the stables, passed the tennis courts and pool, and set out along a jogging trail when they saw Sam waving them back toward the house. Sandra thought he'd finished, but when they arrived back it was to look at a file Sam had printed. It was a correspondence file with letters to Lance Desque and notes chronicling various meetings between Lance and Chip.

Lance knew everything about Project Eagle. He might be able to help them. He was the undersecretary. He had access to any military installation including the Pentagon. If she could get to him, convince him their plan was the best thing to do with the stones, he might help them.

It was worth a try. Lance had been a friend of the family since she was a child. He'd want to help her and her father get out of this mess. She'd called his office only to be told he'd left for the day. Then Sandra knew she had to see him. If she was going to enlist his help she'd have to do it in person.

"I don't like this," Wyatt said as they headed back toward Washington. "That guy wants the stones only to further his own career. He'll never help us."

"Wyatt, I know Lance is ambitious, but after I explain how his helping us can net him the same results, why wouldn't he help?"

"It sounds good, but I . . ."

He left the sentence hanging. Sandra knew he just couldn't say his intuition told him. Men didn't say those kind of things. They avoided the words, even the existence of such a feeling. She knew he was concerned for her.

"Wyatt, you'll be close by," she reminded him. "If anything happens, I'll scream and you can come running; like my knight in shining armor." She laughed, hoping to lift the mood in the car. Wyatt smiled, but it did nothing to change the heavy atmosphere.

They reached Lance's house. Wyatt parked on the street. "Well, it looks as if he's home," Sandra said. His car, with a personalized Maryland plate reading DESQUE, was parked in the driveway.

"Wish me luck," Sandra said as she unlocked the door. Wyatt grabbed her arm.

"You've got fifteen minutes. If you're not out by then, I'm coming in."

She nodded. She wanted to laugh. He sounded like some TV cop who only gave his female partner a few minutes to handle the bad guys. Then he'd come barreling through the door, guns drawn and blazing. The credits would roll while the entire police department came and the hero and heroine kissed, having finally saved the day. She didn't think that would be her fate, but she'd go for the final kiss and the saving of the day bit.

Her heels clicked on the driveway, then on the inlaid brick walkway that led to the front door.

The day was finally over. It had been long and trying and Lance Desque couldn't wait to get to his gym and work the kinks out of his muscles. Later, he had an invitation to an embassy party. He had stacks of invitations. Someone always had something to celebrate. Lance attended as many as he could. Being known in the world community could only help him when it was his turn to shape world power.

Tonight he would be dining with the ambassador of Finland. Tomorrow it would be the Japanese, then the French and the Pakistanis.

He fingered the imperial jade carving of a dragon that sat on the foyer table in his hall. Green fire extended from the open mouth of the three-foot-tall piece of Japanese civilization. It had been a gift from the Prime Minister of Japan.

Most people thought the dragon represented evil, but evil and good were often misunderstood. To him it meant strength and power, a power that would soon be in his hands. All he had to do was find Senator Randolph and Sandra Rutledge.

Lance was thinking of the two people who could derail his plans for power when the doorbell rang. He went to it and peeped through the beveled glass. With a wide smile on his face, he swung it open.

"Sandra, what a surprise. Come in, come in." He greeted her like a friend he hadn't seen in years instead of the woman who had been uppermost in his thoughts. Sandra stepped across the threshold into the white colonial house on a quiet cul-de-sac in Chevy Chase. Lance glanced around outside, wondering if his luck was good enough to include the senator, too. He saw nothing, no cars parked at the curb or in driveways he didn't recognize.

Closing the door, he turned back to Sandra. He hadn't seen her in nearly a week and needed to know what she and Randolph had found out. They, neither of them, were the kind of people to sit around and twiddle their thumbs. They would have been busy trying to find out what they had and what it was used for. He needed to know what they had learned.

Wyatt Randolph was a Boy Scout, fine, upstanding, and honest. How he ever got elected to Congress was a mystery.

He was sure Chip Jackson had sent him the part because of his honesty. And that was what had caused him to lose control of the project. Jackson was livid when he discovered a second system had been built without his knowledge. Lance had managed to placate him on that, but he insisted on seeing it and being involved in its installation. It was Jackson who discovered the discrepancy in the inventory records.

It was up to Lance to recover the stones. He'd been working with Senator Rutledge, and everything appeared to be under control until the senator's daughter had joined forces with Randolph.

Then Everett Horton had stuck his hands into the pie and control was slipping. Lance had to get it back.

"What brings you up here?" he asked when she was seated in the living room. "I didn't expect to see you," he explained honestly.

Lance went to the bar and poured himself a drink. He took a gulp of it before offering to make her one. Sandra refused anything more than bottled water.

"I need your help, Lance," she began when he'd handed her the glass and seated himself across from her. "I know you have your hands in every aspect of Defense. That you know everything there is to know about what goes on in the DOD."

Lance waited. It was a technique he'd learned from Sandra's father. He'd wait a moment and see if she continued. He almost smiled when she did.

"Wyatt . . . Senator Randolph and I have been looking at some files we found on Chip Jackson's computer in the Pentagon."

Sandra scrutinized him. Not even an eyebrow lifted at her words. She was sure Wyatt's opinion of him was wrong. She'd known him since she was a child. If they needed his help he would give it. Wyatt had been right about her father. Sandra decided to be cautious. Before asking him to help them break in to the Pentagon and activate Project Eagle, she'd try a little test.

"What did you find?" he asked.

Sandra wondered if his voice wasn't a little tight. She dismissed it.

"According to the notes and letters Chip had on his computer, you were the person who discovered he was working on the communications system and suggested he make it a Pentagon project."

"I may have been," Lance said without committing himself. "I suggest a lot of projects. It's part of my job."

"Later, he suggested that you were behind the theft."

Lance was out of his chair. "What!"

"A piece of news like that getting around Washington could ruin a man's career."

"Where is this file? It doesn't exist. Why have you come here with these lies?"

Sandra stared at the man in front of her. The Lance Desque she knew had somehow disappeared. The man in front of her was different. Wyatt had been right. Thank God he was outside waiting for her.

"Where are the stones, Sandra?"

"I don't know." She stood up. Fear gathered around her heart. She checked the distance between herself and the door. A sofa stood between her and the exit. A table by the door had a Japanese pagoda on it. She looked at the lamps and knickknacks, seeing what she could throw or pull down if she needed to run. Could she make it? Would Lance let her go? She didn't think so. Lance was fit. She knew he worked out each day, knew he prided himself on how his body could rival that of a seventeen-year-old.

"Don't give me that. I know you have them. I know you gave them to Jeff and you got him killed over them. Is that what you want to happen to everyone who comes in contact with them?"

Sandra's throat was so dry she didn't think she could speak. "The stones don't belong to you."

"They're more mine than yours. I worked for them. Week after week I had to find some story to keep that geek working. For three years I held his hand while he developed this system. I kept him in the dark, telling him we weren't going to do anything more than direct satellites with the system. Then he got together with Parker. They weren't even supposed to know their work had anything to do with the other, but Taylor knew. He knew the code. He was the one who linked them together. Of course he denied it, but I know he planted the code on Jackson's system and left the decoded system there."

Sandra looked around the room. She felt trapped. Lance was no longer talking to her. He was ranting, angry with Chip and Jeff and Sam Parker. Sandra judged her distance again. She took a small step toward the door. She didn't want to call any attention to herself.

"Then you," he shouted, swinging around to stare at her. She jumped. "You gave him the stones. He had them on him that night, taunted me with them."

Fear skittered up her spine. "You killed Jeff." Sandra took another step toward freedom. She wondered how long it had been since she came in. Would Lance kill her? Would Wyatt come barging through the door like he'd said?

She took another step and looked for a clock. There was one on the mantel, next to a framed Japanese print. She suddenly noticed all the Oriental accents in the room. Was that going to be her last thought?

"Killed him?" Lance shouted. "I didn't touch him. But no matter. Tomorrow everything will be over. I'll have the stones and the . . ." He trailed off without completing the sentence.

"What about tomorrow?" she asked.

"No matter," he smiled. She could see venom in that smile. "In a little more than twenty-four hours the stones and Senator Randolph's location will be known."

He was planning to activate the second system. How? Where was it? Twenty-four hours. What did he mean? Wyatt had the stones. They only worked with one system. Had Lance found a way to duplicate them or to make the system work with a different set of stones? She knew it wasn't impossible. They worked on light beams. Refracted light beams. A good technician using computer optics could adjust light until it produced the correct angle. They'd had time. She'd only been involved for a few weeks, but the system had been stolen ages ago.

Sandra had to get out of here. She needed to let Wyatt and Sam know about this. She had to let the President know. Time had run out. They had to act and act now!

She dashed for the door. Lance anticipated her flight and blocked her before she made it past the sofa table.

"Going somewhere?"

She backed off. He could see the fear in her eyes. It pumped him up. He'd like taunting her, keeping that look in her beautiful brown eyes. She looked behind her. There was no escaping.

"There's no way out, Sandra." He walked toward her. She backed away, shifting her glance from side to side. "The only door is behind me," he told her. Then she did the unexpected. She grabbed an egg-shaped paperweight from the table and aimed it at his head. He ducked. It shattered against the wall. At the same moment she bounded over the table and sofa and headed for the window. Lance discovered her intention just in time.

She had the element of surprise on her side and she ran as if she were wearing tennis shoes instead of high heels. Head first, she hurled herself, hitting the pane and shattering it as her body went through both the inside and storm windows. Lance was only a second behind her. She rolled forward on the ground, but didn't come up as steady as he did.

His arms closed around her and dragged her back against him. He slapped his hand over her mouth stifling the scream he felt coming from her belly. She kicked and scratched at him, trying to free herself. Lance laughed at her efforts, running his free hand over her. He needed to know if she had the stones on her person. She continued to kick at him. He avoided most of her strikes, but it was getting tiresome. Grabbing her hand, he twisted it behind her back until she groaned against the hand at her mouth. It hurt. He wanted it to hurt, wanted her to know he was in control and that she would do what he told her.

"Where are the stones?"

Sandra didn't say anything. The pain in her arm prevented her from doing anything but groaning. She wouldn't tell him anyway. The stones were safe. Sam had them. Thank God he'd been telling the truth. For a moment she felt guilty over her mistrust of him.

Lance pulled her to her feet keeping his hand over her mouth and holding her arm behind her back.

"Where are they?" He wrenched her arm up an inch. Her entire body went up until she was standing on the tips of her toes. Pain raced up her arm. Where was Wyatt?

"I don't have them," she said through clenched teeth.

"Randolph, where's Randolph?"

"I don't know."

"Now, why don't I believe that. You and he have been thick as thieves for the past few weeks. You didn't walk here. He's got to be here somewhere."

"He's not." A new fear attacked Sandra. "I came in a taxi."

"Maybe . . . but I doubt it. Well, we'll see. We'll see how long it takes for him to find you, and maybe if he wants you back—alive—he'll turn over the stones."

With that, he punched the back of her legs with his knees. The sudden forced bending made him wrench her hand and the pain made her move forward. He guided her to his car. She fought him. She needed to stay there until Wyatt arrived. Where did he go? He said he'd only give her fifteen minutes. How long had it been? It certainly seemed longer than fifteen minutes.

Lance forced her to the car. With her arm still painfully high behind her back, he opened the driver's door and spun around. She couldn't see what he did, but she heard the garage doors rising. Then he was pushing her fast. She struggled, but the pain in her arm made her eyes water in her attempt to slow him down until Wyatt could get there and help her.

Inside the garage he opened the door to a Mercedes and pressed a button. Sandra saw the trunk open.

"No!" she shouted, but the sound was muffled against his hand. She fought hard, with all her strength, but his hold on her arm was at the breaking point. He'd either break her arm or pull it from its socket. She was helpless. She hated the feeling. Any effort to fight him only increased the pain in her arm. He lifted her and threw her unceremoniously into the dark trunk. The lid came down before she could turn over.

In seconds the car was in motion. She cried, screamed, banged against the dark side of the metal cavern.

"Wyatt!"

CHAPTER 20

Wyatt parked off the street and waited. Chip had lived in Chevy Chase. His house was only a few miles from where Wyatt waited. He checked his watch. He had meant what he said. He didn't want Sandra in there a moment longer than fifteen minutes. He didn't trust Lance Desque. Chip's file had suggested he was the inside man at the Pentagon. To Wyatt, it made sense.

With the security Sam had told him about and Sandra confirmed from her tour, personally conducted by Desque, there was no way the parts to a system could be removed from the building without someone on the inside being the pointman. That someone had to be high up in the chain of command and he couldn't be working alone.

Enter Bradford Campbell Rutledge. He had to be the other partner. Together the two of them had everything they needed, access, opportunity, and motive. For both of them it would be phenomenal wealth and prestige, depending on how they used it.

It would also mean Everett Horton would topple in the popularity polls. Either Lance or Rutledge could run against him and he wouldn't even get his own party's support. Together Rutledge and Desque could run for office on the same ticket. Both were popular among the people. With Everett out of the way, they had the best chance of securing his office and then putting Project Eagle to the ultimate use.

Wyatt shuddered at the thought of the country under the control of power-hungry men and control of a weapon like Project Eagle.

He checked his watch. Ten minutes had passed. Five more and he was on his way in. He checked behind him, thinking he heard something. The neighborhood was quiet and the wind was low tonight. The sky was clear with a bright moon.

Checking his watch again, he noted the time. He still had three minutes. He couldn't wait any longer. He'd parked on a side street. When he opened the door, he heard a car. Quickly, he closed the door and ducked out of sight waiting for the car to pass. Then he left the small sports car and walked to the end of the cul-de-sac.

There was no answer at the door. Wyatt rang the bell three times. Then, with one foot, he kicked the door. It was heavy, very secure, and had been set with deep pieces of side wood to prevent unlawful entry. But Wyatt had both anger and fear for Sandra on his side. The second kick tore the door from its hinges, and Wyatt rushed in low and rolling.

When he stopped, he had the feeling of emptiness. The house was deserted. He knew that without checking, but he searched anyway. He stumbled over the broken egg that had shattered against the wall. He found the broken window, glass on the ground outside. Drops of blood slid down the jagged glass sticking out of the hard putty. Wyatt's heart lurched. Was she all right? Had Lance thrown her through that window? It couldn't have been long ago. The blood was still wet, still flowing. She must have fought with Lance Desque.

Wyatt was too late. Sandra and Lance were gone.

"Damn," Sandra cursed. The car turned, banging her head against the inside of the trunk. She'd never been claustrophobic, but being inside the darkened trunk disoriented her and made her feel as if the darkness had form and was closing in on her. The car smelled new. She wondered if it was rented or if Lance had purchased it recently. Why hadn't he taken her in the other car? She remembered the license tag. It had his name on it. Wherever he was going he didn't want anyone to identify him. That thought sent a tremor of fear through her.

Forcing herself to concentrate on something else, she closed her eyes and counted the number of turns the car made. At least when Lance finally stopped she'd have an inkling of which direction to run.

Escape! The word brightened in her brain. How could she get out of a locked trunk? Lance had pushed a button to open it. That meant it was electronic. There had to be an inside release, but where was it? She wasn't up on trunk locks these days. Espionage 101 was taking all her time.

The car turned again. This time it went left. That made two rights and a left. She opened her eyes, but the appearance of absolute blackness smacked her as clearly as if she'd been hit. A strange vertigo seemed to wave in front of her eyes. She snapped them closed. What kind of car was this? Not even the taillights reflected inside the trunk. She felt for the place where the lights should be. She came up against metal plates. There were screws holding them in place. It could be a normal arrangement, she'd never noticed the inside of her own car. The plates would prevent any packages placed in the trunk from bumping into the lights and breaking them.

How much time had elapsed since he'd driven out of the garage? she wondered. Had Wyatt passed them and not known she was screaming inside the back of just another car? She couldn't see her watch. She'd known what time it was when she went into Lance's house. She couldn't have been inside more than ten minutes or Wyatt would surely have made good on his promise.

Was he following them? She didn't think so. Lance wasn't driving as if he were being pursued. He was taking his time, following the rules of the road as he drove her to whatever destination. She wasn't going to be able to count on Wyatt. He had no idea where she was. Lance had killed Jeff. Very likely he'd killed Chip, too. Another murder wouldn't mean anything to him. She had to get out on her own.

She opened her eyes, surprised at the sliver of light that penetrated the moldings around the trunk lid. Biting her lip, she forced herself to think about the locking mechanism. With hands she couldn't see, she felt for the connector. She found it. A lot of good that did. She'd opened and closed a trunk thousands of times, but she'd never looked at the mechanism. As long as it worked, why should she concern herself with how it worked? She made a mental note to be more observant in the future, provided there was a future.

It was a simple matter of applied mathematics, she told herself. Knowing that would do nothing to help her. There had to be two interlocking pieces. Her hands found sharp edges and she identified the screws keeping it attached to the ceiling of the trunk. Although it was impossible to see, she closed her eyes and concentrated. Like a blind person, she used her sense of feel to try and *see* the lock.

Several moments and three more turns, one right, two lefts, she was no closer to working the lock. Her fingers caught on a small, flat piece of metal. She thought it might be the release an outside key would turn, but from inside the trunk she couldn't get a good enough grip on it to budge it. She needed a pair of pliers. Did Lance have any? Was there a toolbox in the trunk?

Using her hands, she carefully patted the flooring within her reach. Without the ability to see, her mind made every kind of monster only an inch from her questing hand. She found nothing. No toolbox, nothing at all, not even an umbrella for unexpected rainstorms. What about a crowbar? Every car has a crowbar. She must be lying on it. It would be under the rug and screwed in with the spare tire and jack. Did she have time to undo it? She didn't think she was going to get out before Lance stopped.

He could be taking her somewhere to kill her. When he opened the trunk, she'd have no chance at escape. The knowledge made her turn over and rush to find the tire iron. Her head cracked on the roof of the trunk in her efforts, and Lance's execution of two more turns threw her off balance. Finally, she had it in her hand. She felt around the tire for another piece of metal, anything. She hoped she'd find the wanted pliers. No luck.

Now, how was she going to strike him when he opened the trunk? Should she lay on her back and come out swinging or should she play dead and take him by surprise? He'd doubtless be ready for her to try something. She knew his strength and she knew she couldn't overcome it. She had to do something that Lance wouldn't expect. But what?

Another turn. This one sharper. She grasped for something to hold on to to keep from banging her head. Her fingernails scratched the metal lock, but her hand closed over empty air. When the car straightened, she raised her hand to touch her head. Her fingers hit a wire. She stopped. It was small and covered. Could this be the signal wire? What else? she asked herself. The taillights? That's what it was. But taillight wires were concealed. They ran under the rug and came up right at the light. She'd pulled the rug up. She'd exposed them.

What about the release wire? It would do the same thing. It would logically run from that button inside the car under the rug and come up directly at the lock. A glimmer of hope flared in her. She felt for the lock again. This time she went below the connectors. Her hands felt it. There was a piece of narrow metal. Her fingers felt the lip where it had been screwed to the inside of the trunk. At the top of it she found the wire.

Sweat broke out over her entire body. Her fingers were suddenly clumsy. She had no fingers. Only thumbs. She fought the wires, fought to hold on to them. She stopped moving, knowing she'd get nowhere in her excited state. Taking deep breaths, she tried to calm her suddenly thudding heart. Her fingers went numb as she let go. Sandra swallowed hard. For several moments she concentrated on relaxing, telling herself she would get out of this. She would find the wires again. *What will you do with them?* she asked herself. Does hot-wiring work for locks? It was her only chance. She'd find the wires again, pull them up and shave . . . how was she going to shave the insulation off? Her heart started again, loud and thundering.

Stop it! she told herself. *If you panic, you'll die.* Biting the inside of her lip, she found the wires a second time. She needed a knife. Something to cut the rubber covering. Gently, she pulled them, experimenting to find out how much play she had. They came forward about an inch. That wouldn't do. She needed more. The only weapon she had was the tire iron. It was too big and clumsy, and she couldn't see to cut the wires with it. Her fingernails were broken and torn and they were no match for the soft rubber.

"Ouch!" she cried as her teeth sank into the flesh of her inner lip. Teeth! She'd bite it. She had to move.

Lance turned again. Sandra had lost count of the number of turns. Her mind was totally involved in freeing herself from the locked cavern. She was too tall to lie straight and the trunk wasn't high enough to allow her to crouch on her knees. Using her fingers, she separated the two wires without pulling them free or dislodging them from their connection. Then, with her feet cramped against the car wall and her head wrenched back as far as her neck would allow, she bit the wire. Her tongue tasted the cold metal through which the wires were threaded. She refused to think about what might have been on that metal. The trunk was clean and the car smelled new. She concentrated on that.

Sandra worked at the rubber tubing. She didn't want to bite through the casing and into the copper wire. She worked at it until finally a small piece of plastic came away in her mouth. She spit it out. Feeling the tubing for raw metal, she felt only more tubing. Working diligently and trying not to think about when Lance would stop and open the trunk, she finally came away with a sliver of wire in her mouth.

"Thank God," she prayed.

Turning around, she started on the other wire. After an eon passed and her body was bathed in sweat, both wires were down to raw metal. She could only imagine the copper fibers that were rough to her fingers.

"Please, God," she pleaded. "Make this work."

With her eyes wide open, she stared at the place where her fingers should be. Slowly, she brought her hands together. The small spark was like a blinding explosion. Involuntarily she yanked the wires apart, ripping them from the unseen source. Bright lights hurled before her eyes like gold stars as they approached supernova. Then light! The light of the outside. She could see. The trunk was opening. The door was going up. Suddenly, she grabbed for it, pulling it back, then sticking her hand outside to prevent it from locking her in again.

Fresh air rushed in making her blessedly cold. She'd done it. *She'd done it!* Now she had to get away. She peeped through the slit. What road was this? She didn't recognize anything. Trees ran along both sides, their branches waving in the wake of the wind created by the speed of the car. They were moving fast. Too fast for her to jump out and run for it.

The best plan would be for her to get out, close the trunk, and run without Lance knowing she was missing. If she raised the trunk he'd see it in his mirror. If she jumped at this speed she'd be sure to break her ankle or her neck. Either way, Lance would catch her with only a minimum of effort.

Sandra didn't have a choice. She had to wait for Lance to slow the car down before she tried to get away. She wished she could see through the front windows. Then she could get some warning that a stop sign or a stop light was coming up. Raising the trunk enough to see would mean he'd notice its unlocked condition.

Enough light reflected off her watch for her to tell the time. Forty minutes had passed since she'd left Wyatt in the comfort of the Jaguar and walked up Lance's drive. If she'd spent ten minutes in the house, they'd been driving for thirty minutes. Lance lived in Chevy Chase. Thirty minutes was enough time to get into DC if he'd gone that way. Sandra knew he hadn't. There weren't any streets in DC that looked like this, which meant he'd gone further into Maryland.

Alarm bells went off in her head. He was taking her to some remote location and no one would ever hear from her again. Sandra's heart fluttered, then lodged in her throat. Her hand got so weak she nearly let go of the trunk. Could Lance really do that to her? In cold blood? Could he kill her and go on without the slightest bit of conscience?

She remembered him when she'd been a child. He'd come skiing with her family. He'd been influential in her father's bid for the state legislature and had supported him through all his campaigns. Would he stand at her gravesite and mourn with her parents and Annie? Would Annie even come?

The car slowed. Sandra snapped her thoughts back to survival. She wasn't ready to die. She grabbed the crowbar and prepared for her final fight. Sweat broke out again. She had to decide. Whatever he was going to do, he would do it soon. Was she ready? Her shoes would be useless. Why wasn't she wearing sneakers, something she could sprint in? With these she'd be lucky if the heels didn't sink into the soft earth and pitch her into the ground face first.

The car stopped totally. Sandra gripped the tire iron tighter. She would throw the trunk up and swing the minute she felt he was near enough to it. She waited. Nothing happened. She expected to hear Lance's door open and close, but it didn't. Then she heard it, the low whistle of a train. They must be at a crossing, one of those places where the black-and-white arms came down and blocked the road until the train passes.

Sandra knew this was her chance, possibly her only chance. Her timing had to be perfect.

The sound of the train grew. She heard the whistle again and the slow, labored clanging of the engine. Louder. Louder. Until it was upon them. Now, she thought. Raising the roof a mere foot, only enough to accommodate her thin width, she rolled out of the trunk. Hitting the ground, she quickly reversed and grabbed the lid as it started an upward swing. She pulled it down until she heard the click that locked it.

She nearly smiled. It was the kind of trunk that needed only a slight push. Then it electronically lowered itself until the line of the lid was congruous with that of the car. Exhaust went up her nose and made her want to cough and sneeze. She held the urge in.

The train passed. Seconds later, some unseen computerized switch sent a signal and the gate started its rise. Again, she needed to time her movement. Flattening herself to the ground, she waited for Lance to start forward. A small incline lay in front of the car. It would take it up over the tracks and down again. When it started up she'd be at the most vulnerable, but Lance wouldn't be expecting her to be lying in the road. If he hadn't seen the movement of the trunk when she rolled out of it she was sure he thought she was still securely locked inside.

She had to wait for the car to start down the small depression in the road. It was too slight an angle to be called a hill or even an incline. It was just the point where the ground was leveled to meet the tracks, but for Sandra it was her point of escape. The angle of the mirrors would be too far back and too high for him to see her. She'd roll into the bush and wait until he was gone.

The car moved. It went up. Sandra held her breath as dust and exhaust blew into her eyes and nose.

It moved down.

She rolled.

Wyatt had known going to Desque's wasn't a good idea, but he'd given in to Sandra's pleas and driven her there. Now he could kick himself. The scene at Desque's house looked like she'd struggled with him. The broken window glass and blood made him cold. Was it her blood? Was she all right? Where had he taken her?

He drummed his fists against the steering wheel. He'd searched Lance Desque's house looking for something that would give him a clue where he would take Sandra. He found nothing. With the exception that Desque was extremely fond of Oriental artifacts, he found nothing that could help him.

He rifled through drawers, closets, even his mail, but there was nothing that could help. Frustrated, Wyatt had returned to the rented car. He was inside before he realized he was holding one of Lance's letters. It was an invitation from the embassy of Japan. He'd seen one like it at Sandra's sister's hotel room. Staring at it as if it could answer him, he finally threw it aside and forgot it.

He'd driven around trying to find a direction that Lance might have taken. The phone rang and he snatched it up.

"Sandra!" he shouted, but it wasn't her. It was Sam Parker asking him to meet him downtown.

Wyatt didn't want to leave, but there was nothing he could do holding vigil outside Lance Desque's except bring attention to himself and have a jumpy neighbor call the police.

Sam got into the car as Wyatt sat on Pennsylvania Avenue across from the J. Edgar Hoover building. Wyatt had thought it ironic that Sam had asked to meet him in the shadow of the FBI. With probably a hundred agents looking for them, no one was checking the front window.

"I've got good news," Sam said. "I managed to completely defuse the bomb chip."

Wyatt nodded.

"You could sound a little enthusiastic," Sam said. "For a while there I thought my friend Wagner would return from Europe to find his house gone and I wouldn't be around to explain what had happened."

Wyatt told him what he thought had happened to Sandra and that he had no clue to where Lance could have taken her.

Sam picked up the invitation from the floor of the Jaguar. He glanced at the emblem, then at Wyatt.

"I found that at Desque's. I didn't even realize I was still holding it until I got into the car."

"Desque has been very friendly with the Japanese for years," he volunteered.

"I believe that. You should see where he lives. The place is packed with Oriental furnishings."

"What are we going to do now?" Sam asked. "We can go on with the plan—"

Wyatt knew he'd planned to say "without Sandra," but stopped himself in time. "I suppose we'd better do what we have to do." Wyatt spoke but there was little conviction in his voice.

Without Sandra. He didn't want to be without her. He wanted to know where she was. He didn't want to feel as if the worst had happened to her, but seeping into his bones was a weary feeling that there was nothing he could do for her. Even if he went to the President and turned over the stones, he'd still be without Sandra.

He sat up and reached for the key. He started the engine, then glanced sideways. Suddenly, he stopped, his hand frozen on the gearshift.

"What?" Sam asked.

Wyatt stared straight ahead. He blinked, not believing his eyes. Sam looked in the same direction, but couldn't possibly see what Wyatt saw.

Standing across the street, in the shadow of the monolithic building that stood for law and government in the United States was its director, Clarence Christopher. But he wasn't the man Wyatt stared at. It was the other man. The one smiling as if talking to a friend. The one shaking hands with the director.

"Now what could those two possibly have in common?"

"Who?" Sam asked, but Wyatt wasn't talking to him. He no longer even knew Sam was in the car.

The tall, lanky man who acted as his friend, who'd lent him clothes and shoes. "What is Jordon Ames doing with the director of the FBI?"

Sandra took a deep breath. She placed her hand over her heart and waited for it to calm. The lights of the car had disappeared. She was free. Lance would be furious when he discovered she'd escaped. He'd come looking for her, and the most logical place would be right here, where the car had come to a full and complete stop.

She came to a crouch, spitting leaves and twigs that had gathered when she rolled into the ditch. Brushing her clothes off, she got up. She couldn't walk along the road the way she had come. Lance would find her in no time.

Into the woods. The trees along both sides looked dark and ominous. The last turn Lance had made was a left. She ran to the right side of the road and disappeared into the woods. She walked not knowing where she was or where she was going. She looked at her watch. An hour. How far could he drive in an hour? Even if the speed limit wasn't at the maximum she could be thirty, forty miles from town. Walking through the woods it would be even farther.

She tried to run, but her shoes prevented it. If she twisted her ankle she'd kill herself. Every B movie she'd ever seen where the woman hampered her own escape attempt by falling and twisting an ankle came into her mind. She vowed never to put on another pair of heels as long as she lived. Trudging on, she walked, hoping she'd find a road, a sign, a phone, something to give her a hint of where she was.

Sandra would never have told any of her students to run around a dark forest without knowing which direction they were traveling, but that's exactly what she was doing. The thickness of the trees and bush made it almost as dark as the inside of the trunk. Branches slapped her in the face and caught at her hair. The sky was almost obliterated. If this were June instead of January she wouldn't be able to see any of the light or stars that could help with her direction. She pushed on trying to find some point of reference. The only thing she knew for sure was she was walking on a diagonal when she started out. If she stayed on a straight line she should come out on the road where Lance had turned left.

Wyatt! What must he think had happened to her? She pushed faster. She needed a phone more than anything. She had to call him, tell him she was alive, that she'd escaped and she needed help.

Sandra kept going. The next time she looked at her watch she'd been walking over an hour. Her feet hurt and were frozen. Her hands were cold and her legs were tired. Her whole body ached from being crammed in the trunk and then trying to walk through a forest. She refused to admit she was lost. Lost was a state of not knowing where you were and how to get back. She didn't know where she was, but she knew if she kept walking, she'd eventually come to the road. And the road would lead to people.

Another hour passed and she was still in the woods. She stopped. Gazing around, everything looked the same. She could have been walking around in circles. She wanted to cry but refused. The tears would only make her face colder. And they wouldn't help her.

She was lost.

CHAPTER 21

Lance was nearly there. He didn't have to improvise often. Usually he had every detail planned and he executed them in order. Then he'd come up against Senator Randolph and Sandra. When she walked into his house tonight he knew he'd never let her leave it. She was too much of an asset. With her he could get to the senator and ultimately to the stones. He needed them before the reception tomorrow night.

He'd stash Sandra at the house. He would have taken her to the embassy, but he wanted her away from the system. She was smart and if she got loose she could cause untold problems. Thank God he owned this place. She'd be safe here and she'd be so far away from anyone that it wouldn't be necessary to lock the doors to keep her in.

He wondered where she and Randolph had hidden the stones. By now they knew about the fifteenth stone, but there was still number five, his favorite number. Stone number fifteen had been put there as an obvious bomb. It was large enough and complex enough to give an expert serious duty in defusing it. But it was a camouflage to cover stone number five. That's where the real bomb sat. Between contact points eight and ten on the chip. As soon as the system was activated and the stones came within striking distance, he could either get them or destroy them.

Sandra didn't have the stones with her. He'd searched her as he held her against him after she leaped through his living-room window. That took guts. He wished he had time to convert her to his way of thinking. She'd aligned herself to Wyatt Randolph, and with him there was no hope of conversion.

She might not have the stones with her, but she knew where they were. Or the senator knew. He'd make sure word got to both senators, Rutledge and Randolph, that ransom for her was the stones. She was in love with Wyatt Randolph, and Lance assumed the feeling was mutual. The two of them had been inseparable since he'd gone up to that mountain. Why couldn't he have died in that alley? Then Horton would already be packing his bags and vacating the White House.

Lance thought he was lucky. He'd dropped by Senator Rutledge's office the morning Randolph had called and mentioned Project Eagle. Waring had taken the message and left the pink message slip on the edge of his desk. Lance knew then. Randolph knew nothing about what he had. Lance intended to keep it that way, but things had gone wrong. The senator had gotten away and he'd had to devise other methods of trying to find him and retrieve the system components.

Lance only had one more day. By this time tomorrow it would all be over. Horton would be disgraced, Rutledge would have no explanation for anything, Jackson and Taylor were already dead, Parker was too scared to come out of hiding, and he had Sandra in his grips. The only wild card was Randolph, but Lance had his bed partner. Sex! It had been the downfall of more than one man. Too bad Randolph had never learned that.

"Mr. Desque, we were not expecting you tonight." Henri Patterson, his caretaker, friend, butler, and confidant opened the door as Lance pulled up to the house and stopped the car.

"Something's come up." Lance yanked at his tie as he brushed past the man. Henri wasn't his real name, but Lance had ceased thinking of him as anyone else. He was a short man, with a square build and muscles as solid as rock. Lance liked that about him. Henri had been in trouble, accused of killing a man with his bare hands, during a student protest over the Vietnam War. Henri had been a soldier. He'd come home during the height of the antiwar movement. When people called him murderer and spit at him he retaliated like any good soldier. The government had taught Henri to kill, and he liked killing.

Lance had helped him get away from the law, helped him change his name and face and given him a job. In return, the man gave him his loyalty and occasionally did an odd job or two.

"Henri, there's a package in the trunk. I need it kept safe until after the reception tomorrow night. When I get what I want, we'll need to dispose of it."

"I understand, sir."

Henri knew exactly what he meant. He'd taken care of Jeff Taylor, only he hadn't gotten any information before he killed the bastard. That had been one of the few mistakes he'd ever made. Lance had been angry, but he'd calmed quickly. He had other ways of finding out what he needed to know, and one of them was in the trunk.

"Would you like me to retrieve the package, sir?"

"Yes. I'm going to have a drink, then a shower. I'll have dinner here, but I'll be driving back to Chevy Chase tonight."

"Yes, sir."

As Henri turned to go, Lance headed for the stairs. He'd only gone two rungs before thinking he should tell Henri to be prepared for a surprise when he opened the trunk.

Henri was thorough, but Sandra Rutledge was a little spitfire. She would surely come out swinging. Turning around, he ran down the two steps and headed for the door.

"Henri!" he called, stopping the butler just as he inserted the key in the lock. "Be careful. She'll fight you all the way."

"Yes, sir," Henri smiled. It was more a leer than a grin. He turned the key. The lock gave with a click and he opened the trunk. Looking up at Lance, he said, "It's empty."

Lance couldn't believe his ears. He rushed to where the butler stood, shoving him away. He reached inside, pushing aside the disheveled rug, tire iron, and jack. His breath came in ragged gasps. He breathed hard in the clean air. His heart knocked against his rib cage and instantly gave him a headache. Henri had to be wrong. His eyes had to be wrong. She couldn't have escaped. It was impossible. Then he saw the wires; a red one and a black one. They had almost sunk into the recesses of the metal bracket that led them into the trunk lock. His shoulders dropped in defeat.

The urge to order Henri to get the other car and begin a search was strong, but impractical. This part of the Maryland countryside was wooded and undeveloped. Finding her would be pure luck in the daytime. In the dark, it would be a wasted effort.

Lance calmed himself. He still had the upper hand. His heartbeat returned to normal. Losing her was a small setback, but he wasn't beat. He still had a trump card. And this one only he knew about.

"Have you seen her?" Wyatt was at a near shout when Suzanne Rutledge opened the door.

"Don't tell me she's lost." Sandra's sister was in a bad mood. Wyatt had never seen her in any other kind of mood. Tonight he didn't care. His own mood was bad and getting worse by the minute.

"Has she called?"

"No," Suzanne said.

Wyatt came inside and Suzanne closed the door. Sam was waiting downstairs in the garage. Wyatt didn't want to have the stones on him in case Jordon was there.

Jordon *was* there. Both he and Suzanne were dressed, as if they were going out or had just come in. Wyatt couldn't decide which one.

"You," he sneered at Jordon. "Have you done something to get her kidnapped?"

"What are you talking about?" Suzanne asked.

"I saw you tonight."

Wyatt was angry. He paced the room like a big cat who wanted to get out of a cage. He felt like an animal. Sandra was missing, had been missing since she went into Lance Desque's house, and he had no inkling where to look for her.

"Sit down, Wyatt," Jordon offered. "I'll get you a drink." He was playing host again. Wyatt didn't trust him. There was something he was hiding, and Wyatt wanted to know if it had to do with Sandra.

"I don't want a drink and I don't want to sit down. I want to know what you and Clarence Christopher have to talk about?"

"Who's Clarence Christopher?" Suzanne asked.

Jordon stared at her. He didn't say a word. He poured a drink and took a long swallow. The stillness in the room could be touched, cut.

"Claren—"

"Clarence Christopher is the director of the FBI," Jordon interrupted the senator.

"You know the director of the FBI?" Suzanne asked incredulously.

"We're old friends."

"Old enough for you to report that Sandra had been here; that I had been here and that you knew where we were, that we had the stones and—"

"Stop." He put his hands up. "My business with the FBI has nothing to do with you."

"You don't expect me to believe that?" Wyatt accused. "Sandra is missing."

"Well, I had nothing to do with it," Jordon shouted.

"Then what were you doing with him?" Wyatt returned the shout.

"I had . . . other business." He lowered his voice, taking another drink.

"Jordon," Suzanne called. "Did you turn her in?"

He shook his head. "Annie, I could never hurt anyone you loved."

"Then what were you doing there?"

"Can I talk to her alone?" He stared at Wyatt.

"No," Wyatt said. "Not until you tell me what you told the FBI."

"Go on, Jordon," Suzanne said. "Whatever you have to say, I'm sure he can hear it."

Jordon shrugged and poured brandy into a small snifter. He recognized Suzanne's mood. She was scared. With both drinks in his hands, he walked around the bar and handed Suzanne one of the glasses. "Sit down?" he asked, the word "please" implied in his tone.

Suzanne took a seat on the sofa and Wyatt leaned against the windowsill.

"You told me Senator Rutledge was your biological father."

Suzanne recoiled. "You didn't tell that to the FBI?"

"Only in the strictest confidence. Clarence Christopher can be trusted."

"The FBI? You think the FBI can be trusted? Jordon, I told you that in a moment of weakness. I never gave you permission to tell anyone else. You should have asked me before repeating it."

"Let me finish," Jordon said.

She flashed him a hostile look but remained quiet.

"I love you, Annie. I've always loved you. This week I got the impression that you might love me, too." He glanced up at her, then back at the glass he held in his hand. "I know you remember the days when you were poor. You think sooner or later someone is going to pull the rug from under your world and plunge you back into that life of poverty. You have so much hate bottled up inside you, Suzanne, I wanted to relieve it. You can't live with that kind of hate and you can't love freely with it."

"Jordon, it's not your business."

"You're right, technically, but I'm in love with you and that makes it my business." He stared directly at her. Wyatt felt as if he were intruding on a confession. "I want to marry you, but I want you whole, not the half person who dissolves into tears whenever you see or hear from your parents."

Both of them went quiet. Wyatt didn't know if he was hearing a true confession or if Jordon had just concocted this story and was making it up as he went along.

"Go on," he prompted.

Jordon glared at him, but continued. "I asked Clarence Christopher to find out your true parentage."

"I told you my true parentage."

"I know," he said. "I wanted all the details. I wanted to give you the real facts of your life before he adopted you. If I found out exactly what you'd told me, I'd keep the knowledge to myself."

"And if you didn't?"

"I'd decide then what I should do."

"Well, Jordon?" Suzanne lifted her head. If Wyatt hadn't been watching he wouldn't have believed the transformation in her. She went from insecure weakling to a stately queen before his eyes. "What did you find?"

Jordon put his glass on the table and stood up. He went to a case sitting by the door. Opening it, Wyatt saw cameras and lenses, each stored in a compartment. Jordon pulled the foam backing from the top and extracted a manila folder. He brought it back and handed it to Suzanne.

She took it. "Before you open it," Jordon cautioned, "prepare yourself. Bradford Rutledge is not your biological father."

Wyatt was impatient. He needed to know what had happened to

Sandra. He wasn't here to learn whether Brad Rutledge had adopted his own daughter. He didn't even know if it was true and didn't care. He only cared about finding Sandra.

Suzanne opened the folder. Inside were three sheets of paper. They were typewritten, double spaced, and included three photographs. One was of her mother. She was smiling, sitting on an old tire swing that hung in the backyard. Suzanne smiled at the memory of that long ago day. She was in the second photo. Her hair was in braids, three long ones that draped over the side of her face and down her back. She wore her church dress, her only dress. Her mother had made it. Back then all her clothes were handmade. If she bought a handmade dress today it would cost thousands of dollars! She remembered the red dress she'd loved so much. The last picture was that of a man she'd never . . . no, not never, she'd seen him once, twice.

She could almost remember the sound. It was an organ grinder with a monkey. He'd come that day. Suzanne closed her eyes, trying to remember, trying to place herself back in time, into the memory of this man. Yes, she thought. He'd come. He wore a light-colored hat with a brown band. His suit had been pressed and his shoes shined like sunlight on water. Her mother had been happy to see him. He'd taken them out . . . to the circus. That was it. She remembered. She was only seven years old. She'd never seen a circus.

She sat between them. He talked to her, telling her everything about the rings she could see below. He bought her cotton candy and popcorn. Each time she looked at him, his mouth smiled but his eyes had hurt in them. She wondered how a person could do two things at one time.

It couldn't be her mother making him sad. He held her hand and put his arm around her waist when they walked. With his other hand he held on to her. Then he was gone . . . until the train.

She frowned. Where was the train? There were no trains where they lived. But she could see him. He was at the window. She had to look up a long way to see him. He was old. He waved his big hat. It was black with a white band. He waved it and waved it until all she could see was the waving of the hat. The train disappeared but the waving hat hung in her memory.

"Who is he?" Suzanne opened her eyes. Jordon blurred before her and she realized she had tears in her eyes. She blinked them away.

"His name is Curtis Pittman."

The name meant nothing to Suzanne, but it made Wyatt Randolph stand up straight. She stared at him, then back to Jordon.

"He was a young lawyer in Atlanta. He had a wife and four children and was making a meteoric rise in politics. He'd been elected to the state legislature with little opposition. People thought he was headed all the way to the White House. Then at thirty he suffered a heart attack while campaigning. Two years later, he was found dead on a train heading to Atlanta."

"A train?" Suzanne choked. Had that been her memory of him? The big black hat; the old man.

Suzanne sank back against the cushions. "If this man was my father," she stared at the picture, "why does my birth certificate have my da—someone else's name on it?"

"Your father and Brad Rutledge were best friends," Jordon answered. "Likewise, your father was a friend of your mother's. He introduced your parents and frequently visited her after Pittman left. He was unmarried and not interested in politics at the time. She couldn't put your real father's name on your birth certificate for fear his wife or his political enemies would discover it. So she used his friend's name."

Suzanne and Wyatt stared at Jordon.

"How do you know this?"

"Curtis Pittman left a diary. He has a sister, Janey Goodman, still living in Atlanta. She told the agent the story."

Wyatt left his place by the window and came toward them.

"You have this diary?" he asked.

"Curtis Pittman's sister has it. She's willing to give it to you. In fact, the agent says she wants to see you."

"What does it say about me?"

"It mentions you by name; says that you were his child but because of his political career and family he couldn't acknowledge you. He tells about your mother, using Bradford Rutledge's name as the father instead of his."

Tears gathered in Suzanne's eyes, but she fought them. She'd been sorely wrong and her father had never said anything. He'd protected his friend's memory because of her and her volatile nature. He probably thought she'd accost the Pittmans, demanding to be recognized. She thought about her anger and realized he might have been right.

"Janey Goodman told the agent that your father was furious when he found out, years later, what your mother had done. You must have been four then," Jordon went on. "There was nothing that could be done about it. If he had the records changed it would surely be picked up by some reporter or news service and two men's careers would be at stake. The best course of action was to let it lay."

"Then when my real father died and I was adopted, all records of my birth were sealed," Suzanne concluded. "Then there was no way Brad Rutledge's political opponents could find out that on paper he had an illegitimate daughter."

Jordon left his seat to come and sit next to her. He put his arm around her shoulder and pulled her close. "According to the report, that is not the way things happened, Annie."

She shook her head and laid it against him.

"I feel so guilty," she said.

"When you've had time to let all this sink in, I think you should visit Mrs. Goodman. She's your aunt. She can tell you everything you want to know."

Suzanne thought of the man who had given her a home and loved her as a daughter. "He was a wonderful father," she said aloud. "Both of them were wonderful parents." Suzanne remembered the terrible things she'd said to them, how badly she'd treated Sandra. How Sandra kept coming back, refusing to give up even when Suzanne told her she hated her. God, she was a fool. Where was Sandra? Where was her father? She had to talk to him, tell him how wrong she had been.

Wyatt felt like a fifth wheel. He was also a little guilt-ridden. He'd been so wrapped up in his own problems he'd forgotten there were other people with their own difficulties. He was glad Suzanne had found what she needed. He knew her superior attitude was only a defense, but he'd seen her do things for her sister that even she didn't understand. They were mired in the love they had for each other, steeped in the common background they shared.

He only hoped Sandra was all right and that the two sisters would have the opportunity to reconcile. Wyatt didn't want to interrupt the moment between the two people on the sofa. Clearly they were no longer aware of his presence. He'd found out what he needed to know.

"Wyatt?" Suzanne called his name as he headed for the door. "Do you know where she is?"

"No." He shook his head. "She went into Lance Desque's house last night. Fifteen minutes later I broke the door down. No one was there. I've been searching for her all night."

Suzanne got up and went to him. "She's all right, Wyatt. I know it."

"I hope so," Wyatt said without conviction.

Suzanne reached up and took his face in her hands. Gently, she kissed him on the cheek. "You'll find her."

He hoped so. He knew how much he loved her. His heart was heavy in his chest, and each time he thought of her he remembered something she'd said or done. He remembered her hair coming loose when she pulled it out of the ponytail and combed her fingers through it, the funny way she laughed, the way her eyes looked when she smiled, even the serious way she bit her lip and the skin around her finger.

She'd been the best thing that had ever happened to him and he needed her back. Anger flared at Lance Desque. If anything happened to her he'd pay for it.

A knock at the door had the three of them turning toward it.

"It's probably Sam Parker. I left him in the car downstairs," Wyatt explained.

Crossing to the suite door, he checked the peephole. On a single breath his lungs were drained. His heart burst against his chest. He grabbed the knob with strength enough to pulverize metal. Yanking it open, he saw her.

"Sandra!" he cried.

For three seconds no one moved. Then Suzanne and Jordon rushed to the door.

"Wyatt," she moaned, weaving back and forth like a drunk.

She was cold and wet. Her feet were bare, bleeding, and nearly blue with cold. There were scratches and dried blood on her face, her clothes were torn, and her hair looked as if it had barbed-wire knots in it.

Wyatt didn't think she could walk. Taking a step through the door, he scooped her up and carried her inside.

"The bedroom," Suzanne pointed as she went toward it and opened the door. Suzanne rushed forward and pulled the cover down. Wyatt deposited her on the sheet as if she were a precious heirloom. To him she was. She was the woman he wanted to marry, the one who gave him reason to live and breath to fight for his beliefs.

He held her to him, smoothing her hair back and whispering her name. Suzanne called to him, but he ignored her. He needed to be near Sandra, needed to know that she was real and that she was all right. He never wanted to let her go.

"Wyatt, she needs help. Let me get to her."

Wyatt shook his head. He kissed Sandra's cheek.

"Call a doctor," Suzanne said behind him.

"No!" Sandra cried for the first time. Wyatt loosened his grip. "I'm all right."

"You're not all right," Suzanne contradicted. "Look at your face . . . and your *feet.*" Blood stained the white sheets. Sandra eased them under the cover.

"Please," she pleaded. "No doctor."

"There's a first aid kit in the bathroom," Jordon said. "I'll get it."

He came back with a bowl of water and the kit.

"Wyatt, move." This time it was an order. "We've got to get her cleaned up enough to see what she needs."

Annie paid no attention to her evening clothes. She administered to her sister as if she'd been practicing nursing for years. When she finished, Sandra had one bandage on her forehead. The bruises on her face stood out like dark-purple smudges. Her feet were the worst. The skin on her soles had been rubbed off in spots deep enough to bleed. Her heels had cuts on them and her ankles were bruised and swollen.

Jordon managed to get Wyatt out of the room long enough for Suzanne to help her bathe and get into a nightgown.

"Here, take this." She handed her a glass of water and a single white pill.

"What is it?"

"A pain pill. You probably hurt in all kinds of places." Sandra swallowed the pill. "It will also help you sleep." Suzanne pulled the covers up to her sister's chin.

Wyatt knocked on the door and returned. Concern and love vied for dominance in his eyes.

"She'll survive," Suzanne announced. "A few days in bed and she'll be as good as new."

"I don't have time for that," Sandra said. "We have to activate Project Eagle before tomorrow night."

Sandra reached for Wyatt. He took her hands and sat down on the bed. Sandra yawned. "Wyatt, I don't know where he was taking me." She told him about her attempted escape through the living-room window and Lance forcing her in the trunk. He smiled at her ingenious method of getting out. "I climbed a big tree to find out if I could see any lights in the distance. That's the way I walked. When I got to a road, I tried to hitch a ride, but no one picked me up. I can't blame them; look at how I looked." Gingerly, she touched the bandage on her forehead. Her head ached, but it was beginning to feel better. Her eyes were getting heavy, though. She yawned again and closed her eyes.

"Sandra."

She opened her eyes and looked at Wyatt.

"What happened then?"

"Oh," she said, a giddy laugh escaping. "I got a ride on a panel truck."

"Someone picked you up?"

"No-o-o," she yawned.

"No?"

"I saw it coming and I hid in the bush." Another yawn.

"Saw what?"

"The truck. When he started to move, I jumped on the back and held on."

"Sandra, you could have fallen off and been killed."

"I did fall," she yawned again and turned on her side. "I . . . didn't . . . get . . . kill . . ." She was asleep.

Wyatt adjusted the covers. He could watch her all night. He was so glad to see she was all right. He knew what had been on Lance Desque's mind. He'd ransom Sandra for the stones. Wyatt sighed. He'd have had no choice but to give him what he wanted to get her returned. He'd have paid any price to do that. He wanted to wake her and have her explain the importance of tomorrow night. Obviously, Lance had said something to make her aware that time had come to a head. Wyatt couldn't say he wasn't relieved. One way or another it would be over tomorrow night.

"Mr. President—"

Everett raised his hand and stopped the senator from further explanation. "Brad," he said. "Let's stop this dance. I'm too tired to keep it up."

The Japanese ambassador had led him around for the better part of the last week. Tomorrow he'd probably do the same thing and then stand in front of a reception of honored guests and act as if everything was going well. Everett was too weary from his day with the prime minister to engage in a tug-of-war with the senator over the state of Project Eagle.

"I need to know the status of Project Eagle and I need to know now. The truth is your daughter and Senator Randolph have the parts and—" He stopped. He was being unfair to the senator. He came around the desk and joined Brad on the sofa. "Brad, I apologize. I think I'm getting too old for this job."

Everett slipped his feet from his shoes, something he only did when he was comfortable. "My life is falling apart and I'm taking it out on everyone else." Word of those parts had been kept secret for longer than he thought it could in a city where careers lived and died on secrets and nothing was secret. He knew he was over the limit for keeping his career intact. If he didn't nail down the location of the parts and get them into his own hands, the lid would blow up in his face.

Brad pushed himself back in his chair. "I haven't seen my daughter in days. When I did see her she did not have the stones. I can only assume that Randolph has them. If he does, getting them is going to be a problem."

"What about Parker?"

"He's a technician. I doubt he has enough desire to engineer an action as sophisticated as this. If he had them, he'd turn them over for the asking."

"Then we had better hope it's Parker we'll be dealing with."

"We can hope it, sir," Brad told the President. "But be prepared to go head to head with Wyatt Randolph."

CHAPTER 22

Sandra awoke with a groan. She hadn't dreamed anything she could remember, but her head felt heavy; too heavy to raise. She hadn't felt this bad since her eighteenth birthday when she'd celebrated by trying to drink as many beers as Annie and her boyfriend, Mark. This was worse. Not only did her head pound like it was full of tiny men with jackhammers, but every bone and muscle in her body screamed for attention.

The light hurt when she opened her eyes. She blinked, letting them adjust to the sunlight. She was used to awakening in strange rooms. She remembered this one. She was in Annie's suite, in the guest room. Wyatt lay next to her. He cradled her in his arms. She couldn't stop the smile that hurt her mouth.

She'd seen the look on his face when he saw her last night. She must have looked a sight. She wondered what she looked like this morning. Was it morning? What time was it? How long had she slept? Suddenly, she had the feeling that she'd slept through it. That she hadn't had time to tell Wyatt what Lance planned to do, that she'd slept right through the day and this was another morning. Panic made her breathe hard. She tried to push herself up on her elbows. The action made her cry out. Her elbows felt as if she had burns on them. Then she remembered falling off the truck. Her left elbow had taken the brunt of the fall. Her sweater had caused brush burns to bleed through the fabric. She couldn't see them but she was sure they were bruised and scarred with the remnants of her own blood.

Wyatt was instantly awake. "Are you all right?" he asked, pushing himself up and looking at her.

"I'm fine," she lied. There was so much concern in his eyes she didn't want to destroy it by telling him the truth.

"You're not," he told her. She should have known he could see through her and read the truth.

"You're right. I feel like I fell off a truck."

"You said that last night. I thought it was the pill Suzanne gave you."

She combed through her hair with her right hand. "That's why I feel so groggy. She told me it was a pain pill."

"You needed the sleep."

"Wyatt, I have to tell you about Lance." Her eyes were heavy and her head felt as if it were surrounded with cotton wool. She rolled onto her side and threw her legs over the edge of the bed. Her muscles shouted their displeasure at her movement. She ignored them. She had to wake up. There was little time. She looked at her arm, but her watch was gone.

"What time is it?"

"Ten o'clock." Wyatt got out of bed and slipped into his jeans. His chest remained bare as he came around to sit next to her. He held her close and pushed her head to his shoulder.

She let herself be pampered for a moment. Sandra liked being next to him. She wanted nothing more than to stay where she was and let the world go away. She couldn't. She knew it was temporary. They had to get to the Pentagon and find out where the other system had been taken. Only a few hours remained. She didn't know how many. Lance had thrown the information at her, sure she would be unable to do anything to stop him. She wasn't sure they had time, but they had to try.

"What about Desque?" he asked. His voice was low but she heard the underlying hate in it.

"He's going to—" A knock on the door interrupted her. At Wyatt's call the door opened. Annie rushed into the room. For the first time in years she wasn't perfectly groomed. Taking one look at Sandra, she rushed toward her.

"Are you all right, Sand?"

"Sand?" Annie hadn't called her that in years. The last time had been when they were still friends, still sisters. Could her accident last night have made Annie forget that she'd told her never to return? Sandra stared at her. She was clearly nervous. The cup and saucer she held visibly shook and she'd sloshed coffee over the rim of the cup. Wyatt stood up and took it from her. Sandra stood, too. She winced. Her feet hurt, but she remained standing. She didn't want Annie or Wyatt to know how much effort the small act took. She reached for the cup and took a drink of the coffee. It was the most wonderful drink she'd ever had. Taking another gulp, she replaced the cup.

Annie picked up the robe that matched the nightgown Sandra wore and helped her into it. "Breakfast is waiting. You must be hungry."

She was. She couldn't remember the last time she'd eaten, but she wanted to talk to Annie first.

"Annie," Sandra said as she turned back to her sister. "How are you involved in all this? The stones? Grant Richards? You seem to know a lot you haven't told me."

Annie didn't immediately answer. "I don't really know a lot. I suppose it was just a matter of being in the wrong place at the wrong time. I'd just completed an assignment in Japan and was on my way back to the US when I overheard a conversation in an airport that seemed to have something to do with national security. The two men were Americans but they spoke in Japanese. At first I thought I was reading more into it than was actually there. Then I was frightened. Suppose what I heard was true?" She stopped and looked from Sandra to Wyatt. "When the men left, one of them dropped a small scrap of paper on the floor. I picked it up and slipped it into my purse. I got on the plane and when I got here I went to see Dad and told him what I'd heard. The next morning the FBI came to see me and I was brought here to repeat my story. I met Grant Richards there."

"What was written on the paper?" Wyatt asked.

"Eagle's span," she said. "The paper was a map of the world. The words were written over all of it."

"What happened?" Sandra asked.

"The FBI asked me a lot of questions. I was there for hours. When it was over they flew me back to New York, thanked me, and I never heard from them again."

"Didn't they tell you what Eagle's span meant?" Sandra asked.

"They didn't have to. There was a folder on the desk. It had Top Secret written on the outside. They didn't know how well I could read upside down. I read what was on the pages and I knew all about Project Eagle even before you and the senator here got mixed up in it."

"Why didn't you say something?"

"At the time I didn't want to."

Sandra knew why. Annie wanted nothing to do with her. She knew if she mentioned it, Sandra would begin asking questions. Sandra wondered why she'd changed her mind.

"Come on, our breakfast is getting cold."

Jordon Ames was already seated when Wyatt and Annie helped her limp to the table. Sam Parker sat at the desk, a laptop computer open in front of him. The desk was cluttered with papers. He looked as if he'd been at work a long time.

Annie lifted the silver cover off the hot dish in front of Sandra as if she were a waitress. Sam left his work and took a seat near Jordon.

"Sand, there is so much I have to tell you." She sat down, excitement showing in her body. "Jordon, Wyatt . . ." She glanced from one to the other. Sandra looked at them for the secret they were obviously sharing.

"They know about Lance?" Sandra asked.

"It's not about Lance. It's about Dad."

Sandra knew about Dad. She knew he was working with Lance. "I already know about Dad," she told her sister. "He and Lance are activating the system tonight."

"What!" Sam spoke. He pushed his plate away and sat forward in his chair. "Are you sure?"

"Lance told me."

"When, where?" Wyatt asked. "We've got to stop him."

Sandra felt inadequate. "I don't know where. He said that this time tomorrow everything would be over. That was last night. Which means he's planning to do it before the night is over."

"We've got to find and stop him." Wyatt directed his comment at Sam.

"That's not going to be hard," Annie said.

Everyone turned to stare at her. "Why not?" Sandra asked.

"Tonight is the reception at the Japanese Embassy. Lance is very friendly with the prime minister. He wouldn't miss it." No one disputed Annie's information. "It's in today's paper." Sam picked up the copy of the *Post* and scanned the front page. He confirmed the fact that Lance was known for attending embassy functions.

"Dad mentioned the Japanese wanted the system," Sandra said flatly. "Why would he tell me that?"

"It could have been a ruse," Wyatt suggested.

"I don't think so," Sam said. "Information on the disks that Jackson left mentioned the Japanese more than any other country or person. With what Sandra tells us, our time frame has been cut to the next twelve hours. We have to decide which place is better to crash. Getting into and out of the Pentagon would be risky at best. Getting in there during broad daylight is like passing rifles out to your own firing squad. It's a better risk if we try the embassy."

Sandra poured another cup of coffee. She'd eaten the eggs, bacon, and toast ladled with orange marmalade. She felt better after eating and the coffee was working on clearing the sleeping pill hangover from her head.

"*We* have the stones," Sandra reminded them. "We know they are the only ones that will work with the system. How can Lance possibly claim something he can't deliver? He could have been trying to confuse me."

Wyatt nodded agreement.

"Where are these stones?" Annie asked.

"In my briefcase," Sam said. He got up and went to the case sitting next to the sofa on which he'd spent the night. When Wyatt hadn't returned to the car, he'd become concerned. Locking the stones in the trunk inside his briefcase, he came to investigate. He found Wyatt hovering over Sandra Rutledge. Discovering nothing had happened to Wyatt, he'd returned to the car and brought the case up. It hadn't been out of his sight since.

Unlocking the combination, he retrieved the navy-blue velvet case and brought it back to the breakfast table. Like a jeweler displaying his new prize, he opened the lid.

Sandra gasped.

It was empty.

The limousine Jordon ordered pulled into the semicircular driveway of the Japanese Embassy. The chauffeur got out with practiced ease and opened the door. Jordon exited first and helped the two sisters out. Wyatt and Sam Parker followed.

Sam's anger at the loss of the stones had not cooled since they were discovered missing at breakfast. They had only been out of his sight for the time he'd gone to check on Wyatt's lengthy visit to Sandra's sister's suite. Only fifteen minutes and the stones had somehow disappeared. The car showed no signs of being broken into. The briefcase was untouched, but the stones were nowhere to be found.

Wyatt knew Sam felt as if everyone was accusing him of taking the stones. It was natural to doubt his story. The stones had been entrusted to his care and no one had seen them since he'd taken possession of them. Wyatt couldn't help his doubts. He'd doubted and mistrusted everyone since this adventure began. Tonight it would come to an end. Either they retrieved the stones or they turned themselves in. He knew a life of running wasn't for him.

When Sandra had stumbled through the door last night, cold and frightened, he knew he could no longer subject her to the strain of trying to find the system. He would appeal to Everett Horton, tell him the whole truth and see if the President had enough power to get Lance Desque to tell him what he'd done with the stones.

Wyatt knew he'd been behind the theft. Whether Sam had been involved he would not judge. Sam's behavior since the discovery had been controlled anger. While Suzanne and he had argued with Sandra that she was too ill to leave, Sam had paced the room like an animal chained to a pole.

His only reaction had been when Sandra told them there was a duplicate necklace and earring set. He'd turned to her as if she'd handed him a governor's reprieve at the hour of his execution.

Sandra took Jordon's hand and alighted the limo. She stood a moment with the fur cape around her shoulders while the others got out. Sandra felt scared. This was a show they had not rehearsed. Their plan for getting into the Pentagon had been detailed and discussed. Going to this reception had been the product of an afternoon's speculation. Most of the discussion took place after the duplicates arrived. Sam detailed the financial information Annie had found on Lance.

The suite had been littered with clothes ordered from the hotel shops on the ground floor. Annie had taken over the grooming of everyone. She'd ordered tuxedos and shirts and every conceivable accessory needed for the event.

She'd also remembered to order something for Sandra's feet and her bruises. Sandra was afraid to ask her why she was being so nice. Only a day ago she'd told her she never wanted to see her again. Today she was bathing her feet and asking her if her head still hurt.

When they'd left the suite thirty minutes ago they looked like a party of five out for a wonderful evening. Sandra wore a black velvet gown. Its fitted bodice and full skirt covered all the places on which she had bruises. Her feet were cushioned inside gold sandals that Sandra had ordered to prevent any irritation to her tender and swollen feet. The duplicate necklace hung around her neck and the earrings cast shadows on her neck as they danced from her ears.

Annie took Jordon's arm and smiled at him. She was a golden girl, dressed in a gold pleated gown that flowed and swirled like liquid when she moved. Its brilliance had a light, but it wasn't bright enough to cancel out the light in her eyes as she looked at Jordon.

Sam Parker joined Wyatt on the pavement. He'd been an angry bull all day, and she feared that he'd do something to play their hand before they were ready. Wyatt had assured her his military training would win out and he would act according to plan. She didn't find that comforting since the plan was weak at best. When they should have been on a search and destroy mission they had little more advantage on their side than trial and error. But Sam was supposed to be their backup. Lance wouldn't expect him to be there. Obviously, if she and Wyatt were there, they would need someone outside waiting to spirit them away as soon as they found the components. Wyatt had told her he could hide in plain sight. She wasn't sure he was right. Sam was too much the bull in a china shop.

Annie and Jordon entered and joined the reception line. Sam skirted it. When they reached the prime minister, Annie spoke to him in rapid Japanese. The prime minister laughed as did his wife. Then they switched to English and she introduced Jordon, Wyatt, and Sandra. They all bowed. Mrs. Nagano admired her earrings and moved on.

"Now what?" Sandra asked Wyatt. "Do you think the earrings meant anything to her?"

"I'm not sure. I'm suspicious of anyone who takes an interest in those stones."

Sam moved about the crowded room, searching. If he intended to be inconspicuous, he'd already failed. If he wanted people to believe he was there to enjoy himself, he'd never pull it off.

Wyatt guided her toward a bar and ordered a glass of mineral water. They needed nothing to dull their senses.

"I think you should dance with Sam."

She took a sip of her water and glanced at Sam. "You're right. He looks rather . . . intense," she smiled, hoping the strain she felt wasn't as apparent as Sam's. Handing her glass to Wyatt, she said, "Don't get too far from me."

"I won't."

She stepped lightly on her cushioned soles and went to the colonel. "Dance with me, Sam."

He turned to her, his expression stern.

"You look as if you're searching for someone."

"I am."

Sandra took his arm and placed it on her waist. She led him to the floor. Surprisingly, he was a good dancer. He took over the lead and guided her around the crowded couples.

"When you find him, what are you planning to do?"

Sam's head scanned the room. Like a periscope, he swung around searching. Then he gave her his attention. "I want to break his neck."

"That won't help us," she told him. "Remember, we need to stick to the plan if we're to discover if the system is here. When we find it, we simply exchange the stones and bid the prime minister and his lovely wife good night."

Sam swung her around. The execution made her lift to the balls of her feet and turn. She winced at the pain.

"Excuse me," he said. "I forgot about your feet." He moved slower with wide, easy turns.

Sam knew she was right. His instincts were warlike, but he had to be practical. For the welfare of the country they needed to retrieve the stones, but for himself, for the way he'd felt when he opened that case and found the empty depressions, he'd take unbridled pleasure in beating Lance Desque to a pulp.

Annie and Jordon danced among the throngs of visiting dignitaries. Every country's representatives came in native garb. The Africans wore bright-colored fabrics, including headdresses wrapped into intricate designs that looked as if they had fabric flowers embedded in them. The silk of the Indian sari blended with the stylish western gowns and everywhere there were Japanese kimonos.

Annie kept track of her sister and the senator. She watched everyone who took an interest in them.

"Too bad we didn't have more time," Jordon whispered in her ear. "I could have called the FBI back and seen if we could have gotten the floor plan to this building."

"Jordon, this is foreign soil. We might as well be in Japan."

"They probably have the plans to the US Embassy in the Japanese version of the FBI."

Annie stared at him. "Do you think he would have given it to you?"

"If he knew the stakes, I think it would have been no question."

Jordon danced well. Suzanne had danced with him for years. They'd been paired through his camera, but tonight was the first time she'd danced with him where she could admit more than casual friendship. She loved the way his strong arms held her close and guided her through the steps as the two of them moved in the same time and space.

They kept dancing and kept looking. Lance had not put in an appearance yet. She wondered where he was. He was known for being on time and staying until the end of an event. He never overstayed his welcome and never did anything that would be considered rude. Lance would study the culture, its mores and rules to make sure he did nothing to insult his hosts.

Wyatt and Sandra disappeared through a door at the end of the room. Sam Parker, no longer with murder in his eyes, casually went through an archway at the opposite end of the room.

"Did you see them?" she asked.

"Yes." Jordon danced her through the crowd toward the door where Wyatt and Sandra had gone.

They had agreed to try the basement first. Sam was going to keep an eye out for Lance. Wyatt hoped he was moving in the right direction. Basements were usually close to kitchens. The kitchen would be bustling with activity. Sandra would say she had to have a glass of milk if anyone stopped them. They would get the opportunity to look around, see if there were any doors.

If luck was with them they'd find the right one immediately, but they could end up in a closet or pantry. They could always say they couldn't find their way back if they were seen. Play as you go and make it up when needed, Wyatt thought.

With his arm draped around her waist, they passed waiters carrying dishes of canapés and drinks. One or two nodded at them. Wyatt took a champagne glass from an offered tray, then shook his head and patted Sandra's stomach. The look on his face told the waiter she could not have the alcohol. He smiled knowingly and continued on his way to serve the rest of his tray.

Three doors stood closed off the hallway leading to the kitchen. The kitchen double doors were wide open. White-clad cooks moved at speeds too great for the small amount of floor space. Food covered every available space. Gleaming copper pots steamed on the stove and wonderful aromas floated through the air.

Wyatt checked the people before opening the first door, which turned out to be a broom closet. He closed it quickly and took Sandra's hand. The second door was a small bathroom and the third a closet. The coats hanging inside belonged to the kitchen staff. The clinging odor of food locked inside the fabric was overwhelming.

They were going to have to go into the kitchen to see if any other doors could be found. He didn't like that. It meant being discovered faster if they actually found a basement. Their presence would be missed if they came in and no one saw them leave. *It's a risk we're going to have to take.* The words came back to him from the afternoon's activity of formulating a plan.

"May I have a glass of milk?" Sandra asked a man in the center of the room. She'd walked straight into the room and stopped at a vantage point that gave them full view of the front and back of the room.

The cook was shaking his head and speaking in Japanese. Wyatt didn't need an interpreter to tell him the man did not speak English and did not understand her question. Sandra knew it, too. She rubbed her stomach and frowned at him. Then, with universal sign language, she posed as if she had a glass in her hand and drank from it.

"Ohhh," he said. He started to lead her to the door through which they had come.

Taking his arm, she stopped him. Pointing to a white liquid, then to the double-door refrigerator, he reversed his direction and went toward the area to which she pointed.

Wyatt looked for a door. There was none. He followed Sandra, and while she got the milk and waited for a glass, he checked the back of the room. There was a door leading to the outside, a huge pantry with stores of canned and dried foodstuff, but no door that could have led to a basement.

Giving her a signal, Wyatt saw the imperceptible movement of her head. Her hair shone with a healthy glow. Suzanne had washed, blown it, and curled it into a sleek style that hung to her shoulders before gently curling under. With curls that dripped down the side of her face, the bruise was effectively hidden from any prying eyes. The rest of her face had been covered with a makeup that evened her skin tone and completely covered the other marks. If Wyatt hadn't seen Suzanne performing her magic, he'd never have believed that the woman who had fallen into his arms last night could look this beautiful twenty-four hours later.

"Thank you." Sandra bowed and smiled. The Japanese cook bowed in return and they left the kitchen. At the turn back to the main hall, they ran into Sam.

"I found it," he whispered. "It's the first door under the back staircase on the left side of the ballroom. There is no guard, but the maids store the coats in a room near it."

"What about Lance?" Sandra inquired. "Did he make an appearance yet?"

"I haven't seen him and I think that's a plus for our side. If he sees us, our escape route could be effectively cut."

Colonel Sam Parker was back. The military mind was operating at full capacity. Gone was the emotional man who was angry and ready to bash in his enemy's head.

"Let's go," Wyatt said. He took Sandra in his arms and danced her back to the place where Annie and Jordon stood drinking glasses of bottled water.

"Sam found the basement," he whispered. "We're going there now." He danced her away.

At that moment the music ended. The couples stopped dancing and quiet applause rippled through the room. Wyatt stopped. It wouldn't look natural for them to continue until the band started up again.

"Hello, Miss Rutledge, is it?"

Sandra turned toward the voice. Prime Minister Nagano stood before her. He was a short man with graying hair and a smile on his lips. He wore a black tuxedo with a red sash draped across his torso. He reminded Sandra of a tennis coach she'd once had who taught her a backhand that produced a winner every time. The prime minister stood straight, looking her directly in the eye. She wondered if his backhand was as good.

"I believe I am acquainted with your father, Senator Rutledge."

"Yes," Sandra smiled at him. Wyatt eased away, apparently going to join another conversation group. "He has mentioned you several times when he's returned from Japan."

"He has often mentioned his beautiful daughters."

She wondered where Annie was and if the prime minister knew they were sisters. Annie had spoken to him in his native language. They had laughed as if they were old friends. Sandra wondered what she'd said.

The band started to play again. By mutual consent she danced with him. He was quiet for a while. Then he said, "I have only been in your country for a short time. Do all American women have such beautiful jewels?"

Antennae seemed to spring out of her head. Why was he interested in the necklace and earrings? The question was too casual for her. He'd met many woman from many countries. In this room alone were many American woman. All of them wore various amounts of jewelry. The other women also had on many different kinds of decorations.

"I can't say, Minister Nagano."

"Were these a gift, perhaps?"

"Sir, I'll let you in on a little secret." She put her lips close to his ear. "They're just for show. They're not real." He laughed at her words. "Go on, take a look," she told him.

With just the right amount of hesitation he stopped dancing. They were close to the left side of the ballroom. He examined the stones. Sandra thought he looked at them with the eye of an experienced jeweler.

"I am told you cannot tell the difference between real and not real any longer. I cannot tell."

His words rang false in her ears, but she smiled at him. The music ended and he bowed to her. A group descended on him and carried him away, each person vying for his attention.

Wyatt stood near the end of the room talking to a man dressed in a bright-blue African pants outfit. Sandra started toward him, but was asked to dance by another man. She complied so as not to call attention to herself. This man mentioned how familiar she looked and asked her if she was a television anchorwoman. He released her at the end of the dance with a comment that he would remember where he'd seen her.

Two dances later, her feet sore, she finally reached Wyatt. They slipped away unnoticed and met Sam at the door to the basement. It was almost too easy. They found only one locked room down there. In no time Sam had it open. Going inside they closed the door and switched on the light. The room was massive; a control center. Computer servers hummed in the quiet air. A console, tables, displays, rows of digital printouts. All of the equipment was state of the art. Some of it she recognized. Other items were foreign to her.

"There it is," Sam stated. He went to a relatively small machine standing near the back wall.

Sandra stared at it. She couldn't move. Her head ached with relief that they might pull this off. Her heart hammered and her hands turned to cold globs of ice. This was what they had come to find. This was what Wyatt had been stabbed over, what people had shot at her helicopter over. Through this innocent-looking piece of almond-colored metal and plastic millions of people in the world could lose their right to a basic freedom.

"Give me the stones!" Sam's voice, at the strength of a stage whisper, boomed in the air-controlled room.

Wyatt unhooked the necklace while Sandra removed the earrings. The heavy stones left a light feeling about her head and chest. Sandra shivered more from fear than cold. They were in deep now. Anyone finding them here would have the sole advantage. They were on foreign soil. Nothing done to them could ever be prosecuted in an American court. There were no other doors. No escape from here by biting her way through wires and opening a locked door.

Sam was staring into the machine. He'd produced a screwdriver from his inside pocket and quickly unscrewed the housing. Now he examined the inside. It took less than five minutes for him to get the jewelry out. He pulled a second item from his pocket. She didn't see what it was. Working calmly, quickly, and efficiently he completed his work, set the fake necklace in place and covered the machine. The magic screwdriver flew through his hands as he replaced the screws. Wyatt hung the real necklace around her neck. She touched it, thinking about its worth, remembering Jeff Taylor and feeling grief for Chip Jackson. No one would ever know they'd given their lives to protect free speech.

"Now," Sam said with unconcealed concern. "I suggest we get the hell out of here."

Wyatt wiped the sweat from his brow and returned the silk handkerchief to his pocket. Blood surged through his system. His ears flamed and he could taste fear in the back of his throat. Getting into the embassy had been a cakewalk. He had the invitation he'd taken from Desque's last night. As a top model Suzanne Rutledge had been legitimately invited. They had bowed and shook hands with various guests and dignitaries, but at that point they had nothing of value. Now they had loaded stones dropping from her ears and hanging around Sandra's neck.

His instinct told him to make a beeline for the door. Get her out of there and whisk her away from anyone who might want to stop them. He knew that would certainly raise eyebrows. They were going to have to run the gauntlet. Dance slowly, work their way to the front door, and slip out unobserved.

The color had drained from Sandra's face and her eyes were huge chips of black ice.

"Smile," he whispered, turning her into his arms. "You look as if you've just stolen a defense system." His attempt at lightness was more for himself than her, but it broke the ice and a smile turned her mouth up. It didn't light her eyes.

Wyatt remembered to hold her lightly and that her feet were tender and raw. He couldn't swing her around in wide circles which would get them to the door with the least amount of steps. They had to take the long way around.

Spotting Jordon and Suzanne, he signaled them and kept moving. They'd made it. The front door stood the space of the foyer away. It opened to admit more guests and closed. A laughing party of four came inside, sweeping the cold January air in with them. It felt like a burst of heaven to Wyatt. As the maid took their coats and directed them into the main salon, Wyatt's hand on the small of Sandra's back guided her to the exit.

Alone, when the guests moved away and the maid, weighed down with fur and wool, headed for the back room, Wyatt grabbed the ornate handle. He didn't have to pull it; the door was being pushed open.

"Going so soon, Senator?" Lance Desque stood in front of him. Another man, shorter and meaner looking, stood behind him. They came into the foyer. Wyatt and Sandra immediately backed away. "And without your coats. You could catch your death of cold." He'd emphasized the word "death."

Neither Desque nor the man who'd entered with him wore overcoats. Wyatt knew they weren't just arriving. They'd been there all along, waiting for this moment.

Turning to Sandra, Desque smiled broadly. "Sandra, how nice to see you . . . again. Our last meeting was, shall we say, short-circuited."

Wyatt felt the fear that fissured through her body. Her hold on his arm tightened to a vise grip. Desque taunted her with his double-edged words.

"I see you survived it," Sandra said, her backbone straightening and her chin lifting a bit.

Desque laughed. He glanced at the man behind him. He had closed the door, but remained mute.

"Henri, I'd like you to meet Senator Rutledge's daughter, Sandra. She rudely avoided meeting you last night. And this is the much sought-after Senator Wyatt Randolph. He's skillfully managed to have his life spread over the daily papers. Dead bodies appear, and what do the police find but fingerprints leading to our esteemed senator."

Henri didn't say a word, but nodded in Sandra's direction. His big hands went to the button of his tailored jacket. He released it and rebuttoned it. The action was designed to let them see the black handle of the gun that was wedged between his pants and shirt. Sandra stood her ground, staring at him as if he were the instrument of death, but valiantly showing no fear.

"Henri, why don't you go with the senator. I'm sure the two of you have things to discuss."

"No!" Sandra spoke, backing up a step and pulling Wyatt with her.

"I believe, Sandra, this is our dance," he went on as if she hadn't spoken.

"I won't dance with you."

Henri reached for the button on his coat. Sandra's gaze involuntarily followed it. She swallowed hard.

Henri stepped forward and grabbed Wyatt's arm. He propelled him through the hall in the direction the maid had gone.

Lance took a step. She recoiled. "I wouldn't do anything stupid, Sandra. We are on foreign soil. You certainly wouldn't want to provoke an international incident."

"You can't create an international incident between two Americans," she told him. "No matter whose soil you're on."

He smiled venomously. "I see you not only excelled in mathematics, but you're up on your government policies, too." The smile left his face. "What about computer science and jewelry making? Have you mastered those yet?"

Sandra felt the earrings brush her neck, but refused to look down at the necklace. Squeezing her hands, she forced them to stay at her sides. The maid returned and more guests arrived. Lance took the moment to encircle her in his arms and carry her into the dancing crowd. He held her tightly, making her muscles and bruises hurt.

"You should have known you couldn't get away with it," Lance whispered in her ear.

"Get away with what?" she asked, wondering where Wyatt had been taken. The black gun stayed in her mind. A new rush of fear took hold of her. Had Lance's gunman taken Wyatt somewhere to kill him?

"With that lovely piece of jewelry you're wearing as if it were only dazzling pieces of man-made stone."

"Isn't that what they are?"

She scanned the room. Where was Sam? What had happened to Jordon and her sister? Wyatt had nodded to them that the exchange had been made. They should get their coats and get out of there. Had they gone without seeing Lance arrive?

Lance stopped dancing when he reached Prime Minister Nagano and his wife. He greeted them in Japanese, keeping a firm hold on Sandra.

"I didn't know you could speak Japanese," she commented when he'd bowed and danced her back onto the floor.

"I began studying it a few years ago."

She knew he was lying. He spoke the language too well. She'd heard her sister speaking and knew that Lance's command was much more refined than Annie's and she'd spent two years in Japan, traveling and modeling but making Tokyo her home base.

"What are you planning to do with us?" Sandra plunged headlong into the real reason they were there.

"You always were one to go straight for the jugular, Sandra. No dancing around the subject for you. I must say, getting out of that trunk was a stroke of genius. I didn't think you could do it. But I know now never to underestimate you."

Lance had maneuvered her to the back stairs. The door to the basement loomed in front of her. With his hand still on her arm, she felt the unmistakable feel of a gun pressed against her back.

"Up," he pushed her.

Her breath rushed out of her lungs on a painful gasp. She stepped on the first rung. "Where are you taking me? Where's Wyatt?"

"Don't worry about the senator. I'm sure the two of you will be seeing each other soon."

His voice had an ominous tone to it. Sandra's blood turned to ice water and shivered through her with a paralyzing fear. Lance pushed her up another step. Pain rocketed from her feet. She bit her lip to keep from crying out. He nearly dragged her to a room in the attic.

"Keep her here," he ordered an Asian woman of about forty as he released his hold on her arm. The woman bowed more than nodded. Sandra rubbed the spot where his hands had been. It was already sore from the constant tangle of bush and branches she'd stumbled through last night during her escape. Tonight she didn't think she'd have the same degree of luck.

Lance took a step toward her. She shrank away from him, hating herself for the cowardly act.

Lance reached into his pocket. Sandra's heart logged in her throat. She forced herself to breathe. Cutting off oxygen would make her pass out and she refused to do that. Lance grinned at her. She hated that grin. His hand came out holding the fake stones they'd left in the machine downstairs.

"The jewelry," he demanded, his hand outstretched. "Mine for yours."

"What good is it to you? It's man-made, you said so yourself."

"I don't have time for games. There are things I have to do, and I need the necklace and earrings. Now give them to me or I'll take them by force and, believe me, you won't like my kind of force."

Sandra clinched her teeth together to keep from shaking. His voice was evil to the core. It seeped into her and sapped her of strength. The Japanese woman came from behind Lance and exchanged one necklace for the other. Sandra removed the earrings and handed them to him. He smiled, a sincere smile of accomplishment, then took her hand and pushed the fakes into it.

"Thank you, Sandra. You'll never know what you've done for your country."

Sandra cringed.

Lance turned and left. The Asian woman, dressed in a western-style business suit and high heels, locked the door after Lance. Her hair was pulled into a topknot that allowed tendrils to fall down her face and soften the look of it. She turned back to Sandra and leveled the barrel of a gun between her breasts.

CHAPTER 23

Sam slipped behind a huge potted plant when he saw the short, squat man leading Wyatt down the hall. Something had gone wrong. Where was Sandra? He could only assume Desque had caught them before they got out and had separated them.

It had to mean he also had the stones. Sam could have kicked himself. He should have destroyed the machine when he had the chance, but at the last minute he changed his mind. It was more than a small box with computer-wired chips. It had been the better part of his life for several years. He took pride in it and couldn't intentionally destroy it.

Now that they knew where it was, he thought the government could put pressure on the Japanese to return it. Now he knew he'd made the wrong decision.

He moved away from the plant, noticing that Randolph had been taken back to the basement. As soon as he discovered where Desque—

He saw him. He was talking to the prime minister and dancing with Sandra. Sam shrank into the darkness of the corridor. He found an empty room and stole inside it. With the door cracked, he could only see the basement door and the back stairs. He waited. Finally, he heard Sandra's voice. She challenged Lance. What a gutsy woman, he thought. Desque pushed her up the stairs.

After all she'd gone through she was here, disregarding her physical pain, to try to get the part that could save not only his hide, but that of the entire world. He had to admit that maybe women in the services wasn't as bad as he'd thought. He'd never had to work with a woman under pressure. Sandra Rutledge had behaved admirably. Wyatt was a lucky man.

Desque came down the stairs—alone. He'd left her up there. He looked around the hallway, then went directly to the basement door. He checked in front and behind him. Seeing no one, he opened the door and disappeared through it.

Sam left his hiding place and went up the stairs. He didn't have time to locate Suzanne and Jordon. He needed to know where Sandra was, then they'd get Wyatt. He hoped.

The room was temperature controlled for the computer equipment. Wyatt was generating his own heat. He wanted to know where Sandra had been taken. Was she all right? She'd been ill and in pain most of the evening. What had Desque done with her?

Wyatt looked at the Neanderthal holding him. The man had not said a word. He'd let the implication of the gun speak for him. Wyatt was under no illusion that he wouldn't use the gun if necessary.

He could hear the party going on upstairs. Band music filtered through the door. He wondered where Sam was and if Jordon and Suzanne were still looking for them. He grabbed the thought as his only means of a possible escape.

There was suddenly a loud applause. Both Wyatt and Henri looked at the ceiling. Something happened. He wondered what. Maybe Jordon and Suzanne had discovered them missing and done something to try to find them. Desque opened and closed the door. The sound resounded and receded.

The look that passed between Desque and the silent man told Wyatt they were involved in the commotion occurring on the floor above.

"They're here," he said to his silent partner.

"What do you want with us?" Wyatt opened. "You've got what you need. Why don't you let us go?"

Desque walked like a man who had everything he'd ever wanted. He went to the desk and sat down. Pulling a small black device from his pocket, he dropped it on the desk. Wyatt thought it was a hand-held tape recorder and that it would begin to play a recorded message. Then he noticed it was a remote control. What did it control? What was Desque's game now? Why did he want him to know?

"I want the last chip, Wyatt."

Wyatt didn't like the way he pronounced his name, as if the two syllables should be dragged apart.

Desque pulled the jewelry from his pocket. He dropped it on the desk. It joined the remote control, giving Wyatt added cause for concern. Where was Sandra? What had he done to her?

"I don't know what you're talking about." He looked at the set stones.

He couldn't tell whether these contained the chips or not. The machine it fit into was open and empty. Sandra had been wearing the real ones. The fakes had been in the machine. Now nothing was in the machine and Desque had danced away with Sandra.

Desque stood up. "I'm talking about the fifteenth stone, Senator." His voice raised. "You had a copy made," he grinned. Adjusting his suit as if he was getting back to his customary state of perfection, he lowered his voice. "It's a good copy." He lifted the necklace. The solitaire swung like a pendulum in a short arc. "To the naked eye there isn't any difference. But," he stopped the swing. "It won't work and I'm going to have it."

"What do you think I can do? I don't have it." Wyatt shrugged. The gesture might have looked as if he didn't care, but he did. He felt his palms growing moist.

"The only person who's had possession of the stones, other than Jeff Taylor, has been you and Senator Rutledge's daughter."

"Where is she? What have you done with her?"

Desque picked up the remote control and leaned back in the chair as if he were relaxing. Wyatt's nerves stretched to the breaking point. "Ah, yes. Senator Rutledge's daughter. You're in love with her, aren't you?"

Wyatt didn't answer.

"You don't have to answer. I could see it the first time I met you." He twirled the small instrument in his hand. "Why don't we talk about Sandra. I've known her for years, since she was a child."

Wyatt stared straight ahead. He wanted to pick up one of the pieces and examine it, find out if the jewelry lying on the desk was the real thing or the copies Sandra had had made. Desque picked up an earring. Wyatt consciously controlled his breathing.

"You're wondering which ones these are?" Desque seemed to read his mind. "They're the real ones, the ones Jackson designed and had made. The ones that fit into the slots of that system and the ones that Sandra Rutledge had gracing her beautiful ears and throat." He paused.

"Desque, if you've done anything to hurt her . . ."

"Hurt her?" His eyes opened in mock surprise. "I wouldn't hurt her. I wouldn't even deprive her of her jewelry." He let the earring drop to the desk. Stretching out his arm, he checked his watch. "It's nearly time," he said to the other man. Then Desque handed him the stones. "Put them in."

"Time for what?" Wyatt asked. He knew time was running out for him, too. Desque was playing some game and he didn't like it, but he had to continue until he found out where Sandra was. Had he taken her out of the building or was she upstairs someplace? Where was Sam? Had he seen Desque and Sandra? "Time for what?" he asked again.

"Time to activate the system, Senator." He glanced at Henri who was busy slipping the stones into place.

"I thought you said it wouldn't work without the fifteenth stone?"

"I'll have the fifteenth stone. You're going to give it to me."

"I don't have it," Wyatt reminded him.

Desque made a display of checking the remote in his hand. "We allowed you in here earlier, Randolph. You and the colonel. Did you think you were safe? You'd replaced the stones with fakes. Having them set into a necklace and earrings . . . that was good," he smiled. "I like that. Was it your idea or the senator's daughter? Maybe I should say the farmer's daughter?"

Wyatt almost lunged for him. He stopped himself in time. Desque was trying to provoke him and he wouldn't let him. He had to stay calm, stay in control until he told him what he'd done with Sandra or until Sam or Jordon and Suzanne found him.

"We let you take the real stones, but we couldn't let you leave. The duplicates were a good touch. Whose idea was that?"

"What difference does it make?"

"Oh, it makes a difference. You see, we . . . modified the duplicate necklace. We . . . added something to one of the stones. We made it a fifteenth stone."

Wyatt shook. He couldn't stop the tremor.

"That got your attention. Good. Let me tell you what we did with it and where it is now."

Wyatt knew.

"Sandra has it. She's upstairs." He looked up. Wyatt couldn't stop himself from following Desque's gaze. "In the attic. Around her neck is the duplicate with a stone that contains a—" He left the sentence hanging.

"You've put a bomb around Sandra's neck?" Wyatt could hardly speak. He squeezed his eyes shut, then opened them. "You're lying," he said. "That bomb would level this building." Sam had told him that when he'd defused it at the mansion in Virginia. If it went off it could turn the building into a small pile of stone, he'd said. Desque wanted to reap his rewards in this life. He'd no more set off a bomb than shoot himself.

"That bomb would," he agreed. "I said we'd modified it. All it will do now is take her head off."

Wyatt weaved at the mental picture created. Desque gave his attention to the black control in his hand. Wyatt pulled himself together. He was going to have to talk his way out of this if he was going to save her life.

"It's done, sir." Henri spoke for the first time. Wyatt looked at him. His face was stony. Wyatt had the feeling that Henri would enjoy killing him. A coldness ran through him as bone-chilling as a winter plunge in the Potomac River.

"Good," Desque told him. "Leave us. Make sure no one enters or leaves without my permission."

Henri nodded and left. Wyatt could have kicked himself. He should have been trying to figure out how to get the remote away from Desque. Instead, he'd followed Henri's movements without thinking of anything else. Sandra was his responsibility. He'd gotten her mixed up in this and she'd nearly been killed for the service. He couldn't let all her effort and work go to waste.

Was Desque telling the truth or was this a good game of poker? Wyatt really didn't know if the fifteenth stone wasn't the same. Who'd changed it? Sam? Sandra? The jeweler?

"I told you I don't know anything about that stone. If it's the wrong one, then Chip sent the wrong one to me."

"Don't give me that!" Desque hit the desk with his fist. A pencil cup toppled over and the green-shaded banker's light skidded to a new location. "You had it and you'll tell me what you did with it." Again he adjusted his clothes. Wyatt realized Desque hated losing control. He liked speaking softly and being in control, holding people with the quiet hostility of his voice. "You've noticed this, haven't you, Senator." He held the remote in plain view.

Wyatt's knees grew weak. He wanted to sit down, but he knew his best position would be to stand and be ready for whatever came his way. He breathed slowly, keeping himself alert.

Desque pushed a button. The machine close to the wall started up. Lights came on, went off, then came on and stayed steady. The whir of the fan made him jump as if it had exploded.

"Don't be so jumpy, Senator. It's this button." He pointed to the white one. The others were black. Only one button had a different color. "When I get to that one, imagine what will happen to her." He pressed a second button. Apparently, nothing happened. "This one just locked the door to a limousine, Senator. Do you want to know who's inside that limousine?" Desque waited for an answer, but Wyatt didn't give it to him. "Of course, you want to know. A certain photographer and his model. They were going to help you and Sandra in the rescue of the world. Too bad things didn't go according to plan."

"What is the plan?" Wyatt asked. He took a step closer to Desque. He couldn't just stand there and wait for him to go through the eight buttons on the control.

"The plan, Wyatt?" He separated his name again. "I thought you'd figured it out by now. Sandra did. She knows exactly what I'm planning to do. I'm going to control the world. All I need is the stone." He pressed another button. Lights at the end of the room went out. "That's three, Wyatt. There are five left. All of them might not have functions. How much longer do you think it will be before I reach the final button? How much time do you think Sandra has?"

Wyatt tried not to think of Sandra's headless body, but Desque kept talking. "Stop this now, Desque." He took another step forward. He was close to the desk.

"She won't even know it," he continued, ignoring Wyatt. "The blast will come as a total surprise. She won't have time to think about you. Her life will be over before it can flash in front of her eyes. She'll probably open her mouth to scream. Do you think she'll be able to, Wyatt? Her head will be gone, Senator. It'll whirl in the air like a ball, blood spurting everywhere. Then it'll crash—"

Desque looked down at the control. Wyatt lunged for him. Momentum over the desk had the two of them crashing to the floor. The remote control skittered away. It clattered over the tiles out of reach. Desque rolled over and reached for it. Wyatt grabbed him. He rolled back, fighting him. His fist connected with Wyatt's jaw. Wyatt was dazed for a moment. He saw the second punch coming and blocked it. Raising to his knees, he pulled Desque with him. The man used his legs to punch Wyatt in the kidneys. Pain exploded in his back. His grip released and Desque pinned him to the floor.

The fist coming toward him was huge. It grew larger and larger as it approached his face. Wyatt shifted his head in time. Desque's hand hit the computer floor. He screamed as pain went through his knuckles and up his arm. Wyatt used the force of his shoulder to connect his fist with Desque's jaw. He went sideways off him. Dazed but not out, Desque shook his head, trying to clear it.

Wyatt rolled away from him and went for the remote control. He picked it up and turned back to the undersecretary. Wyatt stopped in the act of rising. Pointed directly at him was the front end of a loaded gun.

"I think you have something that's mine," Desque huffed. They were both breathing hard. "Lay it on the desk slowly, and I wouldn't try anything stupid, Senator."

Wyatt hesitated. What should he do? He wasn't going to get another chance to surprise Desque.

"I'm waiting, Senator. On the desk." He punctuated each word. "Or I shoot you in the knee."

Wyatt had no choice. He placed the remote on the desk and backed away.

Desque picked it up. He placed his hand over the white button. "Time's up, Senator. Where is it?"

"All right, I'll tell you. It's at the hotel," he lied. Anything for time. "We left it in the safe so it wouldn't be mistaken for one of the others."

"I don't believe you." His finger moved.

"I swear," Wyatt shouted.

"You think I'm stupid. We searched that room the moment you left it. There's nothing there but clothes spread all over the furniture, enough makeup to open a store, and financial reports on some of the most influential men in Washington. That was a major find, Senator," he smiled. "Thanks for providing it."

Wyatt knew he was telling the truth. "Sandra has the stones. She hid them. I don't know where, but take me to her and I'll get her to tell you."

"That's good, Senator. That's rich." He laughed now that his breathing was back to normal. His clothes were slightly disheveled and dusty from their roll on the floor. "You're out of chances, Senator." His finger depressed the button.

"Nooo!" Wyatt shouted. He grabbed for the remote. The explosion resounded in his ears like shock waves that played and replayed against his brain. Desque looked surprised, stunned. The gun slipped from his fingers. Wyatt watched it fall in slow motion. It hit the floor and bounced. He watched it slide toward the wall and come to a stop. Then Desque was falling. His mouth worked feverishly but nothing came out. Wyatt couldn't hear him.

Wyatt's knees gave. He sank to the floor. "Sandra!" he cried over and over. "Sandra!"

"Wyatt, I'm here." Sandra rushed across the room and fell to her knees. "Everything is all right." She put her arms around him and repeated that everything was fine. "Sam found me. He found you and shot Lance."

Wyatt stared at her with eyes that did not see. She kept calling his name, hoping he was all right. She felt his back and looked at his arms. Had Lance shot him? When Sam had burst through the door and seen the gun pointed at Wyatt, he'd taken the first shot. It hit Lance in the arm. The gun fell from his hand.

Wyatt had begun to scream and fell to the floor. "It's over, Wyatt. It's all over."

Wyatt smelled her hair. He was losing his mind. Desque had killed Sandra, yet Wyatt smelled her hair. He could even feel her arms around him, hear her sweet voice.

"Sandra!" he cried.

"I'm here, Wyatt. I'm here."

He wasn't dreaming. He pushed her back. It was her. She was real. "Sandra! You're alive." He pulled her against him, squashed her, pulled her off balance, and crushed her against him. Then his mouth was on her face, seeking, touching her, kissing her eyes, her cheeks, her mouth. The two of them were on their knees. Wyatt moved back a moment to look at her, make sure he hadn't made a mistake. Then he took her mouth again. This time he wanted her to know he'd never let her go again, never let her out of his sight and never put her in the kind of danger that had scared him to death.

"Sam saved me," she explained, when he'd slipped his mouth from hers and just held her. Wyatt had no idea what she was talking about. How could Sam have saved her? "Lance locked me in the attic with a guard, but Sam forced one of the maids to tell her Lance had sent food. She opened the door and he overpowered her. Both of them are upstairs, tied up."

He pushed her away and stood up. "What are you talking about?"

"I'm talking about how I got out of the attic." She glanced at Sam.

"What about the bomb?" He touched the earrings, almost caressing them. "Why didn't it go off?

"Because I switched it," Sam said. Wyatt looked around. Sam was in the room. Jordon and Suzanne had also arrived. Everyone was smiling at them.

Sandra went to the machine and pulled out the real set of stones. She kept them in her hand as Sam finished explaining what had happened.

"I discovered a second bomb in the chips. It's an old fail-safe device that's used to make sure if the first method fails, a second will be there to complete the job."

"If there was one, there was probably another," Wyatt stated.

"Exactly. I also wanted to make it difficult if we actually lost the stones, so I substituted one of the experimental ones we'd used. Desque must have tried to activate it and found out one was bogus."

Wyatt looked at the body on the floor and then back at Sam.

"When I saw him take Sandra upstairs and that big guy take you downstairs, I knew something was wrong. Then Desque comes back alone and I couldn't find Suzanne and Jordon."

"We were locked in the limo," Jordon told him.

"Getting Sandra was easy," Sam continued. "When I saw the earrings, we discovered the bomb and had to defuse the chip. That's what took so long. Sandra went to check the limo while I dealt with Desque's henchman. He's tied up and gagged in one of the basement closets."

"How do you know there aren't more?" Wyatt said. "I can't believe he executed this thing with only a few lackeys."

"Nor did I."

Sandra and Annie gasped at the voice. They turned to find Lance standing, the gun in his hand pointed at them. "I thought you were dead," Sandra said. Blood covered half of him. Sandra was reminded of Wyatt and the amount of blood he'd lost when she found him. She frowned. Lance's face was a pale white. She could see the blood seeping through a point in his chest just under his collarbone.

"I'm harder to kill than that. Now move over." He waved with the gun. They all moved in the direction he pointed.

"You, Colonel. Throw the gun over here. Nice and easy," he said. "Don't think my left hand makes a difference. Any funny business and I'll drop you first." His voice was menacingly cold.

Sam did as he was told. "I should have shot to kill," Sam said.

"Lance, it's over. You can't get away with this," Sandra said. She drew his attention. He stood steady and dangerous. She knew he couldn't last long. Wyatt had tried to stand up at the cabin and he'd wobbled badly enough to fall over. It was only a matter of time before Lance came to the same fate. The blood looked thicker as it soaked into his tuxedo. His right arm was bleeding. He held the gun in his left.

"Hand me the jewels," he ordered.

"No," she said.

He pointed the gun directly at her. "If I shoot this, Sandra, it will put a small hole in your chest, but it will take the back of your body and throw it into the next room. Now hand me the stones."

"Lance, have you wondered what happened to the signal you thought would kill me?"

For a second she saw panic in his eyes. It was quickly replaced with an evil stare. "I don't care."

"You should," Sam told him. "We relayed it. Do you want to know where?"

"You have lots of money," Suzanne joined. "I checked your finances and found very interesting data. I'm sure the IRS wants to discuss income and expenses with you."

"Shut up!" he shouted. "I want those stones."

"You have a private account in a Swiss bank," Suzanne went on.

"It's been opened, breached," Sam went on. "You did it yourself. You pushed the button. Right now funds from that account are being electronically restored to the US Treasury Department. Imagine their surprise when they arrive for work Monday morning, Desque, and find the generous deposit."

"They're particular in Treasury," Wyatt taunted him. "They have to account for every penny. They can't let your kind of balance go without investigation."

"I said shut up!"

He was clearly shaken. "There's more," Sam told him. "Photographic documents of your illegal transactions are being sent to the Treasury Department."

"Drop the gun," Jordon told him. "You haven't a chance."

Lance shook visibly. Sandra wondered if the blood he'd lost was making him weak. She remembered how weak Wyatt had been when she'd found him. Loss of blood would give him double vision and destroy his ability to hold on to the gun. If they could keep him talking, he might pass out.

"Haven't I?" Lance answered Jordon. "Have you forgotten where we are? I'm on foreign soil. I have many friends here. You can't touch me, the government can't touch me."

"Drop the gun, Mr. Desque."

An unfamiliar voice had the entire entourage shifting the attention to the door. Two armed guards pointed guns at Lance. Behind them stood Prime Minister Nagano and Everett Horton.

"Prime Minister," Lance began. "I wish to seek political asylum in the Empire of Japan."

There was clearly a plea in Lance's voice.

"Mr. Desque." The prime minister bowed slightly as he pronounced Lance's name, accenting the last syllable. "The United States does not have political prisoners. The Empire cannot offer you sanctuary against crimes to your own country." He smiled and bowed again. "I wanted to bring President Horton here to assure him that Japan had recovered his property." He glanced at Project Eagle. "We wish for continued relations with the United States. Returning their property is a gesture of mutual friendship." He bowed slightly.

Anger showed in Lance's face. His options had run out. Quickly he turned and trained the gun on the prime minister. Wyatt moved with lightning speed. He kicked the gun out of Lance's hand before it could go off. The guards fired, catching Lance in the chest. He staggered backward, fell against the wall and slid down it leaving a trail of blood.

CHAPTER 24

The Oval Office in the west wing of the White House had pale-yellow walls and a beige rug. The seal of the United States was woven into the rug that sat in front of the *Resolute* desk. Everett Horton had photos of his children on the credenza behind him. Casey's photo sat on the desk facing him.

He stood when Wyatt wheeled Sandra into the office.

"Welcome," he greeted, shaking hands with Jordon and Wyatt and kissing Sandra and Suzanne on the cheek.

Melanie West and Casey Horton, who were already in the room, stood, too. Casey smiled widely. "How are your feet?" she asked Sandra.

"The doctor says they should be completely healed in about two weeks."

"Until then, I'd let this guy carry me around." Everett gestured toward Wyatt as he whispered in a voice only she could hear. She laughed.

When they were seated and had been served cups of coffee, Everett said, "I'm glad everything turned out all right last night."

"I am, too," Sandra said.

"I also congratulate you, sir," Wyatt told the President, "on completing the trade agreement this morning between the US and Japan. It's something the country needs."

"You'll never know how right you are, Wyatt."

Wyatt did know. Nagano and Desque had been in each other's pockets. When Desque proved unable to deliver what he claimed without creating an international incident, Nagano pulled up stakes and threw Desque to the wolves.

"It's over now," Everett said. "And we have you to thank for saving the country."

Everett put his cup down and went to his desk. "I suppose I should get these signed and delivered." He picked up several pieces of paper and took a pen from the blotter. He sat down, the pen poised above the first page.

"Mr. President," Sandra stopped him. "Before you sign . . ." She turned her wheelchair to look him directly in the face. He put down the pen and gave her his attention.

"I thought you and I were on a first-name basis."

"We are," she said. "When I talk to my friend. Right now I want to talk to the President."

"Go on," he said, his voice changing to that of the strong, no-nonsense commander.

"Project Eagle. The system. The stones. What are you planning to do with them?"

Wyatt came and stood next to her. He took her hand in his. Annie joined her on the other side and Jordon stood next to her.

"I see you've all discussed this and have come to some conclusion." He looked at each one of them individually. "Well, who's acting as spokesman?"

"I am, sir," Wyatt told him. "We've discussed the power of Project Eagle, the worldwide implications of a machine so strong no one has any privacy, any freedom to speak freely even in their own homes or on the streets."

"What have you concluded?"

"We agree with you, Everett," Sandra said. "As citizens of the United States, we think Project Eagle will turn the United States into a world dictator. It should never be activated."

He came around the desk and stood in front of it. "What you're saying is you think we should destroy it?"

"No, sir," Jordon took up the explanation.

"Then what?"

"We want to divide it."

"I don't understand." He studied them carefully.

"Sir," Wyatt started. "Chip had some good uses for the project before it became a weapon. We suggest those remain. The rest should be divided for safe-keeping."

"I take it you," he spread his arms, encompassing the group, "are to be the holders of the pieces."

"No," Annie said. "If we kept them we could be picked off one by one until we gave them up."

"Then where do they get stored?"

Sandra looked at Wyatt with a smile. He returned it. Jordon's face broke into a grin and Annie's dazzling smile teased the Commander in Chief.

"We thought, Mr. President," Wyatt said, "the space shuttle would be the best place."

Casey Horton broke into laughter. The group looked at her. She joined them, but didn't stand with Everett. She took the space next to Jordon Ames. Melanie, too, left her position and came to stand next to Wyatt.

"Are you two joining this mutiny?"

Casey nodded. "I think it's a wonderful idea."

"We'd put the stones in the next satellite to be launched. Since no one will have all the pieces, and since an orbiting satellite is impossible to compromise, the stones will be safe and the earth will be rid of a machine that could enslave the world."

Horton took the suggestion and weighed it. It was better than the ones his advisors had come up with. The military wanted it back and wanted to go into mass production. The FBI wanted sole access to it. The State Department wanted a joint program for all areas and Senator Rutledge wanted it destroyed. Everett was in favor of its destruction. He knew the power it could command and he knew that kind of power was both heady and corrupt.

"Everett, I think they've got the best solution," Melanie West said. "I stand with them."

Sandra smiled and looked up at the President. "Everett?" she said.

"You know, Sandra. I asked Casey once for her opinion of you. She said you'd make a great President. I think I'm going to have to agree with her."

"Thank you, sir."

He went back to his desk and picked up his phone. A second later he said, "Marsha, get me Daniel Carmichael at NASA. I need to know when the next shuttle goes up."

Amid the celebration that took place after Everett made his decision, the doors opened and Bradford Campbell Rutledge came in. Sandra saw him first. She stiffened in her metal chair. Her hand began to shake and she placed her glass on the sofa table. Finding Wyatt next to her, she took his hand.

"Brad," Everett called. "I'm glad to see you."

Brad came forward. Sandra's heart beat fast. Her hands were suddenly cold. She looked at Annie. Color had drained from her face.

"I'd like to propose a toast," the President said. "To Brad Rutledge, who in the past couple of weeks has had to lie to his family." Everett's gaze was trained directly on Sandra. "He's been the informant, investigating the undersecretary of defense. Under my direct orders, Brad has been able to tell no one what his assignment was, thus hurting his family and putting his daughter's life in peril." He raised his coffee cup. "Here, here."

Sandra didn't drink. She looked at her father. Tears clouded in her eyes. He'd been working for the President. He wasn't a traitor and she'd doubted him. Water spilled down her cheeks. She felt guilty. How could she ever face him?

"Sandra," he kneeled in front of her. "Can you forgive me?"

"Forgive you," she said. "Dad . . ." Then she was in his arms, hugging him. "Forgive me, Dad. I doubted you. I thought you were trying to sell the stones. I never thought—"

"It's behind us, Sandra. We each doubted the other. I said things about Senator Randolph to get you to leave him. I wanted you safe, and while you were with him there was nothing I could do. I beg your forgiveness . . . and yours, too, Senator."

Sandra moved back and looked at Wyatt. She held her breath. The two men she loved most in the world stood in front of her. She wanted them to be friends.

"I can't very well hold a grudge against my future father-in-law," Wyatt said.

Again the quiet before the storm. Suddenly, everyone was hugging and kissing, congratulating her and Wyatt and asking if they'd set a date.

Annie was the only person who hung back. Sandra knew she hated their father. Yet, when she looked at her sister, what she saw was fear. She'd rarely ever seen that emotion in Annie's eyes.

"Annie, what's wrong?"

Jordon stayed near her. He whispered something Sandra couldn't hear.

"I'm scared," she answered.

"Why, Annie?"

"I can't tell him."

"Hello, Annie," Brad addressed his oldest daughter.

Sandra looked up to see her father and her mother.

"Mom," she said. Her mother reached down to hug her.

"I hear you know," Melissa said.

She was talking to Annie. "Will somebody please tell me what's going on?"

"Annie discovered who her real father was," Jordon answered her question. Brad and Melissa Rutledge looked as if they were about to faint. "It's all right," Jordon assured them.

"I know about the birth certificate," Annie said. "I found it a couple of months before Sand got married. I thought you'd chosen Sand and left me to live in poverty. She got the advantages and I got nothing."

"Annie, that birth certificate—"

"I know," she interrupted her father. "My real father's name was Curtis Pittman. He was from Atlanta."

"How did you find out?" Melissa asked her.

"I have a friend," Jordon answered, "who's an investigator. He told us. And I found Curtis Pittman's diary. Everything is recorded there."

Brad stared at Jordon for a long time.

"I'm sorry, Dad. I said some terrible things to you . . . and to you, Sand."

Tears looked as if they were imminent. The sisters hugged, the parents hugged. All the pain and fear seemed to heal and they stood together.

"We better get out of here," Wyatt suggested. "After all, that man," he pointed at the President, "has a country to run. And I'd like to visit my office and go home."

"You wouldn't want to leave without these," Everett said, holding up several sheets of paper.

Sandra accepted hers. The last few weeks had been a nightmare and this one sheet of paper made it all right. With this she could resume her life.

By order of the President, it began. Everett Horton had by executive order issued her a presidential pardon.

EPILOGUE

Sandra stood looking through the window. Grass rolled away from the cabin like an emerald carpet. The trees were thick with leaves and she could barely see the road. She stood here often, thinking back on the day Wyatt had come into her life.

He was asleep. She'd awakened early and come to the window. They didn't get to the cabin much with his work in Congress, but when an opportunity opened they'd run off to the mountains. Everett began calling it the Pocono Senate.

"What are you doing there?" Wyatt asked. "You can't even see that road."

She turned around. Wyatt sat on the steps. It was one of the memories she had of him. The first time he came downstairs, that's where he'd stood.

"I know it's there." She went and sat next to him. He put his arm around her and cradled her against him. "I love this place."

"I love you," Wyatt said. He kissed the top of her head. "You know what I remember most about the cabin?"

She shook her head and looked at him.

"That table over there." He pointed to the polished wooden table where they usually ate. "When I woke up that first day after I'd come downstairs, I was on the sofa. You were sitting at the table. Your hair had been in a ponytail, but you'd pulled it loose. The light made a halo around your head and I knew I was in love with you."

Sandra couldn't speak past the lump in her throat. That had been eight months ago. She reached up and kissed him. He gathered her close and passion took hold of her.

"Thank God I found you," he whispered against her mouth.

"You didn't find me," she contradicted. "I found you."

Wyatt lifted his mouth and stared at her. "You're not going to start that again." He lifted her onto his lap and kissed her cheek. "I came looking—"

"For my father—"

"And found you."

Wyatt stood up with her. He carried her up the stairs to the bedroom they shared. He lowered her to the floor. Sandra saw passion darken his eyes.

"Wyatt, we don't have time for this." His mouth touched hers as she spoke. "We have to get to the wedding rehearsal. Jordon and Annie will be waiting." He kissed her again. Her insides melted.

"We'll get there. You can drive." Wyatt moved the strap of her nightgown and kissed her shoulder. "It's your helicopter."

"We'll be late," she murmured.

"It'll be all right," he said, as he nipped the skin under her ear. "They were late for ours." He lifted his head and looked at her. "What do you think they were doing?"

"Wyatt, they weren't late for ours. Ours is tomorrow," she reminded him.

"In that case they can't start without us." He took her mouth.

Sandra went up on her tiptoes, forgetting everything except the man she loved. She returned his kiss with all the fervor that gripped her. His hands took her waist and spanned it. Her arms climbed about his neck. She melted against him. His arms tightened, fitting her to his shape and devouring her mouth.

Wyatt made her feel alive. After eight months, when their lives no longer ran from minute to minute, when the press no longer hounded them for stories, she still loved being with him, learning the little things that made him happy, learning how to take his pain away, and sharing in everything that was him.

She liked telling him her secrets, having him there when she needed someone to talk to or someone to hold in front of a warm fire.

Wyatt removed her gown. It pooled at her feet. He stared at her. She should be used to him by now. It had been eight months since they'd left the Oval Office. Yet, she felt like it was their first time. Her breath came in short gasps and her breasts rose and fell in anticipation of his touch. Warmth poured over her as his hands moved deliciously over her skin.

He ran his hands up her back and into her hair. Her body aligned to his from shoulder to thigh. "Will you marry me, Dr. Rutledge?" He spoke as he angled her face to kiss her mouth.

"I am marrying you, Senator. Tomorrow."

"Good," he said, his voice low and intoxicating. "I need a wife and I've picked you." He lifted her and laid her on the bed. He joined her there. She came alive when he touched her. Her skin burned, glowed, melted under his hands. The world shrank, became only two people, her and Wyatt.

He looked at her. In his eyes she'd always be beautiful. She moaned as his body covered hers, moaned as he entered her. Like mirror images they fit together perfectly. Wyatt slipped his hands around her. He worked them over her hips and lifted her to meet him as he joined himself with her, combined his hard thrusts with her soft folds.

He knew she'd undo him. It happened every time he touched her. This time was no different. He looked at her face in the clear morning light. Rapture showed there and he'd done it, he'd put the glow in her face and the dark passion in her eyes. As he moved back and forth, the emotions crossing her face were as erotic as the hands raking down his back, making him arch into her. Throaty guttural sounds pushed him forward as her body rose and fell to meet his.

He didn't think he could hold out much longer. He wanted to give to her, let her know that he loved her, that this was how he felt, how she made him feel, but the smoothness of her legs, the velvety soft feel of her skin, the way she moved against him, taking him in and holding him just long enough before she let him move out snapped his control. He fought for control, knowing it was a losing battle, knowing that with Sandra he could no more control his emotions than he could control the way his heart beat when he looked at her.

"Sandra!" he shouted one final time in an effort to hold them in that one erotic place for a moment longer. Then he exploded inside her and together they plunged over the edge of the world.

Sandra's breath was ragged when she came back to earth. It was past time when she and Wyatt should be in Starfighter and on their way down the mountain, but they were still entwined in each other's arms.

Wyatt reached over her and grasped the remote control. He pointed it toward the television and turned it on. Live pictures from Cape Canaveral at the Kennedy Space Center in Florida came through clearly. The countdown was on the screen. They watched, their hearts pounding. This particular shuttle was scheduled to carry a very special satellite which it would launch before returning to earth.

"Ten . . . nine . . . eight." Sandra and Wyatt counted with the commentator. They were sure there were several other people also watching and counting along. Everett and Casey Horton along with Bradford and Melissa Rutledge were on site for the launch. Jordon and Annie were waiting for them in Washington, Sam Parker was at the Pentagon, and Sandra was cradled in Wyatt's arms.

"Three . . . two . . . one . . . liftoff."

Legacy

To William D. Bennett, who taught me math and chemistry but left me with a legacy that can only be expressed in words, if accompanied with friendship and happy tears.

PROLOGUE

"Money, Erika, like poverty, is one of life's true burdens." Carlton Lipton-Graves fell back against the pillows. He was pale white and small, never having stood more than five-feet, five inches, even in his prime. Now a withered, old man in his nineties, he looked like a dwarf in the huge bed, its headboard stretching nearly as high as the ceiling. Erika St. James sat on the white coverlet, watching him die. She'd been doing it for nearly a year, and the strain took its toll on her energy level. "Some want to take it from you," he continued. "Swindle it from you, con you out of it, even steal it. They'll try any means." He slapped the bed weakly with his fist. "Some want you to *give* it to them, as if somebody gave it to you." He muttered the last. "Others criticize you for what you do or what you don't do with it." He closed his eyes and took a deep breath. His small rib cage expanded and contracted. Erika thought he'd dissolve into wracking coughs as he'd done in days past, but surprisingly he remained calm and coherent.

"Carlton, what are you talking about?"

"It's no favor I've done you, Erika." His gaze was steady, although his eyes were faded and aged. "You or Michael."

"Michael?" she frowned. "Who's Michael?"

"I'm sorry, Erika. I'll tell you that now." He continued as if she hadn't spoken. "It'll probably do him good. Get him off that damn hill. Been up there too long. Time for him to join the living, not the dying."

Erika thought it a strange comment from a man who probably wouldn't last the night. She berated herself for thinking such a thing.

She and Carlton had been friends since she was a child of eight, for twenty-six years. He was sixty years older. Together they had formed a special friendship. A bond existed between them that only the very young and the very old can understand. She had lived in California for the past eight years, and her visits were frequent, but never had he mentioned anyone named Michael. When had he met him? For a moment Erika thought Carlton might be senile, but quickly abandoned the idea. At ninety-four, Carlton had a mind as sharp as it had been when she first met him. He was rambling, but he was entitled, and she was obliged to listen, tired or not. Tonight was possibly his last night on earth. He could do whatever, say whatever, he wanted. Erika didn't mind. Tears gathered in her eyes. Carlton had called her a year ago, almost to the day, and asked her to return. She knew he was ill. There had been nothing to keep her in California, certainly not Bill Castle, her former fiancé, a man who'd run off and married another woman without the courtesy of breaking it off with her first. Carlton's request was a blessing, a chance to escape the sympathetic eyes and hushed whispers that had followed her entrance into a room.

Bill Castle, an entertainment lawyer, was invited to the best celebrity parties, and Erika joined him in his high profile lifestyle. His abrupt marriage had left her reeling and emotionally stung. He was no better than her mother. When Carlton called, needing her, she came here—home. The only place she'd called home since they'd met.

Carlton closed his eyes. She remembered the day she'd met him. She'd been running from some horror, long since forgotten. Without thinking, she'd run through the hedges and over the lawn. There wasn't a gate then. Nothing had impeded her need to get as far away from her mother as possible. She ran through the front door and smack into him. He wasn't as tall as her father had been—he was only half a giant—but his strange white hair and scowling expression put fear in her heart and closed her throat, even to the scream that lodged there. Then he laughed. Not a booming, from-the-belly-laugh, but a happy laugh. She hadn't relaxed even then. Grown people often began with a laugh, but ended being angry. Carlton hadn't. He invited her to tea. They drank it in his garden, a wonderful place full of flowers and smelling of sunshine and fall. She remembered that smell to this day. He invited her to come back whenever she was free, and she'd left smiling. Only her father had ever treated her like that.

Erika came back to the present. Carlton lay quietly, his eyes closed, his breaths even. Brushing a nostalgic tear away, she moved to get up. She wouldn't leave him. It was her duty to stay, a duty she considered more an honor than a command. Erika had resigned herself to the fact that he wouldn't recover from his illness. It had been diagnosed as heart disease, but his body was simply giving out from use. Another tear escaped her.

He stopped her. "Where are you going?"

"I thought you were asleep," she said, resuming her position on the spread.

Erika wore a satin robe. It was a luscious green and contrasted with the white spread. Carlton had given her the robe for her last birthday.

He took her hand. His fingers were thin and felt bony against her flesh. "I won't sleep again. I know that now. When I close my eyes it'll be for the last time."

Tears sprang to Erika's eyes. She didn't contradict him. The doctor had said to keep him comfortable, agree to anything he said, and give him whatever he wanted. Medical science had done everything it could. It was up to a higher authority now.

"I did want to see Michael again, but . . ."

Erika thought he was talking more to himself than to her. Who was Michael? Maybe she could call him. Have him come as quickly as he could.

Carlton interrupted her train of thought. "I guess you'll have to tell him for me."

"Tell him what?" she whispered. "Who is Michael?"

"My grandson."

Grandson? This was the first she'd heard of him. She knew Carlton had had a son. He died three years before Erika met Carlton, the same year her father had died. The commonality gave them the foundation for their alliance. It was rare for the old man to mention his son. Erika thought about him. She understood. She hadn't been able to explain her pain after her father died. But a grandson!

"Where is he?" Erika asked, unable to keep an incredulous note out of her voice. "He should be here." She had known Carlton for twenty-six years. How old was his grandson? Thirty? Thirty-four? He had to be at least as old as she was. What had happened to him? Why had he never come to see his grandfather? Why, when Carlton knew he was dying, had he called for her, and not his own flesh and blood? Of course she'd been glad to come back. Not just because Carlton was her friend, but because her life in Los Angeles had gone sour. Bill was no longer a consideration. Her position as Vice President of Marketing for a manufacturing company that made polyurethane products and sold them, mainly to the fantasy factories of Hollywood, meant nothing, and she was fed up with the shallow personalities of the west coast.

Returning to Philadelphia to help Carlton had seemed a perfect reason to leave the stares behind and begin anew. But even knowing Carlton was ill hadn't prepared her for his dying. She knew she'd have to help him at Graves Enterprises, and she'd looked forward to the opportunity. Carlton had been her teacher more than any of her college professors at UCLA. When applying for jobs, she'd stood heads above other candidates in her ability to analyze a market and understand the dynamics of trending and competitive advantage. From the time she was a small child, Carlton had taught her how to run a diverse business.

"He should be here. Doesn't he know . . ." She stopped, realizing what she was about to say—did he know his grandfather was dying? "I'll call him, Carlton." Erika leaned forward. A phone sat on the nightstand next to Carlton's bed. The ancient black instrument sat incongruously among brown plastic bottles of prescription drugs and a silver pitcher of water. The ice inside caused droplets to form on the shiny surface. Erika noticed a drop slide down the side to disappear into the white cloth at its base.

"No phone. He's stuck on that mountain and no one can get him off." Then Carlton looked at her. His eyes cleared and he stared as if he was seeing her for the first time in years. "Maybe *you* can, Erika. I'm counting on you. Get Michael to come back."

Erika felt manipulated. She wouldn't promise a dying man she would do something she wouldn't. She couldn't. Promises were the most sacred things one person could offer another. She'd had enough of them made to her and broken. No matter what Dr. Mason had said, she was not going to promise Carlton anything having to do with his grandson.

"Carlton, I didn't even know you had a grandson."

"He needs someone, too," Carlton said.

Erika swallowed. She knew exactly what Carlton meant. When she was eight she'd needed a friend and Carlton had been there. Erika, at thirty-four, knew that need didn't go away with adulthood.

"Promise me, Erika?"

She hesitated. "Carlton—"

"Promise me," he interrupted, grasping her hand in his bony one.

Erika peered into his eyes.

"Promise me!" He raised his voice, a shuddering, weak imitation of the voice she remembered from childhood.

She nodded, hating Carlton for forcing her to do something she didn't want to do.

"Get me the book." Carlton pointed toward the large, ornate desk in the corner of the room. It had been used by generations of Graves since the 1800s. Erika went to it. She didn't see any book. "In the drawer," he whispered, his voice weak.

Erika pulled a drawer open and found file folders, each neatly labeled by Carlton's secretary. She closed it and opened another. "Bottom," he said, raising himself up on his elbows as if the effort cost him all his energy.

She found it, a leather-bound photo album with the name Michael Lawrence Lipton-Graves embossed on it in gold letters. It was obviously old and well-worn. The leather was soft, with small creases from being opened and closed.

"Bring it." He reached toward the album.

Erika took it back to him and placed it within reach. He lay back against the pillows, clutching it to him as if holding something precious. His eyes softened and clouded for a moment. Erika had never seen him look so vulnerable. She'd seen him weakened by age and pain, but this photo album had added a weakness that only love could cause.

Erika only barely remembered that kind of love. She never got it from her mother, but her father had loved her unconditionally. She knew Carlton, too, loved her, but not with the same passion as for someone whose bloodline was the same as his and flowed in his veins. Michael Lawrence Lipton-Graves alone held that distinction. When Carlton left this earth, left behind him would be a piece of himself.

Carlton opened the soft leather album, using his gnarled, arthritic fingers, which must be in pain. Turning the book toward Erika, he pointed to a photo. A small black child of about ten years old looked up from the time-encased shot.

"Michael," Carlton said . . . and died.

CHAPTER 1

Michael woke with a start. It wasn't the dream this time—but the crate against his back had fallen away. He lay on the small wharf next to the rowboat. The bobbing had relaxed him and he'd fallen into a light sleep. Pulling the crate back into place, he repositioned himself. The August sun warmed his face, but fall came early in the mountains and winter's snow would soon follow it. Michael liked winter. He liked the freshness in the air, even when he'd lived in the city. Winter days were fresh, biting sometimes, but always clear enough to get his mental juices flowing. Maybe this winter he'd finally get rid of Abby's image.

Michael looked up. Birds, in the standard V formation, flew southward in the sky overhead. Trees swayed in the light breeze. It was quiet, relaxing. Yet he felt disturbed. He'd dreamed of Abby last night, and since then hadn't been able to shake the helpless feeling that he should have done something. Over and over he'd replayed that dream in his head. He couldn't have done anything, didn't have time to react before everything was over. Yet she haunted him from time to time. Just when he thought she was going away, she'd show up again.

A movement from the side caught Michael. He saw her. For a millisecond he thought Abby had stepped out of his dream, but watching her come forward he realized she was just another lost tourist—tourist or weekend camper coming up to the mountains for the weekend who couldn't find the campgrounds. Why did they think camping meant going to a park and plugging in all the amenities they had at home?

She came toward him, one hand raised against the sun. She wore pants, not jeans like most of the tourists but slacks like women wore to offices, and shoes, not tennis sneakers. Her blouse was white, long-sleeved, and soft. The breeze pressed it against her breasts. Her gait was confident and purposeful. Despite her shoes, she didn't tiptoe over the stones that defined the path to the jetty where Michael had a small rowboat. Something stirred inside Michael. For the first time in a long while he felt the beginnings of arousal. Michael gauged her gait. She walked as if she knew where she was going. She reminded him of a fast car, dark and sleek, with underlying power. He'd had a car like that once.

She had to be from his office. Although he'd never set eyes on her before, somehow he recognized that corporate control, that I-can-do-the-impossible attitude.

Stopping in front of him, she studied the mountains in the distance as if she were assessing the place, looking it over with thoughts of buying it. It wasn't for sale.

"Are you Michael Lawrence?" She asked the question without looking at him.

He eyed her, not moving from his position. She had long legs and short hair. If he stood up she'd probably come to his shoulder. He was six foot two. That made her tall for a woman. Her skin was flawlessly smooth and as richly brown as a thoroughbred's coat. No one had come looking for him in the year he'd been here. Except for the last week, when a car had come three times to deliver telegrams he hadn't bothered to open, he'd seen only lost tourists. Now this woman had come specifically for him.

"Who are you?" he asked. His voice came out gruff. He didn't want to be found. He wanted to be left alone.

"I'm Erika St. James."

The name meant nothing to him, and she hadn't said it as if it should. "Do I know you?"

"No." She shook her head. Wispy curls were caught and kissed by the wind. Michael frowned at the thought of how that hair would feel. "I sent you three telegrams about your grandfather."

Michael didn't move, but he eyed her closely. So she'd sent the telegrams. "You've got the wrong guy. I haven't got a grandfather"

"You're Michael Lawrence?"

He nodded.

"Carlton Lipton-Graves told me you were his grandson."

"Not to my knowledge." He shrugged. The name meant nothing to him. Both his sets of grandparents were dead. He'd never known any of them. He squinted. What was she doing here? She knew his name. Why did she think this Carlton was related to him?

Her eyes captured his attention. They were brown, huge, and fringed by dark lashes. He wanted to keep looking into them, but forced himself to look away.

"You didn't read the telegrams?" she asked.

"I have no use for telegrams, newspapers, TV, telephones, or fax machines, for that matter. Whatever you've come here for, I'm sorry it was a wasted trip. Good day, Ms. St. James."

He went back to his position against the crate, closing his eyes, dismissing her. She didn't leave. He would have heard her footsteps on the gravel. What was she waiting for? He opened his eyes. She was standing in the same position, her hands on her hips, her breasts rising and falling with controlled breathing. From his position on the wooden wharf his gaze was drawn to her.

"Is there something else you have to say?"

"Yes . . . no," she corrected.

"Then have a nice trip back to the city."

She turned away, then stopped. Michael could see her hands curl into tight balls. Every line of her body was stiff as she stood still. A moment later she looked back at him. He thought she was about to say something, but changed her mind. She turned again, starting up the slight incline that led back to his cabin and eventually to the road. Michael watched the sway of her hips as she moved away from him. It had been a long time, he thought since he'd wanted a woman, but God, he could want her. Closing his eyes, he shifted his body to relieve some of the tightness in his loins and went back to himself.

He should have asked how she knew his name, and why she thought his grandfather was still alive, but he hadn't. He didn't want to. He didn't want to talk to anyone. Since he'd come here he wanted only solitude, and up to now he'd had it. When the telegrams arrived he'd thought they were from his office or his mother, or Malick, his old friend. Only they knew where he'd gone when he left the city. He'd dropped the telegrams in the drawer with the unopened letters he'd received shortly after coming here. He wasn't going back then, and he wasn't going back now. No telegram would get him off this mountain.

Erika turned back and checked over her shoulder. Thank God she'd known he was older than that picture Carlton had shown her. The album was full of pictures of Michael at various stages of his growth and development. She'd gone through the whole album before embarking on this trip. Carlton had captured the high points of a man's life to this point: his school days, sporting events, graduations, law school acceptance—a mini-world inside the pages of a hundred-page book.

Michael, she estimated from the pictures, must be in his mid-thirties. He fascinated her. He hadn't moved. She knew he could still see her, yet his gaze was as fixed as if he were the only person on earth. He'd made her angry. She had nearly told him right then and there. Before the words tumbled out she'd caught herself, though, thought better of it. She remembered her mother telling her that her father was dead. She hadn't thought to soften the blow. She'd just blurted out the words. "He's dead. Your father's dead." They'd hit her like sharp rocks.

Michael had made her angry enough, but she held her tongue. Since he hadn't read the telegrams, he didn't know. Obviously, there was bad blood between Carlton and his grandson. Denying that he existed was only a defense mechanism. It was probably tied to the reason he was hiding out at this place. She'd wondered what he was doing here during her drive into the Maryland mountains, but she hadn't thought to ask the attorney about it after the will had been read. She was too stunned. First she'd found out Carlton had a grandson, and on the heels of that she'd been confounded by the terms of his will.

Still, no one deserved to hear of the death of a loved one without concern for its impact. There would be time for that later. It wouldn't be dark for another four hours. She had made a reservation at the only motel she'd seen in the last seventy miles. She had some time, but not that much. It had taken longer to negotiate the narrow, winding curves to find him than she expected. She didn't relish the idea of driving down this mountain without the benefit of daylight. Once she'd talked to Michael, she could go back there and spend the night before driving back to Philadelphia.

She had hopes of him returning with her, but now that she'd come up against his hard exterior she knew he'd need time to get used to the idea. Hadn't the general store owner, where she'd stopped to ask directions, told her he came in to pick up food, spoke sparingly, and kept to himself? She could see how his attitude could put people off.

His look reminded her of the old mountain men—dark, unkempt beard, broad shoulders that spoke of hard work despite the heavy, plaid jacket he wore. His denim-clad legs were long, and she couldn't help notice the strength of his thighs. His hair was long, and his clothes were covered with paint, oil, and something else she didn't want to define. Yet his eyes made her breath catch. Deep set and ringed with signs of lack of sleep, they were light brown mirrors that spoke of great pain. It was probably his eyes that pulled at her compassion. They also stirred passion in her. She had no doubt of that. After Bill, though, she'd have nothing to do with a man for a long time, even if she wanted to.

Erika looked at the cabin as it came into view. She glanced at the clear, blue sky and took a great gulp of clean, mountain air into her lungs. When she was in grade school she'd dreamed of living in a cabin like the pilgrims did, fishing in the nearby stream and cooking her own food. This place seemed to have everything her youthful mind had thought of. Then she got closer, and her dream shattered. It looked as rustic as

Michael did, made of logs and covered with a rusty tin roof. She wondered if it leaked during rainstorms, and was glad she wouldn't be here to find out. The perimeter of the small structure was cluttered with old tires and junked auto parts. She wondered how long they had been there, since the only vehicle in the area was her Bronco. Everything had a rusty, discarded look about it as if things were dead, things with no hope of returning to useful life. Weeds overran the path to the door. What could have happened to Michael Lawrence to bring him to this kind of life?

At the Bronco she picked up her phone from the front seat and dialed the office.

"Erika, thank God it's you," Jeff Rivers, her chief financial officer, greeted her after his secretary put her through.

"Is everything all right?" she asked, climbing into the seat.

"For the time being. The stock market closed at three, so nothing more can be done until Monday."

"How was activity?"

"If I said brisk I'd be putting it mildly," he told her.

"It will calm down, Jeff. The market needs to get used to the idea of me sitting in the CEO's chair."

"You've been in that chair for over a year now."

"I know, but Carlton was always there to lean on, and the market knew it."

"I think we still need to keep an eye on this."

"I agree. We don't want any surprises."

Erika could almost see the financially savvy brain spinning in Jeff's head.

"I'll get to work on it. Meanwhile, what did you find out about Michael Lawrence?"

Erika took a deep breath and turned to look back toward the lake. She couldn't see Michael from where she sat, but she assumed he was in the same position he'd been in minutes ago. The news of Carlton's grandson had gone through corporate headquarters like a tornado over flat ground. Morale dipped to an all time low, and she was responsible for raising it.

No one at Graves Enterprises knew Carlton had a grandson, and they were naturally nervous to suddenly find he held their fates in his hands. They looked to her to protect them.

"So far I haven't been able to talk to him," she went on to explain. "He didn't read any of the telegrams I sent."

"Does he even know Carlton is dead?"

He doesn't even know Carlton's his grandfather, she thought, but didn't say. "I don't think so."

Jeff let out a long breath. Erika could hear it through the cordless phone. "I don't envy you."

"How long do you expect to be there?"

"I figure I'll wait around and talk to him, then spend the night at a motel where I made a reservation. In the morning I'll drive home."

"If I find out anything else, I'll leave a message on your answering machine."

"Thanks, Jeff."

Erika pushed the off button and snapped the antenna down. Someone was trying to unseat her, gain control of Graves Enterprises by a hostile takeover, and they hadn't been able to find out who or why. Jeff Rivers was a good man, and she knew he was loyal. If anyone could find the true culprit, it was Jeff.

Carlton had left Michael and her more than enough stock for control of the business, but someone coming in could ruin her plans, force a seat on the board and, with enough influence and charisma, sway the other board members.

Erika was confident in her position at Graves. She knew what she was doing. Carlton had taught her the business from the ground up, but his death, a possible stock problem, an unexpected grandson, and the morale issue were more problems than she wanted to deal with.

Erika wished she were at the office helping Jeff. There had to be something she could do. They should be searching out this problem together. Graves Enterprises was her company. Yet Carlton had forced her to come up this mountain and talk to his grandson.

Erika shivered. Without heat, it was cold in the Bronco. Maybe she'd wait in the cabin. Michael needed time to think about why she'd come looking for him. He'd know she hadn't left if he didn't hear the Bronco motor start up and the sound die away in a fading Doppler effect. When he came in, she'd tell him. In the meantime she was starving. Maybe she'd fix him something to eat. She'd promised the general store owner she'd deliver his groceries. She hoped he wouldn't mind her sharing some of them with him.

Erika got two heavy bags from the back of the truck and elbowed the cabin door open. She stopped suddenly, stepping backward and propping her shoulder against the doorjamb as she tried desperately to hold onto the bags. Breath left her body. The place was filthy. The main room of the cabin was littered with dirty clothes and the remnants of food in various stages of decay. Erika wrinkled her nose as the odor of filth and sweat assaulted her.

"Oh my God!" she gasped, grateful it was too cold for flies.

The urge to turn and run gripped her. Waiting in the truck seemed infinitely more appealing. Then she remembered Carlton. Michael was his grandson, and she'd made a solemn promise to comply with his wishes. From what she could see, after a five minute conversation with Michael Lawrence, he needed family support. At the moment she was as close to family as he could get. She was obligated to Carlton to at least tell him about him. She also needed his help to carry out Carlton's wishes.

Erika hoisted the bags a little higher and went inside. How could he live in this filth? The place had two rooms. There was an area that served as a kitchen and another with a sofa she would have called a living room, except no living creature should enter it. Along one wall was an open door. An unmade bed sat inside.

Pushing aside the debrís, she set the bags on the kitchen table—if it could be called that. It was four foot square, and every inch of it was covered with some kind of crud. Erika frowned, refusing to even think of what it could be. Two spindle-back chairs sat on one side of it. All the spindles were missing from one, and only two remained in the second. Their seats were both covered with a sticky goo.

She tried to remember how long Carlton had said Michael had been on this mountain. Hadn't he ever cleaned this place? She went about opening the two windows in the main room and the front and back doors. She didn't enter the bedroom. Cold air swept through the place, ridding it of some of the smell.

Erika had left home at sunrise. She'd had an almost inedible tuna sandwich and a cup of oily coffee at a truck stop, her only meal of the day. Facing her was a teeth-gnashing trip to the motel. She wasn't about to do it on an empty stomach. Despite the state of the place, she was still hungry.

Wrinkling her nose, she picked up one of the open containers of old food between two fingers. Holding it out in front of her, she went to the trashbasket. It was overfilled with garbage. Dropping the container inside, she pulled the plastic bag up and tied the ends before going in search of a replacement. She found a dust-encrusted box of bags under the sink. With her face in a perpetual frown, she went about picking up the containers of decayed food and dropping them in the trash. She couldn't cook, let alone eat, in a kitchen this dirty.

Starting with the open containers of food, she raked each of them into the trash bin. When she finished the kitchen area she continued, searching for more trash in other areas of the single room. Returning to the kitchen she stacked the full trash bag next to the other one. Then she attacked the kitchen, washing dishes, wiping down counters and scrubbing the table and chairs. Why she was doing this, she didn't know. Something seemed to drive her. Carlton had been more than a friend. He'd treated her like a granddaughter, and she looked on him as a relative. From the way people treated her at the funeral and afterward, she knew they saw her as a part of his family, too. Erika wiped moisture away from her eyes.

Carlton was her final link to a loved one. Accepting that she was alone in the world was taking a toll.

Erika scrubbed harder at the stain on the table. She called it therapy. In the week since the funeral she'd been too busy writing notes and seeing to Carlton's affairs. The long drive had afforded her some time alone, time to think—until she started the ascent to the cabin. Now she needed to be unemotional when she talked to Carlton's grandson. She couldn't show her grief or loss. She couldn't dissolve into the tears that had been close to the surface of her emotions since she'd been called back from California. Keeping her hands busy was a way of controlling her thoughts.

Memories of Carlton came to her, anyway. For twenty-six years they'd shared a friendship that transcended their races. He'd been more a parent to her than her own mother. He'd taught her, consoled her, and praised her accomplishments. The only secret he'd kept from her was about Michael and the contents of his will. How was she to know he'd left her a fortune, but she'd only get it if she and Michael could work together?

Time passed and Michael did not return to the cabin. Hunger overcame Erika. She went through the bags the grocer had given her. Everything was in a can or a box, except for the two steaks and four sweet potatoes he'd thrown in with a wicked wink when she'd offered to deliver the food. Obviously, Michael never had visitors, and the old man in the store was surely matchmaking. Little did he know she wasn't there due to any romantic interest in the man she'd found by the water's edge.

She tried the gas stove but it didn't work. She could hear it, but nothing came through. She was sure nothing worked properly here. Did Michael ever make himself a meal? The open cans she'd picked up looked as if he'd eaten directly from them. *Well, not today,* she thought. Pulling the stove units free, she dropped them in the pan of soapy water she'd changed three times in her effort to make the place habitable. Ten minutes later she used a pipe cleaner to free them of the dirt preventing the gas from flowing properly.

By the time the kitchen was spotless Erika's stomach growled with anticipated hunger. She ached for the microwave oven sitting among the possessions she'd stored when she left California. With it she could have a meal cooked in minutes. As it was, instead of baking the potatoes, she cut them up and dropped them in boiling water. When they were nearly done, she put the steaks on, prepared broccoli, and brewed a pot of decaf coffee. From the look of Michael's eyes, he didn't need caffeine.

Using chipped plates and silverware that must have been forged in a munitions plant, Erika set the table. Michael had yet to make an appearance, but it was time to eat now. She would wait no longer. If she wanted to get down the mountain by nightfall she'd have to leave within the next hour. Smoothing her hair back, she turned toward the door. She'd go get him.

As she reached the door Michael came through it, practically bumping into her. Surprise registered in his eyes. Erika jumped back and her heart thudded and her breath left her. She gasped, filling her lungs with air a moment later.

"What the hell are you doing?" he asked.

"I've made coffee," she told him, recovering. She kept the emotion out of her voice. "I've prepared something for us to eat." To keep herself from having to endure the intensity of his stare she went to the stove and checked the food. "We need to talk."

"I don't want you here." He came toward her.

Erika sidestepped him. She moved to the sink and picked up two mismatched cups and saucers. Her heartbeat accelerated, but she kept quiet. She'd promised Carlton.

"What are you doing?" Michael followed her.

"I'm sure you can see what I'm doing."

"Is there something wrong with you?" He grabbed her hand, taking the cup and stopping her actions. "Don't you know when you're not wanted?"

She snatched her arm away, taking a step back and staring at him. She certainly understood when she wasn't wanted. It had been drummed into her since she was very young. Quickly she snatched the cup away from his hand and turned back to the table, making unnecessary adjustments to the knives and forks.

"Look," he said. "I'm sorry. I didn't mean that. It's just that I don't want . . . could you stop that?" After a moment he added. "Please?"

Erika straightened and faced him in the only clean area in the place. She forced herself to remain still. He looked older than she had thought at first. When she'd seen him by the river she'd thought he was asleep, but judging by the look of him he hadn't slept in weeks. He had large bags under his bloodshot eyes. The episode at the door had brought her close enough to smell alcohol, if there had been any on him. She hadn't smelled it, so she attributed his state to some form of insomnia. She didn't know if it was voluntarily or not. His eyebrows were thick and bushy. By the stream she'd seen defined muscles, but now his clothes appeared baggy, hanging on his body as if he'd lost a lot of weight.

"Say what you want to say and leave me in peace." His voice jarred her. "I don't want you cleaning my house, and I don't want you cooking meals for me."

"You certainly look like you need someone to do it. How can you live in this filth?" Her gaze swept the room. Michael's didn't follow it.

He put his hands up, palms facing out, to stop her when she would have gone on. Erika saw him weave as if he wouldn't be able to stand up for long.

"Are you all right?" Involuntarily, she took a step toward him.

"I'm fine. Just go!"

She jumped at the force of his voice.

"Sit down." She took another step toward him but stopped when his head came up and his look pinned her in place. He staggered to the sofa, now devoid of extraneous clothing, and sat down.

"When was the last time you ate? Or slept, for that matter?"

"I'm not your responsibility," he shouted. "My rituals are none of your business." His hand went to his stomach, rubbing it as if he were in pain. Erika recognized hunger.

"You ought to be somebody's," she muttered. "You obviously haven't eaten in way too long." The food was ready. She made the plates at the stove and placed them on the small table. She called him, instinctively knowing he'd hate it if she came to help him.

"Would you like to eat there?" She hadn't done more in that area of the room than remove dirty clothes to get at the decaying food. She wanted to talk to him, but she preferred the cleanliness of the kitchen area.

Michael didn't want her here. She was too much a part of another world. He'd left that world behind and wanted nothing more to do with it. He didn't want her food, either. Even though it smelled like a piece of heaven and he hadn't eaten in longer than he could remember, he wanted to be alone. The aroma made his stomach juices churn, protesting the fact that he had not given them proper attention. He was weak with the need to taste the food that smelled so good. She was smart, though. She wasn't going to come and get him. She was asking him to give a little. The carrot she was hanging over him could be considered cruel and unusual punishment.

Michael stared at her. Something about her stance told him she wasn't leaving until she'd talked to him about this grandfather she claimed he had. He wasn't in the mood to fight with her, and he *was* hungry. He could eat with her and then send her packing.

Michael had never set eyes on Erika St. James, yet she knew how to broil his steak to perfection. She'd made delicious potatoes. He'd never cared for broccoli, but hers was covered in a liquid cheese sauce that added a wonderful taste to the crunchy vegetable. Even the iced tea tasted heavenly. He'd helped himself to seconds and thirds. Pushing his plate aside, he felt much better. He'd forgotten what a home-cooked meal tasted like. For a moment he considered how quickly he could get used to meals like this. Then he remembered they entailed returning to the city, and he'd vowed he wouldn't do that.

Erika took his plate away and washed the dishes. He watched her without comment. She wasn't his type of woman—too tall, her features too sharp. Yet there was something about the way her waist curved in and her hips flared out that drew his gaze and had him shifting in his chair.

The sun set in the August sky and twilight settled over the cabin. It had a generator for the electric lights, but he hadn't used it in the year he'd been there. The yellow glow of kerosene lamps he'd never noticed bathed the room, and Erika, in a soft hue.

"Can we talk now?" she asked, placing the wet dishtowel over the sink and bringing the coffeepot to the table. Pouring two cups, she set the pot on the stove and returned.

"Who is Carlton—" Michael raised his eyebrows in question.

"Lipton-Graves. Carlton Lipton-Graves," she supplied.

"Are you related to him?" In the back of his mind Michael wanted to know. If she proved a relationship between him and Carlton Lipton-Graves, would there also be a blood connection between the two of them? Ironically, he hoped not.

She shook her head. "He was my friend. He practically raised me." She smiled and Michael thought her memories must be happy.

"Was?" he asked.

She hesitated, taking a breath. "Carlton died ten days ago."

"I'm sorry," he said. She didn't bow her head or lower her gaze from his, but he could see her eyes fill with tears. She blinked only once and the tears receded. Michael took a drink from his cup, feeling at a loss for what to say. "What do you want with me?" he asked.

"Before he died," she said quietly, "he told me you were his grandson."

"He had to be talking about a different Michael Lawrence."

"He showed me your picture."

"He's wrong. I have no grandparents. They all died years ago." Michael remembered wanting grandparents. Every other kid had them. They had programs at school when he was a child that involved inviting them. Some kids went to stay with their grandparents, and some of them got presents. Michael had wanted that, longed for it, but he'd never said a word to his parents. It wasn't to be his—he knew that—not then, and not now.

"What does a picture prove?" he asked. His picture had been in the papers for months. Cameras flashed in his face all the time. Anyone could have taken a picture.

He looked back at Erika. Why didn't he show her the door? Why did he feel as if there was something intriguing about her, something she wanted to tell him and he wanted to hear? Darkness fell fast on the mountain and the roads were steep and unlighted. It would be hospitable for him to invite her to stay the night, but he didn't want her here. If she planned to get anywhere tonight, she should leave soon. He should remind her of that. Why didn't he?

"Carlton's lawyers had a file on you—birth certificates, blood test results. There is no mistake. Your father was Carlton's son, Kevin. He married Edith Edwards thirty-eight years ago on May seventh. A year later you were born, and before your first birthday Kevin Lipton-Graves died in a plane crash."

"My father's name was Robert Lawrence. He taught Honors English at the local high school in New Brunswick, New Jersey, where I grew up. He died of a heart attack when I was seventeen."

"Robert Lawrence married your mother when you were three years old. He adopted you, had your name legally changed to Lawrence, and raised you as his son."

Michael didn't believe her. His mother wouldn't keep this kind of secret. She would never have done anything like keep information away from him. Erika St. James had either concocted this elaborate practical joke, or she had the wrong man.

"You don't believe me." She stated it as fact.

"My parents would have told me."

Erika thought of her mother. Mothers didn't always do what they should, what was expected of them. "They should have," Erika said quietly.

"You have the wrong man."

"There were blood tests, DNA matches." She shook her head slowly. "There are no mistakes."

He frowned. "When were these tests done?" Michael knew blood tests were used to identify paternity. DNA matches were like fingerprints; no two were the same. He'd used them himself, to get child support payments for children.

"Right after your father died."

"Why?"

He already knew the answer, but he waited and let Erika swallow while she formulated the words.

"Apparently, someone wanted to prove Kevin Lipton-Graves was your father."

"Maybe they wanted to prove he wasn't." He smiled, slipping easily into the role of prosecutor.

Erika gasped. Her eyes opened wide. Michael couldn't stop the immediate response that gripped him when he surprised her. She obviously hadn't thought of any other reason for the tests.

"Does it make sense?"

"I—I don't know," she stuttered, then recovered. "If Carlton wanted to prove you weren't his grandson, why would his dying words be of you?"

Michael thought about that. He didn't have any idea what he should feel. Carlton Lipton-Graves meant nothing to him. He tried to think of what he'd feel if his mother died and her last words were of him. Suddenly Abby's face crowded in on him. What had been her last thoughts before she died? Had she called her children's names? He couldn't remember.

He got up and walked to the door. The sun was completely gone. Stars dotted the sky like silver glitter. The air, cold enough to penetrate his shirt, caused goose bumps on his skin. He thought about what Erika had said. Why should he even consider it? Could she be right? Was there any truth to what she'd said? Had his mother kept this secret from him for the past thirty-seven years? Had his dad not been his real father? Were his brothers only half-brothers? He'd known he was different from them. While the three of them were unmistakably related, he hadn't looked like them at all. He looked like his mother. That was the explanation he'd given himself, never voicing a question except in anger, as all children do. Erika's story would support his . . .

He stopped. It wouldn't. She'd given him a suggestion and he was letting it push its way into his thoughts. His grandparents were dead. He'd seen pictures of them, both sets of them. He remembered thinking his genes had to reach back further than their generation. Believing her would explain why he looked so different from those on his family tree, why he could see none of his father in his own face. Michael closed the door and turned back. She was wrong. She had to be.

"It's dark now. I think you'd better finish up if you plan to get off this mountain before morning." He was angry. She'd thrown his equilibrium off the moment he'd seen her, and now that he'd been in her company for over an hour, he found he liked talking to her, hearing her voice. There was something about her, something deeper than the face she showed to the outside world. It was power, like in his car engine, underlying and apt to break free with the slightest touch of his foot on the accelerator. He wondered if she'd respond in the same manner. Where was her accelerator? Then he didn't want to know. He wanted her gone. He wanted to be alone, to extinguish the lamps so he couldn't see the places where she had been. Somehow he knew that even when she no longer sat at his table, no longer stood at his sink, he would be able to see her there.

She stood up, glancing toward the window over the sink. "I made a reservation on my way up. I need to get there before too long."

"Where?"

"A motel, a few miles back."

"The closest motel is at least a two hour drive down this mountain. You stopped there?" His eyebrows were raised in surprise.

"No, I saw the sign and called."

"Phone in the car?"

She nodded. "You're right. I should be going, and I'm not looking forward to the drive." She took a breath. "Michael, it's important that you believe what I've told you."

"Why?"

"I need your help. Carlton's will left everything to us."

"What! Why? He didn't even know me."

"You're his grandson."

"I'm not his grandson. I have no grandparents." He stopped, taking a long breath. "I've enjoyed talking with you tonight. I liked your food. But you've done nothing to convince me that Carlton Lipton-Graves and I have anything in common."

"I've told you about the blood tests and the DNA. What do you want?"

"You said he practically raised you. What does that mean?"

She smiled. Michael leaned forward. He liked the way her cheekbones made a picture of her face. Her eyes lit up.

"I went to Carlton's every day after school from the time I was eight years old. He helped me with my homework, taught me values, refused to let me hate or love too quickly."

She looked down as she said the last part. Michael wondered what that meant, but didn't interrupt her.

"He met my boyfriends when I began to date and treated me as if I were his grand—"

She stopped.

"He treated you as a granddaughter, but he never once came to see me. Why is that?" He took a step toward Erika. She moved back.

"I don't know. We may never know the answer to that, but I can tell you, he was the kindest man I've ever met."

"You said he was your friend. Are you a distant relative? The daughter of a cousin or an old maid aunt, or even an old war buddy?"

Erika shook her head. "We're not related in any way."

Michael stared at her for a moment. Erika felt as if she were on the witness stand. "You are in no way related to Carlton Lipton-Graves, yet you're the person who shared his life, acted as his granddaughter, presided over his house and funeral, even administered his will?"

"It's not like that," she began.

"But I am his grandson, according to you. I am a blood relation who has no knowledge that he even existed. When he was dying did he call for a relative? No, he called for you." Michael stopped a moment, then continued. "I don't believe anything you've told me. If I had a grandfather alive, my mother would have told me about him. And even if she hadn't, what prevented him from coming to me? It's not like I'm an impressionable child. I'm thirty-seven years old, certainly capable of understanding the information."

"I can't explain Carlton's actions. I only know that he told me you were his grandson, the lawyers confirmed it, and he left his estate to us."

"Well I don't want it. Now you've delivered your news. You can take it back to his lawyers and tell them to leave me alone."

"You mean you won't help me?"

"Exactly." He came to stand directly in front of her. "I'm not sure about you. I haven't decided if you're telling the truth or if you have another reason for being here."

"What other reason could I have for driving all the way up this mountain?"

"You could have been sent by my firm or my family to get me to leave here. They've tried everything and nothing has worked."

"I don't know anyone in your family other than Carlton. It is my purpose to get you to leave here," she confirmed. "I'd hoped you'd return with me."

Erika thought he must make a worthy legal adversary. He even looked different. Gone was the gaunt looking man she'd fed. In his place stood a strong opponent.

"Michael—" She took a step that brought her within arms' reach of him. Her hands came up. She'd been about to touch him when she saw what she was doing. Stepping back, she brought her hands down. Her eyes locked with his, and for the space of a lifetime they stared at each other.

Michael cleared his throat, breaking the bonds that held them suspended. Erika turned to face the sink and let her breath out.

"If you're planning to get to that motel, you'd better leave." Michael was behind her, but close.

She turned back, looking about confused as if she couldn't find something. When she arrived she'd left her jacket in the truck. It was still there.

"Please think about what I've said." Her voice was weak to her own ears. "Carlton's will has some terms that are a bit strange. No matter how I questioned his attorneys they remained adamant about the conditions."

"Conditions?"

She swallowed. "Carlton left us in control of his company. We must work together for a year to keep his business—"

"Stop," he said. "So that's it. That's what this is all about. Another ploy to get me back to the firm. Who is it really? My mother? The firm? Who hired you to act this role?"

"No one." She looked genuinely startled.

"I won't do it. I like it fine here, and I'm not leaving. I'll bet there is no Carlton Lipton-Graves. You're here on behalf of my brothers. They want me to come back to the firm. Well, you can climb in your little truck and hightail it back to wherever you came from and tell them your acting was good, but not good enough."

"I'm not acting. Carlton did leave us his estate."

"Even if he does exist, he cared nothing for me in life. Why should I suddenly adhere to his wishes?"

"You get half the estate at the end of a year."

"I don't want or need his money."

Erika looked around. Suddenly the cabin he'd rarely ever noticed looked rundown and shabby. It was little more than squalor, except for the section she'd cleaned.

Michael let out a breath. "I think you'd better leave."

Erika hesitated, then walked to the door. She opened it. The stars were close enough to touch. Their nearness startled her, but she stepped into the night, anyway. She went to the Bronco and yanked the door open. Pulling herself into the driver's seat she started the engine, then quickly killed it. Next to her sat the album she'd brought. Grabbing it, she went back inside.

Michael had dropped into a chair at the kitchen table. He looked up when her shoes made a noise on the bare wooden floor. "What now?" he asked.

Without a word she walked to where he sat. He looked at her as if at any moment he might get up and bodily remove her. She dropped the album on the table. Opening it, she pulled a large manila envelope out and placed it on top. Turning, she left the cabin, and Michael, to himself.

Michael pulled the envelope and album to him after he'd heard the crunch of gravel the tires had spun up when Erika made her angry getaway. Pushing the envelope with a legal return address aside, he pulled the heavy book onto his knees. His name was embossed on the cover. It fell open at a page that revealed him in full smile. His arms were spread wide. He smiled at the memory. It was his graduation from law school.

How had she gotten this? Where could she have been to take this without his knowledge? Michael looked at the door as if she were still outside.

"Damn," he cursed. She had to be wrong.

CHAPTER 2

The road curved tighter than Erika had anticipated. She was speeding a little too fast for the Bronco to master the turn. Her heart leapt to her throat as she fought for control of the truck. It careened toward the edge of the mountain. She prayed it would stop in time. Things seemed to speed up and slow down in the same instant. The rail came frighteningly closer to her. Gravel crunching under the size fifteen tires and the music of Whitney Houston coming from the CD changer were combined in a discordant symphony.

An inch short of the guardrail, and a three thousand foot drop, the Bronco came to a stop. Erika let out her breath and rested her head on the steering wheel. Switching off the engine, she sat in the dark breathing through her mouth.

Michael had made her angry. Why had Carlton put her in this position? Why, in the last twenty-six years, hadn't he once mentioned a grandson? Why did he leave them everything? And why now, when she needed to be in her office, was she running around a mountain after a man who couldn't care less about Graves Enterprises?

Well, she'd done what Carlton asked her. She'd come up here and she'd tried to get him to return. He refused—refused to help her, and refused Carlton's requests. She couldn't be held responsible for his actions. The lawyers would certainly understand that.

She'd return to Graves Enterprises and resume the position she'd held since she'd come back from California. After all, she had run things. She had taken care of all the problems and kept Carlton informed of her decisions. They had discussed everything for a while, but Carlton's strength ebbed. More and more he'd told her to handle it in her own way. She had. At night she hadn't wanted to burden him with the details of the day, so she'd sat with him and read or talked about the world. She'd let him remember his wife and his son. Yet in those states of memory he'd managed to keep Michael Lawrence a secret.

Michael's face came into her mind. How long had he been here? Carlton had said it was a long time. By the look of him, he needed care, and the way he'd eaten she thought he was going to make himself sick. She hadn't told him they had only thirty days left to begin the terms of Carlton's last will and testament. If she couldn't persuade him to leave this mountain and return to Philadelphia, she'd lose the company.

She sat back and stared through the dark window. She had a long drive ahead of her. She had wanted to head home tomorrow, but now it looked as if she'd have to return here and see if he was more willing to talk. She'd left the album and a copy of the will. If he looked at them, he might be willing to listen to reason.

Erika started the engine. Suddenly the door of the Bronco was yanked open. She screamed as she turned to face her assailant. Michael stood, angry, in front of her.

"We need to talk," he said.

"I have been talking," Erika told him. She slumped back against the seat. While she wanted to tell him everything she knew, she was tired. "Tomorrow," she sighed. "I'm absolutely drained now." She closed her eyes for a moment, feeling the effects of nearly going over the side of the mountain. "It's a very long drive to the motel."

"One you'll never make. Move over."

Michael pushed her, but her seatbelt kept her in place.

"I beg your pardon," she said, resisting his effort.

"You can't stay at that . . . motel." He grinned.

"Why not? I have a reservation."

"I'm sure you do, but it's probably gone by now."

"Why?"

"Move over." He again tried to climb into the cab, and she again pushed him back "You can stay at the cabin," he told her.

Keeping him at bay, she said, "You think that's an enticing advertisement for me to return? I'm looking at clean sheets and the absence of a man who thinks I'm a liar. I should give that up for—"

"It's not a motel," he interrupted her.

Erika turned toward him as if he'd lost his mind.

"It's not a real motel."

"I supposed I imagined it," she said. "I suppose I imagined the man I talked to on the phone, too."

Michael shook his head. Erika could see a faint smile on his face. She wanted to encourage it. She hadn't seen anything but a scowl since she found him by the water.

"It's a guest house, Erika."

"And I'm a guest."

"A tourist home—a place you rent by the hour, not by the night." He paused. "Don't you know what a guest house is?"

Her eyes must have grown as wide as dinner plates. Realization dawned on her. She hadn't heard of a guest house since she was in high school and her first boyfriend tried to coax her into having sex with him. He knew where there were guest houses in Philadelphia, places where they could go to have sex and no one would question their ages or the fact that they signed the register as George and Martha Washington.

"Seventy miles *is* a long way to drive," she said helplessly.

"I guarantee you there won't be an empty room in that house."

Her shoulders dropped. "What am I going to do now?"

"You can stay at the cabin. You can have the bed. I'll sleep on the couch." Michael looked down a second. "I apologize, but I do need to talk to you." He paused. "Please."

Erika stared at him for a long time. His eyes, though still bloodshot, had a life to them. She knew she needed to talk to him, and she didn't look forward to making this drive twice tomorrow. But, as she'd told him, the prospect of spending the night in the cabin with him was no enticement. She couldn't say she'd stayed in worse places. She didn't know if he was lying about the motel being a guest house, but if she drove seventy miles only to find he'd told the truth, she'd have no place to go. Sleeping in the Bronco wasn't something she wanted to do unless she was prepared for it.

"I'll drive," she said, making a decision.

He hesitated a second, then slammed the door and went around the back to climb in on the other side. Erika backed away from the guardrail and turned up the mountain.

"How did you get here?" she asked.

"I knew you wouldn't get far in the dark and I know these hills. I cut through the trees. My heart nearly stopped when I saw you heading for the guardrail."

Erika wanted to smile. Her heart swelled at the thought that he was concerned for her safety. Then she remembered the album. He was interested in how Carlton had gotten those pictures, and admitted to herself, she was his only source of information.

Michael closed the album. The name on the cover was his, at least part of it. He'd looked through the book three times and still found it difficult to imagine a grandfather. The pictures were definitely of him. He remembered the situations; high school basketball games and the parties they'd had after them, graduation, the class trip, his first day of law school, and his last. Michael couldn't help smiling at the happy memories. Erika sat across from him at the table she'd cleaned, and on which he'd had a meal.

"He took these?" Michael asked.

"I don't know. Until a week ago I'd never heard of you."

"He never mentioned my name?"

"Not until the night he died." She spoke softly, reverently. "We must have been growing up at the same time. Since I was thirteen I lived at Carlton's house. He travelled a lot. It wouldn't have been difficult for him to attend one of these events without me knowing about it."

"Tell me about him?"

Erika got up and went to pick up her purse. She took her wallet out of it and slipped out a snapshot. She handed it to him. "This is a picture of Carlton Lipton-Graves."

Michael took it. It was a Christmas shot. Erika, in a red dress with white fur collar, sat on the floor in front of a man in a winged chair. Behind them was part of a decorated tree and a roaring fire.

"We took this last Christmas." She swallowed hard, reseating herself. "It was our last."

The man was small. He looked directly into the camera, giving Michael a clear view of his face. "This is Carlton?" Michael asked.

Erika nodded.

"This man cannot be my grandfather." Michael stood up.

"Why not?"

"He's white. I can't have a white grandfather."

"Surprise, Michael, but we don't get to pick our parents . . . as much as we might like to."

"But—"

"Look closer at the picture," she interrupted. Reaching across the small table, she touched his hand and pushed the photograph a little closer to him. "Can't you see the resemblance between you and him?"

Her touch was soft and warm. Michael wanted to grasp it and hold it for a while. He had to concentrate on performing the action she'd requested. When her hand left his he did as she asked.

"When I saw you by the stream, it was like seeing Carlton again, before age and illness took his strength."

"We might have some of the same features," he agreed. "But everyone can find a resemblance if they look for it."

Erika sighed. She was tired and he knew it, but she'd come to him with these "facts" and he wanted to know the truth.

"What was your association with him?"

"He raised me. We met when I was eight. When I was a teen, he kind of adopted me. I guess I've been kind of a granddaughter to him. I knew he had a son, but he died before I met Carlton."

"How old are you?"

"Thirty-four," she said.

"I'm thirty-seven. Why didn't he ever come to see me? If he took all these pictures, attended the events that were important in my life, why did he never let me know he existed?"

"I can't answer that. Knowing Carlton, I do find that a bit strange."

"Why is that?" Michael asked.

"Carlton insisted I visit my mother. I'm surprised he had a grandson whom he never acknowledged."

Michael didn't reply. Erika had mentioned her mother. Michael needed to talk to his. If even a bit of what Erika said was the truth, Ellen Lawrence had some explaining to do.

Michael gasped in the humid air. It was heavy and hard to breathe, pressing against his chest like an invisible hand. He ran up and down streets he'd never seen. His lungs threatened to burst from exhaustion, yet he trudged on. Every breath burned. His legs, like iron appendages, weighed him down.

Disorientation gripped him as he whirled around trying to find something familiar; something that would tell him where she was hiding. He started running again, pulling at the tie around his neck. It came loose. He sucked air into his lungs. It didn't relieve his distress. The hand on his chest pressed harder.

"Abigail!" he called. "Abigail! Where are you?"

He stopped, listened . . . nothing. He ran again, seeming to get further behind with every agonizing step.

Then he saw her. She was frightened, screaming, running away from him, and away from *Frank*.

"Frraannnnkkkk, nooooo!" she screamed, her face contorted, her words drawing out several syllables as if she were speaking in slow motion.

Frank Mason chased Abigail, a gun in his hand. Michael dragged his heavy legs in pursuit. Frank pointed the gun at the scared woman.

"Noooo . . ." he shouted. The shot rang out. "Noooo . . ."

Erika sat up straight. Someone was screaming. For a moment she didn't know where she was. Then she remembered the cabin, and Michael. Pushing the blanket aside, she ran barefoot into the cabin's only bedroom.

She went straight to the bed. Michael fought her as she tried to calm him. His face was bathed in sweat, and his arms flailed madly in the air.

"It's all right, Michael," she said, keeping her voice calm. "Stop, Michael."

"Abbyyyyy," he called. His legs raced under the sheets as if he were trying to run lying down.

Erika didn't know who he called, but she decided the only way to get him quiet was to let him have his wish. "I'm here, Michael." He still fought his unseen demons. His strong arms batted at them. She grabbed for them but missed. Several times they played an air game of arms missing arms. Erika reached again. Michael's fist connected with her jaw, knocking her to the floor. Pain reverberated up her face, through her ear, creating a flash of light before her eyes, then blurring them with tears. Holding her jaw she waited, watching him thrash about in the sheets as if he fought the devil himself.

Testing her jaw, Erika opened and closed it several times. The pain abated but did not go away. She went back to the bed, resting her knee on the mattress and grabbing at Michael's arms, careful to keep her face sufficiently away from his wild throws.

"Michael!" she shouted. "Wake up. It's me." She was about to tell him, "It's Erika," when she remembered the woman he'd called. "It's me, Abby," she said. The name calmed him this time. All the fight left his arms, and they grabbed her, pulling her down on top of him and burying his face in her neck. Erika lay weakly against him. His sweat soaked through her shirt. She felt the heat of his body. Hers warmed in response. His hands massaged her back and held her secure. His ragged breathing pumped air through her short hair and around her ear. Erika let him hold her. She didn't move. She was too afraid. She lay like that until his breathing quieted. She raised her face to look at him. Michael's even breathing told her he was asleep. She let her breath out in a long sigh. Trying to pull herself free, she moved, and her attempt caused his arms to tighten around her.

Biting her lip, Erika went still. The pain in her jaw made her relax her muscles. She didn't want Michael to wake up and find her in this position. She didn't want the feelings running through her to emerge. He was nothing like her ideal man. She wanted someone educated, with a good job, a sense of humor, and a ready smile. So why was her body going soft and warm over a bearded mountain man who couldn't take care of himself and had horrible dreams about a woman called Abby?

Erika breathed in slowly. She was sure the thumping of her heart would wake Michael even if his nightmares didn't. Despite the state of the cabin and Michael's clothes, he smelled like clean air and sunshine.

Reaching behind her, she caught his arm and pulled it. His hand banked over her buttocks, and sparks rushed up her spine. Involuntarily she arched her back, bringing her into closer contact with his nearly naked body. The pain in her jaw was no competition for the pleasure that flowed through her under his hands. Groaning she rolled off the bed. Holding her stomach, she hobbled to a chair, where she supported herself, forcing herself to breathe in and out. What had happened to her? She'd come in here because Michael was having a bad dream. How had she ended up sprawled across his body, and why did such emotions riot through her? She never felt like this with Bill, and she'd been engaged to him.

She had to get hold of herself. She'd come through more than one bad relationship and she knew she didn't ever want to be involved in another one, no matter how her body reacted. He'd been in pain. She'd come inside because of her compassionate nature. She hadn't counted on the raw sexuality he'd aroused in her.

Weak-kneed and breathless, Erika pushed herself away from the chair and went back to the sofa. She was sure she'd spend the rest of the night in open-eyed terror. She didn't want a relationship with Michael. She never wanted a relationship again. Hadn't her mother written that epitaph for her long ago? Relationships weren't her forte and she wasn't even attracted to Michael Lawrence. So why had she reacted as she had? Erika would be glad to see daylight come. She couldn't wait to get off this mountain and away from Michael. She bit her lip at the paradox of her thoughts. If Michael didn't agree to return with her, she'd lose the company. If he did, she'd have to work side by side with him for the next year.

Would these feelings erupt again? Erika swung her feet to the side of the sofa and sat up. She was certainly capable of controlling her feelings and the situation. She'd been in his bedroom, in his bed. That would certainly not happen again.

Why had Carlton done this? There was no reason to give her an overseer for a year. She was capable of running Graves Enterprises alone. She'd done it for the past year with a degree of success.

What was Carlton's purpose in making a will that forced them together, and what was her part in it?

Michael turned over. Light streaming through the window cut across his eyelids. He smiled. He felt refreshed. He'd had the dream—he remembered that—but then he'd slept well, better than he had in months.

The smell of coffee wafted through the morning air. Where was it coming from? Then he remembered Erika. She'd stayed the night, refused his bed, and slept on the sofa in the next room. He listened to her movements. He wondered what she looked like this morning. Was she grouchy before her first cup of coffee or was she easy to talk to? Michael sat up, pulling his jeans on and walking barefoot to the door. After last night's dinner, his stomach growled at the smell of an anticipated breakfast.

Erika stood at the stove, her back to him. She no longer wore yesterday's clothes, but had on navy blue stirrup pants. Her blouse had been replaced with a long white sweater. A wide blue line angled across the back, beginning at her shoulder and crossing her back to her hips. Her hair had less curl on the top, and the sides were straight and ended in sharp points, yet he wanted to run his hands through it.

"Good morning." She smiled, turning to face him.

He swallowed, thinking how lovely her smile was and that he'd like to see it more often. His insides started a slow melt, and he wished he'd put on more clothes than a revealing pair of jeans, which he had only zipped part of the way up.

"Would you like some coffee?"

He came into the room and took the cup she offered.

"I found some syrup and enough ingredients to make pancakes. I had to use dried milk, powdered eggs, and water, since there's no refrigerator. I don't think they taste too bad. Of course, there was no bacon or ham."

She put a plate in front of him. It smelled wonderful. She sat down, her own plate before her.

"You look a lot better this morning."

"I slept well," he told her. She had no way of knowing the dreams that tortured his nights, how he'd wake in the middle of the night and not be able to get back to sleep. Michael took a fork and dug into the plate of food. "How about you? Did you sleep all right?"

"Most of the night," she said, bringing the coffee cup to her lips. Her eyes almost closed as she looked down to the cup. Michael noticed her long lashes.

"You should have taken the bed."

Her hands shook as she placed the cup on the scarred table. She checked her watch.

"I have to leave soon." Her lip twitched slightly. "Are you sure you won't go with me?"

She wasn't looking at him. Her gaze was trained on the broken cup handle. Her fingers played with it. Michael found it unnerving. He could talk to her better if she looked at him. He'd been trained to make eye contact, to stare at his opponent on an even scale and deliver his message. With Erika looking down he had only her body language to respond to, and it told him she was disappointed in his reply.

"I'm sorry," he said. "My returning to Philadelphia won't accomplish anything. I'll get in touch with the lawyers and turn everything over to you."

"You know that won't work. We're talking about a will. Carlton's lawyers are as adamant as he was. They'll make sure the terms of that will are followed to the letter. If we don't do as requested, all Carlton's money goes to the defense fund of someone named Frank Mason."

Michael stopped eating. The fork in his hand stopped halfway to his mouth. Erika stopped talking. Time on the planet ceased. The only thing that moved was the thumping of his heart, which threatened to jump out of his chest. That damn old man Graves. The sonofabitch, who'd never seen him face-to-face in life, would try to manipulate him in death.

Swallowing the mouthful of food he hadn't chewed, Michael scraped the chair back and stood up. He went to the door and out of it. His bare feet stepped onto the cold ground outside the cabin and he went into the woods toward the stream.

He didn't know how long he stood there, the past running through his head like a old movie. Erika came to stand next to him. She remained quiet. He couldn't talk to her. He couldn't tell her that after the dream and after the first peaceful night he'd had in months, that some unknown relative he couldn't care less about was trying to force him to return to a life of defending people like Frank Mason.

"Who is he?" Erika asked quietly.

Michael turned to her. He liked Erika St. James. He wished he could meet her sometime in the future when he'd made peace with the demons, if that ever happened. She had an underlying compassion about her. He wouldn't invite her into his nightmare, though.

"I won't return, Erika. I'm not sure Carlton Lipton-Graves was my grandfather. My life is here, and here is where I stay." He took her hands in his and looked at them. They were cold. She had long, slender fingers with a strength that was evident in them. "I think you'd better go now." Impulsively he pulled her forward and kissed her on the mouth.

Erika closed her eyes. It was the lightest feather of a kiss, yet she felt as if he'd lifted her off the ground. Her body trembled with reaction. She put her hands up to take hold of his bare arms, but he pushed her back and released her. Her eyes came open. The world was back in place, exactly as she had left it, yet she felt as if something about *her* had changed. She'd stepped over some imaginary line which she could never again retreat across. She stared at Michael, looking for some sign that he felt the trauma that had gone through her, but he'd turned away. His body was stiff, impassible. She knew nothing she could say or do could change him. He was no longer in her world. He'd retreated into the one he'd been in when she arrived a lifetime ago.

Erika placed her fingers on her lips. They still tingled from the memory of Michael's kiss. She was nearly back to the main highway. His short kiss remained at the top of her thoughts. Not even the swerving mountainous roads or the need to get Michael to return to Philadelphia could replace the feel of his mouth against hers. Why hadn't she stopped him? She'd seen it coming, but wanted it. Since she'd found him in the throes of the nightmare, she'd wanted to kiss his hurt away.

The sensation was new to her. She'd never wanted to mother anyone, to fight anyone else's battle. She had too many of her own to fight to take on a stranger's. Yet Carlton had told her about Michael. She'd promised him she'd try to get him back to the city. He'd said Michael had been on the mountain too long. Had he thought she could get him off of it? Well, she'd failed in that, too, just as she'd failed in everything else she'd ever tried except running Graves Enterprises. Her mother had been right. She was no good at anything, and no man would ever want her.

Suddenly Bill Castle's face came into her mind. What was he doing now? It had been almost two years since he'd abruptly married Jennifer Ahrends, her secretary. Just before she'd boarded the plane leaving California she'd heard Jennifer was pregnant. Her baby should be born by now. Erika's eyes were dry, her body numb. She couldn't imagine herself with a child, a baby. She'd loved Bill, but she couldn't see herself as the mother of his children. She couldn't see herself as a mother at all. Some women just weren't cut out for nurturing, she told herself.

Then she remembered Michael's nightmare. Her mouth tingled again. Her tongue darted out to wet her lips. She raised her hand to touch them. Michael's mouth had been soft, undemanding, warm, and tasting of the morning coffee she'd brewed in the ancient coffeepot.

Why could she still feel it? Why could she still taste him? And why did a feeling deep in her belly tell her she wanted more than a taste?

"Damn!" Michael cursed as he pulled the starter cord for the ninth time. What was he doing? It wasn't going to start. In the last three hundred and sixty odd days he hadn't once tried to get this generator to work. He'd never felt the need for electric light. Yet tonight he wanted to flood the cabin with it. He'd already cleaned the chimney and started a fire in the seldom-used fireplace. The glow was yellow-gold, and he needed more light. He needed these damn electric lights to work. Why didn't he light the kerosene lamps? A voice inside his head spoke to him. *She lit them, that's why.* He didn't want to think about her or the way that yellowed light cast golden shadows across her face.

As he tried the cord again the mechanism groaned, then died completely. Michael pulled one of the spark plugs, dusted it on his pants legs, which were black with the soot of the chimney, and replaced it in the generator. He grabbed the cord and yanked. His index finger caught between the frayed nylon cord and the metal casing, ripping through the skin.

"Ouch!" he shouted, sticking his finger into his mouth. He tasted soot, dirt, oil, machine grease, and rust. Quickly he snatched it from his mouth and inspected it. He'd live, but it was her fault. If she'd stayed away from here he wouldn't have to be reminded of the world below the mountain. He wouldn't have to remember Abigail Mason.

Michael glanced one more time at the generator and grabbed for the cord with his uninjured hand. Stubbornly the mechanism refused to perform its intended purpose. It was the belt. The machine needed a new one. The one there was cracked and brittle, and refused to hold the required RPM's to begin the generation of electrical power. *Mr. Hodges would have a belt,* he thought. Mr. Hodges, over at Hodges General Store and Mercantile, stocked everything from aspirin to cure a simple headache to supplies to fully outfit a mountain climber.

The walk was at least two miles uphill. Michael stared at the road—the same road that Erika's Bronco had taken when she left that morning. He took a step. The walk would do him good. A climb up the mountain would be better, but it was dark and that made it dangerous. He'd get his exercise on the way to the store. He hoped the walk would keep his mind off her and that kiss.

It didn't. His mind replayed it over and over with each step he took. Why had he done that? Many woman tourists had come by in the last year. He'd never wanted to kiss any of them. But he'd wanted to kiss her the moment he'd seen her in the afternoon light. And later, in the cabin, when he'd come upon her by surprise, his heart had jumped in his throat at the way she looked with the gold, autumnal effect of the kerosene lamps. When she'd followed him to the stream he could no longer resist. She was leaving. He never expected to see her again. It was his request that she leave. Then he'd looked at her, with the sun behind her, her brown hair showing highlights that framed her head with a red-gold aura. His head had just tilted. His mouth touched hers softly and the shock of heat which attacked him—he couldn't think of another word to describe the sudden impact on his body—had told him to run—quick and fast. If he didn't, she'd have him back where he didn't want to be, down the mountain, in a dark suit with red suspenders and a white shirt. She'd have him seeing clients and going to court, and he'd be right back where he was before he'd ever heard of Abigail Mason. And that's exactly where he never wanted to be again.

Michael unbuttoned his jacket. He was warm despite the cool mountain air. Late August in the city would produce warm nights, but on the mountain it was cold. He wondered if it was warm where Erika had gone.

The air here was cool and crisp, but he was sweating. He told himself it was from the exertion. The store was just up ahead. He could see the roof of the building. It was no more than a rustic log cabin with a wide porch. The overhead covering protected barrels of various seasonal items. In summer one of them was filled with pickles, with dill seed and spices floating in the dark water around them. Winter saw barrels of salt to control the ice that seemingly grew on the steps leading to the door. Since it was August he was likely to find the last remnants of summer seed packets and trays of vegetables.

He wasn't disappointed. Michael smiled to himself for being right. Also present were wooden cases of sweet potatoes, string beans, and fresh broccoli. Michael remembered last night's dinner, and the way Erika had draped his vegetable with melted cheese. She was back—in his mind. His walk hadn't produced the desired effect.

"Hullo, Mr. Lawrence." Gerald Hodges came toward him with an outstretched hand. Michael took it and shook hands.

Michael had little contact with any of the full-time residents on the mountain, but he had met Gerald Hodges and knew that he'd lived all his life on this mountain except for a two year stint in the Army during the Vietnam Era.

"She found you, I take it," he said.

Michael looked blankly at him. How could he know about Erika?

"The Lipton-Graves heiress," Gerald went on to explain. "She come in here looking for you a couple of days ago. I gave her your order. Didn't you get it?"

"The food, yes," Michael told him. "She brought it."

"She's quite a looker."

He had to agree with that. Although she wasn't beautiful, not the way Michael liked his women, there was something about her. Something that had made him kiss her.

Abigail Mason had been beautiful. When he'd first seen her he'd been struck by her beauty. With Erika there was something more than beauty, some deep inner loveliness that touched him deep inside. The word *compelling* came to him. She compelled him to remember her.

"I never met an heiress before," Gerald was saying when Michael brought his attention back. "At least not one with as much money as she has. I did meet Milton Hershey's grandson once, but I don't think he—"

"Would you have a generator belt?" Michael interrupted. If he let Gerald go on he'd be there until closing. Talking was the only thing Gerald liked more than listening to gossip. Michael knew that whatever the inhabitants of Highland Hills, Maryland, population 140, knew about him they'd gotten from Gerald Hodges.

"What kinda belt?"

Michael suddenly felt like a fool. He'd been so intense in his thinking about Erika he hadn't even looked at the make and model number of the generator. "I don't know," he said.

Gerald checked the ceiling as if it knew the answer. "Let's see, I believe ole man Nelson bought that generator back in . . . must be ten years ago." He brought his gaze back to Michael. "Don't worry, Michael. I have one." He turned to leave, presumably to go and get the item, then stopped. "I've been saving something for you," he said. Going to the counter he pulled a newspaper from beneath it and pushed it across to Michael. "I thought you'd enjoy reading about her."

Michael picked up the paper. Gerald smiled, nodded, and went toward the back of the store. Michael studied the grainy photograph of Erika St. James. Again her eyes captured him. Even from the paper she called to him. Next to her was the photograph of a man. William A. Castle was written under the picture. A streak of anger sliced through Michael. It came unbidden and unwanted, but was there nevertheless.

"Erika St. James, longtime friend of Carlton Lipton-Graves, will walk away with the lion's share of the corporate giant's estate," Michael read. "The thirty-four-year-old former vice president of La Canada Manufacturing Corporation near Los Angles returned to Philadelphia last year and took over the operation of Graves Enterprises from the ailing owner."

Again Michael lifted his gaze to the photograph. It pulled at him, forcing him to look into those eyes. He looked away, checking the back room to see if Gerald appeared. Michael was alone, except for the presence of Erika. Michael bent his head back to the paper, whose date was two weeks old.

"Ms. St. James was engaged to William A. Castle, noted entertainment lawyer, also of Los Angeles, in September of last year when (in a surprise move) Mr. Castle married his fiancée's secretary, Jennifer Ahrends."

She's been engaged, jilted, Michael thought. He looked at the photograph of William A. Castle, irrationally disliking the man. How could he hurt her so? The man was a coward, running off and marrying someone else, without the backbone to tell her. *In a surprise move,* he read again. How often had he seen those words? They were lawyer's words. Michael was a lawyer, too. No wonder Erika St. James looked so sad. She probably also hated lawyers. *Good,* he thought, but his heart wasn't in it. He had been a lawyer once, but not anymore, and he'd never be one again.

The rest of the article detailed Erika's education and qualifications. It also touched on the direction of Graves Enterprises and ran a few quotes from Erika. His name wasn't mentioned, but it did allude to some details of the will which had not been disclosed.

Yeah, Michael thought, *like he was an equal partner in everything Carlton had left behind.*

Gerald startled him when he came in. "Sorry to keep you waiting, Michael. It took me a while to find the thing." He held up a hard rubber oval partially hidden inside a faded cardboard rectangle. The word "generator" could easily be read through the watermark circle, indicating it was nearly as old as the one on the dead machine back at his cabin.

The bell over the door rang. Michael and Gerald turned to see a young woman come into the store. She smiled at Gerald and came over.

"Hi, Gerald," she said, but kept her eyes on Michael. Suddenly he wished he didn't look so much like a bum. He'd been working all day, dirty work, and his clothes showed it.

"Amy Foster, this is Michael Lawrence."

"Please excuse my appearance," Michael said.

"You're at the old Nelson cabin," she said.

Michael nodded. Twenty-four hours ago he would have called it a house, but the moment he found Erika there he knew it was only a cabin, meant to be used for weekends, for city people coming up for a back-to-nature weekend before they returned to the world of modern conveniences.

"You planning on staying a while?" Amy asked.

He'd been there over a year, but he'd learned that a while meant different things in different parts of the county. Here it probably meant a lifetime.

"A while," he said. Turning to Gerald, he asked him to put the generator belt on his bill. Gerald sent a monthly invoice to the offices of Lawrence, Barclay, West, and Lawrence. His brothers made sure they were paid. He nodded at Gerald and said goodbye to Amy. At the door Gerald stopped him.

"It's about dark, Michael. Why don't you let Amy drive you back to the cabin?"

"It's no trouble," Amy said before Michael could refuse. Twenty-four hours ago he would have refused and thought nothing of it. Now he felt the need to explain.

"Thank you, but my clothes would leave a permanent mark on your car," he said.

"Don't worry about that." Amy smiled, waving her hand in a nonchalant gesture. "You should see the stuff Jake brings in."

Michael didn't ask who Jake was.

"Now, Amy," Gerald asked. "What can I get you?"

Michael waited by the door and followed Amy out of the store when she'd bought milk, bread, ice cream, and diapers. On the short ride back to "the old Nelson" cabin, as she called it, he learned she was married and had a three-month-old at home. Jake was her husband and he loved to hunt and fish.

Michael thanked her at his driveway and walked the short distance back to the generator and his thoughts of Erika St. James.

CHAPTER 3

The twin bed, with no head or foot board, was slightly over an inch longer than Frank Mason. He folded his body into the fetal position whenever he slept, which wasn't often. Tonight he lay on his back staring at the cracked ceiling. He'd read about people who did that, prisoners with nothing to do night after night but count the cracks in the ceiling. He'd counted two hundred and sixty-seven. He'd done it nineteen times, with never a variance. Exactly two hundred and sixty-seven cracks. His bed had fourteen lumps in it, seven of which were in the spot that cradled his back.

Light filtered in from the hall. He knew Smiley Curtis was on the desk. Smiley came every night at exactly eleven forty-five. He was never a second later. As the chime on the clock in the distance outside his window went through its rendition of St. Michael's Serenade in twelve notes, Smiley Curtis would come through the door. Under one arm he carried the early edition of tomorrow's newspaper. To this he added a cup of coffee and a wide smile. By midnight the exchange of duties had been accomplished. Smiley knew who had taken their medicine calmly, and who had fought against the small white pills the patients had to take. He knew who had spent a pleasant day and who had been a royal pain for the past sixteen hours.

At five minutes past midnight Smiley would make his rounds, speaking to the insomniacs and smiling at the sleepers. Then he'd settle into his chair, switch on the wall-anchored color television and open the paper.

Frank had watched this routine, sometimes pretending to sleep, sometimes acting as if he couldn't. With Smiley it never wavered. He was there on time and he left promptly at the end of his shift. Frank waited. Sooner or later his chance would come, and he figured it would be during Smiley's shift. During the day there were too many people there, too many nurses and doctors, too many patients wandering in and out, for him to remain unnoticed for any length of time.

He'd been here three months. First the jail cell, then the mental ward of the prison, and now this hospital. He grunted in the darkness. This was no hospital. It was a prison. Frank knew a prison when he saw one. The walls might be sheet-rocked, and the windows covered with curtains, but there was nowhere he was allowed out without an escort. He couldn't take a walk alone. Everyone had to have a "buddy." He was thirty-seven years old. What did he need with a buddy? But he didn't expect that to take much longer. He'd be out of here soon. He'd planned it and soon he'd be home. Home with Abby.

A blue moon. There really was such a thing. Michael had always associated blue moon with the cliché, with thoughts of going back to the city and returning to his firm. Now he looked at the shining disk and thought of Erika St. James's eyes. He stared at the silver-blue color as he walked along the road for the second time in as many days. Cloud formations hugged the sky; flat, grey bottoms supporting a puff of gold-tinged cotton, turning the road into a black ribbon meandering through the landscape.

This should be a leisurely walk after dinner, but it wasn't. Michael had only half eaten his meal. Erika had left the will along with the picture album, and what he read there had led him to this road. He held himself stiffly, his hands stuffed in his pockets, shoulders hunched, his gait determined and purposeful. He needed a phone. He needed to call his mother. Find out if there was real truth to Erika St. James's story. He'd told her he didn't believe her. But he did. Now he wanted confirmation. He wanted his mother to tell him the unguarded truth; that she had been married to Kevin Lipton-Graves, and that he was the product of that marriage.

He wanted to call his brothers and have them investigate Erika and her claims, but he knew better than to involve them. There was only one person he could ask to confirm her story—Malick Wainscott.

Michael's breath congealed in the cold air. He dug his hands further into the pockets of his parka and continued his uphill climb. The trees were mere dark images along the side of the road. Michael's attention wasn't on the trees. He was thinking of Malick. Their friendship went back to his law school days. Malick had been his professor, his mentor, and later his friend. Separated in age by twenty-five years, Michael and Malick had formed a strong bond. Malick ran a practice in Philadelphia and taught Criminal Law at the University of Pennsylvania. He'd help him. All Michael had to do was ask. Michael had tried all day to forget the will, forget Erika St. James, and return to his quiet existence, but neither would leave him alone.

He'd climbed the mountain this morning, keeping his concentration on his ropes and spikes and conquering the task before him.

Now he walked up this ribbon of road on his way to Hodges General Store and Mercantile to use the phone. With each step his anger mounted instead of abating. The will stated he'd have to return to Philadelphia and share the legacy Carlton Lipton-Graves had left him with Erika St. James. That legacy included a house and joint management of Graves Enterprises. The name was vaguely familiar, but it meant nothing to Michael. What stuck in his craw was the contingency. *If either of the main parties fail to adhere to the terms of this will, barring death or catastrophic injury, the entire estate bequeathed jointly to Erika St. James and Michael Lawrence will be awarded to Frank Mason.* . . . The words had been unwittingly committed to memory. If he didn't adhere to the terms of the will the entire estate would go to Frank Mason.

Michael's hands balled into fists at the thought of Frank and what he'd done to Abby and her children. Reaching down, he picked up a stone and threw it as far as his pitching arm would let him. Why Frank? Had Carlton known Frank? Did he know what he'd done to Abby? Or was he just a manipulative old man trying to get his way, even from the grave?

Michael could see the light ahead. Hodges General Store and Mercantile had the only streetlamp Michael had seen since he'd come to Highland Hills. He stopped a moment, staring at the pool of light cutting into the engulfing darkness. Tiredness seemed to rush into him. It had been a long day. He'd worked hard today, not just with his hands but with his mind, trying to keep it off Erika St. James and trying to forget the terms of the will lying on the clean wooden surface of the table where he'd eaten only this morning.

Why should he go back? He'd fought his fight and lost. He never wanted to see the inside of a courtroom again. He never wanted to return to a world where people like Frank Mason could say one thing and do something as frightening as—.

Michael stopped the thought. Forcing his feet to move, he continued toward the store.

"Malick, this is Michael," he said several minutes later when he'd completed the walk to the store and Gerald had let him use the private phone in his office. Around him were order slips, stacks of cases with vegetable names written on them; corn, peas, lima beans, string beans. The general clutter reminded Michael of his desk back at Lawrence, Barclay, West, and Lawrence.

"Michael!" The surprise in Malick's voice was clearly evident. "It's good to hear your voice. When are you coming back?"

Malick never beat around the bush. Each time Michael had spoken to him, all three of them, in the last year, he'd begun the conversation in the same manner.

"My plans are unclear," Michael told him, and that was the truth. If he could confirm the validity of the will, he would either return to the world beyond the hill or let Frank Mason walk away with whatever estate had been left to him.

"Do you need anything?" Michael heard the concern in his friend's voice.

"I'm fine, Malick. My health is excellent." Except for his weight, he was as fit as he'd been when he arrived. And even with the dreams, his state of mind had improved. "I want you to do me a favor, something I want to keep quiet."

"What is it?"

Michael could almost see the older man sit forward in his chair, pulling a yellow legal pad close, as he crunched the phone between his ear and shoulder.

"Ever heard of a woman named Erika St. James?"

"Who hasn't?" Malick said. "She's been all over the news since Carlton Lipton-Graves died two weeks ago. A real Cinderella story. The press is eating it up. How do you know her?"

"I don't," Michael replied, then thought of her warm mouth opening under his. Quickly he clamped the lid on that area of memory. "She came to see me."

"Why?" Malick's question came out on a long, incredible breath. "The press has been trying to interview her, but so far she's been behind closed doors. Every newscast ends with 'Ms. St. James was unavailable for comment.' "

Michael groaned. He wanted no part of the press. He'd had enough of them a year ago, when they'd made his life unbearable. Now he might have to return to the same game.

"Malick, I need you to make some discreet inquiries about her and Carlton Lipton-Graves."

"Exactly what are you trying to find?" Malick asked, his voice as dry as sandpaper.

Michael explained the conditions of the will Erika had left with him and the alleged parentage.

"She claims there are DNA tests confirming this. I need to know if it's the truth."

"Why would she lie?"

"I don't know. I don't know if she's even the real thing. Her picture was in the paper, but that can be faked."

Malick described the photo he'd seen and Michael had to agree it was the woman who'd spent the night on his sofa.

"Why don't you do the obvious thing, Michael? Call your mother and ask her."

"I plan to. I just want to know that I have the facts straight before I do that."

"All right," Malick sighed. "Can I reach you through the store?"

"Yeah," Michael told him.

"Give me a couple of days."

Michael knew he could count on Malick. He'd put an investigator on it in the morning and by dinnertime he'd have a report on the heiress to the Lipton-Graves millions. He smiled, replacing the phone. *Millions. He should be so lucky.* He'd never heard of Carlton Lipton-Graves. It wasn't like he was J. Paul Getty or Howard Hughes, dying and leaving a fortune. Malick *had* said the press was carrying the story. He knew the press. They carried anything that sold papers and commanded air time.

If Carlton Lipton-Graves had left a fortune, Michael wouldn't know it. He admitted he'd been single-minded when he practiced law. He'd resided in New Brunswick, and he hadn't concerned himself with much outside of the law and court. If Erika had inherited millions she would surely be courted by the press. Even if she hadn't, her elusiveness would be enough to make them hound her. The more she remained unapproachable the longer the story would play out. Secretly Michael hoped the whole thing would blow over. Then he pictured her, saw her standing by the stream in the misty morning light, staring at the mountains in the background. She looked as if she loved the stone facades, as if she belonged on the hill as much as the evergreen trees and the deer that kept a discreet distance from him. Too bad he hadn't taken their cue and stayed away from Erika.

Erika tapped the head of her pen against the marble-edged blotter on her desk. She should be working. She should be doing something about the takeover. But her mind wasn't on it. She glanced at the phone again. It must be the hundredth time today she'd thought of calling Michael Lawrence. It had been a week since she left him; a week for him to read the will, to get used to the idea of Carlton being his grandfather.

She knew it had to have been a shock to him. She'd grown up with Carlton. He was her friend, and like a good friend she'd grown used to him. Finding out that the man you thought was your father wasn't, that in his place stood a man who didn't even share the same heritage, had to be a revelation that he needed time to assimilate.

She checked her watch. It was only a few minutes past six. The office was quiet, so no one would disturb her, and she was sure Mr. Hodges would still be minding his store. She could call and leave a message for Michael. She could ask him to call her, and then they could discuss the future.

Lifting the receiver, she punched in the number she'd printed on one of her business cards. *Maybe Mr. Hodges isn't there,* she thought when the phone went through its third ring.

". . . bye, Ed. Say hello to Helen."

She heard his voice as he picked up the phone without ending his conversation. She had the feeling that Mr. Hodges was always in the middle of a conversation with someone.

"Hello," he said, speaking to her.

"Mr. Hodges, this is Erika St. James. You may not remember me."

"Not remember an heiress? They'd pull my friendship license if I forgot a beautiful woman like you."

Erika laughed. A little of the tension which held her shoulders stiff lessened, and she relaxed.

"I wanted to leave a message for Mr. Lawrence," she began.

"Sorry, he's gone."

"Gone!" Her grip on the handset tightened. "Where did he go?"

"Said he had some things to see to. I suppose he'll go back to the city. Newcomers never last long up here. He lasted longer than most."

"How long ago did he leave?" Erika interrupted.

"Yesterday, about four o'clock. Dropped by to tell me to rent the cabin if I wanted to."

"He's not coming back?" Erika found her heart sinking. How could she find him if he'd left the cabin?

"He'd didn't say. He left me an address in case you called."

Her heart lurched. He'd assumed she would call. He knew she would.

"Here, I've got it." She knew he was holding it up as if she could see it.

"Would you read it to me?"

Seconds later a frown changed her facial expression from elation to incredulity. Mr. Hodges read Erika's own address, to her. For a moment she thought it was a joke. He knew she'd try to reach him again, and intentionally he'd given a false address. If he'd been coming to see her, he would have arrived late last night or early this morning. The house was full of servants. If Michael had arrived, one of the maids would surely have called to let her know.

She didn't have any idea where he'd go. Maybe he went to talk to his mother. She thought that might be the normal thing to do, if his mother was still alive. Would he get the information he needed? An image of her own mother came to mind. Erika knew Alva Redford would be the last person she'd go to for confirmation of something important in her life.

"You got it?" Mr. Hodges asked, calling her back to the phone she held in her hand.

"Yes, Mr. Hodges. I have it. Thank you very much."

"You're welcome. Come back and visit us when you're out this way again."

She smiled. She liked the old man. "I'll certainly do that, Mr. Hodges."

Erika replaced the receiver in the cradle. She faced it for only a second before punching in the numbers to her own house. As expected, the maid informed her no one had come looking for her all day. Erika thanked her and hung up.

Pushing herself back, she faced the windows and watched the sun drop on the distant horizon. Where was he? She had to know. Her time was running out. There were barely three weeks left. She turned back and looked at her office. Remnants of Carlton's presence haunted the room, but she was also there. Her desk was a huge structure of carved mahogany. She felt comfortable behind it. The walls had pictures she'd chosen. The étagére in the corner held several of her awards and a collection of crystal figurines she'd been collecting for years. The desk held a new computer, something Carlton couldn't stomach and she couldn't live without.

She loved it here, loved this company and her role in it. She'd loved it since her sixteenth year, when she applied for a job in the shipping department without telling Carlton. She hadn't wanted anyone to think he got her the job because of their friendship. She'd worked there for six months before he found out. She thought he'd be angry, but instead he'd begun teaching her things. She worked in every department from the ground up, and by the time she left for college she'd worked there three years.

Then she'd gone to California and stayed there, until Carlton called her home. She wanted to keep this company, run it the way she'd been doing since she returned. She wanted to keep it alive for Carlton. Of course, it offered her wealth, more money than she'd ever dreamed of having, and power. But beyond the wealth and the power, Graves Enterprises offered her the chance to prove that she could do the job. Now she didn't have Carlton showing her, sanctioning her decisions, or guiding her along as if she were his student. She needed to prove she could stand on her own feet. The only person she needed to help her was Carlton's grandson, and at the moment she was without clues as to his whereabouts.

Erika pulled herself closer to the desk and picked up the phone again. The clock on the desk read seven o'clock, but she knew Steven Chambers would still be in his office.

"Chambers," he answered on the first ring.

"Hello, Steven, it's Erika."

"Erika, what can I do for you?" His voice held the no-nonsense tone she was accustomed to hearing whenever she talked to the seasoned lawyer.

"I need to know more about Michael Lawrence."

"I'm afraid I can't tell you anything I haven't already." He sounded distracted, as if he wasn't really concentrating on her.

"Steven, stop whatever it is you're doing and listen to me."

She could hear his sigh. "All right, Erika. You have my full and undivided attention."

"Michael left the cabin he was occupying in the mountains and I don't know where he's gone. He told me his father died when he was seventeen. Would you know if his mother is still alive, and where she lives?"

"I'm afraid I don't."

"Can you find out?"

"I can put an investigator on it if that's what you want."

An investigator. She hadn't thought of that. "Yes." She seized the opportunity. "I need information fast. I only have a few weeks left."

She knew Steven was aware of that.

"Do you think this investigator can find out where he is?"

"If that is what you want him to do."

"I do," she said.

"All right. I'll have someone on it first thing in the morning."

"Thank you, Steven." Erika hung up again. This time she felt better. An investigator. Steven knew her dilemma, knew she would lose everything, including his enormous fees for services, if the estate fell into the hands of Frank Mason. Who was he? She wished she'd asked Steven to have his investigator find out something about Frank Mason, too. But finding Michael was more important. She could concentrate on Frank Mason later, if need be.

"How much did you say?" Michael asked. He stared at Malick Wainscott from across the dinner table at Bookbinders in central Philadelphia. He and Malick hadn't seen each other since the Mason trial. Always well dressed, Malick wore a dark suit over his custom-made shirt. His shock of white hair reminded Michael of the photo Erika had shown him of Carlton Lipton-Graves.

"You might have lost weight, Michael, but your hearing is not impaired. Carlton Lipton-Graves's personal net worth, including pending stock options, is over forty-seven million dollars. If you want to know about Graves Enterprises, the pharmaceutical division alone grosses four billion dollars in sales."

Michael lifted his brandy snifter and swirled the liquid before taking a drink.

"No wonder she wants me to exercise the will."

"I don't blame her—even if Frank Mason wasn't a contingent benefactor."

Michael's hands clenched at the sound of Frank's name. "Why did he do it?" he asked, almost to himself.

"Frank?" Malick asked.

"No, Carlton."

"Obviously, he wanted to get you off that mountain and this was a surefire way of doing it." Malick leaned forward, grasping his brandy in both hands. "He dangled a carrot in front of you, Michael. Granted, it's a forty-seven million-dollar carrot, but that much money can certainly change a lot of opinions."

"What do you mean?"

"If you don't comply with the terms of the will, and Carlton's lawyers closed every available loophole, Frank Mason becomes the richest convicted mental patient in the world. It won't be long before some lawyer, smart, and extremely well paid, convinces a medical board and a court that Frank was only temporarily insane and he should be freed, that he was not responsible for his acts and he's truly been rehabilitated."

Michael studied the window, staring at but not seeing the street outside or the neat rows of parked cars along both sides of it. His mind was on Frank. So much in his life had changed since Erika St. James walked into it, beginning with his father.

After his call to Malick he'd gone to see his mother. He hadn't wanted to ask her about Erika's claims over the phone. From her reaction, maybe he should have. He'd tried to hold onto the belief that Erika could still be wrong, that his mother hadn't concealed information from him his whole life, but the expression of horror on her face told him in the first five minutes that everything Erika had said was the truth. Robert Lawrence wasn't his biological father. His father was a man named Kevin Lipton-Graves, and his grandfather was Carlton Lipton-Graves.

"Why didn't you tell me?" he asked.

"Michael, I couldn't. It was so long ago and when I met Robert, he loved you. It didn't seem important."

"Not important, Mom? Not important that I had a family and you concealed it from me?"

"Michael, I wasn't trying to hurt you. Carlton didn't want me to marry Kevin. He didn't even believe you were his grandson. He had all those tests done when Kevin died. I hated him. I didn't marry Kevin for his money, and I didn't want anything from his father."

Well, Carlton must have wanted something, Michael thought as he swirled the liquid in the brandy snifter. He'd wanted a part of Michael, even from a distance.

"Did he ever attempt to see me?" Michael had asked.

"A few times." Ellen Lawrence swallowed.

"You refused him the right." It was a statement. His mother nodded.

"You had a father," she said. "Our life was comfortable. There was no need to confuse you by introducing him into your life."

"Did his color have anything to do with it?"

Ellen hesitated. "Yes," she said. "I'd been married to a white man. I loved him, Michael, and I would marry him again if given the chance. But I know the horrors we went through, and I didn't want you to have to go through those things."

Michael wondered what that would mean now. The press had to find out about this sooner or later. A man leaving an estate worth forty-seven million dollars to a black man would have to be newsworthy.

"What are you going to do?" Malick's question brought his attention back to the restaurant.

"Do I have a choice?" Michael frowned. "There's no way I'm going to let a person like Frank Mason wangle an easy way out of jail."

"What about returning to the law?" Malick asked.

"Not a chance."

Born in St. Peter's Medical Center thirty-seven years ago. . . . Erika picked up one of the reports and stared at it. She'd received them weekly from the private investigator Steven had hired on her behalf. She knew facts about Michael Lawrence, but the facts didn't tell her where he was. She checked her watch again. It was after eleven o'clock on the final day, and though she'd gone to bed she couldn't sleep. She had returned to the library and these reports.

If Michael didn't show up in the next forty-seven minutes, the entire estate went to Frank Mason. It looked as if Frank Mason would be a very rich man within the hour, and she would be homeless.

She knew he didn't know yet. Steven had told her Carlton's instructions stated that Frank Mason was not to be informed until the expiration of the time limit, a limit that hovered close by.

She'd tried, she told herself. She'd thought he would come. She also thought she'd have more time to try to make him help. But she hadn't figured he would leave without giving an address, or that he wouldn't call to let her know his decision. He knew her address. Carlton's law firm's address was printed on the papers she'd left with him. If he'd wanted to find her, he had all the information. He obviously hadn't.

Erika dropped the papers on the desk and stood up. She wrapped her satin robe closer around her, feeling cold even though it was warm in the room. Why had Carlton played this game, she wondered. He was usually quite up front with his requests and beliefs. She knew Michael had held a very special place in Carlton's heart. He told no one about him, yet attended his ceremonies and vicariously basked in his glory. For some reason Michael had retreated to the mountain, and Carlton wanted him off of it. This was one method of getting his way. Only Carlton wasn't here to see if his plan worked. He was leaving it up to her to resolve, and she'd failed.

"I'm sorry, Carlton," she said. "I tried." She just wished he'd told her what he was up to before he died. Erika felt beaten. Her shoulders drooped with the weight of the burden she'd carried for the last month trying to locate Michael, all for nothing. Tomorrow she would go to the office and make the announcement. Within a week she'd have packed everything, turned over the reins to the new president, and left.

She was a little angry at Carlton for tangling her with Michael, although he hadn't left her penniless. If Michael refused to comply, she would still have a trust fund that paid her $50,000 annually until she died.

It was enough to live on but it wasn't what she had, what she'd become used to and considered her own. She wanted Graves Enterprises, but that looked like something she wouldn't get.

Erika paced the room, feeling lost and disconnected. She should be concentrating on what she would do tomorrow and the rest of her life. But she couldn't. She was too angry. People didn't just disappear these days. There were computers, credit cards, the Internet. How could Michael Lawrence leave a rustic cabin on a Maryland mountain and disappear into thin air? Why couldn't Steven's investigator get his law firm and his brothers to tell him where Michael was? He had to be somewhere.

She walked back to the desk and slammed the file closed. Then, in frustration, she sat down. Ten minutes to midnight. The clock didn't make a sound, but Erika felt as if it were ticking her life away. Michael held her fate in his hands, and it meant nothing to him.

Erika put the file in the desk drawer. She reached for the desk lamp and extinguished it. The darkness closed in around her, but she didn't move immediately. She let her eyes adjust to the darkness, waited for the images of furniture and lamps to settle into place. Finally she pushed her chair back and stood up. She knew this room as well as she knew all the rooms, and she'd be heartbroken to leave it. She walked through the room, neither touching nor bumping into anything as she went toward the splash of hall light spilling through the entry door.

She noticed the time as she passed the grandfather clock on her way to the stairs. Three minutes to midnight. Stopping at the base of the huge staircase, Erika remembered sliding down the curving banister when she was nine. She remembered standing there to have her picture taken when she graduated from junior high school, and going through the front doors with a nervous date on her way to her high school prom. Tomorrow she'd leave a lot of memories behind.

Erika started up the stairs. On the fifth step she stopped, sniffling, trying to hold back tears that were threatening to fall. At the top she turned toward her room.

"Is it all right if I use this part of the house?"

Erika whipped around, her heart thudding. The upstairs hall was long, branching off into two wings. The lights were off and she couldn't see anyone, but she'd heard Michael's voice. Her gaze searched the darkness. Did she really hear him? Was her mind conjuring him up? Then he stepped into the light.

"Any objections?" he asked. Not waiting for a reply, he turned and disappeared into the darkness again.

Her breath was expelled, and her vision blurred. *I'm going to faint,* she told herself. Her knees went weak and rubbery and she gripped the banister to hold herself up. The clock chimed behind her. Tears clouded her eyes as Erika waited, counting the number of gongs on the clock until it reached twelve.

Her body went numb. Mechanically, she started up the stairs. She occupied the third room on the left, next to the one in which Carlton had died. She opened the door and fell against the wood panels as it closed. Her knees give way, and she slid down along the wall to the floor.

He's here.

CHAPTER 4

The night passed. Erika remembered every hour of it as she filled her breakfast plate with eggs and toast. She'd wavered between elation and fear. He'd come. He had to be here to help her. There could be no other reason. What would he want changed? Would he try to usurp her position and take over the day-to-day running of the operation? He was a lawyer and they were presently looking for a legal counsel. Maybe he would be willing to take over that part of the business. Of course, the will said they shared everything. She would certainly discuss anything with him that he wanted to know about. She wasn't planning to exclude him from anything. Carlton wouldn't have forced her to share the company with someone he considered unqualified. Then she remembered the Michael she'd met at the cabin. He wasn't the same man she'd seen in the upstairs hall last night.

"Good morning," he said.

She started, hitting her coffee cup, but luckily it didn't spill. His gaze still went to that nervous act. She'd thought she'd be prepared for him this morning, but his presence sent her blood careening though her veins. He was clean-shaven and wearing a business suit. It fit his strong shoulders as if it had been custom-made. The haggard look about his eyes was still present, and in the shadow his eyebrows looked slightly sinister. Other than that, he was devastating, and every part of her body knew it.

Holding herself erect she said, "Good morning. The coffee's hot and I alerted the cook that you would be here for breakfast."

"That was nice of you." He went to the server and heaped food on his plate. "I take it I won't be enjoying any of your cooking while I'm here."

Erika felt her face warm as memories of the cabin flooded into her brain. A place setting had been set to her right. Michael slipped into the chair in front of it. The gesture was as comfortable as if he'd been doing it for the past twenty years.

"I suppose we should discuss just how long you plan to stay."

"According to Mr. Steven Chambers, this arrangement must remain intact for twelve months. Apparently my . . . grandfather thought you and I should carry on after his death."

So that's how he'd gained access to the house. Steven had given him the packet of information left for him, which included a key and the security codes for the front door. Unfortunately, neither of them had bothered to call her and let her know.

"I believe we are to share everything, including this house," Michael said.

"That's what it says in the will."

"Twelve months from today we have the right to do whatever we want with the companies, the house, and our lives."

Erika nodded.

Michael bit into a crisp piece of bacon. Erika dangled like a puppet.

"Have you agreed?"

"I signed all the necessary papers. I suppose you'll show me around the offices, beginning this morning."

"It would be my pleasure," Erika told him, but it was no pleasure. It took half an hour to get to the offices of Graves Enterprises. A company limousine picked her up each morning. She and Michael sat in strained silence during the drive to downtown Philadelphia and the corporate offices.

She showed him the office she'd picked out for him, which adjoined her own and had been recently decorated. Anything he didn't like his secretary would have redone. Michael looked around approvingly and followed her on the office tour.

"Graves Enterprises major business is pharmaceutical," she explained as they entered the accounting department. "We also own several cosmetics companies and a few hotels. We have our own fleet of cargo ships and use them to transport our products to manufacturing sites which are located in South Carolina, Georgia, Puerto Rico, and Germany. We have a full fleet of trucks that carry our manufactured goods to distribution centers all over the country. We also have marketing and sales organizations in twenty-seven countries around the world."

Michael listened attentively, asking questions, smiling and shaking hands when she introduced him to people in the departments they passed through. He was good-looking and charming. Without turning to look behind her, she knew people were nodding their agreement that he'd make a good addition to the family of companies.

"You appear to know a lot of people here," he observed when they were back in her office.

"I've been here a while."

"You never told me how you and my grandfather came to know each other." This time there was no hesitation when he referred to Carlton.

"I was only eight," she told him. "One day I ran through the hedges and into him." She smiled. "He invited me to tea and we became very good friends."

Erika didn't tell strangers about her childhood. Michael didn't yet qualify as a trusted friend.

"And he didn't tell you about me until—"

"Until the night he died," she finished for him. "He had me bring him the photo album. He pointed you out, called your name, and died." Erika swallowed the lump that formed in her throat whenever she talked about Carlton. "I thought you were a small child until the will was read. After that I looked through the album and found a full history of your accomplishments."

Michael watched her. She wasn't the same as she'd been in the mountains. Last night when he found her in the hall, dressed in a peach nightgown, he'd wanted to scoop her up and carry her to bed. Today she'd receded behind a corporate uniform—navy blue suit, white blouse, low heeled shoes. He preferred her in the sweater and pants she'd left the cabin wearing.

"I went through Carlton's things." She swallowed. "Most of his clothes have been sent away. He left some of his jewelry, gold watches and rings, to the servants, but there is a box of things you might want to go through when you have time."

Michael could see her distress. He changed the subject. "How do you propose we begin this year of sharing?"

Erika took the seat behind her desk. "We are in need of a corporate counsel and—"

"No," he interrupted too quickly and loudly. "I'd prefer something else," he said in a lower voice.

"If you want to learn the business, it might be a good idea if you visited one or two of the plants, to see how the process begins."

Michael nodded. It was a good idea. It would take him out of town for a while. Yet strangely, he didn't want to go. "How about I do that later? Initially, I suppose I could just find my way around. You could explain what you do, and maybe I can help carry some of the burden."

He thought he saw a flash of fear in her eyes, but quickly it disappeared. "Of course," she said. "We can begin tomorrow morning."

"What's wrong with today?" He checked his watch. "It's nearly lunchtime. How about directly after lunch?"

Erika hesitated, then nodded her agreement. "Where shall we eat?"

"I'm afraid I already have a luncheon engagement."

To Michael's retreating back, Erika's mouth dropped open.

The day had been exhausting. After Erika returned from lunch, in which the discussion revolved around a competitive product that would carve into their hard-won market share, Michael had stuck as close as her shadow. She'd pulled up reports on her computer screen and shown him how to access data from the system. She'd explained their product lines, profit margins, and sources of information. Erika explained the rules to him and told him he had the right to request reports or gather information from any of the data sources in the company.

They'd returned to the mansion in the same car and she was now in her room, feeling the first sense of relief she'd felt in twenty-four hours. She showered and stood before her closet dressed in a terry cloth robe.

She'd been standing there for ten minutes, trying to decide what to wear to dinner, when it occurred to her she was trying to pick something that would impress Michael. What was wrong with her? She shouldn't care what he thought of her clothes. Closing her eyes, she reached inside the closet. Her hand came to rest on a black dress. She frowned when she opened them, then shrugged and began dressing. The dress clung to every curve she had and the bodice seemed a bit low, showing off her small breasted cleavage. Hooking a three-strand pearl choker around her neck and applying drop earrings to her ears, she stepped into her three-inch heels and left the bedroom.

Erika entered the salon where she'd always met Carlton before dinner. Michael had not come down yet and for a few minutes she had the room to herself. The grey September day had fallen into a dark night that reflected her appearance through the long windows that faced the courtyard at the back of the house. Across the stone patio the yard was ringed by a low brick wall that had made Erika feel safe when she was small.

She didn't feel safe now. In fact, since Michael's unexpected arrival she'd felt trapped—trapped in space that was her domain, places where she should have the advantage. Somehow he seemed to have taken it.

Leaving the window she went to the bar and poured herself a glass of wine, something she rarely did. Tonight she needed to relax. Except for the brief period at Penns Landing, while Michael attended his luncheon engagement, he had been her constant companion. She had to get through dinner and the evening with him in the house. It was strange, she thought, that all the while she lived here with Carlton and the staff she'd never felt the presence of anyone as much as she felt Michael's.

Lifting the glass, she sipped the chilled liquid. It was smooth, and warmed her as it went down. The door opened behind her and she turned. Michael stood there dressed in a black suit and a white shirt that contrasted with his skin, making him look like some handsome movie star. She was no teenage groupie, but at that moment she prayed her knees would hold her up, for she wanted to melt to the floor.

Finding her voice she said, "I should have told you. We don't dress for dinner."

"I didn't," he said, advancing into the room. When he stood only a step from her he replied, "We were so busy this afternoon I forgot to tell you I wouldn't be here for dinner."

"You have a date?"

"Yes," he said, flashing her a smile.

Something as sharp as an arrow pierced her heart and Erika fought to keep her expression noncommittal. She should be relieved. Only a moment ago she'd been telling herself she had to get through dinner and the evening with him. Why was she disappointed that the problem had been resolved?

"I see you're going out, too." Michael's glance covered her from head to foot. Then he moved around the bar and poured a glass of mineral water.

Erika looked down at her dress. "No," she told him. "I have no plans for the evening other than some reading."

"Then can I assume that lovely little number is for my benefit?" He raised an eyebrow.

Erika felt the blood heat her face and ears. "You're a lawyer, Michael. I'm sure you know what assume means."

Immediately she regretted her words. The playfulness he was having at her expense was suddenly gone. She watched the friendliness in his eyes disappear, replaced by something she thought must hurt him deeply. She wondered what it was, and why the mention of the word "lawyer" had changed him. This morning, when she suggested he take over the legal counsel position, he'd flatly refused.

"I apologize," she said.

"For what?"

"I don't know."

Her answer, though a statement, was an open question for him to answer, but he didn't, and he wasn't going to. He didn't want to think about the law and all the entanglements involved in practicing it.

He changed the subject. "You're quite comfortable at Graves Enterprises?"

She nodded. "I am."

"Rumor has it you've been there since you were a kid."

"I was sixteen and—"

"And what?"

"Afraid, like most sixteen year olds are, I suppose."

Michael didn't believe her. She'd been about to say something else when she caught herself. When he'd been sixteen he hadn't been afraid of anything, except maybe a girl turning him down for a date to the junior prom. He smiled, remembering that time in his life and wondering what Erika's had been like.

"You said you met Carlton when you were very young."

"Eight," she answered, her gaze level on him as if she were suspicious of his motives.

"How did you come to live here?"

"My mother gave me up for adoption and Carlton adopted me."

"When you were eight?" That was highly unusual unless a child was being abused and the courts stepped in and removed the child. Then they tended to get lost in the foster care system, which changed them for life—and for the worse. He couldn't see Erika like that, but suddenly wondered if she had been abused. Some people were good at hiding bruises, but invariably they were revealed in some way.

"Your mother is still alive?"

"Yes." Erika's voice was as dry as a desert. "She is."

"She gave you up when you were eight?"

"I was fourteen, and can we stop with the Twenty Questions?" Erika turned away, going to the windows and staring out into the darkness

"Now it's my turn to apologize." Michael put his drink on the bar and went to her. He wanted to put his arms around her, but every line of her body told him not to touch her. "I didn't mean to pry."

Erika lifted her head and stared at him. Her eyes were enormous but dry. Somehow he thought she never let anyone see anything vulnerable about her. She was a tower of strength to the world, but Michael knew from firsthand experience that those kind of people hurt deeply in the confines of privacy. He didn't like to think of Erika hurting.

"You'd better leave," she said, interrupting his thoughts as she checked her watch. "You wouldn't want to keep the lady waiting."

Michael didn't move. There was that impulsiveness again—the action that had made him kiss her good-bye at the cabin, and the one now that nearly had his hands moving to take her in his arms. He lifted one hand and touched her arm."Good night," he said with a gentle squeeze. "Enjoy your evening." With that he left.

As the cold, wintry air hit him Michael tried to tell himself Erika St. James was not his problem. The two of them had a one year agreement. After that they were both free to do what they would. His intention was to sign over Graves Enterprises to her, take his share of the settlement and walk away. He would return to his mountain or go to Timbuktu, but whatever his decision it had nothing to do with the walnut-colored woman inside.

Her heels clicked hollowly in the cavernous foyer as Erika closed the door and walked across the gleaming black and white tile. She thought she'd heard someone knock. Had Michael already forgotten the set of keys he'd been given? No one was there when she opened the door. Since Carlton died, there seemed to be a steady stream of people coming and going. By now she thought they would have gone on with their lives and forgotten about him, but she found that Carlton had more friends than she remembered. Tonight she wished at least one of them had dropped by. Her lonely dinner gave her time to think about Michael and who he might be having dinner with. How could he have a date so soon? He'd been here less than twenty-four hours, and already he'd met someone.

Ripping her attention away from Michael, Erika thought over her position in this house. Rarely had she ever thought about it. She'd come first here as an intruder, then as a friend. It was her refuge, her haven of sanity when her mother flew into her rages. Eventually, she'd clashed with her mother and run away so much that the judge allowed her to stay here permanently, visiting her mother on holidays for short periods of time. Carlton had insisted that she keep some association with Alva Redford. He said family was important, and when you lost family you could never replace them. She wondered about that now that she knew about Michael. Carlton had not done what he'd forced her to do.

People treated her as if she were a grieving granddaughter. She felt like a granddaughter, but she wasn't one. Carlton had a grandson. What had happened to keep them apart? Why did Michael not know about Carlton? Why had Carlton never mentioned Michael?

Erika slipped into the living room. The coffee service was there and hot. She poured a cup and went to the sofa. Slipping out of her shoes, she curled her feet under her and settled into a comfortable position.

Her mother's house had been gloomy, not dark, but unfriendly. Here there had been no fighting and arguing, no screaming. She sipped the hot liquid, remembering her childhood. Carlton had helped her with her homework, and come to see her in school plays and assembly programs, programs she hadn't even mentioned to her mother. He was always there to talk to her, never too busy or too tired to take an interest in anything she had to say. Now he was gone.

Erika's heart felt tight in her chest. She'd forgotten the deep sense of loss that accompanied death. Balancing the cup on the edge of the sofa, she hugged herself as she shivered in the warm room.

Carlton had been her sanctuary when she was a child and when she needed to come home after Bill. No, she wouldn't remember, not tonight. She stared into the large fire burning in the huge grate.

She needed a vacation—an escape. This just wasn't the time. There was too much to do at work. She had a meeting scheduled with Jeff Rivers tomorrow and she expected it to last most of the day. Even though she'd been at Graves Enterprises permanently for the past year, Carlton's death had left morale low, and people feeling uneasy about a possible restructure. With Michael's arrival and a possible takeover looming, things would invariably get worse before they got better, and she couldn't leave in the middle of that. She needed to be there to show them they had no reason to feel nervous. Carlton was a visionary. She'd learned much in the past year about the pharmaceutical industry. She also had her past experience and the firsthand experience of working at Graves Enterprises. She planned to keep on the same track Carlton had begun. They were releasing a new product and they had a healthy pipeline. With the steady growth of market share in several divisions, they were sitting comfortably. She hadn't discussed conditions with Michael, but she could see no reason why he'd disagree with her.

Michael, she thought. Who was he with? He'd only kissed her, she told herself. He hadn't asked her to have his children. Maybe the way he kissed her good-bye was the way he said good-bye to every unattached female who slept on his sofa.

Erika smiled. Thoughts of him warmed her. Involuntarily her hand went to her mouth.

Erika lifted her cup from the sofa arm. The liquid was cold now. She got up and placed it on the silver tray. Reaching down, she lifted her shoes and headed barefoot for the staircase and her bedroom on the second floor. Before she reached it the doorbell rang. Instinctively, Erika checked the time on the grandfather clock.

Maybe she'd been right before, and Michael had forgotten his keys. If it was him, his date was rather short. She smiled at the thought that he might have not enjoyed himself.

Erika changed direction and started for the door. One of the maids came through the kitchen and met her in the hall. Erika signaled she'd answer it, and the woman left. With her shoes dangling from her fingers Erika went through the foyer. The heavy, carved wooden door had a beveled glass window in the top portion. Through the clear facets Erika saw the last person on earth she expected to find. Hesitating for a moment, she drew in her breath and pulled the door open.

"Mother!"

Alva St. James Redford stood under the portico, her body wrapped in mink, her red Mercedes sport coupe behind her. The light flatteringly bathed her skin tones. Erika's surprise at finding herself face-to-face with her mother took her power of speech.

"I never expected to cross this threshold again," Alva said, pushing past her daughter and entering the foyer. She turned back to Erika, her stance as dramatic as that of an actress from the old black and white movies. Gloria Swanson, with long black hair and a mole on her chin, came to mind. Alva pulled her mink coat closer around her as if the room were cold, instead of comfortably warm for this time of year.

"What brings you here?" Erika asked as she closed the door and started for the living room.

Alva paused at the entrance to the high-ceilinged room full of high, draped windows. The facing sofas shared a beige and rose color scheme and sat on a carpet that picked up the rose color. Erika watched her mother take in the room as if looking for something. After a moment she slipped out of the coat and dropped it on a chair by the door. Advancing, she came toward her daughter.

"Is there something I can get you to drink—coffee, a soft drink?" Erika wouldn't willingly offer her mother alcohol. She remembered all too well her moods after she'd bent her elbow on one too many scotches. "This is cold, but I can make a fresh pot."

"Why don't you ask someone to get it? After all the years you've lived here, haven't you learned how to have servants serve you?"

"The servants work a full day, Mother. At this hour they are afforded time to themselves."

She could see Alva Redford would never stand for this kind of treatment. Erika knew she should make the suggestion again, but sat down, putting her shoes back on and refusing to do so.

Alva sat on the facing sofa, stretching her arm along the back and studying her long, blood-red fingernails in a decidedly feline manner. "I see nothing much has changed here." She lifted her gaze to the life-size portrait of Carlton's wife, Loretta, which hung above the dying fire in the fireplace. She pointed to the far wall. "I'll bet you if I opened that chest over there, there will be a collection of Fabergé eggs and some precious stones."

Erika was obviously surprised at her mother's knowledge of the house. Except for one incident, when Alva had stormed into the house demanding her daughter be returned to her, Erika couldn't remember her ever being here.

"This isn't my first visit," she said, as if she could read Erika's thoughts. "I've been here many times. I can even tell you the color of the wallpaper in your bedroom."

"That won't be necessary," Erika said. "You can tell me what you want, and then we can end our visit the way they always end."

"Erika—" She stopped. For the merest second Erika thought her name sounded strange coming from her mother's lips, as if the woman hadn't said it in so long she'd forgotten the sound of it. "Erika, I only wanted to make sure you were all right."

Erika stared her straight in the eye, looking for any hint of insincerity and finding none. *She's a good actress,* Erika thought. *Who is she playing today, and why?*

"After all," she went on, "Carlton died more than a month ago. All the people surrounding you must be gone. I wanted to see if you needed my help."

Erika stood up and turned away. The thought of her mother offering help was so ludicrous that she nearly laughed out loud. She turned back, her arms folded across her. "Mother, thank you for your concern. You've done your duty. I am not lonely, alone, or in need of your help."

"Erika, don't sound so angry. We are related, and family is the most important thing in the world."

She'd heard Carlton say that. It was the reason he insisted she visit her mother at times. Erika remembered the visits, the arguments over how she looked, what she wore, how she combed her hair, or made up her face. In Alva Redford's eyes, her daughter was a sore disappointment.

"I think I'll have that coffee now," Alva said.

"Mother, you didn't come here for coffee." Erika raised her hands to prevent her mother's protests. "And you aren't here to inquire about my state of health."

Alva rose from the sofa as if she were Cleopatra about to deal with a disloyal subject. "Why, dear, am I here, then?"

"You're here about the money." Erika was rewarded with a small gasp from her mother. "I know about the checks Carlton had been paying you. Just what service did you provide that afforded you that kind of payment?"

"Don't be disgusting!"

"I'm not, Mother. My mind and my conscience are clean. Can you say the same thing about yours?"

"Why, you inconsiderate little wretch! You're just like your father, stubborn and—"

"Leave Daddy out of this. You can't go on blaming him for everything that's happened in your life. And you can't blame me, either."

"Forget your father."

"I'll never forget him, but you certainly have. You probably drove him to killing himself."

Erika knew she'd gone too far. Her mother's hand was suddenly in the air, and the slap that swiped across her cheek stung like an entire hive of bumblebees.

"Hey, what's going on in here?" Michael stood in the huge archway. Both women started as he spoke, and turned toward him. Neither of them answered him. Michael walked into the room. Erika blinked, trying not to let the tears her mother always drew from her spill over.

"Michael," Erika found her voice. It was tight and formal, but she got the words out. "I'd like you to meet my mother, Mrs. Alva St. James Redford."

Michael turned to the older woman and nodded. Alva smiled as if she were sizing up a new conquest. Erika's stomach wrenched and she swallowed the bile in her throat.

"Mother, this is Carlton's grandson, Michael Lawrence."

Alva laughed, a throaty sound. The laughter escalated and went on and on while the two other occupants of the room looked on.

"You . . . you," she said, hesitating, using her fingertips to wipe tears from the corner of her eyes. "You must have been a real surprise to Carlton . . . and Erika." She stopped and pointed toward Erika as the smile on her mouth wore away. "A grandson. Wait until the reporters find out about this one. They are going to have a field day."

Erika had a sudden mental picture of her mother being interviewed by the *Philadelphia Inquirer.*

"Mother, I warn you." Erika spoke through clenched teeth.

"Darling, daughters should never warn their mothers. It's not done." She sauntered toward the door, where her coat lay on the chair, but stopped in front of Michael. She looked up into his eyes for a long moment. Then she went to the chair and pulled on her coat. With an exaggerated flourish she turned back to Michael, delivering her parting shot with the best Gloria Swanson imitation Erika had ever seen. "Erika told me she wasn't alone . . . or lonely."

CHAPTER 5

This time Michael didn't think about what he was doing. His legs took him across the room and he turned Erika into his arms. She resisted only a moment before giving in to his comfort, but she didn't cry. Her arms went around his waist and she buried her face in his shoulder, but no sobs came from her. She needed to hold onto someone. Michael understood that. How many nights had he awakened in a cold sweat and wanted someone to hold him?

He didn't say anything, and didn't expect her to do anything more than cling. After a while he walked her to the sofa and sat down, keeping her cradled against him. She was soft and smelled of a sweet perfume. He swallowed at the sensations she aroused in him.

"Do you want to talk about it?" he asked.

She shook her head against his shoulder. Michael cradled her closer and she settled against him. Invariably his thoughts went to Abby, and the time he'd comforted her in almost the same way. Turning his head, he brushed his mouth against Erika's hair. He didn't like to see her hurt, and her mother had hurt her. When he'd walked into the room he knew the only thing keeping Erika from breaking down was sheer will. He thought she was holding something back. With her mother throwing daggers at her, Erika inherently felt something for her. In her eyes had been a raw plea for love. Michael had seen it before—once, in Abby's eyes. But it hadn't been for him.

Michael looked down at her. She breathed easily and he knew she'd fallen asleep. He thought of her sleeping at the cabin, her face clean of any makeup and wearing a flannel nightshirt. Here she was a queen, always on duty. Michael pulled his arm free and slid away from her. Easily he let her fall backward until she was stretched out on the sofa. He turned the lights off in the downstairs rooms and checked the doors. Coming back, he lifted her into his arms and started for the stairs.

"What are you doing?" Erika jerked awake when his foot touched the first step.

"Shhh," he said and continued up the stairs. She was thin in his arms, light and warm. He enjoyed holding her, smelling her perfume and soap. She rested her head on his shoulder. He forced himself not to put his head on top of hers. At her door he let her slide her feet to the floor. "Are you all right?"

She nodded.

"Good night," he said, then lifted her chin and kissed her lightly on the mouth. Before either of them could respond further he broke contact, turned, and walked toward his own wing.

She called to him. "Michael." Her voice was low, quiet and sexy. It surrounded him, stopping his retreat. He didn't want to stop. He knew if he turned back her eyes would be dewy and inviting. Why had he let himself kiss her? Why did she stir feelings in him that to date he'd been able to control? "Michael." Her voice cracked as she said his name. He turned to look at her. "Thank you," she said. "I mean, thanks for coming." Michael shrugged and turned again.

That night the dream came again, stealing into his subconscious and robbing him of the ability to rest. Michael ran, panting, following Abby and Frank up the hill, toward the building. His lungs burned as they tried to contract and expand. A fiery pain swelled in his chest until he knew his lungs would burst. Yet he kept going. He had no choice. He had to get to Frank, get the gun, and keep him from—.

Michael bolted upright, his teeth clenched, his muscles tight, hands balled into fists. Sweat poured down his face and over his chest. The room seemed hot and stuffy. For a moment he was disoriented, wondering where he was and where Abby had disappeared to. Then he let his breath go and sagged against the pillows. He hoped he hadn't screamed out in his subconscious rage. Pushing the covers aside he left the bed, which looked as if it had been an unwilling participant in a prizefight. Going to the window, he opened it. Leaning against the frame, he sucked in the cold September air, letting it cool his fevered body.

Taking a chair when his breathing returned to normal, he wondered when the dreams would end. Tonight after leaving Erika he would have welcomed dreams of her, but Abby and Frank had invaded his dream state and devastated his ability to relax. When this happened at the cabin he'd do something physically exhausting—chop wood, row the boat, or climb the mountain. There was a full gym here. He could go there and work out. Then he remembered the pool. Dressing in a pair of trunks and hooking a towel around his neck, he headed for the indoor pool. He felt better already. This would be a pleasure. In college he'd been on the swim team, and never tired of the sport. With a pool inside he could swim in any weather and at any time of the day or night. Tonight he intended to exhaust himself until he could do nothing other than sleep.

The water glowed green and inviting under the lights of the Greek style bathhouse. Michael entered the room, smelling the chlorine and feeling the eighty degree heat, and stopped. Erika cut through the water with sure, easy strokes. She swam effortlessly as a water nymph, at one with her environment. Michael wondered if she'd had a bad dream, too. She reached the end of the Olympic-size pool, ducked under the water, and pushed off toward the end closest to where he stood. Her reversal had all the skill and elegance of a choreographed dance. She raised her head out of the water to breathe at regular intervals, but she didn't see him, not until his shadow fell across her and she stopped, finding him directly in front of her.

"Couldn't you sleep?" he asked. The argument he'd interrupted between Erika and her mother came back to him. It pushed his own sleeping problems to the back of his mind.

She angled herself out of the water, wiping her face and smoothing her hair back. Michael noticed how big her eyes looked and how her nearly naked body curved. She wore a royal blue, one-piece suit that had him wishing he'd worn a robe.

"Whenever my mother and I fight, it ruins my sleep. I thought I'd come here and exercise for a while."

"Do these fights occur often?"

She picked up a towel and began drying her face and arms. Michael couldn't stop his gaze from following the towel as she stroked it against her skin. "She and I usually try not to cross paths, but it *is* a small planet."

Michael smiled. He knew a fighter when he saw one. When she'd arrived at Highland Hills he knew she'd be a worthy adversary. She'd come to the cabin to take him on, when no one else had been able to make him budge. Tonight he'd seen her in action. Yet the emotional drain took its toll on her subconscious. He wondered at the methods they each chose to solve their problems.

He wanted to ask her more questions, but decided against it. He'd told himself he wouldn't get involved with her or anyone else. And he was sticking to that rule, despite what his body told him. Despite the fact that when her mother left he'd kissed her and he wanted to kiss her again. Right now.

"How's the water?" he asked, glancing over his shoulder and dragging his attention away from the fact that she looked beautiful soaking wet. He hoped the water was cold. He needed it to be cold now.

"I'll race you to the deep end," she said.

Frank panted, breathing through his mouth. He never thought it would be this easy, and during daylight, too. He knew he'd escape during Smiley's shift. He'd planned it, studied Smiley's routine until he could follow it as well as Smiley could. Then the unthinkable happened. The gate was open—not wide open, just a little ajar, not even noticeable. It was visitors' day. Outsiders, the normals, crowded about the place. Frank never had visitors. He usually spent these kinds of days sequestered in his room. The day staff didn't bother him on these days.

Leaving would be no problem. He already had clothes. They were hidden in a tree at the north end of the compound. He'd collected them a piece at a time and taken them to the tree. He knew he'd need them when he was finally free. And today was freedom day.

Frank waited. The nurse at the station stacked folders on the counter. He nearly smiled at what he knew was about to happen. His heartbeat accelerated, and he consciously willed it to return to normal. He'd practiced his escape, knew every detail of it. All he had to do was remain calm and his plan would work. Finally, as Frank expected, the folders reached critical height and tumbled over. The nurse cursed, then stooped to retrieve the mess she'd made. At that point, Frank eased through the door. Carefully he pulled it closed, listening for the slight click as it locked, while his gaze remained on the white-clad nurse. She was trying to make order out of the chaos when he turned and walked down the hallway, taking the first turn to keep out of her view. He knew the way to the yard. Frank reached it without incident. Outside, he appeared to be one of the patients returning to his weekly visitor. Frank walked easily, smiling at people he'd never seen before.

He kept his gait short and easy. He didn't want anyone to notice him. Following his usual route, he kept going until he reached the clump of shade trees in the distance. He stopped, taking a moment to look back and see if anyone was looking at him. All was calm. *This is just too easy,* he thought. He wondered how long it would be before someone noticed he was missing. Visitors came and went all afternoon. Lunch ended before the visitors arrived. It could be dinner before they thought to check on him. By then it would be dark and he would be miles away from here.

Frank checked the ground. He saw no footprints. The ground varied between pine needles and packed earth. The warm, dry air of the past few weeks acted as an unwilling accomplice to his escape. Frank found the tree where he'd hidden the clothes, and climbed. From inside a hollow knot he pulled a green plastic bag. Refusing to take the time to change now, he forged ahead. The trees became denser and darker until he reached the wall.

Thirty feet high, made of solid, tan brick, it looked as impenetrable as the locked door. Frank knew there was no such thing as a locked door. If you wanted to get through it bad enough, all you had to do was find the key. He looked up, his gaze stretching from tree branch to tree branch. Out here maintenance wasn't performed with as rigid a regimen as it was near the front gate. No sentry held duty here. The guards were more nurses than wardens, and the height and breadth of the wall was a deterrent in itself.

Frank had stood in harder places than this. Often he stepped aside when dividing the men and boys, and he rarely came upon a problem without a solution. Frank moved back several yards and exchanged his hospital whites for jeans, a sweatshirt, jacket, and sneakers. He looked like any other visitor now. No one would notice him. Putting the hospital clothes inside the bag, Frank hooked it onto his beltloop and climbed the first tree.

He went as high as the branches would hold him. Then, using moves that could kill him if he fell, he jumped to the next tree and the next, and one more. Finally, he was one tree from the wall; six yards from freedom. With his arms spread out like a tightrope walker, Frank balanced himself; step by step he moved along the branch until he could reach the next tree. He grabbed the branches. They were coarse against his hands and swiped at his face like scratchy fingers. Holding his breath, he pumped the branch and swung his weight to the last tree. He prayed this would hold him and he wouldn't die from a thirty foot fall over the side of the wall.

Frank crouched for the final trial. Crawling backward along the dark wood, he moved with care. The branch dipped under his weight. Frank held his breath. For the space of a lifetime it dipped downward. Frank squeezed his eyes closed, expecting to hear the snap of wood and know his life would end in seconds as he fell to his death only a few feet from freedom. Finally it stopped. Frank hung over the side, his hand slipping along the leafless branches, his feet fighting for footholds along the smooth wall.

Finally he stopped. His heart beat so fast he thought it would surely stop soon. Frank closed his eyes and waited a moment. Then he looked down. It must be twenty feet to the ground. Vertigo attacked him as the ground bobbed back and forth before settling in place. Frank took a breath. His hands slipped again. The skin on the inside of his right hand tore, and blood dripped into his face as he looked up at it. It was time, he thought. Taking one more deep breath he let go of the branch and fell the remaining feet to the ground. The impact bent his knees and he landed in a sitting position. The branch snapped back into position. It waved for a second, then settled into place as if no human had ever hung from it.

Frank looked up and down the road that followed the outside wall for any sign of trouble. He saw nothing. The other side of narrow strip of blacktop held another clump of trees. Frank went into them and waited. If luck was with him, he'd hop a ride on the first truck or van that came up this road.

He didn't have to wait long. The first car was a low compact job, its rear bumper so low to the ground that Frank would have had to drag himself. He waited. The next vehicle was a minivan. He could have jumped on that, but the driver traveled so fast Frank would have killed himself trying to get a grip on the back.

A quarter hour passed before another car came by. This time there were four in a row, and no time to come out without someone seeing him in a rearview mirror. Frank settled back to wait. Then he heard it. One of his night sounds. The engine labored on the hill, out of sight. He knew it was the bus. The bus that brought patients to the hospital and sometimes transported visitors to the facility. It didn't run on a schedule, and came at odd hours. During the day, with other noises, it was difficult to hear it until it turned into the driveway. At night, with the crisp air magnifying the sound, Frank could hear the engine missing as the driver shifted well-worn gears.

The blue and white bus had long ago lost its fresh paint job, and the mirror on the passenger side had never been replaced after it was broken.

Frank waited for it to completely round the curve before he left his hiding place. Jumping on the back fender, he held on, his fingertips in the crease created by the rear door. Frank rode along the road, following the wall until it ended. When the bus turned onto the connecting road and stopped, Frank jumped clear. He walked to the next road and hitched a ride with a tractor trailer driver.

He was free.

The steady and monotonous droning of cold rain awakened Erika the next morning. Despite her lack of sleep and the promise of a grey, dreary day, Erika felt wonderful. She had enjoyed swimming with Michael. Yesterday she had dreaded his company, been unsure about his presence on a daily basis. This morning she knew everything was going to be all right. She had help.

Carlton must have known that when he wrote the will. She smiled, pulling a red suit from the closet and dropping it on the bed before heading into the shower.

Several minutes later Erika walked into the breakfast room to find the table set for one. She wondered where Michael was. Wasn't he having breakfast this morning?

"Tess, isn't Mr. Lawrence having breakfast this morning?" she asked when the maid came in to bring coffee.

"Mr. Lawrence ate earlier and left, Ms. St. James."

Erika didn't ask why, or when he had told them he was leaving. She felt a little awkward that Michael hadn't told her. They'd swum for nearly an hour, then talked a while before going back to their rooms. The clock had chimed three o'clock as Erika put the light out. Had Michael still not been able to sleep? Had he gone for good? Erika nibbled on her toast and sipped her coffee, trying to remember if he'd said anything to let her know he wasn't satisfied. She could think of nothing.

At Graves Erika checked his office. It was empty, and no one had seen him that morning. She shrugged, still not understanding, but then the pressures of the day required her attention and she didn't have time to dwell on Michael's absence. She found herself thinking of him over and over. Why hadn't he told her he wouldn't be in today? Why had he acted so friendly last night and then disappeared this morning?

At three o'clock, as she prepared to go to a meeting, Erika knew he wasn't going to show up at all. She phoned the house and was told he had not returned or called. Earlier she had been angry, but that was slowly turning to concern. Had something happened to him? He could have been involved in an accident, and no one had notified her.

They hadn't been partners long enough to be responsible to each other. They had set no rules about accounting for their time. It was truly none of her business where he was. However, he was supposed to share this business with her, and during business hours she didn't consider it too much of an imposition to expect him to tell her when he would, and would not, be available.

Erika gathered her folder and walked to the door of her office. She opened it and stopped. The room was full to capacity.

"Ms. St. James, is it true you share this company with the man who won the custody battle for the Mason children?" a woman in a grey suit asked. Flashing camera lights blinded her. Questions hit her like bullets. She'd been through this before. Bill Castle came to mind, and she wanted to shrink back into her office and slam the door.

"Ms. St. James, where is Mr. Lawrence?"

"Ms. St. James, is Mr. Lawrence in Philadelphia?"

"Ms. St. James—"

Erika didn't hear any more. She turned to her secretary. "Call security," she shouted. "And call the police. I want this office cleared."

"Michael! Michael Lawrence!" June Ferrell unplugged her headset and came around the receptionist's station at Lawrence, Barclay, West, and Lawrence. "How have you been?" she asked, catching him in a bear hug.

"Fine, June," he told her. "It's good to see you." June Ferrell had been receptionist at the law firm since Michael and Evan Barclay began it only three years after graduating law school. Michael liked her immensely. "I see you've changed—lost weight, less grey hair. There must be a man in your life."

June laughed. "Don't I wish?"

"Is my brother in?"

She nodded, going back to her station and plugging into her board. "Won't he be surprised?"

"Don't call him. I *want* to surprise him."

June smiled conspiratorially. "Go on. I'll see you soon."

Michael passed his own office on the way to his brother's. Several people gaped at him in open-mouthed surprise. He smiled and waved, but didn't stop to chat. As he approached his brother's secretary he put a finger to his lips to keep her from calling his name.

"How have you been, Margaret?" he asked when he was within whispering distance.

"I'm just fine. But look at you. You've lost weight, but you still look good enough to eat. Are you coming back?"

"No." He laughed, shaking his head. "I just need to talk to Bobby."

As if on cue a soft buzz sounded from her phone. They both looked toward the desk.

"He's calling me," Margaret said.

Michael smiled and went through the door to his brother's office.

"Margaret, I need the Bennett file. I just talked to him and he'll be in tomorrow at four." Bobby hadn't looked up when the door opened and closed. He'd continued making notes on the yellow pad and begun giving instructions. "Also, would you call Mrs. Anglender and ask her the status of her Case Information Statement? We'll need to get that into the judge's office by the end of the week. And I need—"

Michael interrupted his list. "I don't think I'll be able to help."

"Michael!" His brother shouted and jumped up from his chair. The two hugged, patting each other on the back, then shook hands and smiled. Bobby wasn't prone to outbursts of emotion. He was the calm, controlled lawyer, able to quickly analyze the situation and act. What Michael had just witnessed was a side of his personality he generally hid from the world. Bobby must be truly glad to see him.

"I'm so glad you're here. You're coming back," he stated. "We've been so busy since you left. It will be good to have another hand to carry the load."

"Bobby," Michael stopped him. "I'm not returning. I have something else to do. Maybe after it's done I'll consider coming back."

Bobby's shoulders dropped, the exact same way their father's had when he was disappointed. Michael stared at his brother. He could see a lot of his father in Bobby. He'd never liked to compare how much they looked like their parents. However, when Erika entered his life, she caused the foundations on which he lived to crumble.

"How long is it going to take? We could really use you here."

A pang of guilt ripped through Michael. "It's a year contract." Apparently, their mother had said nothing to her second son. Otherwise he'd be aware of where Michael was living, and the details of the will that had been left by his grandfather. "How about hiring another lawyer if there is work to keep another one busy?"

"Actually we have been discussing that, but so far we haven't really had time to interview anyone."

"You will," Michael assured him. "I really came by to talk to you and Peter. I had hoped Mom would be around."

"She's up visiting Aunt Irene in Boston. It was a spur of the moment thing. She called about a week ago and left the next morning. I asked if everything was all right. She said she hadn't seen her in a while and wanted to go."

Michael well knew why. His mother didn't want to deal with him. He'd seen her once when he confronted her about Carlton Lipton-Graves and his true parentage. After that she'd obviously packed her bags and headed north.

"Can you spare a few minutes for lunch?" Michael asked. "Peter's agreed to meet us at The Pub." Michael checked his watch.

"I suppose I can spare time for a brother I haven't seen in a year."

Bobby got up and pushed his arms into his suit jacket. He took a moment to let Margaret know where he was going while he slipped into his overcoat. Moments later they were on the street, walking toward the restaurant. Peter met them at the door with a friendly handshake and a wide grin.

The more outgoing of the three, and certainly the best looking, as he liked to tell them, Peter worked for a local cable company in the newsroom.

The Pub was an old building in downtown New Brunswick. The inside was dark and the seats wooden and hard. The tables had the marks and indentations of the names of hundreds of college students who'd attended Rutgers University, only a few blocks away. Miniature trains ran around a track mounted overhead. Their father used to bring them here as children on Saturday afternoons for lunch. Michael remembered those times.

When they were seated and the waitress had taken their order Michael asked his first question. "Have either of you talked to Mom lately?" None of them lived with their parents any longer. Bobby was married and Peter lived with his girlfriend. Before Michael had left for Maryland, he'd lived in his own condominium in East Brunswick.

"I talked to her this morning," Peter said. "She seems fine, enjoying Aunt Irene's cooking."

Michael looked at Bobby. "Last Sunday," he said. "We called her."

"Did she mention anything about me?"

The brothers looked at each other, then at Michael. Each shook his head.

"Have either of you ever heard of a man called Carlton Lipton-Graves?"

"Sure," Peter said. "I reported the news of his death about a month ago." Peter anchored the New Jersey News. On weeknights at six he could be seen on WNJN. "His substantial holdings in this state prompted the station to do a story on his passing," Peter went on to explain.

"How about Erika St. James?"

"I believe she was Acting CEO while the old man was alive." Peter paused, seeming to pull his memory into focus. "If I'm remembering correctly, she walked off with the lion's share of Graves Enterprises."

"The pharmaceutical company?" Bobby asked.

"That's the one," Peter told him.

"I remember this now," Bobby said. "What's all this got to do with whether we talked to Mom recently?"

The waitress arrived with their lunches. Michael waited for her to set the plates out and leave before answering his brother. "What I'm about to tell you I've already told Mom. I thought she might have let you know, but I will admit when I left her I was pretty angry. I wanted to put as much distance between her and me as possible. Later I regretted it, and returned to apologize."

Peter and Bobby stared at him. He wasn't making much sense.

"Michael, what are you talking about?" Bobby asked.

Michael took a sip from his water glass and began. "About a month ago a woman came to see me. Her name is Erika St. James."

"You let *her* on that mountain, when you wouldn't let any of us come and talk to you?" Bobby asked.

"You haven't met Erika." Michael remembered the picture of her that day, straight, tall, and representing a past he didn't want to confront. Her words and the will she delivered had taken his choice away from him, and he was back. "I didn't let her come and talk to me. She took that initiative herself."

"What did she have to say?" Peter asked. His attention was fastened on Michael, and the playfulness of his tone was completely gone.

"What she told me has a direct effect on all of us." Michael stopped assessing their expressions as he would a witness in court, memorizing what the look was like so he could compare it to the look that would come when he finished his interrogation.

"Come on, Michael," Peter said. "Stop keeping us in suspense."

"Yes," Bobby agreed. "What does the Lipton-Graves heiress have to do with us?"

"Erika St. James isn't the sole heir to the Graves legacy," Michael said.

"You're not going to say he left part of it to us?"

"No," Michael smiled, feeling a little of the tension leaving his body. He went on to explain the exact terms of the will and the news of his true parentage. He told them everything, from Erika's first visit to his day at corporate headquarters. When he finished, his two brothers hadn't eaten a bite, and were looking at him in amazement.

"Mom knew this?" Bobby asked.

Michael nodded. "I told her about the will a couple of weeks ago."

"In all these years she never said a word to you? Never told you you had a living grandfather?"

"She said it didn't seem to matter. My real father was dead. I had no memory of anyone other than Dad. So she just let it go." Michael paused. "I don't blame her. What would have been the reason to tell me? She'd never received anything from Carlton in the way of support, emotional or financial. From what she told me, Carlton didn't believe I was his true grandson. He had unauthorized blood tests performed in an attempt to prove I wasn't part of his bloodline."

"That must have gone over well with Mom," Peter said.

Michael nodded, knowing his mother's explosive nature when one of her children was in danger. She'd have gone up against Carlton Lipton-Graves and his millions if the need had come, but apparently it hadn't.

"You said he had a photo album of you," Bobby said, unconsciously retreating to the confuse-the-witness technique that all lawyers use. "Where did he get these pictures?"

"I don't know. According to Erika he could have been there, taken them himself."

"What do you think?" Peter asked.

"I'm not sure. I don't think he would have left me half his estate if he'd never laid eyes on me."

"Did Mom say anything about him wanting to see you?" Bobby asked.

"He'd asked to see me a couple of times. Her reasons for refusing made sense, but he never demanded any familial rights, and he never acknowledged that I was his grandson."

"At least, not until the will came to light," Peter commented.

"Mom thought it best to put everything behind her and go on, and there was Dad, providing everything we needed, never treating me any differently than he treated you two."

Michael thought of his father. He could never replace Robert Lawrence with the figure of any other man. He'd loved him as a son, and even the knowledge that he had not fathered him didn't change the important part of his life that he'd given him—time, guidance, emotional support. Looking at his brothers, he knew his father would be proud of them all. He didn't know what he would think of Michael's retreat to the mountains, but he would certainly be supportive of his decisions.

"Michael," Peter said. "What are you doing about the conditions of this will?"

"I've given up the cabin in Maryland," he began. "I'll have to stay in Philadelphia for a year and co-manage the companies Carlton left."

"After that, you become one of the most eligible bachelors in the United States and you're free to do as you wish?" Peter had sized up the situation

"Yes." Michael nodded. "Only *you* would put it like that."

"Why hasn't this been reported in any of the papers?" Bobby asked.

"All the details of the will were not disclosed, but I have reason to believe they might be soon." He remembered Erika's mother and her veiled threat to go to the papers. But even without her as a motivation, he thought his brothers should know. They had grown up as family, and he didn't want them to find out through the local news.

"Damn," Peter said. "I feel bad.

"Why?" Michael asked.

"All those times I said you weren't my brother. Now I find out it's true."

Peter's words were refuted by the wide smile that creased his face. Bobby joined him with a grunt that turned into a laugh, and soon the three brothers were laughing, hilariously.

"It doesn't change anything between us," Bobby said when they could speak again.

"So tell us about *her,*" Peter said. "According to the reports she'd worked at Graves Enterprises for years and had been running it solely for the last year. How did she take to you suddenly having a say in things?"

"We haven't clashed over anything yet," Michael hedged. "We're working out which one of us is responsible for what, so we can make this a good relationship."

"Is she beautiful?" Peter asked. The smile on his face showed definite interest. "Even the newspaper pictures were good."

"Why should you care? You have a girlfriend."

"Not any more," Bobby told him. "Peter and the beautiful Cassandra parted company six months ago." He paused to glance at his brother. "Our dear brother here is on the loose."

Peter smiled. "Maybe I'll come stay with you for a while."

"The commute to make the six o'clock news might be a little steep," Michael told him.

The three of them laughed like old times. Michael was glad. By some trick of fate he'd been given the best family in the world. He knew that, and he never wanted it any other way.

"How's Catherine?" Michael changed the subject to Bobby's wife.

"Pregnant," he said. "She should be delivering in the next two weeks. You're going to be an uncle."

"Congratulations!" Michael said, reaching across to shake his brother's hand. "You will call me when the baby is born?" Michael grabbed a napkin and wrote the address and phone number down. He passed it across the table, but Peter took it.

"Isn't this where Erika St. James lives?"

Michael suddenly remembered his brother's uncanny ability to hold details in his head.

"We share the company *and* the house. It was a condition of the will."

Peter's eyebrows went toward the overhead trains.

"She has her wing, and I have mine," he explained, but Peter didn't seem to understand that, from the smirk on his face.

For a moment the three of them didn't say anything. Then Peter sobered and commented, "I suppose that mess in California is all behind her now."

What mess? Michael wanted to know but didn't ask. He knew about her engagement to William A. Castle. The newspaper Gerald Hodges had saved him detailed a little of her association with the entertainment lawyer—that Erika had been in Los Angeles, that she'd worked there before returning to Philadelphia. What had happened that his brother knew about? He didn't want to ask, to reveal he didn't know, and if it was something Erika wanted to forget, he could respect that. Michael knew everyone had secrets. Erika was no different.

He had the sudden urge to talk to Erika. He'd enjoyed their time last night by the pool. They didn't know each other very well, but maybe they would by the end of the year and she would trust him enough to tell him about California. He might trust her enough to tell her about Abby.

"Michael, you didn't answer me. Is she really as beautiful as her pictures?" Peter asked.

Michael couldn't tell him how beautiful she was. A picture of Erika in her blue bathing suit crowded into his mind, and Erika smiling, Erika talking to him in the pool area, Erika at the cabin, her hand raised against the glare of the sun. "Yes, she's beautiful," he finally said.

Suddenly he wanted to leave. He wanted to see her, wanted to go back and have dinner with her. Michael stood up. "I have to go," he said.

"Michael," Peter stopped him. "When do we get to meet her?"

"I'm not sure I want her to ever meet you," Michael teased his youngest brother. He actually felt a tingle of jealousy. He felt more for Erika than he'd realized.

"How about bringing her to Thanksgiving dinner?" Bobby was saying when he brought his attention back. "It's at our house, but Mom is cooking."

"I'll let you know."

Michael left them. He didn't spend time thinking about his brothers and what they would discuss after he left. He wanted to know what Erika was doing. Had she missed him? He wanted to stop the car and call her, but he didn't. He drove straight to the house. It was too early for her to be home from the office.

Michael went to his rooms and dressed for the pool. Within minutes he was swimming laps in the Olympic-size bathtub. His mind was free and happy, anticipating her coming.

He was on lap number fifty-seven when he heard something and looked up. Erika stood at the end of the pool where he'd stood the night before. She had on a red business suit and high heeled shoes. It appeared to be the right color—with her hands on her hips, every line of her body said she was angry.

"How dare you," she said, moving toward him. "You let that story hit the papers and you disappeared into oblivion, leaving me alone to answer the questions."

"What story?"

"That's good," she grunted. "Really good. You heard my mother last night, and today the story is all over the television. My office has been besieged by calls and reporters and you . . . you swim." She stopped as her voice cracked. "I thought we were supposed to share everything. Wasn't that how you said it, *everything*?" She imitated him. "Where were you today, while I was sharing your infamy?"

CHAPTER 6

"What are you talking about?" Michael caught up with her halfway down the hall. Grabbing her arm, he turned her to face him. "What's happened?"

Erika tore her arm from his wet grasp. "What do you think happened? I was assaulted by an army of reporters over your status, and you weren't there to help."

"I didn't know."

"Where were you? Why didn't you tell me you weren't going to be in the office today?"

He couldn't tell her. It would sound trivial. He'd been on the receiving end of battering by the press, and he knew he should have been there. Last night after their swim he had known he needed to see his family. He had to go and tell them the news before they found out from someone else. According to Erika, he'd done that only moments before it became common knowledge. However, he hadn't been there when she needed him. That he regretted.

He hadn't been there for Abby, either. The thought suddenly popped into his head without warning.

"Tell me what happened," he said, pushing the thought aside.

Michael and Erika stood in the hall. The water dripping from his body formed a wet splatter on the light-colored rug, but he refused to postpone the interview to go for a towel.

Erika took a deep breath and looked at him. "Somehow the complete details of the will were discovered today, and my office filled up with reporters like a war room. I opened the door to find lights flashing in my face. People fired questions at me so fast I couldn't possibly have answered them even if I intended to do so." She turned, pacing back and forth. " 'Where is Mr. Lawrence?' they asked. 'Is it true he owns half this company? Is it true Carlton Lipton-Graves was his grandfather? Is it true the two of you are living together?' "

She stopped and stared at him as if waiting for him to say something. Before he could, she came to stand in front of him, anger making her vibrate.

"And where were you? Out somewhere, completely oblivious to the chaos going on in the office?" She answered her own question. "What do you think this is, some cabin where you can decide not to work if you don't want to? Well, Michael Lawrence, this is not the Maryland mountains. Your word means something here, and when you make a promise I expect it to be kept."

Michael stared at her. For some reason he had the impression she wasn't talking about something that had happened today, or even when Carlton died. Erika was angry, angry over something that happened far longer ago than this afternoon. He wondered if it had anything to do with what Peter had mentioned? Something that happened in California.

Michael folded his arms across his chest and waited for her to finish. "What did you do?" he asked quietly.

"I called security and had my secretary calling the police if they didn't vacate the building."

Michael hid his smile. He knew she was a gutsy woman, but she was frightened, too. He wanted to find out what was behind the anger, what had caused it, and he knew her day at work was only a catalyst that brought back painful memories.

"Why didn't you tell them the truth?"

"Truth!" she exploded. "They're not interested in the truth. They want sensationalism." Her hand flew up in disgust. "They want a few words so they can misquote you and print lies because it makes better copy and sells more newspapers."

"Is that what they did to you?"

As if she'd turned to stone, Erika stopped. All motion about her ceased, and she stared at him with ice in her eyes. For a long moment she held his gaze. Then, turning on the balls of her feet, she strutted away from him. Michael watched for a moment, then followed her. He hadn't intended to deliver another blow. Obviously she'd had a bad day and he'd fueled it trying to find out something about her. It was an unfair tactic. How easily he'd done it didn't surprise him. He'd been trained to rout out concealed information, to find the truth wherever it lay, and without thinking he'd done that to Erika.

Erika started up the stairs at a trot, but she wanted to run. She wanted to dash up them at full sprint. She wanted all the reporters to leave her alone and she wanted to put distance between her and Michael Lawrence. Going straight to her room she slammed the door closed.

"Erika!" he called.

Disregarding her privacy Michael charged in after her.

He'd brought it all back. The memories of Bill Castle and the incessant press. Cameras pointing at her, flashes lighting in her face. The questions, the neverending, embarrassing questions that had her hiding in her own house. Everywhere she went people recognized her, whispered behind her back, until she could no longer stand it. If Carlton hadn't asked her to come home, she would have left Los Angeles, anyway. She'd held herself straight, refusing to let them get the better of her.

It was happening all over again. She'd thought the initial news of Carlton's death and her inheritance had come and gone, lost behind more sensational news than the passing of a rich old man. She didn't realize there was something about Michael that would have them hounding her again. Something about Michael and Frank Mason.

"Erika," Michael called again.

She turned to face him, her arms at her sides, her face blank and unreadable.

"When I left they were in the parking lot, waiting," she began. "They followed me home. I assume they're at the end of the driveway, probably with a full television crew, waiting until we come out and give them what they want."

Michael glanced through the window over her shoulder as if he could see the reporters from here. They were out there somewhere, on the other side of the beveled glass door, down the winding driveway and outside the wrought iron gate.

"Where did you go?" Erika asked him. Her voice had softened. She stared at him with hurt in her eyes. Michael felt guilty. He hadn't intended to have her take the full brunt of what he knew would happen. His heart constricted, and he knew he was going to take her in his arms. In a second he'd crossed the room and pulled her against his bare chest. His arms were around her, and with only a minimal amount of resistance she relaxed against him.

"I went home. I needed to talk to my brothers."

"Mother!" she pulled back, concluding this awful day had been the results of her mother's threat. "I forgot all about her. I've got words for her that will turn her roots grey." She went to pull out of his arms, but he stopped her.

"Not now," he whispered, placing his hands on either side of her face. He stared at her. Her eyes were huge and confused, but her gaze was direct. He understood—he was as confused as she. Between them something was happening and he didn't know if he wanted to stop it, or even if he could. Heat swirled around them, drying his skin and cocooning them in a world where only they existed. He lowered his head and brushed his mouth over hers. Her lips were full and soft, yielding. A sound crawled in his throat at the pleasure of her touch. He continued the easy, brushing motion. This could be his undoing. He'd been without a woman for a long time. And Erika wasn't just any woman. He didn't want just any woman. He wanted her. She'd been on his mind since the moment he saw her. Even without the motivation of thwarting Frank Mason, Michael wasn't sure he wouldn't have come to Philadelphia just to see her again.

It wouldn't take much for him to crush her against him, devour her mouth, peel this red suit from her brown body and take her on the bed only a few feet from where they stood.

He wouldn't do that. He *couldn't* do it. There was something about her that told him she was fragile and could easily break into a million pieces. He kissed her tenderly, cradling her head between his hands. She returned his kiss with equal gentleness, opening her mouth to his enticing persuasion, accepting the fullness of his tongue as it swept inside and tasted the sweetness of her being.

Her arms circled his waist, her hands spreading about his naked back with a silkiness that made him shiver with need. His body was warm, hot, melting, and hard. His lack of clothing left her in no doubt about his state of arousal. She was aroused, too. He felt it in the boneless wonder of her arms as their mouths left each other's and her head sank to his chest.

Michael had never experienced a kiss like this before. He'd known plenty of women. He understood passion and sex, uncontrolled and wild, but the tenderness she evoked in him was a new experience. With her in his arms he wanted more than kisses, more than sex. He wanted to be tender. He wanted to know her, understand her hurt and her compassion. She was different from every other woman he'd ever met. He wanted to understand how she could drive him crazy with her look. He wanted to protect her from the reporters outside and from the world that threatened her.

He'd thought he wanted to escape from the world, not interact with mankind or the entrapments that contact invariably caused, but with Erika he wanted to be her champion. She mattered. Why, he couldn't say. He hadn't known her long, but somehow her good opinion of him meant something.

He lifted her chin. Her eyes were full of passion and he knew he'd put it there. His body wanted hers. He wanted to bury himself inside her and make love the rest of the night. They could forget the reporters, forget their pasts, however bad they had been, and only live for the next few hours. But Michael wouldn't do that.

He would kiss her again. That he couldn't stop. Her look pulled his head down, and his mouth took hers. This time the passion he'd held in check fought for release. He kissed her hard, sliding his arms around her waist and pulling her body into close contact with him. His mouth devoured hers as his hands rode low on her hips, pulling her into intimate contact with him. He wouldn't make love to her, but he wanted her to know he could.

He heard the throaty sound of pleasure that escaped from her mouth into his, and he felt her body mold itself around him. He was losing it. In seconds he'd forget his vow and have her naked on the bed. Michael tore his mouth from hers. Her arms tightened around his neck, and he held her for another agonizing moment before pulling free.

He stared down at her, both of them trembling, both of them breathing raggedly. "Make no mistake about this, Erika," he said in a voice thick with emotion, "I want to make love to you." She started to say something. "Shhh . . ." He put his finger to her lips.

Her tongue darted out and licked his finger. Michael nearly lost his power of speech. A spiral of emotion fissured through him.

"Erika, this isn't part of our agreement. We're both rational people and we're awfully close to stepping across a line that hasn't been defined. We might want to think clearly before doing something we could both regret."

Erika sat in her office the next morning, one hand holding her head. For two nights straight she'd had little or no sleep. Her other hand gripped the coffee cup as if it were a lifeline. She drank the hot liquid, black. Usually she added sugar and cream, but this morning she needed something to cancel out the men with sledgehammers inside her head.

Michael hadn't been at breakfast today, either. Erika didn't know whether she should be glad or sad about his absence. He'd only postponed their next meeting. It had to take place sometime. The will pitted them together for the next twelve months. They'd only been together for forty-eight hours, and already they'd been only a hair away from being intimate.

They were strangers, she told herself. How could she act like this? She knew better, knew it was disastrous, but in his arms she didn't think . . . that was the problem. If she were to go on with this for the next year, she had to think clearly, and that meant staying away from him.

Michael was right. The agreement didn't call for them making love, and they certainly would have if he hadn't stopped them. She couldn't believe the way she'd acted. He'd kissed her and the only thing she'd been aware of was the dark heat of his skin, the smell of the dried water, and the contours of his chest. She pictured herself close to him, kissing his male nipples and removing the only barrier he wore between the world and his nakedness.

Erika shook her head. What was she doing? She needed to concentrate on sales levels, on strategy for increasing their market share ratios. But her concentration was gone. Just as it had been last night. One minute she was arguing with Michael over the reporters, and the next she'd been trying to climb inside him.

This time there was no doubt in her mind about his motive. On the mountain he'd been saying good-bye, and the other night he'd been comforting her, but last night, last night was raw, unleashed, sexual excitement, and she'd wanted him to take her to bed. She wanted him to make love to her. The urge was stronger than she'd ever known it could be. But he'd told her he'd regret it, regret making love to her.

Rejection! She knew it when she saw it. How many times would she set herself up for this kind of disappointment? Hadn't she learned anything? Hadn't the trauma with Bill taught her to tread lightly? Or the years with her mother, a woman who didn't want her and had never done one thing but push her away? Obviously, she hadn't, if it took so little provocation and even a smaller amount of resistance on her part before she was lost in Michael's arms.

"Erika?"

She heard her name. Heard Michael's voice. Her head snapped up. He was standing in front of her desk. Erika clenched her teeth. She'd hadn't heard him come in, but a quick glance at the door connecting their offices told her he'd opened it and come inside. How long had he been there?

"Are you all right?"

"I'm fine," she said, trying for a smile. She looked at him. Unlike her, he appeared fresh and rested this morning. A flash of anger went through her. The kiss they'd shared had to have some effect on him, but he must know how to handle the situation better than she did. She admitted she didn't have much experience. Barring Bill, there had only been three other men in her life, and she'd handled none of those relationships well.

"I called a press conference for ten o'clock this morning."

"You what!" She stood up so fast her chair careened backward and hit the wall.

"We can't let them hound us. I know what it's like . . . and hiding doesn't work. It only intrigues them more. If you're not up to it, I'll handle it alone, but I'd really like to have you there."

Erika stared straight at him. She hated the press. There were things Michael didn't know. If she went to that conference they'd drag her through the Bill Castle story again. She'd have to sit there and go through the humiliating questions. She'd have to remember that her fiancé married another woman. Bill Castle was as famous as some of the rock stars he represented. His name was a household word. How could the press let her get away without asking for every intimate detail of her relationship with him?

"Why can't we just issue a press release?" she asked, knowing it wouldn't be enough to satisfy the hungry mob.

"If I thought that would work I'd suggest it, but after seeing them as I left this morning I know that won't keep them from following us around. The only way to get rid of them is to give them what they want."

"They want blood!" she told him, anger stealing into her voice. *Mine,* she added to herself.

"It's not going to be easy," Michael said. "They're bound to bring up Frank Mason."

Frank Mason was nothing compared to William Castle. Erika let out a sigh. When Carlton died she'd avoided the press, but it didn't deter them. They'd hounded her until she finally granted an exclusive interview to a lesser known reporter whom she figured wouldn't have the gall to ask her about Bill.

She'd been wrong.

"More than likely, they're also going to remember your California incident."

She stared at him. "You know about that?" Her throat was dry. A pain lodged in her chest.

Michael shook his head. "My brother mentioned it yesterday. I let him think I knew what he was talking about."

He waited for her to explain. She'd only heard a few questions yesterday about Michael and Frank Mason having a history together. She didn't know the truth of it. But he was asking her to tell him why she'd left California.

"I was engaged to Bill Castle." She checked to see if he recognized Bill's name. Anyone who knew popular music knew of Bill Castle.

"I've heard of him," Michael confirmed.

"He ran off and married my secretary," she said without emotion. Her stare never left his face. She couldn't see any change in his features—pity, concern, or judgment. "The press followed me everywhere. I became a prisoner in my own house. Every time Bill made the news, someone tried to interview me." Erika dropped her gaze to the desk, remembering the hounding nature of the unrelenting press. "They'll ask intimate questions, pry into my life as if they had a right. I'm not sure I want to go through that again."

Michael admired her. She didn't say she couldn't go through it, just that she didn't want to. He didn't want to go through it again, either, but he knew neither of them had a choice. The press was an estate unto itself. Like the army, it would continue to come. The longer the two of them avoided the media, the more people would be assigned to find out the truth.

If they didn't want a small story to escalate into front page news, they had to go through the bad and get it over with.

"This time you won't be alone, Erika," Michael said. "Carlton left us everything to share. We can begin with the press."

She looked at him with a hardness in her eyes. Michael held her gaze until it softened.

"Neither will you," she said.

Michael squeezed Erika's hand as they stood outside the seminar room where the reporters had assembled.

"Let's get it over with," she said.

He took a deep breath and nodded. Michael wasn't looking forward to this, either, but he'd run away before and he refused to do it again. He knew they'd ask questions about Frank Mason and Abby. As much as that would bring back memories, he had to get through it.

Erika grasped the doorknob and turned it. The door swung inward and she walked through. He followed her. Conversation, which had been at a thirty decibel level, deceased to zero. For the space of a moment no one said a word. Then they all tried to speak at once. Michael couldn't make out any questions, but he could hear his name and Erika's being shouted from the sea of suits, cameras, and microphones.

Without a word he and Erika took seats in front of the crowd and waited for them to be seated. The room returned to order and Michael spoke.

"Good morning." He cleared his throat, adjusting the microphone. "I'm glad so many of you could make it on such short notice." A ripple of laughter went through the room.

He glanced at Erika. Her expression was professional, giving nothing away as to how she really felt—which, Michael knew, was scared as a kid on her first day at kindergarten. He felt much the same way, knowing that behind more than one of the many faces in the audience lurked the questions he didn't want to answer.

"I'd like to say something before we answer your questions," he went on. "You all know the terms of the will, if today's papers can be believed." Another ripple of laughter. "I have confirmed to my satisfaction that Carlton Lipton-Graves was my grandfather." He expected a reaction, but all he saw was the nodding of a few heads. "His legacy to Ms. St. James and myself is that we share the running of Graves Enterprises. We have discussed this." He looked again at Erika. Her gaze met his this time. She nodded her confirmation. Somehow he thought her actions reflected a well orchestrated script. Maybe she was relaxing. "Ms. St. James and I plan to fulfill the outstanding contracts of Graves Enterprises and to lead this corporation into the twenty-first century."

Erika turned to look at him. Questions were in her eyes. Michael didn't have anything more to say. He knew he should defer to her, but he wasn't sure she was ready, especially after the way she looked at him. He'd called this conference. He had time to prepare for it. She'd only had ten minutes before she had to go on.

"I'd like to add something," she said, surprising him. He kept all expression off his face, as if they had decided beforehand how to handle the press. "Mr. Lawrence and I have not completely worked through all the details of responsibility, but like any growing organization we'll find the right fit."

She's a trooper, Michael thought. Her voice was controlled, authoritative, and calm. She spoke as if she gave orders, and knew how to get results.

"Now, if there are any questions concerning the business and our roles in it, we'll be glad to answer them."

He almost smiled. She was good, cunning. She'd told them to stick to the point. Of course, he knew they wouldn't, but it would give them a way of deflecting unwanted questions. For as much as she'd feared this arena, Michael somehow didn't think Erika was.

She nodded at a man with his hand raised.

"Did you and Mr. Lawrence really inherit over forty million dollars?"

Erika smiled, a wide grin that reached her eyes. The first question generally set the tone for the rest of the meeting. Michael was grateful to the man.

"Our lawyers are still determining the exact amount of the estate. However, I'm sure the company is in sound financial condition. The third quarter reports will be available to you in a few weeks, and we're expecting to post a profit for the year."

Deflection One.

"Mr. Lawrence, you're a lawyer. Are you taking over the legal affairs of the company?"

"While there is a position available for a general counsel, the requirements are those of corporate law. My expertise in law is in another area."

Michael thought he did well, but he knew there was a gaping hole in his answer. If there was a smart reporter out there, he or she had a perfect opening to ask him the Frank Mason questions.

They didn't come. For half an hour the questions were business oriented, and Michael began to feel they were going to pass this without running into any problems.

Then a man rose from the back of the room. "Ms. St. James, did you know that Bill Castle's marriage is on the rocks, and he's mentioned you in several recent interviews?"

"I haven't spoken to Mr. Castle in over a year." She paused. "And, as you probably already know, Mr. Castle didn't keep me informed of intentions when we were . . . an item." Many in the room laughed, and Erika cut the reporter a look that said he should not pursue that line of questioning.

Unfortunately, the door had been opened, and the entire room seemed to pour through it. Question after question dragged out details Michael was sure she would just as soon forget. But she kept up with them, never flinching, answering the questions with wit and professionalism, managing to keep them from making her look like a fool.

"Were you surprised to find Mr. Castle had married your secretary?"

"No, Mr. Lahey." She obviously knew this reporter. "I usually discuss the marriage plans of my fiancés when they decide to marry other women."

Uproarious laughter spread through the room. Erika also smiled. Michael wanted to laugh out loud, but he controlled it.

His turn came as soon as the laughter abated. A pretty, young reporter in the front row rose and looked directly at him. He could tell. She was the smart one he'd thought of earlier.

"Mr. Lawrence." She looked directly at him. He held her stare, knowing this was his turning point. He'd either get through the rough part or he'd crash and burn right here. "Did Frank Mason know he was a contingent beneficiary?"

"I have no idea," he answered truthfully.

"Have you had any contact with him?"

"Not since that last day in court."

"Frank Mason vowed to make you and everyone else pay for sending him away."

"I heard that," Michael said. "I never saw Frank in person after his children . . . died." Michael couldn't help the slight catch in his voice.

"We're getting a little off the mark," Erika interjected. "Could we bring the discussion—"

"Did you know," the woman interrupted Erika, "that Frank escaped his prison and is on the run?"

Michael's heart missed a beat. How could he escape? He was psychotic. Why wasn't he watched every moment, awake or asleep? He appeared normal, logical, even rational, but he wasn't. He was the most dangerous man Michael had ever come across, and he'd met some beauties. He'd been in and out of court with some of the lowlifes of society, men who beat their wives and girlfriends, women who abused or neglected their children. But when he'd met Frank, he'd thought the man was sincere. He'd taken his custody case, because he appeared to be genuinely in pain at the loss of his marriage and the forced estrangement from his children. Michael had fought hard for Frank and he'd won, but Frank had duped him in the worst way, and now four people were dead. He'd told him lie after lie, and Michael had drunk them in like a smooth cognac. The man seemed sincere, charming, but it was an act. His true colors were shown two weeks after Michael had successfully petitioned the court to give him full custody of his three children. He'd taken them away from his crying ex-wife, and at their first visitation meeting he'd put bullets through their heads. Weeks later, in a state of depression, Abby had taken her own life. Michael was left to deal with the aftereffects of his actions.

How the hell could Frank have escaped?

CHAPTER 7

Champagne, caviar, crystal wineglasses, diamond rings—the accoutrements of the rich and famous. Well, the rich and famous died exactly like the poor and destitute. Frank Mason refilled his glass and dropped the empty bottle into the brown paper bag next to him. He sat on the boardwalk, far away from East Brunswick, where he'd completed his task. The place was deserted, the T-shirt, souvenir, and food stores closed for the season. Frank was alone, remembering the Gilfords. Angela and Jason Gilford. Angela had been Abby's lawyer. She'd said some pretty horrible things about him, brought out all the terrible things that had happened in his marriage. He couldn't forgive her for that.

She'd pleaded for her life, begged him. Frank smiled. She'd been wearing a purple sweater, looking regal and aristocratic, just as she'd looked in court. Well, she'd gotten hers, and that husband of hers, too. They both lay in their East Brunswick house with the high ceiling and walls of glass in the entryway, dead as scared mice, while he sat here, drinking their champagne and eating their caviar.

He dropped the crystal glass into the bag. It clinked against the empty Dom Perignon bottle and broke. Frank pushed the paper bag down until the plastic one covered it completely. Then he tied the end of the plastic bag and stood up. He'd throw the bag in a river. It was already weighted down with stones. The ocean wasn't as good as a river. A river didn't have waves, or adhere to the changing tides. The ocean could throw it back, wash it ashore, but in a river it would sink for all time. And even if it were found, he'd be safe. He knew fingerprints were mostly water, and that water would wash them away, but he hadn't left any. There was nothing in the bag to connect him with Angela and Jason Gilford.

He headed for his car and his next target.

"Who's Frank Mason?" Erika asked the moment she and Michael left the conference room. She recognized his name as the contingent beneficiary, and had made a note to find out who he was while she was trying to find Michael last month. When Michael had shown up she'd forgotten about Frank.

"I'd rather not talk about him," Michael said.

Erika glanced sideways as they walked back to her office. Michael had visibly stiffened when the reporter interrupted her and told him Frank had escaped. She hadn't known Michael very long, but she recognized the tight posture of a man who was retreating into himself. She didn't want that to happen.

Who was Frank Mason and what did he have to do with Michael? Where had he escaped from? What had happened in court?

At the door to his office, Michael left her without a word. She watched him enter. He was tense, as if every nerve in his body had coiled into a tight spring. Erika wondered if she should go to him. She thought he needed someone to talk to, but she didn't know if she should interrupt or let him work it out himself. It would have helped her if he'd told her what he and Frank Mason had in common.

Erika opened the door to her own office. Inside she called Carlton's attorney, Steven Chambers.

"Steven." She smiled when his voice came over the line. "It's Erika St. James."

"How are things going?"

She knew he was asking how she and Michael were getting on. "We're slowly becoming comfortable with each other," she lied.

"Then what can I do for you?"

Steven was great at coming to the point. He didn't have time to waste, not even on clients who paid him well.

"I wonder if you could hire that private investigator again."

"What for?"

"I want to find out about Frank Mason."

"Frank Mason?" he repeated.

"He was the contingent beneficiary in Carlton's will," she said, hoping Steven would know something and volunteer the information she was seeking. "Do you know who he is?"

"I was surprised when Carlton wrote him into the will, especially after what happened."

"Steven," she said, trying to keep the agitation out of her voice. "What happened?"

"Michael Lawrence was Frank's attorney in a child custody suit. The case went on for weeks, and was quite notorious in this part of the state." Steven went on to relate the events of the case. Erika listened in open-mouthed horror as he related the reasons that had caused Michael to escape from the world and retreat to the Maryland mountains.

"So you think the will was Carlton's way of getting him to return to the world he'd rejected?"

"He never told me that, but what else can I infer?"

"Frank's escaped."

"My God!" he said. "When?" Steven was nearly as surprised as Michael had been.

"I don't know. A reporter told us this morning at a press conference. Michael didn't take the news well."

"I imagine he wouldn't," Steven said. "The press hounded him after the children were killed. Some of the not so ethical papers had blaring headlines blaming Lawrence for what happened to the Mason children, and to Frank's ex-wife."

Erika remembered her own moment of notorious fame. She couldn't blame Michael for retreating to the mountains. She'd done practically the same thing in returning to Philadelphia. Her return had been after the press stopped pursuing her, but she gathered Michael had bailed out before that.

"Erika," Steven said, calling her back.

"Do you still want me to hire an investigator?"

"No," she said. Steven had told her what she needed to know. "Thank you." She hung up the phone and stared at the door to Michael's office. The information she'd just heard told her a lot about the man behind that door. He felt deeply about what he'd done. So deeply that he'd turned his back on his profession and his family and retreated to a lonely mountain where he could be alone.

For a year he was there with only his thoughts and the nightmares. Since the storekeeper, Mr. Hodges, had told her Michael kept to himself, she knew today's news must have hit raw nerves. In the mountains he'd been alone, but now he was on the other side of that door with his thoughts of Frank Mason and what his actions had led to, however indirectly.

Erika went to the door of Michael's office. Her hand curled around the brass knob, and she hesitated. Opening the carved oak door that separated their offices, she heard him speaking and realized he was on the phone.

"Is he all right?" Panic was evident in the voice she heard. While eavesdropping wasn't Erika's usual method of gaining information, she was concerned about Michael after the surprising news he'd received at the press conference.

Erika pushed the door open. Michael stood, clutching the phone, his back to her, his body stiff.

"Where?" he asked.

Rapidly he scribbled something on a piece of paper.

"I'll be right there." Hanging the phone up, Michael grabbed his coat and headed for the door.

"Michael?" Erika came forward. Something scared her. "Is everything all right?"

He faced her. "A friend of mine is in the hospital. I have to go."

Erika wondered who she was. A surprised streak of jealousy raced through her at the way he'd stood, and the way he was about to run out. She wondered if he'd run to her this fast if she were ill. Immediately she felt ashamed of herself.

"Is there anything I can do to help?"

The corners of Michael's mouth turned up slightly and he walked over to her.

"Thank you. I don't know how bad he is yet."

It was a he. She couldn't account for the relief that flashed through her.

"Will you call me when you know?"

A brief smile curved his lips again. His hand came up and touched her cheek. He nodded.

Erika put her hand where his had been when he left the room. Two scares in a short period of time. She wondered if he were really all right. First the trauma of Frank Mason, and then a friend suddenly taking sick.

Michael was certainly a complex man. She recognized the strained look on his face. He was worried—about his friend, or the press conference revelation?

She wanted to know him, but he pushed her back each time she got close to him.

Last night he'd kissed her so tenderly she'd thought her feet would never touch the ground again. Then he'd rejected her, walked away, leaving her alone, lonely, and without an understanding of what had just happened to them.

This morning she was more in control, and more confused than she ever thought she'd be. Sharing everything with Michael was light years more complicated than Carlton could have possibly known, if his only intention was to get Michael off that mountain. She wondered if Carlton had thought about her, about the effect Michael's personality and constant presence would have on her.

Had Carlton planned this? Was he trying to manipulate them both? Michael was off the mountain, and she—who'd vowed never again to fall in love—was falling in love with Carlton's grandson.

* * *

The University of Pennsylvania Medical Center housed a first class trauma center. A tan brick structure, built to be functional rather than aesthetically beautiful, it covered several blocks of prime real estate. Michael pulled into a parking space in the hospital garage and made his way to reception.

"How do I get to ICU?" he asked a young, blond woman in a pink and white striped jumper.

"Follow the blue arrows." She pointed to the wall on her left. Michael's gaze followed her finger. The pale yellow wall was bisected by a blue, green, and brown stripe which ran to the end of the room and disappeared through a windowed door.

Michael followed the lines on the walls through a maze of hallways that took him into another building before ending at a set of tan-colored doors.

Pounding in his ears, his heart seemed to stop as he scanned the beds for Malick Wainscott. Michael approached him slowly, breath coming in shallow puffs.

Malick lay under a white sheet, pale as kindergarten paste. His silver hair was tousled against the pillow. Michael stood stock still while tubes dripped clear solutions into his friend's arms and machines beeped around him, monitoring his vital signs. Oxygen tubing was wrapped over his ears and around his face to help him breathe.

"Malick?" His voice croaked. Malick didn't stir. Clearing his throat Michael called him again.

Malick opened his eyes and closed them. A second later he opened them again. A frown creased his brow and his eyelids closed. Michael waited, breathing easier now that he'd confirmed his friend was still alive.

Stepping forward, Michael leaned over the bed. "Malick," he called.

Malick opened his eyes.

"Michael, you made it," Malick said in a weak voice.

"What are you doing here?" Michael tried to cover his concern with a joke.

"I needed a rest." Malick returned his playfulness, but Michael could see the strain in his face and the effort it took for him to talk.

"Don't talk," he said. "Go back to sleep. It's probably good for you."

Malick didn't argue with him. He closed his eyes and was immediately asleep. Michael stayed for a few minutes, noticing the even breathing and the steady sound of the machines flanking his bed. Leaving the room, he went to the nurse's station.

"May I speak to the doctor in charge of Malick Wainscott's case?"

"Are you related to him?" the white-clad woman asked.

"I'm as close to a relative as he has."

"May I have your name, please?"

"Michael Lawrence."

"One moment, please." She dialed a number and spoke into the mouthpiece. When she replaced the receiver she said, "Dr. Washington will be with you in a moment."

Michael paced the floor, waiting for the doctor to arrive. He turned back, glancing into Malick's room. He slept undisturbed.

"Mr. Lawrence?"

Michael turned toward the voice. A black man about his own age faced him. He had dark, steady eyes, and kept one hand on the folded stethoscope in his pocket.

"I'm Dr. Washington."

"I'm Malick Wainscott's friend. He has no relatives. Could you tell me how he is?"

Dr. Washington walked toward the exit and Michael fell into step with him. They crossed the stenciled hall and went into an office. The doctor sat down behind the desk and Michael took one of the two chairs in front of it.

"In simple language, Mr. Wainscott has had a mild heart attack. That's an area between minor and massive. It's a serious condition. The walls of his heart are not damaged, but his stress factors are very high." He paused. Michael thought he was waiting for the familiar family reaction, which Michael held. He'd felt his stomach fall, his hands went cold, and he wanted to grip the arms of the chair in which he sat, but didn't want to admit that Malick might not recover. "We think with proper rest and less stress he will recover," the doctor went on.

Michael let go of his breath. "Thank God," he said wiping his hand down his face.

"We're keeping him in ICU for a few more days, just to make sure he responds to the medication and regains his strength."

Michael was relieved. Malick was a mainstay in his life. He'd never thought of him dying. They'd been friends since his days at Catholic University Law School where Malick had taught him Criminal Law. Michael assumed he would be around for a long time. Michael rarely thought about the differences in their ages. Malick was in his late sixties, still young by today's standards. This sudden attack let him know how mortal Malick was.

"Is there anything else I should know?" Michael asked the doctor.

"Not that I can think of. We're doing everything we can."

"Thank you." Michael stood, shaking hands with the doctor. He left the office and returned to sit with his friend. Malick slept for an hour while Michael waited. Nurses came in and changed his IV bag. The equipment continually monitored his condition with monotonous precision.

Michael thought of Erika and knew how she must have felt when

Carlton was ill. He was helpless. There was nothing he could do to help his friend.

Malick woke just before dark. "Michael, is that you?" he asked. His voice was groggy and slurred. "You're still here."

He remembered he'd been there before. Michael took that as a good sign. "I thought you'd want company when you woke." Michael achieved lightness this time.

"You'd better go home," Malick said. "Erika might need you."

He remembered he hadn't called her, and she didn't know which hospital he'd gone to.

"Erika is a strong woman. She can handle anything that comes her way." He was suddenly surprised by his character assessment. Erika *was* strong, and he knew she could handle things without him. Hadn't she proved that this morning, when the reporters had brought up her past? Then she'd stepped in and tried to bring the discussion back to business when the attack turned to him. She'd defended him, even when she didn't know the impact of the reporter's revelation.

When she'd asked him to explain he'd put her off. He glanced at Malick, who'd fallen asleep again. He needed to call Erika. He admired her, and right now he wanted to hear her voice.

Darkness had fallen and only a small lamp illuminated a corner in Malick Wainscott's ICU cubicle. Erika stood in the doorway, her body casting a shadow on the floor. Michael looked up and saw her.

He sat on the opposite side of the room in the darkness. In a single movement he was on his feet, but he didn't come toward her. She couldn't see his expression in the darkness, and uncertainty about invading his privacy caught her.

"I—I'm sorry," she stammered. "I thought you might need some company." When he'd left the office this morning on the heels of the press conference, she'd been concerned.

For an awkward moment they stared at each other. Then Erika took a step forward. Michael reached for her and she put her hand in his. His grip was surprisingly strong. Erika forced her gaze to the sleeping figure in the bed. Michael must be extremely worried about him if he'd stayed here all afternoon.

The man reminded her of Carlton. He didn't look like him, but he was small and white, and in a medical bed. This was the first time Erika had been in a hospital since Carlton died, and she had the feeling of death about her. Fear gripped her and she clamped her teeth down on her lower lip. She'd come here for Michael, to keep him from the feelings she'd lived with for the long year before Carlton's death. He'd had nurses in the house twenty-four hours a day and the staff was always present, but she'd felt alone. She'd come so Michael wouldn't feel lonely.

"How did you know where I was?" he asked, his voice nearly disembodied in the darkened room.

She glanced at him. "Your secretary told me. When the call came in they identified it as the ICU department at the University of Pennsylvania Hospital."

Michael nodded and continued to hold her hand.

"Is he a good friend?"

"He was one of my law school professors. After I graduated we kept in touch. He's my best friend."

Erika stepped closer and curled her hand in his. "Have you eaten?" she asked, already knowing he'd sat there since he arrived, keeping vigil.

Michael shook his head.

"Would you like me to get you something?"

Michael stared at her for a moment.

"We could go to the hospital cafeteria," she suggested. "I know you haven't left this room since you arrived. The walk will do you good, and you have to eat."

Michael slipped his arm inside her coat. It went around her waist and he pulled her to him. Erika went easily, turning herself toward his body. He needed someone to hold onto. She knew the feeling, and she was glad she was there. She put her arms around him and held him for a moment. She heard his sigh as warm breath against her neck. His arms tightened, and she felt as if he were a small boy needing his mother. Erika didn't mind. She let him hold her until he loosened his grip and stepped back.

"Something to eat might be a good idea," he said.

Minutes later they sat in the hospital cafeteria, a room with sterile white formica tables and blue and white tiled walls. Before them sat buff-colored trays with a hospital version of a turkey club sandwich, hot coffee, and a piece of apple pie. Michael ate in silence, finishing all the food on his plate.

"Talk to me, Michael," Erika said. "I understand what you're going through. I went through it with your grandfather."

He didn't answer immediately. The moment stretched on and Erika didn't think he was going to answer her. Michael got up and took her cup and his. He refilled them both and returned to the table.

"I suppose Malick was my Carlton. We met when I was in law school. I was a young, brash kid who thought I knew everything." He laughed at what must have been a memory of a younger Michael. "Malick quickly made me aware of how little I actually did know." Michael paused, his gaze staring through Erika as if he'd retreated into a past life. "After that he became my unofficial mentor and advisor. We spent hours discussing cases, present and past, politics, art, music. I don't think there's any subject we haven't covered."

Erika wondered if that included her.

"By the time I graduated I was renting a room in his house." Michael laughed and sipped his coffee. "I never actually paid for that room. It was kind of an agreement. I had a lease, but Malick never accepted the money. He said I was a poor law student and I should use the money to buy books."

Erika smiled at him. "Does he still teach law?" She knew from the investigative report Steven Chambers had given her that Michael had gone to Catholic University Law School in Washington, D. C.

"Yes." Michael nodded. "Five years ago he took a job here." Michael spread his hands, encompassing the room. "The University of Pennsylvania had tried to get him to come for years. Finally they made an offer he accepted."

"You must have been practicing by then."

"I was. My partner and I began our firm in New Brunswick. I'd go down to D.C. three or four times a year and stay with him, and we'd talk long into the night. He'd return the favor by coming to New Jersey. When Malick moved to Philadelphia, we met even more regularly."

"Is he going to be all right?" Erika asked the question softly. Michael leaned back in his chair.

"The doctor says he should recover."

Erika could hear the "but" in that statement. Impulsively she reached across the table and took his hand. He caught it and squeezed. "I'm sure he'll be fine," Erika told him.

As they walked back to ICU, Erika thought of the man next to her. This morning they'd sat before news media people, and tonight he stood vigil over a friend's bedside. She recognized there were many sides to Michael Lawrence, the man. Erika thought of the rude mountain man and tried to compare him with the tenderhearted one who held her hand. He had strength and compassion, and Erika had never met anyone like him.

Malick was awake when they entered the room. He looked tired, his eyes half open and his shock of white hair mussed by the pillow. Erika preceded Michael.

"You . . . must . . . be Erika." He spoke slowly and tried to smile. Erika returned it. Surprisingly, her eyes filled with moisture. "I am very pleased . . . to meet . . . you."

"How do you feel?" she asked.

"Better," he said, yet somehow she knew he wasn't telling her the whole truth.

"How are you and Michael getting along?"

Erika stopped herself from looking at Michael although he still held onto her hand. Michael had talked to him about her. She wondered what he'd told him. Did he know about their kiss?

"We're," she said, clearing her throat, "we're having growing pains, but I'm sure we can work them out."

"Growing pains." He grunted, trying to laugh. "Michael will do that to you," he said, as if talking about a child. "But hang in there. He's worth it."

Erika felt strange. Why had he said that? It sounded as if they were engaged. Erika wanted to pull her hand free, but it would look too obvious.

"Malick, you're embarrassing her," Michael said, dropping her hand to move closer to the bedside.

A nurse came in then and told them visiting hours were over. Michael was reluctant to leave.

"Go, Michael. There's no reason for you to sit here watching me sleep. You've been here for hours. Go home."

Malick sounded tired and Michael looked at Erika. He seemed to need her approval. She nodded.

"I'll come back tomorrow," Michael told him.

"It was good meeting you, Malick." Erika took his hand and squeezed it.

"She's prettier than her pictures," Malick said, looking at Michael.

CHAPTER 8

Jilted Fiancée And Mason Children Lawyer Head Graves Enterprises. The headline greeted Erika as she set her briefcase on the polished surface of her desk the next morning. So much had happened last night that she'd nearly forgotten about the press conference yesterday morning. The story in the supermarket rag detailed just enough of the facts of her engagement to Bill Castle and of Michael's involvement in the custody battle for the Mason children to keep them from being sued. It wasn't that the facts were distorted that bothered her so much as the tone of the article, and the implication that they were incompetent to head the conglomerate.

Erika picked up the paper with two fingers and dropped it in the trash can as if it contained three-day-old fish. She didn't expect the papers to be kind to them. Her history didn't regard her kindly and reporters wanted to sell papers, just as the pharmaceutical division wanted to sell medicine. The difference was that her products were ethical. They had been developed, tested, gone through clinical trials, and approved by the Food and Drug Administration before being given to the public. Newspapers were supposed to print the truth, keep the public informed of the facts, but she knew in her case the facts had been distorted.

Erika looked at the letters on her desk. Most of them were marked *Personal.* She didn't recognize the return addresses. Taking a letter opener, she slit the first one and pulled out a single sheet of paper. It was a proposal. Someone actually asked her to marry him. How on earth had word gotten out so quickly? Then she remembered television. She'd never turned the set on yesterday.

The second letter was an attack on her and Michael. It was unsigned. The next one held another proposal, this time for Michael. She put that one aside to give to him. The mail didn't surprise her. She'd gotten the same kind of mail after Bill Castle jilted her. Proposals, attacks, people telling her she was the real winner in that triangle. Except for the ones addressed to Michael, she dropped them all in the trash and decided to go for coffee before reading the other newspapers.

The small kitchenette was crowded with people discussing the days' news when she walked in. Her entrance ended the conversations, each person suddenly remembering a previous engagement requiring their immediate attention. Filling her cup, she knew it was time to do damage control. Michael might not have wanted to go on a site visit, but it was time she left her ivory tower and returned to the trenches.

Back in her office, she saw the *Inquirer* had been kinder to her. *Financial Wizard Has Hollywood Past,* the banner over the two columns read. They'd put her story on the financial page, listed her training, her previous work experience, her history with Graves Enterprises, but had led with her broken engagement to Bill Castle. Michael's had been about the same as hers, with the exception related to his being Carlton's grandson. *Black Lawyer Heir Graves Enterprises* topped his story.

Sipping her coffee, she dropped that paper into the wastebasket, too, wondering if Michael had seen them yet. They seemed to be on different schedules. He wasn't at breakfast and she thought he might need the rest after spending yesterday at the hospital. He still looked tired and he was obviously worried about his friend. She wondered if he were still having nightmares.

A tap sounded on her door. She looked up as it opened. Michael strolled in, looking refreshed, better than she'd seen him since they met. He came straight toward her, a cup of coffee in his hand.

"Have you seen the papers?"

"Yes." she nodded, glancing toward the trashbasket.

"The stories could use some editing, but the photos were good." He made light of the misleading facts.

"You're in rare form this morning. I suppose you're going to tell me it'll pass in a few days."

"It will." Michael lounged in the chair. "Something else will come along and we'll be old news."

"I certainly couldn't tell by that pack of wolves that met me as I drove out of the gates, and the one that met me at the elevators."

Michael held his cup in both hands and drank, but his eyes were trained on her. Erika wanted to smile, but forced herself to keep a straight face.

She changed the subject. "How's Malick this morning?"

"He's wide awake and talkative."

Erika understood Michael's mood. Yesterday his friend had been close to death, but today Malick was recovering. She'd gone through the same stages with Carlton, but in the end Carlton had died. A sudden emptiness developed in her. She missed Carlton. Her talks with him were some of the best. Michael had the same kind of relationship with Malick Wainscott. She envied him.

"Are you leaving to go see him?"

"I'll go tonight. I thought I'd stay around here and settle in. I see my desk is piled high with books about the company."

"I hope you don't mind. I think it helps when you know the history of where we've been and where we plan to go."

Michael nodded.

"Because of the newspaper reports, I think it would be a good idea to take a stroll through the company. Would you like to come with me?"

By mutual consent they left Erika's office and began a slow process of walking through the various departments. Michael had met most of the vice presidents, but he didn't know the majority of the people who made Graves Enterprises a successful company. Erika introduced him to most of the people they came into contact with, taking time to answer their questions and concerns about what they'd read in the papers. This was so much more personal than calling a conference. Erika truly liked the people who worked for Graves. She knew most of them by name, and with some she even knew their families' names.

Michael was charming, answering questions in a quiet, nonconfrontational manner. Erika noticed he had a wonderful memory for names. When introduced to a group of people, he managed to remember all their names and address them that way. She heard positive whispers each time they passed from one department to another.

The damage hadn't been as bad as Erika'd thought it might. The publicity department staff was doing a fine job of answering questions and issuing press releases about the direction of the company. Michael had calmed the fears of the people they talked to. All she had to do was keep a calm head, no matter how much she disliked being the center of media attention.

The tour ended in Jeff Rivers' area. The usually smiling face of the chief financial officer was grim this morning.

"I need to see you, Erika," he said after he'd shaken Michael's hand and introduced him to some of the members in his department.

Erika stared at him. His blue eyes had a nervous look. Erika walked into his office. Michael and Jeff followed her. They took seats at the conference table, which sat in the corner between two sets of windows. The day was bright and sunny, but Erika knew the coming news wouldn't be good.

"How many more?" she asked.

"Ten thousand," Jeff answered.

Erika stared at him.

"Ten thousand what?" Michael asked.

Erika turned to face Michael. "Shares of stock. For the last several months there's been increased activity in the number of shares of Graves stock trading the market. Jeff seems to think there could be a takeover in the making."

"Who's it registered to?"

"We don't know. The shares are made to companies that collapse, and then are transferred to another name. As soon as we find them, they move. It's as if someone is making a job of keeping us out of the loop."

"Do they have enough shares for control?" Michael asked.

"Not yet."

"Can you counter them by exercising options? I remember the lawyers saying something about that."

"We're locked out. Until our year is up we can't exercise any options, sell any current shares, or buy any more on the open market."

"I don't understand. Why would Carlton do that?"

"Money, Erika, like poverty, is one of life's true burdens."

Michael looked confused.

"It was one of Carlton's favorite sayings," she explained. "He felt that too much money too soon didn't give a person enough time to learn how to handle it. By preventing us from using too much power, he took out our ability to amass large amounts of cash."

"It's also a safeguard," Jeff explained. "Carlton ran this company for decades. He knew his death could trigger all kinds of stock activity. To prevent you two from creating a decline in stock value, he took the options out until you were fully aware of the ups and downs of the market."

"Unfortunately," Michael said. "He didn't consider that by tying our hands he might make it easy for someone else to step in and take over, while we stand by helplessly."

"They won't be able to take over—" Erika explained, "between us we have control of the company—but unexpected activity can create either good or ill."

"How so?" Michael asked.

"An unwanted shareholder can force his way onto the board, and once there create havoc by arguing against programs, swaying other board members, holding up discussion, being generally disagreeable," Jeff answered.

"But whoever it is can't really do anything?"

"That's correct," Erika said. "On the board he can't do anything, but the activity in the stock market could cause the stock to drop in price."

"Wouldn't it cause it to go up, if activity is suddenly increased?"

"Maybe," Jeff said. "The market is so fickle that it's difficult to predict what will happen. Even with the solid foundation Graves Enterprises has, people are still uncertain about its continued success since Carlton's death. Sudden activity in the market and rumor could cause our customers to begin buying from our competitors."

"So even if this phantom stockholder isn't trying to gain access to the board, he could erode market share and ruin the company."

"Exactly," Erika said.

"So what are we doing about it?"

"First, we don't even know if there is a real threat. If we're wrong, we want to be on the cautious side."

Michael nodded.

"We have a broker tracking the buying and selling," Erika went on. "So far the number of shares moved in one day clouds the fact that a single individual is buying in great numbers. We don't want the information to get out to the financial community, or it could create the very thing Carlton wanted to avoid."

"You're not going to be able to hide this for long," Michael told them.

"I'm surprised we've been able to keep it covered this long," Erika agreed. "Stock analysts are very astute. Graves Enterprises is no mom-and-pop operation. Like those reporters yesterday, there is some smart analyst out there tracking the buying and selling patterns, looking for his chance to be the next financial wizard on Wall Street. With the introduction of you, as Carlton's grandson, and me as . . . as part of the Hollywood scene, they're probably going to keep keen records on transactions as a measurement of our ability to run a company this large."

"How much time would you estimate we have?"

"Two weeks," Jeff said. "Three, if we're lucky."

The thought of a possible takeover was still on Michael's mind when he walked into the hospital later that day. He wanted to talk to Malick. SEC regulations weren't in Michael's area of expertise, but he knew that he and Malick could come up with a plan to uncover the culprit.

The arrows on the wall ended and Michael went toward the room where Malick had been the night before. He looked much better tonight. He was awake and sitting up when Michael came in. The clear tubing still supplied him with oxygen, and fluids passed through other tubes, to disappear under adhesive tape that covered his right hand.

"You look much better," Michael said, taking a seat in the chair next to the bed. "How do you feel?"

"Much better." Malick's voice was stronger than it had been the night before and his coloring, though still pale, had begun to return to the red, ruddy color that often made Michael think of people who try to tan their white skin in one day. Malick's skin tone looked even more striking against his silver-white head of hair.

Michael felt better today, too. He'd had a real scare when the hospital called, and now he felt as if Malick would recover.

"Have you talked to the doctor today?"

"He was here about an hour ago."

"What did he say?"

"The usual stuff they tell heart patients." He waved his hand as if it were nothing.

"What would that be?"

"That I need to take it easy, avoid stress, eat better, and get plenty of exercise. He even suggested golf would be good." Malick frowned. Michael well knew Malick's view of golf. It was too quiet for him. While he often went to the games in person, most of them he spent as a very vocal television spectator.

"That's good advice, Malick."

Malick stared directly at him. "I know it's good advice," he said harshly, but Michael knew he didn't mean it. "But who ever does what's good for them?"

"You're going to have to."

Malick sighed, then shook his head in agreement. Then he sized Michael up, and he suddenly had a cord of fear running down his back.

"What?" he asked.

"I need you to do me a favor."

"Anything," Michael said.

Malick raised his left hand, favoring the right one, which had the IV needle hidden in it. "It's a big favor."

Michael leaned forward. "Go on," he said.

"I need someone to take over my class—"

Michael was out of his chair. "Malick, you know I can't do that!"

"Why not?"

"I can't go back to the law. I want nothing to do with it." He'd sworn after the Mason children died he'd never go back. It was because of him they were dead. If he hadn't been there, the children would be here today, with their lives in front of them. Michael wouldn't, couldn't, go there.

"Michael," Malick interrupted his thoughts.

He could hear the fatherly nature of Malick's voice and knew what was coming.

"I'm not asking you to return to practice, just to train some first year law students. I have coverage for the day classes. It's only the one night class I need you to teach."

"It's too much." *Too close,* he thought. First year students were the most eager. They knew nothing, but argued every point as if they were before the Supreme Court. He didn't want to stand in front of them as they hung on his every word. And quite possibly they'd know about the Frank Mason case. Was there anyone in America who didn't know about it, with the possible exception of Erika? He doubted it.

"Michael, don't make a decision now. Think about it. Weigh both sides of the argument and make a decision then."

How often had Michael heard Malick say that to a class where he was the student? "I'll think about it," he said.

Erika preferred the library as an office to the upstairs study Carlton had used. As a child she'd spent hours in there doing her homework and reading. The leather-bound volumes along three walls had been her friends during many sleepless nights after she first arrived. Erika only occasionally suffered bouts of insomnia today.

She sat in the library, papers spread around her, as she waited for Michael to return from the hospital. She couldn't believe he'd only been here a few days. It seemed that so much had happened, and was happening—the press conference, his friend's heart attack, and the conglomeration of reporters that camped outside her walls. She stared unseeing at the pages before her—numbers of shares of stock sold in the past month. A graph of the amounts going to the top fifty purchasers lay in a blur on top of the desk.

Erika heard the door, then Michael's footsteps across the tile foyer. She smiled, recognizing the rhythm of his steps. Her heart thumped in anticipation of seeing him. She'd left the door open and the lights on. Standing, she waited for him to come into the room.

"How is he?" she asked when he appeared in the doorway.

"He looks a lot better and he says he feels better."

"Don't you believe him?"

Michael nodded.

"Then, why do you look like someone died?"

Michael slipped his overcoat and suit jacket off. Coming forward, he hooked them over the back of one of the leather chairs before the massive fireplace and sank into the soft cushion. Carlton had often sat there, and in this light Michael reminded her a lot of his grandfather.

She left her position next to the desk and came to perch on the end of the chair next to him.

"What happened?" she asked quietly, forgetting the stock papers on the desk and her own set of problems.

"I'd do anything for Malick," Michael said. He stared blankly into the unlit fireplace. "He asked me to take over one of his classes."

"Michael, that's wonderful!" Erika slipped onto the seat. "I taught briefly right after college and I loved it." Erika didn't think Michael shared her enthusiasm. "Are you worried about being away from Graves Enterprises?"

"It's only one class and it meets during the evening. There won't be any effect on Graves Enterprises."

"Then what's the problem?" She tried to keep her voice level and non-threatening.

"It's teaching the law," he said after a long pause.

"Don't you think you know it well enough to teach?"

He looked into her eyes. She didn't see doubt there about the subject matter, but she did see fear.

"I can't teach law."

His statement seemed final, as if it were explanation enough. It wasn't enough for Erika.

"What does that mean? I think it's wonderful he has enough confidence in you to ask. He didn't impress me as a man who does things without giving them sufficient thought."

"You're right," Michael agreed. "Malick thinks through all his decisions."

"You should be honored he asked you."

Michael looked at her with no enthusiasm in his eyes. "You think I should do this?"

"I can't decide for you, but you did go to law school, and I can't believe you can turn your back and walk away from something you studied years to do and were apparently very good at." She paused. "And it will help Malick, take some of the worry away from him until he's out of the hospital."

"I told him I'd think about it."

Erika could tell he'd been thinking of nothing else during his drive back to the house. She wondered if the real problem was that he really wanted to return to the law, but had told himself he shouldn't. If he truly wanted no part of the law, why was he wrestling with Malick's request?

"If you really don't want to do it, you must know other lawyers who'd be qualified to take over one class. Why don't you suggest this to Malick? Either way, the pressure of trying to find solutions for things beyond Malick's control will be removed."

Michael leaned back in the chair and closed his eyes. He looked tired. "I'll think about that, too," he agreed. He changed the subject. "What did you find out about the stock?"

"Nothing," she said. She hadn't been able to concentrate, and nothing had been done tonight. The man they hired would probably find the answers soon. Erika thought she'd look over some of the papers, hoping a different set of eyes would see what might be hiding between the lines, but she'd seen nothing. She'd been too busy worrying about what Michael was doing.

"I think I'll go to bed," Michael said, getting up and folding his coat and jacket over his shoulder.

Erika stood, too.

"Coming?" he said.

For a moment the two of them going up the stairs together flashed into her mind. "No," she said. "I have to clean up here first."

Michael nodded and left her. At the door he looked over his shoulder. Erika had turned to the desk. He knew she was concerned about the problems at Graves Enterprises. She was also hiding something from him. He wondered if her supporting Malick's idea had anything to do with it. Quickly he dismissed the idea. She'd offered him another solution to teaching. He could find a replacement himself, or surely the university would find one. Michael didn't think he was the reason for Erika's secret. He remembered thinking there was something more to her when they were in the cabin. She needed this year. It was important to her. Michael didn't think it was the money. Not once during her day and night in the cabin had she mentioned the worth of the estate. And to date she hadn't mentioned its value. The numbers alone should have been enough to make anyone leave his home and come here. Yet she hadn't used the obvious trump card she held.

What was it Erika St. James wanted?

How long had he been running? Michael's legs felt like they were tied to weights. He went as fast as he could. His lungs pumped, breath congealing in puffs as he followed Abby up the hill. What was she doing here? She never came here. She always went up toward the building. There was no building here. She climbed, surefooted. How come she didn't seem to have a problem with the ascent? Why was she climbing the mountain? Where was she going, and what did she plan to do when she got to the top?

Michael saved his breath and pushed on after her. His legs and lungs screamed for him to stop, but he pushed on. Then he saw Frank ahead of him, between him and Abby. Fear stilled his heart for a beat, then forced him to push harder. He found it more difficult to breathe. Each time Abby checked over her shoulder he could see the fear on her face. Her long hair unfurled in the wind. Michael felt the wind's raw fury against his face.

"Abbyyyy!" he called. "Stopppp." The wind took his voice. He knew she couldn't hear him but he kept calling her. Frank pursued her with deadly intent. Michael knew Frank would reach her before he could. Either that, or she'd tumble off the other side of the mountain. There was nothing there, no gentle incline, just the sheer face of a cliff and an unrelenting drop. Three thousand feet of open air, then jagged rocks. Her body would be cut to shreds as it pounded into the stone. The mental picture made him run faster. He hoped he could reach Frank, and Abby would know there was nothing to fear.

Then he saw the gun! Frank stopped, took aim. The woman above him didn't know, hadn't turned to look over her shoulder. She was a perfect target.

"Noooo!" he shouted. "She's innocent, Fraaaaank."

Abby moved around a rock as the first shot rang out. In the wind its sound was blunted. Frank started moving again. Abby turned. She looked different. Michael tried to see her but Frank blocked his view.

Michael didn't think he would make it. His legs felt as if he were trudging through a rough sea at high tide. Suddenly Abby moved higher than Frank. Only she wasn't Abby. Michael's heart stopped. It was Erika!

Frank took aim again. The gun was pointed directly at Erika's back. In a second she'd be dead. The shot rang out, reverberating in Michael's head.

Michael screamed.

Erika heard him as she reached the top of the stairs. She knew Michael was dreaming again. Without thinking she headed for his rooms. The second scream sounded like a man in agony. She opened the door at the end of the hall and found him fighting the covers, the same as he had at the cabin. Erika remembered what had happened when she tried to subdue him.

Approaching the bed, she stayed clear of his flailing arms until she could grab them. With her knee on the bed, she wrestled with him for several seconds before he collapsed. Like the time in the cabin, Michael hugged her close. His breath was heavy against her neck, and she could feel his heart hammering against her breast.

Erika stayed, holding him long after he'd relaxed and fallen into a restful sleep. He lay heavily against her, and his head fell back onto the pillow. Erika stared at his sleeping form. He was a beautiful man, but he was made ragged by demons. She didn't know how deeply they were buried. He'd never be a full person until he exorcised them.

Erika knew about demons. She'd lived with them. Her mother had had demons, still had them. Alva St. James Redford had suffered with her enemies day and night. Her life was a living hell, and she'd made Erika's the same until Erika ran to Carlton and refused to ever go back there.

Standing up, Erika straightened the covers over the sleeping man. She laid the back of her hand on his forehead. He was warm but not fevered. She should go to her rooms now, but she felt a reluctance to leave. As tired as she should be, she felt like staying the night and making sure Michael slept comfortably through the remainder of the dark hours. She knew it wasn't the rational thing to do, but that didn't make it any less her wish.

She moved toward the door, thinking how much he had to contend with—the news media and their incessant dredging up of long forgotten stories, his friend being sick, his guilt over refusing to take over his classes, the added pressure of a new job, new people, and *her.* A man used to staying by himself, he must be going through several adjustment problems with her in the same house, albeit a big house.

She certainly knew she had adjustment problems with his presence, and not all of them were bad.

CHAPTER 9

Michael cleared his throat and answered the question the student in the last row had asked. When he finished he checked his watch. Class was over. It had ended fifteen minutes ago and every student was still there. He'd forgotten the time, too.

"Thank you, class. We'll meet again Thursday."

People began putting their books away and filing out of the room. When they were all gone Michael sat down. It hadn't been as bad as he expected. In fact, it had been better than he could have dreamed. He loved talking to them, discussing the points, the logic of it all.

He was exhilarated. He wanted to rush home and talk to Erika, tell her how well things had gone. Snapping his briefcase closed, he drew on his coat and left the room. Chalk on his fingers reminded him of the class he'd just left.

Erika was in the library when he arrived. She wore a dressing gown and had her feet curled under her as she read. Michael liked the picture she made. It surprised him how much he enjoyed finding her waiting for him. He wanted to run to her, pull her into his arms and kiss her. He wanted to take her to his bed and make love to her.

He shrugged off the thought. They were together for one year to run Graves Enterprises, he reminded himself. Then it was over. They would both be free to go their own ways. Romantic entanglements could get messy.

She hadn't turned when he entered. Maybe he should leave her to her reading and go to his room. But he watched her. The light highlighted her hair, giving her natural brown an auburn glow. Michael wanted to run his fingers through it, just as he'd wanted to that first morning when she stood above him.

"Hi." She smiled, looking over her shoulder. "How was it?" She uncurled her feet and stood.

Michael didn't know what to say.

"You liked it?"

"It was better than I expected," he conceded

"You *liked* it."

He paused a long moment. "I liked it."

Like a birthday girl getting a present, Erika ran to him. Instinctively he opened his arms and caught her. Whirling about the room, Michael felt as if *he'd* been given the present. When they stopped he just held her, knowing there was more he wanted to do, but he didn't trust himself. After a moment he stepped back. She was smiling.

"Tell me all about it."

She drew him to the sofa, where she pushed her book aside and sat down. Michael joined her.

"You can't imagine how scared I was walking into that room," he began. "It was like my first day in court—no, worse than my first day."

"But you relaxed," she prompted.

"After a while. Malick had wonderful notes and I started by following them, but shortly into the discussion the class seemed to take on a spirit of its own." Michael told her everything. He couldn't help talking. He'd had a great night. He felt like a kid bubbling over after a great day. Finally something felt as if it had a purpose. *He* had a purpose. He could do this, delve into the law and be safe, away from changing anyone's life.

When he stopped, Erika didn't move or say anything. She just stared at him with an I-told-you-so smile on her face.

"I'm glad you enjoyed it."

Michael actually thought she was glad. It made him feel good. It had been a long time since he thought anyone really cared how he felt.

"It's late," she said.

They stood. Michael reached for her hand and drew it through his arm. Together they left the library and walked to the steps. At the top of the landing Michael let go of her. He didn't want to. He wanted to fulfill his fantasy of lifting her from the floor and carrying her up the remaining steps toward his rooms. Instead, he gently touched his mouth to her cheek and whispered a thank you before turning and heading toward his suite.

That night the dreams came back. This time they were different. He ran and ran, but couldn't reach Erika. Abby wasn't there. Frank Mason raised his gun and pointed it at Erika as she went up the mountain.

Michael shouted. He sat straight up in bed. His body was covered in sweat and his breath came in ragged gasps. Putting his feet over the side of the bed, he leaned his elbows on his knees and held his head in his hands. He tried to calm himself, calm his rapidly beating heart.

Why was Erika in this dream? This was the second time she'd been there. And it was more real. Often, he didn't waken. The dream would end and he'd fall asleep without ever fully awakening. Tonight, though, he'd been so sure Frank would kill her that he'd screamed enough to wake himself. He still had the feeling Erika was in danger.

Then he remembered that Frank had escaped. As much as he tried, Michael couldn't shake the feeling that Erika was in danger. Grabbing his dressing gown, he pulled it over his naked body and padded, barefoot, toward her suite. Michael didn't exactly know where it was. He'd only seen her go that way, not which door she opened.

He tried the first door on her side of the stairs and found the room empty. The second door must have been to Carlton's room. It was huge, dark, and austere. He couldn't image Erika living in there. The third door was hers. He opened it quietly and looked inside. The walls were light beige or yellow. There was a sitting room with a fireplace, and several sofas and chairs making a warm conversation area. The fire had been lit, but had died during the night. Only a few embers snapped on the hearth. Michael went through to the bedroom. Erika lay in the big bed.

Michael should have turned and left then, but he didn't. Her bed was a tall four-poster with swags of fabric giving it an air of openness. Her sheets and comforter were white satin, and she lay between them like a small child. Michael went across the room. Quietly he stood watching her even breathing. She was all right. Michael let go of the breath he didn't know he was holding. His dream had been just that, a dream. He should return to his own room. Why didn't he move? Why was he standing there mesmerized by the sight of a woman sleeping? What would he do if she woke up? Could he explain his presence?

He knew all the answers to these questions, yet he didn't move. He remained staring at the darkness of Erika's skin against the whiteness of the sheets. She was beautiful. She seemed to get more beautiful each time he saw her.

Erika moved. She turned over. Michael froze in place. When she'd settled herself, he let go his breath and stole out of the room.

Erika couldn't shake the feeling this morning that something was wrong. She showered and dressed the same as she did every morning, but today she felt uneasy, more so than usual. Maybe it was the past few days of stress-related incidents, Erika thought. She'd been under stress before, though, and never had the feeling that had awakened her during the night.

Maybe it was Michael. He was new in her life. Maybe she'd just imagined he'd been there. She shrugged, trying to shake off the feeling. As she left her rooms and headed for breakfast she hoped this feeling wouldn't persist.

Michael met her at the landing.

"Good morning," she said.

They fell into step together. "Are you ready for another day?"

Erika nodded. She wasn't her usual self and she wanted to ask Michael a strange question. She just had no way of saying it. She'd always had a good memory and sleep had only been a problem when she'd had a run-in with her mother, but since he arrived her routine had been disrupted. Last night had been . . . more *real,* was all she could call it, more real than ever before.

"I'd like to ask you a question," she began, needing to clear her throat.

Michael shrugged. "Go ahead."

Erika hesitated. They'd reached the bottom step and she still hadn't said anything.

"What is it?" he asked again.

At the door of the breakfast room Erika stopped and faced him. "Were you in my room last night?"

"Now there's a very interesting question."

The door swung fully open. Both Michael and Erika turned to face the person who'd spoken.

"Good morning, Mrs. Redford."

"What are you doing here?" Erika asked, anger dripping from her words.

"Obviously, I've come to protect my daughter." She looked at Michael. "Young man, did you sleep in my daughter's room last night?" She lowered her head and looked at Michael, like a schoolteacher peering over her glasses.

"No," he said decisively. "I slept in my own room."

"Too bad," she said, a smile showing her even, white teeth. "It might be just what she needs." Alva Redford threw a look at her daughter. Erika walked away and poured herself a cup of coffee. She didn't want her mother here this morning. She'd wanted to have a leisurely breakfast with Michael before they went to the office. After she'd asked Michael her question, depending on the answer, she couldn't have predicted how leisurely their breakfast would be. Now she'd have to contend with another of her mother's requests.

"What do you want?" Erika asked again.

Alva took her time. She strolled to the server and lifted a plate as if she were the owner of the house. Piling it high with food, she then poured a cup of black coffee and walked to where Michael stood.

"Would you mind if I talked to my daughter alone?"

"You promise there will be no blood?" Michael glanced at Erika.

Alva laughed. "I can only speak for myself, Michael." She said his name with all the emphasis of a Southern belle.

Michael smiled and accepted the plate and cup. "I'll be in the library," Michael said and left them.

Alva closed the door.

"All right, Mother. We're alone now. Why are you here?"

Alva returned to the server and made herself a plate of fruit and croissants. She then took a seat in front of a cup that already had her lipstick on one side. Obviously, she wasn't going to speak until Erika sat down. Erika remembered this and wondered why she'd let herself fall into her mother's trap. Alva wanted the upper hand, and this was a small measure of her showing Erika she still had the ability to make her cringe.

Erika took a seat opposite her mother.

"Score one for Alva St. James Redford," Erika said. "She won the battle of the chairs. Now what do you want?"

"You know, Erika, Carlton and I had an agreement."

"What kind of agreement?"

Alva lifted her cup. The rings on her fingers shone in the morning light coming through the open curtains.

"An agreement that I believe has been overlooked in the period since his death."

Erika took a deep breath and placed her palms on the table.

"You're back about the checks."

Alva picked up a butter knife and began adding a film of butter to her croissant. "Yes, darling, I'm here about the checks. Why are you holding them? They are mine."

"Mother, I've been running this company solely for over a year. Carlton never mentioned owing you anything. What were you blackmailing him with?"

"Not blackmail, Erika," Alva said sternly. "I never blackmailed Carlton."

"Then why was he paying you, regularly and systematically? It certainly looks like blackmail to me."

"Well, it wasn't."

"Are you an employee of Graves Enterprises?"

Alva didn't give an answer and Erika did not expect one.

"Did you sell something to Carlton?"

Again silence met her question.

"Did you lend money to Carlton, and this was his method of repaying you?" Erika stood up. She went toward her mother. "He'd been paying you every month for how long, Mother? Two years, three, twenty-five? Hasn't Carlton been paying you since I left your house and came to this one?"

"Erika, it's a trust fund."

"Why, Mother?" Erika asked, the menace in her voice made more terrifying by the restrained quiet evident in it. Erika leaned on the polished surface of the dining table, her face only inches from her mother's. "Why did Carlton, who had nothing to do with you, establish a trust fund to take care of you?"

It had been a long time since she felt like an adult in her mother's presence. Then Alva St. James Redford stood up, taking back all the ground Erika had won.

"All you need to know, Erika, is that the fund *was* established. Carlton's will did not restrict, limit, or dissolve it. It's there, and it's mine." She took a step, bringing her to within a foot of Erika. "I'll expect my regular and systematic check to be in the mail this afternoon. And furthermore, I expect a check each and every month, and without the need for me to arrange my day in order to join you for breakfast."

The two women stared at each other as anger remained the only force speaking in the room. After a second Alva turned to leave.

"Mother!" Erika stopped her. "There's one more thing before you leave."

Alva lifted her chin, facing her daughter as if she were an enemy.

"I'll give you the benefit of the doubt and not outright accuse you," Erika began, but she had no doubt that her mother was guilty. "The last time you were here, you intimated that you'd go to the press with Michael's story."

The smile that crossed Alva's face told Erika her mother knew she had the upper hand.

"Are you responsible for the reporters we're having to deal with?"

Erika couldn't read the expression on her mother's face. She had no idea what the smile meant. As the seconds ticked off and Alva offered no response, Erika realized she wasn't going to get one.

"Make sure that check is in the mail," Alva said, and left.

Erika had known she'd lose this fight. When her mother appeared suddenly at her door several nights ago, she'd known the woman had come to discuss her finances, but Michael had interrupted them. Erika purposely had not let the check be mailed. It sat in the drawer of her desk. She wanted to know the reason for the fund. It had been established while Erika was still a teenager. From what she could tell, it appeared Carlton had made some deal with her mother. Erika hated the thought that formed in her mind when she'd heard about the fund. Had her mother effectively sold her to Carlton?

Earlier and earlier, Frank thought, standing at the window watching the Christmas scene. It wasn't even Thanksgiving yet and the Christmas decorations were everywhere in the mall. Mounds of cotton, representing snow, adorned a scene of moving mice, dressed as people and sliding about on a track. Both adults and children smiled as they stood for a moment to watch the wonder.

Frank thought of his children. They would love to see this. Maybe when he was done. When all the people responsible had paid, he and Abby would bring the children and they would see the mice and the red-cheeked Santa. Frank would take them for pictures with the bearded old elf who sat at the center of the mall and asked every child what he wanted for Christmas.

Frank liked waiting to shop. He wouldn't buy anything today. He'd look, get ideas, make lists, and on Christmas Eve he'd buy his gifts. On Christmas morning they would get up and have a family event opening their presents, like when he was a child. His children's Christmas morning would be like his, complete with a warm fire and lots of presents.

All he had to do was complete his work. He'd be finished long before Christmas Eve. Even today's setback hadn't bothered him. He'd missed the judge. The man must be out of town. He'd camped out for three days waiting for him but he simply hadn't appeared. No mail was delivered, no garbage appeared for pickup, and no newspapers gathered in the driveway.

Frank wasn't concerned. He was a cautious man, a patient man. He had time. He could wait and plan until the time was exactly right. All of them would pay for what they'd done to him and his family. Then he'd shop for his children's presents.

CHAPTER 10

The two women at the reception desk were different than the ones Michael had seen on his other trips to visit Malick. He passed them with a nod and a smile and made his way to Malick's room, which had been upgraded to a regular one.

Malick sat up in bed watching television. He switched the set off as Michael came in. He looked years better than he had only a week ago.

"How was class?" Malick asked without a greeting.

"I got through it," Michael said. He didn't want to tell Malick that he had been right, that he liked teaching. Erika had seen it the minute he walked into the room, but then he was coming directly from the classes. Tonight he'd had time to compose himself. He knew he'd tell Malick what he really felt about the class, but he didn't want his friend gloating too soon.

"I'm sure you did more than that."

"I didn't follow your plan very long. We began discussing The State of Pennsylvania vs. Adams but then other precedents were cited and we were off on a tangent. I thought it was an important path for the students to take, so I didn't stop them."

"Good," Malick said. "It's exactly what I would have done. What time did you finish?"

"What?" Michael said, trying to buy himself some time.

"Did you finish before the class ended, or was the entire class still there after the time they should have been gone?"

Michael knew why Malick was such a good lawyer. He'd cornered him into this question and Michael could see where he was going with it.

"Only fifteen minutes," he said.

"Fifteen minutes beyond the time. I knew it! I knew you'd be good. Students are a hard lot and if you got them to forget the time, especially on your first night, they had to be interested in what you were saying."

"I suppose I'll be all right until you return," Michael conceded.

"If the press doesn't discover you're there."

Michael looked confused.

"I've been watching the news. You and Erika made the headlines two days in a row. How's she taking it?"

"She's weathering it." Michael remembered the haunting look on her face when he'd told her about the press conference. Yet once she got there she'd taken control and held it until the end.

"What about you?"

"I'm fine," Michael shrugged.

"Are you really? You've had a lot of stress points in the past few weeks."

"I'm all right, Malick. You don't need to spend your time worrying about me." Michael knew his friend had thought of him constantly when he'd gone to Maryland. Coming back could be just as stressful as the events which had sent him there. "Except for Erika, I'm the same as I was before I went to Maryland."

"You and Erika aren't getting on?"

Michael hesitated. He didn't know how to explain it. "It's not that we don't get along. Quite the opposite. We get along very well."

"Then what's the problem?"

"I'm not sure there is a problem."

"Is she all business? No woman under the business suit?"

Michael remembered holding her close. He shook his head. That was certainly not the Erika he knew. If anything, she was all woman.

"I know I was a little groggy, but she appeared to have a pleasing personality. Isn't that the case?"

"She's fine, Malick. I can't think of any faults or complaints to brand her with."

"Do you want to brand her with something else?"

"What do you mean?"

Malick started a smile that burst into a laugh.

"What's so funny?"

"Michael, you have all the symptoms of a fourteen-year-old, and you don't even know it."

Oh, he knew it—and that was his problem. He was falling for Erika.

"Michael, she's a beautiful and obviously intelligent woman. Why are you fighting the fact that you have feelings for her? I'd think you should question yourself if you didn't."

Michael hadn't come here to talk about his feelings for Erika. Yet he talked to Malick about everything else. Why should Erika be any different?

"It's Abby, isn't it?"

"I suppose everything comes back to Abby. I wonder what will happen to every woman I meet. Will I be the reason some man hurts her?"

"Michael, you can't keep blaming yourself for Abby's death. You didn't kill her."

"I know, but I'm responsible for her death."

"And just how did you manage that? Were you there? Did you provide her with the means?"

"No, just the motive. I'm as much responsible as if I'd poisoned her myself."

"Stop that!"

Michael's head snapped up at the anger in his friend's voice and the sudden crash of Malick's hand against the bed table. His plastic pitcher and cup danced, then settled.

"You didn't poison Abby. If anyone is responsible for her death it's her husband. Now, you get any thoughts like that out of your head and keep them out."

Malick's face was beet red, and Michael knew his blood pressure must be off the scale. If he didn't change the subject he'd be responsible for Malick returning to ICU.

"Let's not talk about Abby any more."

"Fine by me," Malick agreed, settling back against the pillows. "I really want to talk about Erika, anyway. I liked her. She seems like a very nice woman."

"You figured that out from a few groggy minutes in her presence?"

"She came back to see me."

"When?" Surprise made Michael raise his eyebrows. She hadn't mentioned it, but he had done most of the talking. She'd listened to him, shared his happiness.

"Last night while you were in class. We had a nice chat. She's a very interesting woman. Haven't you noticed?"

Michael couldn't have helped noticing. "What did you talk about?" He wondered if they'd discussed him. His feelings were mixed on the answer. Did he want Malick to tell Erika about him? Did she even feel enough for him to ask? She had to. She couldn't have kissed him the way she had, and feel nothing.

"We talked about the shape of the economy, what's happening to the youth of America, would the Phillies win the National Championships . . ."

Michael frowned. Malick obviously didn't plan to help him out.

"Malick?"

His friend stopped talking and looked innocently at him. "I think she likes you, too."

"Did she say that?" Suddenly Michael wanted to know the answer to that question.

"She didn't have to. I could read it in her eyes."

"Then you're better at reading than I am." He'd looked into Erika's eyes many times. Most often he'd gotten lost in the liquid brown pools.

"So you have looked into her eyes?"

Michael could have kicked himself. He'd set himself up for that, and Malick had an open court for his return.

"Where is this leading, Malick?"

"To a grandson, I hope, or the next best thing."

Michael's jaw dropped open. "What are you talking about? Erika and I are only friends."

"That sounds like something her ex-fiancé would have said."

"You know about him?"

Malick nodded.

"What do you know?"

"Don't change the subject. We're talking about Erika and you."

"There is no Erika and me. We're doing a job, and when it's over, we're over." Michael gave his friend a piercing look. "And I didn't miss that comment you made practically assuming we were engaged."

Malick laughed. "You could do worse."

"Malick, I'm not in the market for a relationship."

"Then what was all that talk about getting along and working together? You two wouldn't be the first couple who met on the job."

"Malick, when this year is up I plan to return to Maryland and never leave that mountain again."

Malick smiled. Not the reaction Michael expected.

"She's getting to you," he paused. "Well, Michael, I'm not a betting man." Malick stretched his arms over his head and rested them behind his neck. "Leastways, not outside the courthouse. But I'm willing to put money on you and Erika St. James."

"Then you'll lose your money."

Michael couldn't help staring at Erika. Even now, as they sat in a meeting of area vice presidents, all he could concentrate on was how great she looked. Malick had planted the seed in his mind and each time he looked at her he thought of *them,* a couple, a family unit. He'd shake himself to bring his concentration back, but it never did any good. The only time she wasn't at the top of his thoughts was when he stood in front of the eager faces of his law students.

Erika seemed to grow more beautiful with each passing day. Michael could hardly keep his mind on work with her in the same room. He smelled her perfume and he wanted nothing to do with business. She'd explain competitive action programs while he concentrated on keeping his hands from shaking.

Erika appeared not to notice. She continued to point to her charts and explain every aspect of the presentation. Even outside these meetings she would ask his opinion and keep him informed of every detail. He couldn't fault her. She wasn't trying to push him out of the company.

"Any more questions?" Erika asked. When none were forthcoming, she smiled. "Thank you," she said.

The meeting broke into small groups, each discussing something that had happened at the meeting. Little by little they all left the room. Erika gathered her notes and prepared to leave.

"Erika," he said.

She looked up at him. "Yes," she said, and took a seat.

He was looking at her again with those eyes that made her soul melt. She'd tried hard to concentrate during this morning's meeting, but it was hard with him looking at her. Sometimes he scribbled on his pad, but she knew he missed nothing.

"Are you free for dinner tonight?"

A date? Was he going to ask her for a date? It was the last thing she expected from him. They had dinner together most nights when he wasn't teaching. Even when he went to visit Malick she waited for him. It was the one indulgence she allowed herself.

"Yes," she finally answered. Her heart hammered in her chest. Why? She'd been asked out before, and she'd wanted to go before, but never had she wanted to spend time with a man as much as she wanted to spend it with Michael.

"Would you have dinner with me?"

It was business. He wanted to discuss something he didn't understand about the meeting. Then why couldn't they talk about it now . . . or in the dining room at home?

"Erika, you had dinner with me in the cabin. Is there any reason you won't go to a restaurant?"

"The reporters," she said, remembering, although there had been fewer of them lately. A large arsenal, discovered in the basement of a local business, and the bust of a high ranking official in the police department had pushed them off the front page.

"I think we're safe enough now."

"What brings this on? We have dinner together every night that you're not teaching or visiting Malick. This sounds like a . . . date." She had to swallow to get the word out.

Michael dropped the pencil he'd been playing with and lounged back in the chair. "It is a date."

"Why?" she whispered.

"There's too much going on. We both need a break. I thought going out would give us time to relax and forget about our problems for a few hours. How about it?"

Erika nodded.

"Is that a yes?"

"Yes," she said.

Erika's bedroom looked like an explosion in a clothing factory. She'd changed clothes five times and still she wasn't satisfied about her looks. It was just a date, she told herself. It wasn't like it was her first. Why couldn't she decide what to wear? She and Michael saw each other every day. Why couldn't she put something on and be done with it?

Picking up a green velvet dress, she slipped into it and pulled the zipper up. Barefoot, she stepped in front of the mirror and looked at her reflection. Frowning, she dragged the zipper to its base and let the dress slither to the floor.

Erika kicked it away in frustration. She was no further toward being ready than when she'd entered the house over an hour before. Going back to the closet she pushed dresses aside one by one, rejecting everything until she came to a grey lace. She stopped, remembering the last time she wore it—the last time she and Bill had gone out together. The day before he flew to Las Vegas and married Jennifer Ahrends. Why hadn't she thrown that out? Maybe she shouldn't go out with Michael. How did she know he wouldn't turn out to be another Bill? She knew she was already falling for him. If she went out with him, socialized, got to know him, then the year would end and he'd go off and leave her, too.

"This is the wrong decision," Erika told the dress. She couldn't go out with Michael. Hadn't she learned anything in the last thirty-four years? Didn't she realize these things never worked out for her? The best thing she could do was to run the company and forget about personal relationships. In that, her mother had been right. She'd never find a man who'd want her. She proved that time and time again, and Michael Lawrence was no different.

Erika swatted the dress as if hitting out at a person. Grabbing a bathrobe, she pulled it over her underwear and left her room. She'd decided and found no need to put off telling Michael. Marching to the steps that junctioned the house into wings, she took purposeful steps down and then up the other side. Michael's room was at the end. Going straight there she stopped outside the dark wood panel door and took a deep breath. Then, not giving herself time to think, she knocked.

Michael whirled toward the door at the knock. In the month he'd been here no one had ever knocked on that door when he was in the house. Tonight it could be no one other than Erika. He'd assumed they'd meet in the library. And she was early. *Why?* he wondered.

Quickly checking his clothes he pulled the door inward. She stood there looking beautiful but a little frightened, and she wasn't dressed.

"Has something happened?" he asked.

Erika's hand went to her throat as if she'd only just realized she was wearing a bathrobe. "No, it's just that . . ." she stopped, staring at him. He looked down. His clothes were fine. He looked back at her.

"Come in," he said, taking her arm and drawing her inside. He left the door open as he guided her to a chair near the massive unlit fireplace. "What's wrong?" he asked when she was seated. "Why aren't you dressed?"

Michael took the facing chair. He was physically separated from her, and knew he needed to be. He could smell the clean scent of the soap she'd used in her shower. Her hair wasn't perfect, the way he'd seen it in the past, and she wore no makeup, but she looked better than he could remember—except for that morning in the cabin when she'd come out to look at the mountain in the early light.

Erika looked at him and nearly lost her nerve. He had on jeans and a blue shirt, unbuttoned at the neck. His short cropped hair lay neatly in place, and he smelled good enough to taste. She had mingled with some of the most beautiful people in the world, at least those in Hollywood. Women trying to be the next soaring star. Men with looks, physiques and drive, but never had a combination affected her more than that housed in the rich, brandy-skinned body of Michael Lawrence.

"Erika?"

"I—" she stammered. Looking at him made her tongue-tied. "I can't go out with you."

"Why not?"

"I thought about it and . . ." Lying wasn't her usual way of getting out of things, but this time she had no choice. She couldn't start something with Michael when she was sure from the beginning that she would be the one hurt in the end. This time the publicity would be more than she could handle, since she knew her heart would be involved. "We're partners, and I think it's best if we kept our relationship a business one. When our year is over we can go our separate ways with no entanglements."

"Tonight you believe we—" he pointed from her to himself, "we will become an entanglement?"

Erika was boxed in. She didn't want to answer that question. She was already tangled up with him and she didn't trust herself to keep the secret inside her heart. "Maybe not after one time, but there's no reason for us to begin something that can only lead—"

"Lead where?"

"I'm sorry. I didn't mean to say that," she said. She should have thought about what she'd tell him before she got here, but she hadn't and now she had to escape. She knew Michael would see through her. It was his profession to get the truth out of people, and she'd put herself in his path. Erika stood up. "I'll get something to eat from the kitchen." She moved toward the door. Michael stood up. "And I have some work that needs looking at." Erika moved away from him. She was nearly at the door when Michael stopped her.

"Erika." He was directly behind her. She could feel the heat of his body and wished she'd put on some clothes. "Tell me the truth," he whispered. "Why won't you go out with me?"

Erika dropped her shoulders, but she said nothing.

"I'm not Bill Castle," he said.

Erika turned around, then backed away. "I never thought you were Bill."

"Didn't you? Don't you still?" He came toward her. Erika backed up. "Don't you think every man who tries to get close to you will treat you like Bill Castle? Isn't that the reason you don't have any dates, don't even entertain the idea of having a man around? Isn't that why you run each time I get near you?"

"I don't run."

He took another step. She moved away.

"Don't you?"

For a long, long moment Michael held her stare. He could detect no fear in her eyes, but he knew he frightened her. Bill Castle had done a first class job of making her afraid of another relationship. He'd sworn off women, too, yet here he was practically badgering her into going out with him.

He'd wanted to spend time with her, time alone, without Graves Enterprises between them, without thinking there was anything in the world that prevented them from meeting and talking, sharing a meal. Yet she'd had second thoughts. She'd opened the door to allow him to retract his invitation without complicating conditions. Why wasn't he accepting it?

You don't want to, a voice inside his head told him. It was all he needed.

"Don't move this time, Erika," he said. He took another step. She remained still, lifting her chin in defiance. Michael only looked at her. Her hands were at her sides. There was little tension in her features, yet he knew her knees were knocking. He wanted her. He was only a step away from getting what he wanted. If he touched her, she'd be his. Then he knew he couldn't do it. When he touched her, she had to want his touch.

He stepped back. Erika's breath came out in a slow sigh. He saw her shoulders move slightly, the only outward sign that anything had changed within her.

He went to the door and pushed it to its widest point. With his hand extended he offered her escape. "Good night," he said.

Michael closed the door after she'd left. The telltale smell of her soap lingered. He wanted to grasp it somehow, hold it a little longer than the air would allow, but it was as elusive as the depth of mistrust in her eyes.

She intrigued him more than any woman ever had. He enjoyed talking to her, listening to her. Yet she only wanted a business relationship. Well, he could give her one.

"One business relationship, Ms. St. James, coming right up."

Thirty-seven. Erika banked under the water, pushing off the deep end wall, and began her thirty-eighth lap in the pool. She hadn't been able to forget Michael's comment. The worst part was that he was telling the truth. She did avoid men. She hadn't wanted to trust anyone again. She knew relationships weren't for her but with Bill she had tried one last time, and that had resulted in chaos. She wouldn't try it again, even with Michael. She'd know from the beginning it was headed nowhere.

Thirty-nine, she counted, swimming harder and faster than she'd ever felt the need to before. She was right, she told herself. They should maintain a business relationship, and only that relationship. It would be the best thing for both of them, for their futures. Then why was she here swimming lap after lap instead of working on the papers she'd brought home or merely reading a book? Why was she battling this water as if it were her enemy?

Michael wasn't Bill. She knew that. He could hurt her a lot worse than Bill did. Her feelings had been mostly embarrassment when Bill jilted her. If she let herself fall in love with Michael her emotions would be involved, deeply involved, so deeply that when he left she would have no recovery.

He would leave. He'd told her that when he came. This arrangement was for a year. He wanted to prevent Frank Mason from inheriting Carlton's money. When the year ended Michael would have more money than he could possibly spend in a lifetime, and with it came responsibility.

Money, Erika, like poverty, is one of life's true burdens. How often had she heard Carlton say that? When Michael had his half of the estate, he'd have the burden of women, many women. Not that he didn't have that now. He was an attractive man. She was attracted to him. She'd seen the women in the office reacting to him, each one of them trying to get his attention.

Forty-three. She dipped under and reversed again. If they wanted his attention, she vowed, they could have it. Beginning tomorrow he would be her partner . . . and nothing more.

CHAPTER 11

Rain had drizzled over the city for the past four days. It was raining hard when she woke, and had continued through her shower. Erika had the feeling the heavens were crying for her. For two weeks she'd kept her vow of a business only relationship. Time should have made it easier, but it had become harder each day to maintain her distance where Michael was concerned.

Today was Saturday. As large as the house was, she was bound to run into Michael. She could go to the office, but there was no reason for her to be there. Going in would make it obvious that she was avoiding him. Maybe she could call a friend and suggest they meet for lunch. Suddenly she couldn't think of a soul she wanted to visit who wouldn't question her about Michael's presence, and in her state of mind she was apt to spill her feelings.

She could begin her Christmas shopping, but her heart wasn't in it. She never liked to shop before Thanksgiving, anyway.

She wasn't a coward, she told herself. She could certainly have a conversation with Michael that had nothing to do with business and didn't border on their personal lives. Leaving her bedroom, she headed for the breakfast room. Skipping down the stairs she realized she had on the blue and white sweater and stirrup pants she'd worn in the mountains. At the bottom of the steps she stopped. She'd been wearing this outfit when Michael first kissed her.

Erika grabbed the newel post. Maybe she was a coward.

* * *

Blood. The human body held between four and five quarts. Frank Mason released the leather belts he'd used to secure Judge Raymond Baldwin to the dining room chair. The last blood his heart pumped had squirted through the slits in his wrists twenty minutes ago. Frank had stood behind the judge, watching the arc of blood as it squirted, until it petered into a trickle.

The judge acted like the lawyer. He pleaded and begged, telling him he could help him. How could he help? He'd had his chance, and what had he done? Confined him to that place. He'd die before going back.

Look at him. The judge didn't look so tough now. He had no robes, no high chair above the rest of the crowd. He was just a man. Just a dead man.

And Mrs. Baldwin. She was tougher than her husband—she was still alive—but not for long. Frank pulled her straps free, and her bulk made her body fall out of the chair. Frank wouldn't touch her anymore. He wanted to be careful not to get any of the blood on him. He checked his white coat and shoes. He'd posed as a doctor and they'd trustingly let him in. As white as when he stepped across the threshold. Frank smiled at his handiwork.

"Good night, Judge Baldwin," he said. The smile left his face, replaced by a look of hatred. "See you in hell."

Michael looked at himself in the bathroom mirror. He'd slept in this morning, since most of his night had been spent listening to the silence after the dream. This couldn't go on. His eyes were red and the bags under his eyes would soon be as large as those of the Cowardly Lion from *The Wizard of Oz.* He looked as if he'd been on a dead drunk, but he hadn't. He simply couldn't sleep without nightmares of Frank Mason and Erika. She'd totally replaced Abby in his nocturnal mind. The dreams had become so frequent he would soon have to go to a doctor. Malick had noticed his state, but Michael had been able to attribute it to the strain of the office.

He wasn't far from the truth there. Since he and Erika had established their plan the strain of being close to her had intensified. Each time he saw her at meals or during the business day he'd wanted to convince her to change their plan, but he knew better. He knew a relationship between them was out of the question. He couldn't sustain it. Yet his body didn't quite agree with him. He wanted to touch her, hold her, feel her come to life in his arms as they both let the throes of passion lead them to the place that only a man and a woman can understand. Erika, though, was logical and strong enough to keep the conversations structured around Graves Enterprises.

They'd discussed the pharmaceutical division's product pipeline and new drug applications being filed. There was a lot of excitement about a new AIDS drug awaiting approval. The reports of the stock sales were still being watched, but the buying patterns seemed to have cooled.

The only thing that hadn't cooled was him. Pushing himself back, he entered the bedroom as the phone rang.

"So tell me, is she coming or should I find my own date?" His brother, Peter, laughed in his ear.

"Peter!" He was glad to hear him. "What's going on?"

"Not much. I was wondering if you were free for lunch and we could meet later."

Michael sighed with relief. He needed a method of leaving the house and Peter provided it. "Lunch will be fine."

"Good. If I invite myself there will I get to meet Erika St. James?"

He wanted to come here. Peter had mentioned Erika before, and he knew his brother. He probably only wanted to come to meet Erika. Suddenly he was jealous of his own brother, jealous of his easygoing manner and his ability to attract the opposite sex. They'd never been rivals before, but with Erika it was different. He remembered watching her sleeping and wanting to climb into bed and hold her, make love to her.

"Michael, are you still there?"

Michael cleared his throat. "I'm here."

"Well, how about it?"

"I don't know what Erika's plans are, but I'm sure she'd love to meet you."

"I'll see you in about an hour."

Peter hung up before Michael could say anything. His brother couldn't have picked a worse time to come. His relationship was strained. His physical appearance showed his lack of sleep. He knew Erika was attracted to him. Right now, though, they were at a crossroads and he didn't need a handsome TV personality showing up to tilt the scales.

Michael dressed quickly in jeans and a sweater. He needed to find Erika and let her know about Peter.

He found her in the library, ensconced in papers. She spent all her time working. What was it that drove her? She had to know she was doing a wonderful job. The stock had stabilized. They no longer thought anyone was trying to gain a hostile seat on the Graves board of directors.

Even with that, with market share showing a steady climb and a pipeline of products looking good enough to keep them profitable into the next century, Erika drove herself as if her last meal would be served if she didn't supervise everything herself. She let nothing get in the way of her and Graves Enterprises.

"Good morning," Michael said.

Her head snapped up. She looked tired, too, tired but beautiful. The light was subdued this morning due to the rain outside, but even without the highlights falling on her hair she was beautiful.

"Hello," she said. Her voice appeared unusually low and sexy. She put her pen down and sat back. Her body was stiff and businesslike. Michael suddenly wanted to haul her out of the chair and make her melt into the woman he knew her to be. But he did none of the things his mind told him.

"What are you doing?"

"Going over some of the reports I never get a chance to read in the office."

"Anything I can help you with?"

"You have the same reports. Have you read them all?"

He had read most of them but he still had a desk full of papers that needed his attention. Something about her eyes disturbed him. "Do you work all the time?"

"No," she said. He could see defensiveness creep into her body language.

"Why don't you date?"

"I don't think that's any of your business."

"It is if it affects your performance at Graves Enterprises."

Erika's eyes opened wide. "My dating or not dating has no effect on the company."

"I disagree. If you get out and socialize it makes you a more informed person, someone who understands what is going on in the marketplace, how real people feel. You can't get everything from a report." He spread his hands at the array of papers on her desk. Erika followed his lead.

"Are you trying to get me to go out with you again?"

It hadn't been his intention when he walked into the room, but the thought of her on his arm as he squired her about town—dinner, a show, conversation in a small jazz club—was tantalizing.

"All right." Erika stood up. "If you think the health of Graves Enterprises hinges on whether or not I date, then I'll find myself a date."

She moved to push past him. Michael caught her by both arms and turned her to face him. "That's not what I meant, and you know it." Then he did something he'd promised himself he wouldn't do. He pulled her into his arms and clamped his mouth to hers. She resisted for the merest second but he wouldn't let her go. He couldn't even if he'd wanted to. He'd wanted to taste her again since that first kiss, dreamed of her, pliant in his arms, and now that he'd maneuvered her into them he wasn't going to let go so easily.

Oh God! Michael thought, feeling her hands on his waist and then reaching around him as she pressed her body close. Her breasts, small and firm, pushed against his chest, sending a jolt of need straight to his knees, which threatened to buckle with the onslaught. He shouldn't have done this. He should have let her walk away. He should release her now, let her go and apologize, but he couldn't. He needed more. He wanted more. He couldn't settle for this one kiss alone. He needed massive doses of her, and preferably several times a day. He didn't know that he could survive without her now that the floodgates were open and the wave had swept them away.

Erika stopped her struggle and her arms climbed up his back. She refused to think. If she thought, she'd push herself away, and the way he made her feel she didn't want to be logical. She wanted to rip the thin barrier of clothing between them away and feel his hard nakedness against her soft skin. She wanted to remain in his arms, with his mouth sealed to hers, with his tongue deep in her mouth and the sensations rioting through her body like lightning fissuring through the unresisting sky.

Erika gave as much as she took. She went up on her toes to get closer to him. His hands raked her body, combed through her hair, cupped her face and hips, pressing her into him as if he could merge the two of them into a single being. No one had ever made her feel like this before.

Then Michael's hold changed. The passion in his mouth slowed, teased, and turned to reverence. He held her lightly, gently, as if his hands were too big, too rough, for her delicate features. Erika had never been held like this. His mouth slipped from hers, and his hands cradled her head. He pushed back to look at her face. His eyes were darker and filled with a passion that spoke volumes. Her breath caught and she couldn't speak.

Then she was free. Michael stepped back and the moment was gone—gone but not lost. Erika didn't think she'd ever be the same again. When Michael looked at her for that half second she'd felt as if their souls had linked and she would never again be complete without him. No one had made her feel as if she were the single most important thing in the world.

But the man who had held her in his arms was gone. In his place was another Michael. He looked like the same man, but he was different. She felt as if she'd suddenly lost something, something important, and that she'd never have it again.

"I came in to tell you my brother called this morning. He's invited himself to lunch. He wants to meet you."

He was stiff and formal, as if the interlude in his arms had never taken place, as if the need she knew dwelled inside him had been arrested and placed in solitary confinement. A chill ran through her. She felt cold, as if a sudden wind had passed through her or someone had walked over her grave.

Peter couldn't have been more charming, and Michael had never wanted to strangle his brother as much as he did right now. Erika delighted in talking to him during their meal. She laughed at his jokes and asked questions about his job.

Could this be the same woman he'd held in his arms only an hour ago? The woman he'd seen dressed in only a bathrobe, without makeup, and dripping wet as she came out of the pool? She was confident, in control and an excellent hostess.

Michael felt left out. Peter dominated the conversation—but then, he always had. A ready smile and the right words were always at hand for Peter. And Erika was eating it up.

"Nut brown?" Erika's laughter tinkled when Michael brought his mind back to the conversation. "Really?"

"It's my color," Peter was saying.

"And you really let them put it on you?"

"The lights are very hot and the makeup artist is very good."

Erika looked at Michael. "Can you imagine Michael doing the news?"

Peter turned his attention to his brother. He shook his head. "Michael's much too serious. He'd want to fix all those problems he reported."

Michael tried to join the conversation. "Maybe not *all* of them."

Peter continued to talk about the methods of broadcasting the news and Erika looked genuinely interested in everything he had to say. Finally the conversation wound down and Erika pushed her chair back and stood. Peter stood up, too. She walked to where he was and offered him her hand. Peter took it in both of his. Michael noticed he did not release it.

"It's been nice talking to you, Peter, but you probably want to talk to Michael." She glanced at Michael. "I hope to see you before you go."

"I'm sure Peter didn't come all this way to see me," Michael said, hoping he could keep the jealousy out of his voice.

"Actually, there is something I'd like to talk to you about," Peter contradicted him, finally dropping Erika's hand.

Michael stared at his brother. A beautiful woman was about to leave the room and he wasn't pursuing her. Whatever Peter had to say must be serious.

"I'll leave you then."

Erika turned to go, but Peter stopped her.

"I've had a wonderful lunch, and mostly because of you." Michael couldn't believe these lines worked, but the expression on Peter's face was genuine and Erika looked as if he were telling the truth. "I hope to see you again on Thanksgiving," he finished.

"Thanksgiving?"

"Didn't Michael tell you?"

They both turned to look at him. He felt as if their questioning stares were tangible. He'd forgotten about Thanksgiving. So much was happening to him—the office, Frank Mason's escape, the dreams, Malick. He'd completely forgotten about the invitation. In light of his previous invitation, he doubted she would have accepted even if he had remembered.

"Michael was supposed to invite you to the family dinner."

"I suppose it slipped his mind," Erika said. "It was nice meeting you. I'll have your coffee and dessert sent in."

Quickly she left the room. Michael tried to catch her eye, but she purposely didn't look at him. She couldn't be hurt. She'd told him they should only have a business relationship. A forgotten invitation from him couldn't mean anything to her. Could it? She'd refused his previous offer of a date. He had to be wrong. She was just leaving the room as she'd planned. He wanted to go to her, but the maid came in with the coffee and poured it into their cups. When she left, Peter started to talk.

"People say this all the time and I never thought I'd find myself saying it, but she's much better looking in person."

"Back off, Peter," Michael said. There was no mistaking the warning note in his voice.

"So it's like that, is it?" Peter asked. "I've been trying to figure that out."

"It's like that."

"Then why haven't you invited her to Thanksgiving dinner?"

"I've had a lot on my mind," he answered weakly. "I forgot."

"You could forget a woman like that?"

"Peter, can we drop it?" His tone was harsher than he intended, but Erika had completely thrown his senses out of kilter this afternoon and he hadn't completely recovered them yet. "I apologize. I didn't mean to sound so—"

"Jealous." Peter supplied the word he'd been groping for.

When Michael started to protest his brother stopped him. "Don't worry about it. Jealousy is healthy." Peter added sugar to his coffee and drank. Setting the cup back in the saucer, he said, "I came to talk to you about something that looks rather odd to me."

"What's that?" Michael sat forward in the chair. His brother's expression had changed from happy-go-lucky to serious.

"How much have you heard about Frank Mason since he escaped from the mental hospital?"

"Only that the police are still looking for him."

"Do you remember what he said at his sentencing?"

Michael didn't think he'd ever forget the words, or the expression on Frank Mason's face as he turned in the crowded courtroom and stared him directly in the eye. "Peter, where is this going?"

"Frank Mason swore he'd make you pay for what you'd done to him," Peter said. "He swore he'd make everyone pay. And now he's on the streets."

"What are you saying?" Michael was intrigued, but he didn't have time for a feature-length story.

"Got a VCR handy? I have something I want you to see."

They both stood. Michael took his coffee cup and started for the door.

"I think you'll want to leave the coffee," Peter stopped him.

"What do you have, dirty movies?"

"Absolutely," he said. "The gruesome kind."

There was none of the usual playfulness in Peter's face. He looked like the serious newsman who sat at the anchor desk five nights a week and read the evening news.

Michael ran his hand over his eyes half an hour later, when the screen went blank. Leaning forward he hid the emotion that gathered in his eyes and made him want to cry. Except for the Mason children and Abby, he hadn't cried since he was a small boy, but seeing the pictures on the video tape—Judge Baldwin, Abby's attorney and her husband, the blood, the sadistic method of killing—he hadn't thought anyone could be that crazy.

"Where did you get these?" Michael asked. The emotion wasn't fully out of his voice. "These are police tapes."

"I have a friend on the force. I reported the mystery of the lawyer's death, but didn't put him together with the Frank Mason case until the judge's story broke."

"What are you thinking?" Michael stared at his brother, the bloody pictures still in his mind.

"I think Frank Mason is making good his threat, and you're in his direct line."

"Why should I be there? I was *his* lawyer . . . much as I regret it," he added.

"Michael, I don't think he's going to remember that. I think he's crazy. How could a man do what he did and be sane?"

Michael stood up, feeling the need to walk. He went to the windows and looked out on the brown grass. The rain hadn't let up. Michael felt the weight of Frank's crime on his shoulders.

"Peter, I'm safe here. This place has its own security force, and Frank Mason doesn't even know where I am."

"You've been well publicized. It wouldn't be hard to find you, especially for a person who wants to, and remember how persistent he could be."

Michael remembered. Many times Michael had suggested that Frank accept other terms to full custody of his children, but he'd been relentless and Michael had been his puppet, getting him what he wanted, only to have him betray the innocent children.

"There's also Erika."

Michael turned abruptly at the mention of Erika's name.

"Notice who he's killing," Peter began. "The wives, husbands, families of the victims."

"You think—"

"If he comes looking for you, she's in danger, too."

Michael's stomach knotted. He hadn't considered Erika. Frank was his problem, not hers. He needed to protect her.

"Michael, I think you should leave here. Go someplace else until Frank is caught."

He could hear the concern in his brother's voice. Peter was afraid for him. "I can't leave," he told him. "Erika and I are bound by the terms of Carlton Lipton-Graves's will."

"Your life is in danger. I'm sure if you went to court and explained to the judge, he'd grant you special dispensation."

"He might, but I doubt it."

"Why?"

"Frank hasn't been caught, and according to you only circumstantial evidence connects him with the crimes. They could be coincidences. The perpetrator could be another of the judge's enemies. He need not be Frank Mason."

"It's still worth a try." Peter's face was drawn and Michael knew his brother was concerned about his safety.

"Even if I did go before a judge, there's still Erika. If Frank is looking for me and comes here, he'll find Erika. He could hurt her in order to find me. I can't leave her here alone."

"Don't you think she'd be willing to come with you?"

This was a huge house. Michael could see the two of them confined to a small apartment or hotel room. After what had happened this morning he knew being confined with Erika would be like throwing a match in a vat of nitroglycerin.

"I'll have security doubled, alert them to be on the lookout for Frank, and make sure Erika is protected at all times."

Peter was quiet for a moment. Michael knew he was processing information like a human computer, trying to find a more acceptable alternative.

"You're in love with her," Peter stated softly and truthfully.

Michael nodded.

Erika prowled in the library. She remembered thinking how big this room was when she first ran into it. Carlton had caught her arms and stopped her. He was big, too. Now the room was smaller. She felt caged in, and wanted to throw open the French doors at the end of the room and make the space larger.

The rain stopped her. It beat against the panes like steady smacks. Yet the smacks didn't blot out what had happened earlier, when Michael had touched her, kissed her.

Could he be the one? she asked herself. *The man who would want her, love her? Was there any man who could fall in love with her?* She'd asked herself that question for years, ever since her mother told her she'd never find anyone who'd really love her. Each time Erika had been asked on a date or met a new man, she'd ask herself if he was the one.

Then she'd met Bill Castle. He was the closest she'd come to believing he was the one. Look where that had led her. At first she'd been blinded by his lifestyle; parties every night, mingling with the rich and famous. For a while she thought she could survive in that world, but she knew better now. She didn't like the limelight. She found it too hard to let reporters print lies about her and not respond. The world of pop music was a world in which no one was real. Each person had a mask, and was trying to climb over someone else to get what he wanted. Isn't that what had happened to her? Hadn't Jennifer Ahrends climbed over her to get to her fiancé?

Erika sat down at the desk and stared at the rain. So far, every man she'd ever met had left her, beginning with her father. Michael would be no different. He might have kissed her until she couldn't think straight, until she couldn't distinguish between reality and fantasy, but she knew now, in the cold light of day, that he would be gone in less than a year.

Why should he want her? She wasn't beautiful. She wished she was, but she knew better. Michael was the best-looking man she'd ever seen. Women must fall all over him. The ones at her office certainly would, given the chance. So far she hadn't seen him give anyone a chance—except her. But she was merely convenient. They occupied the same house, met for meals, and found it necessary to talk constantly during the workday.

He didn't really want her, not for the long-term. No one had in the past, and Michael was no different from Bill Castle or any of the other men she'd ever met. When their year was over Michael would go. He'd be a rich man, a very rich man. He could have any woman he wanted. Erika knew she wouldn't be the one he chose.

"Erika."

She whirled around, startled, standing up like a child caught doing something she'd been expressly forbidden to do. Michael walked into the room. He was alone. She'd been thinking of him, and his sudden presence made her pulses beat.

"Where's Peter?" she asked.

"He asked me to say good-bye for him. He had to get back."

Erika was dismayed. She liked Peter and would have liked talking to him again. He'd also provided a buffer between Michael and her. Since this morning she had felt as if electricity flowed around her whenever Michael entered the room. Her heart fluttered out of control when Michael whispered her name. With Peter, she'd be on safe ground.

"I want you to promise me something," Michael began.

"What?" Erika asked.

Michael took the seat in front of the desk. His face was serious, more than when she'd first seen him at the cabin. Erika was suddenly afraid. What had his brother told him after she left?

"Before I ask for the promise, I need to tell you something."

Erika's heart beat fast. Michael was scaring her.

"I was Frank Mason's lawyer. His wife's name was Abigail Mason. She sued him for divorce and I represented Frank in the custody battle over their three young children."

Erika knew this. Carlton's lawyer had given her the overall details, but she didn't tell Michael. She wanted to hear what had happened from him. He'd called Abby's name in his nightmares. She wanted to know how well he knew her and if they had been lovers. It was masochistic, she knew, but she wanted to know, anyway.

Michael got up and paced the floor before the huge fireplace. He dug his hands in his pockets, then took them out. Erika got up and went to stand behind one of the chairs that stood before the fire. The crackle of dry logs was the only sound in the room.

"Frank gave me details about his wife, and I used them. I believed what he said—that his wife was the one who was the unfit parent, that she had a string of affairs, left the children unattended, and was responsible for their accidents."

"Michael, a lawyer is supposed to believe in his client."

"They always lie," he snapped. "At least they omit part of the truth. A lawyer knows that. But I let it go. I let it go, and three children are dead!"

"Michael, it isn't your fault. You couldn't have known what he would do."

"I should have. I should have listened to what his wife's lawyer was telling me, but I was too busy. I had other things on my mind."

"What . . . what other things?"

"I'd been asked to run for state office, and I was considering it. This case was highly publicized. I did my damndest to make Abigail Mason the devil, and she wasn't."

The last two words were almost a cry. Erika's heart clenched at the pain Michael was feeling.

"After the judge awarded the children to their father everything seemed to be in my favor. The political heavyweights courted me, the press followed my movements, the papers hailed me as the next state senator." Michael paused. He wasn't talking to her. He was remembering.

Erika had the feeling he'd never talked about this to anyone. She waited, not wanting to interrupt him.

"Then one day Frank agreed to let the children see their mother," he continued. "He called me to meet him for the exchange. He said he didn't want to be alone, didn't trust himself around Abby."

"You agreed to go?"

Michael nodded. "He was to meet her at one of the shopping malls. I got there and parked. I saw Abby get out of her car and we both got to the entry door at the same time."

He closed his eyes as if he could blot out the memory. "I'll never forget the look she gave me, the vile names she called me. She went through the door before me. The place was crowded with back to school shoppers. When Abby saw the children they were at the end of a long corridor. I saw Frank. He watched her come toward them. He waited until she was close enough to see everything, but too far away to do anything. The children saw their mother and began to run toward her. Then Frank took out a gun, and with the precision of a marksman put a bullet through each one of the children's heads."

Erika gasped, her hand going to her heart. She knew the children had been killed—Steven had told her—but Michael's version was so much more immediate. The impact hit her like a dynamite blast. She could feel the horror of the children dying, of their mother trying to get to them, of knowing that Michael felt he'd been part of the crime.

"I was his witness." Michael hung his head. Erika knew now why he'd retreated to the mountains, and why he never wanted to return to being a lawyer. Hadn't she wanted to do the same thing? What would she have done if her problem had resulted in someone's death? Tears sprang to her eyes and her chest felt hollow.

"Suddenly I was bad news," Michael went on. "No one wanted to talk to me except the press. They wanted to skin me alive." He looked at her. "I graciously withdrew my name from consideration."

"Is that when you left?" she asked.

Michael shook his head. "I testified at Frank's trial, then stayed around until it was over, foolishly thinking I could go on. The day Frank Mason was sentenced I went to court. He swore he'd escape, that no jail or hospital could hold him, that he'd get even with everyone who had made his life miserable."

"That wouldn't include you," she told him, wiping her eyes with the tips of her fingers.

Michael hesitated for a moment. "He looked directly at me when he said it."

"Why?" Her voice was no more than a low rush of air.

"I don't know. The court remanded him to a psychiatric hospital. He blames everyone who had anything to do with his case."

Erika sat, stunned. Then she got up and walked to the fireplace. Frank Mason had escaped. She remembered the reporter at the press conference telling them, and she remembered Michael's reaction to the news. She shuddered as a sudden chill skittered through her. Wrapping her hands around herself, she tried to hold in the nervous tension that knotted her stomach.

"He's been in that hospital for how long? Years? He could have forgotten all about you."

"That's true," Michael said, but he wasn't convinced, and neither was she. If Frank Mason was looking for Michael, he'd be easy to find. Erika suddenly went to him, grasping his arms.

"Michael, you have to leave here," she said.

"That was Peter's suggestion."

"It's a good one."

Michael shook his head. "I've already explained to him the many reasons leaving won't work, only one of which is Carlton's will."

Erika dropped her hands and turned away. She'd forgotten about the will. It seemed that every time they turned around Carlton's will tied their hands.

"Michael, your life could be in danger. Isn't there anything we can do?"

"I'm not the only person in danger."

Erika stared at him. "What do you mean?"

Michael explained what Peter had told him about the families of the other victims.

"We're not related."

"I don't think he's going to stop to check genealogy."

Erika couldn't keep her face straight. She was scared suddenly. Someone could kill Michael and her.

"It's going to be all right, Erika. Let me handle it."

"What are you going to do?"

"Add more security here. And I promise I'll be careful."

"That's all? Shouldn't we call the police or something?"

"What would we tell them?"

"That Frank Mason is trying to kill you."

"We don't know that."

"Yet," she said. "Michael, we can't wait for him actually to—" She stopped, unable to complete the sentence.

Michael came to her. "Erika, I need a promise from you."

She waited for him to continue. Michael told her about the people Frank was alleged to have killed. "I want you to promise me you'll be careful, that until Frank Mason is caught you will take care to always be with someone."

"Someone? Like who?" Erika stared at him. "You think I should get a bodyguard?"

Michael hadn't thought of a bodyguard, but he had to admit it was a good idea. It would solve his problem of how to protect her when he wasn't around.

"Yes," he said, seizing the idea. "We'll hire one tomorrow."

"Michael, I'd feel silly with a bodyguard. Frank hasn't even been spotted near here and we don't even know it's him for sure. With the increase in security, we should be safe enough."

"I'd feel safer knowing there was someone protecting you."

"Me!" she said. "Frank doesn't know anything about me. He'd be looking for you. If anyone needs protection it's you, not me."

"I don't need protection from Frank Mason."

Erika shivered at the coldness in his voice. He spoke as if he wanted to meet Frank. Erika knew there was unfinished business between them. They represented good and evil, black and white, and inevitably they had to meet and take a stand. Erika could only hope that meeting occurred on the opposite sides of a courtroom table and not a .357 Magnum.

CHAPTER 12

The clock chimed midnight in the distance before Erika climbed the stairs that night. At the landing that separated her wing of the house from the one Michael used, she stopped and turned back. She hadn't really looked at the house in years. Tonight she turned before the stained glass window and surveyed the bottom floor. Life had been different since Michael had come, but she'd become used to his presence, his habits, even his bouts with nightmares.

Tomorrow they would add different elements to the household. Even though they wouldn't have bodyguards immediately, it was only a matter of time, if Frank Mason really wanted Michael dead. She, too, would have to accept one if she insisted Michael take one on. Erika didn't know how she felt about having a stranger around all the time. She put her hand on the large newel post and stared into the semi-darkness. For so many years it had been Carlton and her. The servants maintained the household, kept the grounds, and cooked the meals. While Erika knew them intimately, they'd been there for years and she was used to their presence. Then Michael had come, on the heels of Carlton's death. Somehow he had a connection to the house. Strangers—she didn't know what to make of them. Someone always with her, protecting her from possible harm. She shivered in the warm air.

She sighed, accepting that change was part of life. Carlton was gone and she never thought she'd be able to get over the hurt his death caused, but she was doing fine. Then Michael had come and her routine had changed. She smiled to herself. She couldn't say she hated the routine. Day by day he'd wormed his way into her heart until the thought of him could take her breath away.

Maybe having more people around would give her something else to concentrate on and she could get her emotions in order.

She glanced in the direction of her room, but she saw something move from the corner of her eye and turned toward Michael's wing. He stood at the top of the stairs dressed in a silk robe. Erika opened her mouth to speak, but her throat went so dry she couldn't. The hallway behind Michael was dark and she couldn't see his face, but something wouldn't let her move, wouldn't let her breathe.

The memory of another night came back to her. She knew the robe—she'd seen it before, lying at the foot of his bed during one of his nightmares—yet she thought she'd never seen him wearing it. Somehow, she had seen that robe on him, contoured to his dark body as he turned and walked away. It was the dream, what she thought was the dream. Had it been?

"You were in my room," she stated it as fact, as if he knew she meant the night she'd had the dream that he was there.

Michael started down the stairs. Erika took a step back when he reached the bottom step.

"Yes," he said softly. "I needed to know you were safe."

"Safe from what?" she whispered, feeling anything but safe at the moment.

His hands slipped around her waist. Erika didn't think to protest. Indeed, it was the most natural thing that had ever happened to her. Heat swept through her blouse where his hands touched her and instantly her entire body became an incinerator. She didn't know what kept her from dissolving into a puddle of chocolate syrup at Michael's feet.

Michael took a step closer to her. Erika's gaze was fastened on his collarbone. She swallowed and looked up. Light filtering through the stained glass crossed his face with planes of blue and yellow. The garish light turned his features into harsh lines, giving him a sinister look. The dimension increased Erika's excitement. She'd never felt so hungry for a man. His eyes were dark with passion. The heat of his body mingled with hers, cocooning them in a world only they could create. His arms slid around her, pulling her length into contact with his. Every part of them touched—arms to arms, breasts to breasts, thigh to thigh. Everything made contact except their lips.

"If you don't kiss me, I'm going to die," she rasped in a voice she didn't recognize.

Michael stared at her, his eyes reverently memorizing her features. Then his mouth lowered and took hers in a kiss that might have been soft and persuasive, but was hard and hungry and sent the blood rushing to her ears. The ensuing sound was deafening.

Michael's arms pinned her to him. His mouth was greedy in its possession. Erika wouldn't have had it any other way. Her arms went around his neck, the two of them caught in a primal dance as ageless as time.

Michael felt everything about her. His hands had taken on a life of their own. They covered her, touching her everywhere, pulling her into closer contact with him. Her legs lifted against his thigh. Her jeans, rough against his silk-covered leg, sent heat straight to his loins. His mouth couldn't get enough of her. She tasted wonderful, lusty, full of life, and he wanted to touch, feel, learn, every part of her slim body.

Hooking her leg over his, she swung herself into his arms, both legs circling him. Michael lifted his mouth at the boldness of her action. Businesslike, made for the boardroom crowd, Erika St. James was the passionate type. He'd known it, tested her, pushed her until they'd come to this juncture, this charge-building explosive that was bound to detonate this very night.

Michael turned her, taking a step up, never letting his mouth leave hers. It was a slow process climbing the eight stairs to the landing, but it was the most exciting climb he'd ever made. He wouldn't let her go, wouldn't break the contact as he carried her to his room. Inside, he kicked the door closed and let her slide over his body to the floor.

They stared at each other, both raggedly breathing, heaving air into their lungs as if it were a scarce commodity. Her chest rose and fell in rapid succession. Michael reached forward and undid the top button of her blouse. He felt a quiver run through her when his fingers brushed her skin. In this light she was dark as berry wine, and he wanted to drink.

The second button opened and he felt her tremble. Her bra came into view with the third button. Michael couldn't wait any longer. He pulled her forward, her head lolled back, and he kissed her neck, her cheek. His tongue followed the curve of her ear. The shudder that passed through her pushed him on. He wanted her, he had to have her tonight. Carefully, he peeled her blouse down her arms. Each tender amount of flesh exposed drove him insane with need. His hands went to the snap on her jeans. It came free in his hands. Then he was pulling them down her legs. She stepped out of them and her shoes in one movement, standing before him in only a lace bra and panties. She couldn't have been more sexy if she'd been naked. Michael wanted to look at her, commit her to memory.

She reached for him, taking the knot of his robe in her hands. The silk gave way easily and she opened it. For the longest moment she looked at him. His body was aroused, hard and pulsing. She could be in no doubt of how much he wanted her. The last of her clothes dropped to the floor and, walking her backward, he lowered her to the bed.

Michael joined Erika, threading his fingers through her soft hair. Curling his hand around the back of her head, he kissed her softly, holding himself in check. He felt as if this would be the first time he'd ever made love to a woman. He'd had sex, but tonight he was going to make love. This time would be for keeps. There would be no going back.

Erika had never known herself to be as aggressive as she was with Michael. She pulled him to her, leaving not even enough space for air to get between them. His kisses drugged her and she only wanted more. Quickly, passion gripped them and the last of her control snapped. Michael climbed on top of her and she opened her legs to accommodate him. She groaned as he entered her. Pleasure rocketed through her, feelings so strong, so sensual that she thought the overload would kill her. Her fingers dug into Michael's skin as his body rocked into her. Forces greater than the two of them aligned, setting the pace, the rhythm that culminated into a sexual dance shared by only the two of them.

Waves of rapture rioted through her. "Michael!" she screamed over and over as he dug harder, deeper, into her. Erika abandoned anything that could hold her back. She wanted Michael to have everything. She didn't care if he found out she loved him. She wanted him to know. With her body she told him. She opened the temple, crying out as the pinnacle of allowable pleasure racked her body and together the two of them released in mutual satisfaction.

Michael collapsed onto her, their bodies gleaming with sweat. He craved air, dragging it into his lungs in huge mouthfuls. Sex had never been this satisfying, this rich or poignant. Erika had done this to him. She'd showed him what it was like to be in love. He'd never recover from something like this. He wanted to hold her forever, keep her close and protected and never let anything hurt her. He wanted to live for her, to love her, to be with her morning and night, to make love to her and feel this way for the rest of his life.

The room had the unmistakable smell of sex—sweet, electric, and hot. Erika hugged Michael. He felt her hands on his back, loving the feel of them, loving everything about her. He gathered her close, slipping his weight to the mattress. He gazed into her love-dazed eyes and wondered how he could have come this far in life and never experienced the true meaning of love.

This was going to be fun, Frank thought. He hadn't been to the mountains since he was a child. His whole family had come—his mother and father, his brothers. Early in the morning they'd get up and go fishing in the stream, just his father and him. The others had been too lazy. They wanted to sleep. But not Frank. Frank could do anything. He and his father caught fish in the small stream and brought them back for breakfast. His mother cooked them and they all ate. In the mountains they didn't have any rules about eating in the kitchen or what constituted breakfast foods.

In the mountains they could explore. Frank liked exploring. He'd climb the hills, better than his brothers. He could get to the top of any cliff long before his two brothers could reach him. And his father praised him. Those were the only times Frank could remember his father giving him praise.

He'd make his dad proud today. Frank touched the gun concealed under his jacket. It was a new revolver—he'd ditched the one he'd used on Abby's lawyer—automatic with chambers for eight, brass-encased bullets. Each chamber was filled, although Frank didn't expect to use more than one. He was a neat man and he liked things tidy. Killing the judge and his wife had been messy business. Blood seeping into the carpet. The entire room would have to be replaced. There was no way to get that kind of a stain out.

Today Frank wouldn't have to think about carpets. He had the entire outdoors. Today he was on a hunt, and he had the upper hand. The prey didn't even know about him. Frank grinned. Adrenaline pumped through him. He'd be finished before morning and he could join Abby and the children. Maybe they'd go camping, fishing with his girls. Abby would cook the fish they caught, and they could eat them for breakfast, too.

Tomorrow, Abby, he thought. *We'll do it tomorrow.*

Michael jerked awake. Sweat poured off him. His knee hit something and he stopped. Something warm. His eyes snapped open. Erika was there. She stirred next to him, her short hair mussed, her features relaxed. Memory came back and he went still, not wanting to awaken her.

He'd had a dream, not the nightmare that usually disturbed his sleep, and it was morning. The nightmares usually came in the middle of the night.

Michael lay back, his arm propped under his head, the other hand gently holding Erika's. It had been a long time since he'd awakened next to a woman. He savored the moment. He wanted to kiss her awake, make love to her again, but the dream was nagging him. Erika had been there, smiling at him, her arms open and inviting. He'd been running toward her. Then she'd suddenly disappeared. Nothing awful had happened. Dreams often dissolve into nothingness. Yet Michael had the unnerving feeling that there was danger in the dream. Danger for Erika.

He watched her sleeping. Her dark skin contrasting against the whiteness of the bedcovers touched him in an elemental way. He wanted her safe. He wanted to know that she wouldn't be harmed for anything he'd done. Hadn't they spoken about Frank Mason? Hadn't Peter shown him films of crime scenes? Wouldn't it be natural for him to have such a dream? Michael knew the answers to all these questions. It was natural that he should have a dream that might include all the conversations he'd had in the past few hours, but he couldn't shake the feeling that Erika was somehow involved, or would be involved, and he'd be unable to help her.

She stirred again, her hand groping for him. She ran it across his bare belly and the first intoxicating thrill of arousal warmed his loins. Abandoning the dream, Michael ran his hand over Erika's arm and pulled her against him. He held her as if she were a baby. She was safe for the time being, and he'd get her a bodyguard, someone who'd make sure nothing happened to her.

And he'd be there whenever he could.

Erika opened her eyes. Fear made her heart beat fast. She looked around. She was alone. She could hear the sound of water running in the bathroom shower. Michael must be in there. Erika sat up quickly. The sheet covering her nakedness fell away. She grabbed for it as if someone would see her. She had to get out of there. Pushing the sheet away, she got out of bed. Seeing Michael's robe lying on the floor, she grabbed it, stuffing her hands in the overly-long sleeves. Her clothes were strewn over the floor. She snatched them up as she practically ran from the room. At the landing, she skipped steps going down and up the other side.

In her own room she slammed the door and pressed her back against it. How could she have let last night happen? She remembered standing on the landing and deciding to go to her room. Then Michael was above her, looking into her eyes, and from then on everything became a dream. But it wasn't a dream. She'd actually slept with him. The stiffness in her body told her, and her mind remembered. Her nipples got hard at the flash of memory that went through her mind of them making love. Nothing had ever happened like that before. She'd never abandoned herself so freely, demanded so much of a partner, wanted to please so desperately, and been so fulfilled.

What would happen now? He'd leave her, like all the rest. This time would be worse. At least in the past she hadn't had to see them day in and day out. But Michael lived there, worked with her. There was nothing she'd be able to do except die a little each day.

Hot tears spilled from her eyes and rolled over her cheeks. She could never let this happen again. If she did, it was unlikely she would survive when he left. Erika slid to the floor, pulling her knees to her chest and resting her head on them.

She wept.

"Michael, I'm so glad to see you," Malick said when he came into the room. Malick sat in a huge chair next to the hospital bed which had been installed on the first floor of his house. A uniformed nurse smiled at him and left the room carrying a tray with medicines on it. "I've been watching the news and—"

"Malick, this is not good for your blood pressure. I'm going to have that television removed."

"Michael, have you heard that Judge Baldwin and Angela Gilford are both dead?"

"I know that."

"You know? Have you called the police?"

"No," he said. Malick was obviously distressed. Michael sat down on the chair opposite him and explained everything that had happened in the past few days, except the night he'd spent with Erika. That he was keeping to himself. He wanted to hold the memory like a stolen piece of art, that only he could take out and look at. "I want to call Connie Forester."

"Hand me the phone," Malick said, his hand reaching toward the instrument. "She's one of the best. You couldn't do better."

Michael picked up the cordless instrument. "I want her to protect Erika." He paused. "But Erika can't know about it."

"That won't be a problem for Connie, but what about you?" Malick held the phone, no dialing.

"I'll need someone else. Someone discreet Erika won't notice or think is following either of us." He didn't really want anyone. He could handle Frank if he showed up, but he knew if he didn't take a guard Malick would spend time worrying over him. He also thought the two of them could work to protect both him and Erika, if need be.

Malick dialed. "I know just the person."

Malick had been a force in his day. Many people owed him favors—more than a Capitol Hill politician. When he finished one call he immediately dialed another. At the conclusion of the call he smiled and looked at Michael.

"It's all set. Connie will arrive tonight to guard Erika and Adrienne Dantley will be your guard."

"Adrienne?"

"She's just as good as Connie. Don't worry. Until Frank is caught I need to know you're all right."

"I can take care of myself—"

"Don't assume that's true," Malick interrupted. "We've had many assassinations of people who thought they could take care of themselves." Malick smiled. He looked more relaxed than when Michael had first seen him. "How is Erika?"

Michael tensed, hoping Malick didn't notice. He couldn't even think of Erika without remembering last night. It was incredible, what had happened between them. Yet when he'd returned from his shower she was gone. He didn't get to see her before coming here. His thoughts continually returned to the most spectacular night of his life. "She's fine," he said. "I left the maids looking after her and told the guards to admit no one."

Michael felt better, now that he knew Connie would be coming and that Erika would be protected. He'd seen Connie's work. She was expensive, and often sought after, yet Malick had been able to get her to drop whatever she was doing and come to do him a favor. Michael wondered what Malick had done to make her indebted to him.

"Michael," Malick called his name. While Michael had been wondering about Malick, his friend had obviously been observing him. "What about Highland Hills?" Malick paused, giving him a steady gaze. "Have you changed your mind about returning there?"

Erika's face immediately popped into his mind. Michael didn't know when it had happened, but recently he'd been thinking of the future. Whenever he did, his thoughts always came back to her. And after last night he knew he couldn't imagine spending his life on that mountain without Erika. She'd gotten into his blood and he was happy to have her there, but at the moment he wasn't ready to admit it, even to Malick.

"I haven't decided," he finally answered.

CHAPTER 13

Fresh air. Frank expanded his lungs, filling them with the cold mountain air. He wore no shirt or shoes, only his pants. The dirt and gravel under his feet cut into his flesh, and the dew-misty morning cloud glistened on his skin. Frank bent one knee while extending his leg backward and stretching. He loved mornings in the mountains. He'd been camping for a week, climbing the mountains and jogging through trails that only animals saw. It made him tough, like his father had wanted him to be.

Grabbing two large stones, Frank used them as weights, extending his arms backward to flex his triceps and rolling upward to strengthen already developed biceps. He sucked oxygen in and pushed out used air. His father couldn't have survived the past week outdoors but Frank had, and he'd be able to survive more. The police were looking for him, but they'd never find him. After he was through with Michael Lawrence he and Abby would disappear. No one would ever interfere with them again.

Finishing his morning routine, Frank picked up a sweater and pulled it over his head. He slipped his arms into his jacket and cleaned his feet before clothing them with socks and hiking boots. Frank was hungry. His food supply was nearly gone. He had no choice but to go to the store and get more. He'd be discreet. If anyone asked, he was a businessman, spending a few days in the mountains before the weather got too cold for camping. He pulled a baseball cap on his head. He didn't want to be recognized. He'd make sure he didn't look directly at anyone, so they couldn't identify him.

Frank went to the edge of the hill on which he camped. It appeared Michael Lawrence had taken a vacation. Frank had been to the cabin. The place was clean, but there were definite signs that he was still living there. No smoke came from the chimney, and Michael was too soft to stay up here without heat. Frank felt safe in leaving to get more supplies. Michael could take his time. Frank could wait. Abby could wait. Soon it would be over, and then they'd have their whole lives together.

The general store wasn't far. At this time of morning, only mothers needing diapers and true mountain men would be out. Frank didn't think there were too many mountain men running around in November, so that only left mothers.

There were no standard aisles of food, canned goods, or cosmetic products. The place was a mess. There didn't seem to be any order to the products for sale, just a mass of items sitting haphazardly about the floor or littered about on tables. Frank took a wire basket from a stack by the door and forced himself to leisurely walk about in the disorder, putting things in it. In five minutes he had everything he needed and started for the counter.

A white-haired man wearing a black sweater and wool trousers waited for him. Frank bent his head as if checking out possible items to add to his basket on his way to the front of the store. He set the basket on the counter, continuing to check out the space in front of him. His purpose was to keep his head down and his face away from the store owner.

"Anything else?" the man asked.

"That'll be all," Frank said. He reached in his back pocket for his wallet.

The old cash register clanked as the man rang up his purchases.

Frank noticed the wall behind the man. He almost laughed out loud. *Serves me right for not being a reader,* Frank told himself. There, on the wall, was a yellowing newspaper article and Michael Lawrence's picture.

"Used to live up here," the man said.

Frank was so startled he looked directly at the store owner. "Used to?"

"Moved back to the city, must be two months, almost three now," the man supplied.

Frank tried to read the clippings as the ancient cash register went through its designed purpose.

"She come up, and a few days later he followed her back to Philadelphia."

Frank didn't say a word, just continued trying to read the newsprint.

"Can't say as I blame him. She's a looker."

Frank had to agree with that. "Graves Heiress," he read in hopes of keeping the store owner talking.

"She inherited the fortune after Carlton Lipton-Graves died. Then what do you think?" The man stopped long enough to scratch his head. "His grandson turns out to be living right here with us."

"That must have been a surprise."

"Yep," he confirmed.

Frank paid his bill and said good-bye. Outside he dropped the bag in the jeep and climbed inside. So Michael Lawrence wasn't away on vacation. He'd permanently left the cabin to go and claim his fortune. He and Erika St. James.

Frank threw the gearshift into reverse and backed down the drive. He turned the jeep down the mountain and headed toward Philadelphia, abandoning his campsite. There was nothing he needed there. He sought Michael Lawrence. The groundhogs could have everything else.

Erika closeted herself in the library. Papers covered the desk in front of her, but as far as her comprehension was concerned they could have been written in Chinese. Her thoughts were on Michael. She was going to have to face him sooner or later. How was she going to act? she asked herself. They were both adults. There was no reason she should feel uncomfortable. People met and fell into bed together all the time. But not her. And it wasn't as if they had just met. Michael had lived under the same roof with her for almost three months. Then last night had happened. She'd looked up and he'd been there. She didn't know how to explain her feelings, even to herself. She wasn't in love with Michael, was she? Yet their time in bed had been so . . . overwhelming. She swung around to stare at the door of the library. Her body was suddenly hot, flashing heat, the way she'd felt when Michael had held her in his arms.

What would she say when she saw him? They'd spent the night in bed, making love. She couldn't pretend nothing had happened. Something had definitely happened. Her life had been changed, irrevocably. Had his? She didn't think so. He was up and gone before she'd dressed and come down to breakfast. Maybe he didn't want to face her, either.

What were they going to do? They couldn't live here for the next nine months tiptoeing around each other. She certainly couldn't let herself fall under his spell again. She knew where that would lead. She'd be left virtually at the altar again. Reporters would hound her, she wouldn't be able to concentrate on Graves Enterprises, and she'd never be able to raise her head or appear in public again. It was much better if she adopted a more professional attitude. She could control her thoughts, her feelings, and she'd never let herself be pulled into fantasy again, even if the fantasy was the best one she'd ever felt.

Erika turned back to the papers on her desk. It took a while but she immersed herself in the work and forgot about everything else.

When the outer door opened and closed she knew he was back. Her hands shook slightly, her breath went shallow, her mouth dry. She anticipated his approach and stood up, but his footsteps on the tile floor passed her by.

Quickly she went to the door and flung it open. Michael turned at the base of the staircase.

"Hello." He smiled. "I missed you this morning."

His smile was dazzling. She felt herself falling for it. What was it about him that made her all soft and jelly-like inside? She'd just made a decision and now she was considering forgetting it and running into his arms.

He came back toward her. Erika wanted to move but her feet were rooted to the floor. He took her chin in his hand and bent to kiss her. Erika's eyes closed. She refused to fight the fingers of pleasure racing through her. *Just this one time,* she thought. She'd remember later to stop him, but just this one time she wanted to feel his arms around her again.

Stepping into the space separating them, she molded herself to him. Her arms circled his neck and he crushed her to him and kissed her passionately, like he had last night. Erika kissed him as if her life depended on it, as if it were the last time.

Hard bodies. That was the only term Michael could think of to describe Connie Forester and Adrienne Dantley. Even through their clothes he could see the strength of their outline. They shook hands in a small restaurant where the grease smelled old, but the Philly steaks were unmatchable.

Both women had strong grips, but only Adrienne looked as if she could handle a man of Frank Mason's height and weight. She was only a hair shorter than Michael with toned muscles and skin the color of aged teak. Her hair was short and her features angular and hard, but when she smiled every part of her seemed to soften.

Connie, on the other hand, couldn't be more than five feet tall. Her hair was long and fine and she wore it pulled back in a ponytail that hung to her shoulder blades. Streaks of grey strands ran through it like snow trails. She looked about forty. She was compact, muscular, and dressed in pants and a sweater. The sweater had a dragon on it made of gold sequins.

"I know this is a little too cloak and daggerish, but I couldn't meet you at the house. I don't want to upset Erika more than necessary."

"We understand," Connie said in a voice as soft as cotton candy.

"I got these pictures from my brother." Michael handed them both a news photo of Erika. He went on to explain the situation. He told them nothing was certain and he wasn't prone to jumping to conclusions, but two people involved in the case were now dead and he didn't want any surprises if Frank Mason did have something to do with these recent murders.

Connie leafed through the folder. "I'll need more if I'm to be properly prepared. I want to know everything there is about him, from the time he was born until yesterday," she said.

"I'll get you everything I can."

"Transcripts of his trial and the custody battle, where he grew up, his neighbors, church groups, if any, everything."

"I'll have my brother send you everything you want," Michael told her. "Just make sure Erika is kept safe."

Connie nodded. "She'll never know we're around," Adrienne told him.

"Good," Michael said, and finished his steak and cola. He didn't even see them following him back to the mansion. Security had been notified of their presence and given photos of them, so if they needed to get inside there wouldn't be a problem.

He felt a lot better letting himself into the house after meeting the two women. Erika would be safe. He could sleep well.

He was wrong. The dream stole into his sleep like a filmy cloud. Everything was shrouded behind it. He couldn't see clearly, but he recognized Erika. They were in the gym. She climbed the ropes, up and down, hand over hand, pulling herself up. Then the room dissolved into the mountain. Erika ran up the hill, behind bushes and trees. Frank pursued her, cutting the distance between them with his wider gait. Michael screamed to her, hoping she would hear him in time to protect herself. Her motions were slow, yet Michael couldn't get to her, couldn't scream loud enough for her to hear, couldn't reach Frank in time to stop him.

Frank stopped. His face swirled toward Michael in a grotesque mask of determined horror. Then he turned back. Erika ran on. Frank took aim, both hands holding onto the gun. The sound deafened Michael as Frank fired.

The bullet hit Erika in the back. Her hands opened out on impact. The bullet pushed her off balance as she ran. Michael could hear her scream, yet he could do nothing to stop the horror unfolding in front of his eyes. He screamed loud, anguished, gut-wrenching cries until someone began speaking to him. He could hear the calming voice, but not distinguish whose it was. It was a woman. She smelled sweet and felt soft. He grabbed her and held on, wanting it to be Erika, wanting to change the events he'd just witnessed, knowing he had no way of doing so. He buried his face in her neck, ran his hands through her hair and took long, hard breaths. He held on, gasping the air.

Michael came awake holding someone. He opened his eyes, telling himself she was part of the dream, but she didn't disappear. He smelled her perfume and felt the sheer fabric of her nightgown. "Erika!" he said in surprise. Pushing himself back, he looked at her. "You're here?" He hauled her close, hugging her to him.

"You were screaming my name," she said. Her voice was no more than a whisper and Michael loved it. He felt her feather light breath on his neck.

"I'm sorry," he apologized after a moment. "I didn't mean to wake you. I have bad dreams." He released her and fell back against the pillows, one arm covering his eyes. He needed to get control of his breathing and the thudding of his heart. The dream had caused part of it, but finding Erika in his arms was the part that had him unnerved.

"Are you all right?" she asked, leaning toward him.

"Yes," he said.

Erika pushed herself off the bed and stood up. Michael thought she was leaving, but she came around the bed and sat next to him. "Do you want to tell me about the dreams?"

He moved his arm and looked at her. Moonlight flowed through the windows, the only illumination in the room. It turned her gown into a shimmering robe of silver, making her skin golden in contrast. Michael wanted her. He'd made love to her once, and she had been all he could think of since. He wanted her again and again, thinking he could never get too much of Erika St. James.

"Are they always the same?" she asked.

"Most of the time."

"They're about Abby?"

"How did you know?" He wondered if he'd had a dream the night they were together. He remembered waking after one, but she was asleep, and he hadn't cried out.

"At the cabin," she told him. "You had a dream there. Since you came here there have been two other times that I know of."

He stared at her, hoping she didn't know, that she hadn't heard him calling her name more than this one time.

"Is that why you picked this room, the last one in the wing, so I wouldn't hear you in the night?"

Michael knew she was perceptive. He nodded, but didn't think she could see him in the dim light. "They don't come often," he lied. Since he'd met her it seemed the dreams had accelerated, but then Frank Mason had come back into his life at the same time. Erika had been the messenger. Michael assumed that was the reason she often appeared in the nightmares instead of Abby.

"How often is not often?"

"Erika, you're not a psychiatrist."

She reached for his hand and slipped her smaller one into it. "I hope I'm a friend."

Michael stared at her in the darkness. He closed his hand around hers and urged her forward. She came without hesitation. He pulled until she lost her balance and fell against him. Slipping his hand around her head, he threaded it through her short curls, staring at each minute part of her face—her eyes, her forehead, her nose, her lips. At the distance of a kiss he whispered, "You're more than a friend."

Michael closed the millimeter separating them, taking her mouth in a searing kiss. Her mouth was hot, wet, and demanding. Michael felt like a man of fire and Erika an oxygen source. His mouth ate up the life-giving air, consuming it, until the two of them were part of the singular.

Erika's gown, under Michael's hands, was cool against her hot body. He ran his palms over the fabric as if it were a liquid. Her mouth opened to him, giving him her taste as their tongues met and mated. Sensations flashed through Michael. He pulled Erika over him, then turned her over his body until he lay on top of her. Her arms reached for him, caressing his back with long fingers that drew trails of fire over his skin. Michael took in a long breath, raising his head to gaze down at her. Erika's eyes were passion-filled, her lips swollen from the impact of his mouth on hers. She was the most beautiful woman he'd ever seen, and he liked seeing her in this light.

She was driving him crazy and he liked it. Michael had never expected his dream to lead him here. He didn't expect Erika to come to his room. He knew he wanted her here. He wanted her here every night and every morning. What would she think if he told her that?

"Michael," Erika said. The low, sexy quality that entered her voice whenever they made love was there, unraveling him. He'd never heard it so deep and sensual. The one word seemed to wrap around him, pull him closer to her like a haunting saxophone playing in the background.

"Am I too heavy?" he asked.

"Nooo." She stretched the word out, her hands sliding down his body and over his buttocks. He nearly shouted at the sensations of pleasure that began at his toes and reverberated through every nerve in his body. He hardened against her. Erika seemed to like the feeling against her leg. She shifted, trying to accommodate him. Michael placed his hands on either side of her head and looked into her eyes. Carefully he kissed her eyelids, the tip of her nose, her mouth. Erika opened like a rose to rain water. He'd begun slowly, but in seconds he was devouring her mouth as if she were his final hold on life.

Erika couldn't help the noises she made. They were natural, as natural as the way Michael made her feel. She was alive and female—all female. To think she could have spent her life, and never known these feelings. Michael pulled the strap of her gown down and kissed her shoulder. Slowly he moved to the other side, removing that strap and kissing the other shoulder. Erika trembled. He lifted her forward until the gown fell to her waist.

"Don't," he said quietly when she went to cover herself. Instead he touched her. Her skin was hot and his hands sent excitement spiraling through her. Her nipples hardened into dark cherries. Her throat was parched, and she had to breathe through her mouth. Erika closed her eyes, letting her head fall back. She arched herself closer to him, closer to the sensations, to the erotic effects of his hands.

She reached for him, needing to touch, needing to feel. He was hot. She didn't understand why he didn't melt, why she didn't melt. He wore nothing. She could see his fully aroused state and knew that she had done this. He wanted her as much as she wanted him. Michael lifted the body of her gown, and inch by inch raised it up her legs. Bending, he kissed her skin. Her muscles quivered at his touch, her stomach clenched, and hot juices flowed to her core. Her breath came in hard gasps, her breasts heaving. Michael reached across her and opened a drawer. Quickly he pulled out a foil-covered condom and covered himself. Erika watched in anticipation and fascination until he pushed her back and kissed her.

His body covered hers, each contrasting the other; her softness against his hardness, her smooth skin against his roughness, each complementing the other; Michael's body beginning where hers left off.

In a smooth effort Michael entered her. Erika cried out as if it were her first time. Her arms flailed a moment at the attack of sensuous pleasure that created bedlam within her system. He set the rhythm and she followed it, her legs circling him, trying to pull him into her, make him a part of her, letting there be no difference between them, letting them merge into a single entity. Erika's body thrashed below him. All thought, rationality, and reason had long since been replaced by the elemental pleasure created by the joining of a man and a woman.

Erika knew she was going to scream. She felt it coming, felt it with the rising level of tormenting pleasure that Michael instilled in her. He carried her toward a pinnacle that had to be the beginning or end of her existence. Together they created the wave of sensation, and in a flash fire of heat and light the two of them crashed through the barrier between life and creation.

CHAPTER 14

"Ms. St. James, your mother is here to see you." Erika's heart suddenly beat like a tom-tom. What did she want? Why did she continually show up, when she'd been silent for years?

"Send her in," she said, keeping the dryness out of her voice.

Alva came through the door in a short, mink jacket and a long skirt. A large smile curved her mouth, and for the first time in her life Erika saw herself reflected in her mother's face.

"Good morning, Mother. Please sit down."

Erika offered her a chair in front of the desk. Alva relinquished the jacket in her usual nonchalant manner, throwing it across the back of an empty chair. She dropped down in the other and crossed her legs.

"Mother, why are you here this time?"

"Erika, aren't you going to be hospitable and offer me some coffee?"

"Of course, Mother." Erika picked up the phone and spoke into it. "Stephanie, would you do me a favor and bring my mother some coffee, black with one sugar—"

"No sugar," Alva interrupted.

"No sugar," Erika repeated. She replaced the phone and returned her attention to her mother. "Now, what is it?"

Alva took a breath and looked around the large office. Carlton had occupied this office, but Erika had made it hers in the last year.

"I want you to spend Thanksgiving with me."

Erika's mouth dropped open. It was the last thing she expected to hear. She and her mother hadn't spent a holiday together since she was thirteen years old. She went there, but invariably they'd get into an argument and Erika would storm out of the house.

What was she after? Erika had sent her the check and she knew the monthly arrangement was still in effect, although she didn't know why.

"I thought you could bring Michael and we could all spend some time together."

Erika couldn't help her suspicions. Her mother had never wanted her around. Why would she want it now? Was it Michael she really wanted?

"Mother, if you want to invite Michael over, you don't need to drag me along for the ride."

"It isn't Michael I want to spend time with. I only suggested we invite him because he has no relatives here."

Erika didn't ask how she knew that. "It's not as if his family lives on the other side of the world. They're barely an hour away."

"I just thought you'd feel more comfortable having someone else around."

"You want to spend time with me? Why?"

"Erika, I'm your mother. For too long we've been at . . . odds with each other."

Was she saying she wanted to make up?

Stephanie tapped on the door and came in. Alva thanked her politely and sipped the steaming liquid.

"What's going on over at the house?"

Erika stared at her mother. She wasn't used to trading confidences with her mother. "What do you mean?"

"I came by. The place has enough guards to secure Fort Knox."

"You are exaggerating, Mother. We have added a few guards, but there is nothing to be concerned about."

"I'm glad to hear that."

Erika frowned. "Are you, Mother? Do you feel anything for me?"

"I love you, Erika."

Erika felt as if someone had punched her in the stomach. She'd longed to hear her mother say that to her, but she couldn't remember ever hearing her speak those words. She never thought they would have a impact on her life. She never thought she'd even hear them, let alone consider them.

"Mother, are you dying?"

"What would make you ask a question like that?"

"You come here, out of the blue, you make demands one minute, you don't explain anything, and suddenly you're inviting me to a family dinner. I want to know what's going on."

"There's nothing going on. It's a friendly invitation."

Erika hesitated, trying to find some inference, some degree of insincerity, in her mother's expression, but there was none.

"I believe Michael has plans for Thanksgiving," she said.

"Then you come. I'll even cook. You can help me."

For a moment Erika flashed back to a childhood fantasy. She'd wanted to do those things with her mother, but Alva never had time for her. Carlton had cooked with her. They had made a royal mess and the housekeepers had to clean it up, but Erika remembered it fondly. She also remembered wishing her mother had loved her enough to want to cook with her. Even now, Erika wondered whether she would fulfill the fantasy if she went, or would they end up screaming at each other, as they had at every previous encounter?

"Will you think about it?" her mother asked.

Erika hesitated, then nodded.

Alva stood and smiled. "Good." She paused. For a moment Erika thought she saw something flicker in her mother's eyes, something that looked strangely like regret. Did she regret asking her? "I'll call you."

With that, Alva St. James Redford made her exit. She grabbed her jacket and slipped it over her shoulder, then opened the door and went through it with all the panache of a seasoned actress knowing when to end a scene.

That walk was unmistakable. Michael saw Mrs. Redford walking toward the elevators at the end of the hall. Even with a daughter over thirty, she could still turn a head. Michael wondered if Erika knew how similar the two of them were. He smiled as she stepped into the elevator. He turned to Erika's office. She was usually put out when her mother visited. Michael thought he'd go console her. He'd been thinking of her since they woke up this morning. She was there when he woke, and he couldn't help making love to her again.

He knocked, then opened the door. Erika stood by the window. She didn't turn when he entered. *This one must have been bad,* he thought. Michael knew Erika refused to let her mother reduce her to tears, but the effort took a lot out of her.

Quietly he went to her, stopping close enough to feel the heat coming from her body. He wanted to hold her again, share her pain, make love to her again. Would this feeling ever go away? He hoped not.

"She invited me to cook with her."

"What?"

Erika turned around, leaning against the sill. "She invited me to Thanksgiving dinner. You, too. She asked me to come early so I could help her cook."

"Erika—"

"I told her you already had an engagement."

Michael wanted to spend Thanksgiving with her. His brothers had told him to bring her to dinner, but he'd never asked her. Now she was going to her mother's.

"I told her I'd think about it," she said.

Michael could see she was nervous. He didn't know what had happened between the two women. Every time they approached each other the electricity between them could singe hair. Michael knew it wasn't a good idea for the two of them to be alone.

"How do you feel about it?"

Erika waited a moment, composing herself. "Kind of numb."

"Do you want to go?"

Her gaze was direct. "To tell you the truth, I'm scared."

"Are you going?"

"I don't know. My first instinct is to say no."

"But—" he prompted.

Erika walked back to her desk. She leaned against the carved wood frame and stared at the carpeting. Michael waited, not wanting to rush her. He wanted to know what caused the rift between mother and daughter. He had the feeling Erika didn't talk about her mother, but he knew Alva Redford had a profound impact on her daughter.

Erika moved again. She sat down on the chair in front of her desk and looked up at him.

"In all the years and all the fights we've had, I always wanted my mother to love me."

"Erika, I'm sure she loves you." Michael didn't know that for sure, but he couldn't believe Alva Redford couldn't be proud of and love her own daughter. Erika was a wonderful person and he knew how much love she had to give. He couldn't believe she could have been a terrible child. People didn't change that drastically. If her mother had never loved her, it couldn't be because she wasn't a lovable person.

"She's blamed me all my life for my father," Erika said.

"What about your father?"

Her eyes were glassy, but she smiled. "He was the best father a child could ask for, and we did everything together." Erika spoke in this room, but Michael could see her gaze. It went past the windows and out into her childhood. "He'd take me to work on Saturdays. We'd go to the zoo and the movies. I suppose we did all the things normal kids and fathers do, but with us there was a special relationship, one in which my mother didn't participate. When my father died she blamed me."

"You! What did you do?"

"Nothing. He was in a car accident while he was on a business trip. He'd gone to buy me a teddy bear, and a drunk driver hit him while he was crossing the street. She told me if I hadn't asked him to bring me something back, he never would have been in that store and the drunk driver wouldn't have hit him."

Michael took the chair next to her, drawing it close enough to take her hands in his.

"Erika, you have to know you had nothing to do with your father's death."

"I never asked my father for a teddy bear. I didn't even know he was bringing one. It was my birthday, and we'd seen a movie about a bear. I guess that's where he got the idea."

"Did you ever tell her this?"

She shook her head. "What good would it have done? She didn't listen to me. She'd scream that it was my fault we were poor, that no man would look at her because of me, that I was an ugly child, and no man would ever want me. And she was right."

"That's not true," Michael said. "Don't you know the effect you have on men?" Didn't she understand how he felt? Hadn't their time together proved to her the depths of his feelings, the power she had over him?

"Yes," she laughed. "I know it. Look what happened in California. That time I went as far as getting engaged, and look how that turned out. My fiancé ran off with another woman." She stopped again. Michael still held her hands. "All my relationships turn out like that. I'm simply not cut out for the married with children lifestyle."

"God, are you wrong. You just haven't found the right man."

She stared at him then.

Dropping his hands, she continued, "I don't think he's out there. But we were talking about Thanksgiving."

"You don't have to go."

"What if she's trying to make up for the past?" Her confusion showed. "I don't know that I want to be the one slamming the door."

Michael smiled. After all the years and verbal argument her mother had given her, Erika was still willing to give her the benefit of the doubt. Michael had never known a fully beautiful person before, but Erika St. James had that inner beauty he'd read about but never expected to find.

"You want to go?" he asked. Confusion marred Erika's features. "I'll go with you," Michael said.

"You will? What about your family? Peter said you were all getting together for dinner."

"I'll send my regrets. This is obviously important to you, and I'd like to be with you."

Michael didn't know if she heard the emotion in his voice, but he'd suddenly gone soft inside and he couldn't do anything about it. Erika did that to him, and when he thought of her soft body pressed against his he didn't want to do anything except be with her.

She wanted her mother's love. It was natural to feel like that. He'd grown up in a loving family and couldn't imagine the life Erika must have had. Michael didn't want anyone to hurt her again, not even her mother. He'd be there to protect her. If Alva Redford had another agenda, Michael wanted to be there. If she had other plans, she'd have him to deal with.

Wanamaker's Department Store opened its downtown store at Thirteenth and Market Streets decades before any of the mall stores opened. Erika liked the Market Street store best. The building was old and distinctive, with chandeliers and huge display cases. Carlton had taken her here on her first shopping trip. The salesclerk had made her feel comfortable as she bought several pairs of jeans, three sweaters, and a jacket.

Today she needed a dress for dinner with her mother on Thanksgiving. Although she had a closet full of dresses at home, she needed something new to wear, something that would make her feel comfortable, less nervous. Dinner wasn't for another week, yet she was nervous already, and it didn't help that Michael had insisted on coming with her. He'd gone everywhere with her for the past few days. She admitted she loved being with him. All her vows of staying away from him, never allowing him to make love to her again, turned to water the moment he looked at her.

Erika checked her reflection in the three walls of mirror before her. She'd tried on seven dresses, and had narrowed her search to two—a black, straight gown covered with sequins and a green velvet. The one she had on was Christmas green with simple lines. It had a stand-up collar and long sleeves, and fit her to the waist, where it flared out into a full skirt that stopped short of her knees. She turned, inspecting the back. Her pearls would look great with this. She opened the door and stepped out of the dressing room. Michael waited for her in the dress department.

"What do you think?" she asked moments later. He had his back to her, walking near the after five dresses like a man lost in the lingerie department. His eyes opened wide when he saw her.

"You're . . . it's beautiful," he said.

"Do you think it looks all right?"

The look on his face gave her his answer. He came close to her so no one could hear what he said and whispered, "You look so good I could make love to you right here."

Erika blushed, bowing her head and feeling the rush of excitement that coursed through her at the prospect of making love. "I'd better change," she said, going back to the dressing room.

Ten minutes later Michael took her box under his arm and led her away from the department. Erika noticed him looking around.

"Michael, stop doing that."

"Doing what?"

"Looking over your shoulder as if you're expecting someone to be there."

"I'm just being cautious. If Frank Mason has traced me here, I want to be prepared for him."

"If he did kill the judge and the lawyer, then he's probably miles away from here by now."

"You'd think any sane man would be, but Frank Mason isn't sane."

Erika didn't want to discuss Frank Mason. She wanted to have a good time shopping and spending the afternoon with Michael. "Let's go to the shoe department," she said, changing the subject. Michael didn't argue. He led her to the elevators and together they found shoes and other accessories she'd need for her monumental dinner.

When Michael had added three additional boxes and several bags to his load they went to the restaurant for lunch. They were shown to a quiet table in the back, away from the view of the entrance. Michael seemed to approve of the table, but he sat facing the room.

"You're enjoying this, aren't you?" Michael asked.

"I'm having a wonderful time."

Michael could see it. Her expression was animated and happy. He only wished he could feel just as carefree as she did. Erika had the advantage of never having met Frank Mason. Michael had seen the destructive nature of the man, and knew that he didn't care about killing in public.

The police had found nothing more to connect Frank with the two deaths, but Michael didn't like coincidences—Frank escaped and the judge and lawyer associated with his case had both been gruesomely killed.

"Michael," Erika said, calling him out of his musings. "You're ignoring me."

"I couldn't ignore you if I tried."

The four-wheel drive jeep, with mud covering it from his mountain trek, would have looked out of place on the quiet street where Michael Lawrence now lived. Frank knew that, and drove down the street in a rented Lexus. He saw the towering iron gates that protected a house too far from the street to be seen. He smiled. *Neither the gates nor the guards will save Michael Lawrence,* Frank thought. He and Michael had unfinished business, and they were on a collision course in which Frank knew he'd be the victor.

He drove several miles until he found a place to eat, then stopped to kill time. He ordered a short meal and ate it leisurely before turning back toward the house again. He took in the six-foot stone wall that stretched for a mile before reaching the iron gates. The wall was easy enough to scale. The very length of it made it difficult to guard. Although there could be camera surveillance, Frank knew he could get around it. Michael Lawrence's time was coming.

And coming soon.

But first he had other business. He needed to talk to someone. Frank speeded up as the mansion wall disappeared from his rearview mirror.

The lights of Center City came into view within half an hour. Frank drove down Broad Street to Chestnut, then headed over to the university. Parking was at a premium there, especially during the day. He parked in a nearby lot and walked the distance to one of the small, cramped houses along Thirty-eighth Street.

Getting inside was a snap. He knew the timing, knew the nurse would be away and he'd be alone. He sat in the living room, reading.

"Good afternoon, Counselor."

Malick Wainscott raised a white eyebrow at the unexpected arrival of an uninvited guest.

"I see an introduction would be unnecessary," he paused. "You can calm down. I'm not here for you."

"What the hell do you want?" Wainscott's face turned redder than its natural ruddy color.

"I have a message for Michael Lawrence, and I need you to give it to him."

"Do I look like a delivery boy?"

Frank thought the old man had guts. He was too incapacitated to do anything to protect himself if it had been Frank's intention to harm him, but he held his ground—or his chair, Frank thought.

Frank wasn't angered in the least, although there was a time he would have beaten a man into submission for making a comment like that. Today he didn't need the old man's heart giving out before he'd completed his mission.

"Michael Lawrence. You know him." Frank stated fact, but the old man nodded, anyway. "He went to the mall today. Little shopping expedition. I guess they're getting a jump on the Christmas crowd."

Malick Wainscott's face gave nothing away at the news Frank had just given him. Frank had never seen him in court, but he thought he must have been awesome. Frank had watched the lawyers. It was a hobby of his, people watching. He'd studied his own lawyer and Abby's and the lawyers pleading other cases, cases he knew nothing about. He'd become an authority on who would win, who had the better argument, and who could keep their cool even when surprises were presented. Which one was getting through to the judge, and which one had only part of his attention. Malick Wainscott was the kind of lawyer who would win nine times out of ten.

"What's the message?" he asked.

"Tell him I know where he is and he can't escape me. Adding guards to the estate won't save him or that pretty little heiress."

"Why do you want to harm Michael? He represented you."

"I'd love to stay and debate the pros and cons of Michael Lawrence's ability to represent me, but I have a previous appointment and your nurse should be back in . . ." He consulted his watch. "Five minutes," he finished. "Don't forget to give Mr. Lawrence my message. You have a nice day, now."

"Appointment where? What are you planning to do?"

Frank smiled. He loved seeing the strong grovel. It wasn't something he thought he'd see in Malick Wainscott, but then he was a loyal friend to Michael Lawrence, and Frank held loyalty high in his estimation of a person's worth. He liked Malick Wainscott.

"Don't worry. I'm not ready for Michael Lawrence yet, but soon. Soon." Frank saluted him and retraced his steps to the front door.

Malick reached for the phone the moment he heard the door close. Checking the window he saw Frank Mason walking down the street. His steps were even and unhurried. Malick may have had a reasonable doubt before, but it was gone now. Frank was definitely stalking Michael, and he had to let him know.

Dialing Michael's number he reached the maid, who told him Michael and Erika had not returned yet.

"I need them to call me the moment they return," he told her, unable to keep the excitement out of his voice. "No matter what time. I have to talk to Michael."

"I understand, Mr. Wainscott," the maid said.

Malick said good-bye and replaced the phone receiver. Frank Mason had a lot of nerve. He'd killed four people in the last three weeks and he walked around the streets as if he had a perfect right to mingle with law-abiding citizens. He didn't, and he had no right to leave messages for Michael. Malick felt his heart accelerate and he grabbed for his pills. Taking one, he waited for the pressure to calm down. Then, remembering his duty, Malick lifted the phone and dialed 9-1-1.

The blue and red flashing lights on the cars with Philadelphia Police Department written on the sides like a huge blue stencil caught Michael's attention the moment he and Erika turned the corner. Within seconds he was running toward Malick's house, Erika in tow.

He didn't stop to knock, but burst through the front door and looked around quickly.

"Is he all right?" he asked the nurse who stopped as he'd made his entrance.

"Yes," she said. "He's in there with the police." She pointed toward the living room area.

Michael immediately headed for it. Malick sat up in his favorite chair. Three uniformed policemen and two detectives stood in the room.

"Michael!" Malick called when he noticed him.

"What's going on here?" Michael addressed the question to the room.

"Are you Michael Lawrence?" one of the plainclothes men asked him in a voice that told him he was the leader of this small assembly.

Michael nodded.

"Mr. Wainscott here tells us he had a visitor this afternoon. It appears Frank Mason has been here."

"Here! Malick, are you all right?"

"I'm fine. He didn't harm me. He wanted me to deliver a message to you."

Erika, still holding his hand, squeezed it tighter.

"What message?"

Malick related the details of Frank's earlier visit while the policemen checked their notes to see that the story remained unchanged.

When Malick finished, one of the detectives said, "The murders referred to by Wainscott are out of our jurisdiction, but we'll be reporting the details of this incident to the New Jersey authorities."

"Is that all?" Erika spoke up.

"No, Ma'am. Mr. Mason is an escaped convict and we'll do everything we can to find him, but we don't have much to go on."

The second detective addressed Malick. "Do you have any idea where he might have been going when he left here?"

"No," Malick answered. "But he told me he was going to kill Michael. I suggest you give him some protection."

"We'll add more patrol cars to the areas around your house and your estate." He glanced at Michael and Erika. "But that's about all we can do."

"Thank you, Officer," Michael said. He knew there was little the police could do. They had budget problems, huge case loads and the size of the city were all public knowledge.

"If you remember anything you haven't told us," the detective went on, "please call." He handed Malick and Michael cards, then said good day.

"I'll see them to the door," Erika said. She led the way and the officers followed. Michael sat down across from Malick when they were alone.

"You look tired," he told his friend. "It must have been a long afternoon."

"It has been," said a voice from the door. The voice was strong and authoritative. Both men turned. The nurse, holding a small tray, stood there. Erika stood next to her. They came into the room.

"Mr. Wainscott has had too much excitement for one afternoon."

"Don't mind her," Malick said. "She's just feeling a little guilty. Frank came while she was out having the prescription filled."

The nurse looked hurt for a moment. Then she regained her composure and handed Malick a glass of water, followed by a small white cup with two pills in it. Malick took them without comment and drank the water.

"He's going to take a nap now," she said, leaving no area for argument by any of the room's participants. "I'll have to ask you to leave."

"We understand," Erika said. Michael stood and she came to him, taking his arm.

"I don't think she'll ever leave me alone again," Malick said.

"Malick, I think you like the attention," Erika told him. She bent and kissed him on the cheek.

The old man smiled.

CHAPTER 15

Erika turned in front of the mirror in her bedroom. Finally Thanksgiving had arrived, and they were going to dinner at her mother's. She wore the green velvet dress, a single strand of pearls, and pearl drop earrings. Her hand went to her belly and she took a deep breath. The butterflies had greeted her when she woke this morning and threatened to stay all day.

For the past week she hadn't had time to think about her mother, with Frank Mason at the top of her mind. Every day she and Michael had gone to see Malick. Each time they stepped outside the house or the office Erika had the uneasy feeling of being watched. Although she never saw anyone, she knew someone's eyes were always on her.

She shrugged it off, telling herself she had transferred Malick's experience to herself. She hadn't seen anyone and if Frank Mason knew what was good for him, he'd be long gone by now. She hadn't told Michael. It was just a feeling. There was nobody there.

Erika took one last look in the mirror and picked up her coat from the bed. Leaving the room, she went down the staircase. Michael met her at the bottom.

"You look grand," he said. "Your mother will like the dress."

He was the most perceptive man she'd ever met. He knew even more than she did that she wanted the dress for approval.

"Did you talk to your brothers?" she asked as he took her coat and held it while she slipped her arms inside it.

"They all send their love, and said you are missing the best walnut stuffing in the world."

Erika smiled. "It's not too late, Michael. I can go to my mother's alone. You can spend the day with your family."

"I spoke to my mother, too," he said, ignoring her comment. "She's still with my aunt and will not be returning until the holidays. We can miss one Thanksgiving, or if we leave early we can always show up for the sweet potato pie."

Michael held the door open for her and Erika walked out into the cold November afternoon. The wind hit her and she pulled her coat closer around her. Michael closed the door and they got into the car.

The staff had been given the day off except for the guards, so they drove themselves. Alva Redford lived in Springfield, a distance of about forty miles from central Philadelphia. Traffic was slow going through the city. Michael took Route 95 to the Blue Route. The road, a superhighway of rolling hills, generally packed with commuters on any other Thursday, was surprisingly deserted. Michael relaxed and the needle on the speedometer edged up a notch.

Erika was too nervous to talk. She sat quietly next to him and watched the scenery whiz by. What was going to happen at her mother's? Did Alva have an ulterior motive in inviting them to dinner, and what was it? Every other time Erika had been with her mother the results had been disastrous. Why shouldn't she think they would be the same today? And be prepared for them? Yet she couldn't think of anything her mother would want from her. Alva had plenty of money, with the checks that Graves Enterprises sent to her each month.

Could she want her love? Erika shivered at the thought. At this stage in her life, could her mother really want to make amends? A numbness went through her. If that was her mother's intention, Erika didn't know if she could handle that. She'd never had any practice. Her mother had been out of her life since she met Carlton. His wife was already dead when they met. The only women in the household were the maids and cooks. Erika had gotten to know some of them, but none of them took on the role of substitute mother.

Erika's attention came back to the car and Michael's driving. She felt, more than saw, the change in him. Panic caught in her throat as she watched him pump the brakes and felt the car accelerate.

"What's wrong?" she asked stupidly.

"The brakes aren't working."

"Try the emergency brake."

Michael stepped on it. Nothing happened. The car careened forward at an extraordinary speed. The road had been sparsely travelled, but now there were cars everywhere. Michael weaved in and out of traffic, avoiding one collision after another. Erika's heart beat like a drum. The guardrail sailed past her in a silver blur.

"Erika, I want you to climb over the seat and get into the back."

"What are you going to do?"

Michael didn't answer. He shifted onto the shoulder past an eighteen wheeler, then shot back onto the paved road. The truck blew its airhorn in protest of such a foolhardy act.

"Put the seatbelt on and lie down."

Putting her trust in him, she didn't waste time arguing, but climbed over the seat and fell into the back. Righting herself she put on the seatbelt.

Looking up she saw a stream of traffic coming in at Exit Two. Both lanes ahead had cars in them. They had no place to go.

"What are you going to do?" she whispered.

Michael switched to the fast lane, cutting off cars and eliciting a blare of horns. Reaching the left shoulder, he sped past a parked highway patrol car at ninety miles an hour. The car immediately began following him. The blue and red flashing lights did nothing to help slow down the car. More and more traffic seemed to come into the roadway.

"Lie down Erika. I'm going to stop this thing."

"How?" she asked. "How are you going to stop? There's nothing in front of us but other cars."

"I'm going to use the wall. Now lie down."

Erika looked to the side. The sound wall built alongside neighborhoods to cut down on the traffic noise stretched ahead. Michael cut in front of a truck and got on the opposite shoulder. The police car followed them.

"Michael, do you know what you're doing?"

"No, but I don't have a choice!" he shouted. "Now get down."

She huddled behind Michael and waited. The car seemed to go faster when she couldn't see what was happening. Then she heard the sound of metal against stone. Erika had never heard anything more frightening in her life. She clenched her teeth and squeezed her eyes shut. The car bumped and grated against the wall, then it appeared to strike something. She rolled against the restraint, bumping her head on the back of Michael's seat. She heard the "whooshing" sound of the air bag being released. The car bumped over uneven ground, throwing her around like a rag doll. Finally, it came to a halt.

For a moment she didn't move. While the air had rushed by the car, creating a harsh sound, all she heard now was the faint ticking of a crushed engine.

"Michael," she called. He didn't answer. Erika released her belt and sat up. Through the windows she saw only sky. The car had passed the sound wall and hit the guardrail. It teetered there. Michael lay unconscious against the air bag, which had opened and pushed him back in his seat.

She shifted to see if he was all right.

"Don't move!"

Erika faintly heard the shout from outside the car. She turned her head, but it was too late. The car pitched forward. She gasped as it went over the railing and picked up momentum as it careened through the brush. Erika screamed as she was thrown back and forth over the seats. She didn't think the car would stop. When it did, she felt like a crash dummy. Her body was thrown against the window. A blinding pain ripped through her head, bringing tears to her eyes. Reaching up, she tried to touch her head. Everything hurt, and she groaned. She felt blood in her eye and tried to wipe it away. Everything was a blur. She blinked, trying to focus, but her head was heavy and she couldn't see. Resting her head, she fought to remain conscious, but she felt her head spinning. She wanted it to stop, but she couldn't stop it. Then she was falling, falling down a long tunnel. She couldn't fall, she told herself. Michael needed her. She needed to know that he was all right. She fought the darkening light closing in around her. It hurt and the dark felt good, cool, and welcoming.

"Michael," Erika moaned.

She lost the fight and fainted.

Michael groaned at the pain. He tried to open his eyes, but the pain was too much. Moving his hand, he found something restraining him. He forced his eyes open. The hospital room was unmistakable. Then it came back. The car, the accident, Erika.

Where was Erika? He searched the bed for the bell that would summon a nurse. The pain made him groan again.

"Michael," he heard his name.

Michael opened his eyes again. This time the pain was worse. He thought he saw Malick, but he couldn't. Malick wasn't here. Then the darkness came. He couldn't remember what he'd been thinking of, just that the darkness felt good and he let it take him away.

When Michael woke again, it was daylight. It hurt even more to do anything—open his eyes, raise his arm, clear his head so he could think clearly—but he forced himself.

"Peter?" he called, squinting. The man sleeping in the chair by his bed looked like his brother.

The man in the chair moved and was instantly at his bedside. "Michael, you're awake." It was Peter. "How do you feel?"

"Like I fell off a mountain."

Peter laughed. "You aren't far from the truth. Do you remember the accident?"

He tried to nod, immediately realizing that it wasn't a good idea. "Yes," he said. "Erika? Is she all right?"

"She'll be fine. She has a concussion, some cuts and bruises. Otherwise she's as good as new. Malick and her mother are with her."

"Her mother?" Michael touched his head. "Oh, yes, we were going to have dinner with her tonight."

"I'm afraid that was last night. We got the news just as we were sitting down to eat. Everyone picked up and left."

"They're all here?"

"Including mother. She flew down last night."

Michael looked around, wondering where everyone was.

"They're in the waiting area," Peter explained. "I'll let them know you're awake."

"Not yet." Michael knew his brother well. Even though yesterday was Thanksgiving, he knew Peter would have found out something about the accident. "What happened to the car?"

"It had so little brake fluid in it, it might as well have been empty."

"That's why they didn't work." Michael found the control for the bed and raised himself to a sitting position.

"That was only part of it," Peter explained. "The brake line had also been slit. If the low fluid didn't give out, pumping it onto the ground surely would have."

"What about Frank Mason? Has anyone spotted him?"

"No luck there. I talked to the policeman who took the report. At my insistence they checked the car for fingerprints. We only found yours and Erika's."

Michael was beginning to feel better. "I suppose that means Frank is confident that everything is under control. He was always like that, knowing he had the upper hand."

"He doesn't have the upper hand here," Peter said, anger in his voice. "Michael, you've got to hire someone to look out for you."

"I've already done that. I hired two bodyguards."

"Where are they?"

"I don't know. I had them tailing Erika. I haven't seen them in a while, but I know they're close by."

"They surely aren't doing their job."

"I still have confidence in them," Michael said. "Erika is all right and they were hired to guard her person, not to check on the vehicles. In fact, they are rarely on the estate."

"Why?"

"Erika didn't want a bodyguard. I hired them without her knowledge."

"She's going to have to find out now."

"I don't think that will be a problem after the accident."

Peter became very quiet for a moment. Michael was getting tired, but he wanted to see Erika, see for himself that she was fine. He checked the

IV in his hand and followed the clear tubing up to the plastic bag hanging over his head. He didn't think he could get out of bed.

"Michael, have you considered that there might be another person, other than Frank, behind this?"

"What? Peter, you were the person who noticed the connection between the judge and the lawyer's deaths."

"I know, but I want to make sure we're not focusing so much on Frank Mason that we overlook someone else."

"Who?"

"I have no idea." Peter spread his hands. "Maybe someone in Erika's past."

Alva Redford's face came to mind. She'd come from nowhere and invited her daughter to dinner. While the two of them had been estranged for years, she suddenly decided to break bread with her daughter. When Michael had first met her, she and Erika had been in the middle of an argument. One other time that he knew of, Alva had appeared and an argument resulted. Then she invited them to dinner.

"Peter," Michael finally said. "I want you to check out Alva St. James Redford."

"Erika's mother?"

"The two of them don't get on." Michael told him his concerns and Peter agreed to check into the files and see what he could find. "Also, find out what connection Alva Redford had with Carlton Lipton-Graves."

Michael yawned and closed his eyes. His eyelids grew heavy. The effort to keep them open taxed his energy. Peter didn't speak and soon Michael entered a warm, fuzzy world where Erika waited.

"Malick, you should be in this chair," Erika admonished.

"Shhh," he quieted her. "This is against all the hospital rules and if we get caught they'll probably keep our dinner from us."

Erika snickered behind her hand. Malick wheeled her through the hospital corridors toward Michael's room. Erika hadn't seen him since they were brought in, two days ago. She didn't remember the ambulance ride. She was afraid Michael was seriously hurt, that Malick hadn't told her the truth and he was unconscious, in a coma, unable to speak or see. Malick stopped the wheelchair in front of a door that looked much like the door to her room. He turned her around and pulled her into the room. When he wheeled her around, she saw that Michael stood near the window.

His room was the same as hers, with standard hospital furniture, but every space in hers was covered with flowers. She wondered how so many people could have heard about the accident so quickly and immediately sent flowers. A lot of them were from people in the office, but several were from her friends. She felt a little guilty that she hadn't had time for them in the past, and resolved to correct that in the future.

Michael wore a blue velour robe, matching the pink one she wore. Malick's nurse had followed instructions in buying them something other than hospital nightclothes, even if she had dressed them like His and Her bookends.

Michael turned as the door closed.

"Erika," he said, coming to her and kneeling next to her chair. "I've been going out of my mind with worry."

Erika didn't notice Malick leaving them. She'd completely forgotten him when she saw Michael. His face had brush burns from the air bag. His skin was raw in places and looked painful. Other than that, his features were as handsome as she remembered. Then she thought of her own state. Without makeup and bruised, her hair flat to her head, she must look like a monster.

"How's your head? Peter told me you had a concussion." He touched her. Erika's hand covered his.

"He came to see me. Your whole family came in one by one. They're very nice people. I liked them."

"I hope they weren't too overwhelming. They can be."

She smiled. "They were concerned about you."

"I was concerned about you."

Erika's heart swelled large enough to lodge in her throat. "The doctors say the headaches will go away in a few days. I'll be as good as new before you know it. And you, what have they said about you?"

"I'm being discharged tomorrow morning."

Erika's heart dropped. "They haven't told me when I will be able to leave."

"It will be soon."

Michael stood up. He opened his hands and she put hers in them. With him helping her, she stood up. He led her to a chair and sat her down. Then he took the other chair.

"Erika, it's time for the bodyguards."

"I agree," she said.

Michael thought he was going to have to argue with her, but she eliminated the need for his well-planned speech. "Two of them will be here when you're discharged, and from then until Frank Mason is caught."

Erika began to shake. She gripped his hands tightly. "I've never been so scared in my life. When I saw you . . ." Her voice cracked. "I thought you were—"

"Erika, stop. We're both fine. And nothing is going to happen to us."

She took a deep breath. "I didn't really believe it could happen until we were in the car. Even Malick's house seemed unreal, but you pumping that brake made me think I was going to die."

Michael left his chair. He pulled her into his arms and held her. Erika trembled against him. He cradled her head against his shoulder. He was angry. Frank had made her scared, and Michael didn't like that. He didn't like him putting her in danger. She could have been killed. He had to do something. He had to find Frank. This cat and mouse game had gone on long enough.

It was time for them to have their stand.

Frank laughed, threw his head back and bellowed. Michael Lawrence was as predictable as night falling. He'd played right into his hands, as if he didn't know the cards were stacked against him. Of course, Frank had thought he'd only have an accident in town. Going over a ravine and spending a couple of days in the hospital was a far better script than the one he'd written. And he gladly accepted the revision.

Michael's little accident had forced his family to join him. From the smallest child to the oldest adult, they'd all run to his rescue, like they could do something. And they must have left in an incredible hurry. From the looks of things, they took only enough time to clear the dinner dishes.

Frank walked about the dining room, a sneer on his face. This looked like a lawyer's house. He hated lawyers. If he could have one wish in life it would be to eradicate the world of lawyers. If he was lucky, by this time next week there would be at least one less in the world, maybe two if they came home together.

Frank looked around, went through the kitchen. The door to the garage was unlocked and the car was missing. He looked up. The garage door was controlled by a remote. More than likely they would enter through this door. To be on the safe side, he wired both doors.

He went to work then. The wires matched the molding, as if he'd had a blueprint of the interior of the house. No one would notice it if they came in, but they weren't going to get the chance. Opening the door would arm the device. Ten minutes later, when everyone was safely inside the folds of their own home, it would blow. The ensuing explosive would travel through to the other door, either by wire or heat, and it, too, would flare up like an exploding rocket.

He was sorry he wouldn't be here to see it. This kind of an explosion was a work of art, and Frank enjoyed art. But he knew better than to be anywhere near this when the candles were lit. This wasn't his primary target. He needed to concentrate on Michael Lawrence. It might not be as easy to penetrate the grounds of that estate, but he could certainly draw him out into the open. The two of them knew they had to meet sooner or later, and Frank wanted it to be sooner. This was his method. His family had run to him when he was hurt. Michael would certainly return the favor. Would he be surprised at his welcoming committee.

"Kaboom," Frank said, then laughed, laughed to the heavens. The sound echoed off the furniture, the woodwork, the kitchen sink, and gleaming refrigerator. It was a wicked laugh, the kind that Frank had given the judge when he'd sentenced him to a mental hospital. Well, the judge was certainly not laughing now. His time had come. Now it was Michael's time, and it was almost out.

CHAPTER 16

Erika's discharge came twenty-four hours after Michael's. The company limousine came to pick her up and drive her to the house. Stiffly she got out of the backseat, leaning heavily on Michael for support.

"I don't think I'll be able to return to work for a few days," she joked.

Michael turned around and swung her into his arms. "Michael," Erika said in surprise. "You shouldn't be carrying me. You were in an accident, too."

"I had on a seatbelt and from what the officers told me, you didn't."

Erika placed her head on his shoulder and hugged him. He smelled good and she wanted to kiss him at that moment. She settled for holding him close.

Inside, Michael took her directly to her room, but he didn't lower her to the floor. "I'm not very tired," she said.

"Is that an invitation?"

Erika blushed, lowering her head.

"As much as I'd like to oblige you, I'm sure it would delay any healing you have yet to do."

He set her on her feet and kissed her briefly. Erika didn't believe she'd said that. She did feel giddy, but then she felt that way each time Michael came near her. He'd been here for months. She should be used to his presence. Yet she couldn't control her emotions whenever he was around.

"If you need to rest before lunch I can have it postponed," Michael said.

"There's no need," she said.

"We have guests." Michael raised his eyebrows.

"We do?" She braced herself for the news that her mother was downstairs. At the hospital Alva Redford had acted as if her own life was in danger.

"My family and Malick. They refused to go home until they knew you'd be all right."

Erika smiled. She wasn't sure if she was relieved or upset. "They probably wanted some time with you." He hadn't really spent any time with them since he returned from Maryland. She was just an excuse for them to get to see him. Erika had wished for brothers and sisters when she was a child—she used to imagine her life with many relatives—but her mother never had any other children.

"I'll clean up and come down in a few minutes."

Michael kissed her on the forehead and left the room. Moments later Tess came in and helped her shower and change. She was stiff, and the effort took a lot out of her.

"Would you like me to call Mr. Lawrence?" Tess asked when they stood at the top of the massive staircase. Erika heard voices coming from different areas of the house. It had been a very long time since they had guests. Certainly not in the year since she'd returned and Carlton had been sick. Only Carlton's lawyers and an occasional friend dropping by, nothing like the sounds she could hear now.

"I think I can make it down if you let me lean on you." Erika didn't want Michael knowing how stiff she still was. She had the feeling he'd confine her to bed if he knew.

At the bottom of the steps she thanked Tess, and the young maid went toward the kitchen. Erika went to the salon. Hoping it was empty, she needed a moment to prepare herself. She went inside.

She thought she'd been lucky until a strong, musical voice said, "Hello."

Erika turned toward it. Sitting in one of the reclining chairs was a brown-skinned woman with soft features. She nursed a baby in her arms.

"I'm Catherine, Bobby's wife. You must be Erika."

Erika nodded and went to sit next to her.

"I couldn't come to the hospital with the baby, but I'm glad you're all right."

"Thank you," Erika said. She couldn't help looking at the child in Michael's sister-in-law's arms, dressed in a pink outfit. Erika assumed it was a girl. "How old is she?" she asked.

"Three weeks."

"I've never seen a baby that small," Erika said in wonder.

Catherine leaned forward, adjusting her clothing. The child was asleep. She looked like a small doll.

"Can I touch her?" she asked cautiously.

"Sure," Catherine said. "Would you like to hold her?"

Erika's eyes opened wide. "I'd love to . . . but . . . I never . . . I never held a baby."

Catherine looked at her kindly. "You must have been an only child."

"I was," Erika said.

Catherine slid forward in the chair, then stood up. "I had three brothers," she told Erika, "and I was the oldest. I got to hold many babies."

Catherine took a step toward her.

"What do I do?" Erika asked, scared but wanting the experience.

"Didn't you ever have a babysitting job?" Catherine asked her.

"No." Erika suddenly felt as if she'd missed out on something.

"Just be sure to support her head." Catherine laid the baby in her arms. Erika held her breath.

"She's so light," Erika said, staring at the sleeping child. "Will she wake up?"

"She's a good sleeper. She won't wake for at least an hour."

Instinctively Erika rocked the baby. She put her finger in the tiny hand. The child curled her perfect little fingers around it, and Erika smiled as if a miracle had occurred. "What's her name?"

"Roberta Ellen," she said. "After her two grandmothers."

Erika glanced up. "They must be very proud."

The door opened and Michael came in. He'd changed into grey slacks and a fishermen's-knit white sweater. He came forward and kissed Catherine on the cheek, then sat next to Erika on the sofa.

"Is lunch nearly ready?" Catherine asked.

Michael nodded. "As soon as everyone gets here we can go in."

"If you'll be all right, I'll go hurry them up."

"I'll be fine," Michael answered.

Catherine laughed at him.

Erika nodded to her and she left the room. As soon as the door closed Michael took her chin and turned her to face him. He kissed her on the mouth. "I missed you."

"I missed you, too."

He kissed her again and was still kissing her when the door opened.

"Excuse me, but you two keep that up and you'll have one of those of your own." Erika and Michael looked up. Peter walked over with a smile on his face. "How do you feel?" he asked.

Before she could answer, the rest of the family arrived—Bobby, Catherine, and Michael's mother, Ellen—all of them asking the same question. Erika had met them at the hospital. Ellen Lawrence was shorter than anyone in her family. She was a petite woman who reminded Erika of a college professor she'd had her freshman year in college who was stern and competent. Ellen Lawrence had the same manner, and Erika thought she didn't like her.

Michael stood up. "We're all here now. Why don't we go in?"

"I'll take her," Michael's mother said, scooping the baby from Erika's arms as if she were more competent than Erika. She turned and led the assembly toward the dining room. Michael helped her up and they followed everyone into the room.

Lunch may have begun on a strained note, but it quickly turned to fun and laughter. The brothers began with stories of small accidents in their childhood. Most of the incidents included things they hadn't told their parents about. Soon everyone was laughing, including Ellen Lawrence. Her face was marked with laughter at the antics of her children. The only time it changed was when her eyes were shining with love over her grandchild, still sleeping in a bassinet near her mother, and when she looked at Erika.

Erika couldn't help looking at Ellen. The woman didn't like her. Erika could tell by the way she never made eye contact. She looked away each time Erika's gaze found her. Did she blame her for the accident? Was it her fault that Michael's life was in danger? They both could have died in the accident. Didn't she see that? Erika didn't think so.

When everyone was nearly through with the coffee, Erika was visibly tired. Malick noticed it and suggested she go to bed. At that point, everyone decided they needed to begin their trips home, and the party broke up.

"There's no need for you all to leave," Erika said. "I'm sure Michael would like you to stay for a longer visit."

"I have to go, anyway," Bobby said. "There's work tomorrow."

The rest of the party echoed his excuse and soon they were kissing each other good-bye.

Catherine came over to Erika as she stood at the door. She carried Roberta. "I enjoyed myself," she said.

Erika looked at her and at the baby. "I'm so glad you came," she told her. She liked Catherine. "Thank you for letting me hold her." Erika ran her hand lightly over the baby's arm. The child's hands were covered, but Erika let her grasp her finger, anyway. Tears gathered in her eyes at the tiny hand holding hers. Catherine kissed her on cheek, whispering good-bye and going to the car where Ellen Lawrence already sat. Michael leaned over his mother and kissed her. They seated the baby in the child's seat and waved as they started down the driveway.

"Good bye, Erika," Peter said. "I hope to see you soon."

She waved and he, too, left.

Michael came back to her. "You're dead on your feet," he said. "Come on." He pushed her inside and closed the door. They walked to the steps before Michael lifted her and carried her to her room. This time he didn't send Tess in to help her. He unzipped her dress and took it off. In moments he had her in a gown and under the covers. The bruises on her body were dark patches of blue blemishes. Michael didn't mention them. He got her some water and two white tablets.

Leaning her against him, he watched her take the painkillers and drink the water.

"Sleep now," he said, laying her back. Michael turned the lights off and left the room, but she didn't sleep. She wondered about his mother. She had come to her hospital room the day Erika woke up, but she'd hardly had a word to say. What had she done? She wasn't trying to marry her son. Some mothers found that a threat. She was friendly toward Catherine, but Catherine had given her a grandchild, and that could be the difference.

Smiling, she thought of the baby. She hardly weighed anything. Erika loved holding her. She'd never wanted to have a child. At thirty-four, she'd never held a baby in her arms before. She hadn't wanted to give the child up. If Ellen Lawrence hadn't taken her, Erika would have been content to hold her the rest of the afternoon.

How could a mother hold her child, then not want it around? Erika thought of the way her mother had treated her as a child. A single tear formed in her eye and fell onto the pillow.

When Erika woke it was dark. The house was quiet and she felt much better. Getting up she had a slight headache, and took a pill for it. She went downstairs. Voices came from the living room. She recognized Michael's deep voice. Erika wondered who else was there. She went to the door.

"Here's Erika now," Michael said. He stood and came toward her. "Let me introduce Connie Forester and Adrienne Dantley. They're the bodyguards I've hired."

"Hello," Erika said.

"We know about the accident," the shorter woman, Connie, said. "We'll make sure nothing like that happens again."

Erika sat down. "What will you do? I mean, what do bodyguards do?"

"One of us will be with you at all times," Adrienne replied. "We'll make sure the cars are checked, and that no one gets in to see you that you don't want to see."

"What about Michael?" She glanced at him.

"I'm your bodyguard," Connie told her. "Adrienne is Michael's."

Erika didn't know if she liked that arrangement. When she'd agreed to bodyguards, she'd expected men; big, muscular, bouncer types. Not two women, two pretty women.

Michael could see that Erika looked uncomfortable. He understood. Even though it was for her own good, she was giving up her freedom, her ability to come and go as she pleased without the need for a third party looking over her shoulder.

"Has Michael shown you to your rooms?" she asked.

They nodded.

"You were asleep, but I need to get into your room now so I can check out alternative accesses," Connie said.

"Alternative access?"

"Windows, balcony, even vines on the outer walls," she translated.

"Why don't you do that now? You know where the room is?"

She nodded and the two of them left.

"I'm going to hate this," Erika said the moment the door closed.

"Give it time, Erika," Michael said calmly. "We both know this is necessary."

"I don't know that," she argued.

"Erika, you can barely move after that accident. You could have died, because Frank Mason tampered with the brakes of that car." Michael paused to come around to her. "Erika, it will be all right. After a while you won't even notice they're there."

Erika sighed. She knew they needed to protect themselves, but she hadn't expected to have to account for her time to another person, and that's exactly what she'd have to do.

"You'll be home for a few days. The two of you will have time to become friends."

"While you and Adrienne become . . . *friends,"* she said, sneering.

"You're jealous," Michael stated.

"I am not," she denied.

Michael came around the sofa and stood in front of her. It made him feel good that she was jealous. "You have no need to be," he said. Placing his hands on either side of her head, he leaned over her, and her head fell back against the sofa. "I'm already in love with you."

Michael kissed her, hard and deep. Erika reached for him, and his hands went to her waist and he pulled her forward. The two of them fell back and ended on the soft carpet. Michael raised his head to look at her.

"Am I hurting you?" he asked.

She took his face in her hands and pulled him close to her. "Yes," she whispered just before their mouths melded. Michael lay across her, and even though her answer meant he wasn't hurting her, he didn't want her to carry his full weight. He shifted, slipping his arms around her and pulling her close to him. His tongue swept inside her mouth and he felt himself trembling in the wake of the rapturous love that poured from him. She wasn't like any woman he'd ever known. She made him think of families, of loving, of wanting nothing more than to please her for the rest of his life.

"Michael," she said against his mouth.

"Hmmm," he said, refusing to break contact. He couldn't. She tasted too good. And she had him. His mouth left hers and he kissed her cheek, her chin, her bottom lip.

"Michael, if we don't stop—"

He took her mouth again, cutting her speech. He knew he should listen, but he was too far gone. He wanted her too much. She'd frightened him when she'd been in the hospital, and this afternoon when she looked so weak. She didn't look weak now, and she didn't feel weak. She felt wonderful and her perfume drove him crazy. He reached for her sweater and slipped his hand under it.

"Stop," she said, pushing herself back. "Michael! The guards. They could walk in on us at any moment."

It wasn't the guards that came in, but Tess, the maid. She sized them up. Michael checked Erika. The blood in her face colored it a shade darker.

"Did you fall?" Tess asked, coming to her.

Michael helped Erika to her feet.

"Yes, Tess, she fell." He could hardly keep the laughter out of his voice.

"I'll help her, Sir." Tess took hold of Erika's arm. "Your brother is on the phone. There's been an explosion."

The two of them looked at each other for a moment, then quickly got up and rushed to the library. Erika got there only a second behind Michael. He was on the phone asking all the newspaper questions—Who? What? Where? When? Why? How?

Erika didn't interrupt him with questions. She studied his face, looking at his expressions, trying to read what was being said at the other end of the phone.

Michael replaced the receiver and hung his head in his hands. He expelled a long breath and looked up at Erika. He sat at the office desk in the library. She moved to sit on the floor in front of him. Taking his hands, she waited.

"Everyone is all right. They've gone to Mom's house, and the bomb squad has been there to check it out," he told her. "Apparently, Bobby's house was wired. Two doors. They were set to go off ten minutes after the doors were opened."

"Enough time for everyone to get inside," Erika deduced.

"If it hadn't been for a neighbor calling to them when they arrived, they would all have been inside the house when the bomb went off."

Erika shivered. She raised herself up on her knees and put her arms around him. "Michael, I'm so sorry. I never thought when I came to see you that I'd draw you into a world where someone is trying to kill you."

He leaned against her, kissed the top of her head. "It's not your fault. Frank's been planning this for years. Just as I had time on the mountain to think, he's had the same amount of time, and now we're running toward each other. He tried to kill my brother and his family tonight."

Erika shivered. Just a few hours ago she'd held a baby in her arms. And this man, this crazy lunatic, had tried to kill that innocent child. How could anyone want to hurt someone who'd never done anything to anyone?

He kissed the top of her head again. "It won't be long, Erika, before he finds his way here."

"Michael." Erika looked up at him. "When I was trying to find you, I hired an investigator. Why don't we hire one now? If the police don't have the resources to track Frank's movements, we do. It's time we started thinking like rich people."

Erika returned to work three days later. The first thing Connie Forester did was to change the methods they used to get to work. Erika and Michael no longer occupied the same car. For the past three days she'd barely seen Michael.

Erika entered the offices to a chorus of "Welcome back" from everyone she and Connie passed. Her office had a huge bouquet of flowers and a card signed by the entire corporate office staff. Connie checked it for bugs, explosive devices, and poisonous containers. Erika imagined she also checked it for timing devices, electrical charges, and exploding ink. By the time she finished, the surprise of finding a present sent to her was gone.

"We had to get a big card," her secretary told her, and she looked in surprise at what Connie was doing.

"Thank you," Erika said. "I appreciate all your kindness. Please pass that along. I'll take a walk this morning and try to thank everyone, personally."

"Connie, security has been alerted in this building. My staff will feel truly inhibited if you search every piece of paper that comes across this desk."

"This is a big package. You can't imagine the things that could be hidden in there."

"You're right, I can't, and I'm sure I never want to know anything about those kinds of devices, but I also don't want my staff feeling like they're suspects."

"I'll be more considerate," she said.

"There's a small office through that door." Erika went and opened it. "You and Adrienne can use it while you're here."

Connie went through it and Erika sat down at her desk. Separate stacks of reports and mail waited for her. She searched the stack for the report from Jeff Rivers. What had been the activity of the stock over the past week? Thankfully the market was closed on Thanksgiving and the weekend. Jeff's report showed no additional unusual activity. She breathed a little easier. Maybe they had jumped to conclusions, and there was no attempt to gain access to the board or to undermine the market share.

She went on to the competitive reports. Nothing out of place there. She felt better. Maybe they had been chasing their tails in the past few months. Erika hoped that was true, but she knew she'd keep monitoring the reports.

"Good morning." Michael came through the door the way he did every morning about this time. He had two cups of coffee. Handing her one, he sat down.

"How come you're enjoying this so much and I'm having the worst time with it?"

"I've always wanted to be followed around by a beautiful woman." He sipped his coffee. "You probably haven't."

Erika picked up one of the letters in front of her and threw it at him. He put his hand up and blocked the shot, laughing at her.

Picking up the envelope, he handed it back. "What are these?"

"More requests for my hand in marriage," she told him.

Michael got up. "Turn them down," he said. "I've got a meeting. I'll see you soon."

He left and she began her usual day of meetings, reports, and market strategies. By five o'clock she was dead tired and ready to go home. She and Connie rode without speaking in the limousine back to the estate.

Erika opened the door to hanging wreaths and garlands. The staff must have been working all day to make the place ready for Christmas.

She went to her room. She felt guilty. It wasn't like her to be angry with someone for no good reason, and she certainly had no good reason to use cross words with Connie Forester. She didn't dislike her. What she disliked was having her ability to move freely curtailed. There were times when she wanted to be alone, and with Connie lurking about she wasn't given that opportunity.

She should feel grateful for her presence. It allowed her to keep her vow of staying away from Michael. But she'd long ago abandoned that vow. Now she wanted nothing more than to be in his company, to be free to make love without someone knowing where she was.

Erika changed into jeans and a sweater and headed down to the library.

"Excuse me!" She heard her mother's voice from the top of the staircase. "I will not be searched."

Erika ran down the stairs. "It's all right, Connie. She's my mother."

"Ms. St. James—"

"I know, Connie," her voice was a little harsh. Erika let her shoulders drop, and the anger she felt went out of her. "I apologize," she said in a quieter voice. "Let her in."

Alva Redford walked past the guard.

"Don't look so smug, Mother, or I will let them search you." Alva followed her to the living room. A tree that reached near to the ceiling stood fully decorated in front of the window. The fireplace mantel held a scene from the Dickens Village lit with small lights. Everything about the room was merry. It should have made Erika happy.

"What's going on?" her mother asked the moment they were in the room. "Who was that?"

"She's my bodyguard."

"You're kidding." She stared at her for a moment. Erika stood with her arms crossed. "You're not kidding?"

"The accident was caused by someone tampering with the car."

Alva's mouth opened and she clamped her hands over it. Erika could only think of her mother and drama in the same breath. "We've added some extra guards, including the woman you met at the door."

Erika took a seat and waited. Her mother sat down, but said nothing. This time she was determined to wait her mother out. It didn't take long. Alva looked around the room several times. Eventually her gaze came back to her daughter.

"The staff is fully awake, Mother. Should I order you coffee?"

"No, dear. I'm cutting down on my intake of caffeine. It isn't healthy to drink too much caffeine."

"So you're becoming health conscious?"

"It wouldn't hurt any of us. We all need to take care of ourselves sometimes."

Again they lapsed into silence. It stretched about the room like a tight rubber band.

"You know, you look a lot like me when I was your age," Alva said.

"I don't think you want to begin any discussion that goes along that line," Erika said.

"Why not?"

"Because, Mother, you know I don't look like you. I look like my father."

Erika watched her mother. Alva had mastered a flinch that would in the past have been invisible to the naked eye.

"I don't want to talk about your father," she said.

"You never want to talk about him. Why?"

"Erika, I didn't come here to argue with you."

"Why did you come? Each time we get within ten feet and two minutes of each other, we're ready to scratch each other's eyes out. Why is that, *Mother?*"

Alva hesitated a moment. Erika didn't know which of them she wanted to calm down.

"Where's Michael?" she asked calmly and sweetly, as if they hadn't been about to explode.

"He teaches tonight," Erika told her. "Except for the guards, we're alone."

"Your injuries, from the accident," she said. "Are they completely healed?"

"Completely," Erika lied. She still had bruises on her arms and legs, but her headaches were gone. "Mother, you're trying to get to a point to ask for something. Come straight out with it. We get on much better when we're honest with each other."

"All right, Erika." Alva leaned forward in her chair. "I want to borrow some money."

"For what?"

"I can't tell you that."

"How much money?"

"Fifty thousand."

"You have to be kidding."

"I assure you I never kid about money."

"You want me to loan you that much money without knowing what you're going to do with it?"

Alva's head bobbed up and down.

"You have got more nerve than a . . ." She couldn't think of an adequate metaphor. "Give me one good reason why I should lend you anything."

"I'm your mother."

"That's not a good enough reason."

"The reason is personal. That's all I can tell you."

"If I give you this money, is there a chance at all that it will be repaid?"

Alva stared at her daughter for a long time. Her face didn't change. Not one thing about her changed except a narrowing of her eyes. "No," she finally said.

"Yet you think I should give it to you, anyway?"

She nodded. "If you ever in your life felt anything for me. I need the money."

"Why don't you go to a bank? You obviously have assets."

"I need it faster than a bank could process it and they would insist on knowing its purpose, and I couldn't tell them that."

"Whatever you're doing, is it legal?"

"Of course," she said, astonished that her daughter would even consider she'd do something illegal.

Erika had never written a check for that much money, not a personal one. She'd had the need to write few checks at all. Carlton had paid her expenses while she lived here, and when she went to school he paid the bills. After her graduation she got a job and lived on her salary. Carlton insisted she have an allowance, but Erika had never used it. The money had been in the bank for eight years, collecting and compounding interest. Writing a fifty thousand dollar check wouldn't even dent it.

"Mother, I'll give you the money." Alva's shoulders dropped in relief. "On one condition," Erika finished.

"What is it?"

"I want to know what the trust fund was set up for, and why it's been paying you since I moved into this house."

"The establishment of that fund was an agreement between Carlton and me. I promised him I'd take its reason for being to my grave." She stared directly at Erika. "You understand a promise, don't you?"

Erika surely understood promises. They were not to be broken. Alva had broken many promises to her, yet she threw up a curtain when it came to this fund.

"Do I get the money?"

Erika didn't move. She thought about her mother. There was no earthly reason why she should give this woman a penny. She'd mentally abused her as a child. She'd given her no moral support or guidance during her entire life, and now when she could go nowhere else she'd came begging for money—money she wouldn't even tell the purpose for. So why was Erika getting up and going to the library to write her a check?

CHAPTER 17

The University of Pennsylvania School of Law was a brightly lit modern building. Michael looked down from his window on the second floor. His class had ended fifteen minutes ago, and Peter was right on time. Adrienne waited for him nearby. Moments later his brother came into the room and closed the door.

His features were grim, not at all like his anchorman look from the six o'clock news.

"What have you found?" Michael asked.

"Your suspicions were right. Alva St. James Redford does have a secret, but it had nothing to do with stock manipulations."

"How can you be sure?"

"Using sources you don't want to know about, I checked the dates of the checks she received from the fund against the surges in stocks. They coincide closely enough, but the funds don't go for stock."

"Are you sure?" Michael didn't want Alva to be behind anything that affected Graves Enterprises. He knew how much it would mean to Erika to discover her mother really loved her, but if Alva had secretly been buying stock, what could be her purpose, other than to force her daughter to do something? But what?

"All my sources say there isn't any stock problem. The increased activity surrounded Erika and you being named co-partners of a vastly successful business. The analysts think the stock is levelling off."

"If there's not a stock problem, what is Alva using the money for?"

Peter looked directly at him, in the same way he did each night when the camera transmitted his face to an unseen audience. Michael waited.

"Medical treatment," he said. "She's dying."

Michael remembered seeing her walking toward the elevator that day she invited Erika to Thanksgiving dinner. He'd never have thought there was anything wrong with her.

"She has a rare disease that causes an imbalance in the chemistry of the brain. It causes mood swings. One minute she can be normal and talking and the next she'll be screaming and shouting. The addition of alcohol accelerates the process."

"Oh my God!" Michael said. "That's why she treated Erika so badly. Her bouts of shouting and screaming. Her moods changing. For a child that would be unbearable."

"It's not inheritable," Peter assured him. "It is longterm, however. Most people who develop it don't even know they have it. To them, their actions are completely normal. It's everybody else who is irrational."

"How long has she got?"

"No one knows."

"Can she be treated for it?"

"She has been. For the past twenty-five years she's been taking medication to control the imbalance."

"And now?"

"I don't know. Maybe she only takes it at times, or maybe the imbalance has grown worse with time. It's such a rare condition that not much is known about it." Peter reached across to his brother and squeezed his shoulder. "I'm sorry, Michael."

Michael nodded. "What about Bobby and Catherine? Are they all right?" He moved the subject to other avenues.

"They're fine. Mom is having the time of her life with Roberta, and Catherine is supervising the building of the new kitchen."

"She's not alone, is she?"

"No," Peter said. "The guard you hired is always with them. Until this maniac is caught, none of us travel alone. Even Mom has agreed to the terms."

"Good," Michael breathed. At least he didn't have to worry about them.

He told Peter about the firm of investigators they had hired to track Frank. He hoped they could find him and turn him over to the authorities. Then everyone could go back to a normal life.

Michael didn't know if his would ever be normal again. It hadn't been normal in years. He'd thought he was on the right track after he'd met and fallen in love with Erika, but he wasn't sure. The night he'd told her he loved her, she hadn't returned the sentiment, and she still hadn't. He knew she was attracted to him. He knew she satisfied him in bed, and he satisfied her. He'd seen the way she looked at him when her eyes were unguarded and filled with passion. Yet he didn't know how she really felt, or what it would mean to her when he delivered his news.

"I have to get back, Michael. Will you be all right?"

"Sure," Michael said. They both stood and put their coats on. Michael picked up his briefcase, and they met their guards in the hall. Outside the law school they separated and went to their waiting cars.

Michael rode in silence to the mansion. Erika always waited for him. Tonight he had news she probably wouldn't want to hear. He didn't want to tell her. He wanted to make love to her. Tomorrow would be plenty of time to give her bad news. He didn't want to spoil her night. He wanted it to be the most wonderful night in the world.

"Good-night, Mr. Lawrence," the limo driver said as he got out of the car. Michael and Adrienne came through the door. Erika stood in the doorway of the library. She looked beautiful. Michael dropped his briefcase on the hall table and left his overcoat on a chair.

"I have to talk to Erika," he told Adrienne. "We don't want to be disturbed."

Michael came to her. She didn't move. He didn't try to conceal anything from the bodyguard behind him. He took her in his arms and kissed her thoroughly. Then he took her hand and led her up the stairs. At the landing they turned toward his rooms and she followed him, looking back to see if Adrienne was standing in the hall watching. She wasn't. She had discreetly disappeared.

Michael closed the door to his bedroom and locked it. He turned back to Erika, who stood before him. The room was dark except for the firelight. He smelled pine and noticed that Christmas accents had been added to the suite. Then his gaze came to rest on the woman he loved. Her short curls glowed with a red tinge as she watched him. Neither of them moved. Only the hammering of his heart through his shirt was visible. Michael slipped his jacket from his shoulders. His tie followed it before he took a step toward Erika.

"Touch me," he said.

Erika's hands reached his chest. Through the material he felt her slim fingers. Heat speared through him. Nimbly she opened the buttons on his shirt and slipped her fingers inside. When she'd opened it completely she kissed his brandy-hot skin. His muscles contracted. Her tongue tasted him, working a slow, hot magic on his nipples. She circled them in long, rapturous strokes. The flat surfaces hardened into sand pebbles.

Michael groaned at her action. He took hold of her head, his fingers softly digging into her hair. He brought her mouth to his in a hard, fervent kiss. She came up on her toes, her arms circling his neck as she held on, pressing her body into his, devouring his mouth as their tongues danced in a wet, warm, erotic dance.

Moving his hands, Michael caressed her back, slowly sliding his long arms down her spine and up again, pulling her hips into his and reveling in the carnal excitement that tingled about them.

Michael found the hem of the sweater and pushed his hands under it. Pushing it upward, he stepped back, breaking contact only long enough to pull it over her head. He gasped at the touch of her hot skin. He slipped his thumbs in the top of her jeans and made a ceremony of sliding them around to the front snap. Erika expelled air into his mouth when his hands touched the core of her being. He opened the snap and slid the zipper to the bottom.

The mounting heat in the room threatened to incinerate them. Erika pushed his shirt down his arms, and one by one he pulled it free of his arms. The white silk floated to the floor, joining the clothes. Her hands were small as they touched his ungarnished skin, bringing it to fiery life. Her mouth again touched his chest, open and wet, seeking, persuading. Michael clenched his teeth at the pleasure she caused to rocket through him. Opening his pants, she slipped her hands inside. He groaned at the bliss that shot through him, the hardness that pulsed in her hands and the sheer need to have her continue the torturous thrill she'd begun. His pants slipped down his legs and he stepped out of his shoes and the material with no effort.

Lifting Erika, he carried her to the bed and laid her on it. In seconds he'd removed her jeans and shoes. He pulled her to a sitting position and kissed the swell of the breasts still encased in the lacy cups of her bra. Her hands drew widening circles on his back. He unhooked the bra, freeing her breasts. He took them in both hands, his thumbs padding over nipples that hardened to his touch. Erika moaned, asking for more. His fingers moved faster. Her breath caught in her throat, and his mouth took it on the exhale.

He never wanted to be separated from her again. He didn't care about bodyguards or family or business meetings. He wanted Erika to himself for the next hundred years or more. Michael slipped his hands inside the matching lace panties and was rewarded by finding her wet and ready for him. Her mouth bit into his shoulder. He slipped the last scrap of fabric down her long legs and pushed her back onto the bed.

Quickly finding his condom and securing it, he looked into her eyes.

"Say you love me," he said.

"I love you," Erika repeated. "I love you." Her words were full of emotion, and they touched a part of him that had never been reached before.

"I love you, Erika," he said, and slipped inside her.

Her eyes closed on a moan of pure pleasure. Michael moved and she moved with him. He touched her shoulders and she arched into him. He touched her breasts and she grasped his arms. Her legs circled him, giving him greater access as the two of them found their rhythm, found that place where light and dark come together, where man and woman merge into one being, and where the two can no longer control what happens. Michael lunged into her, his body strong, hers stronger, as she took his powerful strokes. Need gripped them, and they fed on their mutual selves, gratifying and consuming. Wet and hungry they continued, pushing, pulling, taking, giving, until Michael thought he'd die of joyous satisfaction.

Erika pushed him on. Guttural sounds came from her throat as she held onto him, as time after time they met, separated, and met again. His heart raced, his lungs fought for air, and his body filled with her and his need to go higher until there was nothing to do but fall. Michael reached for that place, that one place that no other couple could find. His voice sounded in his ears like the wind rushing over dry leaves. Groans and deep, incomprehensible words flowed from him as he reached for the light above him, and the world shattered.

Together they collapsed. Michael held onto Erika, knowing that if he let go they'd fall off the world. Slowly, they came back to reality. He turned her into his arms and kissed her.

"I love you, Michael."

"I'll always love you, Erika."

Erika woke up reaching for Michael. He'd filled her dreams, her bed, and her arms. She cradled herself in his arms and snuggled closer to him. Strong arms circled her, drawing her to him and keeping her safe. She wanted to never get up. She wanted to stay here in his arms and let the world take care of itself. Inside his embrace there were no Graves Enterprises, no market shares, no Frank Mason. There were only the two of them, two lovers who'd shared heaven together and selfishly wanted to keep it for themselves.

"We'd better get up," Michael said from above her head.

"I don't want to," she said, sliding her smooth leg over his rough one. "Isn't today Saturday, or something?"

"I'm afraid it's Friday."

Erika groaned.

"I have an idea," Michael said, drawing her hair back to kiss her forehead.

"What?"

"We play hooky today." He paused to kiss her cheek.

"Hmmm, that sounds good." She felt as feline as a stretching cat.

"We could go and get a blood test, and get married on Wednesday."

Erika froze. Michael continued to nibble on her, placing featherlight kisses on her cheeks and her lips, but Erika had ceased moving, feeling.

"What?" he asked. "What's wrong? You want a big wedding with a white gown and penguin suits?"

Erika couldn't find her voice. She was stunned, too surprised by his declaration to speak.

"Erika, we can do that. We can do—"

She put her fingers to his lips to stop him. She'd made him nervous, and she knew it. Her silence had made him keep talking, staving off what he feared she might say, but Erika had to say it.

"Michael, I can't marry you."

He grabbed her wrist and moved her hand, then turned her on her back and imprisoned her against the mattress. "Didn't you say you loved me?"

She nodded.

"Were you lying?"

She shook her head.

"Then why won't you marry me?"

She felt boxed in. Michael's elbows dug into the mattress on either side of her head. "I told you," she began. "I'm not good with man woman relationships."

"Erika, that's bull and you know it."

She didn't know it. "Every relationship I've ever had went sour."

"And I'm no different, is that it?"

"Let me up." She pushed his arm aside and turned over, swinging her feet to the floor while she held the sheet to her. She looked about for Michael's silk robe.

"Where's your robe?" she asked.

"In *your* room. You took it the last time we made love." His soft words made her flinch. Her sweater lay on the floor halfway across the room. She dropped the sheet and walked to it. Her entire body grew hot at the eyes she knew bore into her back. Drawing her arms into the sweater, she pulled it over her head and down her body. It stopped halfway to her knees.

"If you think that covers you, you're dead wrong," Michael said. "You're more sexy now than when you were naked."

Undaunted by his own nakedness, Michael left the bed and walked toward her.

"I should go now," she began.

"Not on your life," he told her. "We've started a conversation and I'm not postponing it."

"What about Connie Forester? She might discover I'm not in my room."

"You really think she doesn't know where you are?"

Erika hung her head. She was sure she knew. Neither of them had eaten dinner last night. After Michael came in from teaching, neither of them had been seen again by their new houseguests.

"Can we get back to my question?"

"Aren't you going to put on some clothes?" Erika found it hard to talk to a naked man. Especially a man as good-looking as Michael. Instead of talking, she wanted to go back to bed. Her body was already hot, and he was deliberately throwing her thinking processes off.

"Do I make you nervous?"

"Yes," she said.

"Good," he whispered and caught her, pulling her close. "Marry me and I'll get dressed."

"Michael, listen to me." He ran his hands down her back, over the sweater until he reached the hem. Then he ran them up under it. "Michael," she whispered, "there's too much we have to think about." Her body burned like a two-alarm fire. Michael bent his head and leaned toward her mouth. She moved back. He followed her until she couldn't go any farther without falling. His mouth hovered above hers. His tongue traced her lipline. Erika felt the heat in the pit of her stomach and knew she was lost. Each time he reached for her, she had no resistance. She didn't want to resist. She was in love with him. She had been since almost the first moment she'd seen him. Her heart told her to forget her head, forget everything except the fact that her insides had turned to pudding.

She moved closer to him, coming up and joining him in the passion he created. She was weak and she knew it. She wanted Michael. On her toes, she pulled him closer to her, hugging him, aggressively taking his mouth and trading kiss for kiss. Erika stopped thinking. She no longer had the ability. The burning in her belly flashed white and hot. She stood against Michael, pressed into the hard structure of his body, liquefying in the heat of their combined fervor.

Breathing raggedly, Erika and Michael separated but remained in each other's arms. Michael squeezed her as hard as he could without crushing her.

"You've got to marry me, Erika. I love you."

She heard the emotion cracking his voice, making it warble in his throat. Her defenses began to crumble. God, she loved him. She wanted to marry him, to love him the rest of her life.

"I don't want anyone else," he said. "I want you to complete my life, mother my children, share my rewards. You could make me the happiest man alive. And I'll die trying to make you happy."

Tears rushed into Erika's eyes. Hot and salty, they rolled over her cheeks. She shifted and Michael pushed her back.

"What's wrong? Why are you crying."

"Micha—el." His name cracked as she said it. "I can't have children."

* * *

The time is now, Michael. Frank had failed in his attempt to kill Michael's brother, rid the world of another lawyer, but he'd sent the message, anyway. It was Michael's time now. Frank had to get home for Christmas. He needed to shop for his children, and Michael was the only thing standing in his way.

Frank saw the police car and slipped down in the driver's seat so he couldn't be seen. He was parked far enough away on a hill, several miles, but from here he had a clear vision of the estate. He couldn't see the house, but he could see over the wall and for several yards beyond it. With a high-powered rifle he'd have a clear shot at any car that came in or went out of the gates.

Every morning two limousines left the estate. They never left together, and their times varied. Frank knew they were trying to throw him off, but he was no fool. He'd planned this for a year but he wasn't locked into a precise date and time. Still, he wanted to get home. Christmas with Abby and the kids would be especially happy this year.

Then he saw it. Frank tensed. He lifted the binoculars and peered through them. Two women in a car. One of them was Erika St. James. The other he didn't recognize, but by the look of her and the way she checked the streets, she had to be hired help. Frank smiled. Adrenaline rushed into his system, his breath came in gasps, and sweat broke out on his skin. This was his chance.

The driver turned left out of the driveway. She wasn't going to the office. Frank spied the license tag and make of the car. Then he started the engine and headed down the hill. He gripped the steering wheel, hoping he'd have time to get there before they turned off or got too far ahead for him to follow.

The time is now, he thought, and began humming "It's Beginning To Look a Lot Like Christmas."

Facing the office was something Erika couldn't do this morning. Michael would undoubtedly want an explanation and she wasn't up to it. She couldn't marry him. She wouldn't be able to defend herself against his insistence. All he had to do was touch her and she'd fall into his arms. This was what real love was like, not what she'd felt for Bill Castle. He'd done her a favor by running off with Jennifer Ahrends. She now knew what it was like at the creation, when the stars were flung into the dark void and the earth was set among them. Michael had taught her that. It was up to her to live with it.

She felt like dying. Erika had a brain, but it was having a difficult time explaining to her heart what she knew was the right decision.

After Erika tore herself from Michael's arms she stumbled from his room, falling on the steps, but pushing on to get to her room. She showered and dressed in record time, fighting the clock to get out of the house. She needed to be alone, but that option had been taken from her. She had Connie Forester as her constant companion.

The limousine waited for them, but Erika wanted to drive herself. Connie refused her request. Erika was in no mood to argue with the woman, but she was going to have her way. She passed Connie and went to the garage. Connie rushed in and stood in front of her.

She tried to make her see reason. "Erika, think about what you're doing. Obviously, you and Michael had a fight. That's no reason to put your life in danger."

Erika stared at her for a moment, then burst into tears. She cried for Michael, for herself, for the love they shared that would die, for the children they would never have, for the babies she would never hold.

"Get in," Connie said. The bodyguard opened the door and pushed Erika into the passenger seat. "You're in no condition to drive."

Erika sat still while Connie quickly did a check of the car. When she was satisfied everything was all right, she got into the driver's seat and started the engine. Connie drove expertly. She turned the car away from downtown Philly and headed west. Erika didn't ask where they were going. She didn't care as long as it was away from Michael.

Fresh tears pooled in her eyes and spilled down her face. She let them run unchecked, no longer caring that Connie was there, she guessed that Connie knew she'd spent the night with Michael. They had argued, argued over getting married. They were in love with each other. Shouldn't that be the easiest decision in the world? Maybe for someone else, but not for her. It wouldn't last, and then she'd die. She could never hold a man. She wasn't pretty. She didn't have what it took for the long run. And children. He wanted children. She couldn't risk it.

Erika didn't notice where they were going. The traffic on the other side of the road was thick and backed up. Connie drove competently and quietly. She hadn't said anything since they left the garage. Erika let her head fall back and her mind go blank, numb. Her fatigue after a night of lovemaking, coupled with the steady rhythm of the road, lulled her to sleep.

The sudden cessation of motion woke her. "Where are we?" Erika looked around, disoriented.

"Strasburg," Connie said. "I was born here."

Erika got out of the car. The air smelled of horses. On the road she saw a small black carriage, pulled by a single horse. Lancaster County. She remembered. This was Pennsylvania Dutch country. Erika looked at the house. It was a white clapboard structure with black shutters.

"It was my mother's house," Connie explained. "She died six years ago, but I still keep it."

Erika heard the catch in Connie's voice. Everyone spoke well of their parents. Why hadn't her mother given her the love that could produce that kind of emotion even after death? Why hadn't she taught her the forever kind of love? Why hadn't she prepared her for a man like Michael? Erika's eyes clouded again, but she brushed them away.

"Come on in."

Inside the place was spotless. Dark, sturdy, handmade furniture filled every room. Not enough to crowd, just to provide places to sit or work. The kitchen chairs were hard and without cushions. Erika sat down on one of them while Connie made coffee in a percolator that sat on the woodburning stove. While the coffee heated, Connie busied herself making breakfast. Erika felt useless. The house reminded her of the dirty cabin where she'd found Michael. She'd cooked there under less than ideal conditions.

Connie's food was delicious. Erika ate hungrily and drank two cups of the hot, steaming coffee.

"We can stay here as long as you like," Connie said, sipping her second cup of coffee. "But your problems aren't going to go away because you do."

Erika agreed with her. She knew she had no choice but to return. She had to go back and face him. She just needed some time alone to think and decide.

"Do you think it would be all right if I went for a walk?" She meant alone, and she could tell Connie didn't like the request. "I promise I'm not trying to make things difficult. I just need some time by myself."

For a moment Connie didn't say anything. Erika was sure she was going to refuse.

"It's not a good idea."

"No one followed us," she said.

"You were asleep most of the way," Connie told her.

"Didn't you check?"

"Of course," she said. "I'm pretty sure we weren't followed. But it's my job to be with you all the time."

"How could anyone track me here? Frank Mason doesn't know about you. He couldn't possibly know about your mother's house. And I'll be within shouting distance," she paused. Connie looked as if she wanted to refuse. Erika knew she was asking her to compromise her principles, but she needed the space.

"When I needed to be alone, I used to go up to that tree over there." Connie pointed through the window. On a hill stood a huge oak. "There used to be a tire swing hanging from it. I'd swing for hours."

"Thanks, Connie." Erika smiled for the first time since she'd left Michael.

Connie smiled back at her. "I'll tell you what," she said. "We'll stay here all night. I'll make us an authentic Pennsylvania Dutch dinner, and we'll drive back in the morning."

"Connie, you're an angel." Erika hugged her.

"Go on," Connie said, probably a little embarrassed.

"While you're communing with nature, I'll be at the grocery store."

Erika left by the back door and started up the hill. The air still smelled of horses, but she liked it. She pulled her coat around her, continuing toward Connie's tree. She saw the car leave the driveway. She waved at Connie and saw her arm waving from the car window. She headed in the opposite direction from the one they had come. Was Connie trying to gain her trust? She hadn't been the best client a person could work for, but she was warming to the short bodyguard.

She looked up the hill toward the tree. She remembered Michael lying by the stream with the mountain in the background. Where was he? Did he go to the office? Should she call him? She hadn't seen a phone, and from the look of the furniture and kitchen nothing invented after 1700 would be in the house, except that ancient coffeepot. Erika thought about Connie. There would be a phone at the grocery store and surely she carried a cellular unit, although Erika had not seen it. Would she call Michael to let him know they were safe? She hoped Connie would. There was no need for him to worry needlessly.

Erika continued toward the tree. She saw a man on another hill and waved. He stood up and waved back. On the other side was a whole family. Erika again raised her hand in the universal salute. Two small children smiled at her. Then the family, all dressed in black, got into a buggy and rode away. She wondered where they were off to this sunny December morning.

She remembered her morning. She'd reacted badly. Michael had surprised her with his proposal. The night had been beautiful, filled with love and magic and an array of color that comprised their own private world. It was the most wonderful night of her life. She should have seen where it was leading. Hadn't he asked her if she loved him? Hadn't she admitted she did? What else could she say when he looked at her with his own love shining in his eyes? She couldn't have lied if she'd wanted to. Then morning dawned and the magic was gone. Reality was back.

The wind picked up and Erika pulled her coat collar closer to her ears. She'd go back now, and when Connie returned she'd ask to call Michael.

Erika turned, then gasped. Pointed at her heart was the barrel of a black gun. Holding it was Frank Mason.

Where was she? Michael paced the office. She hadn't come here, and Connie hadn't called. At least he knew they left together. Connie was good. She could take care of her. But Erika was headstrong, and she'd fought Connie since she arrived. They weren't in the limo with bulletproof glass, but in the Mercedes, which had regular windows.

Calm down, Michael, he told himself. *You're in love, but this is a time for rationality.* He picked up a letter opener, then dropped it. The phone rang and he snatched it up before it completed the first ring.

Shouting into it, he said, "Lawrence."

"Michael, it's Connie."

"Where the hell are you?" His voice was angry, but he was relieved to hear hers.

"We're in Strasburg at my mother's house. Erika's fine. There's no cause for alarm. She just needed some space."

Michael knew Connie well enough to know she'd held her tongue over why Erika needed space.

"I told her we'd stay the night and return in the morning. Is that all right?"

"Do you think that's wise?" He didn't want them staying overnight. He wanted Erika back so he could talk to her, make love to her. If she didn't want to get married, they didn't have to. If she couldn't have children, they could adopt. He didn't care. All he wanted was her.

"No, I don't," Connie replied. "I'd much rather be at the estate with the added guards, but I kept a close check on the drive up here. We weren't followed."

"Where's Erika now?" Michael played with the letter opener. "I'd like to talk to her."

"She went for a walk. I'm calling from a local grocery store. We left so fast, I left my cellular unit in the limo."

"Is there a number where you can be reached?"

"I'm afraid not. My mother was a Quaker, remember. She didn't believe in telephones."

Michael sighed.

"Do you want me to tell her anything?" Connie offered.

"Yeah," he said. "Tell her I love her."

CHAPTER 18

"Where are you taking me?" Erika asked.

"Shut up and drive."

Frank Mason sat next to her in the jeep. She drove according to his directions. He'd forced her to go with him. Connie hadn't returned, and Erika didn't even get to go into the house. They'd immediately climbed into the black Cherokee and taken off.

Friday afternoon traffic was light and Erika couldn't count on it to give her any time to get away or at least call for help. They bypassed Philadelphia and headed north along Route 1. A heavily trafficked route that ran from Maine to Florida, it was sometimes a four-lane highway, sometimes a normal city street. When they connected with it it was a highway, but soon it would go through the business district of central New Jersey.

Frank had her switch to Route 95, then the New Jersey Turnpike. They got off at Route 18 in East Brunswick and went to a quiet neighborhood with manicured lawns. She stopped in the driveway of a pretty yellow house on a cul-de-sac, with vinyl siding.

"Don't try anything stupid," he told her. "If I have to I'll shoot you here and now."

She believed him. Michael had told her how he killed his children. The man was psychotic. He'd kill her in a minute. Inside, he tied her hands and feet to a chair. Erika's breaths came too fast. She forced herself not to hyperventilate.

"What are you going to do?"

"Don't worry, Sister," he said. "Your time isn't right, yet. I need Michael Lawrence. You're the bait."

"Why?" she asked. "What do you want with Michael?"

"I want him dead."

"Why?"

"No more questions," he said, and tied a scarf around her head, cutting her mouth and forcing her to remain quiet. She nearly gagged on it. It tasted of perfume and powder. "I have to go out now," he said. "You wait here."

Erika didn't move until she heard the jeep drive away. Then she tried to free her hands. The knots were too tight and the more she moved, the more they seemed to tighten.

She wondered what Connie had done when she came back and found her gone. Had she called Michael? Were they looking for her? Tears sprang to her eyes. They would have no idea where to look. She didn't even know where she was.

Think, Erika, she told herself. *You're alone for the time being. How can you get away?* Phone. She needed to call someone, the police, 9-1-1. There was a phone on the wall in the kitchen. She could see it from the chair he'd tied her to. It was too high. She'd never reach it to get it off the wall. There had to be another one.

Trying to stand, she found that the ropes cut into her ankles and wrists. It hurt to move. She couldn't walk with the chair tied to her, but maybe she could scoot along in the chair. She tried it, and found pain shooting up her legs and arms. Still, she had to try. There had to be a phone in the other room. Inch by painful inch she moved the chair until she got to the door of the room.

If Erika could have made a sound she would have screamed at the top of her lungs. All she could do was suck on the wet scarf in her mouth. Lying on the floor, in a pool of blood, was a man of about sixty. His eyes were blank and staring at the ceiling. One side of his head had been bashed in, and near him was a bloodstained baseball bat. Tears formed in Erika's eyes and she cried, making guttural noises and choking on her own saliva.

A key stuck in the door and Frank came through the kitchen. "Going somewhere, Ms. St. James?" He grabbed the back of her chair and pulled her back into the dining room. The shades were down in all the rooms except the living room. The house looked lived in, especially with Frank coming and going as if he lived there.

"Getting to the phone would have done you no good," he told her. "The line is as dead as Mr. Thompson." He glanced at the doorway. "Now all we have to do is wait for Michael to come to the rescue."

Erika couldn't speak. She could only use her eyes to question him.

"I sent him a message," he answered. "Your purse."

Erika looked blankly at him. Her purse had been inside Connie's house. They hadn't gone in.

"I got it while you were enjoying the morning air. Black bag, with a gold clasp. Inside was a wallet with your initials on it, a comb, lipstick, more credit cards than any one person ought to have, a checkbook, and a set of keys. I sent him everything . . . but this." He pulled the Christmas picture of Carlton and her from his pocket and showed it to her.

Fear caught in Erika's chest. What would Michael do? Would he come to save her? Did he love her enough to risk his own life?

Oh God! she cried silently. *I love him. Don't let him come.*

Michael had spent the worst twenty-four hours of his life. He couldn't seem to be still, calm down. He'd paced the library practically all night, waiting for the phone to ring, willing it to ring to give him some relief. He needed to know Erika was alive, that Frank had not done anything to her yet. He'd thought seeing the Mason children killed and Abby's suicide had been enough trauma for a lifetime, but now Erika missing was driving him insane. What had Frank done to her? Michael's stomach was tied up in sailor's knots. His imagination brought pictures of Erika killed in grotesque ways. What could he do? What could the police do? They hadn't heard a word. Was she all right?

Connie came in looking as bad as he did. "Has there been any word?"

"Nothing," he said.

"Michael, I'm sorry—"

"It's not your fault, Connie," he cut her off. It was his fault, Michael told himself. He'd been the one to make her angry. He was the one she wanted to get away from. If he'd kept his thoughts to himself she'd be here now. But he hadn't. He couldn't know a marriage proposal would cause her pain and anger. He hadn't thought about the effect her mother had had on her. Alva Redford had abused her, never giving her the complete love she needed, and even though Michael offered it, she couldn't accept that he wouldn't treat her the same as she'd been treated in the past. If she'd just stayed home or gone to the office, he'd have had a chance to explain. She'd gone off in a rage and now he might never see her again.

Michael wrung his hands, wishing he had Frank Mason's neck between them. His back ached with pent-up tension. What should they do now?

"Michael," Connie said. "She'll be all right. The police are looking for Frank. You've got an agency tracking him, and now the FBI is involved. They'll find her."

Michael squeezed Connie's shoulder. They had to find her. He felt helpless. The room had been full of people for the entire day and most of the night. The only person who hadn't arrived was Alva Redford.

"This package was just delivered," Adrienne said, coming into the room. She carried a familiar red, white, and blue Federal Express box. "It has a return label bearing Frank Mason as the sender."

Michael shot across the room, heading straight for her.

"Wait," Connie stopped him. She had to physically restrain him from taking the box and ripping it open. "Has it been swiped?"

"Yes," Adrienne said. "As soon as I saw his name."

Michael had sudden images of finding an ear or a finger inside the box. "Open it," he said, clearing his throat.

Adrienne pulled the paper tape. A rough, ripping sound exploded in his head. She dumped the contents on the desk. Erika's purse fell out, its clasp striking the polished surface. For a moment no one moved. Then Michael grabbed the bag and opened it. "It's hers," he said. He let his breath out slowly, not wanting to reveal that he'd expected a body part to roll out of the box. Looking at Connie, he saw that her face was as pale as his own. She must have had a similar thought.

"What's this?" she asked, picking up a cassette.

"I don't know," Michael answered.

The label read "Play me."

"Where is there a cassette player?" Adrienne asked.

He led them to the salon. There was more music equipment than he'd had as a college student there. Slipping the cartridge into the deck, he turned on the many switches and a voice boomed into the air. Connie reached around him and turned the sound to a more comfortable level.

"No police, Lawrence," the voice said. Michael hadn't heard Frank speak for over a year, yet he immediately recognized the inflection in his speech patterns. "If you want to see your little heiress again, do exactly as I say." There was a pause. "First, no police or she'll be the first one to drop. Second, no bodyguards. If you're not getting this . . . I'm saying I want you, and you alone."

Michael understood. He'd constantly had to school Frank on being precise, leaving no interpretation for his words except the ones they intended. The man had learned quickly.

"Now, you're to go to the old Rutgers boathouse along the Raritan River. The one near the tennis courts off Route 18, just before you get to Commercial Avenue. You know where they are. You played there as a child."

Connie looked at Michael, and he nodded. He knew where it was.

"The boathouse used to be new, but like all things that age it's rundown and boarded up now. There will be a package for you there near the back door. Lawrence, don't try to cross me on this. Come alone. If I even *think* I see a cop, Erika St. James won't live out the day." He paused again. Michael heard him take a breath. "According to Federal Express, this package should arrive before ten thirty Saturday morning. You've got until two this afternoon to get to the boathouse, or her death will be slow and painful."

The tape ended there. The three of them stood in the salon staring at the machine and hearing the dead, mechanical air of the rolling tape. Michael checked his watch. Eleven-thirty. The delivery had been late. Michael started for the door. Adrienne's hand on his arm stopped him.

"Michael," she began. "Don't even consider going alone."

"I don't have a choice," he said. "The area he picked is across from a high hill, with Douglass College sitting at the top. The boathouse and tennis courts are open. Nothing covers them. Any place you could think to hide is visible."

"We need to call the police."

"We can't do that," he said too fast, too forcefully. "Adrienne, he's in New Brunswick, not here or New York. The New Brunswick Police Department might be good for traffic tickets and breaking up a student party, but they're no match for Frank. I have to go alone if there's any chance of getting Erika back."

He pulled loose from her hand.

"Then we call the FBI," she said.

"There isn't time," he told her. "It's Saturday, nineteen days till Christmas. The day is sunny and warm for this time of year. The roads will be mobbed. I'll be lucky to get there on time, and I'm not waiting around for the FBI to come blundering in and get her killed."

"Michael!" Connie shouted. Both women followed him as he started for the front door. He stopped to get a coat and put it on. "Think about what you're doing. You don't want to be the cause of getting her killed, do you?"

That stopped him. "What are you talking about?"

"What are you planning to do when you get there?"

"I don't know. Follow his instructions, I suppose."

"And if he's on that hill with a high-powered rifle pointed at your head, what will you have accomplished?" Connie stopped for a breath. "How will that help Erika? All you'll do is provide him with the ability to kill both of you on the same day."

She got through to him. Michael dropped down on one of the chairs in the hall. "What do you suggest?"

"First, we call the FBI. We can do that from the car. And then we let them take it from there. They're the experts in this. Let them do what we pay them for."

"All right," Michael agreed after a moment. He wasn't sure they should completely put Erika's life into the hands of strangers, but he had to admit Connie's plan made more sense than his did.

The two women got jackets and put them on. "We can't leave together," Adrienne said. "We don't know if he's watching the house or not. If he sees us all together, he'll know something is up."

"Michael—"

"I'm going to drive myself," he said, not accepting an argument. Michael knew the streets of New Brunswick. They could be small and narrow. If he needed to maneuver, he wanted something small and fast.

"Use the front entrance. Connie and I will go out the back. He can't watch them both at the same time. When you get to New Brunswick, pass it and meet us at the beginning of River Road in Highland Park. I want a good look at that area before we let you go into it."

Michael nodded. "I know where it is." He remembered the interchange well. Twenty years ago River Road had been the easiest method of accessing one of New Jersey's highways. It sat on one side of a two lane bridge spanning the Raritan River. Traffic backed up into the center of Highland Park and the heavily traveled Albany Street on the New Brunswick side. In recent years the roads around it had been redone. A bypass had been added on the New Brunswick side, leading to Route 287 and relieving the small towns of snarling traffic jams.

"Ready?" Michael asked.

"Ready," Adrienne said.

At the garage Michael got into his Porsche. It was small and maneuverable, and he'd once compared its hidden power to Erika's underlying passion. He started the engine. It roared to life at the slight turn of the key. He hoped that before this day ended they would be reunited.

Connie came over to his window. He lowered it. "We're going to find her, Michael," she said. "All we have to do is keep a cool head and remember our purpose."

"Connie, I'm playing your way." He wanted her to know he wasn't planning any cowboy tactics. Erika's life was the one thing he was concerned about.

"Then we're going to put this bastard away where not even his mother could find him."

Connie was angry. Frank had ruined her perfect record and she really wanted him. Michael saw it in her eyes. Yet, she was cautious, and not apt to overplay the role. She wanted to make sure he didn't, either.

The food on her plate smelled delicious, and Erika was weak with hunger. Frank had kept her tied up all night. Her arms and legs were numb. He'd only allowed her up one time, to go to the bathroom.

This morning he'd cooked her breakfast—bacon, scrambled eggs, fried apples, rolls, and coffee. He'd untied her and brought her to the table, then tied her left arm to the chair. Erika ate with her right hand.

The food tasted as good as it smelled. Her mouth was sore from the scarf, but she ate, anyway.

Erika ventured to talk. She wanted to try to reason with him. "You move about as if you live here."

"I do live here," he told her. "This is my house. Mine and Abby's."

She stared at him. Frank ate normally. Nothing seemed out of place to him. Suddenly, Erika knew this *was* his house, at least it had been before the divorce and his wife's death. He knew his way around, but Erika had attributed that to his being there for a while.

He seemed in a rational mood, and Erika might not get another chance to question him. Frank could seem so normal. Last night he'd talked to her about politics, what was happening in the East Brunswick area, how global warming was affecting life on earth. If Erika's hands hadn't been tied behind her back and her ankles fastened to the chair she sat in, and if she hadn't known there was a dead body only a few feet away, she would have had to rethink her decision about his sanity.

"How long are you going to keep me here?" she asked.

He stopped eating and looked her directly in the eye. "If I'm lucky it should all be over today."

The intensity of his gaze sent a chill down Erika's back. How long did she have? What had he done?

"What are you going to do to me?"

"I'm going to kill you."

Erika shivered. Every part of her trembled. She could feel every organ, every cell, every nerve and blood vessel vibrating. Frank continued to eat as if he'd told her they would take in a movie after breakfast.

"Why?" she asked when she could find her voice. It was breathy and weak.

"So Abby and I can live without enemies."

"You and Abby?" Erika asked. Unconsciously she tried to raise her left arm. The restraint forced her to remain where she was.

Frank nodded.

He was crazy! Didn't he realize Abby was dead?

"Where is Abby, Frank?"

Frank looked up, and lightning seemed to flash in his eyes. Suddenly, his glass sailed across the room. Erika had only enough time to shift to the side before it sailed past her. Orange juice splattered her as the glass clipped her shoulder and fell to the floor.

"You don't care about Abby. You don't even know her. But he does, and he'll pay for what he did to her."

"Frank, Abby's dead."

Erika knew she'd stepped over the line. Frank stood up slowly. He glared at her, towered like a giant over his kingdom. Every line of his body was granite hard, menacing. She bit down on her lip to keep from screaming. Fear choked her. He was going to kill her now. She tried to stand, but the chair restrained her. She couldn't run, couldn't get away from him.

Erika had nothing to protect her. If she was going to stay alive, she had to convince him not to kill her. She racked her brain, trying to think of something to say. *How do you talk to a crazy person?* she asked herself.

He moved away from his chair and started for her.

"Frank," she said. "It's Abby. What are we going to get the children for Christmas this year?"

Frank stopped. He stared at her, but she knew he wasn't seeing her. She breathed heavily.

"I've looked in the malls and I can't find anything for . . ." *Who?* she thought. *What were the children's names?* She'd never heard anyone call them anything except the Mason children. "For them," she finished. "I thought a doll for our baby."

She gauged his reaction. He stopped, but she didn't know if the rational Frank had returned or the crazy Frank was still standing in front of her.

"Melissa would like a doll," he finally said. "She told me when I put her to bed last night."

Erika let her breath out. Frank's anger seemed to be going. He turned away from her and checked his watch. "I have to go out," he said.

"Where?" she asked before she could stop herself. He'd told her it would be over today. Had he called Michael when he left her yesterday? Had they agreed to meet somewhere? Was Michael coming here? She had to know.

"I won't be long," he said, ignoring her question. He didn't move, but stood facing the hall door. Erika followed his gaze. The dead body still lay on the floor. She wondered who the man was, and why no one came by or called him. Frank had said the phone was dead. Wasn't there anyone who knew this man? Did he live alone? He wasn't that old. Did he still work? Why hadn't the people from his job called to check on him? Why didn't the neighbors think it strange that the jeep came and went at will?

Frank turned back to her and Erika froze. He came toward her. She pushed herself back in the chair as far as she could go. Her hands and feet went dead cold. Frank grabbed her free arm and pulled it behind her. Her back hurt from the strain of sitting in an unnatural position. He untied her other hand and pulled it behind her, securing the two together.

"I'll be back . . . with Michael," he added.

CHAPTER 19

The Raritan River spanned about a hundred yards at the point from the boathouse to the opposite shore. A string of apartment buildings that had been converted to condominiums sat above a run of trees hugging the shoreline. Michael crouched on the ground with a pair of binoculars. The area was teeming with FBI agents. Michael agreed that they were concealed, and even if Frank were looking from the other shore he'd see nothing.

Michael panned the hilltop, the busy roadway, and the boathouse. From his position he saw no sign of Frank. The day was cold and few people walked on this part of Route 18. Cars pulled in and out of the gas station at Commercial Avenue and the one just across from where Michael lay on the ground.

Frank knew what he was doing when he picked this place. There was nowhere to hide, to conceal himself from attack. Frank could pick him off from a number of places and he'd never know which way the bullet had come. Michael checked his watch. He had only half an hour left. He had to go now to get over the bridge and into the yard before the two o'clock hour.

"It's time," one of the agents he'd met, but couldn't remember, said next to him.

Michael pulled back and stood up under the cover of the leafless trees.

"Are you sure you want to do this? We can still put a double in your place."

"He'd know in seconds I wasn't there, and we don't know what he'd do to Erika," Michael said. "I'm going."

"You have the vest?"

Michael touched his chest. Under his coat he wore a bulletproof vest, but he didn't think it meant much if Frank wanted to kill him. Frank's history called for bullets through the head, and they had no vest that would protect him there.

"We have the car bugged, and we can track you through the vest."

Michael nodded. They walked through the trees to the condos and into the parking lots beyond. Michael got in his car and started the engine.

"Good luck," the agent said. "You'll be picked up by our people on the other side."

"Thanks," Michael said, and drove away. He'd never felt so alone in his life.

Frank saw him coming. He recognized the car. It was the same one he'd driven day in and day out during Frank's trial. Small, sleek, powerful. It wouldn't help him today. Neither would the FBI. Kidnapping was a federal crime. The local police would have little to do with it, if he were caught. Frank had no intention of being caught.

Checking around him he saw no one anywhere, but he didn't expect to. Michael was a letter-of-the-law man. He'd follow directions. The two women guards were a different story. They would call the FBI no matter what he'd told Michael. Frank was prepared for that.

Michael came across the Highland Park Bridge and took the ramp for Route 18 South. He stopped at the light and waited for it to turn green. He was going to have to pass the boathouse and go to the Paulus Boulevard jughandle to turn around and get on the north side of the highway. That's where Frank would make his move.

He saw him coming. He drove fast and took the curve at an easy angle. The light was red when he got to it, and he stopped. Frank had concealed himself in the branches that hung from the top of the hill. The ground beyond the rough vines was a ten foot drop to the ground. He took it easily, landing directly next to the car. His gun pointed at the glass, he said, "Open it."

The automatic door locks clicked and Frank got in the car. "Run the light. Make a right," he said, pressing the cold steel against Michael's neck. "Now!"

Michael did as he asked.

"Take the ramp to 1 South," he commanded.

The first exit took him down to Route 1, heading toward Trenton and South Jersey. At the bottom of the hill, they immediately exited into the Sears parking lot. Frank directed him to the back, where he'd parked his jeep. He estimated they had about three minutes before the FBI agents scrambled and converged on them.

In moments they were out of the car. He pushed Michael to the jeep, grabbed his coat and pulled it down his arms, restraining any movement.

"I know they're on their way. You got one minute to strip to your shorts." Michael didn't move. Frank jabbed the gun into his throat. "Fifty-nine seconds," he shouted. "Do it as if you were trying to get to Erika as fast as you could. Or I'll put a bullet through your head and save myself the trouble of dragging you home."

The FBI offices had been set up in an office building at George and New Streets, across from The State Theater. Connie stared out of the window at the main street of the City of New Brunswick. The agent assigned to Michael and Erika was a tall, blond man of about thirty, but he looked younger. He had a cellular unit pushed up against his ear, listening. "Did they get him?" she asked, looking anxiously at the FBI agent.

"I'm afraid not," he said. "They got to Mr. Lawrence's car, but it was empty."

"What about the bug in his vest? Can't you track him?"

"His clothes were lying in a heap next to the car, including the vest."

Connie turned away. What could they do now? There was no way to determine where they had gone. Leaving that lot by the back gave Mason access to all four directions, and they had no idea what kind of vehicle he was driving.

"What about the transmission before they left the lot? Did they say anything that could help us?"

"They weren't close enough for a clear tape. We'll have to send it to the lab for amplification."

"I want to hear it," Connie commanded.

"It's garbled. You won't be able to make out anything."

"Look," Connie told the blond man, "I know more about Frank Mason than his father does. Let me hear the tape. I might understand something you don't."

The agent turned on the machine and she listened. The first time through she heard nothing but background noise. Connie hit the rewind button and listened again. This time she heard something that sounded like "men" but it was too fast. When it ended she played it again, and again and again.

"If only we could filter out the background noises."

"I told you it wouldn't yield anything," the agent said. "The sooner we get it to the lab, the faster we'll get an answer."

"We don't have time for that. The closest lab is in Newark. Frank Mason has both of them now. He isn't going to wait around for us to analyze a tape. We have to do something now."

"I'm open to suggestion," he told her, spreading his hands.

Adrienne, who had been quiet to this point, spoke. "Give me the tape. I can filter the noises."

"You can?" the agent asked. "How? We need equipment we don't have."

"We have the equipment," she said. She pointed to the window.

Connie and the agent looked out. Then Connie looked at Adrienne and smiled.

"Let's go," she said.

"Where?" the agent asked.

"The State Theater. They've got sound equipment."

The automatic garage door mechanism closed the door completely before Frank got out of the car. He unlocked the cuffs on the jeep door and cuffed Michael's hands behind him.

"Get out," he commanded.

Michael stepped barefoot onto the cold concrete floor. Debris and small pebbles cut into his skin. Frank pushed the gun into his bare back and urged him forward. They went into the house. Michael knew where he was. He'd never been here before but he recognized the street address. This was the house Abby had received as part of the settlement, where the couple had lived as man and wife, and where Abby had committed suicide. Frank had told him he was taking him home.

A jab to his kidneys had him stumbling forward. He went through the kitchen and into the dining room. Erika sat there, tied to a chair. It was tied to the decorative column that separated the living and dining rooms.

"Erika!" he called and rushed to her. "Are you all right?"

She had a gag in her mouth, but she grunted his name. Tears formed in her eyes and spilled down her face.

"Don't," he said, dropping to his knees. He moved his hands, but they were confined. Unable to touch her, he leaned forward and kissed her cheek.

Erika dropped her head to his shoulder and sobbed.

"Take the gag off her," he ordered Frank.

Frank went behind her and untied the scarf. Her mouth was bruised when he saw it, and he wanted to kill Frank. Erika kissed him as soon as she was free.

"I love you, Michael," she said. "I didn't think I'd ever see you again."

Michael didn't want to tell her how much that fear had weighed on his mind. He kissed her again. "Are you all right?" he asked a second time.

She nodded and leaned to kiss him, her wet face brushing against his.

"This is a sweet reunion," Frank sneered. "Too bad I'm going to have to break it up." He got Michael a chair and put it next to Erika's, keeping him in line with the gun in his hand. "I got you some clothes," he told him. "Put them on."

Michael looked at the neatly folded pile of clothes on the living room sofa. "Whose are these?" Michael asked.

"The man who owned them no longer has a need for them," Frank said.

"Michael, there's a dead man in the hall." Erika looked over her shoulder at the doorway to the center hall. Michael followed her gaze.

"His wife's upstairs," Frank explained.

Michael stepped into the pants. Everything was there, down to the socks. Only shoes were missing from the pile.

"What was their crime, Frank? Why did you kill them?"

"This is my house," he said. "They tried to say it was theirs."

Erika groaned. "Frank, I need to go to the bathroom."

"Not yet," he shouted. "First I do him, then you."

Michael pulled on a white shirt and buttoned the front buttons. The shirt fit, but the pants pooled at his ankles.

"Sit down."

Michael did as he was told. Frank bound his arms to the chair back.

"Frank, please," Erika pleaded. "I can't wait any longer."

He looked at her. "You're as bad as one of the children," he scolded.

"Please, Honey."

Michael stared at her, but said nothing. What was she up to? Frank also looked different. His mood swung like a fast pendulum. He went to Erika and untied her legs, then her arms. She pulled them around the chair and massaged the flesh. Michael saw the bruise marks the ropes had left on her skin.

She tried to stand, but fell.

"Let me help you, Abby," Frank said. He pulled her arm around his shoulder and supported her while she limped across the room. What had happened here, Michael wondered. What kind of game was Erika playing, and would it get her killed?

Erika used the toilet, then massaged her wrists and ankles. She couldn't stand like this—her circulation had cramped long ago and her foot and hands were numb—but she wasn't going to get another chance. She'd discovered Frank's weakness. She could keep him thinking she was Abby, and everything would be all right. If he lapsed back into normalcy, he'd kill them.

Wiggling her toes hurt, but it was the only way to get the blood back into her feet. Pins and needles the size of ten-penny nails felt as if they were sticking into her feet. Her wrists weren't as bad. She ran cold water over them to slow down the rush of blood, giving her fingers the effect of the bends.

Gingerly she tried to walk in the confined space. She could do it.

Buying herself time to let her body repair itself, she stayed in the bathroom for as long as Frank allowed. Which turned out to be just a moment more.

"Let's go," he said from outside the door.

Erika opened it and walked out. He grabbed her arm the moment she came out. He knew she was Erika again. He pushed her back to the chair and sat her back down.

"Frank, no," she cried. "Please let me have a little exercise. My skin is red from the ropes, and my fingers are so swollen I can't open and close my hands."

"Too bad," he said, yanking her hands behind her. He set the gun on the floor next to him while he tied her up again. Erika looked at Michael. On the floor next to his chair was the rope that Frank had used. He hadn't taken the time to tie him as tightly as he had her, and he'd gotten free, or almost free.

"Frank," Michael said. "Why are you doing this? It doesn't make sense."

"It doesn't have to make sense," he told him.

"Why do you want to kill us?"

Frank stood up when he'd tied her hands. He left her ankles free.

"You killed *her,*" he accused.

"Killed who?"

"Abby . . . my wife."

"Frank, Abby committed suicide."

Erika didn't like this. When she'd confronted Frank with Abby's death he'd acted as if he was going to kill her right then. She tried to get Michael's attention, but Frank stood between them.

"Why Erika, Frank? She didn't even know Abby."

"Erika?" He said her name as if he didn't remember who she was.

"I'll do what you want, Frank. Let Erika go and you can do anything you want with me."

"Michael!" Erika said.

"Why should I let her go? I have you both. I have all the power now. I'm the judge."

"This isn't a court."

"This is your court, Counselor." Frank glared into Michael's face. He swung the gun nonchalantly in his right hand. "This is the last court you'll ever see."

"All right, since this is court," Michael tried another tactic. "What is it you want to tell the court?"

Frank actually looked like he wanted to address the invisible body. "That they're wrong."

"Wrong about what?"

"About separating my family. They have no right, no jurisdiction over taking what's mine."

"Who has that right, Frank?"

"I do."

"What about Abby? Does she have the right to care for her children, to protect them from anyone who tries to harm them?"

"She's their mother. Mothers protect their children."

"From whom?"

"From anyone, everyone who tries to hurt them."

"Even their father?"

Frank thought about that. "It wasn't my father!" Frank shouted. "My father would never hurt me."

His voice had changed, and he sounded like a younger version of himself.

"My father taught me everything. Not my brothers. They were wimps, sissies, but not me. I could kill the little deer, gut it, carve it up, and eat it."

Erika frowned at the picture he was drawing.

"My father didn't have to make me do it. Not like he did my brothers. I was a good boy. I was a man. I did it."

"Your mother, Frank, what did she do when she saw you were doing what your father did? Did she help you?"

"No, she scolded me. She told me it wasn't good to hurt the animals. That if I didn't want to eat the Bambi deer I didn't have to."

"But you were a man, Frank. You couldn't let your father see that you were afraid of the deer, that you wanted to pet the deer, not eat it."

A coldblooded rage entered Frank's eyes. He was no longer a little boy. He'd turned into a soulless killer.

"I lifted my rifle." Frank demonstrated with the gun. He clasped it in both hands, spread his legs and aimed it directly at Michael's heart. "She stood in the misty morning dew, dazed by my silent appearance. I closed one eye and lined her up." He cocked the trigger. "She waited . . . I held my breath. She lifted her head . . . I squeezed the trigger."

"No, Frank!" Erika shouted, breaking the haze he'd worked himself into. She could see Michael had freed the rope from the chair, but his hands were still tied. "You don't have to do this. It's Abby. I didn't die, Frank. We can be together."

Frank turned his head and looked at her.

"We can be a family. We'll take the children and go wherever you want. We'll stay as long as you like. No one ever has to find us again."

"Do you mean it, Abby?"

She nodded, her face wet with tears. Frank rushed to her, hugged her. "Abby," he said, pushing himself back. "What have you done to your hair?

Where is that long, beautiful hair?" He combed his fingers through her nearly straight mane.

"It fell out when I was sick, remember?" Erika had to think fast. "It will grow back. The doctor said it might take a few months, but it will be as long as it ever was."

"Yes," Frank said, more to himself than to her. "It will grow back."

"Frank?" she began. "Can we go now? We can pick the children up from school and leave right away."

"We'll need clothes," he reminded her pragmatically.

"We have clothes in the car. We packed yesterday." Erika made her story up as she went along. As long as she kept Frank diverted, Michael could work on the bands restraining his hands.

"Release my hands, Honey, and we'll go."

Frank reached around her. She felt his hands on hers. The first knot slipped, then he stopped.

"What is it?" she asked.

"Him." He turned back to Michael. "I'll never be free as long as he lives."

"Why, Frank? He's just the man who helped us. We don't want to hurt anyone who helped us."

"He didn't help us."

The old Frank was back. The psychotic Frank. The Frank who remembered she was Erika and he was Michael. The man pointing the gun at Michael's heart.

Oil and water had been Connie's first thoughts about the FBI agent assigned to this case. Yet she had to revise her opinion when she saw them mobilize outside the yellow-sided house on an East Brunswick cul-de-sac. They'd evacuated the neighbors without a single sound to tip off the inhabitants that anything was going on. The place was surrounded on all sides, and there was confirmation that Frank had gone inside separately with a man and a woman.

Connie and Adrienne huddled behind an open car door directly across the street from the yellow house.

"What do we do now?" Connie whispered to the agent.

"We wait," he told her.

She looked about the other houses. Men crouched on rooftops of neighboring residences. The street had been closed to traffic. There was only one way in or out.

"Can we find out if anyone in there is alive?"

He nodded and sent a signal to the agent in a van parked at the end of the opening that started the circle.

"Put your earphones on."

She plugged them into her ear.

"Frank, that's not true." Erika St. James's voice came through the wire and into her ear. She breathed a sigh of relief that she was still alive. Now they just had to get them out of there.

"Lawrence." Frank tested the name. "Michael Lawrence, my lawyer. A man who defamed my wife. Told the court lies, half truths, made my Abby cry." Frank assumed the position for a point blank hit.

Erika saw Michael was still working with the ropes.

"He didn't, Frank. You did." Her voice was strong, authoritative, challenging.

This was their only chance. She needed to buy them some time for Michael to get free. If she could keep his attention on her, Michael could surprise him from behind.

"You killed them. You killed them all. The children, Abby, the judge, the lawyer. It isn't their fault. It's yours."

Connie glanced at the FBI agent. They both pressed a hand to their ear.

"It's going down now," she said.

He nodded. Another hand signal passed to the other cars. Men begin closing in on the house.

"Admit it, Frank. You're a scared little boy, and you're hiding it. The others aren't the wimps, are they, Frank? You're the wimp. You're the one who can't sleep at night because of the things you have to do during the day."

"Stop it!" Frank cried.

"You're the one who can't tell your father that you don't want to kill Bambi. That you don't want to eat the deer meat. Your brothers, they told him, didn't they, Frank?"

Frank whirled around. He pointed the gun randomly. "There he is." Frank aimed and shot. The explosion made Erika's heart stop, then beat fast as an escaping bandit.

"Now!" the FBI agent yelled. Men started running toward the house.

"There." Frank shot again. "Die!" he shouted and sent a third shot into the lamp. "Die." A chip of wood jumped up and hit Erika on the side of the face.

"Stop it, Frank!"

Michael's hands came free just as Frank leveled the gun at him. Erika saw the flash of light in her mind, knowing she had to move now. Michael lunged for Frank, the shot rang out, and Erika charged, chair in tow, split seconds apart. Using her head, she tackled Frank, hitting him low in the stomach. The two of them crashed against the doorway. Erika heard the breaking of wood as they went down. The gun fell from his hand and landed on the carpet.

She hung sprawled on top of Frank, unable to move, her legs free, her arms wrenched and painfully clasped behind the back of the chair. Then

Connie appeared in front of her. Suddenly there were voices, commands being shouted. Someone calling for a medic. A blond man, obviously in charge, stepped in front of Connie and pulled her and the chair easily to a sitting position.

"Untie her," he said with all the authority of an army captain.

"Where's Michael?" Erika asked Connie. "Is he all right?"

Connie didn't answer. Erika turned as far as she could. Michael lay on the floor. Blood stained the carpet near him. Men in white blocked her view. "Is he all right?" she shouted.

Her hands came free and she bolted from her position. Pushing people aside, she got to him.

"Michael," she pleaded. "Please be all right. Michael, I need you. I love you, and I want to marry you. Michael!"

She looked at the medic. Connie and Adrienne pulled her to her feet to let the medics take him to the waiting ambulance.

"He can't die, Connie," she cried. Connie pulled her into her arms and let her cry. "I love him. I told him I wouldn't marry him, but I will, Connie. He's got to be all right."

"Come on," Connie said. "We'll follow the ambulance to the hospital.

Erika started to move. Frank Mason stepped into her path. This time *his* hands were cuffed behind his back. Erika stared into his eyes. Raw hatred clear as glass assaulted her. She'd never hated anyone in her life, not even her mother, as much as she hated Frank Mason at this moment.

"If he dies," she told him. "You'll have me to deal with me, and I'm no Abby."

CHAPTER 20

Erika stepped out of the limo in front of Robert Wood Johnson University Hospital. Her heart sang at the prospect that Michael was coming home today. She had on a new dress, the house was festively attired, and she couldn't wait to have him all to herself.

She thought of the day when Frank Mason's stray bullet had hit him in the chest. If his hands hadn't come loose at that moment and she hadn't lunged for Frank, Michael might well be dead. Putting her hand over her heart, she thanked God things had worked out differently. The medics working on him had looked grave, and there had been so much blood.

Since Michael had come through the surgery and they'd been told he'd recover completely, there had been a steady stream of family visitors each time she'd come. They hadn't been alone for the entire week he'd been here. She looked forward to having him home, alone. She didn't want any visitors. The two of them had so much to talk about, so much to explain.

She looked down the hill at the new section of the hospital. Michael's room was in the old section. Snow kissed her nose and she stuck out her tongue to catch a snowflake. It was going to be a beautiful Christmas.

Erika turned and put her foot on the first step. Then she turned back. A woman wearing a red coat turned the corner and began walking uphill. Erika scrutinized her. She'd recognize her mother's walk during a sandstorm. *She must have come to see Michael,* Erika thought, but when Alva Redford reached the glass doors to the new section of the hospital she went inside.

It was possible to get from the new section to the old without walking up the hill, she told herself. But her mother had walked with a purpose, as if she'd intended to go through those doors.

Michael hadn't mentioned her coming to see him before. If this was her first time, why would she look as if she knew where she was going? On impulse Erika walked down the hill and entered the area with glass doors. Inside, the place was airy and light, not like the old section which was brick and mortar instead of glass and steel.

She walked up the stairs, checking each floor to see if she could spot her mother. On three she saw her being shown into a room. Erika stepped into the carpeted hall and went to the desk.

"My mother, Mrs. Redford, just went through that door," she told the nurse.

"If you'll have a seat over there I'm sure the doctor will want to speak to you."

Erika opened her mouth to speak but decided against it. She turned around and sat down, facing the door through which her mother had gone. Erika wanted to know what she was doing there.

Ten minutes later a woman doctor came out and briefly stopped at the nurse's station. Erika saw the woman look at her, then back at the nurse. She came over. "Ms. Redford?" she said.

"No," Erika hesitated. "My name is Erika St. James. My mother remarried."

"Would you come with me?"

Erika followed the woman. She was young, probably in her early thirties. She had clear brown eyes and skin a shade lighter than her eyes.

"I'd hoped Alva would bring someone with her," she began when they were seated in her office. Erika looked at the degrees covering the wall behind Dr. Megan Bruce. "Until today she's always come alone."

"She never said she needed—"

"I know she wouldn't," the doctor said. "She's been that way for years. But things are changing now, and you'll have to help her."

"I don't understand, Doctor. Exactly what is wrong with my mother?"

The doctor went on the explain Alva's condition while Erika sat in wide-eyed horror. She left the doctor's office holding her stomach and feeling as if she needed to sit down. *Dying?* Her mother was dying. All those years when Erika had fought with her mother, Alva had had a condition that forced her mood swings. She couldn't control them, and wasn't responsible for them. The medication had helped in the beginning, but Alva had built up a tolerance to it over the years and her ability to control the moods grew shorter and shorter.

Erika found a seat in a waiting room and sat down. She felt bereft, full of grief. She'd never expected to feel anything. Why did she? Was this why she'd tried time and again to get her mother to love her? Because all along she'd thought there was an explanation for why her mother acted the way she did? She could be lying to herself, setting herself up one more time for her mother to come in and stomp on her feelings.

"Erika?"

She looked up as the door opened.

"May I come in?"

Alva Redford stood in the door. She looked unsure of herself, not the competent, always right actress Erika was used to seeing. She sat down opposite her daughter. Her hands fidgeted for a moment.

"I never expected to have to tell you. I didn't want anyone to know."

"Not know, Mother? Not know that all these years you've been trying to control something that was a medical condition? You let me think you hated me, that the two of us were like champagne and beer, incompatible, at opposite ends of the spectrum. When the truth would have been so much easier to understand."

"I didn't want you to know."

"Why?"

Alva looked away from her. She checked the walls and the other seats in the room before she answered. "You've always been so strong, so sure of yourself. Even as a child you were decisive, knew what you wanted to do from the beginning and went after it no matter what anyone . . . what I said about it. You frightened me."

"Me?"

"When your father was alive, he took care of me. Then he died, leaving us with so little money. I couldn't afford the medication, and my moods killed any love you might have had for me."

Tears gathered in Erika's eyes.

"You were running from me that day you met Carlton. You ran fast and long and kept going until I couldn't see you anymore. I got in the car and came after you, but you disappeared. I found out you went to Carlton's."

Erika nodded. "We had tea together."

"When you went to live with Carlton, I signed the papers allowing him to be your guardian, it was to protect you from me. I loved you, Erika, and I couldn't go on hurting you."

Hot tears scalded her cheeks.

"Carlton set up the trust fund to pay for my medication. If he died, he didn't want you to find yourself in the same position you did when your father died. The money I borrowed from you is for a special operation. It's scheduled for January fifth."

"Mother . . ." Her voice cracked.

"I know I'm dying, Erika . . . but before I do I want us to forgive each other for the things we've done and said to each other. I love you. I've always loved you."

Erika sobbed aloud. The floodgates opened and tears cascaded over her face.

"Erika?" Alva Redford stood up and opened her arms. Erika let out a loud sob and rushed into them.

They held each other for a long time, both crying, neither wanting to let go.

"Come on, Honey. Let's fix our makeup. My future son-in-law will be upset if he sees you looking like this."

Erika laughed through her tears. Her mother loved her, had always loved her. She wouldn't think about the time they had left. It was good to know they did have some.

Erika's eyes were bright and shining when she walked into Michael's room. She wore winter white pants and a navy blue jacket. A Christmas tree pin with sparkling diamond lights adorned the lapel.

Michael stood at the head of the bed wearing jeans and a light blue shirt. His left arm was folded in a blue and white sling. At the foot of the bed sat a small canvas bag she'd brought with his clothes and toiletries.

"I'll be in class Tuesday night," he said into the phone. When he saw her he opened his good arm and she walked into his hug. "Don't worry, Malick. I'll be there." She kissed him on the mouth. "Good-bye." He hung up and pulled her closer. She kissed him, tenderly and sweetly. He wanted her so much. If the hospital door had a lock he'd consider claiming her here.

"You look awfully happy," he told her. "I hope I'm the reason."

Her smile grew larger. "You're always the reason," she said. "But I have other good news, wonderful news to tell you."

"What?" He pulled her down on his lap and kissed her cheek.

"I'll tell you later. I have a million things to tell you, but let's go home first." She stood up and pulled him with her. Michael clamped his arm around her waist and pulled her to him.

"Just tell me you'll marry me," he said, his voice emotionally charged. "I can wait for everything except that."

"Yes," she replied. "I'll marry you." Erika lifted her mouth to his. She felt lighter than air. Michael loved her and he wanted to marry her, and she wanted to marry him. She knew there was no guarantee that things would last forever. She knew love meant sharing and risking. She'd work at loving Michael, and he'd work at it, too. As long as they shared Carlton's legacy, they had a chance for the forever kind of love.

"Ready to go home?" she asked.

"Ready."

Erika handed the canvas bag to the driver when they reached the front door. Michael got out of the wheelchair the hospital had insisted he ride in for being discharged. Alva Redford came to stand next to them.

Michael tensed and grabbed Erika's hand. She looked at him with a smile.

"Hello, Michael," she said. "I'm glad to see you're better." She kissed him on the cheek, then hugged Erika. Erika returned the open display of affection. When she pulled back, her eyes were bright. Both women looked at each other as if they shared a remarkable secret. Michael wanted to know what it was. He remembered what Peter had told him about Alva. He'd intended to tell Erika the last night they were together, but never got around to it. Since then he'd had no time with her.

"She told you?" he asked when the limo pulled away from the curb and joined the traffic on Somerset Street.

"You know?" Erika said.

"I know she has a disease that causes mood swings, and that she'd had it for a long time."

"It's incurable," Erika said, her voice hoarse. "She's going to die."

He put his arm around her and pulled her close. She smelled of flowers and spring, and the promise of a better time.

"She told me this morning," Erika went on. "How long have you known?"

Michael explained his request to Peter that they check out the possible stock manipulations. The unexplained trust fund payments coincided with the dates for stock activity. It turned out to be coincidental, but in doing one he found the other.

"Are you all right, now?" he asked.

Erika looked up at him. "I've never been happier," she said. "I know my mother is dying, but I also know why she treated me as she did. I won't say I totally forgive her, but at least we have some time to work things out."

Michael smiled and kissed her. He loved her ability to take the best from people, even those who treated her badly.

"If she'd told me years ago I could have helped her, taken care of her."

"She didn't want you to become her nurse."

"I didn't want to be her nurse. I wanted to be her daughter." She paused. "We could have had some good times together. Some of my fears would never have been."

"You're no longer afraid, are you? You understand that she said things she didn't mean?"

Erika nodded. "Some of them cut deeply. I don't know that I'll be able to forget them for a long time."

"Erika, you are a desirable woman. I love you. Don't let that doubt creep into your mind."

She put her fingers over his mouth. "It isn't you. I know you love me and I love you. It's the children."

"Whose children?"

"Yours . . . mine . . . ours."

"We can adopt children. If you don't want them, we don't have to have them. I'll be content—"

"Michael, I *can* have children," she said, stopping his argument. "I mean, no one has ever said I couldn't."

"Then, why—"

"I was scared. I was so afraid of everything my mother had told me." She stopped to smile at him. "I'm not afraid anymore. I'd love to hold my own child. When I held Roberta in my arms, I felt like a miracle had happened." Erika's voice choked.

Michael understood her fears. In time they would all be removed. He'd feared leaving the mountain, returning to the world that had rejected him. Night after night he'd run in his dreams, trying to get away from the things that hurt him. He was no longer afraid, either. He'd put Abby to rest in his mind and he'd help Erika find out she'd be the kind of mother Alva Redford never was. She'd never do to a child what her mother had done to her.

"A miracle has happened. Sharing is a miracle. Your mother only acted like that because of the disease, and her inability to share her concerns with you. You're not that kind of person. We'll share everything, just as Carlton's legacy required. It won't happen to you."

"I know," Erika said. "I know mother leaned on my father. When he died, Carlton was the only person she told about her condition, and he helped her."

Michael cradled her in his arms and held her. "He must have been a wonderful man."

"He was. I'll tell you about him one day. You're a lot like him," she said.

"I love you," Michael said. He shifted around on his sore arm to take her fully against him. The kiss told him everything he wanted to know. All the doubts were gone. He could feel it in her, feel the softness of her body as they united for now and all time. She was free of the fear, free to love him with all her heart and know that she had his love and they would share this legacy.

Erika loved him, too. She loved him more than she'd ever loved anyone, and if it hadn't been for her mother's condition she'd never have run away, never met Carlton, and Michael might not be part of her life. She shuddered at the thought. Michael tightened his arm around her. He didn't know the legacy Carlton had left them. Money might be one of life's true burdens, but with Michael to share her life, whatever burdens came their way were conquerable.